The lady in the stylish black two piece suit, her red hair neat and tidy, her right hand gently holding a dainty parasol, did not look in the least like the swarthy-skinned Mexican peasant girl who, a few hours later, was riding along in a small cart – a cart which appeared to be loaded with nothing more suspicious than vegetables.

And neither of them looked anything like the notorious Belle Boyd!

Only the Ysabel Kid and his father knew that Belle was in fact engaged in the most dangerous exploit of her entire career!

D1627897

Miscellaneous titles

*Title awaiting publication

J.T. EDSON OMNIBUS
Volume 12

THE BLOODY BORDER
BACK TO THE BLOODY BORDER
THE QUEST FOR BOWIE'S BLADE

CORGI BOOKS

J.T. EDSON OMNIBUS VOLUME 12
A CORGI BOOK 0 552 13866 5

THE BLOODY BORDER, BACK TO THE BLOODY
BORDER and THE QUEST FOR BOWIE'S BLADE were
originally published in Great Britain by Corgi Books, a
division of Transworld Publishers Ltd

PRINTING HISTORY – THE BLOODY BORDER
Corgi edition published 1969
Corgi edition reprinted 1972
Corgi edition reprinted 1975
Corgi edition reprinted 1982

PRINTING HISTORY – BACK TO THE BLOODY BORDER
Corgi edition published 1970
Corgi edition reprinted 1974
Corgi edition reprinted 1978

PRINTING HISTORY – THE QUEST FOR BOWIE'S BLADE
Corgi edition published 1974

Corgi Omnibus edition published 1992

Corgi Books are published by Transworld Publishers Ltd.,
61–63 Uxbridge Road, Ealing, London W5 5SA, in Australia by
Transworld Publishers (Australia) Pty. Ltd., 15–23 Helles
Avenue, Moorebank, NSW 2170, and in New Zealand by
Transworld Publishers (N.Z.) Ltd., 3 William Pickering Drive,
Albany, Auckland.

Printed and bound in Great Britain by
Cox & Wyman Ltd., Reading, Berks.

THE BLOODY BORDER

For Daphne and Harry Chamberlain

Chapter 1

Hit Him With Your Parasol

"You sure you'll be all right, ma'am?" the sailor asked doubtfully, looking around the deserted beach illuminated by the beacon fire which had guided them ashore.

"Yes, thank you," the girl replied, trying to sound more confident than she felt. "My friends will be close by. Carry out your orders."

With a Yankee steam-sloop approaching through the darkness and the blockade-runner *Gabrielle* hove-to at the mouth of the bay, she did not dare delay the boat's return. Owned by British businessmen responsible for her presence on the deserted beach some miles south of the Mexican town of Matamoros, the *Gabrielle* carried a cargo badly needed by the Confederate States and must not fall into Union hands. So she stepped ashore and the men unloaded her two specially-designed trunks. After setting the trunks by the fire, the men returned to the boat. For a moment they hesitated, but a brief flicker of light from the *Gabrielle* gave an urgent warning signal. Climbing back into the boat, the sailors set their oars working to turn it and make for the waiting ship.

Watching them disappear into the night, the girl could not hold down a small sigh. Tall, slender, although far from skinny, she had a strikingly beautiful face with strength of will and intelligence in its lines. Despite the hurried departure from the *Gabrielle*, and the fact that a blockade runner offered few facilities for passengers, her red hair looked remarkably neat and tidy. She wore a plain, stylish black two-piece suit, the jacket ending at waist level and hanging open over a dark blue shirt-waist. Apart from a single somewhat strangely-shaped bracelet on her left wrist, no jewellery decorated her appearance. Striking an incongruous note under the circumstances, she held a dainty parasol in her right hand.

Even knowing of its presence, the girl could not make out the shape of the *Gabrielle* at the mouth of the bay. That did not surprise her, for the ship had been designed, built and coloured for the sole purpose of slipping unseen through the U.S. Navy's blockading squadrons outside Southern ports. If Captain Horsfell acted as fast as she expected, within five minutes, ten at most, the boat would be back aboard and the *Gabrielle* moving away from the danger of the Yankee sloop.

With the ship went her last link to safety if anything should have happened to her escort. That possibility did not escape her, and grew stronger with their non-appearance. While Mexico might be neutral in the War Between The States, it had troubles of its own. The French under Maximilian were fighting to hold the country against Benito Juarez's Mexican patriots. Either side in the brutal, bloody conflict might find the presence of her escort puzzling and knew of a swift, effective way of solving mysteries. Nor would the French or Mexican forces look kindly on her arrival. From what she had heard, it might go badly with a lone young woman who fell into either side's hands in such a lonely area.

Hearing a slight sound, the girl turned to see what had caused it. Momentarily her spirits rose at the sight of the six men who came from the blackness beyond the fire; then dropped again as she realised none of them could be her escort. Despite his name, Sergeant Sam Ysabel was no Mexican and all the approaching party could lay at least nominal claim to belonging to that race.

All in all, the bunch approaching the girl struck her as being the most villainous collection of humanity she had ever seen. None wore a uniform, which proved little in a disorganised state of affairs across Mexico. Few of Juarez's supporters enlisted in an official army unit and fought in whatever clothes came their way. If the men before her belonged to a *guerillos* band, their appearances hinted at successful campaigning. Their clothing looked garish, too good, over-done in every respect; such as poor men wore when sudden wealth came their way. All carried hand-guns on their belts, ranging from single-shot, muzzle-loading pistols to an 1860 Army Colt. However the knife each man

8

wore at his waist would be his chief weapon. Tall, short, slim or heavily built, one thing all had in common. Their faces bore the stamp of evil, lust and cruelty.

One possibility for their presence came to mind. Ysabel needed men to help his work. For all their unprepossessing appearance, the Mexicans might be working for him. Smuggling goods run through the blockade across the Rio Grande into Confederate hands did not call for the services of saints.

"*Saludos, senora,*" greeted the short, wiry man in the lead, eyes roaming over her from head to foot in a lecherous, insolent manner.

"*Buenas noches,*" she replied. "Are you the men who lit the fire?"

"There's nobody else here," grinned the small man.

Walking towards the speaker, the girl happened to glance at the ground by the fire. She saw a blackish patch, different in colour to the sand around it. Raising her eyes, she saw the little man also staring at the discoloration. Then he looked at her with a wicked leer twisting his lips. Moving on, he came to a halt before the girl and his companions started to form a half circle around them.

"What you doing here, *senora*?" the small man asked.

"You don't know?" the girl asked quietly, standing with feet spread slightly apart and the parasol gripped at the handle and on the folded canopy.

"No, *senora,*" came the mocking reply. "The *hombre* who lit the fire, he didn't have time to tell us."

"He didn't even have time to pray," another man went on.

Cold shock bit into the girl at the words. Taken with that patch of drying blood by the fire, they meant only one thing. Her escort was dead—and his position might be preferable to her own in the near future. Realising the danger of landing on a deserted Mexican beach, it had originally been arranged that the *Gabrielle* should remain off shore until her escort arrived. But the presence of the Yankee sloop had deprived her of that means of escape.

If frightened, the girl gave no sign of it. Nor did she allow it to take control and induce panic. Swiftly she reviewed the situation and made her plans to counter its menace. As far as she could see, only one course remained open to her. Yet she must time everything right if she hoped to succeed.

"What happened to him?" she asked in an even voice, as if she believed all was well.

"He died, *senorita*," the little man answered, giving her correct marital status for the first time. "That's his blood you're looking at."

One of the men, a huge hulk with a brute's face, pointed to the trunks and commented on them. Then he walked across and knelt by one of them, hands going to the straps buckled about it.

"What're you doing?" the girl snapped in fair Spanish, going towards the big man. "Take your hands off that."

"If he does, he can't open it, *senorita*," the little spokesman put in.

"Why should he open it?" the girl demanded, swinging to face the speaker.

"How else will we know what's inside?"

None of the other men moved. Watching them, the girl realised they were playing with her as a cat with a mouse. Sneering, lust-filled faces watched her every move and she could guess that they hoped she would provide them with some sport. So much the better; her chances of escape were increased slightly by their attitude.

"Tell him to get away from that trunk!" she ordered.

"Jose's a bad boy, *senorita*," the little man replied. "Maybe you'd better tell him."

"And if he doesn't," another of the group continued with a grin, "hit him with your parasol."

"That will frighten him away," mocked a third.

Watching the big man, the girl walked in his direction. Although still crouching by the trunk, his body was tense to spring when she came within reaching distance. He hoped that she would struggle, it was always more fun when they fought unavailingly to escape from his brute strength.

"You watch her good, Jose!" warned the little man. "She's going to hit you with that parasol."

"I heard!" Jose rumbled and started to thrust himself erect.

Considerable experience had turned Jose into something of an expert on the subject of rape and he felt that he could

10

guess at the girl's reactions. She would either stand still, paralysed with fear, turn and flee, or make a feeble, futile attempt to fight him off. On previous occasions, given the chance, his victims did one or the other.

Only the girl did none of them.

Instead she advanced to meet him, approaching before he reached his feet. With a twist of her left hand, she separated the parasol's head from the handle and let the upper section fall. Doing so revealed a small steel ball around which her first two fingers curled. At their pull, the ball slid out of the handle on a short steel rod which telescoped into a powerful coil spring. No longer did she hold a harmless piece of feminine frippery, but gripped a deadly weapon.

Just how deadly she rapidly proved. Out flashed the parasol handle, driven by a snapping motion which imparted a savage whip to the spring. Taken aback by the girl's unexpected action, the burly man hesitated. Coming around, the steel ball caught him at the side of the jaw. Bone cracked audibly and Jose pitched sideways. Limp and unresisting as a pole-axed steer, the big body sprawled on to the sand.

After drawing the striking head of the spring-loaded blackjack from its place of concealment, the girl's left hand flew to her waistband. A tug at a strap freed the skirt, allowing it to fall away even as she struck the man. Taken with the sight of Jose going down, the girl's action shocked the remainder of the Mexicans into immobility. Rapacious eyes followed the skirt as it slid downwards, to be met with disappointment. Instead of seeing what they hoped for, the men discovered that she wore riding breeches and boots under the skirt. While fitting tightly enough to emphasise the shape of her legs, the breeches lacked the attraction underwear and stockings would have offered.

Expecting to be met by friends, or at least supporters of the Confederate States, the girl had decided against strapping on her gunbelt and its Dance Brothers Navy revolver when dressing to leave the ship. She wished to avoid adding to the interest her departure from the *Gabrielle* at such a place aroused among its crew and the gunbelt's contours would have been noticeable even beneath the skirt.

Although she regretted the omission, the girl wasted no time in brooding on it. Unsure just how much of a respite

11

her unexpected actions might have gained, she intended to make the most of it.

Already the little man was recovering from his surprise. Springing forward, he shot out his right hand to catch hold of the girl's back hair. It felt stiff and unnatural to the touch; a fact that barely registered before he received a shock which drove all thoughts of it from his mind. He intended to jerk her backwards, inflicting sufficient pain to make her drop the deadly thing which had felled Jose.

At the pull, the whole head of hair came away in the man's hand. Expecting some resistance, the lack of it caused him to stagger backwards. Boyishly-short black locks now replaced the full covering of red hair which had previously adorned the girl's head.

The sight added to the men's confusion and held them frozen. To their illiterate, superstitious minds what appeared to be a full scalp coming away at a touch—and without its owner exhibiting the slightest discomfort at the loss—seemed miraculous, awe-inspiring even.

"Get her!" screeched the little man.

At the sound of his voice, the other men jolted from their daze; although, fortunately for the girl, not all at once. Snatching at the knife in his belt, one of the men flung himself into her path as she started a dash for the darkness. His other hand thrust forward to catch her right wrist as the blackjack licked his way. Instantly she whipped up her other arm, driving it at her captor's face. Her fist did not strike the man, in fact she appeared to deliberately avoid it doing so. Instead she raked the bracelet down the man's cheek. A screech broke from the man's lips as blood gushed from the gash which followed where the bracelet touched. Releasing her wrist and his knife, he stumbled away with hands going to the injured cheek.

Hoping to take advantage of his companion's efforts, yet another of the Mexicans flung himself forward. The girl pivoted around fast. With the smooth grace of a ballet dancer, she whipped up her left leg in a kick. Unable to stop himself, the man ran full into the rising boot. It smashed with considerable force against his jaw and sent him reeling aside. Only just in time did he avoid going head-first into the fire.

It could not last, of course, and the girl knew it. Once the men threw off their state of surprise, they would quickly overpower her. Then—she did not want to think of that eventuality. So she must make for the darkness and hope for the best. One thing she swore: when she left the illuminated area of the fire, she would make them pay heavily and in advance for anything they might do if they caught her.

Lashing around with the parasol handle-blackjack, she caused a man to make a hurried spring rearwards, and prepared to dart away. With a spitting snarl like a hound-scared cat, the man jerked the revolver from his belt to line it at the girl. At the same moment the smallest of the party slid out his knife and moved forward. There would, she knew, be no time to deal with both threats, even discounting whatever action the remainder of the gang might take.

A shot crashed from the darkness before the man could complete the cocking and firing of his revolver. Nor would he ever manage to do so. Lead ripped into his head, spinning him around and tumbling him lifeless to the ground.

Bursting from the darkness, two armed men dashed towards the fire, the taller—a powerfully-built, black haired men wearing a battered Confederate campaign hat, buckskin shirt, pants and Indian moccasins—held a smoking Dragoon Colt in his right hand. A long-bladed knife hung sheathed at his waist. Although he looked a wild, dangerous figure, the girl welcomed the sight at that moment.

Dressed in the same general manner, the second of the newcomers was tall, slim and looked very young. Bare-headed, with raven black hair, his Indian dark features bore a savage expression. He reversed his companion's system of armament in that his walnut-handled Dragoon Colt rode butt forward in its holster and he held the knife in his right hand; and such a knife. Two and a half inches wide, its eleven and a half inches long blade's top side swooped down at the end in a concave arc to form a needle-sharp point with the convex curve of the cutting edge. Firelight flickered on the knife, adding to the wild aspect of the youngster.

Swinging around, the small Mexican saw the younger figure rushing at him. From all appearances, the youngster was allowing recklessness to over-ride caution. Certainly the small man seemed to believe so. Out licked his knife in a low, driving thrust aimed to disembowel the rash intruder. Even as the girl thought to scream a warning, the youngster swerved in his tracks. The big knife moved, curving around to catch and deflect the blow launched by the Mexican. Then it drove forward. Shock momentarily twisted the little man's face, to be wiped away by pain. Razor-sharp steel sank into his belly and ripped across. As the knife slid free, blood and intestines gushed from the gaping wound it left.

Accustomed to sudden death through she had been forced to become, the girl could not hold down a gasp of horror at the sight. To her ears came the youngster's low-voiced grunt, but she could not understand what he said.

"*A:he!*" he barked, almost as if taking part in some barbaric sacrificial ritual. The word left him before his victim landed face down by the fire.

There was no time to wonder what the word might mean, or give way to the nausea welling inside her. From the corner of her eye, the girl saw a Mexican pulling out his pistol. Leaping forward, she whipped her blackjack in a backhand swing that drove its steel-ball head into his face. Teeth shattered and he reeled back with his mouth spraying blood. An instant later the big newcomer's Dragoon boomed and its .44 bullet struck the man in the left side of the chest. Such was the impact of Colonel Colt's hand cannon that the man hurtled backwards when hit.

Out at sea, something streaked sparking redly into the air and burst into a brilliant white glow of light that drifted downwards again. Knowing it to be an illuminating rocket from the Yankee steam-sloop, the girl felt a momentary alarm. Then she realised that it had been aimed to explode over the beach, which meant that the enemy ship had not become aware of the departing *Gabrielle*. Probably the sound of shooting had carried across the water and the sloop had sent up a rocket to expose whoever did it. Telescopes would be pointing towards the beach, possibly some of them powerful enough to make out the nature of the fracas. In which case, seeing three obvious *Americanos del Norte* fighting with a bunch of Mexicans, an investigation would surely be made. There were sufficient deserters from both sides in Mexico to arouse the interest of the Yankee captain, without him guessing the true nature of the trio, and to cause him to attempt their capture.

Clearly the Mexicans realised the danger, those in a position to do so. At the first warning glow of the exploding rocket, the two men still on their feet—one of them holding his bracelet-slashed cheek—turned and fled. Looking like a charging cougar, the youngster launched himself after them.

"Let 'em go, Lon!" barked the big man.

At the words, the youngster skidded to a halt and turned. While the rocket's glow had died away, the fire still gave sufficient light for the girl to study her rescuers closely. Hard, tough as nails, but without the vicious, inhuman cruelty of the Mexican attackers was how the big man struck her; and she prided herself as a judge of human character. For all his shaggy black hair, buckskins and generally unsoldierly appearance, she felt sure that she could identify him.

Then she looked at the second of her rescuers. All the savagery had left his face. Suddenly it took on a handsome cast of almost babyish innocence, apart from the reckless glint that remained in the red-hazel eyes. Young he undoubtedly was, yet she gained the impression that he had spent hard, wild years of growing that had left an indelible mark. Walking across to the man he had killed, the youngster bent down. Such had been his actions on arrival that, taken with his Indian-dark skin pigmentation, the girl thought he meant to scalp his victim. From what she had heard, although her personal experience did not support it, Western men sometimes took scalps. However the youngster did no more than clean the blade of his knife on the body's clothing, then dropped it back into the sheath at the left of his belt.

Before the reaction to her narrow escape, or to how the small Mexican had died, could strike the girl, the big man came up.

"Southrons, hear your country call you," he said, twirling the Dragoon's four pounds, one ounce weight on his finger and dropping the big revolver butt forward in his holster.

Relief flooded over the girl and the fact that the man's words formed the opening line to General Albert Pike,

15

C.S.A.'s stirringly patriotic version of Daniel B. Emmet's song 'Dixie' did not entirely account for it. Maybe her rescuers looked as wild and reckless as the hairiest of the old mountain men, but the taller of them had given a password known only to a few.

"Up lest worse than death befall you," she replied. "You must be Se—."

"We'd best get going, ma'am," the man interrupted. "There'll be a Yankee ship out thatways, I'd reckon."

"Yes."

"Figures. No blockade runner'd be sending up rockets that ways. Warn't there nobody here when you landed?"

"No. I thought that you would be when I saw the beacon."

"Right sorry about that, ma'am," the big man apologised, sensing the undercurrent of anger in her voice. "See, we'd just lit up when—."

"There's a boat coming, *ap*'," the youngster put in, nodding towards the bay.

Swinging around, the girl stared into the blackness; but could make out no sign that he spoke the truth. However the man appeared satisfied with the warning.

"We'd best get going, ma'am," he said. "Grab a hold of that pannier, boy. I'll take the other one."

"Beach ahoy!" bawled a voice from the bay. "Stand fast there!"

"I'd as soon not," drawled the big man, striding towards the trunks.

A point the girl found herself in complete agreement with. However she did not wish to abandon her property. So she darted to where her skirt lay and picked it up, then snatched the parasol's head from the sand. Just as she turned to follow the men, she remembered the wig.

"Don't like to keep on about a thing, ma'am," the youngster remarked in a conversational tone. "But that boat's coming up faster'n a deacon headed for a new still. If we're going, now'd be a real good time to start, or sooner."

Glancing across the bay, the girl could see a shape darker than the surrounding blackness. Yet her wig lay where the little man dropped it, some distance from where she stood.

"Stand or we'll fire on you!" shouted the same voice,

16

coming from the dark shape on the bay.

"Come on!" barked the big man, swinging one of the trunks on to his shoulder. "Let's get off afore he does it."

"Pappy's right, like always, ma'am!" the youngster stated, turning and darting to the second trunk.

Knowing that it weighed over a hundred pounds, the girl ran up and took the trunk's left side handle.

"I'll help you carry it," she said, holding her skirt and parasol in the other hand.

Even if the youngster intended to argue, a shot from the approaching boat halted his words unsaid. The bullet passed between him and the girl as they lifted the trunk between them. Then they followed the big man, running through the circle of the firelight towards the protection of the darkness beyond. Another shot sounded and lead made an eerie 'whap!' in the air by the girl's head. She felt the youngster forcing her to the left and realised that he wanted to put the fire between them and the Yankees.

Two more shots sparked muzzle-blasts through the night, but where the bullets went was anybody's guess. Certainly neither came near the running trio and a moment later they passed into the darkness.

From all appearances the girl's rescuers had made use of the bay and beach on previous occasions. Without hesitation the big man led the way to a level path which ran up the slope. Bushes closed in on either side once they left the smooth sand of the beach and the path curved through them. Rising into the air, another rocket illuminated the area. However the trio offered such a poor target among the bushes that the crew of the Yankee launch wasted no more bullets. Then the rocket burned out and darkness descended once more.

On drawing close to the head of the slope, the big man turned off the track. Followed by the other two, he moved a short way among the bushes and came to a halt.

"Just hunker down here, ma'am," he said, setting the trunk on the ground. "I don't figure the Yankees'll follow us too far."

Superbly fit though she might be, the girl was breathing heavily as she set down her end of the trunk. Looking back, she saw the thirty-six foot long launch run ashore and its crew, under the command of a midshipman sprang out. Armed with Sharps carbines, Navy Colts and cutlasses, the nineteen men fanned out and moved towards the fire. One of them went up to the small Mexican's body and rolled it over. Jerking back as if struck, he turned and vomitted on to the sand.

Turning to speak to the men, the girl suddenly realised that only one of them was standing by her. The youngster who had helped carry her second trunk had disappeared.

Chapter 2

There's Fifteen Thousand Dollars In Them

"Where is he?" the girl gasped, swinging to the big man.

"Who, Lon?" he replied. "Gone back down there a ways to see what the Yankees make of it."

"But they might catch him!" she protested.

"It'd take more'n any bunch of web-footed Yankee scaly-backs to do that, ma'am," drawled the man with complete confidence. "He learned the game from the Comanche."

Satisfied, at least partially, the girl turned her attention back to the beach. Some of the sailors were examining the bodies, two more had raised the girl's first victim to his feet and were supporting him. Another of the party handed something which the girl could not see to the midshipman. For a moment the young warrant officer stood looking at the object, the sailor between him and the watchers on the slope. Then he swung to stare up in their direction. The girl caught her breath, wondering if her younger rescuer had failed to justify his companion's confidence. Then the mid-shipman gave an order and his men returned to the boat carrying the injured man along with them.

"They're going," breathed the girl, watching the launch withdraw into the darkness.

"Figured they'd not stick around to look for us," replied the big man.

Landing on the Mexican coast in such a manner might be construed as an armed invasion; or at best be regarded as an intrusion against the other country's territorial rights. To be caught doing so by the authorities would bring about a bitter exchange of diplomatic letters, if nothing worse. So the sloop's captain had probably ordered his subordinate only to go beyond the beach if certain he could make a speedy capture. Seeing no chance of doing so, the midshipman wisely decided to return to his ship. While they took the Mexican along for questioning, the act could later be

19

excused on the grounds that he needed medical attention.

For five minutes after the launch departed, the man and girl remained silent. Then he turned to face her and she could see his teeth glinting white in a grin as he spoke.

"Now we've time, I'd best introduce myself, ma'am. Sergeant Sam Ysabel, Mosby's Raiders. Boy's my son, Loncey Dalton."

"I'm pleased to meet you, sergeant," the girl answered and spoke genuinely, not in the formal conventional reply. "My name is Boyd—."

"Boyd!" said the youngster, materialising at her side as soundlessly as he had disappeared. "Belle Boyd—The Rebel Spy?"

Although the voice gave the girl a nasty fright, she restrained herself beyong the one startled gasp.

"I'm Belle Boyd," she conceded, a faint smile playing on her lips. "And they do call me the Rebel Spy, I've been told."

"This's surely a privilege and honour, ma'am," Ysabel stated and his voice held a ring of truth. "Mind you, I should've figured who you be as soon as I saw the way you handled that scum down there."

"Lordy lord!" grinned his son. "I've never seed a feller so all-fired took back as when that short-growed *pelado** laid hands on your head and the hair all come off in it."

Respect and admiration showed in both her companions' voices. While pleased with it, the two men's attitude did not entirely surprise the girl. Through the war years supporters of the South had much for which to praise and honour Belle Boyd's name.

Born of a rich Southern family, Belle grew up in a slightly different manner than many of her contemporaries. While receiving instruction in the normal womanly virtues and subjects, her education extended beyond those bounds. Possibly to make up for being unable to have a son, her father taught her many boyish skills. Being something of a tomboy, Belle became an accomplished rider—astride as well as on the formal side-saddle—skilled with pistol, shotgun, rifle or sword and very competent at *savate*, the combined foot and fist boxing of the French Creoles.

*Pelado: A grave or corpse-robber.

Probably the skills would have been put aside and forgotten had it not been for the coming of the War. Shortly before the attack on Fort Sumpter occurred, a drunken rabble of Union supporters raided the Boyd plantation. Before the family's 'downtrodden and persecuted' slaves drove off the mob, Belle's father and mother lay dead and the girl was wounded outside the blazing mansion. Nursed back to health by the Negroes, Belle learned of the declaration of war and sought for a way to take her part. Her parents' murder left a bitter hatred for Yankees that could not be healed by sitting passively at home—not that her home remained. So she eagerly accepted the invitation of her cousin, Rose Greenhow, to help organise a spy ring for the Confederate States.

At first there had been considerable opposition to Southern ladies sullying their hands with such a dirty business as spying, but successes and the needs of the times gained their acceptance. While Rose concentrated on gathering information, Belle took a far more active part. Often in the early days she made long, hard rides through enemy territory to deliver messages and won the acclaim of old General Stonewall Jackson himself. More important missions followed, while Pinkerton and his U.S. Secret Service fumed, raged impotently and hunted Belle. Despite all efforts to capture her, Belle retained her liberty and struck shrewd, hard blows for the South.

Standing in the darkness, Belle tried to study the two men who had saved her life and would be working with her on the mission that lay ahead. She knew little about them except that the Grey Ghost, Colonel John Singleton Mosby, claimed them to be the best men available for her aids.

Sam Ysabel belonged to that hardy brotherhood of adventurers who pushed into Texas and helped open up that great State. Objecting to the taxes levied by distant Washington on the import of Mexican goods, he became a smuggler running contraband across the Rio Grande. Then War came and he joined Mosby's Raiders, to be returned to Texas for the purpose of resuming his old business when the Yankees took Brownsville. Many a cargo of goods brought in through the blockade and landed at Matamoros found its way to Texas, then on to the deep South, by Ysabel's efforts.

While none of the trio guessed it, young Loncey Dalton Ysabel was to achieve a legendary status equal to the Rebel Spy's in the years following the War.* Left motherless at birth, the boy grew up among the people of his maternal grandfather. His mother had been the daughter of Long Walker, war chief of the *Pehnane* Comanche and his French Creole *pairaivo*, head wife.

With Ysabel away on man's business, the boy was raised as a Comanche and taught all those things a *Pehnane* brave-heart must know.† Under skilled tuition, he learned to ride any horse ever foaled, and get more out of it than could any white man. Ability with weapons, always a prime subject, took a prominent part in his schooling. While good with his old Dragoon Colt, he relied mostly on his bowie knife for close range work and called upon the services of a deadly accurate Mississippi rifle when dealing with distant enemies. In the use of both he could claim a mastery equal to the best in Mosby's Raiders. few white men matched his ability in the matter of silent movement, locating hidden foes or hiding undetected where such seemed an impossibility.

All in all the Ysabel Kid—as white folks knew him—would prove as great an asset to Belle's mission as he might have to a raiding party of the Wasps, Quick-Stingers, Raiders, all three of which names had been given by Texans to the *Pehnane*.

Although interested in her companions and grateful to them for saving her from the Mexicans, Belle wondered why she found herself in the position of needing to be saved. However, knowing how little regard for discipline and orders such men usually possessed, she hesitated to ask a question that might mar their relationship. Almost as if reading her thoughts, Ysabel launched into an explanation.

"Right sorry about not being on hand when you landed, ma'am," he said. "We come down and got the fire started ready. Then Lon allowed he heard something, so me 'n'

* How this happened is told in the author's floating outfit stories.
† Told in COMANCHE.

22

him went back to keep the hosses quiet. Didn't want no French patrol sneaking up and asking fool questions. We left Miguel, one of our boys, to tend to the fire. He warn't there when you landed?"

"Those men told me they killed him," Belle replied.

"The bastards—Sorry, ma'am. Only Mig'd been with us a fair time. They must've been slick to get up close enough without him hearing. Time we figured whoever the boy heard'd gone by, you'd landed and the fuss started."

"You came in time," Belle stated, satisfied with the explanation. Then she looked at the Kid. "What did the Yankee sailors make of it?"

"Figured us to be Mexican smugglers tangling with deserters, from what they said," he replied. "That wig of your'n sure got 'em puzzled, though."

"Damn that wig!" Belle snapped. "I knew I should never have left it."

"Too late for worrying now, ma'am," Ysabel pointed out. "Go fetch the hosses up, boy. We'd best get going."

"But your friend—," Belle protested, looking back towards the darkness around the fire.

"He's dead, ma'am. Scum like that don't take prisoners— except maybe in a pretty gal's case and they kill her when they've done. Sooner we pull out, the happier I'll be. Those shots could've been heard by more'n the Yankees."

"Then we'll get going," Belle agreed, turning back to find that the Kid had made another of his silent, eerie departures.

Soon he returned, leading four horses. All were fine animals, but one of them more than the others caught the eye. A big, magnificent white stallion, it looked almost as wild and dangerous as the youngster it followed; leading might be too strong a word in its case, for it walked free behind the Kid.

"Don't go near nor touch that white, Miss Boyd," warned Ysabel, following the direction of the girl's gaze. "My grulla's bad enough, but I do swear that damned white's part grizzly b'ar crossed with snapping turtle. Not that I need tell *you* anything about hosses."

"He looks that way," Belle smiled, accepting the tribute to her equestrian knowledge. "Which horse shall I take?"

"The bay. T'other's ole Mig's. We didn't bring but him along. Figured the less who knowed what brought us down here the better."

"I agree," the girl said, then a thought struck her. "But you don't know why I'm here, do you?"

"No, ma'am," Ysabel admitted. "We'll put those boxes of your'n on the pack hoss and move out."

"Aren't you interested in why we're here?" she asked.

"Sure I am. Only I figure you can tell us just as easy while we're riding as do it here."

Loading Belle's trunks on to the horse took little time as they had been designed to fit the official C.S.A. pack saddle used by the Ysabels. While the men attended to the loading, Belle approached and gained the confidence of the horse allocated to her. Although a powerful mount capable of speed and endurance, it would not be easy to handle. So she counted the time well spent. Swinging into the low-horned, double girthed saddle—experience had taught her that the Texans rarely used the word cinch—she felt the horse move restlessly beneath her. However long experience and a knack with animals enabled her to control her mount, then gain its confidence. As long as she did not commit any blunder of riding or management, she expected no trouble with the bay.

"Lead the way, sergeant," she said, glancing to where her escort were swinging astride their horses. "Head towards Matamoros and I'll tell you our assignment as we ride."

However the chance did not come immediately. Deciding that they must put some distance between themselves and the bay, Ysabel urged his party on at a fast trot. Not until they had covered two miles and were riding along a path through heavily wooded country did he slow down.

"Nobody's following," he said. "Do you want to camp here for the night, or push on, ma'am?"

"Push on," she replied. "I must go to see our consul in Matamoros as soon as I possibly can. Do you know his house?"

"Sure," Ysabel agreed. "And so do the Yankees. Unless you have to go there, I'd say stay long and far away."

"I have to report to him," Belle insisted. "He'll be in a

"muck-sweat to know whether I've arrived or not."

"That figures," the Kid remarked.

"Not for my sake, I assure you," smiled the girl. "But for those trunks. There's fifteen thousand dollars in them."

"Is there that much money in the whole world, *ap*'?" asked the Kid.

"I'd say just a mite more," Ysabel replied. "You're taking one helluva chance telling a couple of border roughnecks like us that, ma'am."

"Not if all Captain Fog told me about you is true, sergeant."

"You know Captain Dusty Fog, ma'am?" Ysabel said.

"We've been on two missions together,*" she replied. "He spoke highly of the part you played in averting the Indian war those two Yankee soft-shells planned to start in Texas."†

"He's quite a feller, that Cap'n Fog," drawled the Kid. "I'd sure like to meet up with him."

Almost a year later the Kid found his chance to meet Captain Dustine Edward Marsden Fog,‡ rated one of the South's three top cavalry raiders and eventually gaining acclaim in other fighting fields.

Ysabel put off more discussion on the matter of Captain Dusty Fog. Satisfied that the girl trusted him, or she would never have given the information about the trunk's contents, he got straight down to business.

"That's a whole heap of money, ma'am," he said. "What's it for?"

"Have you heard of a General Klatwitter?" she asked.

"Is he one of our'n, or their'n?" the Kid inquired.

"Neither," Belle replied. "He's French. At least, he's nominally French. His command is made up of mercenaries from most of Continental Europe. He's at the town of Nava, do you know it?"

"Sure," Ysabel confirmed. "It's in Coahuila Territory, maybe ten-fifteen miles in from the Rio Grande below Piedras Negras and Eagle Pass."

"That's correct. We have to reach him with the money as quickly as possible. Can you do it?"

* Told in THE COLT AND THE SABRE and THE REBEL SPY.
† Told in THE DEVIL GUN. ‡ Told in THE YSABEL KID.

25

"Five to eight days' ride, depending on you and the kind of trouble we run into on the way."

"The Yankee Secret Service don't know this yet," Belle objected.

"I wasn't figuring on them," Ysabel assured her. "We'll have to stay close to the river most of the way and that's mighty rough country. The French and the Mexicans're apt to start shooting first and ask who you are a long second. Then there're deserters from both sides that've come across the river. They're living as best they can and aren't choosey on where they get their pickings. Top of them, there's the usual run of border thieves, white and Mexican. No, ma'am. I count the Yankee Secret Service least of our worries."

"We must get through," Belle told him.

"What'd be so all-fired important about a French general, Miss Belle?" the Kid put in. "There's some'd say we've got more'n enough of our own without worrying about the French."

"Few of our generals can throw an extra thousand men into the field right now," Belle pointed out.

"And this Klack-wicker *hombre* can?" asked Ysabel.

"So he claims. A full regiment of cavalry, armed, trained and loyal to whoever feeds and pays them," Belle replied. "And with a battery of horse artillery to boot."

"That's a tolerable good bargain, all for fifteen thousand dollars," Ysabel commented. "Unless there's more to it."

"What's he fixing to do, ma'am?" the Kid went on. "Come down with us and help Rip Ford take Brownsville back from the Yankees?"

"No. He will march west, cross the Rio Grande into New Mexico, attack La Mesilla and continue north up the Sante Fe trail."

"A thousand men can't take New Mexico," Ysabel objected. "Ole General Sibley couldn't do it with at least twice that many."

"And they was most of 'em *Texans*," his son continued.

"General Klatwitter won't try to *take* it. His objective is merely to raid, do as much damage and grab what loot he can, forcing the Yankees to divert troops badly needed elsewhere to stop him."

"Why'd we need to pay a frog-eater good money to do

26

that, ma'am?" the Kid demanded. "We could send some of our own fellers—."

"We don't have any men to spare," the girl replied simply. "The War is going badly for us and every available man is needed right where he is. But the Yankees aren't in any better shape. Meeting a new attack will force them to withdraw troops from their field commands, they've no reserves worth mentioning."

"From Arkansas?" asked Ysabel.

"In the first place, probably," Belle agreed. "But that's one battle front the Yankees daren't weaken to any great extent."

Which figured to anybody who understood the situation. Under General Ole Devil Hardin, the small Confederate Army of Arkansas held back a superior numbered Yankee force on the banks of the Ouachita River. Given a significant reduction in his enemy's strength, he might even start to push them out of the Toothpick State. Should that happen, it would boost the flagging spirits of the Confederate States armies meeting defeat in the East and encourage them to stand firm.

"And if they can hang on in the East, even without pushing the Yankees back, it will have an effect," Belle went on after explaining the previous points. "Up North there's a growing feeling among the ordinary folks that the War should never have been started and ought to be ended speedily. They're seeing wounded brought back by the train-load, hearing almost daily of kin or friends killed. If their armies can be halted, with the appearance of the War dragging on, the civilian population will start bringing pressure on their Government to make peace."

"Will *our* Government have sense enough to take it, should the Yankees make it?" asked the Kid, in a voice which showed a complete lack of faith in Governmental intelligence.

"If the terms are acceptable, which they will be, I can't see them refusing," Belle replied. "It's accept, or go down in defeat, L—K—."

"Could say either 'Lon' or 'Kid', ma'am," the youngster grinned. "I get called both of 'em—or worse."

"Mostly worse and allus deserved," Ysabel growled.

"You allow this here frog general'll do it, ma'am?"

"Of course. The fifteen thousand is only an advance payment, to be made if I am satisfied he can carry out his end of the bargain. I also have a bank draft for a further thirty-five thousand dollars, payable only after the successful completion of his share of the business."

"Now I don't allow to be smart, like the fellers who dreamed up this fancy twirl-me-round," drawled the big man. "So I was wondering what's to stop this here general just taking the money, standing us again a wall and shooting us, then soldiering on for France. Fifteen thousand'd go a long ways, further when that's all he need do to get it."

"A series of letters and other proof will be placed in the hands of the French as soon as it becomes apparent that he doesn't mean to fulfil his part of the bargain," Belle answered. "The people who produced this scheme are playing for high stakes, sergeant. They won't hesitate to do it."

"Would I be out of line in asking who's behind it, Miss Belle?" the Kid said, guessing from her tone that the Confederate Government had not formulated the scheme even if they approved of it.

"A group of British businessmen; mill owners growing desperate for cotton. They know that if the South loses, the cotton-growing industry will be wrecked for years and with it goes their source of income. It was they who contacted Klatwitter before he left Europe, made the plans and provided the money to put it through. He received orders to sail before payment could be made. So the businessmen put the delivery of the payment in our Government's hands and they passed it on to us."

"May *Ka-Dih* reward 'em for their kindness to a poor lil quarter-Injun boy," drawled the Kid. "I allus did want to die young."

"*Ka-Dih*'s the Comanche Great Spirit, Miss Boyde," Ysabel explained. "I sure hope he's watching over us. There's been some trouble and the French put a curfew on in Matamoros. We'll not get through to the consul's house tonight."

"Then what do we do?" she asked.

"Stop with friends just outside town and move in tomorrow morning," Ysabel replied. "It's the only way."

Chapter 3

Full Of Men Who Want To Rape Me

Standing naked in the tiny attic room of a small inn on the outskirts of Matamoros, Belle Boyd allowed a giggling Mexican girl to apply an oily liquid to her back. Already Belle had used the liquid on her face, neck, arms and other places accessible to her hands; turning the creamy whiteness of her skin to a brown equalling that of her assistant. With so much at stake, Belle could not take the chance of some unfortunate exposure revealing patches of white skin to arouse suspicions. So, explaining her needs to Sam Ysabel, she received the girl's assistance to coat the parts of her body beyond her reach.

"Is it all right, *senorita*?" asked the girl, putting down the depleted bottle of liquid and taking a mirror from the bed.

Carefully Belle studied the reflection of her back. Then she scrutinised every inch of her body, checking behind the ears, under her breasts, beneath her armpits and between her legs. Not until certain that she bore no white flesh to betray her did she nod in satisfaction.

"It will do," she said in Spanish. "*Gracias.*"

"You take much trouble to look like one of us, *senorita*," the girl remarked. "Is it for a man?"

"Yes," Belle answered, deciding such an answer would be more acceptable than any other to her assistant.

"For *Cabrito*?" the girl hissed.

"No!" Belle replied hastily, knowing *Carbrito* to be the Kid's Mexican name. She recalled how the other had greeted the Kid on his arrival and wanted to avoid stirring up a feeling of jealousy. "He and his father are taking me to meet my—my sweetheart."

Clearly the explanation satisfied the girl and her air of hostility evaporated as quickly as it came. Smiling warmly, she indicated the clothing on the bed and suggested that Belle dressed herself.

While donning the clothing of a poor Mexican working girl, Belle thought of the previous night's events.

Although nobody had followed them, Ysabel had set a fast pace and kept clear of trails during the ride to Matamoros. In addition to a desire to avoid attracting attention, the girl felt the Texans might be motivated by a wish to learn her ability at riding a horse through rough country at night. In which case she believed that she had gained their approbation.

On drawing close to the town, Ysabel halted the party and sent the Kid forward to scout their way. Learning on his son's return that a French picket was watching the trail, Ysabel still stated his intention of pushing on to the inn. Once again Belle felt herself being put to a test, but believed that she came through it to the Texans' satisfaction. Moving on foot among the scattered bushes, keeping the horses as quiet as possible, they passed within a hundred feet of the picket and avoided being detected.

If the arrival of the Ysabels at the small inn were any indication, they were highly popular visitors. The owner greeted them warmly, accepting Belle's presence without question. Leading his guests towards his stables, he avoided the front entrance and made his way to the rear. There he raised a dirt-covered trapdoor and lit the way down an incline to a large cellar equipped for housing horses. With the welfare of their mounts attended to, the innkeeper helped the Texans carry Belle's trunks into the main building. Such was Belle's confidence in her companions that she agreed without a moment's thought to them keeping the trunks in their room while she bedded down in the attic.

Over breakfast, Belle and the Ysabels discussed their future arrangements. First she must report to the Confederate States' consul in the town, but knew that doing so would be far from easy. To appear in her present garb of shirtwaist and riding breeches was, of course, out of the question. Nor could she make use of a dress and wig from her trunks. If she knew the Yankee Secret Service, and by that time she figured she did, they were sure to maintain a watch on the consul's house. The arrival of a strange white woman would be noted and steps speedily taken to identify her. When it became obvious that she had not arrived through the normal channels, conclusions—maybe the correct one—would be drawn. Let the Yankees receive but one hint that the Rebel Spy had returned to Matamoros, and they would spare no effort to locate her. The mission ahead stood to be sufficiently dangerous without needlessly adding complications.

Fortunately Belle had come prepared for some such eventuality. A chemist working for her organisation had produced a body stain of exactly the right colour to give her the appearance of a Mexican; easy to apply, quick-drying and—he swore—impervious to soaking in cold water, while hot water and a special soap would remove it with one washing. That and clothing borrowed from the innkeeper's daughter gave Belle a suitable disguise.

Dressing did not take long, for the clothing of a peon girl consisted of only a shift, blouse, skirt and sandals. That meant, Belle concluded as she glanced in the mirror on completion, she could not carry the Dance concealed on her person. Nor would her parasol, even reassembled, be less noticeable in her disguise. So she would have to make do with the knife-bracelet. It would not be out of place or conspicuous among the bangles of the cheap jewellery supplied to complete her attire.

"There is only your hair now, *senorita*," the Mexican girl said. "I have never see—."

"I don't suppose you have," Belle replied in English.

Her hair was kept cut so short for a purpose. In her trunk she carried six wigs—or had until the loss of the red one at the bay—designed by an expert and used to alter her appearance. To wear one of them so that it appeared almost completely natural, she had to keep her own hair cropped close to the skull. At first Belle felt self-conscious when not wearing a wig, but she grew used to it and no longer worried over other people's attitude towards her appearance.

Selecting a wig from the box brought up, Belle tried it on. She stood before the mirror, altering the long black tresses to conform with the style of the girl by her side. A knock sounded at the door as she completed the work. Crossing the room, she opened it. The Kid stood outside. No longer did he wear his buckskins but was dressed in a torn white shirt, ragged white trousers and sandals. A sombrero rode

31

on his head, while a serape draped over his left shoulder. With his Indian-dark skin, he would pass as a peon provided he prevented anybody looking too closely at his face. Those red-hazel eyes would give him away even if his features did not. Glancing at Belle, he opened his mouth to speak, closed it and stared again.

"Miss Belle?" he croaked.

"Will I do?" she smiled.

"I'd say you'll get by," he enthused. "As long as you don't talk too much."

That, Belle knew, would give her away. While she spoke some Spanish, her accent could never get by. However she did not intend speaking any more than possible on the short journey to the house of the Confederate States consul.

Seated alongside the Kid on the small donkey cart, Belle attracted no more than casual attention from the passersby. However only a coating of vegetables lay on the tarpaulin which covered her trunks. Hidden among them lay her Dance and the Kid's Dragoon Colt, while he carried the bowie knife concealed beneath his serape. Belle hoped that they would not find need for the weapons, but carried them in case of detection.

At first all went well. They passed through the narrow streets of the poorer section, entered an area of greater prosperity and moved at a leisurely pace towards their objective.

"Won't be long now, Miss Belle," the Kid commented, sitting with the brim of his sombrero drawn down to shield his face. "Once we're through this business section, we'll soon be at the consul's house."

"I won't be sorry," Belle replied.

They continued along the street, passing the town's best hotel. Ahead of them, a burly French corporal halted. Studying the approaching cart, he stepped from the sidewalk and blocked their way.

"Hey you!" he said in bad Spanish. "Stop that cart!"

"*Si, senor*," Belle answered mildly, jabbing her elbow into the Kid's ribs as a warning for him to control his temper.

"What've you got here?" the corporal demanded, walking forward and eyeing Belle from head to toe.

"Is only vegetables for the market, *senor* general," the

girl replied, satisfied that her accent would pass unnoticed by the Frenchman. "My brother and I bring them to sell."

"Get down, both of you!" the corporal ordered.

Only a few people were using the street at that moment and none displayed too much interest in the scene. Such sights had become common in Mexico since the French began their occupation and they discouraged undue curiosity in their affairs.

Once again Belle jabbed the Kid's ribs and he dropped from the cart to face the soldier.

"Vegetables," the corporal sniffed. "Maybe there're guns under them."

"No, *senor*!" Belle gasped. "Just vegetables. What would simple peons like us want with guns?"

"You Mexicans are all the same, rebels," the corporal answered, glancing at her.

Then, without any warning, he lashed his hand across the Kid's face. The attack came so suddenly that even the Kid's Indian-fast reactions could not avoid it. Caught with a powerful round-house backhand swing, he went sprawling to the ground. Luckily his knife remained hidden, but Belle knew he would not accept the blow without retaliation. Just let him clear his head, and the Kid would be up with knife in hand. Then either he or the Frenchman would die. Whichever way the affair went, her mission would be endangered. So she decided to lure the corporal away before the Kid recovered.

"*Hijo de puta!*" she screamed, catching up a tomato and hurling it.

Letting out a bellow as the tomato struck and burst in his face, the corporal sprang forward. His hands closed on air for Belle bounded from the cart and fled down the alley by the hotel. Determined to take his revenge, the corporal gave chase. He plunged around the rear of the cart, ignoring it completely, and ran after the girl. Immediately the pedestrians hurried away. Since their arrival in the country, French soldiers plundered, committed acts of vandalism or rape unchecked by their officers. Any Mexican who interfered was likely to be shot on the spot as a rebel and troublecauser. So the few people who saw the incident played safe and got clear of its location.

Hoping that the Kid did not recover too quickly, Belle fled down the alley. On either side rose a high wall, at the end another street where she might meet more French troops. behind her clumped the boots of the running soldier. Hoping to throw him off her trail, she darted through a gateway and found that she had entered a cul-de-sac. It was a small plaza, deserted at that moment, where residents of the hotel could take exercise or dine out of doors in private. What Belle found most interesting—and annoying—about the place was that it offered only two ways out; the gate by which she entered and a closed door leading into the hotel.

Even as the facts registered, Belle heard the heavy footsteps of the corporal drawing closer. She could not chance entering the hotel in search of an escape. Such a fancy place probably housed French army officers or officials and any Mexican peon who entered—even for Belle's perfectly good reasons—would just as rapidly be evicted. Should she manage to raise an objection, the corporal would claim he was suspicious. A search of the cart would reveal the trunks. Belle could not see any French commandant turning away a chance to lay hands on fifteen thousand dollars in gold; even if acquiring it meant antagonising the Confederate States Government. Even if her story and identity should be accepted by the French, they might order her out of Mexico rather than become compromised with the United States. In any event, word was sure to reach the Yankee Secret Service and cause a search to be organised to locate her.

So Belle knew that she must handle the matter herself, dealing with the corporal in a way which would dissuade his intentions. Yet she must not kill or seriously injure him. To do either would start an investigation and hunt for the person responsible. Glancing around quickly, she saw nobody at the windows overlooking the plaza to witness what happened. That made dealing with her pursuer easier.

Turning as she reached a side wall, Belle faced the man. A lecherous grin twisted his face as he advanced with arms reaching out to close on her.

"Damned if the country's not full of men who want to rape me," Belle mused. "I admire their taste, but not their style."

34

With the thought come and gone in a flash, she prepared to defend her honour. Just in time she recalled that she was not wearing her riding boots and knew the sandals did not lend themselves to *savate* kicking.

Twisting aside, she tried to dart by the man. His right hand shot out, catching her arm and swinging her around. Doing so put him with his back to the wall. Taking her other arm in his free hand, he pulled her towards him. At first Belle approached with only feeble struggles and face twisted in an expression of panic which lulled any suspicions he might feel at the easy capture. Measuring the distance, she whipped up her right knee at the exact moment when it would do most good. Steel-spring powerful muscles knotted to give force to the rising leg and the loose-fitting, calf-long peon's skirt did nothing to impede its movement. Coming with sickening impact, her knee struck between the man's spread apart legs. Instantly his hands fell away from her arms. Agony knotted up his face as he stumbled back against the wall and started to double over.

Interlacing her fingers, Belle hooked the cupped hands under the corporal's chin and heaved. Lifted erect, he slammed into the wall hard and bounced from it. Nor had Belle finished. She wanted to make sure that the corporal could not raise an alarm for some time to come. Nobody from the hotel appeared to be aware of their presence in the plaza, so she might easily make her escape and reach the safety of the consul's house before he recovered.

With that in mind she caught the right shoulder of his jacket in her left hand, while the right closed on the open neck. At the same moment her right foot rose to ram into his midsection. As he bounced forward from being slammed against the wall, she shot her left leg between his open feet and sank rapidly to the ground. Her weight and the pull on his torso caused the corporal to tilt forward. When her rump landed on the hard-packed soil of the plaza, she thrust upwards with her right leg. The corporal catapulted over, crashed down on his back, bounced once and lay still.

Hoping that she had not done too much damage to her assailant, Belle rolled over and to her knees. Before trying to rise, she shot her hands to her head and adjusted the wig. Then she saw the hotel's side door open and, as she stood up, a man and woman emerged. They came to a halt, staring in surprise at the scene before them. Belle could imagine just how it looked, the corporal sprawled on his back and her standing dishevelled by his head.

Neither of the newcomers had the skin pigmentation nor features of Mexicans; which could mean they were French. However the man did not seem to be of Gallic origin either. Short, blocky, heavily-built, he gave an impression of rubbery hardness rather than fat. His face had a jovial expression belied by the cold, calculating eyes. Clad in a Stetson hat, buckskin jacket, shirt, string tie, trousers tucked into riding boots, with a gunbelt around his waist supporting an 1860 Army Colt in an open-topped holster at the right side and a sheathed Arkansas toothpick on the left, he looked like an American; but not the type to stay in Matormoros' best hotel. If it came to a point, he hardly seemed a suitable escort for the woman.

In height she would equal Belle, some two inches taller than her companion. Black hair framed a good-looking face somewhat marred by an air of superiority. She wore a mauve shirt-waist and a plain black skirt from beneath which showed high-heeled boots suitable for town wear or occasional riding. Full-busted, she trimmed down to a slim waist and out again for the hourglass figure currently regarded as fashionable. Studying her, Belle guessed she would be in her middle thirties. A fine-looking woman, yet hard and intelligent, were Belle's other conclusions.

None of which worried Belle over much at that moment. She realised that something must be done, and fast, to explain away the dramatic scene into which the couple were walking. If the woman were a French officer's or official's wife, she would not overlook what she saw.

Twisting her face into what she hoped would be suitable lines of fear, Belle lurched across the plaza. Collapsing to her knees before the woman, she began to babble out an incoherent version of what happened. The effort taxed all her knowledge of Spanish, but she hoped that the man and woman attributed mistakes in grammar or pronunciation to fright rather than the real cause. She also kept her face averted, in case she failed to adopt a sufficiently convincing expression to go with the hesitantly spluttering words. Then she received something of a shock herself. So much so that she darted a quick glance at the woman and studied her with extra interest.

"What's she talking about, Mr. Kraus?" asked the woman.

Not in French, but speaking English with a clipped New England accent and the tone of one who had received a good education.

Hearing the words almost made Belle forget her pose. However she regained it quickly as the man replied. From his accent, he hailed out of Texas and he clearly understood Spanish better than his companion.

"She allows the soldier tried to lay hands on her, from what I can make out," he told the woman. "Gal's so spooked she don't talk too clear. Reckons she got scared and run in here. When he caught her, she pushed him off and he fell. Must've caught his nut one hell of a crack. Anyways, now she's worse scared that the soldiers'll come and shoot her. She wants you to talk up for her to your husband. Must allow you're some frog's missus."

Keeping up her scared babble, after the one brief pause, Belle continued to dart glances up at the woman. The guess at the age seemed close enough, for her skin showed the coarsening of time. Although she wore some good jewellery, a wedding ring was not included. Annoyance showed on the woman's face as she turned her eyes in Belle's direction. Just in time Belle dropped her head forward, not wishing to let a Yankee woman see too much of her features.

"Get her out of here!" the woman snapped in the tone of one used to giving orders. "We don't want to be mixed up in trouble between the French and Mexicans."

Clearly neither she nor the man felt any suspicion that Belle was lying. Bending down, she gently helped Belle to stand up. The girl kept her head bowed and allowed her shoulders to jerk as if sobbing.

"Come on, girl!" the man ordered in Spanish, taking her by the arm and turning her towards the gate. "Go back to your people. The lady'll not let them follow you. *Vamos, pronto!*"

Deciding not to push her luck further, the girl stumbled from the plaza. She heard the woman tell the man to give her a head start, which suited her too. Once through the gate, she discarded her terror-stricken pose and started to turn along the alley.

A shape loomed before her, bringing her to a halt. Raising her head, and ready to launch an immediate *savate* attack, she found herself faced by the Kid. Anger showed on his face, while the bowie knife in his hand told what had brought him off the street. Then relief flickered across his features at the sight of the girl. He opened his mouth to speak and Belle saw the danger. If the man and woman in the plaza heard a voice speaking English, they were sure to investigate. Finding only two Mexican peons in the alley would arouse their suspicions. So Belle took steps to avoid it.

"My brother!" she said loudly in Spanish. "It is all right. I am not harmed. A great lady saved me."

Give the Kid full credit; he might be boiling with rage and full of a desire for revenge, but he could still think. Darting a glance at the gate-way, he slid the knife back into its sheath beneath the serape.

"Are you all right, ma'am?" he asked in English, but barely higher than a whisper.

"Yes. Come on, let's get back to the cart. I've quietened him down."

"For good?"

"I hope not. Let's move. There's no time to lose."

"Damn it, that lousy frog-eater knocked me down!" the Kid growled. "I'll just go—."

"To that cart!" Belle ordered. "Believe me, Lon. I've paid him back in full for hitting you."

38

Chapter 4

There'll Be Blood Spilled Afore We're Through

For a moment the Kid stood glaring towards the plaza. To the grandson of Long Walker and a *Pehnane tehnap'** in his own right, it went hard to take a blow without repaying the striker in full. However he studied the grim set of the girl's face and knew she would brook no arguments. Good sense helped him to reach the right decision. Turning, he walked with the girl to the waiting cart. Not until they sat behind the plodding donkey did he ask the questions seething inside him.

"What happened in there?"

"Like I said, I handled the corporal and he won't be bothering us for a spell," Belle replied, turning to look back along the street. Seeing no sign of the man and woman, she concluded they must have left the alley by its other entrance.

"Anybody see you do it?" asked the Kid.

"A man and woman."

"Mexicans?"

"No," Belle answered. "Americans. That's why I stopped you talking to me in English back there."

"I figured there must be some reason," the Kid grinned. "Only damn me if I could see it. Who were they, Miss Belle, some of our folks?"

"No," she said definitely, then described the pair.

"Feller's Charlie Kraus, I'd say," the Kid drawled at the conclusion. "Woman don't come to mind, though."

"She did say 'Mr. Kraus', or some such name," Belle admitted.

"That *posada's* not Charlie's sort of place," the Kid commented. "Fact being, I'm tolerable surprised they let him inside and I sure hope they didn't leave nothing lying loose with him there."

"Who is he?" she asked.

* *Tehnap'*: an experienced warrior.

39

"A border jumper, like pappy and me—only I'd not thank anybody to class us with him."

"What does he do?"

"Anybody," the Kid replied laconically. "Kept out of the Army when the War started. Fought Injuns and bad Mexicans for a spell, so I heard. Then he started running blockade stuff across the river into Texas."

"For the Confederacy?"

"For him and his partner, a skinny-gutted—sorry, ma'am —*hombre* called Joe Giss. They run in the luxury stuff that pays best."

Being operated mainly by private individuals interested in making a profit, the blockade running ships carried more than essential goods for the Confederate States. Luxury items commanded a high price, so much so that the Confederate Government laid down rules as to the proportion that might be brought in. However some of the captains still ran complete non-essential cargoes, relying on unscrupulous men to dispose of them.

"I don't like the sound of this, Lon," Belle admitted.

"Or me. Among other things, Giss and Kraus do dirty work for the French and Mexicans both. If Charlie Kraus's around and gets to hear about that money, there'll be blood spilled afore we're through."

"We'll just have to stop him getting to hear," Belle stated.

"He's got mighty handy ways of finding things out," warned the Kid. "What do you make of the woman? Way you tell it, she's not his kind."

"I don't know. No wedding ring, which means she's not a wife from the Yankee consul's office. Unless she's cheating on her husband."

"Not with Charlie Kraus, or at that *posada*. Might be working for some Yankee ship-owner though."

Belle admitted the possibility. Although New England stood high on the anti-slavery vote that had helped start the War, a number of its businessmen held shares in blockade running ships and indirectly sold goods to the South. So the woman could be acting as a go-between for such people. The number of men called into the Army caused many women to handle what had previously been male work, especially in the industrial Northern States.

Seeing the consul's house ahead, Belle put all thoughts of the woman from her head. If she was no more than a go-between for blockade runners, it seemed unlikely that their paths would cross again.

Donated by a Southern businessman, the consul's house was a fine, large building standing in its own grounds and surrounded by a high wall. Since assuming its new function, broken glass had been fixed to the top of the wall as a bar-rier against intruders. In addition, a Confederate infantry private stood guard at the front and rear entrances. Know-ing that a vegetable cart would not be allowed in at the front under normal circumstances, Belle steered their vehicle around to the rear. As she approached the gate, the sentry moved forward to block her path.

"What's this?" he demanded.

"Vegetables for the consul, *senor,*" Belle replied, not wanting to make her true identity known in so public a place. Across the street were other large houses in their own grounds and she would be willing to bet the U.S. Secret Service owned or rented one from which the consul's prop-erty could be kept under observation. However the sentry showed no sign of moving.

"We've got all we want from our regular feller," he said. scowling suspiciously at the cart. *"Vamos!"*

"I think you should ask the corporal of the guard to come and see our vegetables, *senor,*" Belle answered, hoping the man would have sufficient intelligence to take the hint. When he did not, she continued, "Perhaps the corporal will not like it if you send us away."

Still the words failed to bring the desired result. Annoy-ance showed on the guard's face and he started to move for-ward in a menacing manner. "Damned if I don't take a chance on i—!"

Then he came to a halt as if running into an invisible wall. His bugged-out eyes seemed magnetized to the bowie knife which slid into view from beneath the Kid's serape and lined its needle-sharp point at the centre button of his tunic. Held low and in a position that only the sentry might see it, the bowie knife gave added menace to the Comanche-mean lines of the Kid's face.

"Get the hell out of our way, foot-shuffler," the youngster

growled in a pure Texas voice, "afore I come down and whittle your head top to a point."

And he looked mean enough to try it, what with the incident outside the hotel and a complete lack of patience in face of stupidity.

Nor had the use of a cavalryman's derogatory term for an infantry soldier escaped the sentry's notice, adding to his sudden realisation that the couple on the cart were far more than itinerant vegetable sellers. Having been employed as a guard at the consul for over a year, the soldier could guess what kind of people he was facing. Spies in disguise did not expect to have their identities revealed and possessed sufficient influence high up to make life uncomfortable for any mere private who crossed them. Maybe his present employment lacked the glamour of active service, but he preferred to remain at it rather than be returned to his regiment. So he stepped back and prepared to let the visitors enter.

"Act *just* as you would on an ordinary call like this!" Belle ordered, speaking English for the first time. "If you point out the kitchen, do it. Or take us there if that's what you normally do."

Should there be a Yankee watching, he must see everything done in a normal manner.

"Yes'm!" the sentry replied, but he had sense enough not to make the change in his demeanour too obvious. "I should shout up the corporal of the guard, ma'am."

"Then do it," Belle snapped. "We haven't all day."

"No, ma'am! Yes'm! Corporal of the guard! Back gate for the corporal of the guard!"

On his arrival, the corporal of the guard proved to have a better grasp of the situation than the sentry. Which did not surprise Belle, who remembered him from her last visit. In fact she knew that, despite the two stripes on his sleeves, Rule Shafto drew the pay and held the rank of captain in the Confederate States Army. Of slightly over medium height, he possessed the kind of average build and features which defy description. On occasion he could pose as Mexican, from hildalgo down to peon, a French soldier, or a border drifter as tough and coarse as any of that breed and escape detection.

42

"Vegetables for the consul, *senor* captain," Belle greeted in a low voice. "Hello, Rule."

"Pass them in, Tidd," Shafto ordered, without giving a sign of the surprise he must have felt.

"Yo!" answered the sentry, stepping aside.

"I had less trouble getting in last time," Belle smiled as the cart rolled through the gate.

"You looked different then," Shafto replied, for on the previous visit she had posed as the *amie* of a Confederate 'general'. "Tidd's not the quickest thinker around. Comes in handy if we want the Yankees to know something. There's one of 'em buys him drinks regularly for what can be learned. Not that that's much. I make good and sure he sees nothing."

"How about seeing us?" Belle asked.

"I'll keep him away from the cantina until you've finished your assignment. What brings you back here, Belle?"

"A big one. You know Corporal Ysabel?"

"Sure. Hi, Lon. Where's your pappy?"

"Down to ole Ramon's *posada*," the Kid replied.

"Act natural," Shafto warned. "The Yankees own that house back there and keep a feller in one of the top floor rooms watching us all the time."

"That's bad!" Belle breathed. "I've two trunks in the cart that we have to take inside."

"Easy enough done," Shafto assured her. "We put up that cabin—for the guard—when we took over. The Yankees can't see behind it and we always unload stuff for the kitchen there."

Belle had already noticed the small cabin, obviously of later construction than the rest of the building, standing to one side. Instead of driving towards the rear doors, she directed the cart around the cabin and found it concealed another entrance to the kitchen.

While members of the Negro domestic staff unloaded the cart, the Kid looked around him. Although he received information and instructions from Shafto, this was his first visit to the consul's house. The French knew about the blockade runners using Matamoros, but preferred that the Confederate States consul did not take an active part in it.

43

So all contact with the Ysabel's superiors took place well away from the house.

At the rear of the building lay a small open plaza and a truck garden. Along each side and, he presumed, to the front, were well cared for gardens with a number of thick, flowering bushes scattered around. Too many, to the Kid's way of thinking, for they offered places of concealment a skilled man might use. However the high wall, with its topping of jagged glass, and the sentries at front and rear seemed to rule out the chances of anybody making use of the cover.

"Here you are, Lon," Belle said, holding out the Dragoon Colt. "Let's go inside and see the consul."

Already the trunks were being carried inside. Following them, Belle, the Kid and Shafto passed through the kitchen and to the front hall. The servants set down the trunks by one of the doors leading from the hall and Shafto went through it. Trying to tuck the Colt into his waist band, the Kid found its weight too much for the piece of rope which acted as a belt.

"Damn it!" he growled.

"Leave it on the trunks with mine," Belle suggested. "You're not likely to need it in here."

"Mr. Garfield won't keep you a couple of minutes, Belle," Shafto announced, returning from the room. "He has a visitor. Don't worry, he'll show him out through the library."

While waiting, Belle told Shafto of her run-in with the French corporal. When she mentioned the pair of Ameri-ans, he nodded his head.

"Her name's Corstin, Emily Corstin," Shafto said. "Cousin of Hayter, the Yankee consul and down here on a visit. Or so I heard. Only that doesn't tell us why she'd be with a border rat like Charlie Kraus."

"I think Miss Corstin will bear watching," Belle re-marked.

"So do I, now," Shafto agreed. "I'll see to that."

Soon after, the room's door opened and Winston Gar-field, the consul, came out. A tall, well-built, elegantly-dressed man, he covered ability under a mantle of amiable pomposity.

"My dear Miss Boyd," he greeted, looking her over from head to toe. "I'd never have recognised you-all. Come in, come in. I'm sorry for keeping you waiting, but that was the harbour-master come for his weekly pay-off."

"You know why I'm here?" Belle asked, leading the way into the consul's comfortably furnished study.

"Of course," Garfield admitted. "Have a seat, Miss Boyd. May I offer you a glass of wine?"

"I think I could use one," Belle smiled. "Have you met Corporal Ysabel?"

"Not officially," Garfield answered. "But I've seen the results of your work, young man."

"Thanks," the Kid replied, feeling just a touch uncomfortable in the luxurious surroundings. "Pappy said to tell you he'd bring down some more of that wine on the next trip."

"Hum! Yes!" Garfield sniffed. "And now, to business. I trust everything has gone smoothly so far, Miss Boyd?"

"Well enough," she said. "We ran into a little difficulty on the way to the bay, but it all worked out."

While the others talked, the Kid looked around the room. Then his eyes went to the window which overlooked the gardens on the left side of the building. The upper part of the sash had been lowered to allow a cooling breeze to circulate around the room, but that did not interest him. Even as he looked, he caught the brief flicker of a colour alien to its surroundings in the garden. Constant alertness had been a lesson taught from early childhood and the sight sent a warning ringing in his head.

"Is there anybody working in the garden?" he asked, cutting into the conversation without hesitation.

"Not on this side of the house," Shafto replied. "There never is when the harbour-master calls."

Before the reply was half completed, the Kid started across the room towards the window. He intended to raise the lower sash on his arrival and check that his eyes were not playing tricks, but saw there would be no time. That flicker of colour had been no trick of light or imagination. A man was darting through the bushes away from the house.

Hurling himself forward in a rolling dive, the Kid went through the window in a cloud of shattering glass and framework. Behind him Garfield let out a startled squawk. Equally surprised, Belle and Shafto followed on the Kid's heels. They did not know why he was acting in such a manner, but figured he must have a mighty good reason.

While falling to the ground, the Kid found time to curse his luck in not having the old Dragoon available. The man running away from the window must be stopped and had a good head start to be run down in a foot-race. Then another fact ripped into him. A flicker of dark blue had attracted his attention, but the fleeing men wore buckskins of a tawny colour. That meant there must be two interlopers in the garden. Locating the second of them became a matter of vital importance to the Kid's continued well-being.

Not that the locating took much accomplishing. Catching a movement from the corner of his eye, the Kid swung his head to make a closer examination. To the side of the window, dark blue shirt and all, was the second man, a lean, vicious-looking half-breed armed with a knife and already moving forward to use it. Holding his weapon Indian fashion, with the blade below the hand, the man launched a sideways stroke aimed at the Kid's neck. No white man could have avoided the attack, but the man struck at a part Comanche.

Landing with a cat-like agility, the Kid dropped his right knee to the ground, thrusting his left leg behind him and lowering the left hand for added support. The other's knife almost brushed the black hair as it passed over the Kid's head. Then the young Texan launched an attack of his own. While thinking and acting like a *Pehnane tehnap'*, he gripped the bowie in the fashion of skilled white knife-fighter With the blade rising ahead of his thumb and forefinger, he could thrust, cut, or chop with equal ease. He chose the latter, swinging the knife around like a woodman chopping fire-kindling. A scream broke from the man as the razor-edged blade tore across his body. Designed by a man who had given much thought to perfecting it as a fighting weapon, the bowie knife possessed the deadly qualities of a cavalry sabre. It ripped across the man's body, laying through the flesh and into the vitals below.

"*A:he!*"

Once again Belle heard the deep-throated sound break

from the Kid's lips. Still she could not guess whether it be words or a grunt caused by a strenuous effort. Few white people could have given her the answer, for those who heard that particular sound rarely lived to discuss it. It was the Comanche coup cry, 'I claim it!' given when a brave achieved his ambition of killing an enemy by personal contact.

"Close the gates!" Shafto roared through the window.

Ignoring the stricken man, the Kid rose like a sprinter starting a footrace and went after the second man. Already the other had disappeared around the rear of the building. Mingled with Shafto's warning yell came a startled shout from the back entrance's sentry. Then a revolver barked, followed by the crack of a rifle. The Kid heard a bullet strike the wall of the house and scream off in a ricochet, so guessed that the sentry had been hit and was firing wild.

Belle's hand flew to the top of her skirt as Shafto plunged out of the window. Then she realised that the garment did no possess means of speedy removal; which, in view of the skimpy nature of her sole piece of underclothing, was probably just as well. However a peon girl's attire did not impede rapid movement, so she found little difficulty in leaping out after the man. Then she raced across the garden, following the departing Kid.

Bursting from the bushes, the young Texan looked across the truck garden to the rear entrance. The sentry lay on the ground, his smoking rifle at his side, but the Kid paid little attention to him. More important right then was the sight of the gate closing. Uncaring for the danger he might do, the Kid charged across the truck garden. He reached the gate and grabbed its handle, tugged and let out a low curse. In passing on his arrival, he had seen a key in the gate's lock. It was no longer there. That lean cuss in the buckskins had been a man of some nerve, taking the time to extract the key and using it to increase his chances of escape.

Transferring the blood-smeared blade of the bowie knife to between his teeth, the Kid drew back a couple of paces from the gate. Then he sprang forward and leapt, his hands catching the top. Even as he began to haul himself up, Belle and Shafto appeared at the one end of the building, while the sentry from the front gate came around the other corner.

"Look out, Lon!" Belle screamed. "Drop back!"

Brought from his post by Shafto's shout, the sentry came ready for trouble. When he saw the Kid climbing the gate, he drew an erroneous—if understandable—conclusion. Whipping the Enfield rifle to his shoulder, he took aim and prepared to bring down the absconding 'Mexican'. He heard the girl's yell, but realised he might be making a mistake just too late to halt the final rearward movement of the trigger.

At Belle's warning, the Kid released his hold and dropped back to the ground. Nor did he move a moment too soon. The Enfield's bullet kicked splinters from the top of the gate a scant couple of inches above his head. Spitting the bowie knife back into his hand as he landed, the Kid turned towards the girl.

"He's locked the gate on the outside," he explained.

"I'll go over and open it," Shafto answered. "See to Tidd, will you, Belle?"

"Of course," she replied, dropping to her knees at the soldier's side. "Did you see who the man was, Lon?"

"Not for sure," the Kid admitted. "A tall, lean cuss in buckskins. But I know the *pelado* who was with him. It was one of Charlie Kraus' boys—Damn it! The feller who got away was Joe Giss most likely."

"Get some of the servants out here, sentry," Belle told the soldier who came up. "He's got a crease across his scalp, but nothing worse."

"Joe Giss allus was a lousy shot with a hand-gun," the Kid commented. "Reckons to be something real special with a rifle, though." Then he looked around him. "Reckon somebody'd best start finding out how they got in."

Chapter 5

Now They Know You're Here, Belle

Following on the Ysabel Kid's heels, Belle Boyd watched a masterly display in the art of reading tracks. As he moved across the garden, the Kid pointed out small marks on the ground which she could barely see, much less attribute any significance to. He showed her where the two men had lain hidden among a thick clump of bushes before advancing cautiously towards the window and inadvertently attracting his attention. Then he retraced the route they had taken to reach their vantage point. Close to the wall, he ducked under another bush and pulled out a strange-looking object. It appeared to be a saddle's seat without the horn, cantle, tree or other fittings. A number of scratches and cuts in the leather of the inner side gave a clue to its purpose.

"They used it to climb the wall," Belle said. "Threw it on top to cover the glass and climbed over on it."

"Yep," agreed the Kid. "Come over afore day-break and hid out."

"How did they plan to get out?"

"Same way, I guess, unless something went wrong."

"You mean they'd stay here all day until after dark?"

"Why sure," the Kid answered. "Ole Joe Giss's long on patience and so was the 'breed. Happen nobody disturbed 'em, they'd lie up under the bushes and could watch everything that happened in this side of the house. They've done it afore. Not every day, but regular enough."

"That's going to please Winston Garfield!" Belle commented.

"As long as he don't lay too much blame on Rule Shafto," the Kid replied. "Rule's got more'n plenty on his hands one way and another. And he's from Virginia, they don't get trained right down there. Joe Giss learned watching and not being seen from Injuns."

"It's not for me to lay blame," Belle smiled, recognising

49

a hint of rebuke in her companion's voice.

Certainly Shafto did have plenty of work on his hands, controlling and operating in the Confederate spy ring based on Matamoros and organising the blockade runners. So he might be excused for not having located the two men. Such a contingency would evade most people, although it was easy to be wise and raise points after the event.

"Why'd they risk coming up to the window?" the Kid said, half to himself. "It's not like Joe Giss to take chances."

"Probably they wanted to see who we were," Belle guessed. "Or to try to hear what was said. How long had they been there?"

"I dunno. Not long, but maybe long enough to hear Mr. Garfield say your name. He talks kinda loud and they'd be able to hear him."

"Yes," Belle agreed, realising the implications of what the Kid told her. "Even if the man wasn't Giss, he must be working for the Yankees. No matter what Garfield told the French patrol, the two of them didn't come just to commit robbery."

Almost as soon as Shafto had climbed over the gate and unlocked it, a French lieutenant and half-a-dozen soldiers arrived to investigate the shooting. They belonged to a small force assigned to the task of policing the town and were clearly under orders to prevent open trouble between members of the Confederate and United States consular staffs. Stalling the French long enough for Belle and the Kid to hide in the house, Shafto then allowed them to enter the grounds and offered an explanation for the shooting which Garfield backed up. As the French authorities did not wish to antagonise either of the warring sides north of the border, the lieutenant made only a brief examination of the grounds and left apparently satisfied.

"Reckon he believed the story?" asked the Kid.

"He accepted it," Belle replied. "Can they trace the half-breed to Giss?"

"He's one of their regular bunch. Happen they try at it, they could tie him in with Giss 'n' Kraus."

"I doubt if they'll bother. But, if that man did hear my name, we're in for trouble, Lon."

A view to which Shafto subscribed when he heard the Kid's findings. They gathered in Shafto's private quarters at the rear of the building and he listened to the other two before adding his quota.

Already there had been a noticeable increase in the Yankees' surveillance of the building. By the time he climbed the gate, Shafto could see no sign of the man who had escaped; which led him to believe that the other had entered the Yankee-owned house across the street. On hearing the man's report, the Yankees worked fast. Usually they maintained a watch from only one upstairs room of their houses at front and rear of the consul's property. When Shafto last checked, there had been four observers training telescopes from positions where they could cover almost all of the grounds and building. The increased scrutiny gave mute testimony that the man had heard Belle's name and that the Yankees regarded the Rebel Spy's arrival in Matamoros as being the prelude to trouble.

"They'll cling like leeches now they know you're here, Belle" Shafto warned.

"I know," she replied. "I think we could get by them and on our way in the dark, but they'd soon come looking. If only we could throw them off our trail—." She paused, then went on, "Suppose we make them believe that I've achieved the purpose of my visit?"

"How do you mean?" Shafto inquired; while the Kid sat and listened, ready to give any help he could.

"What's the most significant recent Yankee development, either here or in Brownsville?"

"There was a ship arrived yesterday across the river, with six of those thirty-foot steam launches as its deck cargo. And the *Waterbury*, a steam sloop, came in this morning."

In a trip down the Mississippi River aboard a submersible warship during her second mission with Dusty Fog, Belle had seen one of the U.S. Navy's thirty-foot steam launches. She also knew of them in connection with Lieutenant William B. Cushing's successful attack on the Confederate ironclad war-ram *Albermarle*. Small, fast, carrying up to ten men, armed with a spar torpedo and 12-pounder boat howitzer, the steam launches proved effective craft in shallow waters.

51

"Those launches could mean the Yankees are planning stronger offensive action against the blockade runners," Belle remarked. "Catch them close in, when they're not expecting trouble. Two fully manned launches could deal with any blockade runner, even without using their torpedoes."

"Or they might be planning to raid up the Rio Grande," Shafto went on. "I've been expecting the Mississippi Squadron to try something like that down here ever since the Yankees took Brownsville."

"Either's possible," Belle admitted. "Launches would be ideal for running up the Rio Grande, raiding and hunting for your supply trains, Lon."

"Yes, ma'am," agreed the Kid.

"Then they're what we need," the girl stated. "Let's see if we can make the Yankees believe I came down here to warn you about the launches and help in their destruction. That may throw them off the real trail."

"It might at that," Shafto answered. "And it's important enough for our folk to send *you*."

Belle accepted the compliment without comment; although she could not help but compare it with the open, or thinly hidden hostility that had often greeted her in the early days of the War.

"Can we bring it off?" she asked. "I mean, have we the means of doing it?"

"Sure we have," Shafto insisted. "I've been gathering equipment for a strike at the Yankee shipping in Brownsville harbour when the time was right."

"What kind of equipment?" Belle inquired, although she could guess.

"Torpedoes. I've a couple of keg floaters and one of the new drifting kind hid out down by the river. One of our raiders landed them at the bay where you came in, Belle, and Lon helped bring them here."

"How can you be sure the Yankees'll know you're in the game, Miss Belle?" the Kid put in. "It could be Cap'n Rule here, or ole Rip Ford from across the river doing it."

"They'll know I'm involved," Belle said quietly. "You see, they're going to capture me."

"You'd best tie that a lil tighter for a half-smart lil Texas boy like me to follow," the Kid drawled. "How's you getting captured by the Yankees going to help *us*?"

"It won't," Belle smiled. "Unless I can escape once they've seen and recognised me. I've an idea that might work."

Listening to the girl's scheme, Shafto and the Kid decided that it might just work, given careful organisation plus a little luck. It would be risky in the extreme, but the girl felt that the ends justified the means.

"How do we get a boat in close enough to do it?" asked the Kid. "I reckon the Yankees'll keep some sort of guard out."

"They have a guard boat working the mouth of the bay," Shafto supplied. "And the *Waterbury's* moored well out. Both her and the other ship will have some of the crew rowing guard. It won't be easy to get in close. I planned to send the torpedoes down with the current, let it carry them into the bay and hope for the best."

"We must have something a bit more certain than that," Belle stated.

For a minute almost none of them spoke, each turning over the problem in silence. Then the Kid broke it.

"Didn't I see a big ole tarpon in the kitchen when I come through?"

"It could be," Shafto answered. "The staff either buy them, or go out and catch them for the table."

"Best time to catch 'em's at night," the Kid said, almost to himself; then he looked at Shafto. "How well can you trust those folk of your'n?"

"They've had my life in their hands before now," the man replied. "And you and your father's too when they've carried messages from me to you."

The Kid nodded and grinned. "No offence. It's only that I've got a fool notion that just might work."

After hearing the Kid's suggestions, Belle and Shafto agreed that he had come up with a sound answer to the problem. Then Belle brought up the matter of the weapons they would be using in the attack.

As the adversary mainly concerned with defence, the Confederate States put 'torpedoes' as a major item in their naval armoury. The term covered what would later be known as mines, rather than missiles fired through the water. Showing great originality, the Confederate States Navy's Torpedo Bureau—established early in the War—produced many lethal devices ranging from simple bombs disguised as lumps of coal—which, smuggled aboard enemy vessels, exploded when fed into the engineroom furnaces—to complicated mines detonated in a variety of ways.

To her relief, Belle learned that the torpedoes in Shafto's store were of the uncomplicated variety. That would be of great help in the work ahead. So she went into further details, planning with care and trying to leave as little to chance as possible. Not until satisfied that all had been arranged and fully understood did she give the order for the other two to start. Neither questioned her right to command. In addition to risking her life by allowing the Yankees to capture her, she held the honorary—but no less official—rank of colonel in the C.S.A. Granted to her by the Confederate high command, the rank served when dealing with officious, or conservative members of the armed forces who still clung to the belief that a woman's place was in the home.

The Kid left the house accompanied by Shafto, headed for the *posada* to inform his father of the latest developments. Once clear of the building, they separated—much to the annoyance of the Yankee who followed them—and Shafto went to make certain purchases from a store on the waterfront that catered mainly for the gringo trade.

There being no further point in trying to conceal her identity, Belle did not try. In fact the plan called for her to make sure the Yankees knew she was in the house. So she asked the servants to prepare a bath for her and went up to the room Garfield allocated to her. At her request, he placed her in a room at the front and with windows facing the house from which one bunch of Yankees was keeping watch. The next move in her plan did not come easily to a girl of Belle's upbringing, but she went through with it just the same.

Entering the room, she crossed to the windows and stood where she might be seen yet give the impression that she was trying to avoid letting it happen. At that distance she could only make out a vague shape with the naked eye, but knew a telescope would reveal more. If the Yankees were doing their work properly, one of them ought to have spotted her by that time. So she turned and walked across to where her trunks stood at the end of the bed. Looking back, she could still see the windows of the other house and knew she would be just as visible through the telescopes of the Yankee observers.

"In which case, you're going to see a lot of me," she thought, opening one of the trunks to take out her shirt, riding breeches, boots, gunbelt and other clothing. "I hope your eye-balls bulge out so far they stick in the telescopes."

After which sentiment, she stripped off the Mexican clothing, standing where the men across the street could see her through the window. With any amount of luck they were watching, maybe even passing word for their less fortunate colleagues to come and enjoy the view. When sure that she had given the watchers enough time, she slipped on a robe and sat down to wait until told her bath was ready. By all fair means, her presence at the consulate should be well established already. However she must make certain and continue to let herself be seen around the house.

The Confederate chemist's claims about his skin-dye proved to be true, for it came off in the bath and left Belle looking her usual self. Returning to her room, she repeated the process of cautiously letting herself be seen at the window, then returned to the end of the bed and dressed in her male clothing. If the Yankees across the street had seen her the first time, she dare bet they were watching in the hope of another view. Which meant they would notice the change in her skin's colour and be even more certain that the Rebel Spy was back.

After an absence of almost two hours, Shafto returned with the required purchases. He delivered them to the girl and found that they met with her approval.

"Did you have any trouble?" she asked.

"Not much," Shafto answered. "We picked up a Yankee outside the house and he followed me when we split up. But I lost him before I went near the store to buy the clothes. He was lucky, that Yankee."

"Why?"

"If he'd gone after the Kid, I don't think he'd've come

back. Those Ysabels play the game for keeps."

"I can imagine they would," Belle smiled grimly. "That boy scares me."

"That *boy* scares a whole heap of grown men along the border," Shafto told her. "I went down to the waterfront to see what's happening across the bay and have word sent to Colonel Ford, asking him not to make any moves against the Yankees tonight if he could avoid it."

Belle nodded in satisfied agreement. Despite his failure to locate the two men in the garden, she knew Shafto to be a shrewd, capable agent. Only the fact that he could not be spared from his work in Matamoros, and his absence would probably be noticed, had prevented him from being assigned the task of delivering the money to General Klatwitter. Many men in Shafto's position would have protested, maybe even have acted in a sulky, uncooperative manner under the same circumstances. He not only gave the girl every aid, but showed himself capable of acting on his own behalf when a forgotten point arose.

Across the Rio Grande, Colonel 'Rip' Ford commanded a small force trying to retake Brownsville from the Yankees. Trained in Indian warfare, Ford wore down the superior enemy strength by raids, alarms and darting attacks. If he should launch one that night, the Yankee ships would be on the alert; far more so than might be the case otherwise.

"Will Colonel Ford cooperate?" she asked.

"He always has before," Shafto assured her. "The situation across the bay's still the same. Three of the launches have been lowered from the ship, but haven't left the harbour. Up to the time I left, only the *Waterbury* had put out its chain armour."

As a precaution against attacks by torpedo or war-ram, Yankee ships at harbour or lying off Southern ports often hung a curtain of 'chain armour' around their sides from about eight feet above the water-line and extending some twenty-four inches below the surface. Made of lengths of chain-cable lashed together and suspended from a rod, the 'armour' offered some protection and lessened the effect of a ram's charging impact or torpedo's explosion.

"The new drifting torpedo's designed to go under the armour," Shafto replied. "By the way, I've arranged for a good man to follow that Corstin woman when she comes back to the hotel."

"That's good," Belle said. "I've a feeling there's more to her being here than meets the eye."

They stood in the hall talking and then went on with their plan for confusing the Yankees. Returning to her room accompanied by a Negro maid, Belle changed into a dress. She handed the male clothing to the maid and asked, with gestures, for it to be washed. Sure that the Yankee watchers read her scrubbing motions correctly, and would see nothing wrong in a Southern girl expecting a coloured servant to wash clothes worn only for a short time, she followed the maid from the room. Then, to the maid's surprise, she cancelled the order and took the clothes back again. However, being used to the eccentric ways of white fools, the negress asked no questions.

Shortly before dark the Kid returned, but he came neither in his usual clothing nor as a poor peon. Instead he arrived dressed in the style of a *vaquero* and riding his huge stallion which had turned into a piebald. Clothed in such a manner, he could wear his normal weapons. So the Dragoon Colt hung in its holster, the bowie knife rode its sheath and his Mississippi rifle was in the saddleboot.

"It's an old trick," he explained, seeing the girl studying the black patches on the stallion's white coat. "Some powder a *Pehnane tsukup*, old man, makes up for us. It stands up to a fair washing in river or rain."

"I don't think anybody across there will recognise you," Belle replied, curiosity satisfied. "Are you ready?"

"Why sure," the Kid answered. "Pappy'll be waiting for you when we're all through. With luck, we'll win you a day's head start afore they know you've gone."

57

Chapter 6

Hell's Fire. It's A Woman

Rising to the surface, a tarpon over five foot long sent a swirling eddy in the direction of the Yankee guard boat and submerged again. By that time such appearances had become so common that the sailors rowing guard across the mouth of Brownsville's harbour no longer commented when one occurred. At that early hour of the evening, hardly past eight o'clock, they acted in a far more lax manner than later in the night, or on another station. Further north along the coast, attacks by Confederate submersibles, war-rams or other surface vessels kept the blockading fleets constantly on the alert. No such alarms had come in Brownsville, Colonel Rip Ford being a plainsman, skilled at land fighting but with no knowledge, or means, of making war on water.

However the relaxed performance of duty did not cause the men to overlook the two boats out on the river. One halted some way upstream, hanging in the current, while the other dropped down closer to the guard boat's line of patrol.

"Ahoy there!" the midshipman commanding the guard boat called. "What boat's that then?"

At the same moment he nodded and a man uncovered the head of a bull's eye lantern to illuminate the other boat. Two Negroes lowered heavy weights on ropes to halt the boat's progress and the third held a powerful fishing pole. Turning towards the speaker, the third Negro answered.

"We'ns out fishing for t'pon, sah," he said, holding up his line with a small bait-fish kicking on the hook. "They am running just now."

Seeing the man in his ragged shirt and pants, nobody would recognise him as the immaculate butler from the Confederate consulate. To the midshipman, raised in New England, the trio in the boat looked like any other ragged,

58

ordinary negroes to be seen south of the Mason-Dixie line.

"Guard boat ahoy!" bellowed a voice from the steam-sloop moored just inside the harbour entrance. "What's that boat doing?"

"It's just some coons fishing, sir," the midshipman called back. "Want for me to move 'em on?"

"No, they're doing no harm. If they catch one, have it sent aboard here."

"Aye, aye, sir."

"Could you-all put out that light, sah?" the butler asked. "It am scaring the t'pon and I'd surely not want Cousin Rastus along there to catch one if I don't. When dat happens, his missus done takes on and boasts about it and that gives my woman the miseries and I don't get a lick of peace."

"We wouldn't want that," grinned the midshipman and gave the required order.

Light or no light, the tarpon did not appear to be frightened away and it seemed that Cousin Rastus' wife would have nothing to boast about the following day. Dropping in his bait as the light went out, the butler allowed it to float down the river. Barely had it gone three yards when there came a vicious swirl in the water and the fishing pole bowed over violently. Then a tarpon shot into the air, rising in the kind of leap fast gaining its kind the reputation of being superb sporting fish. Again the tarpon jumped, arching its body high as it tried to throw the hooks embedded in its jaws.

Just about to give the order to resume their patrol, the midshipmen closed his mouth. Sitting back, he watched the spectacular fight, pleased with the break in the monotonous routine.

Treading water in an effort to stem back against the current, Belle Boyd heard the commotion and guessed what had happened. It seemed that the fates looked kindly on her enterprise. At best she hoped that the Negroes would be allowed to carry on fishing, but expected them to be ordered away. Having a tarpon take the bait was a choice, unexpected piece of luck.

Luck or not, she refused to relax and become complacent. Across the bay, Shafto ought to be releasing his keg torpedo towards the second ship by that time. She must wait until sure before turning free the piece of driftwood from which her own device hung suspended below the surface.

Of the two, Belle was handling the more dangerous assignment. True Shafto had swum into the harbour, but sufficient tarpon had shown inside for him to pass unnoticed, or unsuspected. His torpedo consisted of a water-proofed wooden keg containing one hundred pounds of gun powder, with conical pine ends giving a streamlined shape easy to handle in the water, weighted down to the desired level. As long as he avoided knocking the five percussion detonators on the sides and top of the keg, he ran little risk from the torpedo.

Designed to counter chain armour, the device hanging so close to Belle was a more tricky thing entirely. Its firing charge, in a metal cylinder $16\frac{1}{2}$ inches long and with a diameter of $11\frac{1}{2}$ inches, might be less than the keg's but the firing mechanism was more complicated. Attached to the bottom of the cylinder, a propeller operated gears which released a spring-loaded plunger to fire the charge. As long as the propellers pointed forward, the torpedo remained in-operative. When its driftwood support swept against the target, the dangling torpedo swung under the armour, turned and set the mechanism into operation.

A good idea, directing the charge where it would do most damage and explode at the right time. However—and here lay the snag—if for any reason the propeller case turned early, there would be a premature explosion.

Slowly she drifted closer to the steam sloop, seeing its bulk looming up ahead. Then she decided that the time had come.

Using the device by which the two men had entered the consulate grounds, Belle, the Kid and Shafto had left un-seen by the Yankee observers. They passed through the town to where the Negroes and Shafto's man waited with the boats. Already the torpedoes lay aboard 'Cousin Rastus'' boat and they moved into position. With the greater dis-tance to cover, Shafto left first and Belle followed when sure he would be almost in place. The tidal current ran at a good speed, sweeping into the bay in a manner calculated to carry home the torpedoes. Everything went according to plan, without any hitch to delay or endanger its effective working.

Belle released the driftwood, watching it lurch forward and holding down a gulp of concern. No explosion came, so all must still be well beneath the surface. Turning, she started to swim away in the opposite direction and towards the guard boat. At first she went carefully, using a breast stroke and keeping her feet beneath the surface to minimize the noise she made. However, on drawing close to the boat, she struck out and splashed with her arms.

"What's that?" one of the boat's crew asked, turning his head her way.

"Another tarpon," replied his companion on the thwart.

For a moment Belle thought that the men would dismiss her as another of the big fish. However the midshipman looked her way and came to his feet.

"Tarpon, hell!" he ejaculated. "It's a swimmer. After him, men!"

Powerful arms worked the oars, sending the boat leaping in Belle's direction. She continued to swim, giving the impression that she was seeking to escape. Surging up, the boat ranged alongside her and hands reached down to catch her by the arm.

"Come on, mate," said a voice. "Don't struggle or I'll have to crack your skull. You shouldn't've tried to run, you'd never reach the other side."

Just as Belle hoped, the men thought of her as a deserter from one of the ships. She intended to alter that as soon as possible. Another set of arms came down to catch her free wrist. Then the two sailors started to haul her upwards. Bracing her feet against the side of the boat, she struggled against the pull. With a growl of annoyance, the man on her left released her wrist with one hand and grabbed at the front of her shirt. She felt his hand close, loosen, feel at her breast then jerk away.

"Hell's fire. It's a woman!" the sailor gasped.

"Get your stinking Yankee hands off of me!" Belle hissed, sounding as feminine as she could manage.

Excitement welled up among the boat's crew and all thought of the fight between the butler and tarpon were forgotten. Then the midshipman's voice cut through the undisciplined row.

"Belay that bilge!" he barked and waited until silence fell on the crew. "Put a light on her, Torrey. Let's see what the hell we've landed."

'Landed' might be too premature a term, for the two sailors had not yet hauled Belle into the boat. The discovery that their captive was a woman handed them sufficient of a shock that they just sat holding her instead of raising her over the gunwale. Hanging in their hands, both bare feet firmly pressed against the side of the boat, Belle prepared to hand her captors another shock. She felt a slight upwards strain and knew the men had partially recovered from the surprise of their original discovery—and the explosions of the torpedoes still had not come to give the diversion she needed.

"You'll make ensign at least for this, brassbounder," she told the midshipman in a voice throbbing with well-assumed venom. "You've just captured Belle Boyd."

Once again the pull upwards ended and the sailors stared at her.

"The Rebel Spy!" a man announced in an excited voice.

Then he and all but Belle's captors of the crew started to stand up, wishing to take a look at the legendary figure.

Despite all his attempts, Pinkerton, then head of the United States Secret Service, had failed to prevent news of Belle Boyd's activities from appearing in the Yankee press. So her fame had spread and there could be few members of the Federal armed forces who had not heard of the Rebel Spy. Aware of that fact, Belle used it to buy her a little more time. Once in the boat, escape would be far harder than while still outside.

Even as the sailor with the lantern uncovered its face and directed a beam of light on Belle, showing without any doubt—due to the way the soaking shirt clung to her torso —that she was a woman, the required diversion came.

Carried against the side of the *Waterbury*, the piece of driftwood hung against the chain armour. Not so the torpedo which dangled at the end of a six foot triangle of rope fastened to the driftwood. Continuing forward, the torpedo passed beneath the hem of the armour and, as the rope drew tight, lifted until the pressure of the water forced it against the bottom of the sloop. Having achieved its purpose in circumventing the chain armour, the torpedo needed only to complete its work. The current beneath the sloop acted on the torpedo's propellors, causing them to turn, operate the gearing that released the coilspring. Up slammed the plunger, hurled by the released spring, to strike the detonator. With a dull roar, the powder charge ignited. A gaping hole ripped in the *Waterbury's* bottom, allowing the muddy water of the Rio Grande to gush in.

Nor did the effect end there. Still suspended on the side of the guard boat, Belle felt the concussion-spread wave arrive. Unlike the sailors, she expected—or hoped for—the explosion and was ready to take advantage of it. Given time, the guard boat's crew might have realised why the Rebel Spy had been found so close to a Yankee warship and raised the alarm; but that time was not granted to them. Taken completely by surprise, two of the standing men went over the side as the boat rose and pitched on the wave. The lantern flew from its holder's hand, struck the gunwale and flopped into the river.

No less startled than their companions, the two men holding Belle relaxed their grip. Ready for that to happen, the girl thrust herself backwards. Using all the strength in her powerful legs, she tore free from her captors' surprise-loosened hands. She went away from the boat, twisting around and diving beneath the surface of the water. Then she started to swim upstream in search of her companions.

At the same moment that Belle jerked herself free from the sailors, the second torpedo made its presence felt. Caught by the spreading wave from the *Waterbury*, the keg torpedo crashed into the side of the second ship. Crushed against the side, two of the torpedo's percussion detonators sparked their fire into the waiting charge. One hundred pounds of gun powder exploded with a roar that far exceeded the water-deadened boom of the drifting torpedo's detonation. For some reason the ship's captain had not ordered his chain armour to be spread, so the torpedo exploded against the bare side and blasted open a large hole.

Only by an effort of balance and skilled handling did the

midshipman and crew prevent the guard boat capsizing. Horrible oaths ripped the air and gurgling yells rose from the two men in the water. Then the midshipman realised that his prize captive had escaped. Standing up, he glared around him. He saw that the Negro fishing boat was rowing hurriedly away from them, which did not surprise him. No Negro would wish to become involved in the fighting between rebels and Yankees. However there was no sign of the girl.

"Torrey!" he yelled. "Where's that god-damned lantern?"

"Over the son-of-a-bitching side!" the sailor answered.

Although Torrey would never know it, the loss of the lantern probably saved his life. Upstream, in 'Cousin Rastus'' boat, the Ysabel Kid stood holding his Mississippi rifle ready to shoot anybody who used a light in an attempt to locate the swimming girl.

However the attempt could not be made. Nor did the guard boat's crew try to find Belle by rowing upstream. Rockets rose into the air from both ships, flares glowed to illuminate the harbour, rattles and drum rolls sounded the alarm. In the flickering glare of artificial light, the midshipman saw his boat's crew would be needed more urgently than in making a search for their escaped prisoner, even though she claimed to be the Rebel Spy.

Taking in water fast through the gaping hole ripped in her bottom, the *Waterbury* would need every hand at the pumps or for other work if she was to be saved. Nor did the second ship look to be in any better shape, holed at the waterline and already beginning to list. Desperately concerned with trying to keep their vessels afloat, nobody gave a thought to the second boat even though one of the rockets revealed it held two Negroes and two white men. Before the rocket's glow died away, Rule Shafto reached the boat and hauled himself aboard.

"Belle—?" he asked.

"Coming now," the Kid replied, pointing.

A tired Belle reached the boat and once again felt hands taking hold of her. Only this time she knew them to be friendly and did not struggle against their pull. Up she rose, over the boat's gunwale and flopped exhaustedly on to a thwart.

"You all right, Miss Belle?" the Kid asked anxiously, draping a blanket around her.

"Ye—Yes," she replied. "Ru—Rule—?"

"Here," Shafto answered, sounding just as exhausted. "Get going, boys."

Without needing urging, the Negroes started to row the boat at angle upstream and towards the Mexican shore. Already the explosions and confusion in the Brownsville harbour were attracting attention. However the French did not maintain any naval force in Matamoros harbour, so any danger would come from their army patrols.

"Maybe the Yankees'll cut loose with their cannons," the Kid remarked as he and Shafto's white assistant took up two more oars.

"That's not likely," Belle replied. "If they miss, the ball will probably ricochet into Matamoros. They won't risk that."

"I'd say they've got their hands full right now, without bothering about us," Shafto went on. "Make straight for the hide-out, boys."

"We've got clean away," the Kid breathed as the boat pulled alongside a wooden pier.

"Maybe," Shafto answered. "There's still the French curfew and Yankee Secret Service to beat. George, you'd best stay down here for the night."

"Yes, sah, Massa Rule," replied one of the negro oarsmen. "We'll do that."

"How about Amos and his men?" Belle inquired, meaning the butler.

"They'll lay up until morning and then come ashore," Shafto explained. "If possible we want to avoid them being tied in with this raid."

Belle could understand the reason for the precaution. If the Yankees could prove Garfield knew of the raid, he would be discredited. Even if the French allowed the Confederate consulate to continue, it would be so closely watched that its use as a base for further operations would become negligible.

They landed unseen, leaving the boat at its moorings and with nothing to show they had used it. Then they went to the place from which the expedition had been launched.

Ostensibly a warehouse owned by a British trading company, the building served as a base for shipping Texas-grown cotton and other produce, or storing goods run through the blockade until the Ysabels could arrange for their delivery across the Rio Grande.

Leaving the Negroes with the white man, Belle, the Kid and Shafto pushed on through the town's curfew-emptied streets. Guided and aided by the Kid's cat-keen eyes and remarkably keen ears, the trio avoided contact with the French patrols enforcing the curfew. The wisdom of taking an indirect route to the consulate showed on their arrival. Reaching the rear of the grounds, they found the Yankee watchers gone from the street, probably to investigate the disturbance at the river. So they entered the grounds through the rear gate without being detected.

Once inside, however, Belle went ahead with her plan of allowing the Yankees to know that she had taken an active part in the raid. Before going upstairs, she had water tipped over her. Then, in her room, she lit the lantern and felt sure her soaked condition would be noticed. If so, the watchers ought to take the point that she had recently been in the water.

Standing at the foot of the bed, where she knew the men across the street could see her, she steeled herself for a further disrobing. After peeling off the wet garments, she took up a towel and began to dry herself. With that completed she started to dress in the clothing bought for her by Shafto. Pulling the black shirt and trousers on over a change of underwear, she looked around the room. Everything was as she left it. Her trunks stood open, clothing inside. However the money and a few vital items had been unloaded before the trunks came up and were waiting for her down below, packed in a set of saddlebags.

Then, acting as if on an afterthought, she crossed to the window and started to draw down the hanging drapes, but not to the bottom. While the men across the street could still see into the room, their view had been curtailed. For one thing they could no longer see higher than slightly above the girl's waist as she walked about, although they were still able to look on to the bed.

Leaving the room, she found the Kid waiting in the hall.

He also wore a black shirt and pants, they being the only matching garments Shafto could find of suitable sizes. Belle thought the colour distinctive enough for their purpose.

"Reckon I'll get by?" he asked, with a glance at the room's door.

"I think I've a better shape," Belle replied with a smile. "But with the curtains drawn down, it's likely the Yankees won't notice the difference. You'd best not walk around too much though."

"That's for sure," he answered, also grinning. "I'll give you 'n' pappy a day's head start, more if the Yankees look to be fooled."

"And then?"

"I'll come after you."

"Will you be able to find us?"

"I'm *Nemenuh*, of The People, the Comanche," the Kid told her with quiet, reassuring dignity. "I'll find you."

"But two days, or even one day's start—," Belle went on.

"With that pack hoss and all, you'll be travelling like white folks," the Kid pointed out. "I'll be coming after you like an Injun."

With that he turned and walked into Belle's room. Crossing to the bed, he lay down on it as if meaning to snatch a short rest before leaving. If all went well, the Yankees would continue watching him, thinking Belle lay on the bed when all the time she made good her escape.

Chapter 7

That's No Woman Over There

"The Rebel Spy is in Matamoros," Abner Ffauldes told the woman who called herself Emily Corstin as she entered the dining room of the house facing the Confederate States' consulate shortly before eight o'clock in the evening.

Halting, Eve Coniston—the other name having been placed on the hotel's register to hide her true identity—stared at the leader of the United States Secret Service's Matamoros detachment.

"When did you learn that?" she demanded.

"Early this afternoon," Ffauldes replied. "I sent a message to you at the hotel. But you'd left and I didn't know where to find you."

Annoying though it might be, Eve could not argue on that point. After leaving the hotel, she had accompanied Charlie Kraus to start on part of the business which had brought her to Matamoros.

Events in the Mexican town, ranging from Belle Boyd's previous undetected arrival and departure to the Ysabel family's wholesale smuggling activities, had caused serious doubts to be raised in the U.S. Secret Service about the efficiency of Ffauldes' detachment. So Eve Coniston had received orders to investigate the matter while also trying to bring an end to the smuggling.

Although shrewd, capable, efficient and successful, Eve had received little public acclaim and was hardly known beyond her organisation. The lack of recognition sometimes annoyed her, but she also recognised its value. While Pauline Cushman received publicity, being boosted as the North's answer to Belle Boyd, no mention of Eve ever reached the Yankee newspapers. So she went her way unsuspected, achieving far more than the so-called 'Scout of the Cumberland's' often-told exploits.

From the little she had seen since her arrival aboard the

steam-launches' depot ship, Eve knew she faced a formidable task. Guided by Kraus, she rode some five miles upstream on the Rio Grande's southern bank and talked with a number of unsavoury people who made their living along the bloody border between Texas and Mexico. At the end of it, she felt that she was wasting her time. When Kraus brought up the matter of reporting rebel troop movements, for money of course, all agreed; even those who, she suspected, never crossed the river. On the other matter discussed, the results had been far less satisfactory. To be fair to him, Kraus had warned her from the start about that.

When asked to spy on and report the movements of the Ysabel family's smuggling trains, the border dwellers' attitudes changed fast. A few refused profanely and point blank. Others seemed unwilling, frightened almost, to talk about it and their eyes took on a far-away look as they evaded even the question of whether they had seen the Ysabels go by in the past. Only two offered to help and they did so with such blatant insincerity that Eve doubted if anything would come of it.

On the way back to town, she thought about the matter. Even with the aid of the steam-launch flotilla, borrowed from the Mississippi Squadron, catching the Ysabels in the act would be anything but a sinecure. So she decided to concentrate her efforts at the source of the supply. The shipments brought into Matamoros could only arrive because some important French officials were looking the other way. If she produced proof against them, their superiors would be forced to make them carry out their duties correctly. Failing that, she could find evidence of Garfield helping the Ysabels and rebel spies. Then the U.S. consul could approach the French and demand that Garfield be ordered from the city for breaches of diplomatic privilege. Causing the Confederate consul's removal ought to throw the landing organisation into confusion long enough for the steam launches to learn the vagaries of the Rio Grande. Skilled veterans of the Mississippi campaign, they should be able to cope with the problems of blockading a smaller river.

Returning to the hotel, she found Ffauldes' message and visited him after eating with a French colonel who gave much helpful advice and a permit to travel after the curfew hour. She noticed the men keeping watch from the street on the Confederate consulate as her hired carriage drove up and learned the reason the moment she met Ffauldes.

Tall, lean, with a gaunt face that bore a mixture of assumed superiority and an avaricious nature, Abner Ffauldes wore a rumpled town suit and grubby shirt. His attitude showed that he resented the woman's presence. Like all liberal-intellectuals, Ffauldes hated any authority he did not wield himself. Eve Coniston had arrived the previous day with a letter from Pinkerton himself, giving her virtual control of the Matamoros detachment.

"Where is she now?" Eve asked, although willing to guess at the answer.

"Across the street there," Ffaulds replied. "We've had her under observation ever since she arrived. Well, soon after she arrived anyway."

"And how did she manage to reach the rebel consulate?"

"Dressed as a Mexican girl. Hell! She looked and dressed just like one and rode in on a donkey cart."

"You didn't expect her to come down the street in full Confederate Army uniform and waving the Stars and Bars, did you?" Eve said dryly, hoping her own uneasiness did not show.

All too well she remembered the Mexican girl at the hotel's plaza. Something about that whole affair had struck her as wrong from the start. The French sergeant showed, even unconscious, signs of greater agony than would arise from being pushed and falling over backwards to crack his head on the ground. Wishing to avoid becoming involved in French-Mexican affairs, she had kept her conclusions to herself. What if that terrified Mexican girl had really been— Eve did not care to take *that* line of thought any further. So she prevented herself from doing it by resuming the questioning.

"You're sure it was her?"

"Joe Giss and one of his men were over the wall, hidden in the grounds, and heard Garfield call her by name," Ffauldes answered. "As soon as he got out and told me, I put every available man to watching the house."

"You had a man in their garden?" Eve asked.

"And not for the first time," Ffauldes replied, smirking

with smug satisfaction. "One or two of them go over the wall at night, using a leather pad against the broken glass, and lie up in the bushes all day."

"Our men?"

"They work for us. Either Joe Giss or one of his men go in."

"And what does it cost us?" said the practical Eve.

"Fifty dollars a day for one or both of them," Ffauldes answered, losing some of his smirk. "I'm making a list of French and other callers Garfield sees."

"And what they talk about?"

"Sometimes—Look, Giss and the other man take their lives in their hands every time they go over the wall—."

"They're well paid for doing it," Eve pointed out. "Fifty dollars a day! Couldn't any of your own men—?"

"None of them have that kind of experience," Ffauldes told her sulkily. "It paid off today well enough. We know the Rebel's Spy's there."

What Ffauldes omitted to mention was the number of times the watcher in the grounds had failed to bring back any worthwhile information. In his bigoted hatred of the supporters of the Confederacy who dared to oppose his own lofty ideals, Ffauldes overlooked the fact that the watching had, to that day, gained little more knowledge than was gathered by the normal lookouts outside the consulate's grounds. To know he was putting one over on the rebels satisfied him. What he did not know was that only rarely did Giss take the chance of entering the garden, or how most of the watching from within had been carried out by men with only a scanty knowledge of English. That Giss had gone in the previous night had been brought about by Eve's presence in the town. After meeting her, Charlie Kraus had warned his partner that there would need to be an improvement in their service if they hoped for it to continue. So Giss went in with the half-breed and, in trying to gather some information of sufficient importance to satisfy Eve, had been discovered and lost his man while escaping.

"Have you seen her yourself?" Eve inquired, having formed a poor opinion of Joe Giss during their one brief meeting the previous evening.

"I saw her!" Ffauldes replied with considerably more

71

enthusiasm than a mere glimpse of the South's top spy appeared to merit. "She's using a room at the front of the house, upstairs."

"And she's still there?"

"My men are covering the whole building, there's no way she could leave."

Before any more could be said, the door flew open and an excited-looking man dashed in.

"There's trouble across the river, Mr. Ffauldes!" he said. "We saw a flash, like an explosion, then rockets and flares started going up."

Darting to the window, Eve looked through it and saw the glow in the sky. She swung hurriedly to look at the men.

"Is the Rebel Spy still across the street?" she hissed.

"Sure," the newcomer answered. "We saw her once at the dining room window, wearing a fancy gown."

"How long since?" Eve asked.

"Maybe half, threequarters of an hour back," the man replied. "I'm near enough certain she's still in there. Garfield's been talking to somebody just now and I could see the hem of her dress from just in front of him."

"It may not be her," Eve said, half to herself. "I think she's here to—. Come on, we'll go to the waterfront and see what we can learn."

"The curfew—!" Ffauldes croaked.

"I know about it!" Eve snapped. "The French won't enforce it on members of the U.S. consular staff going to see what's happening across the river."

"That's for sure," the lookout agreed. "They've never stopped us being out after curfew yet."

"Who's going with you?" Ffauldes asked.

"Leave the men on watch in the upstairs rooms and get the rest," Eve answered. "If the attack came from this side, I want whoever launched it."

"I'll go harness the coach," the lookout offered. "There're enough of the boys upstairs without me."

While Ffauldes gathered the men and his lookout prepared the coach, Eve went upstairs to interview the other watchers. She found all the men awake and showing considerable zeal in keeping the consulate under observation. However none could state for certain that he had seen the

72

Rebel Spy in the last threequarters of an hour or more.

"Shucks," one of them said. "She come up, put a frock on and give her shirt and pants to a nigger maid for washing."

Listening to the man, Eve realised that the eager scrutiny of the other house had not been caused by news of her arrival. Taking a telescope, she lined it at the consulate and had the window of Belle's room pointed out. While it lay in darkness, she decided that its interior would be visible in daylight or with a lamp lit inside.

"You saw her?" Eve repeated her opening question.

"And how," grinned the man. "She come in there dressed like a greaser. I saw her peaking out of the window. Must've figured we couldn't see into the room or weren't watching, 'cause she stripped, went for a bath and when she come back we knew for sure she was the Rebel Spy."

"Why?"

"She got dressed in men's clothes. Dark shirt, riding breeches, like she's worn afore. Had a black wig on when she come in dressed like a greaser gal and under it she'd real short black hair."

"Could it have been a man dressed in woman's clothing?"

"Lady!" the lookout answered. "Believe me, that was no *man* I saw."

"You mean she stripped standing in front of the window?" Eve asked.

"Naw!" he replied, sounding just a touch disappointed. "Back by the bed. Must've figured we couldn't see that far into the room. But we could. Boy! Those app—* Well, we could see her good, *all* of her."

"Miss Coniston!" Ffauldes yelled from downstairs. "The coach's ready."

Although feeling doubts about what she had just heard, Eve put them aside. She could finish questioning the man later, but if they hoped to catch whoever had raided the shipping a start must be made immediately.

Two men sat on the coach's box, while four more crammed inside with Ffauldes. Hardly had Eve climbed in than the driver started the two-horse team moving. Before they had covered half the distance, a French army patrol stopped them.

* Apples: slang name for breasts.

73

"United States consular staff," the driver replied in answer to the challenge. "We're going to—."

"*Monsieur!*" Eve called through the window and the officer turned her way. "My husband in on a ship in Brownsville harbour. These gentlemen are taking me to see if all is well. I have a pass from Colonel Ponthieu."

"Of course, *madame*," the officer replied. "You may pass."

Continuing its journey through the streets, the coach came to a halt as close to the waterfront as the French would allow. Again an officer came up, a major this time, but he accepted the story of concern for the welfare of Eve's 'husband' and raised no objection to the party going forward on foot.

"I want to take a boat out to the ships, major," Eve went on, after acknowledging the permission. "Will that be possible?"

"It is on your own responsibility, *madame*," he answered.

Like all army officers and Government officials, the major had recieved ambiguous instructions regarding his treatment of important *Americanos del Norte;* no matter which side in the War they served. Faced with the possibility of a long, arduous task in subduing Mexican resistance to their rule, the French high command dare not antagonise either the Confederate or Federal Governments. So they tended to order a blind eye turned to both sides' breaches of diplomatic conduct, or to be obliging to members of each.

More than that, Eve's request struck the major as being perfectly natural. Due to the prevailing conditions in Brownsville, with a hostile population waiting to rise against the occupying forces and constant harassment from Ford's command, the Yankee officers hesitated to bring in their wives. So a number of service families lived in Matamoros. Naturally they would be worried and wish to learn of their husbands' fate. Assuming Eve to be the wife of at least an army colonel or naval captain, the major decided she had been requested by the other wives to gather the required information.

Entering the boat accompanied by Ffauldes and another man, Eve set them to rowing across the river. The rest of her party spread out in an attempt to find the raiders.

Flares and lanterns illuminated the *Waterbury* and depot ship. From all appearances, the raid had been at least a partial success. Water spurting out of hoses and the clanging of pumps aboard the *Waterbury* told of the fight to save her. Even as Eve's boat approached, she saw one of the forward Dahlgren nine-inch cannon tumble over the side through a gap cut in the bulwarks. A further gap at the stern told that the steam sloop's captain had jettisoned some of his armament in the bid to stay afloat. Yet, even with the reduction in weight of four—two from each side—9,200 pound cannon, the sloop lay low in the water. Beyond her, the depot ship listed far over to port and looked in a more sorry plight even than the *Waterbury*.

Kusik, the man rowing at Ffauldes' side, knew naval procedure for he raised his voice in a hail. "*Waterbury* ahoy! Permission to come aboard!"

"Who the hell are you?" demanded an exasperated voice.

"If they're from some stinking newspaper, turn the hoses on 'em!" roared the burly captain, appearing at the rail.

"We're U.S. consular staff from Matamoros!" Ffauldes yelled hastily.

"Lay alongside aft and come aboard!" ordered the captain grudgingly and Eve heard him continue in a lower tone, "A woman! That's all I need right now. A damned woman coming aboard asking stupid questions."

"I'll report him to the admiral comm—!" Ffauldes began.

"Shut your mouth!" Eve snapped. "He's right, but I have to go aboard."

She could sympathise with the captain, doing everything in his power to save his ship and faced by the arrival of what would probably amount to nothing more than useless sightseers. However she wanted to learn if any of the raiders had been seen and might be identified.

Boarding the *Waterbury* presented no problem, for she lay low in the water. Two sailors reached through the gap in the bulwarks, caught Eve's wrists and swung her up on to the deck. Kusik followed by his own efforts and Ffauldes struggled up after the other two.

"You understand I've no time to spare, madam," the captain told Eve, giving her a scowl along with the salute.

75

"You may tell the ladies ashore that there've been no casualties in either vessel."

"Thank you, captain," she replied. "And the damage?"

"We're holed in the bottom, have plugged it with hammocks as best we can but are still making water. The *Grayson* is in worse shape than us. I've had no report from her. You are from the consulate?"

"I'm with the Secret Service," Eve answered, her voice holding just a touch of pride. "Did anybody see the attackers?"

"See them!" growled the captain, sounding more angry than ever. "One of my officers had his hands on her and—."

"*Her*?" Eve prompted. "There was a woman involved?"

"Damn it, can't you see I'm—," the captain blared, then gave a resigned shrug. "Very well. It will come out later anyhow. Mr. Thurley. Lay aft here."

"Aye aye, sir!" answered the abashed midshipman who had commanded the guard boat, running up to the party.

"Tell the lady about your outstanding achievement tonight, Mr. Thurley," ordered the captain. "And while you're at it, tell her about that damned wig you brought aboard with that blasted greaser down the coast last night. I'm going below to inspect the damage."

Slowly the midshipman told of Belle's 'capture' and escape, clearly hating to admit his failure to civilians, especially when one of them was a woman. If he came out of the affair still retaining his commission, he would be lucky; and he knew it. So he spoke carefully, weighing out each word with the view to how it would sound repeated before a court martial. Showing tact and using skilled questioning backed by sympathy, Eve drew out all the details.

"It could have happened to anybody," she finally said with more compassion than she felt. The Rebel Spy had been in Yankee hands and escaped. No member of the U.S. Secret Service could regard that news with equanimity. However she wished to let the young man down as lightly as possible in view of what his superiors would do to him. "What was that about a wig?"

Thurley did not hesitate with his answer. On that matter at least he could maintain a clear conscience, being covered in his actions by the captain's stringent orders.

"That was last night, ma'am. We heard shots from the shore and saw a fight by a fire. Captain sent me ashore with a party to investigate. The fighters ran before we landed. Hey though! One of them was a woman—the same one we caught tonight, I'll bet. At least they both had the same sort of short black hair. The two men with her were Americans, frontiersmen from the look of them."

"What baggage did they have?" Eve asked eagerly.

"Two trunks. They carried them off. The bigger man took one and she helped the youngster with the other."

"And you didn't give chase?" Ffauldes put in.

"That was on Mexican territory, *mister*," Thurley answered, contempt for a civilian plain in his tone. "My orders were not to go beyond the beach. I brought a greaser aboard with me, but his jaw's smashed so bad that he can't talk."

"About what size were the trunks?" Eve inquired.

"About so," Thurley replied, demonstrating with his hands. "I'd say they weighed around a hundred pounds each, they way they carried them off."

Not large enough to carry two torpedoes then, although that proved little, Eve told herself. Then she looked at the young officer and gave him a reassuring smile.

"There's nothing more you can tell us?"

"No, ma'am. Now I'd like to get back to my duties."

"Hell!" Kusik ejaculated, pointing. "Look there!"

Turning, they saw the *Grayson* lurch and then roll over until she lay on her side. She took two of the launches with her, smashing down on them before they could draw away, but the other four hovered around her.

"Jettison two more cannon!" roared the captain, coming up to the deck from below. "Move, damn you. Madam, I'd be obliged if you'd go ashore, make contact with the Mex—French authorities and ask if I can run this ship in for repairs."

Brownsville offered few dockyard facilities. Nor did Matamoros for that matter, but repairs could be carried out more safely there. As long as the *Waterbury* made only such repairs as would render her seaworthy and did not touch her armament, she could enter a neutral port for that purpose under international law.

"I'll see the arrangements are made," Eve promised,

77

knowing that the sloop would be safe in Matamoros even should Brownsville be retaken by the Confederacy. "We'll get from under your feet now, captain."

While being rowed back to Matamoros, Eve turned over her findings in her mind and liked nothing about them. Somehow Belle Boyd's capture and escape seemed too fortunate, contrived almost. Then there had been her behaviour in the Confederate consulate. After suspecting that her presence had been discovered, the Rebel Spy had acted in a peculiarly uncharacteristic manner. Not once, but several times she had permitted herself to be seen, and in such a manner as to ensure a still more careful watch for her would be made. Eve could imagine how eagerly the lookouts had waited in the hope of seeing the girl disrobing again.

A spy as successful as Belle Boyd became cautious in the extreme. Of course she might be growing carelessly overconfident—but not if she had come to Matamoros on the business Eve suspected.

"Hurry!" Eve told the men.

"I'd say we're too late for that," Kusic answered. "The Rebel Spy's done what she came here for."

"I only hope you're right!" she breathed.

On the landing, Eve found two of the men waiting to deliver a negative report. Telling one of them to stay and watch what happened across the river, she sent the other to pass the captain of the *Waterbury's* message to the U.S. consul. Then she went to the carriage and ordered Kusik to go as fast as he could to the house overlooking the rebel consulate.

At the house, Eve threw herself from the coach and dashed inside. She ran up the stairs, bursting into the room where she had interviewed the lookouts earlier. One man lay dozing in a chair, but his companion sat at the window. Jolting awake, the first man joined his companion in meeting Eve's cold gaze with the hang-dog expressions caused by knowing that they had failed in their duty.

"She's back, Miss Coniston," the watcher announced. "Asleep on the bed."

"Damned if I can see how she got out," his companion went on.

78

"But she did!" Eve snapped. "I don't think Allan Pinkerton's going to like this at all."

Which, both men knew, was quite an understatement. There would definitely be a big reorganisation of the Matamoros detachment when Eve Coniston reported to their leader.

"Yes'm," the watcher admitted. "It's not 'cause we didn't watch. Hell, we watched real good."

"Hoping to see her walk into that room there and strip off her clothes again, I suppose!" Eve shouted. "Anyway, I blame the men on the streets more than you in the houses. How was she dressed when she came back?"

"In a dark shirt and riding breeches. Looked like she'd been in the water—!"

"She had!" Eve interrupted grimly. "And then?"

"She undressed," the man replied uneasily. "Dried herself and dressed in a black shirt and pants. We thought she aimed to go out, but she's lying on the bed."

"Did she leave the room at all?" Eve inquired, taking the telescope and focusing it on the room.

First she noticed that the curtains had been drawn down some of the way from the top of the window. Not enough to block all view of the interior, for she could see the shape on the bed.

"After she tried to pull down the curtain and it stuck," the man answered. "We figured she'd gone to get somebody to fix it, but nobody came."

"It stuck?" Eve repeated.

"Shucks," the second man protested. "We could still see her from the waist down at least when she was on her feet and she's there plain enough on the bed."

At that moment Kusik appeared at the door and Eve turned to him. "Describe the Ysabels to me!" she ordered.

"Father's a big, powerful feller. Black Irish from the looks of him—."

"And the son?"

"Tall, slender as a beanpole. He looks about fourteen years old and innocent as a church full of choirboys—only don't let that fool you. Ffauldes hired a couple of Mexican *asesinos* to go after the Ysabels—He only tried it once."

"What happened?" Eve asked, lining the telescope again.

"We never did find out about one of them."

"And the other?"

"We found him leaning against the gate. His belly ripped wide open and an extra mouth—under his chin. After that there wasn't a hired killer would take on the chore. We hired Giss and Kraus in the first place hoping they would, or could find men willing to try."

Most of the explanation passed unheeded as Eve stared at the room across the street. Everything fell into place and she realised the nature of the trick the Rebel Spy played on them. Damaging though it had been, the raid on the shipping was only a diversion made to help the fiction that Belle Boyd was in the consulate building.

"That's no woman over there!" she snapped. "It's a young man, probably the Ysabel Kid!"

"Bu—But the clothes!" protested the watcher. "The Kid allus wears buckskins—."

"Except when he's dressed as a peon riding on a donkey cart, or a *vaquero* delivering a message!" Eve spat back. "Damn it, he can change clothes just like Belle Boyd did, although you probably wouldn't find the sight so attractive. And that's what's happened. While you've been sat here watching him, the Rebel Spy has escaped again."

"Now she's done what she came here for, you mean?" Kusik put in.

"That's what she wants me to think," Eve answered. "Find Giss and Kraus for me as quickly as you can!"

"Yes'm!" answered the second of the watchers, to whom the order had been given and he scuttled from the room.

"Mr. Kusik, be ready to leave in an hour," Eve went on, walking towards the door. "You'll be going up the Rio Grande with one of Kraus' men in a steam-launch. I'll give you the necessary authority for the officer in command of the flotilla. I want the word spreading that we'll pay a thousand dollars for the capture, alive if possible, of Sam Ysabel and the Rebel Spy."

"There's few enough, if anybody, who'll chance doing that, even for a thousand dollars," Kusik objected.

"Then spread the word that she and Ysabel are carrying a large sum, at least ten thousand dollars in gold, with them."

"It's a good story. Every border rat along the river will

be looking for them when I spread it."

"I only wish it wasn't true," Eve thought as she started to walk down the stairs. "Because if they reach that damned renegade Klatwitter, it might easily cost us the War."

Chapter 8

He's Lucky To Still Be Alive

Barely had the door opened and Shafto entered the room than the Ysabel Kid came off the bed to face him. From full asleep, in more comfort than came his way in many months, to wide awake took only a brief instant.

Across the street, the man on watch let out a yell which brought his companion leaping to his side.

"The Coniston dame was right," the lookout said. "It's the Kid and not the Rebel Spy."

"Shafto bursting in like that, took with that feller we just saw go into the house," the second man replied, "I'd say means they know Miss Coniston left town with Giss and Kraus."

A point that Shafto was making to the Kid at that moment.

"They pulled out maybe three hours back, Lon. My man trailed along after them to try and learn what was up. Kusik from over there and one of Kraus' 'breeds left the others, heading towards the river. My man did as I said, stuck with the Corstin woman. She went with Giss and Kraus to the *Posada del Rio*—."

"That's Charlie's favourite hangout," the Kid drawled. "I wouldn't want to be caught dead in there—and you stand a chance of winding up that way even if you do no more than drink the *tequila* they serve."

"So I've heard," Shafto answered dryly. "Well, Kraus, the woman and six of their men come out on good horses. From the way they took, they intended to go up river—."

"Three hours back!" the Kid spat out. "Why in hell didn't your man—."

"They must've seen him. Two of Giss' men took after him and he's been trying to lose them ever since. He had to fight his way in finally."

"There's times I talk a heap too much!" said the Kid

contritely. "He's lucky to still be alive, tangling with Joe Giss' boys on their own ground."

"He caught a knife in the ribs doing it," Shafto replied. "Luckily he had a sword-stick and knew how to use it. Killed one of them and wounded the other. What do we do now?"

"I don't know about you," the Kid growled. "But I'm going after pappy to warn him. There's no point in trying to make 'em think Miss Belle's still here now."

"That's what I think. I've told the cook to make breakfast for you and put up food to take along."

"I'll take the breakfast. But forget the food. I've pemmican and jerked meat that'll last me and be lighter to carry. Which same I'll be moving fast. Say I saw a right likely looking sorrel in the stables. Reckon I can borrow him to ride relay along with my ole Nigger hoss?"

"Take him," Shafto offered, although the horse in question was his favourite mount. The Kid would need the best available animal, the way he must travel to reach his father in time. "Do you want me to go and saddle him?"

"Just a blanket'll do. If I can, I'll leave him someplace safe."

"Don't worry about the horse. Reaching Belle and your father's the important thing right now."

After the meal, the Kid and Shafto went to the stables. Although the youngster had brought his warbag to the consulate, he would not be taking it any farther. No Indian riding on a raiding mission cluttered himself up with more spare clothing or anything but essentials; and the Kid intended to travel in such a manner. So he selected only a partly eaten *awyaw:t* of pemmican and a few strips of jerked buffalo meat which could be rolled in the single blanket that would form his bed on the trail. For the rest, weapons and ammunition were his only other needs. Thirty rounds of soft lead balls for the Dragoon, fifty for the rifle and a flask of powder would be sufficient. Every ounce of weight counted, so he decided against taking along the second Dragoon which lay in the warbag. While the revolver was of the Third Model, with a detachable canteen-carbine stock, the latter device did little to improve its potential for long-range shooting. In case of a fight from a distance, the

Mississippi rifle would be more use. He dispensed with the rifle's saddleboot, intending to carry it in the lighter buckskin pouch presented to him by his grandfather on the day he rode out to fight the Yankees.

Saddling the stallion, he studied its black-patched hide and put aside his thoughts of changing out of the black clothing into his buckskins.

"Reckon you can find me a hat, Cap'n Rule?" he asked.

"I'll see what we have around," Shafto promised.

By the time he returned, the Kid was all ready to leave. The white stallion stood saddled and the sorrel bore a blanket Indian fashion on its back, although with a white man's headstall, bit and reins, the latter of the short, closed type favoured by cavalrymen. The Kid's own reins were Texas style, open in two separate straps and he looped them loosely around the saddlehorn, knowing the white would stay by him tied or free.

Neither of the men realised as the Kid tried on the hats and found a black Stetson to be the only one which fitted, that he had commenced wearing what would become his usual style of clothing. Only rarely in the years to come would the Kid wear other than all black clothes.

"Anybody watching the house, Cap'n?" the Kid inquired, swinging astride the sorrel with deft ease.

"Only the usual lookouts," Shafto replied. "Not that they'd try to stop you so close to the consulate. But they saw my man come in wounded. So they'll try it somewhere along the way."

"Likely," the Kid answered. "Somebody could get hurt if they try. Open up, Cap'n. I'm on my way."

Riding out of the gate, the Kid watched the Yankee-owned house but met with no trouble. Nor did he appear to attract any undue attention while riding through the town. Enough *Americanos del Norte* made Matamoras their home, coming and going in such a manner, to prevent his appearance being out of the ordinary. However the Kid did not relax. Any trouble that came his way in town would be unlikely to start in the better-class areas. Down among the *jacales* of the poor quarter was the danger area. More than one man entered that section and never returned, murdered for his weapons, horse and clothing.

Holding his horses to a steady trot, the Kid noted the empty nature of the street leading on to the west-bound river trail. Instead of the normal swarm of children, men and women gossiping in front of houses, he could see only two figures. Both wore the ragged clothes of ordinary peons and seemed to be following the age-old custom of *siesta*. The nearer man sat with his back against the wall of a *jacale*, sombrero drawn down over his face and serape hung negligently over his shoulder. Further along the street, the second of them took his rest standing with a shoulder propping him up against another adobe building.

Casually the Kid let his right hand fall to be thumb-hooked into the gunbelt close to the Colt's butt. It was a mite early for *siesta* hour, although diligent peons had been known to start before time on occasion. To the Kid's mind, the closer man at least was sitting just a touch too tense to be resting. More than that, his right hand lay under the serape and held a revolver. The Kid could see the glint of metal beyond the brown of the partially-hidden hand. Nor did he miss the unobtrusive way the man inched up the sombrero and peeked from beneath its brim in his direction. However, after the one quick glance, the man appeared to relax. Then, as the Kid came closer, the man took another look. A startled croak broke from him and he began to lurch erect, bringing the revolver into view.

Even as the Kid twisted his old Dragoon from its holster, he guessed what had happened. Coming from the east, with the morning sun behind him, the man had failed at first to recognise him. Riding the sorrel, with the stallion's white coat bearing the black patches still, dressed in the black clothing instead of his usual buckskins, all helped the deception. Recognition came a fatal minute too late for the man, one of Joe Giss' regular helpers. Flame belched from the Dragoon's muzzle and the lead ball drove, by accident rather than lenient aim, into the man's shoulder. Not that the wound it caused could be termed slight, for a soft lead ball opened up on impact and caused tissue damage out of all proportion to its size. Stumbling back, the man let his revolver fall from a hand he would never use again.

At the shot, the second man threw off his pretence of sleeping. He lunged away from the building, bringing a

Colt into view. The Kid saw him as a greater threat than the first would-be attacker. No Mexican, to whom a gun took second place to the knife, but an American—despite the clothes—and one who knew how to handle a revolver.

Some thirty yards separated them, hardly ideal revolver-fighting range. However the man did not hesitate. No matter how he dressed, the Ysabel Kid could not be trifled with at such a moment. With that thought in mind, the man raised the Colt shoulder high, sighted and fired.

An instant before the Colt barked, the Kid brought the sorrel to a halt, tossed his right leg forward over its neck and dropped to the ground. The bullet cut the air where his body had been a moment earlier. On reaching the ground, the Kid sank immediately into a kneeling position, left elbow resting on the raised knee and supporting the right hand as he aimed the old Dragoon. Before the man re-cocked his Colt, the Dragoon bellowed. Lead, driven by forty grains of powder—the most powerful loading possible at that time in a hand-gun—smashed into the man. Flung backwards, he crashed into the wall of the *jacale* and bounced from it. In falling, he lost his hat and it rolled out into the street.

Rising, the Kid darted a quick glance around him. While he saw no sign of enemies, voices raised in the *jacale* behind his first victim told of their presence. So he ran towards the restlessly moving sorrel and leap-frog mounted its back, setting it running while thrusting away the Colt. Bursting out of the *jacale*, the leader of two men threw a shot after the departing Kid and might have made a lucky hit but for one thing. Having need for it at a later time, the Kid leaned sideways from the racing sorrel and scooped up the sombrero dropped by the disguised American. Doing so saved his life, for the bullet hissed just above him as he moved. In passing he looked at the dead man and recognised him as one of the many who lived along the bloody border by any means available.

"Trust Joe to move fast," the Kid mused as he urged the sorrel on, the white stallion sticking close to his side. "He must've hired that cuss as soon as he got the word."

Another bullet made its eerie sound as it hummed by his head. Then he turned a corner which hid him from the shooters. To his ears came the yelled order to get the horses *pronto*.

"Which same means I'm not out of the woods by a long Texas mile," the Kid told himself. "Ole Joe's likely waiting up the trail with more of 'em. Least-wise, I'll be mortal offended happen he figures *four* of 'em was all he needed to take me."

Passing beyond the last buildings of the town, the Kid turned and saw two riders following. However, knowing him to be *Cabrito*, they made no attempt to come too close. That they followed at all suggested they expected Giss and more help to be waiting somewhere ahead.

The point of importance being where would the reinforcements lay their ambush?

Not too far from town, the Kid figured. Close enough to hear shooting and make preparations in case the first attempt at stopping him failed. Too far away and he might turn off the trail to head across country. Prudence dictated that he followed that line of action; but the Kid could not claim prudence among his many virtues.

So he continued to ride along the trail, counting on his trained senses to locate the waiting men. During his childhood he had always excelled at the game of *Nan-ip-ka*, Guess-Over-The-Hill, by which Comanche boys learned to locate hidden enemies. Nor had he ever forgotten the skills gained in those formative years.

At first he rode through fairly open country unsuitable for the laying of an ambush, especially with *Cabrito*, the Ysabel Kid, as the proposed victim. However about a mile from town the trail entered and wound through thickly wooded country.

Looking ahead, he saw a small cart drawn across the trail, its shafts empty and no sign of the driver. So he turned in time to see one of the following men making an obvious signal which ended abruptly on noticing he was being observed.

"Down there, huh," he grinned, eyes raking the ground around the wagon.

A white man might have betrayed himself through anxiety or over-eagerness, but never a *Pehnane Tehnap*; and the Kid was all of that as he continued to ride into the ambush. No longer did he look young or innocent. Lips drawn back in a wolfish grin, rest of face a cold, savage mask, he might have been Long Walker, war leader of the dreaded Dog Soldier lodge, heading to meet an enemy.

Not that he under-estimated the dangers of the situation. Joe Giss claimed few peers in accurate rifle shooting and— as the Kid had told Shafto—had learned the art of concealment from Indians. So he would be hard for even a *Pehnane* to locate. Anywhere within three hundred yards of the cart could be the danger area. Up to that distance Giss allowed to be able to knock out a squirrel's eye and call which one he meant to hit.

"So it's from now to maybe a hundred and not less'n fifty," the Kid decided, gauging the distance with an eye almost as accurate as a surveyor's tape-measure. "Come on, Joe. Show your skinny-gutted hand. There's one of your boys, all hid real careful behind that pepperwood tree. Another hunkered under the deadfall and one laid up between them sassfrass bushes. Where're you, Joe. Come out, come out, wherever you are."

Giving no sign that he had located three of his enemies, the Kid rode on. Still no hint of Giss' presence. Yet he would be there, hidden carefully and squinting along the sights of his rifle.

Watching the Kid draw closer, the man behind the pepperwood tree grew more alarmed. That was no ordinary man approaching, but *Cabrito*, who many claimed to have a charmed life. Gomez had been an *asesino* of high quality, skilled at his work, and everybody knew how he had died when sent after the Ysabel Kid. So, despite Giss' orders that the others waited until he opened fire, the Mexican acted. Burning powder sparked alongside the pepperwood tree and the Kid slid sideways between the two horses.

"I got him!" yelled the man, his voice almost drowned out by other shots.

Finger already squeezing the Sharps rifle's trigger, Joe Giss had received a shock when the Mexican's shot cracked out. Nor could he control the involuntary tightening of his forefinger that set the rifle's mechanism working. Both his remaining men's weapons barked almost at the same moment and the three bullets tore harmlessly over the backs of the approaching horses.

Carefully concealed under the branches of another sass-frass bush, Giss heard his man's exultant yell. At first glance the words appeared to be justified, for the horses raced down the trail with no sign of a rider. The trouble being that the Kid's body did not lie on the trail either. In which case, the Sharps ought to be reloaded and fast. Which raised a snag. To load a rifle, even a breech-feeding Sharps, meant movement sure to draw the Kid's attention to Giss' hiding place. Attracting *Cabrito's* interest at such a moment was as dangerous a pastime as poking one's head into the mouth of a starving silvertip grizzly bear and saying, "Bite it."

Whoops of delight rose from Giss' less perspicacious companions and he could see that none of them thought to reload their rifles. Then they too realised that something must be wrong. The two men from town signalled violently; and not in congratulation for a well-aimed shot. Closer thundered the two horses, still with no sign of the Kid. So the ambushers belatedly reached for powder flasks to begin the business of recharging their rifles.

When he slid from the sorrel's back, a split-second before the Mexican cut loose at him, the Kid caught hold of the white's saddlehorn. He hung suspended between the two horses, guiding the white by word and signal while retaining his hold of the sorrel's reins. Watching ahead, he saw the cart rushing nearer.

"Sorry, Cap'n Rule," he breathed. "But I don't know if I can trust your hoss to come with me."

With that, he let the reins free to hang over the borrowed horse's neck. Dropping his feet to the ground, he used their impact to bound up and astride the white's saddle. A wild Comanche yell shattered the air and the huge horse lengthened its stride. Dropping his rifle, one of the Mexicans sprang from his cover and snatched at the holstered re-volver on his hip. None of the others were even close to being reloaded and could only stare, hoping not to catch the Kid's eye.

Up soared the white stallion, taking the cart like a hunter-spooked white-tail deer bounding over a bush. Gathering itself, the sorrel also jumped, clearing the obstacle and lighting down running alongside the white. Wanting his own horse as fresh as possible for the work ahead, the Kid quit its saddle, dropped to the ground and leapt on to the sorrel's back once more. Although the Mexican drew and fired his revolver, the bullet came nowhere near hitting the fast-moving Kid.

"Get after him, you stinking greasers!" Giss howled, rolling out from under the bush and standing up.

Under the pretence of reloading the Sharps, Giss allowed his men to reach their horses—hidden among the trees—first. By the time he completed the loading, they were mounted and starting after the Kid. However his plan failed, for once by the cart they drew rein and waited for him. Scowling, he rode up and ordered the chase to be continued. Giss never cared to take chances; and neither did his men where the Ysabel Kid was concerned.

Holding his horses to a gallop, the Kid watched for a chance to lose his pursuers. At first he stuck to the trail, not wishing to pass through that thickly tangled woodland when riding at speed. A mile or so fell behind him before he reached more open country. So far his hunters had caught only fleeting glimpses of him on the winding trail and wasted no lead in trying for such a scanty target. However the trail stretched straight and level for almost a quarter of a mile. That meant presenting Joe Giss with too good a mark at which to aim. So the Kid swung his horses from the trail, riding up the slope flanking it to the south through the scattered trees and bushes.

Just as he reached the top, something struck the sorrel. The Kid heard the horse's stricken grunt and the sound of a shot from behind him. Then the sorrel staggered and began to collapse. Throwing his leg across its back, he jumped clear and darted around the white stallion's rump. Even using the Indian-made boot, the Kid carried his rifle Texas fashion, on the left of the saddle with the butt pointing to the rear. So he needed only to grip the wrist of the butt and the horse walking away slid the rifle free.

"That Kid's luckier'n the devil!" Giss spat out, lowering his smoking Sharps.

Seeing the Kid approaching the top of the slope and realising the nature of the country beyond it, Giss felt disinclined to follow the young Texan further. So he swung up his Sharps and chanced a snap shot. At almost a hundred yards, on a fast moving target, he might have counted himself fortunate to come so close to hitting his mark.

Swivelling around, the long old Mississippi rifle flowing to his shoulder, the Kid sighted quickly and took a fast shot. Giss' hat spun from his head and he threw himself from the saddle to dive into cover, a move his men copied with some speed. Once hidden from further bullets, they looked to their leader for guidance. Not for almost two minutes did Giss offer to give any. Then he looked up the slope and sucked in a breath.

"Let's go. Stay with the hosses, Manuel. The rest of us'll foot it."

After shooting, the Kid ran to where his stallion was waiting. He thrust the rifle unloaded into the boot and took the sombrero collected in Matamoros from where it hung on the saddlehorn. Drawing his bowie knife, he slashed open the top of the crown and ripped the brim. Tossing the ruined hat on to the body of the sorrel, he turned, mounted the white and rode off to the south-west.

Advancing cautiously up the slope, darting from cover to cover, Giss and his men approached the dead horse. Halting, their gaze went to the sombrero and noted the damage. Then they exchanged glances as the significance of what they saw struck them. All of the men, including Giss, had worked with *Comanchero* bands and knew something of Comanche Indian ways; enough to read the message left by the Kid.

If a raiding *Pehnane* brave found enemies persistently sticking to his trail, seeking to regain the loot lifted from them, he would destroy an item of their property and leave it in his tracks. That served as a warning of his future intentions. No longer would he content himself with passive flight. If they continued beyond his marker, he would kill on sight.

Some people, considering the Kid's youth and appearance of innocence, might have regarded the hat as mere ostentation left without serious intent; but Giss did not number among them. He *knew*, as sure as spring followed winter, that to follow the dark youngster would be courting quick, unexpected death. So Joe Giss reached a rapid decision.

"That frog-eater colonel in Matamoros wants somebody to scout for him, boys," he announced. "I conclude it'd be easy money. Let's go take on for him."

That meant deserting his partner, but Charlie Kraus had an understanding nature. Anyway, if their expressions were any guide, Giss' companions wholeheartedly approved of the desertion, even if scouting for the French meant working against their own people. Turning, they walked back down the slope, collected their horses and retraced their tracks to Matamoros.

Chapter 9

Keep Your Hands Off My Perfume

"Tired, Miss Boyd?" Sam Ysabel asked, turning in his saddle and studying their back-trail.

"I've forgotten what a bed is," she replied with a wry smile and eased her aching limbs as best she could.

"Rosita O'Malley's place's down this ways a piece," Ysabell told her. "We'll stop off and let the horses rest a spell. You can grab some sleep 'til night-fall and then we'll push on again."

"I'll not argue on that," Belle assured him.

Before Eve Coniston returned to the house, Belle and Shafto had slipped away from the consulate. They carried the heavy saddlebags, containing the money, a change of clothing and few other items Belle felt she might need, with them. Joining Sam Ysabel at the pre-arranged rendezvous, the girl rode out of Matamoros before midnight. All through the night and on towards the following noon they continued to ride at a good pace. Although Belle felt very tired, she refused to show it until Ysabel suggested that they should halt.

At first sight, Rosita O'Malley's cantina and *posada* looked little different to hundreds of other such places scattered through the Rio Grande border country. A two-storey adobe building set on the banks of a small stream, it offered a choice of stables or corrals for its guests' horses. Choosing the former, Ysabel led the way inside.

"Only Rosita's hosses here, and at the corral," he commented and his grulla walked into a stall in a manner which showed that it had done so often before.

Fighting down her tiredness, Belle set to work tending to her bay. Then she went to help Ysabel care for the pack-horse. Brought along more as a blind than for any other reason, the packs were empty and held in shape by light frameworks of twigs. While working on the horse, she saw a shadow at the doors and looked around. A tall, buxom, black haired woman, good-looking although no longer in the bloom of youth, entered. She wore a plain black dress, although of more daring cut than convention allowed. Halting, the woman's smile of welcome died as her eyes turned from Ysabel to Belle.

"*Hola*, Rosita gal," Ysabel greeted.

"Who's she, Big Sam?" the woman demanded in English.

"Fee-ancy to one of Jack Cureton's Rangers, come down the coast by boat. I'm taking her up to meet him."

"You sure on that?"

"Would I lie to you, Rosey gal?" asked Ysabel, sounding pained. "Come here and give a hard-travelled man a kiss."

A request to which Rosita responded with gusto, although throwing Belle a challenging, defiant glare as she commenced. When released, she turned to face the girl once more.

"Who's your feller, sister?"

"Solly Cole from up Tyler way," Ysabel put in. "Go make us some food and we'll want two rooms until night fall."

"I think you're one big liar, Sam Ysabel," Rosita stated. "And if I thought what I was thinking's true, I'd alter the shape of her face some."

"You mean like this?" asked Belle, swinging gracefully into a *chassé*, rear lateral kick which slashed her foot hard into the wall of the stall.

Jerking back a pace, Rosita stared at the mark on the wall and noted it to be at the height of her own face. Nor did she overlook the power with which the kick had landed, and she realised what it would do should it strike home on human flesh. A grin came to her face.

"I hope you 'n' Solly Cole'll be happy, *senorita*," she said. "And I still reckon Big Sam's a liar."

"Only about me," Belle smiled back. "He's loyal and true to you."

"Yeah. I just bet he is," Rosita replied. "As long as he's where I can keep both eyes on him. Come on. Leave the big *Indio* to finish the work and I'll give you a meal. Then you look like you could use some sleep."

Clearly the woman accepted that Belle and Ysabel were travelling together without romantic intentions. However she asked no questions about the girl's real reason for riding the river trail. Nobody, not even a close friend like Rosita O'Malley, inquired too closely into the Ysabel family's business—not twice hand-running, anyways.

"Shall I keep the saddlebags, or you, Miss Belle?" Ysabel asked.

"You, although there are a couple of things I'd like from them before I go to sleep," the girl replied.

For a *posada* drawing its trade from people travelling the bloody border, Rosita's place offered a good standard of cleanliness and the bed in the room allocated to Belle looked comfortable. Tired through she might be, Belle collected her dark blue shirt and riding breeches—dried and ironed hurriedly before she left the consulate—her parasol and, to Ysabel's amusement, a perfume bottle with its spray attached from the saddlebags before going to catch up on her rest. She closed the door, placed her property on the bed-side chair, hung her gunbelt on its back and eased off her boots. Then she lay on the bed and went to sleep.

Practice had taught Belle to wake at any given time. When she opened her eyes, feeling refreshed, she saw that the sun hung low in the western sky. Rising, she worked her muscles and found the ache had left them. It would be time to move soon, so she started to change clothes. While the black shirt and trousers fitted her, they lacked the comfortable feel of her older garments. With the riding breeches and boots on, a precaution against sudden departure, Belle reached for the shirt. She heard the lock click and the door opened.

"Well, now ain't that a sight to see?" asked an unfamiliar male voice.

Swinging around, Belle saw a man and woman entering the room. Strangers to her, they wore filthy clothes and gave an impression of voluntary uncleanliness. Across the passage a man covered Sam Ysabel at the door to his room and a third turned towards the speaker.

"Wha—!" Belle began, darting a glance towards her gunbelt.

"You try it and I'll blow your purty head off, gal!" warned the man at the door, thrusting forward a Le Mat revolver in a threatening manner. "Go take her gun, Amy-Jo."

Standing at the opposite end of the bed to her weapons, Belle knew she could not hope to reach them in time. She she stood still as the young woman walked by her and the man came closer. Despite his eyes ogling her bare shoulders and revealing underskirt, the Le Mat never wavered from its line on her stomach.

"Well I'll swan, Hickey!" Amy-Jo announced, picking up the perfume bottle. "If she don't have some fancy scent long."

"Keep your hands off my perfume!" Bell snapped.

"You hear her, Hickey?" Amy-Jo asked. "Anybody'd think it was her got the gun way she gives orders."

"Don't you put any of that perfume on yourself!" Belle warned.

"Listen here now, quality gal!" Amy-Jo flared back. "Right now I don't have to do one lil thing you tells me."

With that she directed the nozzle at her face and squeezed the bulb. A misty spray of liquid shot out, striking just under her nose. Instantly Amy-Jo let out a strangled, gagging croak, half-dropping, half-throwing the bottle on to the bed as she reeled backwards. The raw, acrid aroma of ammonia rose from the girl as she stumbled around in a circle and dropped fighting for breath to her knees.

Hickey's head jerked around to stare at Amy-Jo and for a moment he wondered what had caused the girl to act in such a manner. After which he became too engrossed in his own problems to care.

Up rose Belle's foot and this time she wore a boot highly suitable for kicking. While Hickey's Le Mat wavered involuntarily out of line, the toe of Belle's boot drove with considerable power under his jaw. Shooting backwards across the room, he crashed into the wall, bounced from it and landed face down on the floor.

At the commotion, the nearer of the men in the passage turned and sprang into Belle's room. His companion foolishly failed to keep full attention on Sam Ysabel. Whipping across, Ysabel's right hand slapped the man's revolver aside and flashed towards his holstered Dragoon. As the man took an unintended pace to the rear, Ysabel bunched and launched his left fist against the side of the other's head. Sent reeling across the passage, the man tried to bring his gun back into line. Thumb-cocked on the draw, the big Dragoon bellowed in Ysabel's hand as it cleared leather. The bullet sliced into the man's head, ending his attempt at shooting immediately. Even before the man fell, Ysabel went leaping towards the door of Belle's room.

Diving on to the bed as Hickey's second companion entered, Belle grabbed the scent-spray. She swung its nozzle towards the man as he lunged with hands reaching for her, and squeezed the bulb. Caught in the face by the spray of ammonia, the man duplicated Amy-Jo's reactions. Belle brought up her foot, ramming it into his stomach and shoving hard. Propelled backwards, the man offered Ysabel a tempting target. Up and down rose the big Texan's arm, smashing the base of the Dragoon's butt on top of the man's head to drop him like a pole-axed steer.

From downstairs came the voice of Rosita O'Malley, raised in a mixture of lurid Spanish and Irish curses.

"Watch 'em, gal!" Ysabel yelled, turning to dash out of the room and in the direction of the stairs.

Looking around her, Belle decided there would be no need to bother about the visitors for a spell. Even Amy-Jo showed no signs of recovery, but still crouched on the floor gagging and trying to breathe.

"I warned you not to use it," Belle remarked as she picked up her shirt.

Deciding that they would be making a hurried departure, Belle donned the shirt, tucked it into her waistband and then strapped on the gunbelt. With the Dance at her hip she felt capable of dealing with anything Hickey's crowd cared to start. Gathering up her belongings, she took them to Ysabel's room. On coming out, she saw Ysabel returning. The big Texan walked towards her, shaking his head as if unable to believe what he had found below.

"I never figured Hickey to have one lil bit of right good sense," he told the girl. "But I never reckoned he'd he hawg-stupid enough to leave just *one* feller guarding Rosey."

"Is she all right?" Belle asked.

"*She's* fine. Only I don't know how the feller'll feel when he gets round to feeling again. That skillet she hit him with sure messed up his face some."

From which Belle concluded that Rosita had managed to cope with the situation unaided.

"What lousy luck," Belle commented. "Picking today of all times to attempt a robbery."

"Like I say," Ysabel drawled. "Hickey's not smart; but he's a whole heap too smart to try a game like that at Rosey's place and again me without real good reason. If he knowed how much money we're carrying—."

"Then he might?"

"He just might get brave enough then."

"But he can't know!" Belle stated.

"He *shouldn't* know," corrected Ysabel. "Maybe we'd best ask some questions!"

"I think you're right,"Belle agreed. "The girl looks to be the only one likely to tell us anything for a time."

Sucking in sobbing breaths of air, Amy-Jo stared with tear-reddened, frightened eyes as Belle and Ysabel approached her.

"We didn't mean no harm!" the girl whined, edging across the floor on her rump away from them and darted a glance at her companions. "I tried to tell Hickey it wouldn't work."

"What wouldn't work, Amy-Jo?" Ysabel asked.

"Nothin'—."

Bending down, Belle dug her fingers into the girl's dirty hair and jerked her head back, looking at Ysabel and saying, "Pass me that scent bottle, please, Sergeant Ysabel."

"No!" Amy-Jo yelped, the recollection of her first tangling with the thing still vivid in her mind.

"What wouldn't work?" Belle demanded.

"H—Hickey'd kill me if he knowed I'd talked!" Amy-Jo wailed.

"You've got troubles from all sides, gal," Ysabel told her unsympathetically "Rosita's all riled up and looking to take it out of somebody's hide. I'll just call and tell her you're the first one woke up."

"Lookee, Big Sam!" the girl yelped, fear plain on her face as she directed another glance at the still form of her leader. "I had to come. You know Hickey!"

"I know him," Ysabel admitted. "And I never figured

he'd be *loco* enough to try a game like this."

"That ten thousand dollars you've got sounded mighty tempting," Amy-Jo answered simply.

Belle and Ysabel exchanged glances. Maybe the sum fell short of the actual total, but it came close enough to arouse ugly suspicions.

"How'd you know about that?" Ysabel growled.

"We was down on the river this afternoon," Amy-Jo replied. "Heard something coming and dog-my-cats if'n around a bend don't steam three itty-bitty boats like I've never seed afore. Like big rowing boats they was, only with chimneys 'n' engines in 'em. Done got cannons in the front—."

"Steam launches!" Belle breathed. "What about them?"

"We was just fixing to get the hell out of there when a feller yells out Hickey's name. It was Golly, that 'breed who rides for Charlie Kraus. Tells us it's all right and they only wants to make talk."

"What did he say?" Belle asked.

"That Big Sam was coming up river with you and for us to go after you. Hickey wouldn't've listened, only Golly allowed you'd got maybe ten thousand in gold along. Said for us to let Charlie have a cut if we got it."

"Who were in the boat?"

"Fellers in uniforms, ma'am. They let Golly come on to the bank to talk to us, that's how he let on about the money."

"Smart," Belle said to Ysabel. "They're sending word up-river and making it look like the people he tells are getting something extra that the Yankees don't know about."

"Smart and tricky," Ysabel agreed. "Charlie Kraus always was. What come off next, Amy-Jo?"

"Golly gets back to the boat and they heads on up river," the girl replied. "Then Hickey allows you'd be sure to call in here, Big Sam, and we should oughta try for the money. Only it didn't work."

"You tell Hickey, when he starts to take notice, to keep well out of my sight from now on," Ysabel growled.

"If you ain't holding me, I'm going to be long gone afore that," the girl stated. "Hickey's not going to forget it was me worked that damned scent squirter."

99

"Light out, gal," Ysabel grinned. "Let's get going, Miss Belle."

Collecting their belongings, Belle and Ysabel went downstairs. By the time they reached the ground floor, the drumming of hooves told that Amy-Jo had made good her promise of departing.

"I let her go," Rosita remarked.

"She'd not help against Hickey," Ysabel answered. "So its as well."

"I'm sorry about making trouble for you, Rosita," Belle went on.

"So'll Hickey be, unless you killed him," the woman replied, nodding to a bunch of tough-looking Mexicans who hovered in the background. "We'll tend to everything here. You'd best start riding."

"Could be there'll be more folks around asking about us, Rosey," Ysabel warned. "Don't get smart should they come."

"They'll get the same as everybody else," Rosita promised. "Food, a place to sleep, and no information. How about Lon?"

"Tell him we're headed south, instead of sticking to the river trail," Ysabel replied. "He'll find us easy enough."

"I agree with you, sergeant," Belle put in. "Those launches can make easily six miles an hour going up-river and will have been moving while we rested."

"They've got engines that don't get tired, ma'am," the Texan pointed out. "Hosses do, and people. Thing is, how did the Yankees get to know about us?"

"They have efficient spies too," Belle replied as they walked out of the building. "I've been afraid they'd find out from the start."

"You mean they brought them launches here especial for this?"

"No. Although somebody acted fast and smart in using them to pass on the message. I don't suppose there's a chance of them meeting some of our troops along the river?"

"Devil the bit this far from Brownsville."

"How about Captain Cureton and his men?" Belle asked.

"They're Rangers, not army. Fellers who didn't want to take sides, some Yankees and some of us rebs," Ysabel explained. "Cureton can only hold 'em together by staying clear of either side in the War. They're trying to protect the homes of soldiers away fighting from Injuns, bad whites and Mexican *bandidos*. There'll be no help from them."

"And the man with the launches can find other men like Hickey?"

"Or worse. Golly knows the river hang-outs. Even if he only tells 'em ten thousand dollars, there'll be plenty wanting to try for it."

"What do we do then?" Belle inquired.

"Like I said. Go south. They'll likely all be figuring on us sticking to the river and looking for a place to cross into Texas."

"How about Rosita?" Belle said as she saddled her horse. "Will she be safe after we've gone?"

"From Hickey?" Ysabel laughed. "She could eat two like him and his whole bunch. And for the rest; well, she's got kin on both sides of the river, tough *hombres* all of 'em, thicker'n fleas on an Injun dawg, who'll come a-running happen she yells, or should anything untoward happen to her. Yes, ma'am. I figure Rosey'll be all right. But we sure as hell won't, unless we put some miles between us and the border."

Chapter 10

You Never Should've Tried A Knife

Seeing a dead animal on the range, a domesticated dog will go straight up to it and investigate. A wolf never does, but circles around the body warily, alert for traps and danger.

So it was with the Ysabel Kid as he rode towards Rosita O'Malley's place at ten o'clock on the night of his father's hectic visit. Instead of riding up to the buildings—owned by a good and loyal friend though they might be—he studied them from a distance and made a circle around to take note of everything. Lights glowed at the downstairs' windows and he could see a number of horses in the corral.

Slipping from the white's saddle, he led it to some trees beyond the house. Although he removed the headstall and bit, hanging them with the coiled rope on the horn, he left the saddle in place. The horse would remain where he left it, tied or free, while a whistle would bring it to him when needed. So he left it in the cover of the trees, with good grazing under-foot. Silently as an owl hunting in the night sky, the Kid advanced on foot towards the buildings. His route took him by the corral and he kept down wind as a matter of simple precaution. Pausing, he looked the horses over. Fine animals, yet their assortment of colours seemed to rule out a French cavalry patrol. Which still left a whole slew of possibilities. No guards around the place made the visitors unlikely to be Juaristas, for such invariably kept watch for their foreign enemies. That left a variety of border citizens, not all friendly to the Ysabel family, who might be calling on Rosita O'Malley.

The Kid moved on, creeping to the side of the main building and moving to where he could see into the big barroom through a window. What he saw surprised him and made him bless the precautions taken.

The visitors formed two distinct groups, either of which might be found anywhere along the bloody border, except in areas with large and efficient law enforcement organisations. Finding them both at Rosita O'Malley's place, noted for its neutrality in the various border feuds, might have been natural enough. What surprised the Kid was the fact that the two leaders shared a table in apparent amity.

No mere chance meeting could bring them together, nor a desire to discuss matters of cultural interest. Tall, slender, elegantly dressed like a wealthy *haciendero*, Ramon Peraro possessed leanings towards education and gentlemanly habits. Which same nobody could even start to claim for Bully Segan. Big, bulky, with cold, hard eyes practically the only thing visible among his mat of whiskers, he wore buckskins and might have been a member of the old hairy Rocky Mountain brigade who opened up so much of the far West. Only one thing linked Peraro and Segan. Each ran as mean a band of cut-throats and killers as could be assembled.

Four of Segan's men, *Americanos del Norte* dressed in buckskins and well-armed, sat at a table behind their boss. While two of Peraro's gang stood at the bar, another four sat over against the wall beyond the *bandido* leader. The atmosphere seemed strained, only natural with the two gangs in competition with each other, and most of the company drank left-handed. Only the two leaders sat together, using the right hand to raise their *tequila* glasses. Watching the others, the Kid was reminded of seeing, as a boy, a cougar and grizzly bear drinking on either side of the only waterhole in ten miles. The two predators showed the same alert, suspicious watchfulness as did the members of the rival gangs.

"Now what in hell's ole Bully Segan doing sat here all friendlied-up with Peraro?" the Kid asked himself. "Last I heard, Ramon was fixing to side with Juarez against the French."

Not to celebrate, or merely have fun, certainly; for the men ignored Rosita's girls and drank sparingly. One possibility sprang to mind. Ever since they started smuggling, long before the War, the Ysabels had built up a name for rugged, effective defence of their property. Few gangs on the border would chance attacking one of their pack trains. Yet it seemed unlikely that such a project would bring together Peraro and Segan. Even less so that their meeting would take place at Rosita O'Malley's *posada*, known to be the Ysabel family's favourite visiting spot.

Deciding to learn more about the visitors before entering, the Kid withdrew and went to the rear of the building. He could see into the kitchen, but made no attempt to approach it. Instead he settled on his haunches and waited in the darkness with all the patience of his maternal grandfather's people.

Almost an hour passed before Rosita entered the kitchen and came close enough to its open door for the Kid's purpose. Cupping his hands around his mouth, he gave a near perfect imitation of an Arizona pyrrhuloxia's mating call. Passing the doorway, Rosita changed direction and walked outside. Again came the twittering whistle. Aware that the bird rarely came into that region and sang only in daylight, she knew the call to be a signal. So she spoke over her shoulder, telling the cook she was going out back and walked into the darkness.

"*Cabrito?*" she asked, speaking barely above a whisper.

"It ain't Benito Juarez," the youngster replied, moving to her side. "You got the cream of so-ciety tonight, Rosey."

"That's no way to talk about my customers," the woman answered, lowering the Remington Double Derringer she had carried concealed on her person since Sam Ysabel's departure. "Way you're fancied up, I thought you'd be coming in. All it wants is for your pappy and that high-quality gal to come along for it to be the success of the year."

A grin twisted the Kid's lips as he realised that his change of clothes had come close to bringing a bullet into his belly. Knowing Rosita, he did not doubt that she would have shot if he had spoken less promptly to identify himself. Not that he blamed her. Anybody who aroused the suspicions of either Peraro or Segan stood a better than fair chance of meeting a painful death. So she could take no chances.

"What's up, Rosey?" he asked, moving to one side as she entered the small backhouse and left its door open.

"I don't know who that high-quality gal was, or what's she's doing; and'd 's soon not find out," Rosita answered. "But she's sure got a heap of real nice folks looking for her and Big Sam."

"Charlie Kraus here as well as Segan and Peraro?"

"Nope. Hickey 'n' his crowd come in earlier. Lone Walt's still here—'fact he won't be leaving."

"Poor ole Lone Walt," drawled the Kid, in a voice which showed no sympathy. "I hope he's not planted close to drinking water or growing things. You mean Hickey come here looking for pappy?"

"*Si!*" admitted the woman. "I couldn't hardly believe it myself. That high-quality gal sure has something."

"That was Belle Boyd, the Rebel Spy," the Kid told her. "What's going on, Rosey gal?"

"Ramon and the Bully's after your pappy and the gal. From what they've said, there'll be more folks looking. So they're working in cahoots and figure to split the money between 'em—."

"So word's got out," the Kid breathed.

"Three Yankee steam-launches've gone up river passing it," Rosita replied. "Big Sam said to tell you he's swung off to the south."

"Peraro and old Bully's got fellers along who can read sign real good," the Kid remarked. "I'd's soon not have 'em dogging my tracks when I go after pappy."

"You want for me to put something in their *tequila*?" Rosita inquired.

"Does that firewater need anything in it?" countered the Kid and grinned at the pungent, obscene defence of the *posada's* liquor. Then he went on, "Nope. Don't you chance it, Rosey. I'll tend to things myself."

All too well the Kid knew Peraro's and Segan's vindictive nature. Let either of them feel the slightest breath of suspicion and no amount of potential family backing could save Rosita. So the youngster intended, if possible, to halt the pursuit in a manner which would leave her free from blame.

"I'll do anything I can, Lon," Rosita promised.

"I know that, you never did have a lick of good sense. Got some Ysabel blood in you, most likely. Only I got me a right sneaky, treacherous notion. Where're their hosses?"

"In the corral, all except Peraro's black stallion."

"That figures. He allus keeps it in a stable if he can."

"And with that Yaqui of his standing guard on it," Rosita

warned. "I could send something out—."

"Damned if I'll chance eating here again," grinned the Kid, "way you're so set on slipping something into the stuff. Nope, Rosey. Happen you want to help, just hint around that Ramon might have some more fellers out 'n' about."

"You'll never get the black—!" Rosita began.

"Likely not," the Kid agreed, although the time would come when he had to steal Peraro's well-guarded favourite horse.* "But Bully's *bayo-coyote's* in the corral and not guarded. Ole Bully sets a heap of store in that hoss."

"It's a good hoss," Rosita answered.

"Yeah," the Kid replied. "And wouldn't he be all riled up happen it's gone comes morning?"

"It's a big chance, *Cabrito*."

"Yes'm. A real big chance."

Silence fell and Rosita realised that the Kid had gone. Sucking in a deep breath, she rose from the backhouse seat, shook down her skirts and returned to the *posada*.

Although he went back to his horse, the Kid did not intend to make a move straight away. There would be no point on going on, for he needed daylight to find his father's and Belle's tracks. More important, he must attempt to prevent the two gangs following them. Trying to do so in an open fight offered too little chance of success to be contemplated. So he planned another way. If one of the gangs found some of its horses missing, the blame would fall on their rivals.

Taking Peraro's horse from the stable would be difficult. So, despite his desire to attempt the feat, he decided against trying. Down in the corral stood a easier mark. Unless his boyhood training had left him—and he knew it had not— he should be able to achieve his ends.

Satisfied, he off-saddled the white and allowed it to roll on the grass while making his own preparations to catch some rest.

Like Belle, the Kid could wake at any time he set himself to. Sitting up, he looked around, darted a glance at the sky and estimated how long he had slept. Then he rose and moved to where he could see the *posada*. No lights showed at any of the windows, although a lantern still glowed in

* Told in THE TEXAN.

106

the stable. To one side the white stallion lay sleeping, but it woke and raised its head as he walked back to his saddle.

"Settle down again, ole hoss," the Kid said quietly, unfastening the coiled rope from the saddlehorn. "I won't be needing you for a spell yet."

Leaving the horse still resting, the youngster made his way through the darkness towards the *posada*. Although not really needing one, he used the light from the stables as a guide and directed his silent feet towards the corral. Eyes and ears worked constantly to catch any slight warning of danger as the Kid drew closer to his destination. Probably as a sign of their trust and faith in each other, neither gang appeared to have a man guarding the horses in the corral. Peraro could continue to do so with his black stallion; for he always did, even in the safety of his hide-out.

Raiding—horse-stealing—always rated high in the ways a Comanche could gain honour and boys received a very thorough training in all aspects of the art. So the Kid possessed all the knowledge he would need to carry out his scheme. In his hand, he held his rope, a most useful extension of his will when properly used. On reaching the downwind side of the corral, he paused to study the situation and decide which horses he wanted to steal. For his idea to work out properly, he must take horses belonging only to Bully Segan's gang.

Selecting the required animals, even in darkness, proved easy to a man of the Kid's encyclopedic equine knowledge. Horse being gregarious by nature, they tended to bunch with those of their kind to which they were most familiar. So the Kid could make out three well-defined groups in the corral. Even without being able to point directly at Segan's big *bayo-coyote* stallion, he quickly learned which of the groups belonged to the white men. Easing around so that the wind bore his scent into the corral, he watched the horses' reactions. Mexican animals gave signs of restlessness at catching a white man's scent; not as much as Indian ponies would, but sufficient for the Kid's needs. With the ownership of the groups established, the rest was easy. Even before he withdrew down wind, he had located the Segan's highly-prized mount.

Before entering the corral, the Kid took out his knife and

107

slit the rope into three twenty foot lengths. Nomally an Indian on a raiding mission took along the ropes ready prepared, but the Kid had not expected the need to arise. However a small matter like that created little difficulty. Swiftly he made running nooses on two of the pieces, the original honda remaining to be used on the third. With all ready, he approached the corral gate openly. A low hissing whistle left his lips, alerting the horses to his presence without disturbing them. Fortunately even Rosita O'Mally's stock saw enough arrivals in the darkness not to take fright at his approach and the gangs' mounts regarded such behaviour as natural.

Carefully the Kid eased out the gate bars, lowering the ends he held to the ground. A quick glance around told him his presence still remained unsuspected and he entered the corral. Keeping up the soothing hissing, he moved among the horses. If any of them showed signs of restlessness, he stopped like a statue until the animal quietened down once more. At last he reached the *bayo-coyote* and it faced him with alert, but not frightened attention. Using the same unhurried, calm manner that had covered his every movement since entering the corral, the Kid raised the rope and slipped its honda-formed loop over the horse's head. Giving a snort, the *bayo-coyote* tossed its head. If the Kid had so much as flinched, the stallion might have attacked; but he stood like a statue and continuing the low comforting whistle. Then the noose drew tight and the worst danger passed. Feeling the familiar touch of a rope, the horse stood fast and awaited the next command. Before attempting anything further, the Kid drew gently but insistently on the rope. As the sleek head lowered, he blew into its nostrils. Back in the days when the Comanche obtained the first of the 'goddogs' from the Spanish explorers, it had been learned that breathing into a horse's nostrils quietened it and rendered it amenable to orders. Nor did the *bayo-coyote* prove any exception, having received the treatment many times since its capture and training. Gently and without fuss, the Kid won the horse's confidence and dominated its will.

Gathering two more of the horses belonging to Segan's gang took less time and presented no problems. As its owner ran the gang, so the *bayo-coyote* led their mounts. Seeing it accept the newcomer, the others stood steady enough. Leading his three captives, the Kid walked slowly around the corral and through the gate. If anybody had been watching, it seemed that the trio of horses did no more than move aimlessly. Only while passing through the gate could the difference be seen. All the rest of the Segan gang's horses followed, but he turned them back at the gate. Three would be enough for his plan and to handle more added noise and risk. Knotting the three lead-ropes together, he left his captives standing while he replaced the corral gates.

"Grandpappy Long Walker'd be proud of me," the Kid grinned as he reached for the knotted lead ropes. "Sure wish I'd a pair of wored-out ole moccasins along—Naw, that'd give the whole snap away for sure."

Often a successful Comanche raider would leave a sign of his presence to mock the people he robbed. A favourite trick was to leave behind an ancient pair of moccasins. Then when the owners discovered their loss they read the message that the raider no longer needed his old foot-wear as he could ride off in comfort on the stolen horses.

Much as the Kid wished he could play the old ending to his raid, he knew it would be impossible and impracticable. He did not have a pair of old moccasins along. Even if he had, using them in such a manner might ruin his scheme. Seeing the old Comanche sign might point out an alternative remover of the horses to Segan. The Kid's connection with that particular Indian tribe being well known, his activities could be understood and the desired trouble between the gangs averted.

So, regretfully putting aside the thoughts, he led the horses around the outside of the corral and, on the opposite side to the stables, off towards where his white stallion waited. Picketing them securely out of sight of the corral, he returned to his interrupted sleep. By the first light of dawn he woke, packed his gear, saddled the white and returned to a position from which he could watch the cantina.

Soon after the Kid took his place, a couple of Segan's men walked from the building and in the direction of the corral. Then the others came out, the gang leaders still apparently on the best of terms even if their men showed the same veiled hostility. Reaching the corral, the first pair came to a halt, staring at the horses.

"Now cut for sign, you stupid yahoos!" breathed the Kid.

Almost as if they heard him, the men directed their eyes to the ground and started around the corral. At last they halted, pointing down. Without attempting to follow the tracks further, they turned and dashed back the way they came.

"Bully!" one of them yelled. "Your hoss's gone. And two more."

"Gone!" Segan bellowed and started towards the corral.

Standing at the door of the cantina to see her guests depart, Rosita decided to add her touch to the Kid's plan.

"Hey, Ramon," she called in Spanish. "I've sent Yaqui his breakfast to the stable. What an appetite. He eats enough for two."

Harmless enough sounding words, but sufficient to raise unpleasant thoughts in Segan's head. Suspicious by nature, he read what Rosita hoped he would in her words. There had been other hints during the previous night that Peraro might have more than the one man outside the *posada*. While accepting that Yaqui was standing guard on the black stallion, in the interests of retaining Peraro's good will until after relieving the Ysabels of the money, Segan drew sinister conclusions from Rosita's innocent statement.

Three of Sagan's gang would be without horses, even if he took one of their mounts for himself. He did not wish to help bushwhack the Ysabels unless sure that he had enough men at his back to protect his interests.

Never known for his tact, but famous as a hater of *gringos*, Peraro's second in command, Perez, could not resist injecting a mocking comment.

"You lose something, *Matón*?" he asked with a grin at his companions.

"You're damned right I lost something!" Segan answered, swinging around to face the Mexicans. "Where are they, Peraro?"

"*Matón*, Bully, *amigo*," Peraro replied. "I don't know what you mean."

However he stood tense, balancing lightly on the balls of his feet. One night's drinking could not wipe away decades of antipathy caused by racial differences and working in

110

active competition. No more than a precaution on Peraro's part, it increased Segan's suspicions and anger.

Quickly Rosita drew the cantina door closed. Not suspicious in itself. Born and raised on the border, she could read the signs. At the first hint of trouble, even without prior knowledge of its coming, she would have acted in the same manner.

"Where's my hoss?" Segan demanded. "Where the hell did your son-of-a-bitch take it to?"

"I'm not sure that I like that question, *hombre*!" Peraro answered with the silky deadliness of a high born Spanish fighting man. "If you can't keep hold of your horses, I am not to blame."

"Keep 'em!" Segan bellowed. "I'll damned soon get 'em back."

Despite having an old Walker Colt hanging in his holster, Segan snatched the long bladed knife from its sheath and sprang at Peraro. Moving even faster, the Mexican also fanned out his shorter but no less deadly blade. With the fluid grace of a matador avoiding the charge of a bull, Peraro side-stepped Segan's rush. As the heavy copy of a James Black bowie lashed harmlessly by him, the Mexican delivered a ripping thrust to the attacker's body. Letting out a croaking cry of agony, Segan staggered by Peraro, dropped his knife, clawed at his belly and crashed to his knees at the porch.

"You never should've tried a knife, Bully," the Kid commented, watching with satisfaction.

One of Segan's men showed a better grasp of the situation than his boss. Whipping the revolver from his belt, he fired. The bullet caught Peraro in the shoulder, spinning him around and tumbling him to the ground. Out came more guns and men dashed for cover to continue the fight.

Satisfied that everything in his scheme was going as he wanted, the Kid returned to his horses. With both leaders incapacitated, the Ysabels and Belle Boyd need not fear pursuit from either gang. Finding his father's tracks took only a short time. Using his newly-acquired horses, the Kid could push on at a better pace. From what Rosita told him and he had seen at the *posada*, the sooner they joined forces the better.

111

Chapter 11

They'll Pay To Get Her Back

Due to nursing his throbbing jaw and thinking what he would do to Amy-Jo when he laid hands on her, Hickey rode through the darkness without his usual caution. Nor did the men with him show greater alertness, being concerned with their own sufferings. Before they could stop themselves or realise the danger, the trio found themselves covered by the guns of three horsemen who loomed out of the bushes.

For a moment panic filled Hickey, then he recognised the stocky shape on the nearest horse.

"Howdy, Charlie," he greeted. "You headed for Rosita O'Malley's?"

"Maybe," Charlie Kraus replied, holstering his Colt. "You been there?"

"Sure. We got your word and figured Big Sam'd likely call in to see Rosey. He was there all right."

"*You* went up against Sam Ysabel?" Kraus asked, his voice showing how he felt on the matter.

"Sure, but him and some of his boys laid for us and whomped us good," Hickey answered.

"What is it, Mr. Kraus?" asked a woman's voice and Eve rode forward from where she and Ffauldes had been told to wait until the approaching riders were identified. "Has he seen Ysabel and Boyd?"

"Sure," Kraus replied. "At Rosey O'Malley's place."

"They ain't there now, ma'am," Hickey put in, sensing the chance of making a little money out of the disastrous affair.

"Who's this, Mr. Kraus?" Eve inquired.

"Name's Hickey. He tried to get that money."

"Tried?"

"That'd be his best, ma'am. What happened, Hickey?"

"Big Sam was waiting for us. Nigh on bust my jaw, beat

Tetch here about the head something evil and done for poor ole Lone Tom. Rosey lay a skillet on Mick's face and when we come too, Big Sam and that high-quality gal'd lit out."

"Where?" Eve demanded. "Along the river?"

"Down south, way Rosey told it," Hickey replied.

"She told *you* that?" Kraus growled.

"Naw. I heard her telling it to Ramon Peraro and Bully Segan."

"Peraro and Segan, huh?"

"Who are they, Mr. Kraus?" Eve put in.

"Just about the meanest, most ornery pair of killers on the Rio Grande," he explained. "Fact being, you'd be hard put to pair 'em anywheres short of hell."

"Then it wouldn't be advisable for us to go to this woman and question her about Ysabel?" Eve said.

"Ma'am," Kraus replied. "It wouldn't be advisable even without them two there. Where Ysabel's concerned, Rosey O'Malley wouldn't tell you the time of day. And with Peraro 'n' the Bully both there, it's be plumb suicide." Then a thought struck him and he glared at Hickey. "How much did you tell Big Sam?"

"Nothing!" the man yelped. "Warn't much talking done when we met up and time I'd got round to feeling like it again, he'd pulled out."

"Where's Amy-Jo?" Kraus growled.

"She—She pulled out," Hickey admitted.

"Afore you come round?"

"Yeah. And when I lay hands on her, I'll make her wish she'd never learned to talk!"

"So she told Big Sam how you got on to him?"

"She told him," agreed Hickey. "You can't blame her, Charlie. Big Sam's got mighty fetching ways when he gets that way inclined."

"That means Ysabel and Boyd know what we've done," Eve remarked. "Here, take this ten dollars and ride!"

Grabbing the money, Hickey gabbled his thanks while putting the spurs to his horse. Followed by his men, he set off through the darkness at a gallop.

"That stupid—!" Kraus began. "A bullet'd been more his needings."

Satisfied that there would be no danger, Ffauldes rode

up to assert himself. He had heard everything said and felt he should give the others the benefit of his superior ability.

"So they've left the river trail—," he began.

"Maybe," Kraus replied. "You can't be sure of anything with Sam Ysabel and less with the Kid."

"Your partner stayed in Matamoros to deal with the Kid," Ffauldes pointed out. "He took our money to hire extra help to do it."

"Staying there's one thing, getting help's easy," Kraus grunted. "Stopping the Kid's another again. It's been tried afore—he's still around even if the folks who tried it ain't."

"Damn it! Your partner—."

"Joe'll do the best he can, mister," Kraus interrupted. "Right now it's Big Sam, not the Kid I'm thinking about."

"We can pick up their trail at the *posada*—," Ffauldes started.

"And while we're following it slow, which's the only way it'll be followed, Big Sam and the gal'll be at the other end making more tracks," Kraus told him. "Top of that, *mister*, Bully Segan and Ramon Peraro ain't going to take kind to more folk trailing along to share the money."

"They'd object to us going along?" Eve asked.

"They'd object to each other going along, happen one of 'em's got enough men to do it," Kraus replied. "We don't have near enough men to tangle with 'em."

"What do you think Ysabel will do?" Eve said after a moment's thought.

"I dunno," Kraus admitted. "He'll know that by now every robbing son-of-a-bitch along the river's heard, or enough of 'em, and'll be hunting for him. I'd say he'll keep to the south, at least until he gets near Nava. You want to try hunting for him?"

"No," Eve decided. "We'll go up the river. I want to contact the steam launch flotilla and, if Ysabel gets through, I'll be there ready to send warning to our garrisons in New Mexico."

Before Ffauldes could make another comment, Kraus gave the signal to start moving. Clearly the stocky man had decided who was running the affair and accepted Eve's suggestions.

There had been a heated scene in Matamoros when Eve laid her plans for the journey and announced that she would take one man along. That was a simple precaution, for she doubted if Kraus would be reliable if things went wrong. Much to her annoyance, Ffauldes had pulled rank and insisted that he be the one to accompany her. That she agreed had been less a tribute to his capabilities than the desire to keep him under her eyes. The French agreed to allow the *Waterbury* into Matamoros for the purpose of repairing her damaged hull. Expecting the Confederate agents to make a further attempt, Eve gave strict instructions to the Yankee detachment for the ship's protection. So she gave in to Ffauldes' demands, taking him with her to prevent his interference or ruination of her arrangements.

Patriotism did not lie behind Ffauldes' insistence, nor devotion to duty. Knowing the state of affairs in the United States, he could imagine the acclaim that would come to the man who ruined the South's desperate final bid. With the War almost over, that man could expect recognition which would still be fresh in the public's memory when the handing out of rewards commenced. So he joined Eve's party and promised himself that he alone would garner the credit. However he soon learned that Eve commanded the expedition. All through the first day's journey Kraus made that plain.

By-passing Rosita O'Malley's *posada* shortly before the Kid arrived, they pushed on a further two miles and made camp. Next morning, following Eve's orders, they continued to go west along the banks of the river. They travelled fast, changing horses as needed. Visiting various gathering-places for the criminal element, Kraus reported on the lack of men present. Twice the party were halted and challenged by armed gangs, to be let pass after establishing their identity. On one occasion they fought off a bunch of Mexicans who objected to another party apparently on the trail of Ysabel and the money. At Nuevo Laredo, Kraus went into town with one of his men while Eve and the remainder stayed outside. He returned with news that both the French and Juaristas were interested in the gold, adding more searchers for Ysabel and the Rebel Spy.

At noon on the day after passing Nuevo Laredo, the

party met up with the launch flotilla and its commanding officer reported on his activities. He had taken his command along the river as far as Piedras Negras, returning without the Texas citizens of Eagle Pass learning of their presence. Telling the officer of her plans, Eve arranged for him to patrol between Piedras Negras and Nuevo Laredo. Then, if they received word about Ysabel and Belle Boyd reaching Klatwitter, it could be acted upon without waste of time.

While Eve was conversing with the U.S. Navy lieutenant, she saw Kraus talking to Golly. The two men stood clear of the others and she noticed that Golly pointed across to the Texas bank of the river. When questioned, Kraus said that he and Golly had discussed the chances of meeting with Texan opposition.

Leaving the flotilla to complete taking on wood for fuel, the party continued its journey. The day went by without incident, so did the next until the late afternoon. By that time they had come close to the town of Nava, although still sticking to the river. As usual Kraus had men ahead as scouts. With the proximity of the danger area, he used two instead of the usual one scout and they returned in some haste. Then followed a conversation in Spanish so rapid that neither Eve nor Ffauldes could follow it. Eve caught one word, 'Danvila', probably because it came several times and was spoken with some feeling.

"What's wrong, Mr. Kraus?" she asked.

"We've got to turn back," he replied. "There's a big bunch of Juaristas up ahead."

"We've no quarrel with them," Eve stated. "And I've a letter from our consul in Matamoros explaining our presence."

"Maybe you won't get time to show it," Kraus pointed out.

"Very well. We'll go and make camp by the river until the flotilla comes by," Eve decided. "With two cannon and a Gatling gun at our backs, they'll listen."

A point with which Kraus could not argue. In fact he seemed more cheerful at being reminded of the flotilla's assault armament. As she had never seen one, Amy-Jo had failed to identify the six-barrelled, .58 calibre Gatling gun the lieutenant's launch carried in place of the usual

12-pounder boat howitzer. Such weapons, especially the Gatling gun, would impress the Juaristas and make them amenable to discussion.

Raising no more objections, Kraus led the way farther upstream until finding a suitable camp-site. Tired from the hard, long journey, Eve removed her boots and rolled fully-dressed into her blankets. She fell asleep almost immediately and deeply. Just how deeply she discovered on waking.

The morning sun hung just above the horizon as she sat up and reached to where her boots should be. Then her sleep-slowed mind registered that something must be wrong. She heard Mexican voices, which did not in itself surprise her for few of Kraus' men spoke English. What came as a surprise was the high-pitched tones of women mingled with the voices of the men. At the same moment she became aware that her boots no longer stood by the bed.

Jerking upright, Eve stared around her. There was no sign of Kraus and his men. Instead half-a-dozen well-armed, hard-faced men in *vaquero* dress and two pretty young women stood around the camp. One of the women was drawing on Eve's boots, while the other petulantly watched a man up-ending Eve's saddlebags.

"If you look for Charlie, *senorita*," said the tallest of the men, walking towards Eve. "He's gone."

"Who are you?" she demanded, glancing to where Ffauldes was sitting covered by one of the newcomers' rifle.

"Joaquim Sandos, *senorita*," the man replied. "Didn't Charlie speak about me, or tell you his fellers saw Pancho there yesterday and know we come looking for him?"

"He didn't. Why do you want to see him?"

"He not tell you much, *senorita*. Didn't he say how I'm Cosme Danvila's *segundo*?" Sandos asked. "Him and Cosme, they not good friends since Charlie shoot Cosme's brother and leave his sister with a little *nino*. I never think to see Charlie this far west. Unless he hear that Cosme across the river in Texas on—business."

"I see," Eve said quietly.

Which she did. Clearly Kraus had only accompanied her that far because Golly had brought him word of his enemy's absence. She remembered the pointing across the river when

117

they met the flotilla. Then Kraus must have learned the previous afternoon that not all Danvila's band had gone on the raid. The story about a Juarista force had been fabricated as an excuse to turn back. Probably Kraus was hoping for the arrival of the flotilla. When it did not come, or possibly because he had learned that Sandos' party was drawing near, Kraus slipped away with his men. Eve could even understand why he had deserted her. Neither she nor Ffauldes could handle horses quietly in the dark, or stand up to a hard, fast flight. So, to Kraus' practical way of thinking, leaving them behind offered the only solution.

"Maybe Charlie leave her as a presen' for Cosme," suggested the man searching Eve's belongings.

"No. He was guiding me to El Paso," Eve answered. "My husband is in the army there."

"You not a *Tejano, senorita;* and you don't wear a wedding ring," Sandos pointed out. "And there're no soldiers at El Paso."

"She's an important member of the United States Government," Ffauldes put in. "So am I. Show them that letter from the consul, Miss Coniston."

"Can I?" Eve inquired and, receiving Sandos' nod, took the letter from the pocket of her divided skirt.

However, if the way Sandos examined the sheet of paper was anything to go by, he could not read the consul's request that Eve be given free passage through to El Paso.

"You got 'nother pair of boots, *senorita*?" Sandos asked, thrusting the paper into his pocket. "Rosa and Juanita never had any before and Rosa wants a pair."

"Look, mister!" Ffauldes put in, standing up and showing that he was not wearing a gun. "She's real important, but I'm not."

"Shut your mouth!" Eve hissed and then smiled at Sandos. "I'm not important at all."

"Is a pity if you're not, *senorita*. If you not Charlie's *amante*, sweetheart you call him, maybe somebody pay good to get you back."

"You can bet they'll pay to get her back!" Ffauldes agreed eagerly. "There're three small steam boats on the river. If you let me go to them, they'll take me to Matamoros and I'll bring you the money."

"I'll just bet you will!" Eve hissed.

"The *senorita* she don' trust you, *hombre*," Sandos remarked.

"What have I to lose?" Ffauldes spat back. "Let me go to the boats and I'll arrange everything."

"Go get on your horse, *senor*," Sandos ordered.

Without as much as a glance at Eve, Ffauldes started to obey. Sandos nodded as Ffaulkes walked towards the two horses left by Kraus. Even as Eve opened her mouth to scream a warning, two rifles cracked. Lead ripped into Ffauldes' back and he sprawled face down on the ground. Letting her breath out in a gasp, Eve tried to go towards the stricken man.

"I think he wouldn't've come back, *senorita*," Sandos remarked, stopping her. "He look like my Uncle Sebastian and he one big liar. Will anybody pay to get you back?"

For a moment Eve did not reply. Then she realised that her only chance of staying alive would be to answer in the affirmative. Resistance would be futile, so she decided to go along with what might offer her a hope of escape.

"Yes. They'll pay to get me back. Or the authorities over the border will give you money for me. I'm a United States agent. If you look for the boats, they'll go at top speed to Brownsville for the money."

"You a spy for the *Estados Unidos*, heh?"

"Yes."

"I think you tell the truth this time. But it for Cosme to say what we do with you."

"Is Senor Danvila hunting for Sam Ysabel?" Eve inquired, suddenly realising that Sandos had not mentioned the matter.

"Nobody goes hunting for Big Sam, *senorita*," Sandos replied. "Not if they want to stay alive."

"Even if he has fifteen thousand dollars in gold with him?"

"You make the joke with Sandos, no?"

"I'm not joking, *senor*. Ysabel and the Rebel Spy, a girl, are taking the gold to the French general at Nava."

"Maybe they won't get it there," Sandos grinned.

"Why don't you go and find them?" Eve asked.

"With six men?" Sandos scoffed and spoke to his companions.

Eve judged that he was telling them the news and all seemed to find the latter part highly amusing.

"If you don't believe me, send one of your men along the river to find the boats," Eve said. "They will tell him, the sailors. Or he could go to Pasear Hennessey's cantina. Kraus' man, Golly, came up river with the boats to tell everybody about Big Sam and the money."

"Nobody from Charlie Kraus would come near us, *senorita*," Sandos replied. "We take you to our camp and I send for Cosme. He say what we do."

They mounted Eve on the sorriest of their horses when ready to move out, one which looked incapable of outrunning a turtle in its sway-backed, gaunt-ribbed condition. Gathering up all they wanted and hiding Ffauldes' stripped body in the bushes, the men and girls surrounded Eve and rode off. Instead of sticking to the river's bank, they rode parallel to it but some distance away. However the country was open enough for Eve to see the water and she scanned it eagerly in the hope of seeing the flotilla.

Manned by veterans of the Mississippi Squadron, who carried Navy Colts, cutlasses and Spencer carbines in addition to the cannons and Gatling gun, the three launches held the means of her escape. Although sailors, the crews knew plenty about land fighting and, if they heard of her capture, might contrive a rescue.

"Look!" one of the men said, pointing towards the river.

The three launches came into sight, going upstream. Instantly the Mexicans gathered closer about Eve and a knife's point pricked against her ribs. Wisely she kept quiet and the launches went by without knowing of her presence. Then Sandos grinned at her.

"You behave good, *senorita* and I think maybe you tell the truth."

Riding on, the Mexicans kept a watch behind them but the launches did not return. The river curved through a valley at that point, the Texas shore rising plainly on the other side. Down below Eve, thick clumps of bushes grew down to the water's edge, interspersed with open patches of sandy beach that would be bays and back-waters in time of flood. Ahead the country became more open than ever and the bushes ended on a large patch of open beach.

A horse whinnied from among the bushes, the sound chopping off as if stopped in some way. Immediately the party came to a halt. An order from Sandos sent three of the men riding cautiously towards the source of the sound and the other three held rifles ready for use. Not that Eve saw a chance to escape, for the two girls flanked her holding knives ready for use.

Suddenly a rider burst into view, racing down the slope towards the river. Eve bit down a startled exclamation at the sight. Dressed in male clothing, with black hair cropped boyishly short, the rider was without doubt a woman. Unless Eve missed her guess, it was *the* woman, the Rebel Spy.

Flame ripped from one of the advancing trio's rifle and the fleeing womans horse went down, pitching her from its saddle. She landed sprawling on the soft sand and, before she had recovered, the three men advanced surrounding her. Bending down, one of the three pulled the Dance Brothers revolver from her holster. Then he waved his companions to join him and the woman sat up.

Eve sucked in a deep breath as she rode with the others down the slope. It seemed that the Rebel Spy had fallen into the Mexican *bandidos'* hands. The problem facing Eve was what to do about it.

Chapter 12

The Fort Is Under Attack

"Lon's coming, Miss Belle," said Sam Ysabel, after making one of his periodic searches of their back-trail.

Relief lay under the laconic tone and Belle mirrored the feeling. Almost three days had gone by since they left the O'Malley *posada*. After the first day, Ysabel clearly expected the Kid to arrive by the hour. Although he never mentioned it, the girl guessed that he felt a growing concern for his son's safety as the time went by.

Turning in her saddle, the girl looked back and saw only small, indistinct specks on the horizon. However she had seen enough of Ysabel to know that he would not make a mistake.

"There's more than one horse," she said after a moment.

"Mebbe Lon borrowed some from Rosey to ride relay," Ysabel replied. "Only he'd've been along sooner if he had. He's coming fast now."

"We'd best wait for him then," Belle suggested.

Nodding, Ysabel led the way to a clump of bushes. By the time they had halted in concealment, the blobs had come close enough for Belle to make out definite shapes. Ysabel saw far more. Enough to bring a low-voiced exclamation from his lips.

"Well I'm damned!"

"That's more than likely," smiled Belle, having grown to like and respect the big man during their journey. While he might lack many of the social graces, at no time had he acted in any but a proper manner towards her. "But why the sudden realisation?"

"If the boy ain't wide-looped Bully Segan's *bayo-coyote* hoss, I'll be a Tejas Injun's squaw."

"I don't know the gentleman—not that I suppose he is a gentleman—but I'll take your word that it is his horse."

122

"Bully won't take happy to losing it," Ysabel drawled. "That means—."

Allowing the words to trail off, the big man made another of his careful searches of the surrounding country. Then he turned his attention to his son. No longer did the white stallion have black patches on its coat. The *bayo-coyote* and the third horse showed signs of hard travel and use.

"Howdy, boy," Ysabel greeted as his son rode up.

"Howdy, *ap*," the Kid replied, using the Comanche term for father. "Howdy, Miss Belle. "Got me some antelope steaks for supper. Reckon we'd best be moving on."

"How about the horses, Lon?" Belle asked.

"Hosses? Which hosses?" the Kid said innocently. "Oh, *them* hosses. I just happened on 'em."

"The Bully likely to be raising fuss about you 'happening' on to his *bayo-coyote* there?" Ysabel growled.

"I'd say 'no' to that," drawled the Kid, eyes darting around him as he spoke. "Seems he got to blaming Ramon Peraro for the hoss going missing. Damned if he didn't try to do the blaming with a knife."

"Well doggie!" Ysabel ejaculated. "If that don't beat all. So ole Bully won't be coming along?"

"Nor Ramon neither," the Kid confirmed. "One of Bully's boys had a mite more sense and started throwing lead. I don't reckon Ramon'll be riding for a spell. I'd've been along sooner, only a bunch of Juaristas got after me and I led 'em around for a spell afore losing 'em."

Which did not tell the entire story. Coming across the Juaristas without their knowledge, the Kid heard enough to know they hunted for his father and Belle. So he washed the stain from the white's coat and allowed himself to be seen from a distance. Then he kept out of sight but left tracks for the men to follow. When sure they would be unable to catch up to his father, he lost his pursuers and resumed his journey. Heading south, he located his father's and Belle's tracks at last and found them. Doing so cost him one of the horses stolen from Segan's gang.

"Saw some smoke this morning," he went on. "Likely you couldn't. Too much for just a camp fire. Figured I'd best catch up fast. Let's go."

Used as she had become to Sam Ysabel's caution, Belle could not help but notice how much more alert he seemed to be when they resumed the journey. She put it down to fears that Bully Segan, whoever he might be, was on their trail. Yet that did not explain why the Ysabels freed their buckskin saddleboots and rode with the rifles still encased but across their arms. Still pondering on their behaviour, she turned to ask a question.

"Drop behind us, Miss Belle!" the Kid said urgently. "And take these hosses."

"Wha—?" Belle began, accepting the reins of the spare mounts and pack horse which he thrust into her hands.

"Do it, *pronto!*" Ysabel interrupted. "And whatever happens, stop back there. Don't make a move or speak unless I tell you."

Although surprised at the man's behaviour, Belle obeyed. She knew they must have good reasons for their actions, so she neither asked questions nor raised snobbish points of social standing, rank or sex.

For almost two minutes they rode on. Then, suddenly, the country before them became dotted with Indians. Squat, thick-set braves seemed to rise out of the ground, seated on their ponies and armed with a variety of weapons.

Immediately the Kid gripped his rifle at the wrist of the butt and end of barrel, raising it above his head. A moment later Ysabel repeated the gesture and Belle became aware that neither of her escort had removed the covering from his rifle. Fighting down a desire to draw her Dance, the girl sat still and waited to see what developed.

One of the Indians, sporting a long war bonnet, raised his war lance in the same manner. Lowering it again, he took his right hand away to make a sign in the trio's direction. Taking his right hand from the rifle, the Kid held it palm downwards before his chest. Then he moved his bent arm to the right in a wriggling motion.

Whatever the sign might mean, Belle could see no change in the Indians' attitude. After a moment they sent their horses leaping forward, charging down on the trio at full speed.

"Sit fast and don't touch that Dance, Miss Belle!" Ysabel growled over his shoulder and the girl guessed he was speaking with the minimum of lip movement.

The next few seconds seemed to be the longest Belle could ever remember. Nearer thundered the Indians, looking meaner than all hell and more deadly than a stampeding herd of buffalo. Then, when there appeared to be no way to avoid being ridden down, the Indians split around them and came to a halt. Belle had never seen such fine riding, although she admitted that most of the finer points were lost to her at that moment.

For a moment nobody spoke, then the war-bonnet chief let out a guttural growl of words. Listening to the Kid's reply, Belle caught only two familiar words, 'Ysabel' and '*Cuchilo*' which she knew to be Spanish for knife. Her quick ears noticed that the Kid spoke more slowly than the chief—much as a Texan's speech differed from a New Englander's—but she put that down to his using a foreign language. She could not fail to notice the depreciating manner with which the Kid waved a hand in her direction, then indicated his father.

More talk followed, some laughter and the Ysabels passed out tobacco. Then the two parties separated. Even so, Ysabel warned the girl to remain behind and not until a mile lay between them and the Indians did he offer an explanation for his and the Kid's behaviour.

"I reckon we can get divorced now, Miss Belle," he said, halting the horse and grinning at her.

"Divorced?" she repeated. "What was that all about?"

"They're *Pahuraix*, Water Horse Comanches, on a raid. Lon saw their scout just in time for us to make things look right. These medicine boots Long Walker gave us let 'em know we belonged to the *Pehnane* band and we allowed that you was my squaw."

"And no Indian would let his squaw ride at his side, or lead the horses with her along," Belle smiled.

"Not on a trail in country like this," Ysabel agreed. "We're through 'em now, but we'd best keep going."

"It was a close call," Belle stated rather than guessed.

"Too close," Ysabel replied. "Happen we hadn't been totting these medicine boots on the rifles, they mightn't've give us time to start talking. With them, the *Pahuraix* figured they'd best see who we were afore they killed us.

125

Lon's Long Walker's grandson, killing him'd start off a blood feud."

Listening to the quiet words, Belle found herself blessing the good fortune which had given her such able companions, and not for the first time since meeting the Ysabel family. She could realise just how dangerous the situation had been. Only the Kid's alertness and relationship to the *Pehnane* war chief had saved them.

As they rode on to the west, Ysabel explained how the Kid had used the traditional sign when the *Pahuraix* chief asked for information as to their tribe. Speaking the slow *Pehnane* dialect which had attracted Belle's attention, the Kid introduced himself as *Cuchilo*, grandson of Long Walker and explained that he and his father were riding on private business, accompanied by the latter's squaw. After an exchange of information and the latest jokes, the *Pahuraix* went on their way.

Despite their belief that the *Pahuraix* had accepted their *bona-fides*, the Ysabels insisted that they made a camp in wooded country that night. A *tuivitsi*, young warrior, might decide to ignore the threat of a blood feud with the *Pehnane* and try to win acclaim by stealing their horses. So they settled down for the night in an area through which silent progress would be difficult.

Always a light sleeper, Belle woke in the night. She saw the Kid and his father standing by the dying embers of the fire and sat up. Turning, the Kid raised a finger to his lips.

"There's somebody out that ways, Miss Belle," he said, coming to the girl's side and pointing into the blackness.

"One of the Indians?" she whispered back.

"Nope. Too noisy and wearing boots. I'm going to take a look, see who it is. Stay put and keep your Dance handy."

With that the Kid turned and disappeared into the woods. He went in silence, flickering out of the girl's sight with his knife in hand. Joining Belle, holding a Sharps rifle, Ysabel nodded after his departing son.

"Knife's better than any gun in the dark and among the trees."

"I suppose so," Belle replied. "We must be close to Nava now?"

"Be there late tomorrow night, or before noon the day after," Ysabel replied. "Depends on who's around."

Five minutes went by, then a whistle sounded in the darkness.

"Lon?" asked Belle.

"Sure," Ysabel answered, putting down his rifle at her side. "Wait here."

Rising, Belle watched Ysabel walk away. In a short time he returned, helping his son to carry a man in uniform. Belle tossed a few sticks on to the fire and its glow allowed them to study the newcomer.

"A French Huzzar," Belle said as the Ysabels lay the man by the fire. "He's been shot!"

"Late this afternoon, I'd say," Ysabel replied. "Lord knows how he's come this far."

"Maybe saw the fire and come towards it," the Kid went on as Belle ran forward to kneel at the man's side. "He's near on bled white and just about gone."

Opening his eyes, the Huzzar stared vacantly around for a moment. Then a flicker of realisation showed in them and he began to speak haltingly. Only by bending forward could Belle catch the words. At first he talked sensibly, then began to ramble. His hand clutched the girl's arm, tightened and went loose.

"He's done," Ysabel said quietly.

"Yes," Belle replied.

"What'd he say?" asked the Kid.

"That the fort is under attack by a large force of Juaristas armed with cannon," the girl told her companions. "Klatwitter sent two of them to fetch help, but the Mexicans killed his companion and wounded him before his horse out-ran them. He doesn't think they can hold out."

For a moment neither the Kid nor his father spoke. Then the youngster let out a low-growled curse.

"That's just about all we need."

"Have the Juaristas any cannon?" Belle inquired.

"The Mexican army has, and a whole slew of 'em are fighting for Juarez," Ysabel replied.

"Can they take Klatwitter?" the girl asked.

"That fort at Nava was built to stand off Injuns, not soldiers with cannon," Ysabel answered. "But if Klatwit-

127

ter's got a thousand men and guns of his own he just might do it."

"Trouble being we just can't go riding up there to see him," the Kid put in.

"That's for sure," Ysabel agreed.

"The Juaristas might let us through if they knew why we wanted to see Klatwitter," Belle remarked.

"Could be," Ysabel said. "Thing being, can we trust the Juaristas? Some of 'em we know and're honest as they come. Others run Peraro and Bully Segan close for ornery meanness. Fifteen thousand dollars in gold'd come in useful to Juarez."

"You don't think we'd be advised to take it with us?"

"I reckon we'd be plumb foolish to take it," Ysabel corrected. "Look, Miss Belle, what I'd say is this. We've got a hide-away down by the river, nobody's found it yet. Let's cache the money there. Then Lon and me'll make a fast ride to Nava and see what's doing."

"We'll go Injun-style, ma'am," the Kid went on. "If there's somebody we can trust with the Juaristas, we'll talk to him. Then, if they'll agree, we'll come back to fetch you."

"That would be best," Belle admitted. "My orders are that this money must not fall into the wrong hands."

"That's how we play it then," Ysabel stated. "We'll take this feller into the woods and leave him. There's no way we can bury him. Comes morning, we'll head for the river."

"Will it be safe?" Belle asked.

"Nowhere's safe for us right now," Ysabel replied grimly. "Only where we're headed's in Cosme Danvila's neck of the woods. Him and Charlie Kraus hate each other like the devil hates holy water. I don't figure Golly'd pass the word about us to Danvila. We'll have to chance it and ride careful."

Dawn found them riding in a north-westerly direction. They travelled fast, but with caution, and saw nobody all day. Towards evening they approached the Rio Grande and Ysabel called a halt while the Kid went ahead as scout. On his return, the youngster said that their hide-out remained undetected. So the party rode on once more.

Coming to a valley through which the river curved, Sam Ysabel led the way downwards. They watered their horses on a wide sand bank and the Kid used a leafy branch to wipe out their tracks. Taking the horses into the thick bushes which grew close to the sand bar, Ysabel ordered that they be picketed. Then he led the girl on foot through the bushes to where a section of the valley side fell in a cliff. Still Belle could see no sign of their destination. Thrusting through some bushes, Ysabel brought the girl to the concealed mouth of a cave. Small the entrance might be, but beyond it lay a large, roomy cavern. Striking a match on the seat of his pants, Ysabel located and lit a lantern.

Looking around her in the improved light given by the lantern, Belle saw a birch-bark canoe and several familiar-looking kegs in the cave.

"We helped Rip Ford raid the Yankees and he gave us those kegs of powder," Ysabel explained. "We sent Mig and some of the boys up here with 'em to be took over to Long Walker. He's keeping the peace with the white folks and Rip figured a present was called for."

Studying the powder and canoe, Belle formed an idea. The safety of the money seemed assured, but she wished to make certain that it would not fall into the wrong hands.

"Is the canoe safe?" she asked, taking the paddle from inside it.

"Why sure," Ysabel replied. "Feller who taught me to make 'em learned from the Blackfeet and Sioux up north."

"Then we could take the money across the river in it?"

"Sure. But it's as safe here as any place."

"I thought that we might put it in the canoe, launched ready, and take it across the river if the Juaristas should refuse to let us see Klatwitter and come after it."

"Might be best, ap'," the Kid remarked. "One thing's for sure. If we get it across, nobody'll follow us."

"Is the current so fast?" Belle asked.

"Nope. The bottom's quick-sand once you get out a ways," drawled the Kid. "Trouble being they might get to us afore we got the boat out."

"I've thought of that," Belle said. "If we could put the money into two or three of these powder kegs and load them into the boat, we could push it off and blow the lot up rather than let it fall into the wrong hands."

"That's smart figuring, Miss Belle," Ysabel told her.

"We can do it easy enough."

By that time the night had come down and so they could not launch the canoe. However they prepared three kegs, emptying out sufficient powder from each to take the money. At dawn they moved the canoe to the river, carried down and loaded the three kegs aboard. Shoving the canoe upstream, to where the bushes grew down to the water's edge, Ysabel fastened it to the bank. Then he and his son cut branches and draped them in position to hide the canoe.

"She'll hold there, Miss Belle," Ysabel finally told the girl. "If you have to get her out fast, yank on that rope and the knot'll slip. Then push her out into the river and use the paddle to go across."

"It's a pity we haven't any fuse or slow match along," Belle remarked, walking back off the sand bar with Ysabel while the Kid removed all signs of their presence. "Then if the worst comes to the worst, we could blow up the powder."

"Should it come to that," Ysabel replied, "a bullet into one of the kegs'll do just as good as a fuse."

"It sure will," agreed the Kid, standing surveying his work. "Touch off that powder and the money's gone."

"I hope it doesn't come to that," Belle said sincerely.

If it did, as they all knew, the mission would be a failure and the South's last hope was gone.

Chapter 13

Work Together—Or Die

After the Ysabels left, Belle settled down. Wanting to travel
fast, the men took all but Belle's mount and the packhorse.
In view of the new turn of events, Belle saddled her horse
and left it tied ready for an immediate departure. Then she
settled down to rest. She did not sleep and heard the sound
of approaching hooves. Rising, she went to the horses and
stood by their heads. The riders were travelling along the
trail at the top of the slope and could not see her. With any
luck, they ought to pass without becoming aware of her
presence.

Blowing down the slope, the wind carried the scent of its
kind to the packhorse. Just a moment too late Belle lunged
forward and caught the horse's nose to silence the whinny
it gave. Seeing the riders turn and three of their number
start in her direction, she knew there was only one thing to
do. Releasing the packhorse, she freed her mount, swung
into the saddle and charged from the bushes. At first she
thought of launching the canoe across the river, then decided
to try to draw away the Mexicans. Before she could turn
the horse, a bullet ripped into it and it fell. Pitched from
the saddle, Belle was winded by the fall and unable to resist when the men came down. With her Dance gone, she sat
on the ground and studied her captors.

Only with an effort did Belle prevent her surprise showing at the sight of Eve Coniston riding with the Mexicans.
At first Belle thought that she had fallen into Kraus' hands.
On second thoughts, she concluded that the Yankee woman
was also a prisoner. The poor-quality horse and bare feet
did not suggest she, Eve, rode of her own free will.

After reaching this conclusion, Belle gave thought to her
own predicament. Whatever happened, she must not let the
others suspect her identity. If possible, she wanted to get
them away from the area before any of them started nosing

around and found the canoe.

"You wait 'til Bully hears what you done!" she screeched in the accent of a poor southerner. "He'll be riled about you-all shooting my hoss!"

"Who are you, *senorita*?" Sandos asked.

"Rosie-May Benstable, that's who!" Belle replied, conscious of Eve's eyes on her. "And I'm Bully Segan's best gal."

"She's got good boots, Joaquim," Juanita put in. "Nearly as good as mine."

"I want them!" Rosa yelled, drawing the knife from her belt and starting towards Belle.

Tensing slightly, Belle prepared to defend herself. She watched the men's faces and decided against making the attempt. Still partially winded by the fall, she could not give of her best. While a *savate* attack might, probably would, take Rosa by surprise, using it was not the answer. To demonstrate her skill would arouse the Mexicans' suspicions. Even if they failed to understand the significance of what they saw, the Yankee woman might. Already 'Emily Corstin' had proved to be a smart, capable adversary and could be relied upon to draw the right conclusions. So Belle decided to avoid drawing too much attention to herself. Tangling in a hair-yanking brawl offered no way out, either. Rosa looked strong enough to make a hard fight. The longer they remained on the sand bar, the greater chance of somebody seeing the boat.

"Hey!" yelped Belle, backing off on her rump with well-simulated fear. "You'll keep her off me, d'you hear!"

"She want your boots, *senorita*," Sandos pointed out.

"Then she c'n have 'em!" Belle wailed, starting to ease the right boot off.

While doing so, she glanced at Eve Coniston and saw the other showing more interest in her surroundings than the Mexicans. Then their eyes met and a smile flickered momentarily on Eve's lips. No matter what the Mexicans believed, Belle felt that she was not fooling the Yankee girl.

"Get the boots on *pronto*, Rosa!" Sandos ordered in Spanish, throwing a look towards the river. "The boats might come back and we don't want to be caught down here."

"What do we do with this one?" another of the gang inquired, indicating Belle with his thumb.

"Take her with us," Sandos replied. "If she's Bully Segan's woman, we'd better keep her for him."

"What's she going to ride?"

"Get her up behind the other *gringo*."

Having spent some of her time during the ride from Matamoros in improving her knowledge of Spanish, with Ysabel acting as tutor, Belle could follow the conversation. However she gave no sign of understanding what she heard. The time might come when her apparent lack of comprehension would pay off.

Escape would be impossible while seated behind Eve on the sway-backed horse, even if Belle could rely on the Yankee to cooperate, so she made no attempt. In his eagerness to leave the river's edge, Sandos pushed his party at a good pace. So they missed noticing the tracks made by Belle and the Ysabels on their arrival.

Swinging away from the Rio Grande, they took a southeasterly direction for something over a mile. At last Sandos directed his horse into the mouth of a draw. As they turned a bend in the wide valley, they came into sight if the *bandido* camp. The fact that only two adobe *jacales* and a pole corral stood before them led Belle to assume the place was not the gang's main headquarters. Probably it served as no more than a temporary hide-out handy for the border. From the general lack of life around the place, no other members of the gang were using it. Which still left six men and two women from whom Belle must escape.

"Put the women in there!" Sandos ordered, pointing to the smaller of the *jacales*. "When we've fed, we'll go across the river, spread out and find Cosme."

"All of us?" Juanita asked.

"You and Rosa stop here to help Ruis guard the gringos," Sandos replied and scowled at the girl. "Keep away from them until we learn what Cosme wants to do."

"*Si*, Joaquim," she answered. "Maybe then we have some fun with them."

"Maybe," Sandos grunted. "Lock them in the *jacale*."

On entering the smaller building, Eve and Belle looked around them. From all appearances the building had been

133

used before for a similar purpose. Since its construction the window had been closed to mere slits and the door made strong to resist being broken open. Trying to do so would make sufficient noise to alert their captors. Belle studied the building, trying to decide how they might escape.

"You thought fast back there," Eve remarked, cutting into the other girl's thoughts. "Trying to lead them off like that. Then giving the girl your boots. If we'd stayed around that sand bar much longer, somebody might have seen that canoe."

"I don't know what you-all getting at, for sure," Belle answered. "When Bully comes—."

"Drop it, Boyd. I know you now, even if I didn't at the hotel in Matamoros," Eve interrupted. "What's wrong, did the Ysabels desert you?"

Realising that her bluff had failed, Belle shrugged. "No. I suppose you're a Yankee spy?"

"Yes."

"Say! You must be Eve Coniston. I've heard about you."

Despite herself, Eve could not hold down a beam of pleasure at the words. That the legendary Rebel Spy knew of her meant her work had not gone unnoticed. Usually when Eve announced her vocation, people asked if she was Pauline Cushman. However she put aside her thoughts and turned her attention back to their present situation.

"I thought one of them might see the canoe," she said. "I did."

"Why didn't you tell them?"

"If I had, we might both be dead, or wishing we were. Where're the Ysabels. Can we expect any help from them?"

"They went to Nava and won't be back until late afternoon at the earliest."

"I don't think we've that much time," Eve remarked. "It looks like you and I work together—or die."

"Why are they holding you?" Belle asked.

"For ransom," Eve explained. "My loyal companion told them what an important person I am."

Watching the bitter twist which came to Eve's lips, Belle could see how she felt and guess as its cause. When word of Eve's capture leaked out, the men who opposed using women for such important work would have another argument in their favour. Remembering the opposition to her own participation, Belly sympathised with Eve. She also realised that the other woman's feelings might make her more willing to cooperate in escaping.

"What happened to him?" Belle inquired.

"They shot him down in cold blood. Lord! I can't say I liked him as a man or a colleague, but even Ffauldes didn't deserve what he got."

"I don't know what you think," Belle remarked. "But I think we ought to try to escape."

"So do I," Eve stated grimly, showing Belle guessed correctly about her feelings. "The odds are steep against us doing it."

"Sandos is taking all but one man and the girls across the river with him to look for their leader," Belle said. "If we don't escape before they get back with him, we'll never make it."

Before any more could be said, the door opened and the two Mexican girls entered followed by Sandos. The man indicated the tin plates loaded with food that his companions carried.

"Eat well, *senoritas*," he ordered. "Cosme Danvila always feeds his visitors good—until he finds that nobody wants to pay to get them back."

Taking the plate, Belle almost held her breath as she waited to see what happened next. Without even waiting for his prisoners to start eating, Sandos walked out of the cabin. Juanita limped a little as she followed the man and Rosa did not look any too happy in the unaccustomed foot-wear. As the lock clicked on the door, Belle looked at the plate. Then she smiled at Eve.

"I've an idea," she said. "Let's eat and I'll tell you about it."

For all the urgency of the business, Sandos and his men took their *siesta* before leaving to search for Danvila. Standing at the window slit in the front of the building, Belle watched the five men take their horses and ride away from the camp. She saw that four horses remained tied to the corral rails, but the man sat on the porch of the other *jacale* where he could see the animals and the front of the prisoners' quarters.

135

"We can't get to the horses with him there," Eve said, after taking a look.

"He'll have to be settled then," Belle answered. "The girls are still in the other cabin. If they don't come out before we're ready, it'll help us."

"Let's get started, they might remember the plates if we don't," Eve said.

Crossing to the rear wall, the two girls began to dig at the newer adobe of the window slit. At first they made no impression, then pieces began to crumble away with increasing regularity. Once started, the work progressed so well that one of them kept watch on the Mexican guard while the other continued digging.

"That'll do," Belle said at last, stepping back and studying the hole. "We don't want it too big or he might wonder why you didn't get through after me."

"He's still out front," Eve replied. "No sign of the girls."

Changing places, Eve went to stand by the enlarged rear window. She looked across at Belle who halted between the door and the slit in the front wall. Then Eve turned and thrust her head through the hole.

"You stinking peckerwood* bitch!" the Yankee girl screeched at the top of her voice. "Come back here and help me!"

While the Mexican probably did not understand English, Eve declined to rely on it and so shouted the words she might have used at finding that her companion had deserted her.

"Ag—!" Belle began, then saw the man leap to his feet and run towards the building. He jerked a revolver Belle recognised as her Dance from his belt as he approached the door. "He's coming. Get ready!"

Twisting away from the look-out slit, Belle flattened her back against the wall on the hinged side of the door. Tense and alert, she listened to the lock click and watched the door open. Leaping in, his revolver held ready, the man glared at Eve as she turned from the rear wall. His eyes went to the hole and he drew just the conclusions they hoped he would. Clearly the two prisoners had attempted to escape, but the slim one had wriggled through the hole before

* Peckerwood: derogatory name for a white Southerner.

making it large enough for her companion. Knowing how he would act under the circumstances, the man saw nothing out of the ordinary in Eve's behaviour.

Letting out a snarl, the man advanced across the room. Again he acted just as Belle had hoped and placed himself in an ideal position for what she planned to do. Thrusting herself from the wall, she followed the man. The loss of her boots ruled out the use of several effective *savate* attacks, but she knew one that suited the conditions. Bounding into the air, she drew both feet up under her. At the full height of the leap, she straightened her legs and drove them at the man's back. With all the force she could manage, she crashed the bottom of her feet into the centre of the man's back. Taken by surprise, he went reeling across the room. Eve sprang to meet him, side-stepping and sticking her right leg between his feet to trip him. Pitching head first into the wall, the man bounced away, landed on his back and lay still.

Rebounding from the man after delivering her frontal leaping high kick, Belle started towards him. She saw that Eve needed no help and turned to face the door. Through it charged Rosa, a pistol in her hand. The girl no longer wore her looted boots and so made better time than Juanita who clung to the foot-wear and was hobbling painfully across from the other *jacale*.

On arrival Rosa found herself faced with a tricky problem. The pistol she held was a muzzle-loading single-shot and two potentially dangerous targets confronted her. While she vaccilated between the gringos, Belle took the problem out of her hands. Even as Eve flung herself past the unconscious man, Belle darted forward. Once again the slim girl leapt into the air, but not in a kick. Passing over the pistol, she wrapped her legs about Rosa's neck. Breaking her fall with her hands, Belle let her shoulders hit the floor. then she twisted her body, pulling and using her weight to flip the Mexican over. A wail broke from Rosa as her feet left the floor, then she crashed down on to her back.

Beaten to Rosa by Belle, Eve still found work to do. Juanita entered the cabin walking awkwardly, which did not increase her efficiency. Springing past Belle, Eve slapped aside the revolver Juanita held. Then her other

137

hand, knotted into a fist, drove hard into the Mexican girl's sizeable bust. Giving a croaking cry, Juanita loosened her hold on the revolver. Eve slammed the trapped hand against the wall, completing the work of making Juanita release the weapon.

Turning her head, Eve saw Belle starting to rise and remembered about the canoe. The time for cooperation had ended and they became enemies once more. Catching the gasping Juanita by the hair, Eve hurled her at Belle. Just too late the Southern girl realised Eve's intention. Juanita crashed into her and they went down in a heap. Swinging around, Eve darted through the door and slammed it behind her. For a moment she hesitated, hand halfway to the lock. Then she swung away without touching it. Maybe the Rebel Spy was an enemy, but Eve could not leave her trapped at the mercy of the *bandidos*. So she turned and ran to the waiting horses. Unfastening the reins of the best animal, she mounted. The stirrup irons hurt her feet, but she ignored the pain and started the horse moving.

With a heave Belle rolled Juanita from her and started to rise. Squealing curses, the other girl clawed at her and caught hold of her waistband. Cold rage filled Belle as she saw Eve's departure. The Yankee girl was not fleeing in blind panic. She knew where to find the canoe and could possibly make her escape along the Rio Grande in it.

"Like hell she will!" Belle gritted.

Despite the weight of the Mexican girl clinging to her, Belle made her feet. Then she dug both hands into the black mass of hair and began to pull at it. Across the room, Rosa started to stir, moaning and writhing. Pain caused Juanita to draw away from Belle, although she still retained her hold. Up rammed Belle's left knee, driving into the Mexican girl's left breast. Twice more Belle sent her knee home before agony made the other release the hold on her belt. With a surging heave Belle threw Juanita from her. Going backwards, the Mexican girl landed on her companion just as Rosa sat up. Pain made the girls oblivious of each other's identity. Hands dug into hair and they began to fight instead of rising to deal with Belle.

Running to the door, Belle tugged at it. Much to her surprise, she found it was not locked. However by that

138

time Eve had mounted and was already galloping along the draw. Anger made Belle act rashly for once. Instead of returning to the cabin and collecting her Dance, she dashed across to the waiting horses. Unfastening one of them, she swung into the saddle and set off after the fleeing Yankee spy.

Chapter 14

A:He I Claim It!

Sitting their horses in cover, the Ysabel Kid and his father studied the fort at Nava. As Sam Ysabel had told the Rebel Spy, the walls, designed to stand off an attack by arrows and rifle bullets, fared badly when assailed by cannon fire. However the defenders were still holding out and there did not appear to be any chance of a rapid end to the siege.

"Can't see anybody we know well enough to trust, boy," Ysabel remarked.

"Nope," the Kid replied. "But there're a few there we know well enough *not* to trust. Damned if that's not old Marcus back there, all fancied up like a regular army officer."

"He was allus ambitious," Ysabel said. "If Benito Juarez does chase the French out, he'll have to watch his back against Marcus."

"Somebody'll chill Marcus' milk if he gets feisty," drawled the Kid.

Little did the Kid know, but he was fated to play a prominent part in the chilling process.*

"We'd best not get down there," Ysabel went on. "Marcus'd shoot us first and ask what we wanted while they buried us. Anyways, I don't feel right about leaving Miss Belle back by the river."

"Or me. What'll she do, *ap*'?"

"Damned if I know. Even if the Juaristas don't take the fort, I can't see Klatwitter having enough men or ammunition left to make their raid on New Mexico."

Turning their horses, they started the return journey. Indian-wise, they knew better than return along the route they had followed to Nava. Should somebody, French, Mexican or Kraus' gang, have come on their tracks, the Ysabels did not intend to simplify matters by going back

*Told in THE PEACEMAKERS.

along them. By riding relay, they had covered the distance to Nava in fast time and intended to return in the same manner. Three miles fell behind them. Then the Kid reined in his white stallion and pointed ahead.

"No Juaristas'd make that much smoke," he said.

"Nor Charlie Kraus, especially this close to Cosme Danvila's balliwick," Ysabel went on, studying the column of smoke which climbed upwards from beyond a rim half a mile ahead. "They'll be French soldiers, I'd say."

Father and son exchanged glances. Several Mexican friends of long standing fought for Juarez, but the Ysabels had their duty to the Confederacy. So they must see if there was any way that relief could be brought to Klatwitter, even though doing so hurt the Juaristas' cause.

"We'd best go tell 'em what's happening at Nava," the Kid finally said.

"It's the only way," his father agreed.

Attacking unexpectedly, even a moderate-numbered French force might drive off the Juaristas. If the siege could be raised, Belle Boyd might yet visit Klatwitter and decide whether to continue with the plan.

As they rode on, the Ysabels watched the smoke. Although they had only just come into a position from which they could see it, both realised that it must have been visible for some time in other directions.

"Those frog soldiers sure must be lucky," the Kid remarked as they drew closer to the rim, "happen they allus make fires that smoke that ways."

"Likely there's no Injuns where they come from," his father replied. "Although a Creole feller I knowed one time allowed they had Apaches in Paris, France."

"I thought all the Apaches was over to New Mexico 'n' Arizona, 'cepting for the Lipans in West Texas," the Kid said. "Happen them French Apaches're like our'n, I don't see how whoever's making that smoke's not wound up with their ears hanging on some buck's lodge-pole."

Topping the rim, they looked down and marvelled still more. Eight French troopers and a sergeant were gathered around a fire, their carbines piled out of reach. Standing aloof at one side of the men, a young lieutenant was smoking a cigar. While four sentries covered the main points of

141

the compass, each held his carbine on the crook of his arm and was doing his work inefficiently. Not one kept truly alert and each was looking in the wrong places. Such lack of caution might easily spell disaster. Discounting an Indian attack, the Juaristas claimed enough wild-country brains to read the signs and take appropriate action from what they learned.

Not until the Ysabels started to ride down the slope did any of the French soldiers notice them. Then the sentry nearest to them jerked his head around, brought his carbine to the ready position and gave a yell. Belated though the warning might be, the soldiers moved with some speed. Dropping coffee cups, the troopers leapt towards their carbines. The officer spat away his cigar and swung to look at the newcomers. Discovering that they were not Mexicans, he barked an order which halted his men before they reached and un-piled the weapons.

Following the dictates of frontier etiquette, Ysabel halted his horse at the edge of the camp. He raised his hand in a peace sign and called, "Howdy. Mind if we'ns come up to the fire?"

"You may come," the officer answered in good English.

Swinging from their saddles and leaving the horses standing with trailing reins, the Ysabels walked forward. Studying the Frenchmen, Sam Ysabel liked little of what he saw. Tall, slim, handsome, the lieutenant's face held a hint of calculated cruelty. Ysabel summed him up as the kind of officer found all too frequently in the French army, a harsh disciplinarian who drove but never led men. Nor did the sergeant strike Ysabel in any more favourable a manner. Big, burly, brutal in appearance, he would blindly back up any order his officer gave.

"You gents headed for Nava?" Ysabel asked, noticing the envious manner with which the officer and sergeant were eyeing the four horses.

"Perhaps," the officer replied coldly.

"Happen you do," the big Texan drawled, "ride real careful. The Juaristas are attacking the fort down there."

"They attack the fort at Nava?" the officer repeated.

"Foot, hoss and artillery," Ysabel confirmed. "Happen there's more of you around, I'd get 'em *pronto*. They're

142

being bad hit at Nava and could use some help."

"Did Colonel Klatwitter send you?"

"He don't even know we're alive."

"Then how do you know of the attack?"

"We was down that ways and saw it."

"And what took you to Nava?" the lieutenant demanded.

"Me 'n' the boy know some folks down there and went visiting. Only when we saw the fighting, we concluded to head back across the river to home."

"Then why did you come to tell me of the attack?"

"You French folks've allus played square with the Confederacy," Ysabel replied. "So we allowed to come and give you the word."

All the time his superior and Ysabel were talking the French sergeant stood to one side studying first the Texans then their horses. Stepping forward, he saluted and spoke quietly to the officer in French. Nodding, the lieutenant replied and then turned back to Ysabel.

"Was the friend you intended to visit General Klatwitter?" he asked.

"Trouble, boy!" Ysabel grunted in Comanche to the Kid, although he never took his eyes from the officer's face or allowed a flicker of expression to show. "Plain folks like us don't get to make friends with generals, mister. So I don't know what you're meaning."

"You don't?" the officer purred.

"Nary a notion," Ysabel answered.

"We have heard that two men and a girl take money to seduce General Klatwitter from his duty to France," the lieutenant explained. "Sergeant Manguer says he believes you are they."

"Don't see no gal along of us, do you, mister?" Ysabel drawled.

"Happen there is one around, you just tell me where to find her," the Kid went on with a grin. "I ain't seed a white gal in a coon's age."

Although he stood in what resembled a relaxed slouch, the youngster was tense with coiled-spring readiness. Like his father, he realised that coming to the French had been a serious error in tactics. Leaving again might prove even

143

more difficult. Before coming to speak with his officer, the sergeant had flashed a signal to the troopers. Already the four sentries were lining their carbines at the Texans and the other men continued their interrupted gathering of piled carbines.

Used to the servile deference given by French enlisted men and Mexican peons, the officer found the Ysabels' attitude infuriatingly over-familiar.

"Don't play games with me!" he blazed. "Not a few of those Juarista pigs have learned that Lieutenant Henri du Plessis is no man to trifle with."

"Mister," Ysabel drawled. "We come here to do you a service. Happen you don't want it, we'll be on our way."

"Not so fast!" du Plessis barked. "I am dissatisfied with your answers and intend to hold you for further questioning. Drop your gunbelts."

While on patrol along the Rio Grande, du Plessis had seen and challenged the three Yankee steam-launches. He had learned of the Rebel Spy's mission and had changed his route in the hope of finding her before she reached Klatwitter. Avarice showed on his face as he studied the Texans and wondered if Manguer had guessed correctly. They did not have a woman along, nor carry saddle pouches bulky enough to hold the large sum of money mentioned by the men from the launches. So he wanted to take them alive if possible and see if they would give useful information under questioning.

Even if they should not be the men seeking Klatwitter, killing them would produce some valuably loot. Four good, if hard-run, horses, a Sharps rifle and two Dragoon Colts—so much more effective than the Le Mat and Lefauchex revolvers issued by the French army—could not be picked up every day of the week. Nor was there likely to be any come-back over the killings. The Confederate States Government could hardly complain at the death of two agents while on a mission to seduce an entire French regiment from its duty. And if the men were not Confederate agents it seemed unlikely that such unimportant people would be missed.

"Damned if we don't oughta make him kill us, so's he'll try to ride ole Nigger there," the Kid remarked to his father, having read du Plessis' feelings towards the white stallion in the avaricious study of it. "Do you see 'em, *ap*'?"

"Just now did. Likely there're waiting to see how things go," Ysabel answered and turned his attention to du Plessis. Much as he disliked the Frenchman, he felt that he must give a warning. "Soldier-boy. Was I you, I'd tell your fellers to set them carbines down, go get their hosses and be ready to ride for Nava."

"You tell me nothing!" du Plessis yelled, wild with fury at the lack of deference showed by the Ysabels. "I will count to three, by which time you will drop your gunbelts and surrender." Then in French he told Manguer of his intentions and added, "Shoot them in the legs when I say 'two'."

"*Oui, mon lieutenant,*" Manguer replied, realising the importance of taking the Texans alive.

Drawing his revolver, the sergeant began to raise it and du Plessis commenced his treacherous count.

"One!"

Something swished through the air, flying from the slope opposite to that down which the Ysabels had come to the camp. Even as his finger squeezed at the trigger ready to carry out his orders, Manguer's back arched in sudden pain. Shock and agony twisted his face as he took an involuntary pace forward. Dropping the revolver, he clawed at the head of an arrow which burst through the left breast of his tunic. Vainly trying to draw the arrow from him, he sank to his knees, collapsed face forward and spasmodically kicked as his life-blood soaked into the Mexican soil.

Attracted by the same smoke that had led the Ysabels to the French, the band of *Pahuraix* raiders reached the scene shortly after the Texans arrived. Seeing the two men who claimed such close ties with Long Walker of the *Pehnane*, the chief did not launch an immediate attack. However it soon became obvious that the Texans were not among friends and the braves moved forward. Neglecting their duty, all the sentries were watching what happened to their visitors and failed to see the deadly advance. Witnessing the sergeant aiming his revolver at Ysabel, the chief took a hand. The short Comanche bow, designed for use on the back of a fast-running horse, packed enough power to sink a thirty-six inch arrow flight deep into the muscular back of a bull buffalo. It proved no less successful when used against a human being.

Showing commendable restraint, the rest of the party let their chief commence the attack. However all held their weapons ready and turned loose a volley as their leaders bow-string vibrated. Arrows, and bullets from the few rifles in the group, tore down into the unsuspecting Frenchmen.

Four troopers and the sergeant died in that first deadly assault, but the rest did not panic and prepared to fight. Nor did the arrival of the Indians cause the French to forget their original visitors.

Throwing up his carbine, a trooper snapped a shot that sent Ysabel's hat spinning from his head. On the heels of the shot, the big Texan drew and fired his Dragoon. Ysabel shot to kill; not only to prevent another attempt on himself but to make sure the soldier did not fall alive into the hands of the *Pahuraix*.

No Comanche worth his salt would be content to stand back from an enemy. A coup counted by bullet or arrow rated lower than one gained in personal contact. So after the first volley, they charged recklessly forward at the remains of the French party.

Out flashed du Plessis' sabre and he flashed a quick glance around. Quick maybe, but it told him all he needed to know. Nothing could save his men and he saw no reason to die with them. Not when the means of escape lay so near. Not his own horse, for that stood picketed with his men's close to where the Indians attacked. However four fine mounts were waiting for him in a position that offered a clear run to safety. Mounted on that magnificent white stallion, he could escape while the remains of his command fought to their deaths.

With that thought in mind, he sprang in the direction of the horses. Before he took three strides, he found his way blocked by an obstacle that must be removed if he hoped to carry on. At first he did not recognise the obstacle. Although still dressed in his white man's clothing, the Ysabel Kid's face looked no less savage than those of the attacking Comanches. Steel glinted in the Kid's hand also, but for

146

once the bowie knife looked almost dwarfed alongside its opposite number.

During his career in the army, du Plessis had fought in several duels and not all of the *au premier sang*—which ended when blood, no matter how slight, was drawn—variety prescribed in regulations. A fine swordsman, he expected no trouble in dealing with the tall youngster. What he failed to take into consideration was that he faced a *man* trained from early childhood in all the rudiments and refinements of fighting with cold steel; yet whose schooling did not conform to the accepted precepts of the continental *code duello*.

Going into the attack, du Plessis launched a cut at the Kid's head and confidently expected to batter down the other's guard to reach his target. However the youngster knew better than try to parry a sabre blow with even a James Black bowie knife. Instead he seemed to go two ways at the same moment. From landing on the ground in a forward step, the right foot thrust backwards and the Kid moved to the rear, outside the sabre's lethal arc.

Taken by surprise at the failure of his attack, du Plessis still caught his balance and returned the sabre with a sweeping inside swing to the head. Again he missed, for the Kid thrust, cut and lunged at the illusive shape before him. oblivious of the fight which was raging behind them, the Kid and du Plessis fought their strange duel. While the Kid's long knife never met the sabre, neither did the *arme blanche* make hit on him.

Leaping over a low cut, the Kid landed inside the blade and his knife ripped across. For the first time du Plessis found need to show his own agility. He tried to avoid the Kid's attack by a hurried spring to the rear. Slicing through the French tunic, the tip of the bowie knife carved a shallow gash across its wearer's chest. Pain stung du Plessis, although he knew the wound to be superficial. However he realised that he must bring the fight to a speedy end, kill that deadly savage who stood between him and the horses. Doing it with the sabre would consume too much time.

Again he sprang to the rear and the Kid started after him. Whipping back his arm, du Plessis hurled his sabre at the Kid. Then the officer sent his right hand flashing towards

147

the revolver at his belt. Shone brightly and looking militarily smart, the holster did not lend itself to a fast draw.

Like a giant dart, the sabre hurled at the Kid, but he went under it in a rolling dive that wound up with him in a kneeling position almost at du Plessis' feet. Up drove the Kid's blade, its point gouging into the Frenchman's belly—always the knife-fighter's favourite target. With a croaking cry of pain du Plessis stumbled backwards and began to double over. Again the Kid struck, almost in a continuation of the move which tore the knife free from its first mark. Coming upwards and back, the curved false-edge, as sharp as the blade itself, sank into flesh. It sliced through the windpipe, veins and arteries of the throat almost to the bone. Gagging in an effort to breathe, blood spouting from the terrible gash, du Plessis went down.

"*A:he,* I claim it!" hissed the Kid.

Behind him a French trooper turned a Le Mat revolver in his direction. Coming up from behind, the *Pahuraix* war chief swung his fighting axe to sever the soldier's spine and drop him instantly to the ground. Springing past his chief, a young brave sank his knife into the dying trooper and claimed the coup.

Then it was all over. Standing with his smoking Dragoon in hand, Ysabel looked around him. With something like relief he saw that none of the soldiers had been taken alive. If any had fallen into the Comanches' hands, there was little enough Ysabel could have done to save them. Nor could he interfere in any way with the aftermath of the victory.

"My thanks, *Soldado Pronto,*" the Kid said, wiping clean his knife on du Plessis' tunic. "The smoke brought you here?"

"Yes," the chief replied. "This has been a poor raid, *Cuchilo.* Everywhere we found soldiers and little loot."

"You have horses, guns and bullets here," Ysabel pointed out, joining his son. Then he pointed unerringly towards Nava. "Down that way is a big fight, many soldiers are going there."

"I think we go and see what we can take," the chief stated.

"And we must ride to meet my squaw," Ysabel answered.

"It's lucky we come back," the Kid said as he and his father rode away and the *Pahuraix* braves set about the business of gathering loot. "They were headed for the border and might've found Miss Belle."

"Yep!" Ysabel agreed. "And with their medicine looking so bad, they might've took their meanness out on her."

Riding on, they swung somewhat to the east of their original line and came into sight of the two *jacales* from which Belle and Eve had escaped. They brought their horses to a halt, ears catching certain significant sounds. Mingled with a scuffling sound and screams from the smaller building was the drumming of rapidly departing hooves. At first they saw no sign of life, other than the horses at the corral. Then the two exhausted, but still fighting Mexican girls reeled through the front door and sprawled to the ground.

"What the hell?" Ysabel ejaculated, starting his horses moving. "This's one of Danvila's hide-outs, but there don't look to be any of his fellers around."

If there had been any of the gang present, it was unlikely they would miss such a prime piece of excitement as what looked to have been one hell of a good girl fight.

"Wonder who it was rode off," the Kid went on. "Two of 'em. Way the hooves sounded, I'd say one following the other and both going like the devil after a yearling."

"Best go take a look and pull them two apart afore they snatch each other bald-headed," Ysabel suggested.

Before the men reached them, the girls rose to their knees and pitched back into the *jacale*. Alert for a trap, Ysabel and the Kid dismounted, drew their Colts and followed the girls. Looking over the fighting pair, the Kid studied the man lying by the rear wall. Then he glanced at the hole and dropped his eyes to the revolver at the man's side.

Forgetting the girls, the Kid darted across and picked up the revolver. At first glance it looked like a well-made Navy Colt. Only the Kid knew different. The revolver bore the unmistakable signs of being made by the Dance brothers of Columbia, Texas. More than that, its ivory handle and superior finish proved it to be the gun they made for and presented to the Rebel Spy as a tribute to her good work.

"Miss Belle'd never part with this unless there was no

way she could help it!" the Kid growled. "They must've got her."

"And she's got away again," his father went on. "Likely that was her running with one of 'em after her we heard."

"Let's get going after her and see!" the Kid barked, thrusting the Dance into his belt and running towards the door.

Although the Ysabels wasted no time in mounting, when they reached the end of the draw they could see no sign of whoever had fled before their arrival. So they pushed on in the direction of the sand bar. With tired horses under them, they could not make as fast a pace as they wished. However they rode on, hoping for a sight of the people they were following. Suddenly they heard shooting ahead. Not just rifles and carbines, but the crack of a light cannon and a harsh staccato rattle that reminded Ysabel of the sound made by an Ager Coffee-Mill machine gun.

Jerking their rifles from the medicine boots, Sam Ysabel and the Kid urged their leg-weary mounts on towards the head of the slope which hid the river—and the sand bar where they had left the money in the canoe—from view.

Chapter 15

Take Her Out Comanche Fashion

By the time Belle Boyd had selected, freed and mounted the best of the remaining horses, Eve Coniston had built up a good lead in the race for the canoe. While a good horsewoman, Eve could not equal Belle's skill. However no amount of ability could off-set the superior mount Eve sat and Belle failed to close the distance no matter how she urged on her horse.

Wondering if the Rebel Spy had managed to make good her escape, Eve fought down a desire to look back. She wished to avoid anything that might jeopardize her chances. To take her attention of the horse and where she rode might cause a fall. As she rode, she decided on her course of action. At the sand-bar she would shove off and board the canoe, then either paddle down the river or allow the current to take her. Either way, the steam launches would find her. Then she could continue down to Brownsville at all speed and deliver the money to the authorities. With it as evidence, the United States Government ought to be able to demand that Great Britain should prevent any recurrence of the attempt.

On Eve rode, keeping the horse at a gallop. At last she saw the sand bar, identifying it for certain by the dead horse lying by the water's edge. Down the slope she went, almost losing her balance. At the foot, she jumped from the saddle and let the horse go free. If all went well she would not need it again and she could not spare valuable seconds to secure it.

Even as Eve reached the canoe and tugged at its fastenings, she heard the drumming of hooves. Turning her head, she saw Belle Boyd galloping into sight. She swung back to the canoe, jerking the knot open and throwing the rope aside. Then she began to haul the canoe out from under its covering, turning its bows towards the centre of the river as soon as she could.

A glance over her shoulder told Eve how little time she had. Riding with reckless abandon, Belle plunged down the incline. The slim Southern girl left the saddle as the horse reached the foot of the slope and ran across the sand. Belle knew she would be too late to prevent the launching of the canoe, but figured she could still destroy its load. Although she had no means of igniting the powder charges, she felt that up-turning the canoe and dumping them into the river would suffice. Under the surface lay quicksands, according to the Kid. Once the kegs reached them, recovery would be impossible.

Realising that she could not hope to board the canoe and escape, Eve did not try. Instead she gave it a hard push and watched it carried forward across the water. Then she swung around to face Belle. What a triumph it would be if she could deliver the Rebel Spy along with the gold to Brownsville. The smug male crowd who insisted that women had no place in the Secret Service would be hard pressed to find an argument to that achievement.

However Eve knew capturing Belle Boyd would be anything but easy. From what she had seen at the *jacale*, and suspected had happened to the French sergeant in Brownsville, the Southern girl could handle her end of any rough stuff that came along. So could Eve if it came to that.

During the ride to the *jacales*, being seated behind Eve and holding on to her waist had allowed Belle to form an estimate of the other's physical condition. So Belle had an idea of Eve's strength. Yet the older woman showed no sign of knowing other than female ways of defending herself. Charging forward with hands raised and fingers hooked like talons, Eve seemed to be wide open for a *savate* attack. Bare footed or not, Belle felt sure a stamping side kick would take most of the aggression out of the older woman.

So Belle skidded to a halt, going into a *savate* fighting stance and swinging herself into position to deliver the kick. As her leg rose, she saw a change come over Eve. Down came the woman's hands, thumbs touching and with the fingers forming a U shape into which Belle's ankle slipped to be halted. Clamping hold of the ankle, Eve swung the leg around and twisted the foot. Belle felt her other foot leave the ground, then she went somersaulting over.

Long training at riding helped her to break her fall on the soft sand.

Springing after Belle, Eve raised her right leg and stamped. Her heel drove into Belle's side as the girl rolled over, instead of striking her stomach. While painful, the stamp did not slow Belle down as it would if it had landed on its intended mark. So she was ready when Eve followed her and tried to repeat the stamp. Twisting herself over in Eve's direction, Belle caught the ankle on which she stood in one hand and placed the other on the knee. By tugging forward at the ankle and shoving back on the knee, she over balanced the older woman. Eve yelled as she fell on to her back on the sand.

Like a flash Belle hurled herself on to Eve, trying to pin down her arms as a prelude to driving home punches at the other's face and torso. Belle knew Eve was strong, and learned the extent of her strength. Heaving herself upwards, until only the soles of her feet and top of her head rested on the sand, Eve pitched the lighter girl off her. Rolling on top, Eve locked her fingers about Belle's throat and began to squeeze. Desperately Belle heaved and shook to try to tip the other woman from her. Eve's fingers clamped home hard, tightening savagely and Belle knew she must escape the grip. Fighting down the near panic which caused her to waste energy striking wildly at Eve's face, Belle reached up and clutched at the front of the mauve blouse. Pain knifed into Eve as Belle's fingers dug into and crushed at her bust. Croaking curses, she tried to raise Belle's head and crash it down again. The effort proved only partially successful, for the soft sand cushioned the impact and Belle's neck muscles fought against it. Nor did the slim fingers relax their hold, but continued to dig into the sensitive mounds of flesh. Giving a screech of agony, Eve tried to rise without releasing her hold on Belle's throat. As Eve stood up, Belle curled both feet between her spread-apart legs, placed them against her mid-section and heaved. Losing her grip on Belle, Eve felt the fingers dragged from her bust. Then she flew over and landed on her back.

That first exchange gave Belle a grim warning. Eve possessed strength at least equal to and probably greater than her own. Tangling at close quarters would be dangerous. So she rolled over to a kneeling position and rose. Sucking in deep breaths of air, she swung to face Eve who had also made her feet. For a moment the older woman stood rubbing at her bust, then she clenched her fists and advanced. No longer did she act like an untrained woman, but came forward in the manner of a trained male pugilist. Belle moved to meet Eve in much the same manner, except that she favoured the stance of the *savate* fighter.

When they came together, it might have been two men fighting. Their fists flew, smacking hard into face, bust, stomach as they circled. Any slight advantage Belle might have gained by her speed was countered by Eve's small strength superiority. Blood ran from Eve's nose and Belle's lip, their breath came in gasping hisses, but they fought on oblivious of everything except each other. Bony knuckles smacked solidly against Eve's already throbbing nose. She stumbled back a couple of paces, screamed and flung herself at the advancing Belle. Swept backwards by the older woman's weight, Belle collided with the dead horse. Still locked together the women fell over it, landing on the sand to churn over and over in a wild tangle. They went at it completely oblivious of everything but each other and neither saw the two riders who came into view on the slope across the river.

"*Madre de dios!*" Sandos spat out as he saw the two women rolling over and over by the dead horse. Even at that distance he could recognise them. "It's the gringoes I told you about, Cosme. How did they escape?"

Middle-sized, stocky and hard-looking despite his elegant clothing, Cosme Danvila let out a low growl, "We'll find out whe—Hey! Look at that canoe."

Carried forward by its light weight and Eve's shove, the canoe had reached the centre of the river. The sluggish current at that point turned the canoe's bows down stream and floated it along slowly. Pleased that something had taken his leader's thoughts off how the prisoners escaped, Sandos decided to try to keep them that way.

"Maybe that other one isn't Bully Segan's woman," he said hurriedly. "She could be the one who was with Big Sam Ysabel, taking the gold to the French general at Nava."

154

"I never knew Bully to have a woman who wasn't fat as a pig and ugly," Danvila answered. "You told me the old one was a spy for the United States; and the other will work for the Confederacy. Get the men, that canoe has the money in it."

While Sandos turned to obey, Danvila looked at the kegs in the canoe. He had guessed pretty accurately what had happened; from the Ysabels hiding the money until learning if the French general could be trusted, through Belle's actions at the time of her capture, to the women's escape— somebody was going to wish they had never been born allowing that to happen—and why they were fighting. One of them must have pushed it off, meaning to escape and the other was trying to prevent her from doing so. On the latter point Danvila wasted no time or thought. Whatever had started the fight, he intended to have the money. A large sum in gold would be a god-send at a time when French and Juarista soldiers were making banditry unprofitable below the border and Captain Jack Cureton's hard-fighting Rangers rendered it extremely unsafe in Texas.

On the sand bar, unaware of the new threat to their existence, Eve expended much of her remaining dregs of energy to heave Belle away from her. The tangle on the ground had been rough, with teeth, fists, knees, elbows and heads used indiscriminately. Their blouses hung in tatters, underwear torn and Eve's skirt had split up its left side. Croaking in breaths of air, they both began to rise. Pain and exhaustion gnawed at Eve, for Belle's youth and superb physical condition had combined to wear the older women down. Eve stumbled back, away from Belle, hoping to gain a respite during which she could gather her flagging strength for a further effort. Sensing the other's condition, Belle clenched her fists and advanced. If she could continue the attack quickly enough, Eve was beaten.

Leading his men down the slope, Danvila saw the three steam launches come into sight around the river's up-stream bend. With almost fifty well-armed men at his back, and the chance of laying hands on fifteen thousand dollars as an inducement, the *bandido* leader saw no reason to call off his attempt. Faced by a body of men on land, be they sheriff's posse, company of Texas Rangers or members of

155

the Mexican *Guardia Rurales*, he could have estimated the danger immediately. However he knew nothing of naval power. While he recognised the cannon, the true potential of the Gatling gun in the leading launch escaped him. Like Amy-Jo, he took the six-barrelled machine gun to be some strange form of cannon, single-shot and not especially dangerous. So he yelled to his men to kill the gringos, jerked out his revolver and fired towards the river.

Seated forward on the gunwale of the launch commanded by the lieutenant, the Gatling's gunner saw the canoe. At his look-out's yell, the lieutenant moved towards the bows. Taking in the canoe and the sight of the two tattered, exhausted women getting to their feet on the sand bar, the officer guessed what might be happening. Even before Eve's assistant in the second launch, or Golly in his own could speak, the lieutenant opened his mouth to give orders. He meant to tell the launch nearest to the Mexican shore to land and bring aboard the women. A bullet, flying down from the Texas bank of the river, struck his launch's funnel and chopped off the words unsaid.

More shots sounded and a sailor cried out, clutching at his bleeding chest as he toppled over the side of the third launch. That drew the crews' attention to the approaching Mexicans. Veterans of the Mississippi Squadron's river campaigns, the sailors knew how to deal with such an attack, whether it be delivered by Confederate cavalry or a rabble of Mexican border thieves.

Without needing orders the gunners sprang to their pieces and started twirling elevating screws to line the barrels upwards. Their assistants leapt forward to throw open the ammunition lockers under the decking which supported the guns. Already the coxswains were thrusting on the tillers to point the launches' bows in the required direction and the engineers cut off the propellers to prevent them being run aground. Other members of the crews grabbed up Spencer carbines or drew their Navy Colts.

Before Danvila and his men fully realised the extent of their danger, the flotilla opened fire. With a sullen double roar, the two twelve-pounders vomitted out their loads. Each cannon was charged with canister, the twenty-seven 1.5 inch balls turning it into a kind of enormous shotgun, deadly up to a range of three hundred and fifty yards. Their detonations mingled with the harsh chatter as the man behind the Gatling gun whirled its firing handle around, turning the barrels in their loading cycle to spurt flame and lead as each muzzle reached the uppermost point of its axis.

Caught in the blast of flying lead, the *bandido* gang suffered badly. Men and horses went down. Flung over its head by his mount's collapse, Danvila fell into the path of the Gatling gun's bullets. His body arched as three of them ripped into him, then went limp and rolled a few feet down the slope. Desperate hands hauled back on reins, trying to swing the horses away from the hail of death. Then the shattered remnants of Danvila's gang plunged back up the slope. They left ten dead and seven wounded behind in their flight. Not until the last of the gang had passed out of sight over the rim could the lieutenant spare a thought for the two women.

At the sound of the shooting Belle stopped in her tracks and started to look around. She had her back to the river, so failed to see the new arrivals. Exhausted she might be, but Eve saw them and recognised that help was on hand. Taking a staggering step forward, she swung a round-house punch to the side of Belle's jaw. Taken completely by surprise, Belle went down to land spread-eagled on her back. Dazed by the blow, she lay motionless. Breath whistling through her mouth, Eve stumbled towards the slim girl. The woman intended to fall knees first on to Belle's stomach and finish her off. Through the mists which seemed to be swirling around in her head, Belle saw Eve's advance and guessed her intention. Yet the girl could not make herself do anything to prevent the move.

Then an explosion split the air, its sound all but drowning out the double crack of rifle fire which wafted down from the rim on the Mexican shore. On the river, the canoe disappeared in a sheet of flame and cloud of black smoke. Tossed up by the blast, a sizeable wave rushed on to the launches. Each boat had men flung over the side by the unexpected pitching and the one closest to the explosion took a considerable amount of water aboard as it rocked violently.

On the bank Eve staggered as the shock wave of air hit

her but did not fall. The halt in Eve's advance gave Belle just that brief moment she needed to recover. Coiling up her body, Belle thrust her legs forward and up with all her remaining strength. Reeling forward again, Eve took the soles of Belle's driving feet full in the pit of her stomach. A strangled croak broke from the Yankee as she doubled over, pitched backwards and crashed helplessly to the sand. All but spent by her final effort, Belle rolled on to her stomach. She could not force herself higher than to hands and knees. Yet she knew that she must try to escape. Weakly, sobbing at the effort, she started to crawl in the direction of the bushes.

At the top of the slope overlooking the sand bar, Sam Ysabel and the Kid watched the result of their shooting. When they came into view of the river, they had seen immediately what must be done. No bunch of Mexican *bandidos* ever born would face up to what Danvila and his men received from the launches. With the gang disposed of, the Yankees could easily catch up with the canoe. So there was only one course left open to the two Texans. Sighting their rifles, they planted a bullet each into the powder kegs. Some of the gold coins might land on the banks, but the vast majority of them sank irrecoverably into the quick-sands at the bottom of the river. That left only one problem needing a hurried solution.

"We've got to rescue Miss Belle!" the Kid stated, coming to his feet.

"Yeah!" Ysabel replied. "We'll take her out Comanche fashion."

Running to their waiting horses, they thrust the rifles into the saddleboots, freed the spare mounts and swung into the saddles. Side by side, the father and son headed over the rim and down towards the sand bar.

Occupied with the work of bailing out their launches and helping comrades back aboard, the Yankee sailors did not notice the Ysabels. Golly saw them first, guessed what they meant to do and yelled a warning.

Painfully Belle dragged herself along the sand. Although she could hear the thunder of approaching hooves, the sound meant nothing to her. Directing their horses to pass on either side of the girl, the Ysabels leant inwards and reached down. Belle felt a hand take hold of each arm and raise her then carry her along. Shouts rang out as the Yankees realised a rescue bid was being made. Golly's revolver barked twice, but its bullets came nowhere near the fast-moving Texans. Other men grabbed at weapons, their excited movements threatening to capsize the boats.

"Belay that shooting!" roared the lieutenant. "Mr. Snaith, run your launch ashore and bring Miss Coniston off. She looks like she needs help."

With the bushes close ahead, there could be no more carrying Belle between them. So Ysabel reached across with his other hand, took hold and swung the girl's limp body up before him. Supporting her in his arms, he used knee pressure to guide the grulla in among the undergrowth. Showing superb horsemanship, the Kid allowed his father to go first and plunged into cover after him. Letting Ysabel ride on, the Kid collected the pack horse and its saddles before following.

Not until they had put two miles between them and the river did the Texans stop. While the Kid made a fire and set up camp for the night, Ysabel helped Belle tend to her injuries. At last the girl lay on a bed of soft grass, her numerous bruises and aching muscles sending knife-like jagged stabs of pain through her. Yet she had barely felt them in the sick, numbing realisation that her mission had ended in failure. The Kid had brought along the packs which held her property and disguised weapons; but the gold on which so much depended lay at the bottom of the Rio Grande. Without it Klatwitter would not make a move, even if he could after the attack on the fort at Nava. Nothing the Ysabels could say offered her any comfort.

"I've failed!" she moaned. "Everything is lost."

Little did Belle know that the failure had probably been the most fortunate thing to happen to her.

The date was April the 8th, 1865. Next day at the Appomattox courthouse, wishing to prevent further bloodshed and loss of life, General Robert E. Lee surrendered his sword to General U. S. Grant as a preliminary to bringing the War Between The States to an end.

BACK TO THE
BLOODY BORDER

For Jerry 'Jesbo' Culley, best plug-maker and third best pike-fisherman in Melton Mowbray.

CHAPTER ONE

THE WAR'S OVER, SAILOR

'What're you fixing to do now, Miss Belle?' asked Sam Ysabel, sitting with his back against a wall of the dining-room in Bannister's Hotel.

Over the years, Ysabel had made sufficient enemies to render the precaution second nature. He always preferred to have a wall behind him, even when eating in a respectable Brownsville hotel.

'I don't know,' Belle Boyd admitted. 'What does a spy do when the war's over and she's served on the losing side?'

'You could always go back home,' suggested Ysabel's son, having selected a chair that allowed him an uninterrupted view across the table at the hotel's lobby.

'Home!' Belle repeated the word bitterly. 'I don't have a home any more. A bunch of Abolitionists saw to that back in '61.'

Tall, slender, although by no means skinny, the girl had coal-black hair cut almost boyishly short. She wore an expensive, stylish, if travel-stained, black jacket and riding-skirt, a frilly-bosomed white blouse and dainty, calf-high boots. Beautiful features, with strength of will and intelligence in their lines, displayed little of the concern she might feel for the future. Her voice, with its well-educated deep-South drawl, expressed unspoken anger as she mentioned her loss.

As Belle claimed, she no longer had a home. Not since the night, early in 1861, when Alfred Tollinger and George Barmain had led a mob, consisting of rabidly violent pro-Union fanatics and ordinary drunken rabble in search of a chance to loot and pillage, against her father's plantation. The family and house-servants had fought back desperately. However, before the Boyds' 'down-trodden and abused' slaves had rallied and helped to drive off the attackers, Belle had been wounded, her parents murdered and the once magnificent mansion de-

7

stroyed by fire. To escape justice, the leaders of the mob had fled to the North. The start of the War Between the States had prevented their arrest and return to Baton Royale for trial.

Belle's wound had healed in time, but it left her with a deep and lasting desire for revenge and a hatred of the Union's supporters that she had not felt before the attack. The brutal, irresponsible and ill-advised actions of a pair of intellectual fanatics was to cost the North dearly in the years that followed. Wanting to avenge her parents, Belle had sought for a way to do so. Learning that a cousin, Rose Greenhow, intended to organise a spy-ring, Belle had offered her services in the hope that the work would bring her into contact with Tollinger and Barmain. Knowing of the girl's unconventional upbringing, Rose had been only too willing to enrol her.

Wanting a son, and learning that his wife could have no more children, Vincent Boyd had insisted on instructing his daughter in several subjects not normally taught to a wealthy Southern girl. By sixteen, she could ride a horse—astride, not side-saddle—and follow a hound-pack as well as any of her fox-hunting male neighbours. At twenty, when the mob had arrived, she was a skilled performer with a duelling sword, a deadly shot with a hand-gun and had also acquired a thorough knowledge of *savate* : French-Creole foot- and fist-boxing.

Belle's lessons in the more usual feminine accomplishments had not been neglected and, but for the raid on her home, she would probably have put aside her masculine skills, taken a husband and lived a conventional life. Instead she made use of her training as a member of the newly-formed, but very efficient, Confederate States' Secret Service organisation.

Not for Belle Boyd the routine and intrigue of making contacts, worming confidences from susceptible males or accumulating information. She had preferred the more active task of delivering her fellow-agents' gatherings to their superiors in the organisation. Coming and going through the Union Army's lines, she had relied upon disguises, quick wits, riding or fighting skills to avoid capture. Her fame grew and she was given the name 'the Rebel Spy' for her efforts in the South's cause.

All through the War, wherever its fortunes carried her, she had looked for Tollinger and Barmain. Rumour had it that they were members of the United States' Secret Service, but Belle had failed to locate them. Despite military hostilities having ended, she felt disinclined to forgive or forget what the two men had done to her parents; although she knew that gaining her revenge would not be easy.

Typical of Belle, while unsure of what the future might hold for her, she also wondered how her companions would make out now that peace had returned to the United States. Yet she guessed that her fears on their behalf might be unfounded. Although their pre-War business would be reduced, if not ruined, the Ysabels were probably better fixed than Belle in the matter of earning a living. They were Texan's frontiersmen, with the great wide spread of the Lone Star State in which to search for a fresh start.

Big, powerfully-built, Sam Ysabel had short-cropped black hair and a rugged face tanned to the colour of old saddle-leather; but was clean-shaven in honour of the occasion. He wore a fringed buckskin shirt and trousers, with Comanche moccasins on his feet. A battered old Confederate Jeff Davis campaign hat dangled from the back of his chair. Around his waist hung a gunbelt, supporting an old Dragoon Colt, its butt pointing forward, at the left side, and on the right a sheathed bowie knife.

Almost as tall as his father, Loncey Dalton Ysabel had a slim, wiry frame that hinted at hidden reserves of strength. Hair as black as the wing of a deep-South crow framed a handsome, Indian-dark face with a young, almost babishly-innocent cast of features. His red-hazel eyes seemed out of place in such a face, being neither young nor innocent, but giving a hint of his true, reckless nature. He wore all black clothing, including the wide-brimmed, low-crowned Stetson hat hanging on his chair and the gunbelt about his lean waist. Reversing his father's style of armament, he carried his walnut-handled Dragoon Colt in a low cavalry-twist-draw holster on his right thigh and an ivory-hilted James Black bowie knife sheathed at his left hip. There were few people along the Rio Grande's banks who would have regarded those weapons as being mere decorations.

Born in the village of the *Pehnane*—Wasp, Quick-Stinger, Raider—Comanche, the tall, slim, young Texan had been brought up and educated as a member of that hardy warrior race. Sam Ysabel's wife, daughter of Chief Long Walker and his French-Creole *pairaivo*,* had died giving birth to their

Pairaivo: favourite wife.

9

only child. With his father away much of the time on the family business of first mustanging, then smuggling, the boy had been raised by his maternal grandfather. War leader of the Dog Soldier lodge, Long Walker had taught his grandson all those things a *Pehane* brave-heart must know.* The boy had grown up skilled in the use of both white and red man's weapons, capable of winning the confidence or mastering any horse ever foaled, able to follow barely discernible tracks and to locate hidden enemies or to conceal himself from the most keen-eyed searchers.

Following his father along the Río Grande's smuggling trails, the boy had put his *Pehane* education to good use. He had also earned himself considerable fame in the bloody border country. By virtue of his exceptional skill when wielding one, the *Pehane* had given him the man-name '*Cuchilo*', the Knife. To the Mexicans with whom he came in contact, he was '*Cabrito*', the Kid. Among the Texans, he was known as 'the Ysabel Kid'. Members of all three races, fighting men from soda to hock, recognised his fatal accuracy when shooting a Mississippi rifle and acknowledged that he could perform adequately with his old Dragoon or knife. All were unanimous in their belief that he made a real good, loyal friend, but was a deadly, implacable foe.

On learning of the War between the States, the Ysabels had travelled East and enlisted in John Singleton Mosby's Raiders. Although the Grey Ghost had thought highly of their ability as scouts, he had been compelled to let them return to Texas. There they had continued to render important service to the South by delivering urgently needed supplies—run through the U.S. Navy's blockade into neutral Matamoros—across the Rio Grande to the Confederate authorities.

It had been during this work that they had met the Rebel Spy. Sent to negotiate with a French general, who had offered to throw his full command into the War on the side of the Confederate States, Belle had been assigned the Ysabels as her escort. Fortunately for her, circumstances had prevented Belle from completing the mission.† Generals Grant and Lee had met at the Appomattox Courthouse, as the first move towards ending the War, on the day that she should have contacted the French renegade and handed over the advance payment for

* Told in *Comanche*.
† Told in *The Bloody Border*.

his services.

That had been just over six months ago. On their return to Matamoros, news of the War's end had not yet arrived. So the Confederate States' consul had asked them to leave as quickly as possible. The ambiguous diplomatic situation in the town had caused him to make the request. Neither of the warring governments north of the border wished to antagonise the Mexican patriots or the European powers involved in the struggle for control of Mexico. Knowing that Belle's mission might be exploited by the Yankees as a means of discrediting his consulate, the consul had taken steps to remove her and her assistants.

Being aware of the consul's motives, Belle had taken a ship to Nassau, the principal port for blockade-runners in the West Indies. It had been her intention to go on to Charleston, or Savannah, from either of which Confederate town she could report to her superiors for further orders. On hearing that the War had ended, she returned to Matamoros with the intention of spreading the news in Texas and ending the fighting between the Rebels and the Yankees defending Brownsville.

On arrival in Matamoros, she had learned that the news was known. The consulate no longer had any official status, but its consul had remained in Mexico as a private citizen. Wanting to learn all she could about conditions north of the Rio Grande, Belle had crossed over and in Brownsville had met the Ysabels. From what they had told her, they had spent their enforced absence with the *Pehnane* Comanche. The Kid had been hoping to locate a boyhood enemy, No Father, and settle accounts with him, but failed to do so.* Coming back to Matamoros, the Ysabels had found that their services were no longer required officially and were making their first visit to Brownsville since the start of the Yankee occupation.

Accepting the Ysabels' offer to have a meal with them, Belle had been surprised when they brought her to Bannister's Hotel. One of the town's best-known establishments, it now appeared to cater for businessmen who had carved a niche during the Union's control. However, its owner raised no objections to the Ysabel family entering with their guest. The food had been good and the disapproving glares thrown their way by the room's other occupants failed to spoil Belle's

* How the Kid settled his account with No Father is told in *Sidewinder*.

appetite. Not until they had finished the meal did the subject of the future come up.

'What will you do now, Sam?' Belle asked, sitting opposite the big man and with the Kid on her left.

'Ain't made our minds up yet,' Ysabel admitted.

'Could start selling maps to where we buried all that money we was taking to the Frog general, *ap'*,' suggested the Kid with a grin, using the Comanche word for father.

'But we destroyed the money,' Belle objected.

'You know it, we know it,' the Kid answered. 'Trouble being, nobody believes us that that's what happened.'

'We've had three different fellers asking us about it,' Ysabel confirmed.

Belle smiled, knowing that the money in question was irrecoverable at the bottom of the Rio Grande.

'I can't see you as treasure-map sellers,' she told the Texans.

'Anyways, we'll make out fine one way or another,' Ysabel assured her. 'Right now it's you we're thinking about.'

'Why don't you stay on here in Brownsville and help us set up again, Miss Belle?' asked the Kid. 'It's not going to be easy for rough-necks like us to do it, is it, *ap'*?'

'Sure ain't, boy,' Ysabel confirmed. 'Most all the folks we used to trade with don't have money no more to buy smuggled wine and stuff.'

That Belle could figure out without needing to ask for an explanation. By its support of the Confederate States, Texas had been left with a worthless currency. The majority of the Ysabels' old customers would be broke, or near to it. For some time to come they would be too busy striving for survival and the recovery of their State's solvency to be able to afford smuggled luxuries.* Yet there were others, people whose loyalties had been with the victorious North, who might possess the means to purchase the Ysabels' wares. As Sam Ysabel had said, contacting such new customers would not be easy.

There was one big snag to Belle accepting the offer and helping the Ysabel family to gather sufficient customers to make their business pay. Even before the assassination of President Lincoln, the liberals, radicals and intellectuals of the Union had been demanding that extreme reprisals be carried out against the supporters of the Confederacy. With the blind,

* The way in which Texas recovered is told in *Goodnight's Dream* and *From Hide and Horn*.

bigoted intolerance their kind always showed against anybody who dared to oppose their lofty ideals, the Northern soft-shells had repeatedly demanded that every Southern leader be hanged for treason. Having caused some of the soft-shells inconvenience, humiliation and loss, Belle had heard that she and Rose Greenhow were to receive the same treatment if captured. So she had no desire to fall into the Yankees' hands until she had discovered how much power and authority the soft-shells would command in the United States' government.

Wondering how she could frame a refusal that would not offend the Texans, Belle heard a disturbance from the hotel's lobby. Raucous laughter and loud talk rose, drawing the attention of all the diners to the door of the room. Turning her head to the right, Belle saw a quartet of sailors had entered the building. Judging by their general appearance of conviviality and the increase to their nautical rolling gait, the newcomers had been drinking steadily and long. Clad in the usual dark blue, round, peakless cap, blouse and bell-bottomed trousers of the United States' Navy, each of them had a cutlass dangling from the left side of his belt and a Colt Navy revolver in a high-riding, close-topped holster at its right.

Before the War, ordinary seamen would not have been encouraged to remain in the Bannister Hotel; and the quartet clearly knew it. Conscious of their status as victors in a conquered city, they showed disdain for the management's prejudices. Halting just outside the dining-room's door, they looked around until their eyes came to rest on Belle, the youngest and best-looking woman present.

Although the Ysabels hardly gave the sailors more than a glance, Belle treated them to a longer scrutiny. All were tall: one a big, thickset, clean shaven stoker, two leaner, dark-headed and bearded—and the last a gangling beanpole with sandy red hair.

Early in her career as a spy, Belle had found that she possessed a talent of the greatest use and did her best to develop it. She had a remarkable memory for faces and, more important, the ability to recall the circumstances which led her to remember them. Stiffening slightly, she halted her right hand as it moved involuntarily towards the parasol leaning against her chair.

'What's up, Miss Belle?' demanded the Kid, having noticed the girl's gesture.

'I've seen that ginger-haired sailor before,' Belle replied, turning her attention hurriedly towards her companions as the sailors' gaze moved her way. 'He was one of the pair who tried to pull me into the guard-boat the night we attacked the *Waterbury*.'

'Reckon he'll recognise you?' asked Ysabel, suddenly realising that it might go badly for the girl should she be identified as the Rebel Spy.

'I hope not,' Belle answered. 'Damn it, they're coming over here.'

Having completed their examination of the room and satisfied themselves that only civilians were present, the sailors swaggered forward. If the man with ginger hair recognised Belle as the girl who had been captured, but escaped, on the night that the U.S. Navy's steam-sloop *Waterbury* had been torpedoed in Brownsville harbour, he showed no sign of it. Instead he seemed to be jockeying for position with his companions. Coming to a halt at the empty side of the table, the quartet eyed Sam Ysabel and the Kid in the challenging manner before turning their lecherous gaze in Belle's direction.

'These land-crabs don't look to be giving you much of a time, gal,' the stoker exclaimed in a loud voice.

'Why they're my uncle and cousin from out of town, sir,' Belle answered, giving the Kid's leg a quick kick as he seemed about to speak. 'We've just finished supper and are going home.'

'They don't look like your kin,' declared one of the black-haired pair and looked at the other. 'Do they, Mick?'

'Not all that much, Joe,' Mick replied.

'She's a niece on my wife's side,' Ysabel rumbled.

'Was you pair in the Reb army?' demanded Joe belligerently.

'The War's over, sailor,' Belle put in, studiously avoiding looking at the ginger-haired man.

'And we won it,' the stoker pointed out. 'Anyways, it's too early for a pretty gal like you to be going home.'

'It sure is, Cully,' grinned Mick. 'And she shouldn't be going home with no kin-folks neither.'

Swiftly Belle looked around the room. Its other occupants showed signs of resentment or concern. They were middle-aged couples, reasonably prosperous-looking and not the kind

14

to become involved in anything as unseemly as the behaviour of the sailors. Knowing there would be no help from that source, Belle hoped to be able to avert trouble.

At which point Belle became aware of the ginger man's eyes on her. Moving around his companions, he halted close to the girl and was studying her with extra interest. To add to Belle's discomfort, she recollected that she had not troubled to don a wig, or any other form of disguise, before crossing from Matamoros. So, apart from being dry, she looked much the same as she had when the sailor had last seen her.

'That's truly true, Mick,' the stoker said. 'And being so, we can't let you do it, gal.'

'Who'd you reckon she should go home with, *hombre*?' asked the Kid in a mild, gentle tone that would have shrieked warnings to anybody who knew him.

'Us, beef-head. Us!' Cully answered. 'So you can push off and leave us see her safe to port.'

'Why I do declare I'm honoured, gentlemen,' Belle gushed before either of the Ysabels could speak. 'But there'd be four of you-all and only the one of lil me. I just couldn't be attentive to more than one of you-all. It wouldn't be proper.'

Apparently that point had not struck the four sailors. Finding the girl willing to accept the company of one of them came as a surprise and raised difficulties. Some of the quartet's hostility was diverted from the Ysabels and to each other as they wondered who should take precedence with the girl. Nor did Belle help matters. Glancing from face to face, she seemed to exude a welcome and promise to each of the sailors and made the recipient feel that he was the one she favoured.

Catching his father's eye, the Kid sank into a casual-seeming slouch on the chair. Both of them knew that the sailors were looking for trouble, so they prepared to deal with it. A quick inclination of Ysabel's head told the Kid how he aimed to make his play should the need arise. Slowly, so as to arouse no suspicion, Ysabel placed the palms of his hands under the edge of the table. Drawing no more attention to himself, the Kid duplicated his father's move. Then they waited, tense as coilsprings under pressure, watching for the first hostile word or gesture from the other four.

For her part, Belle also studied the sailors. She hoped that she had prevented a clash between them and the Ysabels. During her assignment with them, she had seen her companions in action and knew that they had small regard for the sanctity of human life. While she did not doubt the two Texans' ability to protect themselves, she knew that doing so might lead them into very serious trouble. Just let one of the sailors be killed, no matter how much provocation had been heaped on the Ysabels, and a military court would show them no mercy. With that in mind, Belle went on with her attempt at setting the quartet at each other's throats.

'If you gentlemen just tell me which of you I'll have the honour to be escorted home by,' Belle went on, uncomfortably aware of the ginger-haired sailor's scrutiny, 'I'm right sure my kins-folk won't——'

'Hey!' yelped the ginger man, stabbing a finger in Belle's direction. 'I've seen you afore.'

'Don't try that one, Carrots!' Cully the stoker, growled. 'The gal's going with me.'

'She never said so,' protested Mick indignantly. 'I reckon she——'

Stabbing forward his left hand, Carrots placed it on Belle's right shoulder and started to turn her towards him. Before his companions, or the Ysabels, could object, he leaned forward to stare directly into the girl's face.

'It's her, damn it!' Carrots screeched. 'She's the Rebel Spy. I saw her——'

CHAPTER TWO

IF YOU'VE MADE ME LOSE THEM

As soon as Carrots laid hands on her, Belle reached for the parasol with her right hand and her left slipped her reticule's strings free from the back of her chair. Hearing his words, she started to rise. While doing so, she propelled the parasol upwards sharply. Driving towards the sailor's chin, the silver knob at the end of the handle rammed with considerable force against his prominent adam's apple. Just too late to prevent him from making his denunciation, the pain of the impact

16

chopped off the rest of Carrots' words. With hands rising to clutch at the stricken area, he released the girl's shoulder and stumbled back a few paces. Freed from Carrot's restraint, Belle continued to stand up.

Seeing Belle launch her attack, the Ysabel family went into action. Shoving back with his knees, the Kid sent his chair skidding away from beneath him. Then he lunged erect and heaved at his edge of the table. Timing his moves to coincide with his son's, Sam Ysabel also rose. Lifting the table between them, they hurled it at the remaining three sailors.

Turning edgeways to the floor and spraying the utensils and crockery it had supported from its top, the table struck Cully and Joe, hurling them back. Although he was no less surprised by the sudden turn of events, Mick managed to throw himself towards the wall and avoided being hit by the Ysabels' missile. Doing so proved to be a mistake. In fact he might have wished that he had stood his ground and taken his punishment like a man.

Noticing that Mick had not been driven to the rear with his companions, Ysabel swung in his direction. Up lashed the big Texan's left leg. Years of wearing no other covering than moccasins had hardened Ysabel's feet to a considerable degree and made them effective weapons. Caught in the groin by the kick, Mick let out a screech of pain, folded over and collapsed. Almost before his victim had landed, Ysabel was snatching his hat from the chair's back and ramming it on to his head.

'Get out of here!' Belle yelled, turning to do so.

While in full agreement with the girl's suggestion, Sam Ysabel and the Kid knew that carrying it out would not be an easy matter. The table might have forced Cully and Joe to withdraw for long enough to give Ysabel time to render Mick *hors de combat*, but it had in no way incapacitated the other two sailors. They and Carrots were still capable of disputing the three Southerners' departure.

Pitching the table out of his way, Cully bellowed in fury and hurled himself at Ysabel. Stoking the boilers of a coal-burning warship was not a task to be performed by weaklings and Cully was noted in the U.S. Navy for his strength. He used it in a fight to smash down all resistance by sheer force. Looking as huge and dangerous as a charging buffalo bull, he rushed towards the Texan with ham-like hands reaching out to seize and crush.

Being a more cautious man than Cully, even when drunk, Joe was content to let the stoker avenge the attack on his brother. The Kid had sprung into the centre of the room after throwing over the table and looked a safer subject for reprisals than his father. Clenching his fists, Joe went towards the Indian-dark youngster. While approaching, the sailor saw a change come over his intended victim. Up to that moment, the Kid had looked like a very young and harmless boy. Suddenly all the babyish innocence left his face, being replaced by the cold, savage, slit-eyed expression of a *Pehnane* Dog Soldier waiting to take on an enemy. Flashing across, the Kid's right hand closed about the hilt of the bowie knife and started to slide the eleven-and-a-half-inch-long, two-and-a-half-inch-wide, clip-pointed blade from its sheath.

Few people who knew the Ysabel Kid would have given Joe a life expectancy exceeding the time he took to come within striking distance of the other's black-sleeved right arm.

Seeing Belle darting in his direction and transferring the reticule into her parasol-filled right hand, Carrots tore his thoughts from his half-strangled condition. As the girl swerved to go by him, he shot out his hands to catch her by the right wrist and bicep. Having received one taste of the parasol's handle, he had no wish to repeat the dose. With the girl's right arm immobilised, he felt sure that she was helpless. Bringing her to a halt at arms' length in front of him, he started to imagine the commendation and promotion that would come his way as a reward for capturing the Rebel Spy.

For all his bulk, Sam Ysabel could move with surprising speed. Springing forward as if meaning to meet Cully head-on, Ysabel swerved aside at the last moment. Powerful hands clamped hold of Cully's left wrist. Taking a firm grip, Ysabel heaved the stoker onwards. Narrowly missing a collision with Joe, Cully felt himself hauled around in a half circle. Combined with the stoker's own momentum, Ysabel's pull built up an uncontrollable speed. Then Ysabel released his hold. On being turned loose, Cully could not prevent himself plunging across the room. A waiter flung himself hurriedly from the stoker's path. Ahead was a window, but Cully could neither stop himself nor swerve aside. Barely managing to do more than throw up his hands to protect his face, Cully went through the window. Crashing to the sidewalk, he rolled across it to drop on to the street.

Hearing the shattering crash of breaking glass, an infantry patrol farther along the street halted and did a rapid about face to see what caused it. Being assigned to the duty of policing the town, the lieutenant in command knew that he must investigate. He had seen the four sailors before they had entered the hotel and marked them as potential trouble-causers. Having also noted the size and brawn of Cully in particular, he wanted his men as fresh as possible while dealing with the quartet. So he led them back over the hundred or so yards separating them from the building at a quick march instead of on the double.

Despite having her right arm held, Belle was far from helpless. Balancing on her right leg, she shot her left foot behind her. The heel of her boot spiked on to Carrots' kneecap, driven by a powerful set of leg muscles. Pain ripped through the lean man. Letting go of the girl's arm, he hopped back and tried to support his injured knee with his hands. Unfortunately for him, he did not retreat sufficiently far before doing so. Spinning around, Belle used her turning momentum to add force to her knotted left fist. It swung, not in the manner of a frightened girl, but with trained purpose. Hard knuckles met Carrots' jaw with a sharp click. Off balance, he spun around and went head-first into the wall. Bouncing back, he flopped as limp as a rag-doll to the floor.

With his knife half drawn, the Kid recalled his father's orders. Few people in Texas had ever regarded smuggling, as carried out by the Ysabel family, as a serious crime. Even the U.S. military authorities had tended to ignore it before the War and, provided they received their share of the goods, would most likely continue to do so. However, Ysabel knew that no such tolerance could be expected if a Yankee service-man should be killed. So he had repeatedly warned his son that weapons must only be used as a last resort if they were forced to lock horns with their erstwhile enemies.

Restraining his first impulse to produce and make use of the bowie knife, the Kid returned it to the sheath and took his hand from the hilt. Already Joe was closing in and his right fist lashed savagely at the young Texan's head.

Deprived of his favourite close-quarters' weapon, the Kid was still far from being easy meat. While the Comanches preferred more direct, permanent ways of dealing with an enemy, they had not been unmindful of the possibility that an

19

attack might come at a time when no weapon was available. So they had developed various bare-hand fighting tricks to meet such situations. The Kid had received a thorough training in *Nemenuh** wrestling techniques.

Throwing up his left hand inside Joe's advancing right arm, the Kid deftly prevented the punch from reaching his head and caught the other's wrist. At the same time, the Kid started to pivot to his left. His right arm rose, working in concert with the other movements, passing beneath Joe's right armpit and behind the sailor's bicep. Continuing to turn and sinking into a kneeling position on his bent right leg, the Kid heaved on the trapped arm. Feeling his feet leave the floor and body rise into the air, Joe let out a startled wail. Released as he passed above the Kid's shoulder, Joe smashed down hard on his back.

After liberating herself and felling Carrots, Belle swung ready to lend her companions assistance. She gripped the parasol in both hands. Designed for her work, its innocent exterior concealed a powerful steel-spring billy of considerable strength and effectiveness. Seeing that her help would not be needed, she left the parasol intact.

'Come on!' she yelled, turning in the direction of the door.

Although the other guests were on their feet, none tried to interfere with the trio as they ran from the room. The Kid had retrieved his hat before leaving and donned it as he followed his father and Belle from the hotel.

'Hey you!' yelled the patrol commander. 'Halt right there!'

'Like hell!' Ysabel growled, glancing at the unconscious stoker. 'Cross over and go down between Orley's saloon and that undertaker's parlour, Miss Belle. We'll lose 'em easy enough in the back streets.'

Obediently, the girl bounded from the sidewalk and sped diagonally across the street in the direction indicated by the big Texan. Wanting to shield her if the patrol started shooting, the Ysabels allowed the girl to draw ahead. Belle set a fast pace, taking a line that would keep them out of the lighted area before the saloon. While he shouted another command to halt, the Yankee officer did not order his men to open fire. Instead, they gave chase, running as fast as they could in their overcoats, accoutrements and heavy Jefferson bootees and armed with Springfield muzzle-loading rifles.

* *Nemenuh*: the People, the Comanches' name for their tribe.

Approaching the front of the saloon, Belle saw three men walk out. Hearing the sounds of the chase, the trio turned to investigate. A gasp burst from Belle and she skidded to a halt, staring at the men as if she could not believe the evidence of her eyes.

'Tollinger!' she gasped.

Following the direction of Belle's gaze, the Ysabels wondered at her reaction. They had noticed the three men, but attached no importance to them as none wore uniforms or showed other signs of official capacity.

Dressed in town suits, with vests, white shirts and red neckties, two of the men's appearance gave no clue as to who or what they might be. Sporting a derby hat, the taller of them was gaunt, wth a sallow face that a thick-lipped, petulant mouth, hollow cheeks and sunken eyes gave a mean, arrogant expression. Bare-headed, the other had a portly build. His surly, piggish cast of features were not improved by a drooping black moustache and lank, greasy long hair.

The third man hardly seemed likely company for the other two. Middle-sized, stocky, he was a Mexican with an evil face that carried a scar running down its left cheek and along his neck until hidden by the *serape* draped over his shoulders. A grey *sombrero* perched on the back of his head and the *serape* covered him to the knees, effectively concealing any weapons he might be carrying.

Even as the word left the girl's lips, the Kid collided with her. Staggering, she might have fallen but for Sam Ysabel. Leaping forward, he scooped Belle up under his right arm. Without breaking his stride, he continued to run towards the alley.

Glancing at the three men in passing, the Kid recognised the Mexican and saw shock twist at the faces of the two white men. Snarling something that did not reach the Kid's ears, the taller of the pair made as if to move forward. Catching his arm, the other dude spoke quietly but urgently in his ear. Then the Kid raced by, following his father.

'Let me down!' Belle gasped, kicking her legs and struggling in Ysabel's grasp. 'If you've made me lose them, I'll——'

Dropping the girl to her feet as they rounded the corner of the building, Ysabel expected her to follow him. Instead she made as if to return to the street. Grabbing her by the wrist, he jerked her after him. Sanity returned to Belle as she was on the point of resisting and she yielded to his pull.

''Round the corner there!' Ysabel ordered, indicating the rear end of the undertaker's parlour. 'Reckon you can lead 'em off, boy?'

'Nothing easier,' drawled the Kid, drawing and cocking his old Dragoon.

Lengthening his stride, the youngster drew ahead. His black clothing soon rendered him invisible in the darkness. Looking back over her shoulder, Belle half expected to see the men from the saloon following her. Nobody had appeared so far. Changing his hold from the wrist to her bicep, Ysabel guided her around the corner. With the clumping of heavy boots drawing closer, they came to an involuntary halt.

'Hell's fires!' Ysabel spat out. 'He's built a wall since we was last here.'

Rising a good eight feet high, the plank wall extended from the rear of the undertaker's premises for a disconcertingly indefinite distance, merging into the darkness without giving any sign of coming to an end. For some reason, it had been erected from a point about a yard along the building instead of at the corner. So they had failed to notice it until too late.

Already the patrol had reached the mouth of the alley. Climbing the obstruction could not be accomplished silently enough to escape detection; nor could Belle and Ysabel retreat and follow the Kid.

Even as the girl and the Texan became aware of their predicament, they heard the sound of a shot. Not the high-pitched crack a Springfield rifle would make, but the deep boom caused by igniting forty grains of powder in the uppermost chamber of a Dragoon Colt's cylinder. It rang out from the direction taken by the Kid.

'What——!' Belle began, starting to turn as startled exclamations rose and the patrol's boot-thuds came to a stop.

Instantly Ysabel's hands gripped her shoulders, forcing her to face the wall. Another shot boomed from the Dragoon and Ysabel kept Belle motionless while drawing his own revolver.

'There they are!' bawled a voice from the mouth of the valley.

'Stay put!' Ysabel hissed in Belle's ear as two rifles cracked. 'It's Lon's way of making sure they follow him.'

'Stop that shooting, damn you!' barked the officer. 'Come on!'

'Real still now, Miss Belle!' whispered Ysabel. 'Don't turn

and we're safe.'

Suddenly Belle understood her companion's insistence that she remained motionless. If she had turned, the white of her blouse might have caught the attention of the passing soldiers. Hardly daring to breathe, she stood as if turned to stone and followed the progress of their pursuers with her ears. They continued by the end of the building. Waiting to catch any comment that would mean the Yankees' bullets had hit the Kid, Belle gave an involuntary jump as one of them shouted:

'There they go!'

'Get after them!' roared the officer.

When the sounds of the pursuit had faded away, Ysabel allowed Belle to turn from the fence.

'Sorry I had to rough-handle you that ways, Miss Belle,' he said and holstered his Colt. 'Only I didn't want you turning——'

'I know why,' Belle interrupted. 'Lon's still all right.'

'Trust him for that,' grinned Ysabel. 'Say, what was up on the street? Do you know *Cicatriz*?'

'*Cica*—— You mean the Mexican?'

'Yes'm.'

'I've never seen him. It was the other two. They're the men who murdered my parents.'

'The hell you say!' Ysabel growled.

For a moment Belle did not speak. A shudder ran through her slender frame and she shook her head from side to side, as if trying to blot out the memory. Ysabel waited in silence. With an effort, the girl regained control of her feelings.

'Thanks for your help, Sam,' she said. 'I'll be going now.'

'After them?' Ysabel inquired.

'Yes!'

'Leave it a minute, then we'll both go,' suggested Ysabel.

'It's not your quarrel, Sam,' Belle pointed out.

'Maybe not,' the big Texan grunted. 'But with *Cicatriz* sitting in the game, you'll need help. So I'm coming, 'less you say I shouldn't.'

'Tollinger and Barmain may still work for the Yankee Secret Service,' Belle warned. 'And I mean to kill them both.'

'Which I don't blame you for,' Ysabel replied. 'So, if you want it, you've got Lon 'n' me siding you.'

Belle did not reply immediately. During the mission they had shared, she had come to know the Ysabel family very well and formed the highest opinion of their sterling qualities. There could be only one answer to the magnanimous offer.

'Thank you, Sam,' she said. 'I'd admire to have you with me.'

While waiting for Ysabel's minute, Belle learned that *Cicatriz*, the Scar, was a notorious border *bandido*. They briefly debated the reason for the Mexican being with her enemies, but reached no conclusions. No further shooting sounded, which implied that the patrol had not caught up with the Kid. At last Ysabel led the way to the street, but they saw no sign of the three men. Ysabel asked Belle to remain in hiding while he conducted inquiries in the saloon. On Belle agreeing, he went to the rear of that building and returned within five minutes.

'Seems like they was only waiting there for *Cicatriz*,' the big Texan remarked as he and Belle walked off through the darkness. 'Orley don't know anything about 'em; and he's a good enough friend to tell me if he did. Do you reckon they knowed it was you?'

'That's what's been puzzling me, Sam,' Belle replied. 'I'm almost sure that they recognised me, especially as I said Tollinger's name. So I wonder why they didn't tell the patrol who I am, or come with them to help hunt me down.'

'Do they know you're after them?'

'I've never made any great secret of it.'

'We don't know they recognised you,' Ysabel pointed out. 'They for sure didn't tell the puddle-splashers. Them soldiers didn't stop until Lon throwed lead their way.'

Leading Belle through the darkened streets into the poorer white residential section, Ysabel insisted that they should behave in a natural manner. The Kid joined them as they approached a house standing in the centre of a garden surrounded by a picket fence.

'Lon!' Belle greeted. 'You're safe!'

'Why wouldn't I be?' asked the Kid. 'Shucks, I near on had to whistle, whoop 'n' wave a couple of times to stop them bluebellies losing me.'

Pressed by Belle for further details, the Kid explained briefly how he had drawn the patrol to the fringes of the Mexican section before giving them the slip. Although no rendezvous had been arranged, he guessed that his father would bring the girl to Ma O'Grady's rooming house—the family's headquarters in Brownsville—and so had made his way there. Learning of the reason for Belle's behaviour outside the saloon, the Kid disagreed with the summation that she and his father had made.

'Way them two acted, I'd say they knowed you, Miss Belle,' the youngster stated. 'The tall jasper made like he was fixing to come after you, but his *amigo* stopped him.'

'Then *I* don't know what to make of it,' Belle sighed. 'They know I've sworn to kill them.'

'Could be they don't want the Army to know they're around,' the Kid offered. 'Or figure to get you killed without the blue-bellies knowing about it, seeing's the Army's playing fair with folks here in Brownsville and don't want trouble.'

'Either's possible,' Belle admitted.

'If it's the last,' Ysabel said soberly, 'they've got real good help on hand to get you killed.'

'The Mexican?' Belle guessed.

'*Cicatriz*,' confirmed Ysabel. 'You being a woman wouldn't make no never mind to him.'

'If the price was right,' drawled the Kid, 'he'd kill you, or fix it done, Miss Belle. Would them two *hombres* know you're back in town?'

'It's not likely,' Belle said after a moment's thought.

'Anyways,' said the Kid, with the air of one who had solved a difficult problem, and opened the picket fence's gate. 'I don't see what all the talking's about. There's one feller's can likely give us all the answers.'

'Who?' asked Belle.

'*Cicatriz*,' replied the Kid.

CHAPTER THREE

BAD DON'T EVEN START TO COVER IT

Halting just inside the gate, Belle looked from the Kid to his father and back again.

'Do you know where to find him?' she asked.

'We know where to go ask about him, for starters,' Ysabel replied. 'He mostly hangs out around Cisco Castro's *cantina*.'

'Let's go and see if he's there,' Belle said eagerly. 'They might be with him.'

'Not if they've got the sense of a seam-squirrel between 'em,' the Kid growled. 'You can die through just breathing the air in Castro's *cantina*, you don't even need to drink his liquor.'

'Comes to a point,' Ysabel continued, 'I wouldn't like to say who's the most ornery, him or *Cicatriz*. Anyways, you can't come with us, Miss Belle. Castro's is no place for a lady.'

'I've been told that a lady wouldn't become a spy,' Belle smiled. 'So I'm coming with you. I've been in some pretty bad places, you know.'

'Not's bad's Castro's place,' Ysabel contradicted.

'That's for sure,' the Kid agreed. 'Bad don't even start to cover it.'

'I'm still coming with you!' Belle stated, setting her face grimly. 'No arguments, boys. I've made up my mind on that score.'

The Kid gave an overdone sigh of resignation, but his lips curled in an admiring grin as he looked at the girl. If ever he had seen determination personified, it was Belle at that moment.

'Do you have any of them fancy disguises with you, ma'am?' Ysabel inquired, also yielding to the inevitable.

'Only what I'm wearing,' Belle replied. 'My wigs are with my other gear at our consulate in Matamoros. I think I can fix something up, if I've anywhere to do it.'

'I hope finding *Cicatriz's* as easy,' Ysabel told her and led the way along the path.

Before they reached the house, its front door opened. A big buxom, white-haired woman stepped on to the porch. Neatly dressed, she held a Navy Colt in her right hand with casual competence.

'Oh, 'tis you, Big Sam,' the woman greeted, letting the revolver's barrel sag out of line. 'When I heard three of yez coming, I didn't know who it might be.'

'This here's Miss Boyd, Ma,' Ysabel introduced, joining the woman on the porch. 'Can you put her up for the night?'

Before answering, Ma O'Grady looked Belle over from head to foot. The old woman read quality and breeding in the girl's face and bearing. That was no tail-peddler from a whorehouse; not that the Ysabels would bring such a person to Ma's home.

'It's not grand, like you've been used to,' Ma told Belle at last. 'But it's clean and you're welcome to stay.'

'Thank you,' Belle answered, smiling. 'That's very good of you, especially taken with the company I'm keeping.'

'I thought you was trying to improve 'em maybe,' Ma grinned. 'There's room for plenty of that. Come on in, all of you.'

With that, Ma ushered Belle and the Texans into the house and closed the door. Taking them into the small, clean and comfortably furnished sitting-room, she offered the girl the best chair and asked if Belle would care for a meal.

'We already ate, Ma,' Ysabel put in. 'Got to go out again for a spell after Miss Belle's changed clothes.'

'Out?' Ma snorted. 'And where'd you be taking a young lady to at this hour, Big Sam?'

'Cisco Castro's *cantina*,' the Kid answered when his father hesitated.

'Don't you go making fun of a poor, defenceless old body like me, Lon Ysabel!' Ma warned, swinging belligerently towards the youngster. 'Sure and he's lost all his respect while he's been away, Big Sam.'

'He sure has, Ma,' agreed Ysabel. 'Only he told you the truth.'

Giving the woman no chance to protest, Ysabel explained why he and the Kid would be taking Belle to Castro's *cantina*. Listening in silence, Ma kept her eyes on the girl whose name had become a legend during the War years. For her part, Belle stiffened slightly and waited to see Ma show condemnation on learning that she intended to avenge her parents' murders. None came. Instead, Ma nodded approval. When Ysabel stopped talking, the old woman showed that she had not only followed his explanation but also formed conclusions.

'You can't go dressed like that,' Ma declared, indicating Belle's clothes. 'Maybe I can help. Had a gal rooming here in the last weeks of the War. She'd been working in a saloon, but married a sailor. They went off home a month back, but she left some of her work clothes behind. If they're any use to you——'

'Can I take a look at them?' Belle asked.

'Come up to your room and I'll fetch 'em along to you,' Ma replied.

Collecting and lighting a lamp, Ma escorted Belle upstairs

and into a small bedroom at the rear of the building. Like the rest of the house, its furnishings were not new. However, the bed looked comfortable and had clean sheets and pillow-cases. Crossing to the window, Ma drew its curtains together. Then she turned and looked at the girl.

'Will it do?'

'It's the best room I've had for some time,' Belle replied, placing her parasol and reticule on the bed.

'I'll go and fetch up Dolly's gear then,' Ma decided. 'It may take me a while to find it.'

'That's all right, Ma,' Belle assured her. 'I've a few things to do.'

After Ma had left the room, Belle hung her coat in the wardrobe and returned to the bed. Tugging at the side of her waistband, she set free her skirt and it fell to the floor around her feet. Encased in black silk stockings, her legs had a dancer's shapely, well-developed muscles. Removing her blouse left her clad in brief underclothing of a style not usually worn by well-bred Southern ladies.

Gathering up the skirt, Belle turned it inside out. Like the parasol, the skirt had been made with the needs of her profession in mind. Although the outer side had been plain, inside was a lining of glossy material. From the skirt, Belle turned her attention to the blouse. Taking a small pair of scissors from her reticule, she set to work removing the decorous frilly ruffle from its bosom.

On her return, carrying a leather case and a hat-box, Ma slammed to a halt and stared at the transformed Belle. The blouse, turned inside out, was of a shiny white material, sleeveless and with a daring decollete. Drawn tighter, the skirt emphasised the rich curves of her hips but looked cheap and flashy.

'The saints preserve us!' Ma ejaculated. 'How'd you do that?'

'These clothes were specially made for me,' Belle replied, going across and relieving the woman of the case.

Examining the belongings of the departed ex-saloon-girl, Belle found all she would need to make her disguise acceptable. Despite the alterations to her clothes, she had known there were other touches required to make her look the part. So she helped herself to a hat that would conceal the shortness of her hair, some cheap jewellery and a fancy shawl. Swiftly she applied some of Dolly's discarded make-up to her face.

'How do I look?' Belle asked, entering the sitting-room and turning around before the Kid and his father.

'Just like the sort of gal who'd go into Castro's place,' Ysabel praised.

'We'd better go out the back way,' Belle suggested as the men prepared to leave. 'I don't want to spoil Ma's good name in the neighbourhood.'

'Don't let that worry you, Miss Belle,' Ma answered. 'I can out-cuss anybody on this street; and I know enough about them all to make them keep quiet.'

Despite Ma's assurances, Belle and the Ysabels elected to leave by the back door. Doing so gave Belle her first view of the rear-side of the property. Going by all appearances, the old woman ran a livery barn in addition to the rooming house. As she went by the open doors of the big barn, Belle saw her companions' horses in the stalls. Knowing the two Texans' dislike for walking, she expected them to go and collect the animals.

'We'll walk over there,' Ysabel said, interpreting her look correctly. 'It'll be easier'n riding, if we have to leave in a hurry.'

At first Belle could not follow the reasoning behind Ysabel's statement, but understanding soon came. They passed through an increasingly poorer white section of the town, until it merged with the Mexican quarter. The change showed chiefly in the selection of building materials, although the smells which came to Belle's nose grew subtly different. Instead of wooden shacks, the buildings were adobe *jacales*, gradually getting smaller in size and closer together. She could see that riding a horse at speed through the narrow, winding streets would be hazardous in the extreme and how escaping on foot might offer a better chance of safety.

Watching the way in which her companions kept their hands hovering near their weapons, Belle gripped her reticule tightly in her left hand and the right tightened on the handle of the parasol. Closing protectively on either side of the girl, the Ysabels stayed alert for any warning sound or movement. Belle did not blame them for the precautions. Cold eyes watched them from all sides and occasionally a silent shape would flicker across their path then disappear into the shadows.

'There it is,' Ysabel announced, pointing ahead.

They stood on the edge of a small plaza. At the other side, dwarfing the surrounding buildings with its two-storey height and considerable length, Castro's *cantina* glowed with lights, music and rowdy merriment. As the trio crossed the plaza, a pair of bulky Mexicans hauled a smaller member of their race outside and hurled him headlong into the gutter. Dragging himself up, moaning and clasping at a bloody gash on his cheek, the evicted man stumbled away. For a moment the two bouncers stared at the girl and the Ysabels, then turned and walked back inside.

'Maybe he spit on the floor,' drawled the Kid in answer to Belle's unspoken question. 'Ole Cisco's real touchy about folks doing things like that. Other things, he's not so touchy about.'

'Stick close, Miss Belle,' Ysabel ordered. 'But if there's trouble, drop back and leave us handle it.'

Taking the lead, Ysabel pushed through the doors. Following at the Kid's side. Belle looked around in the hope of seeing Tollinger and Barmain. Smoke curled in a billowing cloud beneath the ceiling, but she could see clearly enough. Mexicans and white men, all well-armed, ranged along the bar, dabbled at the various gambling games, or sat drinking around the tables. While coming to the *cantina*, Sam Ysabel had warned Belle of what kind of customers it catered for. The girl read lust, depravity and evil on the majority of the male faces. In one corner, a four-piece band consisting solely of string instruments beat out a fast rhythm to which a girl twirled and gyrated in a high-stepping dance. Other girls of various nationalities, dressed in garish, abbreviated costumes, mingled with the customers.

Unfortunately, as far as Belle could see, the two men she sought were not in the big room.

'Hey, Big Sam!' yelled a voice. '*Cabrito! Saludos, amigos!*'

Even without needing to be told, Belle guessed the identity of the man who was advancing on Ysabel with widespread arms and a welcoming smile that appeared to stretch from ear to ear. Smallish, slender, with a hooked nose above a bristly beard, the man wore clothes in the fashion of a wealthy Mexican *haciendero*; glittering with silver filigree and gold decorative buttons. The deference exhibited by the girls and customers warned Belle that she was looking at Cisco Castro, the owner of the *cantina*.

'Way he takes on, you'd near to reckon he means it,' drawled the Kid sardonically in Belle's ear, watching Castro embrace his father around the shoulders. 'If he figured he could get away with it, he'd knife pappy right now.'

'It has been much too long since you came here last, Big Sam,' Castro stated, stepping back. Then he looked by Ysabel and beamed at the Kid. 'And you have grown since our last meeting, *Cabrito*.'

'You ain't, Cisco,' the Kid replied.

If Castro felt any resentment at the Kid's barely polite comment, he concealed it. Turning his gaze in Belle's direction, he raked her up and down in the coldly calculating manner of a farmer examining an animal offered for sale. While Castro's lips held a smile, his eyes were cold, expressionless, yet seemed to show a wary, suspicious glint.

'And who is this, Big Sam?' Castro asked.

'Name's Annie,' Ysabel answered, without calling Belle forward to be introduced. 'Is the bar open?'

'For you, *amigo*, always,' Castro enthused, taking Ysabel by the arm and leading him towards the counter.

Instead of following his father, the Kid remained at the door. With Belle at his side, he looked around the room. For a moment, Belle felt embarrassed by the lascivious manner in which several of the men present studied her. Then she noticed that the Kid's gaze had come to a stop. Looking in the same direction, Belle's hope that he had located Tollinger and Barmain met with disappointment.

Two men sat at a small table close to the left side door; but not the pair that the girl had hoped to see. Dressed in buckskins, they were leathery old Texans; one tall, lean, heavily bearded and sporting a coonskin cap, the other short, wiry, with bristle-stubbled cheeks and a large moustache under a black Stetson hat that had seen better days, months and years. A Colt revolving cylinder rifle leaned by the taller man's chair and a heavy-gauge, twin-barrelled shotgun rested against the table close to his companion's right hand. Belle felt certain that signals of some kind had passed between the Kid and the ancient duo, but figured she had better avoid drawing attention to the fact. While walking with the Kid after his father, she glanced again at the pair and found that they were following her party's progress with their eyes. More significantly, each of them had picked up his weapon and laid it across his lap.

On reaching the bar, the Kid did not join his father and Castro. Halting a short distance from them, he took hold of Belle's arm in his left hand and kept her at his side.

'And what brings you here, Sam?' Castro inquired, indicating the two glasses of *tequila* poured out by his bartender.

'Pleasure,' Ysabel answered, downing the fiery liquor in one gulp. 'And the gal there.'

'She is not bad looking, *amigo*. Not bad, if you like them skinny. With no offence to you or *Cabrito*, of course.'

'What's she worth, Cisco?'

'You mean——' Castro breathed, eyeing Belle with fresh interest.

'I mean how much'll you pay me for her,' confirmed Ysabel and saw suspicion flicker to the Mexican's face. 'Look, Cisco, I need me a stake to start smuggling again. And that gal strikes me as a good way to get it.'

'*You* need a stake?' Castro asked.

'Aw hell, Cisco. Don't tell me you've fallen for that story that me 'n' Lon's got a pile of Yankee gold stashed away. If we had, would I need to come to you this aways?'

'Of course you wouldn't.'

In his life as a *cantina* owner, Castro had bought and sold more than one girl. However, he had never known Big Sam Ysabel to become involved in such transactions. Being suspicious by nature, Castro had been on his guard for a trap. Now he felt that he knew the big Texan's motive. According to rumours making the rounds, the Ysabel family had hidden away a large sum of money in Yankee gold. By coming to Castro on the pretence of selling the girl, they hoped to convince people that the story was false. Naturally, they had come to Castro, knowing him to be the best market for such merchandise.

'This is something we can't discuss publicly, *amigo*,' Castro declared amiably. 'Bring the girl to my office.'

'Lon, Annie,' Ysabel called, looking their way. 'Come with us.'

While Ysabel turned his head to speak, Belle saw Castro nod sharply to the attentive bartender. Then she noticed that the Kid, acting as if he were taking a quick glance around the room, gave a slight inclination of his head towards the two old-timers. Again she could not be certain if it was a signal. Neither of them showed any sign of having caught it, if it should be. Instead they continued to sit nursing the shotgun and rifle, drinking their *tequila* with complete indifference to what was going on around them.

Still holding Belle's arm, the Kid guided her along the bar. They went to the right and Castro opened a door in the wall at the end of the counter. Politely he stood aside for his guests to precede him through it. Going in, Belle darted a quick look across her shoulder. She saw the bartender go through another door behind the counter.

Clearly Castro loved personal luxury and comfort. A thick carpet covered the floor of his private office. In its centre stood a large, expensive desk with a highly-polished but bare top. For additional furnishings there were a few fancy, upholstered chairs. Big and bulky, a Chubb safe looked almost out of place in a corner of such elegant surroundings. On each wall, heavy drapes hung down to floor level as if covering windows and ensuring the owner's privacy.

'And how goes it, Big Sam?' Castro asked jovially, waving Ysabel into a chair in front of the desk.

'Can't complain,' the Texan answered. 'How about with you?'

'Things haven't been easy,' Castro sighed and sat down facing Ysabel across the desk. 'Maybe things will improve now the War is over. Take a seat, *Cabrito*.'

Crossing to the desk, the Kid hooked his rump on to its end at his father's left. The action drew a slight frown from Castro, but he raised no verbal objection to the dark youngster's behaviour. Instead he launched into a dirty story, speaking clearly to emphasise its point and, while telling it, darted a look at the wall behind the Ysabels.

Nobody had asked Belle to sit down, so she stood by the door and studied her surroundings. Noticing Castro's interest in the left wall of the room, Belle also turned her attention that way. She had already observed that the desk did not face the door through which they had entered and read significance in its position. As the joke continued, Belle saw the left side drapes stir slightly. It was as if a draught of air had blown briefly through a window. Except that there could be no window behind the drapes. The left side wall was internal, separating the office from whatever rooms lay behind the bar. Remembering Castro's signal and the bartender's departure, Belle began to draw conclusions which she did not like.

After the one quick flutter, the drapes hung motionless. Belle might have wondered if her eyes had played a trick on her, but Castro's attitude hinted that they had not. Sitting back in his chair, the Mexican exhibited an impression of satisfaction like a man who had covered every bet. With the story ended and laughed at, Castro swung his gaze to Belle.

'All right, girl,' he said. 'Take all your clothes off.'

CHAPTER FOUR

CICATRIZ IS A VERY GOOD FRIEND

'How's that?' growled the Kid indignantly, tensing and his right hand moving towards the bowie knife's hilt.

'Didn't you tell *Cabrito* of your intention, Big Sam?' Castro asked nervously.

'Sure I did,' Ysabel replied.

'Then surely, *Cabrito,* you and your father have never bought a horse without giving it a thorough examination?' Castro purred. 'It is the same now. Come on, girl. Strip yourself so I can see what I'm buying.'

'Wha—Why——?' Belle gasped, looking flustered.

'Big Sam is selling you to me,' Castro explained. 'Didn't he tell you?'

'Like hell he did!' Belle screeched, sounding as coarse and uneducated as might be expected of a girl dressed in such a fashion. With relief, she saw that the Kid had relaxed slightly. 'You-all allowed you'd get me work, Sam Ysabel. You never said nothing to me about this.'

Until they heard Belle start speaking, the Kid and his father had been on the point of disclosing the real reason for their visit. Seeing Belle's reaction and subsequent behaviour, they guessed that she had seen or heard something which had escaped them. So they held their tempers in check and a-waited developments.

While speaking, Belle began to sidle across the room. Her hands disappeared behind her back and she wriggled in an embarrassed manner, letting her reticule and parasol fall to the floor. All the time, never looking that way, she edged herself closer to the drapes on the left-side wall. A capable poker player, Ysabel read the signs and prepared to help Belle make her play.

'Shucks, Annie,' he said placatingly, 'Senor Castro here'll see you right well settled. Do like he says.'

'I don't wanna!' Belle protested.

Simulating anger, Ysabel lunged to his feet. Starting towards the girl, he spoke in a harsher tone. The Kid remained seated on the desk, looking over his shoulder at Belle.

'Damn it all!' Ysabel snarled. 'You do like you was told, or I'll peel you raw myself.'

'Aw, Sam!' Belle whined, backing towards the wall. 'It ain't I minds stripping afore you gents. I just don't cotton to these jaspers back of here a-peeking at me.'

With that, the girl grabbed at and snatched open the drapes. Doing so confirmed her theory that there was no window behind them. Instead, she exposed a small alcove with a door at its rear end. Inside the opening, three hard-faced Mexicans armed with revolvers formed a living triangle. Spitting out an explosive Spanish curse, the foremost member of the trio lunged forward and lifted his Starr Army revolver to line in Ysabel's direction. In his surprise at being discovered, the advancing Mexican overlooked the fact that somebody other than the big Texan must have pulled open the drapes. He discovered his mistake quickly enough.

Bringing her right hand from behind her back, Belle showed that she had taken apart her parasol and had only dropped its body. As the man burst from the alcove, she raised and slashed down the handle. Out slid the components of the billy. Its ball struck the top of the Starr with a force that ripped the gun from the man's grasp. Nor did his troubles end there. On the heels of the blow, giving its recipient no time to recover, Belle swung her left arm. Her palm caught the centre of the man's shoulders, sending him staggering onwards. At no time during her attack did she step into sight of the other two Mexicans. After completing their companion's discomfiture, she remained concealed ready to help deal with them when they emerged.

Although as surprised as his men by Belle's actions, Castro recovered quickly and grabbed towards the drawer of his desk.

He failed to react quite fast enough. With his suspicions aroused by the girl's actions, the Kid had been ready for something to pop. At Castro's first hostile movement, the youngster swung up his feet and thrust himself into motion. Sliding across the polished top of the desk, he opened his legs and dropped astride Castro's lap. The chair skidded back and crumpled under their combined weights, dumping them on to the floor. Of the two, the Kid came out best from the landing. Before Castro regained his breath, the Kid was sitting on his chest and pricking him under the chin with the point of the bowie knife's blade.

Aware of the type of men Castro hired as bodyguards, Ysabel had no inclination to let the element of surprise slip away from his party. Catching Belle's victim by the front of his shirt, Ysabel brought him to a halt then heaved him back in the direction from which he had come.

Having seen what had happened to the first man, the other two Mexicans had not tried to rush into the office. Instead, they remained in the alcove and hoped to lure the girl from behind the wall. The hope did not materialise. With their companion hurtling towards them, they found themselves further handicapped. The alcove was not wide enough for them to step aside and let him pass; nor could they shoot at Ysabel without the chance of hitting their colleague. So they compromised by catching the man and shoving him out of the opening. That did not greatly improve their situation. By the time they had cleared the obstruction, Ysabel stood covering them with his big old Colt.

'Tell your boys to yell "calf rope", Cisco,' Ysabel ordered.

'You best do it,' the Kid went on in a caressing voice that sent shivers running through Castro. 'If you don't, you'll be too dead to care.'

'Put up your guns, *muchachos*!' Castro commanded, knowing that to yell 'calf rope' meant to surrender and not doubting for a moment that the Kid would carry out the threat.

Scooping up the first Mexican's Starr, Belle backed to Ysabel's side. She waited until the other two bodyguards had obeyed their employer's order, then turned and strolled over to the desk.

'Let him get up, Lon,' she said. 'I told you that we couldn't fool a man of Senor Castro's intelligence and should have been frank with him from the start.'

Coming to his feet in a lithe movement, the Kid stepped away from Castro and sat on the desk with his legs blocking access to the drawer. Eyes glowing hatred, Castro rose and glared around the office. Suddenly he realised that a change had come over 'Annie'. She no longer sounded like an uncouth calico-cat, but spoke with the accent of a refined Southern lady. Closing her billy into the parasol's handle, Belle smiled in a disarmingly friendly manner at the *cantina's* owner.

'I apologise for this trouble, *senor*,' Belle declared. 'Of course I realise that we made you suspicious and I don't blame you for taking precautions. You aren't hurt, are you?'

'N-No!' The word popped like a cork from Castro's mouth as he stared at the girl and rubbed his rump.

'Get Senor Castro another chair, Lon,' Belle ordered and held the Starr to the Mexican. Looking to where Ysabel still covered the bodyguards, she continued, 'You can put your gun away, Sam. Senor Castro knows we don't mean any harm and is going to dismiss his men.'

'Whatever you say, Miss Belle,' drawled Ysabel, returning his Dragoon to its holster. 'Now it's your turn, Cisco.'

For a moment Castro hesitated. Then his curiosity overrode his anger and suspicion. Much to his surprise, the Kid quit the desk and collected a chair from by the safe.

'*Vamos!*' Castro snarled at his men and took the revolver from the girl. 'Here!' he went on, tossing the weapon to its owner with a gesture of disgust. 'Get out of here.'

'That's better,' Belle stated, after the three bodyguards had left.

Sinking into the chair brought for him by the Kid, Castro studied the girl with interest, but no longer as a prospective buyer. Ysabel and the Kid positioned themselves by the girl and so that they could keep the alcove under observation.

'What's this all about, *senorita*?' Castro inquired.

'Big Sam tells me that you are the best-informed man in the border country, Senor Castro. Is that true?'

'It is,' Castro agreed. 'There is little happens that I do not know about.'

'Then I've come to the right person,' Belle told him. 'I thought that I had when I first saw you. I need information.'

'Then why——?'

'Why did I come dressed like this? To avoid rousing suspicion. For the rest, Big Sam suggested that we pretended he

37

wanted to sell me so that we had an excuse to come and talk privately in your office.'

'Ah. So that's why——'

'It was Sam's idea,' Belle said depreciatingly. 'I doubted if it would work and felt sure that you would see through our deception. That was why I exposed your men——'

'You knew about them?' Castro gasped.

'It seemed a logical precaution for an intelligent man to take,' Belle complimented. 'That wall was the most likely place for your men to be hiding and I knew you would have more than one man on hand to deal with the Ysabels.'

'I see,' breathed the Mexican, not hiding the pleasure he felt at Belle's flattering references to his intelligence.

'Fetch my reticule, Lon,' Belle ordered.

'Yes, ma'am,' drawled the Kid.

Watching the youngster obey, Castro felt even more intrigued by his female visitor. Any woman—or man for that matter—who could command such obedience from *Cabrito* must be a person of importance. Castro's interest increased when the girl received her reticule. Opening it, she extracted a thick wad of paper money. Staring intently across the desk, Castro saw that the top note was a United States' fifty-dollar bill.

'I think Sam suggested that we should act as we did because the information I want concerns one of your friends,' Belle remarked, riffling the edges of the bills with her thumb. 'He doesn't understand that business and friendship don't mix.'

'Which friend would that be, *senorita*?' Castro asked, tearing his eyes from the money with an effort.

'The one called *Cicatriz*.'

'The Scar, huh? And you want to know——?'

'Where he is and what his business is with the two Yankees he met tonight at Orley's saloon.'

'*Cicatriz* is a very good friend, *senorita*,' Castro hinted and Belle slid the wad's top bill on to the desk. 'Well, maybe not such a *very* good friend.' A second bill left Belle's fingers. 'But a friend of long standing.'

'This long?' Belle inquired, adding the third fifty-dollar bill and ignoring the Kid's low hiss of disapproval.

'Well, not so long perhaps,' Castro answered, watching the girl's face.

'Is the friendship dwindling?' Belle wanted to know and the fourth bill joined its companions in front of her.

A shrewd trader, Castro possessed a keen judgement for exactly how much any given market would stand. Unless he missed his guess, the girl had about reached her limit in the bidding.

'It's possible I may have mislead you, *senorita*,' the Mexican said, noticing the air of finality with which Belle dropped the fifth bill. He reached towards the money. 'Thinking about it, I find that the Scar is unworthy of my friendship.'

Laying the handle of her parasol across the bills before he touched them, Belle smiled at Castro.

'I *never* pay for a horse until after I've seen if it is worth the money, *senor*,' she warned.

'Of course you don't,' Castro replied, also smiling, if not with his eyes. '*Cicatriz* is taking the two *gringos* to Matamoros tonight. In fact, he has probably already left with them.'

'He's more of your friend than I thought,' Belle sighed and made as if to gather up the money.

'They will be there for maybe a week!' Castro offered hurriedly.

'Why?' the girl demanded.

'I don't know,' admitted Castro. Then, as he saw her lips tighten ominously, he went on, '*Senorita*, I could lie; or make up a reason. But I am dealing fairly with you. *Cicatriz* knows me well. Too well to trust me with much knowledge of his affairs.'

Catching Ysabel's eye, Belle saw him nod agreement with Castro's declaration. So she signified her acceptance of the explanation.

'Matamoros's a fair-sized town, Cisco,' Ysabel remarked. 'So you'll have to narrow it down just a lil mite.'

'For two hundred and fifty dollars,' the Kid went on, 'I'd say it's got to be narrowed down a *big* mite.'

'*Cicatriz* always stays at the *Posada del Infernales*,' Castro elaborated. 'That's where you can find him. You know the place, Big Sam?'

'I know it,' confirmed the Kid. 'Allus sort of reminds me of your place.'

'What if he isn't there?' Belle asked.

'There is a rumour that a renegade general is hiring *pistoleros* to help him set up his own republic south of the border. Again I can say nothing for certain, but I think that the Scar may have been finding men to serve him.'

'Where's this here general at?' demanded the Kid.

'Rumour says at the fort on the Rio Mendez, between Cruillas and San Fernando,' the Mexican replied. 'Haven't *you* heard of him?'

'Could've been more'n the one of 'em at it,' the Kid pointed out and glanced at the money before Belle.

'And you can tell us nothing more?' Belle asked, guessing what the youngster was thinking.

'I wish I could, *senorita*,' Castro sighed. 'As long as *Cicatriz* is in Matamoros, he will stay at the *Posada del Infernales*. As Big Sam and *Cabrito* will tell you, the Scar likes to have friends around him. A man with many enemies must live close to his friends.'

'Which same's way ole Cisco here don't stray far from the *cantina*, Miss Belle,' remarked the Kid. 'Only he's not giving you a whole heap for your money.'

'You pay a poor man poorly, Lon,' the girl explained. 'Senor Castro is rich, so his price is high. But that has its advantages. A poor man would want to make more money and might go to *Cicatriz* and tell him about us.'

'Which Cisco wouldn't think of doing?' the Kid scoffed.

'I don't think he will,' Belle answered. 'For this price, *senor*, I don't expect any warning to reach *Cicatriz*.'

'You have my word as a *caballero*,' Castro assured her, rising and bowing gallantly. Ignoring the Kid's disbelieving sniff, he gathered up the money and dropped it into the drawer of the desk. 'And now, if there is nothing more, I must be getting back to my guests.'

Belle jabbed an elbow into the Kid's ribs as he opened his mouth to speak. 'I'm satisfied, *senor*,' she stated.

Placing the palms of his hands on the top of the desk, Ysabel leaned forward and fixed Castro with his eyes.

'There's just one thing more, *amigo*,' the big Texan said gently. 'Miss Belle's toting a fair-sized roll of cash-money. Only us four in this room know about it.'

'So?' the Mexican ejaculated, looking away from where the rest of the money was disappearing into the girl's reticule.

'So if anybody comes 'round trying to take that money,' Ysabel elaborated, 'there can't be too many ways to share the blame—— If you follow my meaning.'

'Pappy's being real polite, him being white 'n' all,' the Kid continued. 'Me, I'm part *Pehnane* and wasn't learned to talk in circles. So I'm telling you that if we run into fuss 'tween here 'n' where we're going, I'll be coming straight back to tell you all about it. I might even start by tossing a couple of Dragoon balls through them fancy curtains when I come in.'

At the reference to his secret, Castro darted an annoyed glare towards the alcove. Following his reaction and guessing at its cause, Belle smiled coldly. Like her companions, she had not been unaware of Castro's avaricious glances at her bank-roll. She saw a way of avoiding trouble.

'I don't think we need worry about it happening, *Cabrito*,' she said, exuding quiet confidence. 'Any more than Senor Castro needs worry about us telling anybody of what we found behind the drapes.'

'Like Miss Belle says, Cisco,' grinned Ysabel, delighted by the girl's astute grasp of the situation. 'If you don't tell, we won't.'

'If you *do*,' the Kid purred in his most gentle, therefore most dangerous, tone of voice, 'I'll be back.'

During the walk across town to the *cantina*, Ysabel had been disparaging in the extreme about Castro's moral standards, but he had also commented favourably on the Mexican's personal courage. So Belle took it as a fitting tribute to the Kid's reputation that Castro showed anxiety at the soft-spoken threat.

All too well Castro knew that the Kid did not speak idly. If an attempt to rob the girl should be made and *Cabrito* came through it alive, he would return to keep his promise. Ensuring that he was killed would not be easy. To organise the attempt would take time and could only be done after the Ysabels had left the *cantina*. On the streets, alert for trouble, they would be difficult if not impossible to surprise. Handled any other way, those making the attempt would pay a dear price. Which raised another point. Finding men willing to go against the Ysabel family would not be easy. Others who had tried it had never succeeded and mostly failed to return. Even Castro's employers might refuse to take the chance.

However, if the Ysabels gave their word that they would keep quiet about the purpose of the left wall's drapes, Castro knew that they could be counted on to do it. So he decided that the loss of the girl's remaining money would be a reasonable price for the protection of a most useful secret.*

'There will be no need for you to return, *Cabrito*,' Castro declared.

The Ysabels and Belle exchanged satisfied glances, knowing that they had made their point.

Waiting until Belle had collected and reassembled her parasol, Castro escorted them from the office. Curious—and a few hostile—stares greeted their return to the bar-room, causing Ysabel to lay a hand on their host's sleeve.

'Maybe you'd best come across and see us out, Cisco,' the big Texan suggested in a tone that brooked no argument. 'That way everybody'll know we're all still *buenos amigos*.'

'If you insist,' Castro replied.

'We do,' the Kid assured him and Castro yielded to the inevitable.

Once again Belle's personality changed. Hooking her right hand through the Kid's left arm, she became the saloon-girl flaunting her delight at being in the company of important men. While crossing the room, she darted glances around. The two old-timers still sat at their table, but no longer nursed their weapons. They gave no hint of being aware of the Ysabel family's departure. Belle wondered if she had been mistaken about the Kid signalling to them.

Outside the *cantina*, Belle's party exchanged mutually insincere expressions of good will with Castro and left him. Crossing the plaza, she felt satisfaction at her handling of a delicate situation. After impressing Castro with her ability, she had fed his ego with flattery and made him more susceptible to her request for information. Something told her that the Kid, at least, did not share her high opinion of the affair's outcome.

'I'm not sorry to get out of there,' Belle remarked, releasing the Kid's arm.

'We likely wouldn't't've if you hadn't guessed about them jaspers behind the drapes,' Ysabel replied. 'How'd you know about 'em being there?'

'*I* wasn't listening to that dirty story,' Belle explained. 'So I noticed the drapes move. The rest was easy, especially with the way you played along.'

* While the Ysabel family and Belle kept their promise, the Kid later made use of his knowledge to save his life, as is told in *The Bad Bunch*.

'Figured something was up, way you acted,' Ysabel drawled, 'and allowed I should set back until I knowed what.'

'The thing is, did he tell us the truth about *Cicatriz*?'

'Some of it. Only I'd not count on him playing square with you.'

'I don't, Sam,' Belle said calmly.

'Then you sure paid high for the bit he told you,' growled the Kid. 'We could've got that much free after his *pelados* left us with him.'

'I doubt it,' Belle objected. 'And I think it was worth fifty dollars to know where the Scar took Tollinger and Barmain.'

'*Fifty?*' the Kid ejaculated. 'Either you can't count, or I can't see. I saw you give him——'

'Five fifty-dollar bills,' Belle finished for the indignant youngster. 'Only four of them are forgeries, printed for us spies to use during the War.' Her companions' startled and admiring comments made her smile and she continued, 'You surely didn't think I would hand over two hundred and fifty real dollars are easily as all that, did you?'

CHAPTER FIVE

YOU'RE BLOCKING MY TRAIL

'There it is, Miss Belle,' the Ysabel Kid remarked, pointing along the street at the *Posada del Infernales*. 'We'll soon know if you wasted your money.'

'Yes,' Belle agreed quietly. 'We'll soon know.'

'Don't forget what we fixed with pappy,' the Kid warned. 'If they're there, we pull out and wait until he's on hand before you take them.'

'I'll remember,' Belle promised, glancing down at her parasol.

Once more the Rebel Spy had cause to be grateful for the Ysabel family's assistance. They had organised everything so far with smooth efficiency and to her complete satisfaction.

The walk from Castro's *cantina* to Ma O'Grady's house the

previous night had been uneventful. On their arrival, Sam Ysabel had told Ma most of what had happened and the woman had helped Belle return her blouse to a state of decorous modesty by stitching back the removed pieces. When Belle had mentioned the two old men, the Kid dismissed them as 'a couple of worthless, no-account ole goats' who must have seen the Ysabels some place or other.

That morning, dressed as a lady again, Belle had accompanied the Ysabels on horseback out of Brownsville. Going upriver along the Rio Grande, they had crossed into Mexico on a small ferry-boat which had the advantage of operating in secret. Returning to the ex-consul's residence in Matamoros, the girl had collected her belongings and transferred them to an inn owned by a friend of the Ysabels. There had been two reasons for the change of quarters. Knowing something of her original host's plans for the future, Belle wished to avoid jeopardising them by starting her vengeance mission from his home. Secondly, the Ysabels felt that the inn would make a better base of operations, being situated in a less high-toned neighbourhood than the late Confederate States' consulate.

With her wigs and other disguise equipment on hand, Belle had transformed herself into a brassy, flashy blonde saloon-girl. She felt certain that Tollinger, Barmain and *Cicatriz* would not recognise her.

Then a hitch had developed in their arrangements. A Mexican had arrived at the inn with a message for Sam Ysabel. Having learned in some way of the Ysabel family's return to Matamoros, Don Francisco Almonte wanted to talk with them. A good friend—and supplier of much fine wine before the War—his request had presented the Ysabels with a problem. They were torn between their desire to help Belle and a wish to accommodate Almonte. After some discussion, Belle had offered a compromise. While Ysabel visited Almonte, she and the Kid would scout the *Posada del Infernales* and try to discover whether Castro had told the truth. Ysabel had agreed to the suggestion; but with the proviso that if Belle's enemies should be there, no attempt would be made to tackle them unless he was on hand to help.

Being a sensible young woman, Belle had accepted Ysabel's terms. She believed that the visit to the *posada* could be made without risk of detection. Not only did she wear a disguise, but the Kid dressed differently than on his previous visits to the town. Then he had worn a Confederate States Army uniform, or buckskins. In his black range clothes, he might pass as an ordinary young Texas hard-case making a visit to Mexico for private reasons. There seemed sufficient likelihood of it succeeding to make the chance worth taking.

For all her apparent calm, Belle felt the tension rising and seething inside her as she approached the doors of the *posada*. Until she had seen them the previous night, she had forgotten just how deep and bitter her hatred of Tollinger and Barmain was. The memory of their crime had always been with her, but she had pushed it to the back of her mind so that it would not impede her work and chances of survival. Warning herself that she might be headed for a disappointment, she kept walking. Whatever she did, she must prevent her churning emotions from overriding good sense.

'You all right, Belle?' asked the Kid, sensing the mental turmoil that assailed her.

'Yes,' the girl replied. 'Lon. If I start to do anything *loco*, stop me.'

'If I thought you'd do anything *loco*,' drawled the Kid, 'I wouldn't go in there with you.'

Externally the *Posada del Infernales* resembled Castro's Brownsville *cantina*, being two storeys high, made of adobe and timber planks, and dominating the surrounding buildings. The resemblance continued internally, although at that early hour the big bar-room was sparsely occupied. Several bored-looking girls sat eyeing Belle with hostility. Behind the bar, a big, fat Mexican leaned his elbows on the counter and scowled at the new arrivals. A few customers scattered around the room and in its centre four cold-eyed Americans sat in apparent amity at a table with a couple of evil-featured Mexicans. Another Mexican disappeared up the stairs alongside the bar, moving with considerable speed.

All that Belle saw as she and the Kid entered. Then, as they started to cross the room, something attracted her attention. Her eyes went to two familiar figures who were sitting in a corner of the room. Even if she had not been able to see their faces, she would have identified the 'couple of worthless, no-account ole goats' from Castro's *cantina*. While other people undoubtedly owned Colt revolving-cylinder rifles and heavy-gauge shotguns, Belle refused to believe that any other hat could attain a state of decrepitude equalling that of the shorter man's Stetson.

'Something up, Annie-gal?' asked the Kid innocently, following the direction of her gaze.

'I smell a rat, Lon Ysabel,' Belle replied and realised that the levity had suddenly left her companion. A moment later, she knew why.

Although they did not know it, Belle and the Kid had been under observation as they crossed the street towards the *posada*. There had been three Mexicans with the four Americans, but one of them rose and made for the stairs as soon as he saw the couple. The stockier of the remaining Mexicans pointed through the window and hissed the Kid's name to his companions.

'You sure *that's* him?' demanded a middle-sized, heavily moustached American, his voice a hard New York dialect.

'*Si,*' the Mexican agreed vehemently. 'I saw him and the girl come from Villena's *posada* with Big Sam.'

'So this's *Cabrito,*' sneered another of the Americans, watching the Kid approach the doors. 'He don't look so all-fired savage to me.'

'Where is Big Sam?' demanded the remaining Mexican worriedly.

'He went off somewhere,' the first Mexican explained. 'I think *Cabrito* believes nobody will know him, dressed like that.'

'You want him stopping, Yorky?' asked the man who had been unimpressed by the Kid's appearance. In his early twenties, he was tall, well-built and had an air of arrogant toughness. Although dressed in a U.S. Cavalry uniform, it no longer bore official insignia and he carried his Army Colt low on his right thigh in an open-topped, tied-down holster.

'Go to it, Kansas.' the middle-sized American replied.

Since their first meeting, Kansas had been set on impressing the other members of the party with his extreme salty toughness. Yorktown Hoxley had known hard men of one kind or another all his life and, like the fabled character from Missouri, needed a visual demonstration before he believed such claims. So he was quite content to let Kansas make the attempt. If the other failed, the remainder of the party could easily settle that baby-faced Texan's hash. Not that Hoxley expected Kansas to fail, having seen the speed with which he could draw and shoot.

Setting down his glass, Kansas nodded towards the bottle of *tequila* on the table and said, 'Fill her up. This won't take long.'

With that, he strolled forward and halted deliberately in front of the approaching couple. Hooking his thumbs into his gunbelt, Kansas stood on spread-apart feet and a cold, contemptuous grin twisted at his lips. Everything about him rang a warning for the Kid, but it did not cause the Indian-dark youngster to halt or turn aside. Instead, he signalled for Belle to drop back. Disengaging his arm, the girl obeyed. As she prepared to jerk apart her parasol, the Kid walked on with a leisurely seeming stride.

While the Kid did not want trouble, he felt sure that it could not be avoided. As far as he knew, the party to which the man had belonged had no connection with *Cicatriz*. If they did, he would have expected more of them to be facing him. Either way, he would get nowhere by backing down or trying to leave. Unless the Kid missed his guess, that Yankee jasper was spoiling for a fight. In which case, the best thing to do would be oblige him.

'You're blocking my trail, *hombre*,' the Kid pointed out, sounding almost angelically mild.

'Then walk 'round me,' Kansas ordered and his right hand lifted to hang above the Colt's butt.

Conversations died away around the room as the girls and other customers realised that something dramatic might soon take place. Belle held the two parts of her parasol in her hands, giving the Kid and his antagonist her whole attention. At Hoxley's table, the Americans watched with interest and the Mexicans fingered their knives. The latter possessed the advantage of knowing *Cabrito's* hard-earned reputation and lacked their companion's confidence in Kansas.

'I never was no hand at walking,' drawled the Kid, continuing his steady advance. 'You got something better to offer?'

'Nothing you could take, sonny,' Kansas replied. 'Tell you, though. I'll let you come by, but the gal stays with me.'

'Mister,' the Kid said, looking so gentle that butter would be hard put to melt in his mouth, and measuring the distance separating them. 'I'd sooner leave her with a hawg!'

Rage twisted at Kansas' face. 'Why you——!' he snarled and started to make his draw.

Speaking proved to be an error of tactics. At the first word, the Kid immediately changed from passive relaxation to sav-

47

age, deadly movement. Gliding forward fast he ignored the Dragoon. Flashing across his body, his right hand enfolded the hilt of the bowie knife.

To give him credit, Kansas was fast and against most white men he would have achieved his intention. The Kid moved like a *Pehnane* warrior. As the Colt left leather, its hammer drawn back and trigger depressed, the youngster's left hand blurred to slap its barrel outwards. Flame ripped from the revolver's muzzle, but the bullet it ejected missed the Kid by inches. At almost the same moment, glinting wickedly in the bar's lights, the great blade of the bowie knife sprang from its sheath to rise outwards and across.

Despite his early Comanche training, the Kid did not hold his knife in the Indian fashion with its blade below his fist. Instead he gripped the hilt so that the blade extended before his thumb and forefinger, its razor-sharp edge uppermost. Doing so allowed him to thrust, slash or deliver a back-hand chop. He selected the latter method of attack.

To some of the audience, it seemed that the Kid had made a mistake. Striking as he did, the back of the blade would be the part to make contact with Kansas' flesh. The more knowledgeable of the onlookers knew better.

'*A:he!*' grunted the Kid as he struck, giving the traditional Comanche coup cry meaning, 'I claim it!'

Honed as sharp as the edge, the concave section of the clipped point raked at and bit deep into Kansas' throat. Blood spurted in the wake of the shining steel and the man stumbled backwards. Letting his Colt drop, he turned and collapsed on to a table. Coughing out his life-blood, he slid from there to the floor.

Everything had happened with such devastating speed that even the Mexicans in Hoxley's party sat numbed into immobility for a moment. The Kid's sudden transition from a meek-seeming youngster to a savage Comanche Dog Soldier added to the shock and helped freeze the men at a time when they should have been backing Kansas' play.

Letting out a snarl, Hoxley shoved back his chair and started to rise. His action set an example to the others, causing them to emulate it. Feet rasped on the floor and hands reached weapons as the other members of Hoxley's group tried to stand up.

Transferring his knife from the right hand to the left, in a throw reminiscent of a gun-fighter performing the 'border shift', the Kid prepared to fetch out his old Colt. Behind him, Belle made a snapping motion with her right hand. The billy opened, its steel ball drawing out the metal rod and coil-spring ready for use.

A shot crashed from the right side of the room and the *tequila* bottle disintegrated on Hoxley's table. Fiery liquor sprayed, intermingled with slivers of glass, peppering the men painfully. Startled curses burst from them, to be cut off on hearing a cracked, irascibly plaintive old voice from the shot's direction.

'Why'd you go and do that for, Cactus?' it asked. 'You done sp'iled a good bottle of tee-keely.'

Swivelling around still mouthing obscenities, Hoxley jerked his hand away from the butt of his holstered Remington 1861 Navy revolver. Also turning, the rest of the men stiffened and refrained from continuing their hostile movements.

Smoke curled up lazily from the twenty-seven inch long, ·56 calibre, barrel of the Colt rifle cradled against the taller old-timer's shoulder. That alone did not cause the pacifism displayed by Hoxley's party. The second ancient Texan's shotgun lined disconcertingly in their direction, its enormous eight-gauge twin tubes a fine inducement to compliance.

'Do you reckon I meant to hit the blasted thing, consarn it?' the taller man answered indignantly. 'I was aiming at them fellers.'

Swinging her eyes from the dying man to the two old-timers, then in the Kid's direction, Belle felt an uneasy sensation of being watched by hostile eyes. Not from the men at the table, whose attention was divided between the young Texan and his rescuers. Instinct guided her gaze in the right direction. At the head of the stairs stood the menacing figure of *Cicatriz*, the gun in his hand lining downwards.

Not at the Kid!

With a sensation of shock, Belle realised that the Colt's barrel was slanted in her direction.

Desperately Belle twisted herself aside, and not a moment too soon. *Cicatriz's* revolver barked and she heard the eerie 'splat!' as its bullet ploughed a hole through the wide brim of her hat. On the heels of the shot, the Kid completed his draw and the old Dragoon swung up to bellow a reply. Fast-taken, his aim proved adequate, if not entirely successful. Propelled by forty grains of prime du Pont powder—looted from a Yankee patrol during the War—a soft lead, round ball struck the wall after stirring a draught of air before *Cicatriz*'s scarred face. Jerking backwards hurriedly, the Mexican disappeared from Belle's range of vision.

Reaching up, Belle jerked off her hat and wig, spinning them aside with the body of her parasol. Then her left hand flew down to pull at the strap securing her skirt. As that garment fell away from her hips, she saw the bartender's fat face twist into lines of anticipatory eagerness and knew that he was doomed to disappointment. Knowing that she might run into trouble, Belle had come prepared to meet it. Under the skirt, she wore skin-tight black riding breeches and calf-high boots. Although removing the skirt had not left her clad only in under-garments, the skimpy nature of the blouse and figure-hugging fit of the breeches set off her slender, yet eye-catching contours to their best advantage.

'Let's get him, Lon!' Belle shrieked, racing by Hoxley's party and across the room.

Still holding his bloody bowie knife in his hand, the Kid bounded after the girl. Catching up with her, they plunged side by side up the stairs.

The occupants of the room watched Belle and the Kid reach the head of the stairs. In the stillness that had fallen after the crashing of the shots, the men and women on the ground floor could hear the girl's and the Texan's feet thudding over the wooden boards of the second storey. Suddenly a scream, feminine in pitch, rang out, causing Cactus and Rache to take their attention briefly from Hoxley and his companions.

Seeing his chance, Hoxley took it without hesitation. At any moment members of the French occupation troops policing the city might arrive to investigate the shooting. If that happened, Hoxley had no desire to be asked to explain his presence in either the *posada* or in Matamoros.

'Beat it!' he yelled, heaving over the table in the two old Texans' direction and propelling himself in a leaping run towards the front door.

One of the Americans lunged sideways, right hand fanging towards his gun. In an almost leisurely manner, Cactus swung, lined and fired his rifle. Caught in the head with a ·56 bullet, the man's lunge changed to a sprawl and he went down with his revolver unfired.

Pandemonium broke in the *posada*'s bar-room. Faced with the possibility that Rache would turn lead loose from his shot-gun, the remainder of Hoxley's party showed a quick appreciation of the peril. Ignoring their two fallen companions, they set off after Hoxley as quickly as their legs would carry them.

Girls screeched and screamed, flying like hawk-scared chickens towards the safety offered by the bar. The other customers, although not involved in the fracas, showed an understandable desire to vacate the premises. At such times, the French soldiers were inclined to shoot first and ask questions a good second. In one way the confusion proved a blessing to Cactus and Rache, but in another it was a curse. Various inoffensive bodies interposed themselves between the old-timers and the departing men. So, while they prevented Hoxley's crowd from shooting at the ancient pair, the scattering, darting figures ruined any chance of keeping the fleeing men in the building until the Kid returned. Muttering curses in English, Spanish and Comanche, Rache and Cactus watched the batwing doors swing violently as the four men burst through to the street.

'Shall we go after 'em, Rache?' Cactus inquired and a crackle of gun-fire from upstairs supplied the answer.

'Let's go see if *Cuchilo* needs help,' Rache answered, setting off in a bandy-legged, but fast, run towards the stairs.

About to follow his companion, Cactus saw the bartender grabbing under the counter for something. Skidding to a halt, the lean oldster swung his rifle up and laid sights on the Mexican's chest.

'Come up empty, Heriberto,' Cactus commanded and the man obeyed with alacrity, showing his empty hands as proof of his good intentions.

Reaching the head of the stairs, Belle and the Kid darted along the small passage formed by the outside wall of the *posada* and one of its rooms. Where the room ended, another passage ran at right angles between the front and rear rooms. Halting at the corner, the Kid peered cautiously around. Looking over his shoulder, Belle found the passage to be poorly lighted and deserted. However, a door in the centre of the farther side was just swinging shut.

'He's in there!' Belle spat out.

Giving the Kid no time to comment, the girl sprang around the corner and sped along the passage. In her eagerness to reach *Cicatriz* and, if possible discover the whereabouts of Tollinger and Barmain, Belle paid little attention to her surroundings. Coming to a halt before the door, she took a firmer grip of her parasol-handle-billy and prepared to gain admittance to the room. Again she did not wait for the Kid, or let him take the lead. Balancing on her left foot, with its knee flexed slightly, she raised her right leg. Gathering herself as she had learned in *savate* lessons, she propelled her right boot alongside the door knob with the full power of her gluteus muscles behind it.

With surprisingly little resistance, the door burst inwards. Carried on by her impetus, Belle made a discovery horrifying in its implications. No room or floor lay behind the door. Instead it opened on to a gap let into the rear of the building. Twenty feet below, placed so that anybody falling from the doorway could not miss them, a number of sharp-pointed wooden stakes rose upwards.

All that Belle saw as she teetered helplessly at the edge of the drop. An involuntary scream burst from her and she tried desperately to keep her balance.

CHAPTER SIX

I'D SOONER HAD HIM ALIVE

Following Belle, the Kid's keen eyes detected something dangling down the door and across the floor. At first he thought that it might be a strand of cord spun by a spider. Then he realised that no spider he had ever seen could produce a cord of such length and thickness. It might, in fact, be a piece of black cotton thread. Given that much of a doubt, his natural caution and suspicious nature took over. Following the cord to its upper end, he saw that it was fastened to a small hook at the top of the door. That quelled any lingering hope that it had been spun by a spider.

In a flash, the Kid decided that some kind of danger lay beyond the door. Before he could warn her, Belle launched her kick and the terrible peril produced by her action stared them in the face.

Flinging his knife aside, so that its point sank into the opposite wall, the Kid freed his left hand. It flashed up in a continuation of the throw and his fingers closed on Belle's right shoulder. Starting to pivot to the right and pull, he felt his hand slip on the girl's flesh. Then his fingers hooked under the shoulder strap of her blouse. Swinging around, he started to turn and drag the girl away from the sheer drop. The strap broke and the blouse ripped from armpit to waist along its seam, but Belle felt herself drawn to safety. The force of the Kid's pull caused her to release the parasol's handle and it flew along the passage. At the same instant, she became aware of another danger making its appearance.

'Lon!' Belle gasped, staring at the other side of the passage.

A Mexican half-breed holding a knife appeared through a door to Belle's right. Gun in hand, also across the passage, another Mexican sprang out of a room on the left.

Completing his turn, the Kid swung up his Dragoon. From waist high, aimed by instinctive alignment, he touched off a shot. The Dragoon went off an instant ahead of the Mexican's Le Mat; but that proved sufficient. Hurling from the Colt's seven-and-a-half-inch barrel at a velocity of something over nine hundred feet-per-second, the 219 grain bullet churned into the man's chest. Shock and the force of the impact flung the Mexican backwards and his revolver's bullet went harmlessly into the roof. Not for the first time the Kid felt grateful for his decision to retain the heavy old hand-gun, instead of obtaining one of the lighter, more convenient to carry 1860 Army Colts. No other hand-gun of the day packed such stopping power.

Rushing at Belle, the half-breed whipped his knife-hand into the air. His appearance of Indian blood showed to an even greater extent in the way he held the weapon. The blade-below-the-hand grip limited the number of ways the knife could be used to a downwards chop directed to strike behind the recipient's collar-bone and a sidewise stroke aimed at the ribs or stomach.

Ducking her head, Belle flung herself to meet the man. It was an action that took him by surprise, for he was used to more passive or easily frightened women. Belle's head rammed into his belly before he could bring down the knife. With its short-cropped hair, the girl's skull made an effective weapon. All the man's breath burst from his lungs in a croaking gasp and he let go of the knife so that it clattered to the floor without touching its intended victim.

The collision brought Belle and her assailant to a halt, but the girl was ready for it. Wrapping her arms around his knees as he started to bend over her, she exerted all her strength to straighten up. Raising the man into the air, she set his legs free. Passing over her head, he contrived in some way to alight on his feet. Doing so proved to be unfortunate. Combined with the force of Belle's throw, his impetus carried him forward. On his second stride, a realisation of his danger struck him. Desperately he grabbed at the jamb of the door, but missed. Nor could he stop. Down came his advancing foot, but no floor was beneath it. Pitching forward, he let out a hideous scream and plunged down to be impaled through the body on one of the stakes.

As her straining muscles were relieved of the man's weight, Belle staggered back a pace. Catching her balance, she turned and struck the wall by the side of the door. With horrified eyes, she watched the man's departure. Hearing the terror-filled cry, the Kid swung around to see what had happened.

Any relief the Kid felt at discovering Belle safe was forgotten. Once more feet sounded in the passage. Looking over his shoulder, the Kid saw *Cicatriz* burst from the room that had harboured the gun-toting Mexican.

'Behind, Belle!' the Kid roared, throwing himself floorwards in a rolling dive.

Give her full due, Belle reacted with speed. Even without waiting to see what danger lay behind, she twisted and plunged through the air in the direction of her billy.

Although *Cicatriz* emerged holding his Colt, he found himself faced with a problem. Probably his employers would want him to make sure that the girl died, for they had expressed considerable concern over seeing her the previous night; but he knew that killing her might, almost certainly would, bring about his own death at the hands of *Cabrito*. If he turned the gun in the Kid's direction, the girl would have time to reach her weapon and he had seen the speed with which she tackled the half-breed.

Faced with such a problem, *Cicatriz* decided that his best solution would be in rapid, immediate flight. Clearly his plans had gone badly astray on both floors of the *posada*, so he gave his attention to saving his own skin.

Learning that the Ysabel family had brought the girl to Matamoros, *Cicatriz* needed little thought to guess why. His employers had mentioned the possibility of her following them during their departure—flight might be a better word—from Brownsville. Nor did the Scar need to exercise his brain greatly to figure out from whom they had obtained information concerning his whereabouts. For a price, Cisco Castro would tell the girl and the Ysabels where to find *Cicatriz*. So the Scar had made arrangements for a watch to be kept on Villena's *posada*, knowing that the Ysabel family used it as their headquarters in town.

When his scout had brought the news that Belle and the Kid were on their way, *Cicatriz* had organised a suitable reception. Leaving Hoxley and his men in the bar-room to stop the visitors, *Cicatriz* had come upstairs to establish a second line of defence. Maybe all the odds favoured the Yankee's party, but with *Cabrito* in the game a man would be a fool to take chances.

An old customer at the *Posada del Infernales*, *Cicatriz* had access to its secret facilities and prepared to make use of them. With his men positioned in the rooms and his enemies in the *posada*, he had fastened a length of stout black cotton thread to the door of the trap. By pulling on it at the right moment, he had conveyed the impression that somebody had just passed through and closed the door. Although the girl had snapped up the bait, *Cabrito*'s keen eyes and lightning reactions had saved her.

Seeing the trap fail, having been watching through the cracks of their barely opened doors, *Cicatriz*'s companions had made their try and met with an equal lack of success. In the hope of taking the girl and *Cabrito* by surprise, the Scar had made his appearance. Expecting at every movement to feel the Kid's lead rip into him, he tore along the passage ducking and weaving.

Not until he rounded the corner and made for the head of the stairs did *Cicatriz* recall one very important point. According to his scout, Big Sam had not been with the girl and the Kid. Which raised a serious question.

How had they got by Hoxley's men with so little resistance or opposition?

Looking down the stairs, *Cicatriz* learned the answer. It was all so simple, he should have known——

With an almost bestial snarl of rage, *Cicatriz* started to raise his Colt.

Landing on the floor, the Kid pointed his Dragoon after the fleeing Mexican. Holding down his first inclination to use the revolver as a means of halting *Cicatriz*, he thrust himself to his feet. He doubted if he could aim the four-pound, one-ounce hand-cannon with sufficient accuracy to merely bring down and wound the fast-moving, swerving figure. A dead man could not help Belle find Tollinger and Barmain. With that thought in mind, the Kid bounded over and plucked his knife from the wall.

Belle figured out why the Kid did not shoot and marked it as another example of his ability to think straight even in a crisis. Scooping up her billy, she lunged upright. Then she and the Kid started to follow the Scar, watching him turn the corner ahead of them.

A thunderous boom shattered the air, rocking echoes up the stairs and from the walls. *Cicatriz* shot into view, travelling backwards so fast that his feet barely touched the floor. His head was a hideous ruin of lacerated flesh, disintegrated brains and shattered bone. Hardened through necessity by more than one contact with sudden, violent death, Belle still could not hold down a gasp of horror. Skidding to a stop, she swung hurriedly away from the ghastly sight of the Scar colliding with and bouncing from the wall, then pitching forward lifeless to the floor.

'Oh God!' Belle gasped.

'Air you-all right, *Cuchilo*?' called a voice.

'Sure,' the Kid answered. 'Come ahead.'

Holding his shotgun, with smoke rising from its left-hand barrel, old Rache ambled around the corner. He threw a glance at the body, sniffed and turned his gaze to the girl. Concern showed on his seamed, leathery face.

'Right sorry to've done that afore you, Miss Belle,' Rache apologised. 'Only there warn't no other way with the Scar coming at me, when he'd got a gun in his fist. Anyways, he ain't no loss.'

'You did what you had to,' Belle answered, still not looking in *Cicatriz*'s direction. 'I wonder if Tollinger 'n' Barmain are up here?'

'They ain't showed if they are,' the Kid pointed out. 'Let's take a look.' Nodding towards the grey body, he went on, 'I'd sooner had him alive, Rache.'

'There ye go!' wailed the old-timer, bristling indignation. 'There ye just dod-blasted go! Ain't no suiting you Ysabels, pappy nor button. Whyn't you tell me you wanted him on the hoof and I'd've let him shoot me a couple of times while we was waiting for you to sneak up and rope him.'

'Like I told you, Miss Belle,' sighed the Kid in patient disgust. 'Just a couple of worthless, wored-out ole goats.'

'Yah!' Rache sniffed and turned to the girl. 'I'm tarnally damned if I can see how come a smart for-real lady like you gotten tied in with these Ysabel varmints, Miss Belle.'

'It's the fascination of the horrible,' Belle explained, wondering how the old man knew her name.

'That's what it be!' cackled Rache delightedly.

'Where's that other ole fool?' the Kid demanded.

'Down in the bar, keeping ole Heriberto friendly 'n' sociable,' Rache explained. 'Not that I knows who you're ree-ferring to in them disrespecting words. And didn't you say something about us peeking in the rooms to see if them two fellers Miss Belle's after're hid out there?'

'You're just hoping there'll be a gal with no clothes on in one of 'em,' the Kid accused. 'Are you up to making a start, Belle?'

Suddenly Belle realised that the exchange of bantering insults had been for her benefit, designed to take her mind off *Cicatriz* and the other recent events. A momentary annoyance bit at her. Despite all her ability, the Kid and Rache still regarded her as a fragile female who needed comforting to prevent an outbreak of hysterics in the face of violent death. Then her annoyance was replaced by pleasure. The two men, anything but sentimentalists, were deeply concerned about her welfare.

'I'm up to it,' she said.

With Rache spluttering furious denials of the Kid's accusation, they commenced the search of the rooms. The brief spell of flippancy had given Belle time to regain control of her emotions and she was her usual competent self as she accompanied the Kid.

If Rache had hoped to discover a naked girl during the search, he was to be disappointed. Every room proved to be empty, which did not entirely surprise the Kid. He had not expected Tollinger or Barmain to be present and figured that the management would remove any possible witnesses in case the door-trap needed to be used. Cleaning his knife's blade on the blankets of the last room's bed—which did not make them much dirtier—the Kid sheathed it and returned the Colt to its holster. Then he and the girl joined Rache in the passage and delivered their negative result.

'Same with me,' the old-timer admitted. 'Now we'd best conclude to get the hell out of here. I just saw a bunch of Frog puddle-splashers headed this way.'

'How far off?' Belle demanded.

'Along the street a piece. Only we can't get out and away afore they come.'

'Then we'll have to try something else,' the girl declared, leading the way downstairs. 'Not by fighting, either, unless we're forced to it.'

'Let's hope somebody's got something else in mind, then,' drawled the Kid.

'I just may have at that,' Belle admitted, thinking fast.

On reaching the ground floor, they found Cactus seated on the bar with his rifle across his knees. The Army Colt revolver from his belt holster was pointed in the general direction of Heriberto's fat stomach. Several girls were peering through the half-open door behind the counter, having gone through it into the room beyond when the trouble started. Apart from them, the bar-room was empty.

Darting across the room by the two bodies, Belle grabbed up her skirt. The Kid and Rache joined Cactus at the bar and they waited to hear what the girl planned to do. Swiftly she donned her skirt and fastened it into place. Collecting her wig, the hat and the body of the parasol, she returned to the counter. While the Kid assembled the parasol, she replaced the wig and placed the hat on at a rakish angle. During the search of the upstairs rooms, she had managed to fasten her broken shoulder-strap. Pulling it apart again, she allowed the blouse to trail around her waist. Throwing a look at the doors, to estimate how much time she had, Belle swung back to the Kid.

'Slap my face hard!' Belle ordered.

'Wha——?' the Kid ejaculated.

'Do it, damn you!' Belle hissed. 'I'm your wife, kidnapped

by the men you killed and you've come to rescue me. Now slap me hard. *Pronto!*'

Such was the vehemence in the girl's voice that the Kid dropped the parasol and obeyed. Whipping around his right hand, he lashed its palm across Belle's face. The force of the slap rocked her head over and left livid finger-marks on her cheek, bringing tears to her eyes.

Screwing up her face to keep the tears coming, Belle ruined her already smeared make-up and mussed up the hair of the wig. Then, hearing the sound of heavy boots outside, she thrust herself up close to the Kid.

'Hold me!' she commanded, wrapping her arms around his neck. 'Come on. Don't tell me this's the first time you've done it with a girl?'

'I never had to hit her first,' the Kid answered, cradling Belle's slender torso up to his chest.

The door burst open. Followed by six privates armed with rifles, a burly French infantry sergeant entered warily. Coming to a halt, gripping a Lefauchex revolver, the sergeant scowled at the two bodies. Then he raised his eyes and studied the group at the bar. Cactus had already jumped from his perch and holstered his Colt, to stand close to where the Kid was holding Belle in his arms. Slightly clear of the others, Rache rested his shotgun's barrels in a casual-seeming manner on top of the counter. Maybe it looked that way to the French soldiers, but Heriberto knew that the twin tubes aimed straight at him.

'What's all this?' demanded the sergeant in passable English and walking over to look at the dead men.

'It's on account of me granddaughter here,' Cactus replied, indicating the sob-shaken shoulders of the girl. 'Them fellers done stole her offen our ranch over in Texas.'

'We come to take her back peaceable,' Rache went on, without diverting his attention or weapon from Heriberto. 'Only them fellers wouldn't have it that way. Caught 'em roughing her up some, tearing her clothes 'n' all. Had to kill some of 'em a mite to make 'em quit it.'

Stepping by the corpses with the air of finding them unimportant, the sergeant approached the bar.

'Is that what happened, you?' he snarled at the bartender.

Maybe Heriberto had no love for the Kid's party, but he possessed an even greater antipathy towards the European invaders of his country. Not for patriotic reasons, but because

59

they had disrupted his trade and reduced his *posada*'s once considerable takings to a fraction of their original worth. More than that, Rache's shotgun menaced his existence and the old-timer's eyes flashed a grim warning that the bartender took to heart.

'*Si, senor general*,' Heriberto lied, but with an expression of pious honesty that might have fooled his mother. 'They treat her very cruel.'

'Gal's my wife, sergeant,' the Kid said, loosening his hold so that Belle could turn her reddened, tear-streaked face to look plaintively at the Frenchmen. 'You don't hold what I done again' me, do you?'

'I don't,' the sergeant admitted as a low murmur of pity and condolence rose from his men. 'But you'd better leave Mata-moros as quickly as you can.'

'You can count on it, sir,' Cactus promised and, having had some experience with French non-commissioned officers, dip-ped a hand into his pants' pocket. 'Say, can we buy you 'n' your men a drink to show there's no hard feelings and how sorry we be?'

'We can't drink on duty, and a sergeant never drinks with his men,' replied the non-com and winked. 'But if you let me have the money, I'll see that we all drink your good health later.'

'Anyways you wants it, sergeant,' said Cactus obligingly, producing and handing over a U.S. ten-dollar piece.

Accepting the money, the sergeant thrust it into his pocket with such an air of ownership that it seemed doubtful whether his subordinates would ever taste the drinks or toast the giver's health.

'This is a bad place to be in,' the non-com warned the Texans. 'You had better take the girl back to your home.'

'We'll do that,' Cactus agreed. 'Only we'll stay put a spell if it's all right with you. Until she's settled a mite.'

'You can do that,' the sergeant confirmed and glared at Heriberto. 'See my friends come to no harm, you fat pig. And don't throw this carrion into the street or I'll come back and tear your guts out with a bayonet.'

'*Si, senor general*,' the bartender whined.

'And don't let there be any more trouble in this den of thieves,' the sergeant warned, before turning on his heel and telling his men to leave.

'Keep acting like you're real worried about me, Lon!' Belle whispered, feeling the youngster's arms relax as the soldier marched towards the door.

Gambling on the French soldiers being indifferent to trouble that involved only Americans and Mexicans had paid off. Belle had known enough about the occupying troops to have felt sure that they would not be over-zealous in their duties of policing the town. So her plan had worked. However, she did not wish to ruin their advantage by actions that might arouse the sergeant's suspicions.

'There now, Annie-gal,' the Kid said loudly, in what he hoped would sound a consolatory manner. 'Don't you go fretting no more. It's all done with now.'

'That's what you think, Lon Ysabel,' Belle warned *sotto voce*, watching the soldiers pass through the batwing doors.

'How do you mean?' the Kid wanted to know.

'I think you enjoyed slapping my face,' Belle explained with mock grimness, 'because of what happened in Castro's office last night.'

CHAPTER SEVEN

I'D GO THROUGH HELL TO GET THEM

Releasing the girl after the soldiers had left the *posada*, the Kid looked at her and asked worriedly, 'Did I hurt you?'

'No more than that female pugilist I had to fight in New Orleans,'* Belle answered, wryly fingering her cheek.

'Did you lick her?' Rache inquired.

'Finally,' Belle admitted. Then she swung to face the bartender and her voice hardened. 'Where are the two *gringos*?'

Heriberto looked at the girl with interest and some trepidation. Despite the tear-smeared make-up and gaudy, if dishevelled clothes, that was no ordinary saloon-worker. Everything about her, the way she had acted since her arrival, her voice and deportment, the respect she obviously commanded

* Told in *The Rebel Spy*.

from the three Texans, warned him of that. There was a grim determination about her, the air of a person used to being obeyed and capable of enforcing obedience.

Wanting to avoid answering the question, or to prevent anybody knowing of it should he be forced to do so, the bartender turned and snarled at the watching girls. Even after they had retreated and closed the storeroom door, he felt that some evasion ought to be attempted.

'They ran out after you went upstairs, *senorita*. *All* of them that could.'

'I mean the two who *Cicatriz* worked for,' Belle elaborated coldly.

'*Quien sabe?*' Heriberto answered. 'I don't——'

'Go and call the French sergeant back, *Cabrito*,' Belle ordered. 'Tell him that we think this fat one hired the men who kidnapped me.'

'No!' Heriberto yelped, realising what his fate would be if the sergeant returned. Having received ten dollars, he would regard himself under an obligation to help the givers. 'I don't know where they are, *senorita*.' He crossed himself fervently. '*Madre de Dios!* I tell you the truth.'

'Have they been here?' Belle demanded.

'Only once, *senorita*. Last night, late. They came with *Cicatriz*, looked around and didn't like what they saw. So they left and haven't been back.'

'Why didn't *Cicatriz* go with them?'

'He went, but came back, *senorita*. Maybe they're staying at some place that wouldn't have the Scar inside.'

'Which'd be nigh on every place in Matamoros 'n' Brownsville,' Rache growled. 'I hates to talk ill of the dead, but that's the only way with *Cicatriz*.'

'What did *Cicatriz* want with the two *gringos*?' Belle asked, making adjustments to her torn blouse so that it would serve her during the return to Villena's *posada*.

Sweat trickled down Heriberto's fat face and he ran the tip of his tongue across lips that suddenly felt dry. Discussing the customers' affairs had never been a sound business policy, especially when considering the type of trade attracted by the *Posada del Infernales*. Refusing to do so could prove equally dangerous and painful when dealing with *Cabrito* or his two ancient *companeros*.

'He was to help them hire men, *senorita*,' the bartender

replied, having concluded that his present company posed a greater threat than the two *gringos* who had employed *Cicatriz*. 'The *Americanos* your *amigos* ran out of here were some of them.'

'Who were they hiring for?' Belle demanded.

'They said for the French general at the fort on the Rio Mendez,' Heriberto answered.

'Why'd a French general want to hire guns?' Rache grunted.

'I don't know,' Heriberto whined and cringed away as if expecting a blow or worse to repay his lack of knowledge.

'He's telling the truth,' Belle stated after scrutinising the Mexican's face. 'I shouldn't have expected to find Tollinger and Barmain here. Their kind are all for equality, but not to the extent of living among what they regard as the lower classes. We may as well get going.'

Cradling his shotgun on the crook of his left arm, Rache eyed Heriberto as if disappointed that he had not needed to use it. Cactus gathered up his rifle and the Kid handed Belle her parasol. Then they left the *posada*, followed by Heriberto's hate-filled scowl.

'Want for me to stick around, hid out, in case they come looking for *Cicatriz*?' asked the Kid.

'It wouldn't be safe, Lon,' Belle objected. 'Not unless you change your clothes. Dressed like a peon, you might get away with it. We'll see what Big Sam thinks first.'

'Why don't me 'n' Rache nose around a mite and see if we can find where they're living, Miss Belle?' suggested Cactus.

'That's an idea,' Belle agreed. 'Unless they're at the U.S. consulate, they're likely to be at one of the better hotels.'

'We got friends in 'em all,' Rache stated.

'Emptying the spitoons 'n' washing out the chamber-pots,' finished the Kid.

'These gentlemen mean *their* friends,' Belle pointed out, 'not your's. And you might introduce us. Somehow you never got around to doing it last night.'

'I never thought anybody'd want to know 'em,' drawled the Kid. 'Ain't no telling what foolishness women'll want. This here's Cactus Jones and Hor—Hor——'

'Horatio Charles Wilberforce, ma'am,' Rache put in, blazing with exasperation. 'Blasted young pup done forgot me name!'

'With a name like that, it's best forgot,' scoffed the Kid. 'Anyways, that's who they are, Belle, for what it's worth.'

'When I asked about them last night,' Belle pointed out accusingly, 'you told me——'

'I was just showing you that it's not only she-male spies, can play sneaky,' grinned the Kid. 'And who'd want to admit they knowed a couple of ornery, mean ole goats like them?'

'He means us, Miss Belle,' Rache informed the girl sadly. 'Danged *Pehnane*, never did have no ree-spect for age, wisdom, nor beauty.'

'You're sure old,' admitted the Kid, 'but nobody'd give you claim to the other two.'

'Ignore him, Horatio,' Belle ordered, taking the old-timer's arm. '*I* know you're both perfect gentlemen. Not like some of the youngsters you meet these days. Why I bet neither of you would slap a lady's face.'

'They wouldn't,' the Kid agreed with reservations. 'Not less'n she was a whole heap smaller than them.'

Despite the levity of their conversation, Belle and her companions kept a careful watch around them as they walked away from the *Posada del Infernales*. There were a few details the girl wished to have cleared up, so, with wrathful interruptions from Rache at the derogatory comments aimed his way, the Kid satisfied her curiosity.

While Cactus and Rache had been friends with the Ysabel family for several years, the Kid's signal had prevented them from coming over and speaking the previous evening in Castro's *casino*. Instead, they had kept clear, but were ready to lend support should it be needed. On Belle's party leaving, the old-timers had stayed behind to guard against pursuit by Castro's employees. None had come, so they finally followed the girl and the Ysabels to Ma O'Grady's house.

Arriving after Belle had retired for the night, Cactus and Rache had learned her identity. On being told of her vengeance mission, they had insisted on offering their services. There followed a brief, irate and profane string of objections by Rache to the Kid's libellous statement that only blackmail persuaded him to come along. Being assured by Belle that she did not believe a word of the story, but agreed with Rache's comments on the Kid's morals, the old man permitted the explanation to continue.

Crossing the Rio Grande at sundown, Cactus and Rache had reached the *Posada del Infernales* some time before Belle and the Kid arrived. Mingling with the other customers, they had avoided drawing attention to themselves until the appropriate moment to make their presence felt.

'And I'm pleased that you were there,' Belle told the old-timers at the end of the recital.

'Company you was keeping, I ain't see-prised,' Rache snorted, eyeing the Kid malevolently and strutting like a bantam cock with the girl on his arm.

'Ain't it time you pair was headed off around them hotels as is full of all your rich friends?' demanded the Kid.

'It is,' agreed Cactus. 'Happen I can pry Rache offen Miss Belle's arm, we'll get to going.'

'Way some ornery young cusses slap her around, I figured she needed pertecting,' Rache explained, relinquishing the girl's arm with an air of reluctance. 'You let me know happen he does it again, ma'am, and I'll whup him good.'

Watching the two old-timers amble off along a side street, Belle smiled.

'They're real nice people, Lon.'

'Yes'm. And don't let all that bluster fool you. They're a couple of forty-four calibre men.'

Belle had heard the term before and knew it to be one that a Texan did not award lightly.* Continuing her pose as a saloon-girl, she hooked on to the Kid's left arm and strolled at his side until they reached Villena's *posada*. Entering the building, they found that Sam Ysabel had just returned. When they joined him in the deserted dining-room, he looked them over sardonically.

'You run into fuss, boy?' Ysabel inquired.

'Some, pappy. Rache had to kill *Cicatriz*.'

'I'll buy him a drink for it. Were they with the Scar, Miss Belle?'

'No,' Belle replied, trying to conceal her disappointment.

'Rache killed him afore we could ask about it,' the Kid explained. 'Couldn't do nothing else, though.'

'Where're Rache 'n' Cactus now?' asked Ysabel.

'Making the rounds, seeing if they can learn where them two soft-shells're at,' the Kid replied. 'What'd Don Francisco want, *ap'*?'

'I'll go and change,' Belle offered, thinking that Almonte's business with the Ysabels might be private.

'Like you stay on, Miss Belle. You can maybe help some,'

* How the name came into being is told in *·44 Calibre Man*.

Ysabel requested and nodded to the nearest table. 'Let's sit a spell, talking's easier that way.' After they had taken seats, he continued, 'Don Francisco wants our help, Lon.'

'That figures,' drawled the Kid. 'Only Belle don't know who he is.'

'He's fighting for Juarez,' Ysabel explained. 'I reckon you know how things are down here, Miss Belle.'

'I know a little about them,' Belle corrected, for the conditions existing in Mexico, and their causes, were extremely complicated.

Basically, throughout their years of civil conflict, the Conservatives under *Presidente* Miramón and the Constitutionalists led by Benito Juarez had financed their respective war efforts by extracting forced contributions from foreign businessmen and property owners. Enraged by continued outrages and abuses of its nationals, the United States' Congress had withdrawn its recognition of Miramón's government in 1858. Two years later, receiving moral and material aid from north of the border, Juarez had been able to take the offensive. Before the War Between the States had brought an end to the United States' assistance, he had defeated the Conservatives. On assuming office, he had expelled the Spanish minister, the papal legate and various members of the episcopate.

Faced with legitimate debts to various European countries totalling some eighty-two million dollars, the Mexican Congress had voted to suspend paying even the interest due on the money for at least two years. That had played into the hands of the ambitious Napoleon the Third. Desiring to establish a French colony in America, he had negotiated a convention between his country, Great Britain and Spain to enforce demands for payment.

When Napoleon's true purpose had become obvious, the British and the Spaniards had withdrawn their support. Pouring more French troops into Mexico, Napoleon had sought other allies. By arranging a fake Mexican plebiscite that offered to make Maximilian—brother of Emperor Francis Joseph—the country's ruler, Napoleon had obtained support and reinforcements from Austria, Belgium and Turkey. Driven from office, unable to match the superiorly equipped European invaders in open battle, Juarez now fought a guerilla war to try to free his homeland.

'Thing being,' Ysabel said, 'everybody down here wants to

know what the Yankees'll do now the War's over.'

'That's understandable,' Belle admitted, removing her hat and wig.

The fate of Mexico might depend on which side the United States gave its support. During the War, the Federal government had tried to steer a central path and avoid antagonising either side. With a cessation of hostilities north of the Rio Grande, both the French and Mexican authorities would be waiting anxiously to discover what the reformed United States' policies were going to be.

'What do you reckon, Miss Belle?' asked Ysabel.

'I reckon that you should stop calling me "Miss",' Belle replied, wanting a moment's grace to assemble her thoughts. 'It makes me feel awful old.'

'I'll mind it,' Ysabel promised. 'Seeing's Lon's stop doing it already.'

Ignoring the incongruous sight she must present with her facial make-up ruined and general bedraggled appearance, Belle thought for almost a minute before she replied to the big Texan's question.

'You remember why we were sent to General Klatwitter, Sam?'

'Yes'm.'

Belle's last, abortive mission had been a final, desperate throw of the dice for the South. On the verge of defeat before the Union's superior numbers, arms, equipment and economy, the Confederate government had hoped that the renegade general's intervention would prolong the War. Already in the North, public opinion had been growing more and more vociferous in its demands for an end to the hostilities. So the possibility of being compelled to continue the struggle might have caused the Union's Congress to offer peace while the South was still in a position to bargain for terms. General Grant's rapid advance and successes, along with Belle's unavoidable failure to complete her assignment, had prevented this from happening. It was a factor to be taken into consideration.

'I don't think that the Union government will be willing to commit themselves yet,' Belle went on. 'Right now, everybody up North is sick of war with its death, losses, miseries and increased taxations——'

'Knowing Yankees,' interrupted the Kid, 'that last'll bother 'em most.'

'Keep mum and hear Mi—Belle out,' his father ordered.

'If you don't,' I'll sic Rache on to you,' Belle warned, then became serious. 'Congress won't want to give active support to either side until the voters have forgotten how much fighting the South has cost them. So I think they'll try to avoid becoming involved. Being drawn into another war could sweep them out of office.'

'That's about how Don Francisco sees it,' Ysabel admitted soberly.

'Then what's bothering him?' Belle inquired. 'Surely the *Juaristas* didn't believe that the Yankees would come marching straight down here to help them against the French now the War is over?'

'Some of them might have, but Don Francisco figures the same as you.'

'Then——?'

'It's that French general down on the Rio Mendez——'

'I don't follow you, Sam,' Belle stated. 'If he's trying to establish a private republic, it will weaken the French's fighting strength. And there's not much chance of him bringing it off.'

'Likely not,' agreed Ysabel. 'Only it'll weaken the *Juaristas* some as well. You know there're fellers fighting for ole Benito who don't exactly cotton to his ways 'n' notions?'

'The big landowners, you mean?'

'Nope. Maybe some of them don't cotton to a Zapotec Injun being *el presidente*, no matter how smart he is. But mostly they figure he'll play square with 'em if he wins.'

'Then who——?'

'Don Francisco reckons it's the soft-shells. *They* allow Juarez'll be too easy-going on the *haciendenos*. Them's the sort this renegade general's likely to be drawing, along of some of the *bandidos* who ain't making enough loot fighting the French.'

'I see,' Belle breathed. 'And they're willing to throw in with this general to bring Juarez down?'

'Something like that,' agreed Ysabel. 'Anyways, Don Francisco wants us, Lon 'n' me, to go down to this fort and learn who's in the deal, how strong they are, what they're fixing to do, and such.'

'Don Francisco knows the general is hiring gun-fighters,' Belle guessed. 'So he wants you to go there pretending to be looking for work.'

'That's about the size of it,' Ysabel admitted.

Sitting back in her chair, Belle studied the dark, expressionless features of the big Texan. All too well she could imagine his dilemma. He had promised to help hunt down the murderers of her parents and now found himself faced with the possibility of having to refuse an old friend's request for assistance. Yet Belle wondered if the two problems might be compatible.

'*Cicatriz* was helping Tollinger and Barmain to gather men for this general,' the girl said quietly.

'Or so we got told,' growled the Kid.

'*Twice*,' Belle reminded him. 'I think that we heard the truth. The thing is, why are they doing it?'

'We could maybe try asking 'em,' the Kid suggested. 'Only we can't find 'em to do it.'

'Rache and Cactus might attend to that for us,' Belle pointed out. 'If not, the fort on the Rio Mendez would be a good place to start looking for them.'

'You reckon that's where they're going, Mi—Belle?' asked Ysabel. 'They might be hiring help for Juarez and making out it's to fight for this General Caillard so nobody'd know.'

'That's possible,' Belle admitted. 'It might account for why they didn't tell the patrol on Brownsville who I was, or help to chase me. They wouldn't want to have to explain how they knew me as it might arouse suspicions about their reason for being on the border. They wouldn't want it even suspected that members of the Yankee Secret Service were becoming involved in Mexican affairs.'

'Ole Benito don't have much money,' the Kid pointed out. 'And them jaspers we locked horns with weren't the kind to fight for free.'

'There's that to it,' Belle agreed. 'But if Don Francisco's right about the renegade attracting soft-shells, Tollinger and Barmain might be going to help their own kind; perhaps without official sanction.'

'You mean they might not be Yankee spies no more?' asked the Kid.

'They might not. In which case, they're acting on their own. I think that we should go to this fort, Sam. How far is it?'

' 'Bout eighty miles south, along the coast.'

'Two days' ride. Unless we find them in Matamoros, I suggest that we go to the fort and look for them.'

'What if they're not there?' the Kid wanted to know.

'Then we'll do as Don Francisco asks, come back and report and start looking again,' Belle replied. 'Should we find them here. I'll still come along to the fort, if you'll have me.'

'We'd admire to have you along, M—Belle,' Ysabel began.

'You're improving,' Belle smiled. 'You almost didn't say it that time—— But what?'

'Huh?' grunted Ysabel.

'We'd admire to have you along, but——' Belle elaborated. 'That's what you intended to say.'

'Damned if I could ever stand smart women,' Ysabel grinned. 'I don't know what kind of jasper this Caillard is, but I can figure out the sort of fellers who'll be gathering 'round him.'

'So can I,' Belle answered. 'Malcontents, deserters from both sides, plain thieves after loot.'

'As mean 'n' ornery a bunch of cut-throats and *pelados*'* as you could ask to miss meeting,' Ysabel confirmed. 'I'd hate to take a for-real lady like you among 'em.'

'If Tollinger and Barmain are there, I'll chance it,' Belle said quietly. 'I'd go through hell to get them!'

The cold, grim, deadly determination in the girl's voice warned her audience that she would not be swayed from her purpose by any arguments or warnings of possible danger.

CHAPTER EIGHT

LET'S GO IN OVER THE WALL

'There she be,' announced Horatio Charles Wilberforce, pointing through the deepening dusk as he sat his wiry dun horse alongside Belle's *bayo-cebrunos** gelding on the second day after her visit to the *Posada del Infernales*. His entire

---

* *Pelado*: used in this context it means a grave or corpse-robber of the lowest kind.

* *Bayo-cebrunos*: a dun colour, shading into smokey-grey.

attitude seemed to claim that he was responsible for what lay before them.

Despite their excellent sources of information, Rache and Cactus had failed to locate Belle's enemies. The short oldster had complained bitterly over the failure, claiming that he or Cactus should have followed the hard-cases when they fled from the *posada*, until Belle had pointed out that both of them had been needed more urgently inside the building. As it was, they had found the hotel at which Tollinger and Barmain had been staying; but reached it too late. According to their friend at the hotel, a Mexican had arrived and asked to see the two Yankees. Whatever he had told them caused the pair to pack their bags and leave hurriedly. Continuing their investigations, the old-timers discovered that the objects of their search had not taken rooms in another hotel. So they had visited the United States' consulate. Contacting a Mexican friend employed by the consul, they again drew a blank. Tollinger and Barmain were not in residence with their government's representative.

Dressed as a *peon*, the Kid had scouted the *Posada del Infernales*. He had returned to report that neither Tollinger and Barmain nor the Yankee hard-cases were present. Further inquiries had brought to light that Hoxley had taken his men out of Matamoros, but the informant could not say if Tollinger and Barmain had accompanied them.

By that time, it had been too late to think of setting after the men that day. Instead, Belle's party had made their preparations to leave the following morning. The girl found that she would have four companions to back her on arrival at Fort Mendez. As Rache had put it, no self-respecting Texas gentlemen could contemplate entrusting a lady of quality to them shiftless Ysabel varmints; so he and Cactus intended to go along.

The Ysabels had obtained the *bayo-cebrunos* gelding for the girl to ride, claiming it to be a horse with *brio escondido*—hidden vigour, or stamina of a high order—and ideally suited to her needs. In addition, they had produced a sturdy pack-horse to carry the items Belle felt might be of use on her mission. For the journey, she wore her boots, riding breeches, a dark blue shirt and a black Stetson. Butt-forward in a fast-draw holster on her right thigh hung the ivory-handled Navy revolver presented to her by the Dance Brothers, Texas fire-

71

arms manufacturers, as a tribute to her services in the Confederate cause.

Starting early the next morning, Belle's party had headed south. All her companions were well-mounted: the Kid on a magnificent big white stallion that had a nature as wild and savage as his own; Sam Ysabel was afork a large *grulla* stud the mousey-grey colour of a sandhill crane; Cactus sat a leggy, saffron-hued *bayo-azafranados* gelding; Rache's dun looked as small, wiry and aggressive as its master. They rode low-horned, double-girthed Texas range saddles, with bedrolls fastened to the cantles and their shoulder arms in the boots. In such company, Belle had reason to be grateful for her mount's *brio escondido* qualities. She also found satisfaction in the Texan's unspoken approval of her riding skill.

Soon after leaving Matamoros, ranging ahead of the others, the Kid had found hoof-tracks of approximately the right age to have been made by the hard-cases' mounts and going in a southerly direction. There had been at least six horses, which might mean that Tollinger and Barmain had accompanied Hoxley's bunch.

Discussing the discovery, Belle and her companions had decided against increasing their speed in an attempt to catch up with the other travellers. The group ahead might not be the men from the *Posada del Infernales*; and even if they were, the lead they had built up could only be reduced by pushing the horses very hard. So Belle and the Texans had concluded that their best plan would be to follow at a pace which would leave their mounts with a reserve of stamina to meet the needs of any emergency.

Covering almost forty miles that day, they had made a comfortable but carefully concealed camp at sundown. Before turning in for the night, Belle had formulated a plan to cover the eventuality of her enemies having already made contact with the renegade general. Explaining her scheme to the Texans, she found that they considered it worth trying if the circumstances should permit. At dawn they had ridden on and at last, with the sun again sinking in the west, had come into sight of their destination. Keeping back among the trees on the fringes of a large *bosque*, they examined their surroundings with interest.

One aspect of the affair had been puzzling Belle, but she could now see the possible answer. With so many people involved in it, the French high command must have heard rumours of General Caillard's defection. So Belle had wondered why no steps had been taken to deal with him. Looking ahead, she could understand the reason for the French's inactivity.

Built by men who had unlimited cheap labour and adequate materials at their disposal, the fort nestling in a bend of the Rio Mendez was an impressive structure. Through embrasures cut into the twenty foot high stone walls, heavy muzzle-loading cannon mounted *en barbette* covered all the approaches. Belle counted four such guns on each wall and guessed that they would be at least 42-pounders.

While the builders had not troubled to surround the walls with a water-filled moat or a deep ditch, or to provide an outlying earthwork demilune, the place was still formidable. An attacker would be compelled to send his men from any side across almost a mile of level, open ground under fire from the cannon and rifles on the terreplein. Assuming that there was an internal water-supply—which seemed likely—and adequate provisions, a determined garrison could only be evicted by a fully organised and equipped siege. Even then, capturing the fort would be anything but easy. In fact the French had only gained control of it through the Mexican commandant betraying his trust and handing it over. Probably Maximilian's high command did not believe the effort of recovering it justified the high price in lives, material, time and effort that they would have to pay.

Producing field-glasses from their saddle pouches, Belle and Ysabel studied the fort. They could see sentries patrolling the walls. Five in all. Two on the side facing them, working outwards from the main gates, and one on each other wall. Inside there would be quarters for the garrison, stables, storerooms, an underground magazine and, possibly, accommodation for wives. All that showed above the walls was the roof of a large building in the centre of the enclosure, corresponding with the keep of an old-time castle.

'Look up there!' the Kid remarked, pointing.

Following the direction he indicated, the others saw a small group of riders coming downstream along the banks of the Rio Mendez. Through her glasses, Belle found them to be Mexicans, led by a tall, swarthily handsome man dressed elegantly but with cruel lines to his features. He and his companions were well-armed and superbly mounted.

'Well, I'll swan!' Ysabel breathed, also using a pair of battlefield 'liberated' glasses. 'If that ain't Ramon Peraro, I'll vote Republican.'

'Mean ye don't?' Rache sniffed, squinting at the newcomers.

Recalling comments made by the Ysabels during her last assignment, Belle frowned. Ramon Peraro led a particularly ruthless *bandido* gang and he came from a family that had always been prominent in Mexican criminal circles.* Also, he might have reason to dislike her companions.

'Looks like his arm's done healed up,' the Kid remarked.

'I wonder if he really knows what happened the day he was wounded?' Belle said soberly, lowering her glasses. 'Have you heard anything, Cactus, Rache?'

'Only how him and the late Bully Segan locked horns, which's how Bully comes to be "the late",' Cactus replied. 'Do you know something about it, Miss Belle?'

'It was all Lon's fault,' Belle replied.

'It mostly is,' grunted Rache, before she could continue her explanation.

Trying to stop Belle reaching General Klatwitter, members of the Yankee Secret Service had spread the story among the various border gangs of how much money she was carrying. Learning that the Peraro and Segan bands intended to co-operate in an attempted theft, the Kid had stolen some of the latter's horses in a way that laid suspicion on the former. In the fight that followed, Segan died and Peraro had received a wound which prevented him from continuing the hunt for Belle's party.

'Could be that none of 'em knew for sure what did happen,' the Kid said. 'They'd not seen me around. Thing being, what's Peraro doing here?'

'Come to see if this Frog general's worth joining, likely,' Rache guessed. 'His kind drop down like buzzards if there's a smell of easy money.'

'It looks like they're expected,' Belle put in, whipping up her glasses as the huge double gates swung open and Peraro's band rode through.

'There's a fair slew of horses inside,' Ysabel commented. 'McClellan saddles, dinner-plate rigs, a few with just blankets.

* And still are, as is told in *Point of Contact* and *Run for the Border*.

74

I'd say they'd got visitors.'

'So would I,' Belle agreed, following the significance of the statement.

Most Union and Confederate cavalry regiments used the McClellan-pattern saddle and many of them must now be in civilian hands north of the border. The large horn of a Mexican range saddle gave it the derogatory name applied by Ysabel. Horses carrying only blankets hinted at Indian owners.

As the gates swung closed, Belle saw a tall, handsome officer in the elaborate green uniform of the Austrian Hussars walk up and greet Peraro. She lowered the glasses and looked at her companions.

'I'd say Caillard's called folks in to hear what he's got in mind,' Ysabel said, returning his glasses to the pouch.

'It's likely,' Belle agreed. 'We couldn't have come at a better time. I'll be interested in hearing what he has to say.'

'We could ride on over and ask 'em to let us in,' the Kid suggested.

'And might get our heads shot off in return,' Belle warned. 'It's a chance I'd rather not take.'

'You got something else in mind, Miss Belle?' asked Rache, his tone showing that he expected the answer to be in the affirmative.

'Not off-hand,' Belle admitted ruefully.

'Let's go in over the wall,' offered the Kid. 'I reckon that'd do what you want, Belle.'

It had been Belle's intention, if possible, to make a dramatic entrance. One calculated to convince General Caillard that her party would be of greater use to his cause than would Tollinger and Barmain. Having examined the fort, she had doubted if the plan could be carried out.

'It would, Lon,' the girl agreed. 'But can we do it?'

'Likely, comes dark,' the Kid affirmed, patting the forty-foot length of three strand, hard-plaited Manila rope which hung coiled and strapped to his saddle-horn. 'We Injun across there, wait until the sentry goes by, toss a loop over the barrel of one of them cannons and climb up.'

'It could be done, Belle,' Ysabel continued. 'You want to, you, me 'n' Lon'll give it a whirl.'

'What's up?' demanded Rache belligerently. 'Reckon me 'n' Cactus're too old to make it?'

'I know you'd be fool enough to try,' grinned Ysabel. 'Only,

way them sentries keep patrolling, there won't be time for
more than three of us to get over.'

'Hell!' Rache protested and touched his left side. 'We've got
enough knives to hand them their needings.'

'We want to impress Caillard, not rile him by wiping out
half of his garrison,' Belle reminded the bristling oldster, then
smiled in her most winning manner. 'Will you play it Sam's
way please, boys?'

As if to give another reason for the old-timers staying behind, a mountain lion cut loose with its spine-chilling screech
not far away. All the horses moved restlessly. Range-bred, they
recognised the danger heralded by the sound. Rache and
Cactus realised that they could not leave their mounts un-
attended with a cougar on the prowl.

'Aw shucks!' Rache replied. 'Iffen you wants it that way,
Miss Belle, that's how she's going to be.'

'We'll lay up back in the woods,' Cactus went on. 'Then
when you want us, we'll drift on over.'

Belle felt considerable relief at the old-timers' acceptance.
Once inside the fort, she and her escort would be at Caillard's
mercy and might not be permitted to leave. So she had sufficient misgivings over endangering the Ysabel family's lives
without also dragging the two ancient Texans into peril.

'One thing, though,' Rache growled, throwing a disgusted
scowl at the Kid's stallion. 'You take the saddle of that blasted
white snapping-turtle yourself. First time he looks like biting
me, I'll make wolf-bait of him.'

'Shucks,' grinned the Kid, swinging his horse around. 'Ole
Nigger won't hurt you none.'

'You're danged right he won't,' bristled the oldster. ' 'Cause
I ain't fixing to give him a son-of-a-bitching chance. Being
right sorry for saying such words afore you, Miss Belle.'

'That's all right, Horatio,' Belle commiserated. 'He'd make a
saint go to cursing. Don't pay him no never mind.

'Danged if they ain't ganging up on me again, *ap*',' groaned
the Kid. 'I'm going. Saw a clearing by a stream back there a
ways that'd make a jim-dandy camping place for us.'

Withdrawing from the edge of the *bosque*, they made their
way to the Kid's clearing. Once there, no time was wasted on
levity. Swiftly they removed the saddles and saw to the horses'
needs. Belle's *bayo-cebrunos* and the pack animal had to be
hobbled, but the others' mounts could be trusted not to stray

and were left free. Then Belle gave thought to her arrival in the fort. She wondered if she should select other clothing from her baggage, but decided against it. Maybe the garments she had in mind would be impressive, but they were not suitable for the manner in which they planned to enter the general's presence. Nor, if it came to a point, were her riding-boots.

Mentioning the matter to her companions, she announced her intention of making the climb bare-footed. Beaming with pleasure, Rache announced that *he* could solve the girl's problem. Opening his bed-roll, he dug into his 'thirty-year gatherings'* and produced a pair of calf-high Comanche moccasins. Belle accepted them, tried them on and found that they fitted her snugly.

'Let's get going afore that pesky ole varmint swells up and busts,' grinned the Kid, unstrapping his rope and hanging it over his left shoulder. 'Bring your glasses, *ap'*, I'd like a closer look over them walls.'

The Kid had also donned moccasins and debated the advisability of taking along his Mississippi rifle. Reluctantly he concluded that the rifle's usefulness for displaying accurate shooting would be outweighed by its awkwardness during the climb. So he left it in its boot.

When everything had been settled, Belle, the Ysabels and Rache returned to the fringe of the *bosque*. Agreeing to stay and watch over the horses, Cactus had given his short companion a dire warning of severe reprisals if Rache attempted to accompany the others all the way.

Keeping concealed, Belle and her escort spent the last minutes of daylight scanning the terrain and examining their objective. Taking his father's field-glasses, the Kid climbed a tree and obtained a better view over the walls. On descending, he announced that most of the activity inside the walls seemed to be centring on the large main building. Apart from a few soldiers, the rest of the occupants appeared to be converging on it. Supplementing his early *Pehnane* scout training with experience picked up in the war, he had drawn other, more important conclusions. While the left, right and rear walls each had only one sentry patrolling its length, he felt that the front offered the best chance to them. The other sides were too open, with the only steps down from the terreplein placed at the corners.

* Thirty-year gatherings: personal property, carried in a war-bag.

'We'd have to chance moving along to 'em with the guards on two sides likely to see us,' the youngster explained. 'The two sentries on the front wall don't have to walk so far, but them gate-towers'll keep us hid from the feller on the other side. That jasper on the right never comes by the cannon nearest the gate.'

'The front it is, then,' Belle said and Ysabel nodded his agreement. 'And on the cannon next to the gate.'

With the gathering darkness, the soft, melancholy cooing calls of the Coppery-Tailed Trogons among the trees had died away. From the depths of the *bosque* came night noises and a Great-Horned Owl gave its eerie cry as it skimmed through the air in search of its prey.

'Let's go,' Ysabel ordered, coming to his feet.

Handing the field-glasses to Rache, the Kid returned his rope to his shoulder. With a grin at the old-timer, he followed his father and the girl from the shelter of the trees. They advanced cautiously, the girl between the men and watching their every move. Alert for the first hint that the sentries had detected them, their clothing merging into the darkness, taking advantage of every scrap of cover, they approached the front of the fort.

As they drew nearer, and no challenge had been given, they became aware of the noise made by the sentries' feet. Probably there were enclosed casemates, although without mounted cannon, beneath the terreplein, acting as stables, stores or accommodation for the lower-ranked members of the garrison. That would account for the dull echoing effect as the sentries marched their beats. The sound would be of help to Belle and her companions.

At last the trio stood in the deeper shadow thrown by the wall and comparatively safe from detection. Looking up, Belle could just make out the barrel of the cannon nearest to the gate as it protruded beyond the embrasure. It would be a small enough target for the Kid's rope, taken with the awkward angle at which he must make his throw.

Shaking out his loop, the Kid stepped back and measured the distance with his eye. He cocked an ear and listened to the foot-falls of the sentry on their side of the gate. Satisfied that the man was going away, he took aim, twirled the rope and sent it shooting upwards. Missing the barrel, it fell back with a soft, swishing thud. Just as the Kid prepared to throw again, the sentry came to a halt. Instantly the youngster froze and his companions stiffened, straining to discover what had caused the man to stop. Voices drifted to their ears—but conversing in normal tones, not raised in alarm. Apparently the sentry had met his opposite number on the eastern terreplein and paused to have a chat.

At a nod from Ysabel, the Kid tried again. Down fell the rope. Letting out an annoyed hiss, the youngster rebuilt his loop with extra care. A quick whirl and it went upwards for the third time—and did not tumble back. With a flick of his wrists, the Kid caused the loop to slide farther along the barrel. Then he drew it tight and tested its security. On the corner of the terreplein, the sentries continued talking, oblivious of the trio behind the walls.

Gripping the rope in both hands, the Kid set his feet against the wall and started to walk upwards. Hardly daring to breathe, Belle watched him go higher. Then he disappeared and the rope jerked three times. A glance at Ysabel and Belle took hold to follow the youngster.

Although superbly fit, Belle did not find climbing the wall easy. She forced herself to go on and, after what seemed like an age, saw the square opening of the embrasure just above her.

Suddenly the Kid's arm emerged from the hole and made an urgent downwards movement. To her horror, Belle realised that the voices along the wall had ceased and the footsteps resumed.

The sentry was coming back!

There could be no retreating down the rope. If she tried, its movement could betray or she might slip. Either way, the sentry would be alerted and raise the alarm. Setting her teeth grimly, she forced herself to remain still and hung suspended just below the lip of the embrasure.

CHAPTER NINE

WE'VE ONE MISS BOYD TOO MANY

After delivering his warning to Belle, the Kid remained crouched behind the big cannon on its *barbette* carriage. His right hand moved swiftly and silently to slide the bowie knife from its sheath. Heavy boots clumping noisily, the sentry came nearer and nearer. The Kid tensed like a great cat waiting to spring. If the sentry kept walking, he would change the pattern of his previous evolutions by passing the cannon. In which case, he could not avoid seeing the Kid—and would likely wind up dead. The trouble with that being the Kid did not think he could silence the soldier without attracting the attention of the man on the east wall.

'Raoul!' called the other sentry, and continued in French. 'Come here, quick!'

Turning, just one step before he reached a position where he would suffer the consequences of seeing the Kid, the sentry loped back along the terreplein. A brief conversation reached Belle's and the Kid's ears, although only she could follow its meaning.

'What's wrong?'

'I thought I saw something moving out there!'

Bracing her feet against the hard stone of the wall, Belle gritted her teeth and clenched her hands tighter about the rope. For a few heart-pounding seconds, she wondered if the second sentry had seen her. Then she realised that if he had, he would have come to 'Raoul' instead of calling for the other to join him. Nor did it seem likely that he had noticed Ysabel, for the big Texan stood flattened against the wall below her.

Which raised the point of who, or what, the soldier had seen.

'I can't see anything!' Raoul declared after a moment.

'Over there!' the second sentry insisted. 'Shall I shoot?'

Again Belle's heart seemed to increase its pounding. A shot would bring the remainder of the guard to investigate. Fortunately, Raoul also appreciated the fact.

'You'd better not,' he said. 'If it's nothing, Sergeant Poncey will have you in the cells.'

'Come up!' whispered the Kid, leaning through the embrasure and gripping the girl's left wrist. He had sheathed his knife as soon as the sentry turned away.

With the youngster's help, Belle reached the opening. There was room in plenty alongside the cannon's barrel for her to slip through. Almost before she felt the level surface of the terreplein under her feet, the Kid jerked the rope and signalled to his father to follow.

'Let's go,' the Kid hissed. 'Pappy'll come's soon's he's up.'

'It's still there, I tell you!' the second sentry said. 'I saw it move.'

Fighting to hold down the sound of her breathing, Belle tiptoed after the Kid across the terreplein and down the stone steps. At the forward eastern corner, the two soldiers continued to debate the possibility of somebody, or something, moving around in the darkness beyond the walls. They were so engrossed that they did not notice the girl and the Kid cross, or, a few seconds later, Ysabel come through the embrasure and follow them.

'What the hell've they se——?' Ysabel began as he joined Belle and the Kid.

As if in answer, they heard a loud, raucous braying sound shatter the silence outside the fort.

'It's only a donkey!' Raoul snorted. 'Put down your rifle, you fool. The Austrian pig or Poncey would have the hide flogged off your back if you'd turned out the garrison for that.'

'Donkey's right,' grinned the Kid, after Belle had interpreted the sentry's comment. 'It sure is. Only it's got two legs and a droopy misplaced eyebrow.'

'*Rache!*' Belle gasped.

'Danged ole fool,' agreed Ysabel admiringly. 'He must've snuck over that ways and moved around just enough for the sentry not to be sure he saw him.'

'He certainly helped us,' Belle said quietly.

An inner glow of satisfaction filled the girl at this further demonstration of her companions' high regard for her. Without any mention of expecting a reward, making no demands for monetary, material or sexual remuneration for their services, they willingly took desperate chances to help her.

However, one did not stand day-dreaming in Belle's current situation. At a sign from Ysabel, they advanced alongside the gate tower. The Kid peered cautiously around the corner and nodded in satisfaction.

81

'Nobody around,' he said.

'Nor any need for us to keep sneaking about now,' Ysabel went on.

With that he walked boldly forward. After a moment's hesitation, Belle followed on the Kid's heels. As Ysabel had claimed, there was no further need for them to attempt to avoid being observed. In fact, doing it might easily ruin all they had so far achieved. They would attract less attention if they walked openly than by being caught skulking in the shadows. There were sufficient strangers in the fort for any of its garrison who saw the trio to mistake them for guests.

Going by the noise which rose from it, the large building in the middle of the square must be the centre of attraction. It had two stories of solid height, the upper of them apparently being divided into rooms for offices or officers' living quarters. The front half of the ground floor was given over to a mess-hall.

Before offering to enter the big, closed double doors, Belle and the Texans paused and looked through one of the windows. At first-floor level, a gallery overlooked the rear end of the mess-hall. Split into segments, the gallery resembled a row of boxes at a theatre. Half of the segments had drapes drawn across their fronts.

At that moment, however, Belle felt less interested in the gallery than with the ground floor. In its centre, three long tables formed an open-ended square. All of the guests had been seated on the outer sides of the tables so that they received an uninterrupted view of the men opposite or around them.

'That figures,' Ysabel remarked, when his son commented on the seating arrangements. 'I shouldn't reckon any of them yahoos in there'd trust the others behind their backs.'

'No sir,' agreed the Kid. 'I tell you, that bunch in there makes even Castro's regular crowd look good.'

Damning as the statement might be, Belle felt inclined to concur with it. Gazing along the two side tables, she failed to locate Tollinger or Barmain. What she did see was as villainous, cruel and savage a set of faces as had ever come before her eyes. At the right, she recognised Hoxley's white companion sitting glowering around and eating. The other guests were Mexicans, dressed too garishly and well to suit their table manners, Yaquis and a few Indians from more civilised tribes.

82

Showing none of the impressive dress-style of the Plains Indians from north of the border, the latter sported cast-off Mexican or white men's clothing and had their hair held back by cloth bands instead of concealed beneath war bonnets.

Serving the guests were several Mexican and Indian girls. Each wore a wide-brimmed, low-crowned black hat with a red plume trailing from it and secured by white ribbons tied in a bow under the chin. A waist-long blue tunic, in the style worn by the French infantry, extended to the top of a white apron hanging over a knee-long, flaring blue skirt encircled by two white bands. Decorum was preserved by red trousers with a double blue stripe down the seams. Suspended from the right shoulder on a shining black leather strap, a small wine keg hung at each girl's left hip. Belle recognised the ensemble as the uniform of a *cantinière*, now generally adopted by the French Army.

From the flanks, Belle turned her attention to the centre table. There sat the organisers of the plot and the leaders of the various gangs assembled in the hall. Belle identified Hoxley and Peraro, while Sam Ysabel whispered the names of other prominent personages. *Halcón*, Yaqui war chief; Crespo and Yerno, *bandidos* only slightly less prominent than Peraro; Matt Harvey, a British-born ship's captain who combined slave- and blockade-running with piracy along the Mexican coast. Three more Mexicans sat at the top table, but the Ysabels did not know them.

In the centre of the gang leaders sat two men and a woman. On the woman's right side, the tall Austrian Hussar colonel watched the guests' table manners with thinly concealed, supercilious disdain.

From what Belle could make out, the woman was a beautiful blonde who would equal her in height. Even seated, she conveyed an impression of possessing a richly endowed, voluptuous figure. The full swell of her bosom showed to its best advantage under a tight scarlet jacket. Gold hussar braiding graced its front and the sleeves bore so-called 'Austrian knots' of the same material—resembling the 'chicken guts' insignia of the C.S.A. By peering under the table, Belle discovered that the blonde wore matching, skin-tight breeches with inverted 'Austrian knot' patterning. Hessian boots ended just below each knee, with a 'V' notch at the front. The martial effect presented by the blonde extended to her having a sword of some kind hanging at her side.

To the left of the woman sat a bear of a man. Big, burly, with a hard, blue-chinned face, he wore the uniform of a French general. In his late forties at least, he had the appearance of a harsh martinet, a driver rather than a leader of men. There could be no doubting his identity. He must be General Gautier Caillard, commandant of the fort and potential ruler of a separate kingdom.

'Those jaspers you want aren't in there, Belle,' commented the Kid.

'No,' Belle replied. 'They'd be at Caillard's table if they were.'

'How about it then?' Ysabel inquired.

'Let's go in,' Belle suggested. 'And let's make a real entrance.'

At the double front doors, Ysabel took the right side and the Kid went to the left. With Belle between them, they turned the handles. On Belle's nod, they pushed hard. Creaking hinges drew attention as the doors swung inwards. All around the room conversations died and cold eyes stared suspiciously at the newcomers. Belle strolled in, acting as calm and unconcerned as if she were entering the headquarters of the Confederate Secret Service, with the Ysabels forming barbs to her arrow-point. In that formation they advanced across the room.

'Up on the balcony, Belle,' growled the Kid, hardly moving his lips.

Looking up, Belle saw that some of the gallery's drapes had been drawn open. Soldiers stood lining rifles down at her party, but did not fire. Belle sucked in a breath of exasperation at the sight. Naturally Caillard would take precautions when entertaining that class of visitor. Equally naturally, those precautions would include concealing riflemen on the gallery; from which position they could cover the whole of the mess-hall.

Unfortunately, the realisation had come too late. In all probability, only the fact that one of the new arrivals was a woman caused the soldiers to hold their fire. One thing was certain. There could be no turning back. So, ignoring the rifles and the cold stares of the men at the tables, the trio kept walking.

An explosive curse broke from Hoxley's lips and he made as if to shove back his chair. Thinking better of it, he remained seated. Belle saw the gesture, but her main interest centred on the trio in the middle of the table. Surprise flickered across Caillard's face, but he made no move. Losing its supercilious expression, the Austrian's handsome features showed mingled bafflement and anger. Looking Belle over from head to toe, the blonde tightened her lips into a grim line. She snapped her fingers and the two *cantinières* attending to the top table moved to her side. Big, buxom, they were of European descent, a red-head and a straw-yellow blonde, good looking in a large way, but with hard mouths.

'I left orders that nobody was to be let in without my authority,' the Austrian barked in good English. 'Who gave you permission to enter?'

'We didn't ask for it,' Belle replied, coming to a halt facing the trio across the table. 'We climbed the wall.'

'Climbed the——!' the Austrian spat out. 'How?'

'Threw a rope over one of the cannon and climbed up,' Belle explained.

'That's impossible!' barked the Austrian.

'The rope's still hanging on the cannon,' Belle pointed out. 'And we're here.'

'It seems that your arrangements aren't so perfect after all, Count Otto,' Caillard remarked, and Belle thought that she detected a hint of malicious delight at the Austrian being found wanting in his duties.

'Good evening, General Caillard,' Belle put in, speaking fluent French. 'We heard that you need good fighting men, so we came to offer our services.'

'*Your* services?' the blonde challenged coldly.

'My companions and mine,' Belle confirmed, then indicated the Texans in turn. 'This is Sam Ysabel and his son, *Cabrito*. Or, as we say north of the Rio Grande, the Ysabel Kid.'

A brief rumble of talk rose along the flanking tables as the names were repeated. Even the Yaqui chief and the Mexicans from the more southerly districts of the country showed that they had heard of Sam Ysabel and the Kid. Caillard frowned, the Austrian scowled and muttered, while the blonde stared straight at Belle.

'And who are you?' the blonde demanded.

'My name is Belle Boyd,' the girl answered. 'They call me the Rebel Spy.'

While Belle had figured that her name would be known, she

hardly expected it to produce such an effect as the trio from the fort displayed. The blonde, Caillard and the Austrian exchanged startled glances, then turned their eyes to Belle in a mixture of mistrust and disbelief. Taking their attention from the Ysabels, Hoxley and Peraro studied the girl with increased interest.

'So you are Belle Boyd, the Rebel Spy?' purred the Blonde. 'This *is* a surprise. Surely she must join us at our table, Gautier?'

'Of course she must, Sylvie,' Caillard replied. 'Alice, tell the orderlies to bring chairs for *Mademoiselle* Boyd and her companions.'

'Perhaps the Rebel Spy would like to wash up before she eats?' the blonde suggested. 'I will take her to the washroom if she does.'

Something in the blonde's tone disturbed Belle. Just what, she could not decide. Maybe Sylvie did not care for the idea of the Rebel Spy being around. If her choice of clothing meant anything, the blonde liked to draw attention her way. Having a beautiful girl, already famous and with solid achievements behind her, in the fort would tend to distract notice from Sylvie. However, there was nothing to be gained by openly antagonising the blonde. Not, at least, until Belle knew for sure who Sylvie was. A wedding ring and the manner in which she addressed Caillard suggested that she might be his wife.

'Thank you,' Belle said. 'I would like to wash. Climbing your wall was easy, but it did dirty my hands.'

Already the red-haired *cantinière* and two French private soldiers carried chairs from the rear of the room to Caillard's table. Belle and the Ysabels turned, passing through a barrage of interested stares as they walked around the left side table and towards their seats.

Leaving her chair, Sylvie went to meet Belle. Doing so, the blonde displayed her whole figure. Flaunted might be a better word, for her tunic's tight fit set off the mound of her bust, the slenderness of her waist and the curve of her hips; while the breeches emphasised the play of her magnificent thigh and gluteus muscles to the full. An elegant, yet functional rapier's sheath hung from the slings of her mirror-surfaced black weapon belt. She moved with a sensual attention-drawing grace.

'Come with me, Miss Boyd,' Sylvie requested. 'I am *Madame* Caillard.'

'I'm pleased to meet you,' Belle answered.

'Be seated, gentlemen,' Caillard told the Texans, indicating two of the open-backed chairs. 'Can I introduce you to any of our other guests?'

'We know most of these gents,' Ysabel answered. '*Saludos*, Ramon, Crespo, Yerno, *Halcón*. Howdy there, Matt.'

Mutters came back in reply to the greetings and Caillard announced the names of the other three Mexicans; all of whom the Ysabels had heard mentioned but did not know. Then the general indicated the scowling Austrian.

'This is Colonel Count Otto von Bulow.'

'Howdy, colonel,' Ysabel drawled, sitting down. 'Don't get too riled at your sentries. Me 'n' the boy here, we learned sneaky-moving from Injuns. Whites come easy after that. And Miss Belle steps mighty light on her feet.'

Leaving her husband to deal with the Texans, Sylvie escorted Belle under the gallery and towards one of the doors in the wall separating the mess-hall from the rear of the ground floor. Both the European *cantinières* followed the blonde and Belle, walking soft-footed as they watched every move the girl made. Opening the door, Sylvie led the way into what appeared to be a smaller dining-room. Four more *cantinières*, all Mexicans, were sharing the one table with a fifth woman. Although she was sitting with her back to the door, Belle thought the fifth occupant of the room looked vaguely familiar. As the woman rose and turned, Belle's suspicions became certainties.

Although several years older, the woman equalled Belle's and Sylvie's height. Maybe she lacked their beauty, but she was still good looking and matched the blonde in the matter of a rich, hour-glass figure. Her black hair had been cut as short as Belle's. She wore an open-necked mauve blouse, snug-fitting riding breeches and calf-high boots.

Her name was Eve Coniston and, when she last came into contact with Belle, she had been a member of the United States' Secret Service. Which did not explain why she was in Fort Mendez, or the reason for her obvious perturbation at being confronted by the Rebel Spy.

'You seem to know each other,' Sylvie purred and, unseen by Belle, the red-headed *cantinière* freed her flask to hold it in both hands.

'We do,' Belle agreed. 'She is——'

Shoving her chair aside, Eve hurled herself towards Belle. Instantly the girl clenched her fists and prepared to defend herself. Their last meeting had culminated in a fight and, although Belle had just managed to win it, she knew all too well how tough the Yankee could be. Letting out startled and excited exclamations, the four Mexican *cantinières* sprang to their feet.

Before Eve reached Belle, Alice swung up the cask and brought it down on the girl's head. Although Belle's Stetson took the worst of the impact, she still collapsed stunned. Unable to halt her charge, Eve tripped over Belle's body and sprawled forward. Around lashed the blonde *cantinière*'s left fist, thudding against the base of Eve's skull. Plunging helplessly on, Eve collided with the wall and slid limply to the floor. Looking from Belle to Eve, Sylvie snapped orders to the watching women.

Groaning back to consciousness, Belle raised a hand towards her head. Her eyes regained their focus and she became aware that no sleeve covered her arm. As she raised herself into a sitting position and looked down, she discovered that she was naked to the waist and had also lost the borrowed moccasins. Hearing an exclamation, she turned her head in its direction. Clad in nothing but her riding breeches, Eve was being hauled to her feet by two of the Mexican *cantinières*. Hands gripped Belle by the arms and raised her erect, holding on firmly. Both Belle and Eve struggled, glaring at each other.

'Let me go!' Belle gasped, with Eve repeating the request simultaneously.

'Not yet, little chickens,' Alice sneered, standing by the table on which the two girls' removed clothing had been placed. '*Madame la général* has something better in mind for you.' She looked at the blonde *cantinière*. 'Hasn't she, Marthe?'

At that moment the door behind Belle opened, then closed. Sylvie walked into the girl's view and looked at Eve.

'Who are you?' the blonde demanded.

'Belle Boyd!' Eve replied, in an excellent imitation of a Southern drawl.

'Then who is she?' Sylvie wanted to know, indicating Belle.

'I'm——!' Belle began, only to be silenced by Marthe stepping behind her and reaching forward to clap a hand over her mouth.

'She used to work for me in the War,' Eve explained.

88

'Is that true?' Sylvie asked, turning towards Belle.

Meeting Eve's eyes as the hand left her mouth, Belle thought fast. At that moment she held Eve's life in her hands just as surely as Eve had held Belle's when they had been captured by Mexican *bandidos*. Then Eve had held her tongue, saving Belle from torture, if not death. So Belle knew that she could not denounce Eve as a Yankee spy.

'In reverse,' Belle replied. 'I'm Belle Boyd. She was the madam of a whore-house who used to get information for me.'

'It seems we've one Miss Boyd too many,' Sylvie said and her eyes glinted maliciously. 'Fortunately, the solution is not difficult. We have all heard of how tough the Rebel Spy is; and I had promised my husband that I would provide entertainment for our—guests——' Her lips twisted derisively as she uttered the last word. 'You have presented me with a way of doing it and of solving the problem of your identity.'

'How?' Belle asked, although she and Eve could guess.

'You will be taken into the mess-hall,' Sylvie informed them. 'There you will be released and one of you must make the other confess that she is a liar.'

'And if we refuse?' asked Eve.

'I'll have you both handed over to the—guests——' Sylvie replied. 'On the other hand, the Rebel Spy will be made welcome and the liar will be given to our guests for their pleasure. Take them around and bring them in through the main entrance, *cantinières*. If they make trouble for you, cripple them. I doubt if the men we are entertaining will care if they can't walk.'

CHAPTER TEN

I WISH TO SAVE YOUR LIVES

Although the Kid and his father had noticed Sylvie come from the room into which she had taken Belle, they felt no concern. The blonde had crossed to the table and whispered in her husband's ear, then spoken with the orderlies. Nothing suspicious had happened and she retired from the hall. Plates loaded with thick steaks, potatoes and beans were placed before the Texans. Around the room, talk continued while knives, forks or fingers transferred food to mouths. Neither of the Texans paid any great attention to the orderlies hovering in the background, but waited for Belle to return.

Not until the main doors opened and Sylvie walked in did Ysabel and the Kid begin to wonder why Belle had not rejoined them. Advancing to the centre of the open space before the tables, Sylvie halted and raised her hands. What that did to her garments brought silence to the supper-guests quicker than the gesture's meaning alone would have. Watching the blonde, the Ysabels failed to observe the orderlies drawing Lefauchex revolvers and moving cautiously towards them.

'Senores!' Sylvie called and pointed towards the doors. 'For your entertainment——'

Anything more she might have planned to say was drowned by the rumble of excited comment that arose as the cantinières hustled Belle and Eve into the room. Immediately, before the Kid and his father could do more than start to push back their chairs, the orderlies obeyed orders. The Kid felt the hard muzzle of a revolver ram into his back, but still tensed to continue rising.

'Sit still, gentlemen!' Caillard ordered, leaning forward to look at the Texans.

'Do it, Lon!' Ysabel growled, guessing that his son also had a gun boring against his spine.

For all his anger, the Kid could still think. He knew that to resist would not only be futile, but fatal. With an effort, he controlled his impulse to rise. Sinking back on to his chair, he sat without movement. At that moment, he looked every inch a Comanche. Not just an ordinary member of the Nemenuh, but a Pehnane Dog Soldier ready to go on the rampage. Looking sideways, Ysabel knew his son was sitting at hair-trigger readiness. The big Texan hoped that the Kid would not do anything foolish or rash.

'I wish to save your lives, gentlemen,' Caillard announced still facing the Ysabels. 'If you tried to interfere, my other guests would kill you.'

'These two women both claim to be the Rebel Spy,' Sylvie announced. 'So they will fight to see who tells the truth. The loser is for you.'

Savage curses in the slow-tongued *Pehnane* dialect blasted from the Kid's lips, to be swamped under by the raucous, ebullient comments bouncing among the other guests. With the exception of the Ysabels—and possibly Caillard and von Bulow—every man in the room studied Belle and Eve from two separate angles. First, as contestants in a fight on which money could be bet. Second, in the light of what could be done to the loser. Certainly they all figured that the next few minutes might prove to be sensationally entertaining, with the added attraction of venting their aroused sexual stimulations on one or the other of the white women.

Sufficiently good-looking under normal conditions to interest men, Eve had aged well. Exposed to view and unsupported, the twin hemispheres of her breasts thrust out pink-tipped and firm, sagging only slightly despite their size. Her waist slimmed without artificial aids, while her stomach was flat and gave a hint of its muscular hardness. Weight would favour her and she probably had the advantage of strength, for her biceps showed good development, although not to the point of being unfeminine.

By comparison with Eve, Belle's small-busted, slim-hipped frame seemed almost boyish. Yet her high, slightly uptilted breasts and beautiful features dispelled such notions as soon as they came. There stood a gorgeous woman, even in an age when a more buxom figure was considered the acme of female pulchritude. Taken in collation with Eve, for the forthcoming fight, the men noted the muscular effect of Belle's legs within the skin-tight breeches and the steel-spring firmness of her arms and body. Both told of speed and power. Maybe she was lighter, but the Ysabel family's companion might be a match for the other woman.

Reconciled to the fact that a fight could not be avoided, Belle and Eve allowed the *cantinières* to guide them into the open space between the tables. To resist would be useless and merely drain away energy that might make all the difference between victory and defeat later on. Both of them burned with humiliation and embarrassment as they were turned, still securely held, to face each other. On three sides, lascivious eyes and drooling mouths turned their way. They could guess at the thoughts running through the male onlookers' heads, but fought to quell their revulsion and concentrate on what lay ahead.

Thinking back to the savage brawl on the banks of the Rio Grande, Eve tried to decide which tactics would offer her the best chance of winning. The *cantinières* had removed her rings and her fingernails were too short to make effective weapons. While they had also taken her shoes, the same applied to Belle; for which Eve felt thankful. Even barefooted, the slim Rebel girl's *savate* training could be put to use, but not so effectively.

Mingled with the revulsion she felt, Belle experienced a thrill of anticipation. Despite the publicity accorded to the so-called 'Scout of the Cumberland', Pauline Cushman,* Eve Coniston had been the Union's best and most capable female spy. Belle had always been proud of her professional ability, including her skill in the art of self-defence; and last time she had been brought very close to defeat at Eve's hands. Only the Ysabel family's explosive destruction of the bribe money had given Belle the respite she desperately needed by distracting Eve. Often in the past months, Belle had wondered if she could have beaten Eve without it. So she found herself waiting almost eagerly to try conclusions against the Yankee agent once more, this time without interruptions or distractions. Meeting Eve's gaze, Belle realised that much the same conjecture and eagerness ate at her.

While the *cantinières* led Belle and Eve into position, Sylvie had backed out of the combat area.

'Now!' the blonde snapped in Spanish.

Instantly the women holding the contestants' arms propelled them at each other, releasing them and hurrying away to join Sylvie. An anticipatory hush dropped on the room as the onlookers realised that the spectacle was about to commence.

Although Belle had hoped that they would be turned loose and allowed to make their own way at each other, the *cantinières*' actions did not permit it. Instead, she and Eve rushed together on a collision course. Bare feet slapping on the hard-packed earth floor, unable to stop herself, Belle threw a punch with her right fist. At the same moment, Eve's left hand lashed in Belle's direction. Even as the girl's bony knuckles rammed into Eve's mouth, she felt the woman's fist impact on the side of her cheek. The blows stung, but did no real damage; then

* Some of Pauline Cushman's story is told in 'The Major' episode of *The Texan*.

Belle and Eve came together.

Drawing closer, they continued to use their fists. Belle bored in, her hard fists bombarding Eve's bust and midsection. Oblivious of the pain, Eve hooked powerful punches into the girl's stomach, ribs and breasts. In the space of ten seconds at least a dozen blows landed on each of them, ending any remaining compunctions the recipients might have felt about fighting.

Instinct and a desire to escape from the punishing fists caused them to move nearer to each other. Up rammed Belle's left knee, but Eve had either expected it or was lucky. Twisting to the right, she took the attack on her thigh and threw her left arm around behind Belle's neck. Belle's right arm hooked around Eve's torso, linking hands with her left as it passed down over the woman's shoulder. Locked together in that way, they wrestled with spread-apart legs, each trying to throw the other from her feet.

More by luck than intention, Eve hooked her right leg behind Belle's left knee. Still locked breast to breast, they lost their footing and went to the floor. Belle landed on the bottom, with Eve kneeling astride her and driving a punch into her ribs. Heaving upwards, Belle tipped the woman over only to be turned. As she assumed the lower position again, she locked her legs about Eve's waist. Crossing her ankles, Belle strived for crushing pressure and to prevent Eve drawing far enough away to ram those short jabs into her. Riding and other strenuous exercise had given Belle exceptionally strong leg muscles, so the compression they applied to Eve's kidney region was painful in the extreme. Gasping, spitting incoherent threats, Eve tried to free herself. With Belle's arms enfolding her neck, she could not bring her fists into play.

Twice they rolled over, without any slackening of Belle's holds. Then Eve's face pressed against Belle's left shoulder, mouth opening to close on flesh. A screech broke from Belle's lips as the burning sharpness of the bite stabbed into her. Feeling the girl's arms and legs loosen, Eve placed her hands on the floor and forced upwards. Her torso came free from Belle's arms, but the legs tightened again before she could escape. Flashing across, Belle's left fist caught Eve's nose and blood splashed down on to the girl. Eve's hands flailed in return, slapping Belle's face and rocking her head from side to side. When that failed, Eve stabbed her fingers towards the girl's bust. Just in time Belle caught the woman's wrists and held the clutching hands away from the ultra-sensitive region.

Struggling to her knees, shaking and pulling to free her wrists, Eve managed to regain her feet. Still Belle clung to the scissor-hold, dangling in front of her victim with the tenacity of a bulldog nailing on to a beef-critter's nose. Releasing Eve's wrists, Belle spread her arms on the floor to prevent herself being rolled over and attempted to tilt the other off balance. Digging her fingers into the tops of Belle's thighs, Eve also rammed her knees into the girl's back; but was too close to put any force behind them. So Eve balanced herself on her right leg, curling the left around the girl's slender middle. Just too late Belle saw the danger. Thrusting downwards, Eve raked the heel of her foot over the bottom of the girl's right breast. Gasping, Belle opened her legs. The stamp had hurt but not incapacitated her. Swinging her feet from behind Eve, she propelled them into the woman's belly. If Belle could have put her full strength behind the kick, the fight would have been as good as over. As it was, Eve reeled back a few steps before catching her balance and halting.

Yells of encouragement rose from the onlookers as Eve's body literally soared through the air in her eagerness to get at Belle. The woman landed flush on Belle with a loud smack of reminiscent of a side of beef being flung on to a table. Momentarily, the impact knocked the breath from both of them. Then, as Eve's hands dug into Belle's short hair, the girl hooked her right hand under and between the woman's spread-apart, kneeling legs and heaved her over. Rolling on top, Belle felt Eve's legs close about her. Feeling Belle rear back, Eve raised her rump from the floor and used her legs to throw the girl from her. They started to rise, then flung themselves at each other before reaching higher than their knees.

Squirming, contorting and twisting, the two women thrashed over and over on the floor. Gasps, squeals, harsh screeches broke from them, mingling with the constant barrage of excited comment and suggestions rising on all sides. In addition to the impact of flat palms, knuckles, elbows, knees, feet and foreheads against whatever part of the opponent's body happened to be most readily available, their teeth came into play. However, their short hair, especially when it became slick with sweat, offered a poor gripping surface. On more than one occasion, clutching fingers slipped from their hold and threw their user off balance. When that happened, a surging heave would see the recipient of the abortive hair-pull momentarily in ascendancy.

For five minutes with barely a pause, the wild, savage, rolling mill continued. Excited men stood on their chairs, or climbed on to the tables to obtain a better view. Bets were still being made, on which girl would win, how long the fight would last or even who would gain the next brief advantage. Faces twisted with lust as the sexual stimulation, caused by watching the half-naked bodies twirling and gyrating, grew among the male members of the audience.

'Can't we stop it, *ap'*?' growled the Kid, his respect for Belle causing a revulsion that prevented him from sharing the other men's emotions.

Even as he spoke, the Kid became aware that the revolver was no longer boring into his back. Instead, the orderly who had been covering him now stood at his side. The Lefauchex hung with its barrel pointing at the floor, while the soldier stared with rapt attention at Eve and Belle. Reaching out, the Kid gripped the gun. Such was the orderly's fascination in the fight that he did no more than glare furiously at the Kid for a moment before relinquishing the weapon and returning his gaze to the women.

'Not yet, boy!' Ysabel warned as he saw his son tense. 'We'd have to fight the whole blasted boiling of 'em if we tried to stop it. And likely get Belle killed along of us.'

Bitterly, the Kid relaxed. He knew that his father had called the play correctly. So, no matter how much doing it went against the grain, they must allow the fight to go on to the end. One thing the Kid swore to himself, whether Belle won or lost, nobody in the crowd would lay hands on either woman if he could prevent it. Glancing sideways, the Kid saw that the second orderly was also neglecting his duty. Leaning across the table to improve his view, he had actually laid down his revolver. Going by the rapt manner in which Caillard and von Bulow were following the brawl, they had not noticed the soldiers' abandonment of duty.

Returning his attenion to the space between the tables, the Kid saw that Belle and Eve had managed to rise. Still clinging together, they spun around three times. Relinquishing her hold, Belle rained a battery of punches into Eve's body. Gasps of almost breathless pain whistled through Eve's lips. Desperate to halt the impact of the bony knuckles against her stomach and bust, she threw her right arm around Belle's neck and twisted to the left until she was standing alongside the girl. With a ripping sound, Eve's breeches split down the rear seam as she slammed her right thigh against the back of Belle's left knee and heaved on the girl's right shoulder.

Thrown off balance, Belle fell with enough force to roll her along the floor. Running after her, Eve stamped hard on her side. Croaking with pain, Belle tried to crawl away. Eve swooped down, caught Belle by the hair and the left arm to drag her erect. Another rapid exchange of blows followed before pain goaded Eve to repeat the throw. Again Eve followed Belle, the waist band keeping her breeches up with the aid of the material clinging to her sweat-sodden skin. The older woman showed signs of the exhaustion that welled through her pain-filled body as she halted and raised her foot. Bringing it down, she tottered slightly on her supporting leg. She felt her heel strike, but slide from Belle's perspiration-saturated shoulder and finished up standing astride the girl facing Belle's feet.

Sobbing for breath, Belle sat up. She interlaced her fingers and slammed her linked hands behind Eve's rump. Knocked forward by the attack, Eve stumbled and only remained upright with an effort. By the time she had stopped and turned, Belle had already regained her feet and was advancing. With fingers crooked like talons, Eve lunged to meet the girl. Stepping aside at the last moment, Belle inclined her torso to the left. Drawing up her right leg, she swung it in a *savate* horizontal side-kick. Continuing to move forward, Eve took the top of Belle's instep in the stomach. Breath burst from Eve's tormented lungs and she gripped at the nearest table to prevent herself from falling.

Moaning a little, Eve managed to turn towards Belle. By spreading her feet wide apart, Eve contrived to keep her balance. Weakly she raised her hands in an attempt to ward off her younger assailant. Gathering her flagging reserves of energy, Belle leapt into the air. Pointing her toes downwards, she bent her legs and her knees rammed with sickening force into the bottoms of Eve's breasts. A shriek of agony burst from the woman and she spun away from Belle. Hands clutching at the stricken area, she dropped to her knees by the end of the left side table.

Belle thought that the fight was over. Landing from the leaping double-knee high kick, she clutched at the left hand table for support. With a feeling of horror, she watched Eve dragging herself erect with its aid. Pure guts alone raised the woman upright. She stood with her shoulders slumped in exhaustion, face contorted with suffering and legs buckling like candles left standing close to a fire. Weakly Eve pawed in Belle's direction, trying to hold off the inevitable. Catching Eve's left wrist in both hands, Belle carried it upwards. Pivoting under the trapped arm, she twisted it in a hammerlock behind Eve's back. Then Belle stamped her right foot behind Eve's right knee. Forcing Eve down, Belle thrust the woman's left breast against the corner of the table. Although rounded instead of coming to a point, the corner ground into Eve's already bruised, throbbing breast with savage, numbing, sickening pressure.

'Tell them who I am!' Belle demanded, relaxing her grip slightly.

At first Eve made no reply, other than moaning piteously. Once more Belle forced her against the hard, unyielding wood. A scream of torment burst from Eve and Belle repeated the words.

'Sh-She—B-Boyd!' Eve babbled almost hysterically, her body contorting weakly in pain.

With a swinging heave, Belle dragged Eve from the table and released her. Going down, the Yankee spy turned and lay with arms thrown out wide and legs moving spasmodically. All but overcome by nausea and exhaustion, Belle hobbled across the floor towards the other woman. The girl halted spraddle-legged above the nearly motionless figure. Bending, she sank her fingers into Eve's raw-looking left breast. Blood ran from its nipple tract as Belle dragged Eve upwards. Through the swirling mists that seemed to fill her head, Belle saw that Eve's head lolled back, mouth open and working soundlessly, eyes glassy and unseeing. Slowly the exhausted girl released the breast and Eve's torso slumped back limply to the floor.

Seeing that the fight had ended, an Indian standing on the upper end of the right side table let out a wild whoop. Bounding to the floor on the inside, he ran towards where Belle was standing over the unconscious Eve.

Catapulting to his feet, the Kid sent his chair flying behind him. Out came his bowie knife and his right arm swung upwards. Driving down savagely it propelled the knife through the air. Catching the Indian between the shoulders, the point of the blade spiked home. Throwing up his arms, he blundered by the women and tumbled face down beyond them.

From hurling the knife, the Kid's hand dipped, turned palm out and plucked the big Dragoon Colt from its holster. Still completing his draw, he slapped the left palm on to the table's top and vaulted across. As he landed, he saw a Mexican to the left dropping to the floor and reaching for a gun. Swivelling around, the Kid lined the Dragoon and squeezed its trigger. Black powder swirled as the old revolver roared. Catching the *bandido* in the chest, the ·44 ball flung him backwards. Ignoring the sight of his second victim striking the table, then collapsing, the Kid sprinted to Belle's side.

Almost as quick off the mark as his son, Ysabel rose the moment it became obvious the fight had ended. Catching the orderly by the shoulder, the big Texan swung him from the table and sent him spinning across the room. Then Ysabel snatched up the man's Lefauchex and bounded by the chairs of *Halcón* and Yerno to reach Caillard's side.

'Tell 'em to keep back!' Ysabel commanded, ramming the French revolver's barrel into the general's ribs. 'You're dead if you don't!'

For a moment Caillard just sat and stared, still drooling in the erotic stimulus created by watching the fight. The crash of the Dragoon jolted him back to reality and an understanding of his position. Already more of the less-important guests showed signs of going forward to collect what they regarded as their legitimate spoils. If that happened, Caillard knew the big Texan would carry out his threat. A man of Ysabel's kind did not lightly make such minatory statements.

'Gentlemen!' Caillard yelled. 'Stand away. Tell your men to keep off!'

Realising that the words had been directed at them, the gang leaders put aside any aspirations they might have harboured towards Eve. However, all knew that halting the inflamed passions of their men might take some doing. Feeling Ysabel's acquired revolver gouge harder against his ribs, Caillard took a firmer line of action.

'Guards!' the general roared, turning in his chair to look up at the gallery. 'Shoot down any man, other than the American, who tries to go near the women.'

Discipline ingrained by long, hard years of service drove the riflemen to make ready to obey. More than that, they felt admiration and a wish to prevent abuses to the women who had fought so gamely; especially as they would be unable to share in the benefits of Eve's defeat. Seeing the rifles lining downwards, the men around the tables were not so excited that they would risk going against Caillard's commands.

Nor were the riflemen the only factor to make the guests change their minds. Halting by Belle as she sank to her hands and knees over Eve, the Kid swung slowly around. There was something in his appearance that screamed warnings to the experienced *bandidos* and Yankee hard-cases. Even Harvey's British contingent knew that the menacing young figure in the black clothing spelled sudden, unhesitating death to anybody foolish enough to cross him. To the Indians, the signs stood out with complete clarity. No matter how he might be dressed, there stood one of their own race; a name-warrior who had counted coup twice already and was prepared to add to his score.

'Young man!' Sylvie said loudly in the lull that followed her husband's threat. 'We accept that your friend is the Rebel Spy. No harm will come to her, but the other one pays the penalty.'

Although the words seemed to come from very far away, Belle heard and understood them. Slowly she raised her head, shook it and looked around. Despite all Eve had done to her in the course of the savage brawl, Belle could not bear the thought of the loser's penalty being inflicted on the woman.

'N-No——!' Belle croaked, then her pain-drugged mind worked and produced a possible way of saving Eve. 'I—I—want—her—my—ser-servant.'

'Never!' Sylvie shouted as the Kid translated Belle's request into Spanish. 'I said the guests could have the loser.'

Stepping away from Belle, the Kid bent and plucked his knife from the Indian's back. Then he returned to the girl's side. Holding the bowie knife, with its gory blade, in his left hand and the cocked Dragoon revolver in the right, he once more swung around.

'All right,' the Kid said. 'Whoever wants her can have her. All they have to do is get by me!'

For a few seconds the silence hung heavy and charged with menace. Completely spent by her exertions, Belle subsided limply on to Eve and they both lay without a movement.

'By God, Texas!' Hoxley suddenly bellowed, standing up. 'I'm with you!'

'And me!' Harvey went on, also rising. 'Nobody'll touch that woman if I've anything to do about it.'

Instantly Caillard recognised the danger. With the Anglo-Saxons banding together, the Mexicans and Indians might also combine. If so, his meeting could dissolve in smoke, burning powder and roaring guns. That must be prevented at all costs.

'Come, gentlemen,' Caillard boomed, trying to sound more jovial than he felt. 'We've seen a good fight. Now let us drink to the two gallant ladies' health and leave them be.'

'*Cantinières!*' von Bulow went on, ignoring the furious expression twisting at Sylvie's face. 'Pour wine for all.'

'That's a whole heap better,' drawled Ysabel as the *cantinières* moved to carry out the order. Laying the Lefauchex on the table, he continued, 'Now I want Belle and the other gal getting out of here and their hurts tended to.'

'Of course,' Caillard answered. 'Miss B— The other woman has been given a room upstairs. Who is she, by the way?'

'I dunno,' Ysabel lied, for he had recognised Eve but wanted to wait until he had talked with Belle before denouncing the Yankee spy. 'Best ask her, or Miss Boyd in the morning.'

'I will,' Caillard promised, watching the guests resume their seats and accept the wine. Raising his voice, he ordered the two European *cantinières* to take Belle and Eve upstairs and see that the fort's surgeon treated their injuries. He turned to Ysabel and went on, 'Take your seat, sir.'

'I'll be down again after I've seen Miss Belle's all right,' Ysabel answered and walked around the tables to join the Kid.

CHAPTER ELEVEN

I WANT THE LIVES OF TWO OF YOUR MEN

Groaning a little, Belle Boyd swung her feet from the bed in the small room to which she and Eve had been carried the previous night. Daylight streamed in at its window and, going by the sun's position, she guessed the time to be mid-morning. Every muscle of her naked body seemed stiff and protested at being used, while numerous bruises and a few bites sent stabs of pain through her. Her top lip and nose felt as if they were swollen to twice their normal size. Looking down, she studied the discoloured patches caused by Eve's attacks or contact with the floor. A shudder ran through the girl. That had been one hell of a fight and she hoped that she might never have to go through another like it.

With that in mind, Belle looked across the room. Vaguely she seemed to remember that Eve had been brought upstairs with her. Everything after Belle's collapse had been hazy. She recalled that the *cantinières* had bathed her and Eve, then the fort's surgeon had attended to their injuries. After that, Belle had been put into the reasonably comfortable bed and Eve laid on a mattress in the corner of the room.

Forcing herself to rise, Belle crossed and looked down at Eve. Drawing aside the blanket, Belle saw that Eve's naked body carried a mottling of bruising in excess to her own. The swollen, inflamed breasts rose and fell so steadily that Belle felt sure Eve must be under heavy sedation. She would be in too great pain to sleep with such evident ease and soundness.

Hearing the door open, Belle covered Eve and turned indignantly. Marthe and one of the Mexican *cantinières* entered, carrying Belle's pack-saddle trunks. Admiration and not a little awe showed on the women's faces as they found the girl on her feet.

'Your men have brought your baggage, *mademoiselle*,' Marthe announced in French. 'And General Caillard says that we are to attend you.'

'Thank you,' Belle answered in the same language. 'I would like a bath, a meal and to dress. Then I would like an interview with the General if he can spare the time to see me.'

'That one still sleeps, I see,' Marthe commented, setting her burden on the bed. 'The surgeon gave her laudanum to ease the pain.'

'I bet she needed it,' the Mexican girl put in. Clearly she understood sufficient French to follow the conversation. 'You beat her good, *senorita*.'

'*Madame la général* has a *douche*-bathe in her quarters, *mademoiselle*,' Marthe said, glaring her companion to silence. 'She's gone riding with the Austrian. You can use it before she

101

comes back.'

Something in the way Marthe spoke of Sylvie Caillard hinted to Belle that the blonde might be unpopular with the *cantinières*. If Marthe had been alone in her dislike, she would never have used the mocking name *'madame la général'* with the Mexican girl present. It was a point worth remembering, for Belle felt sure that Sylvie would be an implacable enemy.

'Cabrito and the little old one are outside, *senorita,'* the Mexican said. 'They ask if you are all right.'

'Tell them I'm fine,' Belle replied and wished that she was speaking the truth.

Opening one of her trunks, Belle produced a robe. By the time she had put it on, the message had been delivered and the passage cleared for her to go unobserved to Sylvie's room. Accompanied there by Marthe, Belle took pleasure in using *madame la général*'s private shower-bath, knowing that Sylvie would be furious if she learned of it. The cold water refreshed Belle and, for a time at least, soothed away aches in her body. On returning to her room, she found Eve was still unconscious. Although Belle had hoped to learn what had brought the woman to Fort Mendez, posing as herself, before meeting Caillard, she knew that would be impossible. So she made her preparations for the forthcoming interview.

From her second trunk, she took the cadet-grey uniform of a Confederate States' cavalry colonel. She had been awarded the rank for her services to the South and to invest her with authority when dealing with military personnel. Slipping into clean under-clothes and a blouse, she put on socks and the tight-legged, yellow-striped breeches, then drew shining Hessian boots into place. Wincing a little, she donned her tunic. Copied from a style made popular by a Lieutenant Mark Counter*—with whom she and the Kid would become well-acquainted in the future†—it did not blindly conform with the *Manual of Dress regulations*. Double-breasted, it had the formal two rows of seven buttons on its front, the triple one-eighth of an inch gold braid 'chicken guts' insignia of a field officer on the sleeves and three five-pointed gold stars, denoting a full colonel, graced its stand-up collar. However, the

---

* Mark Counter's history is told in the author's floating outfit stories.

† The Kid's first meeting with Mark is in *The Ysabel Kid* and Belle's is in *The Bad Bunch*.

skirt 'extending halfway between hip and knee' had not been included. Instead of wearing a black silk cravat, she knotted a tight-rolled green scarf of the same material about her throat and let its ends dangle free.

An official weapon belt came next, being buckled about her waist just a touch loosely to avoid pressure on her bruised sides. From the bottom of her trunk, she lifted a magnificent rapier. Specially built to suit her, it rode in a sheath designed to be carried on the slings of her belt. At the sight of the sword, Marthe gave a low exclamation. The sound confirmed Belle's suspicions that Sylvie would not approve of her dressing in uniform and wearing a weapon. That only hardened Belle's resolve, for she meant her appearance to be an open challenge to the blonde.

The trunk next yielded a correctly made officer's peaked forage cap. Although that particular style of head-gear had never been noted for beauty, Belle gave it an air of style and attractiveness as she perched it jauntily on her head.

Having been to the kitchen while Belle was bathing, the Mexican *cantinière* returned bearing a large, loaded tray. Belle started to make a good breakfast and Alice, the second of the French *cantinières*, arrived to say that General Caillard wished to interview her as soon as convenient. Alice almost duplicated Marthe's reaction on discovering how Belle was attired.

'Tell the general, with my compliments, that I'll join him in half an hour,' Belle requested. 'And ask my companions if they will meet me here, please.'

'*Oui, mademoiselle,*' Alice answered and left the room.

By the time Belle had eaten her breakfast, Marthe appeared to say that the Ysabel family, Rache and Cactus had arrived. After the *cantinières* had left with the tray, Belle collected a pad of the forged fifty-dollar bills from her trunk and slipped it into her tunic's breast pocket. Giving the motionless Eve a glance, the girl left her room. The waiting men grinned appreciatively as they saw the way she was dressed, for she made an attractive picture.

'I'm all right, I assure you,' Belle replied in answer to her escort's inquiries about her health. 'Rache, will you and Cactus stay on guard here, please?'

'Sure will, Miss Belle,' Rache agreed without hesitation and Cactus nodded his assent. 'Reckon the Frogs'll try to rob you?'

'I doubt it, although they might want to search my baggage,' the girl answered. 'It's the woman I fought——'

'If she comes round making fuss——!' Rache bristled.

'Way she looked after the fight,' grinned the Kid, 'I'd say that's not *real* likely.'

'She's in there,' Belle went on, indicating the door. 'I don't want her harming, or *questioning*. You can let the post surgeon see her, but nobody else.'

'We'll see to it,' promised Cactus. 'What if she wants to leave?'

'As Lon would say, that's not real likely. But if she tries, tell her that I want her to stay until I can talk to her.'

'She'll be here when you want her,' Rache promised.

Leaving the two old-timers sitting outside her door, Belle accompanied the Kid and his father. Due to her condition the previous night, Belle had seen nothing of her surroundings. So she let the Ysabels guide her along the passage and down a flight of stairs to a small hall lined with doors. On the way, she learned what had happened after she was carried from the mess-hall.

'Wasn't much,' Ysabel told her. 'Caillard spouted some about taking over down this ways, and how them's helped him'd do right well out of it. Then he set to getting 'em all drunk and it got sort of forgot about.'

'What's that Yan——' the Kid began.

'Her name's Eve—Caterham,' Belle interrupted quickly. 'She ran a hog-ranch—I think you Texans call it—and used to pick up information for Cousin Rose and me.'

'Why's she here?' the Kid insisted.

'We haven't discussed it,' Belle admitted with a wry smile.

At which point the Texans became aware of how stiffly she was walking and noticed that her face showed occasional hints of the pain she must still feel.

'You sure you're all right, Miss Belle?' Ysabel asked worriedly.

'I was until you started to say "Miss" again,' she replied, then nodded to where a French sergeant-major was coming from the door which bore Caillard's name. 'That's where we're going.'

Showing his surprise at the sight of Belle's uniform, the sergeant-major listened to her request that she and the Ysabels be admitted to the general's presence. Returning to the room he had just left, he emerged after a moment and told them to go in. The Kid and his father saw the girl set her face into a stolid mask, square her shoulders and march by the warrant officer. Following, they found Caillard seated at his desk, with von Bulow standing to his right. Across the room, Sylvie turned from the window. A low hiss broke from the blonde's lips as she stared at Belle then glanced down at her own uniform. Without as much as a flicker of her eyes in Sylvie's direction, Belle marched smartly to the desk. Coming to a halt, the girl threw Caillard a brisk salute that cost her plenty in sharp twinges of protest from stiff, sore muscles.

'Miss Boyd——' Caillard started to say, returning her salute before he could stop himself.

'Colonel Boyd of the Confederate States' Army's Secret Service, general,' Belle corrected and took a sheet of paper from the pouch on the left of her belt. 'My credentials, sir.'

Accepting and examining the paper, Caillard found it to be a document identifying Belle. It also gave a description of her, along with the information that she held the rank of colonel with seniority from January the First, 1862. It was signed by General Robert E. Lee.

'My pleasure, Colonel Boyd,' Caillard said, rising and returning the paper. 'You are over your exertions, I hope?'

'I am, sir,' the girl answered.

'Will you have a chair, colonel?' von Bulow offered, fetching one and ignoring Sylvie's disapproving sniff at the repeated use of Belle's rank.

'Thank you,' Belle answered, throwing a dazzling smile at the Austrian and noticing that it drew a glare of hatred from the blonde.

As Belle sat down, the Ysabels ranged themselves on either side of her and stood with thumbs hooked into their gunbelts.

'May I ask why you came here, Colonel Boyd?' Caillard said and Belle sensed that he used the word to increase his wife's antipathy towards her.

'As I told you last night,' Belle replied, 'we, Sam Ysabel, *Cabrito*, the other two Texans and I, have heard what you plan to do. So we came to offer our services. I think that you will find they are worth accepting.'

'In what way?' Sylvie demanded, stalking across the room to sit on the edge of the desk between Belle and von Bulow.

'I think I proved my identity last night,' Belle said, touching her discoloured left cheek with a finger-tip. 'But if there are still doubts, I will answer them with bare hands, a revolver or a sword.' She paused, looking straight at Sylvie. For a moment their eyes locked, then the blonde swung her head away. Smiling, Belle went on, 'You will have my services as a spy, general; or in any other active capacity you require. In addition, the Ysabels, Rache and Cactus will join you. I think last night they gave you convincing proof of their worth.'

Although Belle could only vaguely remember the Kid's intervention, the fact that Eve Coniston was still alive and unmolested told her that pressure had been brought on Caillard to rescind his wife's stipulations about the fight.

Caillard let out a grunt that might have expressed agreement. When Belle had thrown the challenge at his wife, he had sat back as if expecting her to accept it. Going by his scowl, he had been disappointed by Sylvie's lack of response.

'Besides that, general,' Belle continued. 'I can offer an even greater contribution to your cause.'

'What might that be?' Sylvie hissed.

'Money,' Belle answered, taking out the wad of forged bills and tossing them on to the desk's top before Caillard. 'Or what will pass for it.'

Interest, and not a little greed, flickered across the general's face as he took up and thumbed over the sheaf of what looked like genuine fifty-dollar bills. However, Sylvie let out a depreciating snort.

'That's not much,' the blonde said.

'They're forgeries,' Belle explained. '*Undetectable* forgeries. I can put into your hands, general, the plates, inks and sufficient paper to print between five hundred and seven hundred and fifty thousand dollars. One could buy a lot of arms and ammunition with them.'

'You have them with you?' Caillard breathed.

'You didn't expect me to say "yes", general,' Belle flattered. 'I can have them brought here, after we have come to terms.'

'Terms?' Sylvie repeated.

'We're not doing this for charity,' Belle pointed out. 'Tell the general what you want, Sam.'

'A big *hacienda*,' Ysabel drawled. 'And the right to run anything I want over the Rio Grande without the revenuers bothering me. That'll do me 'n' the boy. Rache 'n' Cactus'll settle for top fighting wages and a share of any loot that's going.'

'And what is your price, Colonel Boyd?' von Bulow inquired.

'I want the lives of two of your men,' Belle announced quietly.

Coming to her feet, Sylvie stared at the girl. Caillard and von Bulow stiffened and gave Belle even greater attention. There was no doubt about her sincerity.

Sucking in a deep breath, Caillard asked, 'Which two, M—Colonel Boyd?'

'I know them as Tollinger and Barmain.'

So did the Caillards and von Bulow, going by their expressions. In fact, learning the identities of her proposed victims appeared to have handed the trio a greater shock than had hearing the price of Belle's enlistment to their cause. Sylvie seemed to be on the point of delivering a vehement refusal. Looking at her, von Bulow gave a slight, but definite, shake of his head. With a thinly veiled show of reluctance, the blonde kept her mouth closed. Belle had seen the by-play and wondered what lay behind it.

'They aren't here at the moment,' Caillard claimed. 'Would I be permitted to ask why you want to kill them?'

'They murdered my parents,' Belle replied.

'I see,' the general grunted. 'This is not a matter I can decide immediately, Miss—Colonel Boyd. However, I will think on it and give you a decision within the hour.'

'Who was the woman who pretended to be you?' Sylvie put in.

'As I told you last night, a brothel-keeper who did some work for us in the War,' Belle answered. 'Her name is Eve Caterham. Probably she hoped to make money from you, general, by saying she was me. I will find out when she recovers and it will amuse me to have her as my servant.'

'She's yours,' Caillard stated.

'How soon can you hand over the forging plates?' von Bulow continued.

'I will make arrangements for them to be collected,' Belle promised. '*After* I have settled accounts with Tollinger and Barmain.'

'If you will wait in your room, colonel,' Caillard said, standing up but not offering to return the money, 'I'll send for you when I've reached a decision.'

'Very well,' Belle answered, rising and saluting, actions

which stabbed agony through her.

Turning on her heels, the girl marched from the room without a backwards glance. Her whole being expressed the belief that her offer would be readily and gratefully accepted. Exchanging admiring grins, the Kid and his father followed her.

'Whooee!' breathed the Kid as they left the office and walked across the hall. 'You couldn't've shook them any more if you'd walked up and slapped that blonde gal in the face with a sock-full of bull-droppings.'

'I may do it yet,' Belle replied. 'I don't like her and she doesn't like me.'

'Thing being, will Caillard say "yes" or "no",' Ysabel drawled. 'They sure looked uneasy when they heard what you're after, Belle.'

'I know,' Belle agreed. 'Did you see anything of the men from the *Posada del Infernales* last night, Sam?'

'Sure. Hoxley, their boss, backed our play to keep them *pelados* offen the Yankee gal. Had a talk with him. Seems like Tollinger hired him and the others up North after their regiment'd disbanded.'

With the War ended, the Union was wasting no time in reducing its Army's size. Many men, unsettled by four years of fighting, would have no desire to return home and might leap at the offer of employment by a revolutionary general.

'Why did he help you?' Belle wanted to know. 'Did he know Eve?'

'Not's he let on,' Ysabel admitted. 'Allowed he wouldn't see no white woman raped by greasers 'n' Injuns. Could be he told the truth.'

'Did he say why he jumped us at the *posada*?' Belle asked.

'Laid the blame for it on the jasper Lon killed,' Ysabel replied. 'We was getting along so all-fired well I didn't push it any further.'

'You did the right thing,' Belle stated. 'Let's wait and see what Caillard decides.'

'Why don't you go rest in your room until he sends for you, Belle?' the Kid suggested. 'Pappy 'n' me'll nose 'round a mite.'

'You don't need to impress us,' Ysabel went on. 'We know you're one tough lil gal. I'll bet Caillard and the Austrian figure it now.'

'That's what I want them to think,' Belle smiled. 'I'll do

what you say.'

Leaving the Ysabels, she went upstairs and found the two old-timers still seated outside her room. Cactus told her that nobody had tried to enter, then asked how she had got on. Quickly Belle went over what had happened downstairs and received her listeners' unqualified approbation and support.

'Count on us to back your play, Miss Belle,' Rache declared. 'Now you go 'n' rest up a spell. We'll stick around here and make sure you don't get bothered.'

'Thanks,' Belle answered gratefully. 'Have you heard anything from Eve?'

'Who?' Rache grunted.

'The woman I fought last night.'

'She ain't showed, nor made no noise,' Cactus declared. 'Who air she?'

'Danged if I see why you're doing it for her,' Rache stated, after Belle had told them Eve's true identity and the story which they should give if anybody else inquired.

'I not sure myself,' Belle admitted wryly and entered her room.

Closing the door, Belle noticed that Eve's blankets no longer had an occupant. More significant, the holster of the girl's gunbelt was empty. Even as the two facts struck home, Belle heard a soft gasp of pain from the left side of the door and the barrel of her Dance jabbed into her ribs.

CHAPTER TWELVE

THEY'D KNOW WAYS TO MAKE YOU TALK

'Put it down, Coniston,' Belle said gently, standing still. 'As soon as you pull the trigger, my friends will burst in and you'll be dead. If I'd wanted that, I could have let it happen last night.'

Looking around the room while she spoke, Belle could see no sign of Eve having searched her trunks. Advancing two strides, the girl turned slowly without the revolver driving a bullet into her. Wearing a dark blue blouse and black skirt, bare-footed and dishevelled, her face showing something of the torment she was enduring, Eve kept the Dance's barrel pointing in Belle's direction. Despite the hammer being in the fully-cocked position, Belle extended her left hand.

Dropping her eyes to the hand, Eve lifted them again to the girl's face. A mixture of admiration crept into the haggard lines of the woman's features. Aware of her own physical condition, she guessed that Belle must be suffering almost as much from the after-effects of the fight. Yet the girl stood, balancing lightly on the balls of her feet, hiding her feelings.

No fool, Eve realised that she owed her life to the Rebel Spy. If Belle, or her companions, had not intervened after the fight, Eve would be dead now—or wishing that she was. Those same companions, at least one of whom stood outside the door, would certainly shoot her, if nothing worse, if she pulled the trigger.

'I could most likely take it,' Belle remarked, reading the woman's indecision correctly. 'But I'd rather you gave it back without that.'

'How much do you want to say that I'm you, Boyd?' Eve demanded, without lowering the revolver. 'I could pay a high price if you'd do it.'

'Even if I trusted you Yankee spies,' Belle replied, 'why should I do it?'

Eve did not answer for a few seconds. Frowning, she looked at the girl as well as she could through the blackened, puffy slits of her eyes. Then she turned the Dance's muzzle, lowered its hammer and reversed it to lay the butt on Belle's offered palm. Releasing the weapon as Belle took hold, Eve hobbled painfully across the room and flopped on to the bed.

'All right, Boyd,' Eve said. 'Let's talk straight to each other.'

'You first,' Belle requested, walking over and returning the Dance to its holster. Drawing up a chair, she sat astride it with the gunbelt hanging before her over its back.

'Why?' Eve asked.

'Last night should have answered *that*,' Belle stated.

'I've more to lose than you have,' Eve pointed out. 'By now they're satisfied that you're the Rebel Spy.' She threw a calculating glance at the girl. 'And I suppose they know who I am.'

'They do,' Belle agreed and, ignoring Eve's exclamation of anger, continued, 'If they believe me, you are Eve Caterham, the madam of a brothel, and used to supply us with information—I thought I'd better give you a character you could play.'

'Thank you, I don't think!' Eve sniffed, but her smile fought to return.

'The Yankees ran you out and you came down here hoping, by pretending to be me, to get hired as a spy.'

'That's what you told Caillard?'

'All but the past part. I couldn't be expected to know that much, could I?'

'What happens now?'

'I'm keeping you here as my maid,' Belle informed Eve with a smile. 'I *hope* you enjoy being in my employment.'

'I'll try to give satisfaction, ma'am,' Eve promised, attempting to sound humble. 'Why *did* you come, Boyd?'

'You'd better get into the habit of calling me "Miss Boyd",' Belle warned.

'Yes, *Miss* Boyd. But why——?'

'With the War over, I'm unemployed. So I've come with the Texans to enlist in General Caillard's revolutionary army. But I want to hear your side first. Talk, Coniston, I can always tell Caillard the truth and let *him* learn why you're here.'

'In which case, you'd have to explain why you lied to him in the first place, *Miss* Boyd.'

'All right,' Belle countered. 'I'll have Big Sam and the Kid take you out of the fort. They'd know ways to make you talk.'

Remembering all she had heard about the Ysabel family, Eve could not hold back a slight shiver.

'They'd do it if you told them,' the woman admitted. 'Lord! I wish I could have worked with men who had that kind of loyalty. Listen, B—Miss Boyd, you're mistaken about Caillard.'

'In what way?'

'His family have always been stout Bonapartists. And he's not a renegade planning to set up his own little kingdom.'

'Go on.'

'He's still loyal to Maximilian.'

'You're saying this revolution business is only a scheme to weaken Juarez by drawing away men who are disaffected with his régime?'

'That's part of it. But I've been sent to learn if there's a deeper motive.'

'Couldn't Major Allen trust Tollinger and Barmain to find

out?' Belle asked, watching carefully for any sign of emotion. to her question.

'So that's why you're here, Boyd!' Eve hissed. 'I'd heard rumours that you'd sworn to kill them. Are they coming here?'

'You mean you didn't know?' Belle said cynically.

'I knew somebody would come, but not who it would be,' Eve replied. 'It could be you've saved my life again, B—Miss Boyd. And if you want them so badly, you'll be willing to work along with me.'

'Keep talking,' Belle ordered.

'What do you know about the assassination of President Lincoln?' Eve asked, settling herself comfortably on the bed.

'Only what I read in the newspapers. And the fact that our organisation didn't send Booth to do it.'

'*We* never thought you did, although we naturally encouraged the newspapers to make the accusation. You'd have done the same.'

'Probably,' Belle grunted.

'Booth and his accomplices were Southern fanatics,' Eve elaborated. 'But they weren't acting in the interests of the Confederate States when they murdered Lincoln. Your high brass knew that he was too wise and tolerant to impose the conditions and penalties demanded by the Northern soft-shells.'

'So?'

'So I think that some of the soft-shells arranged for Booth to be persuaded to kill him and even left the way open for the attempt to be carried out.'

'There either had to be bad management, or help, for Booth to get through,' Belle admitted. 'But——'

'But you don't see what it has to do with Caillard,' Eve finished for her. 'Maybe nothing. Except that things haven't gone the soft-shells' way since the end of the War. General Grant and other moderates are gaining power. Men who are willing to forget the War and let the South rebuild its economy, even if that means pardoning Confederate leaders.'

'I've heard about it,' Belle said. 'They've refused to put our leaders on trial even.'

'Which doesn't suit the soft-shells as you can imagine,' Eve replied. 'General Handiman's taken over the Secret Service, now that Allen Pinkerton's retired. He—and I—believe that some of the soft-shells are involved in a plot to either discredit or overthrow the moderates.'

'Tollinger and Barmain, you mean?'

'They're evidently in it, along with General Smethurst and his crowd. You know of him?'

'He ran your prisoner-of-war camps,' Belle answered. 'Fortunately, our paths never crossed.'*

'Your Captain Fog pulled some of that crowd's fangs when he killed Horace Trumpeter in Little Rock,'† Eve told Belle. 'It's a pity that he didn't get more of them.'

Belle had heard of the events leading up to General Trumpeter's death at the hands of Dusty Fog,‡ then a captain in the Texas Light Cavalry and soon to gain legendary status as a trail-driving, gun-fighting cowhand. She had been on two missions with him§ and in the near future he would share with Mark Counter in changing the course of the Ysabel Kid's life.

'From what we can learn, but can't prove, Smethurst's crowd are conspiring with the French to place our Congress in an embarrassing situation——' Eve went on when the girl did not speak.

'*Your* Congress,' Belle corrected. 'I've sworn no oath of allegiance——'

'Damn it, Boyd!' Eve snapped, trying to rise but subsiding with a gasp and a wince of pain. 'If they succeed, they might get into office and you know what *that* will mean to the South.'

'I do,' Belle confirmed, lips tightening at the thought. 'What's the game?'

'From what I've learned, it's for Maximilian to be able to claim that the United States sent agents to seduce members of the French Army from their duty. Naturally, Congress will refute the claim. Then the French will be in a position to demand that we show proof of our good will by giving active support against the *Juaristas*, which will mean open war with Mexico. If we refuse, the French will declare war on us. And that could easily bring Britain or other European countries in as France's allies.'

'It might at that,' Belle agreed, having followed Eve's reasoning and matched it with her own knowledge of foreign policies. 'Some of the European powers would jump at an

---

* They eventually crossed, as is told in *The Hooded Riders*.
† Told in *Kill Dusty Fog!*
‡ Dusty Fog's history is told in the author's floating outfit stories.
§ Told in *The Colt and the Sabre* and *The Rebel Spy*.

excuse to gain a foothold in America. But what will the soft-shells gain if that happens?'

'The voters up north are sickened with war,' Eve explained. 'They'd not stand for a government that let them be drawn into another one. Naturally the soft-shells will preach peace, lay the blame on Grant and the moderates for the war and they'll probably be in a position to end it. If that happens, they'll be in control. And I don't need to tell *you* what that will mean to white folks in the South.'

'I can imagine,' Belle admitted quietly. 'God! There's nothing so bigoted, intolerant or out-and-out vicious than a liberal-intellectual with anybody who won't conform blindly to his beliefs.'

'Things haven't come to a boil ye——'

The sound of voices being raised in the passage outside Belle's door caused Eve to stop speaking.

'Get out of my way, damn you!' Sylvie Caillard was shouting, her normally sultry voice strident with anger. 'My husband will have you whipped for this impertinence.'

If the threat carried any weight, Cactus' even drawl showed no sign of it as he answered, speaking louder than necessary so that Belle would be able to hear.

'Colonel Boyd's resting, ma'am. I'll just sort. of knock and ask if she'll see you-all.'

'Go and see what the noise is about, Caterham!' Belle barked, loud enough for her words to reach the passage. 'Move yourself, you idle whore, or I'll kick some life into you.'

'You're enjoying this, aren't you?' Eve whispered as she rose and Belle went to lie on the bed.

Limping across to the door, Eve opened it. Outside, Cactus and Rache confronted Sylvie. The blonde's face was almost purple with fury at their disrespectful behaviour. Although Cactus looked over his shoulder, neither he nor Rache offered to move. Instead, the taller Texan went through the pretence of announcing the woman's desire to speak with Colonel Boyd. Upholding the deception, Eve relayed the message. On receiving Belle's permission for Madame Caillard to enter, the men stepped aside. Storming between Cactus and Rache, Sylvie brushed by Eve and stamped indignantly into the room.

'My dear Madame Caillard,' Belle purred, rising languidly. 'I apologise for my men keeping you waiting. Caterham, a chair for Madame. Or may I call you "Sylvie"?'

Watching Sylvie while closing the door and fetching the chair, Eve took malicious pleasure at the blonde's obvious annoyance.

'My husband has reached a decision,' Sylvie gritted, ignoring the chair and Belle's blatantly insincere welcome. 'He accepts your offer.'

'On my terms?' Belle asked.

'He promises that he won't intervene between you and—the men,' Sylvie replied and scowled at Eve. 'Has this bitch told you why she came here?'

'Tell Madame Caillard what you've just told me, Caterham!' Belle commanded. 'Spit it out, or you'll get more of what I gave you last night.'

Looking convincingly frightened and cowed, Eve repeated the story Belle had suggested. Belle watched Sylvie all the time and felt convinced that the blonde accepted the story. However, it raised another point and Sylvie turned suspicious eyes to the girl.

'Why didn't you let the men have her last night?'

'Because I wanted to know what her game was,' Belle answered. 'And I decided it would be amusing as well as useful to have her for my maid. Does the general want to see me?'

'Later today,' Sylvie replied and her disapproval was obvious. 'He said you might wish to rest first.'

'I don't, but he's probably got arrangements to make,' Belle said and raised her right leg. 'Pull my boots off, Caterham. You can clean them and my belt; and be sure you do a good job of them.'

'Yes'm,' Eve replied humbly.

'My husband also feels that you should make arrangements for us to obtain the forging plates even if things go wrong between you and the men,' Sylvie declared coldly, watching Eve straddle Belle's legs and draw off the boot. 'It is not an unreasonable request.'

'Probably not,' Belle replied. 'Anyway, I'll tell *him* what I decide when we next meet.'

Giving a sniff of indignation at the curt dismissal, Sylvie turned and left the room. Smiling a little, Eve tugged off Belle's other boot. After the blonde had left, Rache looked in.

'Everything all right, Miss Belle?' he inquired, favouring Eve with a malevolent scowl.

'Yes,' Belle replied. 'We're hired. Will one of you stay on guard while the other fetches Sam and Lon, please?'

'I'll send me assistant,' Rache promised and withdrew, closing the door.

'What was all that about?' Eve inquired. 'Between you and Caillard, I mean.'

'I offered to replace Tollinger and Barmain,' Belle explained. 'It looks as if they've taken me up on it.'

'Why?' Eve demanded.

'Probably they feel that I, the Ysabels and the other two Texans have more to offer,' Belle answered and described the concessions she had made in return for a chance to settle accounts with her enemies.

Eve still did not look satisfied. Frowning a little as she sat on the bed, she said, 'But why would Caillard do it? I could understand him wanting money, but not forged bills.'

'Unless he's planning to double-cross the French,' Belle suggested.

'How do you mean?' Eve asked.

'Suppose he's considering setting up his own private kingdom after all?' Belle answered. 'He might have decided that it beats being a general in the French army. Especially seeing that he has so much going for him already.'

'His family are noted for their Bonapartist sympathies,' Eve reminded her.

'Perhaps he feels the time's come for a change,' Belle offered. 'Or Sylvie may have persuaded him to do it. She looks the kind who wouldn't be slow to see the advantages of their situation. They've an all but impregnable fort, sufficient men to take and hold a large section of land. And now I'm offering them the means of arming and hiring more men. It could have made Caillard decide to become a renegade.'

'I suppose it could,' Eve agreed, then looked quizzically at the girl. 'What do you intend to do?'

'Play along with them. Learn all I can. Then, when the time comes, I'll make my move.'

'What move?'

'Settle accounts with Tollinger and Barmain.'

'And after you've done it?' Eve demanded.

'I'll face up to *that* when the time comes,' Belle stated. 'Until then, we'll carry on as we've started. If you try to double-cross me, Coniston, I'll make you wish we'd let the men have you.'

'All right,' Eve replied, looking straight into Belle's eyes. 'And to set things straight between us, Boyd, if I find that you're endangering the safety of the United States, I'll do my damnedest to stop you. Even if I have to kill you to do it.'

CHAPTER THIRTEEN

THROW THE SWORD AWAY, BOYD

'*Senorita* Colonel,' the pretty little Mexican *cantinière* said, intercepting Belle as she approached the rear entrance of the mess-hall to join the other guests for supper. '*Cabrito* wants you to meet him on the east wall. He says it is very important.'

Ten days had gone by since Belle's eventful arrival at Fort Mendez. During that time, she and the Texans had been treated as honoured guests. They had been permitted to walk about the fort, with no restrictions being placed on their movements. In return for Caillard's promise that he would allow Belle to deal with Tollinger and Barmain without interference, she had written details of how to obtain the forging equipment. Tearing the paper in half, she had given one portion to the general and retained the other until after the affair was concluded. Nothing the girl had seen or heard after that had supplied proof that Eve was correct about Caillard's motives. Nor could Belle honestly claim that he had openly declared himself as a revolutionary and renegade.

On the morning after the fight, von Bulow had ordered that all the cannon's barrels be withdrawn so that they no longer protruded beyond the embrasures. Inspecting the defences later, in the company of the Austrian, Belle had noticed that each piece was not only kept loaded, but had its friction-primer, with the firing-lanyard attached, fitted in position. Pyramids of cannon balls were heaped on the ground below each cannon's mounting. She had been unable to determine whether this was standard procedure, or a precaution taken to ensure the garrison could meet an attack in the event of Caillard defecting.

Throughout the period, while the girl recovered from her injuries and exertions, there had been meetings with the *bandido* leaders which she and the Texans also attended. Caillard had talked broadly about his plans, offered substantial shares in the loot gained during his conquests and hinted at arms and ammunition being forthcoming; but he had made no attempt to implement activity in his proposed revolution. As food and drink continued to flow freely, the various delegations raised no objections. A few Mexican intellectuals arrived and departed, their interviews with Caillard being conducted in secret.

Cultivating Hoxley's men, Belle had soon reached the conclusion that they knew nothing of their employers' plans. Hoxley expressed open admiration for her and stuck to his story that Kansas and *Cicatriz* alone had been responsible for the attack on the Kid at the *Posada del Infernales*. Not that Belle had expected him to admit otherwise and she did not press the matter.

Turning Sylvie's unpopularity to her advantage, Belle had won over most of the garrison, from *cantinières* to hard-bitten veterans. Showing none of *madame la général's* arrogant, bad-tempered snobbery, Belle had captivated the junior officers. Once the stiffness had left her muscles, she had made regular visits to the *salle des armes* where she further stole Sylvie's thunder by demonstrating her skill at fencing. Although good herself, the blonde had repeatedly refused to cross swords with the girl and lost face by doing so. Nothing Belle had learned led her to believe that the garrison officers, except possibly von Bulow, had access to Caillard's schemes. Also mingling on good terms with the soldiers, the Texans had proved equally unsuccessful in their findings.

Hoping to provoke Sylvie into indiscretion, Belle had openly flirted with von Bulow. While the blonde did not hide her annoyance, she had failed to react as Belle had hoped she would. Discussing the matter with Eve—who continued to play the dispirited, beaten and sullen maid—and the Texans, Belle had concluded that Caillard might be waiting for Tollinger and Barmain to arrive before reaching a decision on which line to take.

The only other item of note had been the interest Caillard and the various gang leaders had shown in the money that

Belle had been under orders to deliver to General Klatwitter. The more Belle and her companions insisted that it had been destroyed, the greater had been the disbelief displayed by their questioners. So far, however, there had been no more than hints. Nobody was foolish enough to try to forcibly extract the location of the 'buried' wealth.

Knowing the *cantinière* to be a very close friend of the Kid's, Belle did not question her about the message. Thanking her, the girl went out of the main building. With a new moon rising, the night was not too dark and Belle's eyes soon became accustomed to it. Left hand resting lightly on the hilt of her sheathed rapier, she strode in the direction of the east wall. Studying it, she saw an indistinct shape standing alongside one of the cannon and looking through the embrasure. Further along the terreplein, a second figure she assumed to be a sentry was also looking out of the fort. Belle wondered why the Kid had sent for her. Perhaps he had seen something of interest and, wishing to keep it under observation, had asked her to come instead of joining her in the mess-hall.

Going up the steps, Belle walked along the terreplein. Beyond the cannon, the dark shape continued to look through the embrasure. Footsteps echoed hollowly as the second figure came towards her. Then, as she drew level with the cannon, the girl realised that the footfalls lacked the solid thud of heavy infantry boots and the man making them walked with a mincing gait that had not been induced by parade-ground drilling. Peering more carefully, she became aware that the approaching man neither wore a uniform nor carried a rifle.

'Lon?' Belle hissed, reaching with her right hand towards the rapier's hilt and wishing that she had strapped on her revolver.

'Guess again, Boyd,' answered a mocking voice that sounded nothing like the Ysabel Kid's pleasant tenor drawl.

With a growing sense of shock, Belle watched the man by the cannon turn her way. Up that close, she could see that he wore a derby hat, town suit and a collarless white shirt. In his right hand, a small revolver was aimed directly at her stomach. Recognition came instantly and the girl tensed ready to leap to the attack.

'*Tollinger!*' Belle hissed, and the one word throbbed with pent-up hatred.

Although the second man on the eastern terreplein started

to run in her direction, Belle knew that she could expect no help from that source. Given so much of a clue, she had identified the stocky shape of Barmain during a swift glance flickered away from Tollinger.

'We've got her, Alfie,' Barmain enthused in the high-pitched, affected tone which had always set Belle's teeth on edge.

'We've got her, Georgie,' Tollinger agreed, then his voice hardened. 'Throw the sword away, Boyd.'

All to well Tollinger and Barmain remembered the way Belle had handled a rapier during the attack on her home. Two of their drunken rabble had gone down, spitted by the flashing blade in the hands of the slim, beautiful girl. So Tollinger wanted to remove such a deadly weapon from her reach.

At first Belle considered refusing, sliding the blade from its sheath and staking all in a sudden lunge. Cold logic came in time to prevent her from making the attempt. Tollinger was standing much too far away for the girl to hope to reach him and prevent the revolver firing. Barmain had come to a halt at an equally safe distance. So she knew that she must obey, playing for a respite in the hope that something might happen to give her a chance of survival.

Perhaps somebody might come from the casemate beneath their feet; although that was a slender hope, the eastern wall being given over to storerooms. Maybe one of the garrison or guests would walk by. Possibly the sentries on the north or south walls might become suspicious and come to investigate. Belle knew that refusal to comply with the demand meant death; and while life remained, there was the hope of a rescue. So she slowly lowered her hands, unbuckled her belt and let it fall at her feet.

'Kick it over the edge,' Tollinger ordered.

'I see that you've still got the same wife, *Alfie*,' Belle sneered as she sent the belt and its burden sliding over the edge of the terreplein.

An angry snarl rumbled from Barmain's lips, for he deeply resented the girl's mocking reference to his homosexual relationship with Tollinger. However, it did not produce the effect for which it had been made. Clenching his fists, Barmain continued to stand beyond her reach.

'You've made a lot of trouble for us, Boyd,' Tollinger gritted.

'And caused some of our friends to be killed,' Barmain went on.

'You'll soon find fresh bed-mates, Georgie,' Belle answered, but once again she failed to produce the required response. 'What now, Tollinger?'

'We heard that you want to kill us,' Tollinger replied. 'So we're going to protect ourselves by killing you first.'

'With a gun?' Belle scoffed. 'The shot will bring the guard out, and the rest of the garrison. I wouldn't give much for your chances of survival when my friends find out you've shot me.'

'She promised us that they'll be taken care of,' Barmain spat out, darting a nervous glance towards the main building.

'But can you trust her?' Belle countered, guessing at which "she" the soft-shell meant and playing on his suspicious nature. 'There are more than the Texans I can call my friends, including a number of the garrison. *She* might not arrive quickly enough to stop some of them blowing your stupid Yankee heads off.'

'She could be right, Alfie!' Barmain wavered. 'We'll have to kill her quietly and get away from the wall before anybody knows it's happened.'

'You're right, Georgie,' Tollinger admitted and slipped the revolver into his waist-band. Dipping his hand into the jacket's pocket, he produced and started to open a long-bladed folding knife.

'If you're going to kill me, *Georgie*, I'll turn around,' Belle mocked at him. 'That's the only way you'd have the guts to kill even a woman.' Exhibiting an attitude of complete disdain, she began to pivot towards the edge of the terreplein. 'Come on, you rotten. cowardly swish. I'll make it easy for you!'

'*Swish!*' Barmain screeched, knowing it to be the derogatory term for a homosexual. 'I'll——'

Words failed the soft-shell. At last the goad of Belle's icy contempt and mockery of his effeminate nature had pricked home. Spluttering off into an incoherent gurgle, he lunged at the girl and his hands drove almost woman-like in the direction of her hair. In doing so, Barmain played straight into her hands.

From a slow start, Belle spun swiftly around on her left foot. Tilting her torso away from Barmain's reaching fingers, she raised and swung her right leg. With a power increased by the momentum of her turn, she propelled the toe of her boot into her attacker's side. A croak of pain burst from Barmain as the kick landed. Staggering, he gyrated and reached the edge of the terreplein while going backwards. Feeling himself falling, he let out a shriek. Down he went, his spine colliding with the uppermost of a pile of cannon-balls. Bone crackled, sounding hideously clear in the silence that followed as agony stilled Barmain's voice. Sliding down the pyramid, his body contorted spasmodically in torment for a few seconds. Then it became limp and still.

With his knife's blade open, Tollinger froze momentarily at the sight of his friend tumbling backwards from the terreplein. Letting out a snarl that sounded a good half fear, he lunged in the girl's direction. From kicking Barmain, Belle brought her right foot down. Using it to pivot, on, she faced Tollinger, took aim and whipped up her left leg. Flying accurately, her boot struck beneath the man's thrusting knife-hand. Tollinger yelped as his arm snapped upwards, fingers opened and the knife flew from them to pass over the parapet.

Bringing down her left foot, Belle slashed a savage punch. It caught the side of Tollinger's jaw and caused him to retreat. For all that, he recovered fast. As the girl followed him up, he brought himself to a halt and whirled a backhand blow to her head that knocked her sprawling. The wall prevented Belle from going down. Hanging against it with her head spinning, she saw Tollinger looming towards her. Before she could regain her equilibrium, he had reached her and his fingers closed about her neck.

Spitting curses, his face distorted with rage and fright, Tollinger tightened his hold. Choked by the grip, Belle grabbed at his wrists and kicked savagely. Although unable to put all her strength into the efforts, the impact of her boots upon Tollinger's shins still hurt. Almost gibbering with the pain, he dragged the girl forward and slammed her against the wall. Belle's moan was strangled into a faint hiss by the clutching hands. Again and again she kicked, raining the attacks against the sensitive area of his shins. Incoherent mutters rose from him and he swung the girl around. Trying to keep his legs clear of her driving boots, he attempted to force her across the terreplein.

Desperately Belle spiked the heels of her boots into the hard-packed earth surface of the terreplein. Such was the strength in her slender frame that she forced Tollinger to halt in the centre of the level area. Mindful of the girl's savage assault on his shins, he concentrated most of his attention on keeping his legs away from her feet. Maintaining his hold on the girl's neck, he opened his feet and edged them to the rear.

Belle did not kick straight away. Like a flash she caught his left wrist from above with her right hand. Equally swiftly, she passed her left hand over his right arm to join its mate on the trapped limb. Already the need for air, she exerted all her will to continuing with what she hoped would prove an escape from the danger of strangulation. With the hold gained, she arched her torso away from him almost like a contortionist performing a back-bend. Not until then did she kick. Up drove her right foot, its toe passing between his separated thighs in the direction of his crotch. Although the speed with which she moved precluded the full use of her power, the kick still landed hard enough for her purposes. Tollinger did not release her throat, but she felt his fingers slacken. That was all the girl asked for.

Gratefully dragging air into her throbbing lungs, she twisted her body sharply to the left. Retaining her hold on the wrist, she thrust downwards with her left elbow and used its leverage against his right arm to wrench her neck free. Continuing to turn until her back was towards him, she carried and held the trapped limb under her right armpit. Doing so caused Tollinger to bend forward and she leaned to the rear so that her weight rested on his left shoulder.

Respiration restored, Belle went ahead with her escape. Gathering herself, she threw her legs into the air and rolled backwards over Tollinger's shoulders. On landing, giving him no chance to straighten up, she turned his arm free and brought up her bent right leg. Smashing into the centre of his face, Belle's knee lifted the soft-shell erect. Blood gushed from his nostrils as he reeled away from her. Turning from the force of the attack, he plunged alongside the cannon towards the embrasure.

Never had the simple, involuntary process of breathing felt so pleasant to Belle as during the seconds immediately following her escape from Tollinger's fingers. Stumbling slightly, she caught her balance. About to follow the reeling man and render him incapable of further efforts, she saw that he was in the process of averting the danger.

Throwing his left arm across the barrel of the cannon, he clutched at it. Feet teetering on the lip of the embrasure, he managed to halt his advance and turn inwards. Doing so brought his chest around until it rested against the muzzle of the piece. Pain and terror tore at him. Being what he was, his self-centred ego recognised only one thing. He gave no thought to the threat to his mission, or avenging his friend. All he wanted to do was escape from the girl. Yet he knew that he must also try to kill her. Even should he flee from the fort unscathed, he would never know a secure minute as long as Belle Boyd lived. With that in mind, still clinging to and leaning against the cannon's barrel, he grabbed at his revolver and the fingers of his free hand closed about its butt.

Even as she sprang forward, Belle knew that she could not get to Tollinger before he completed his draw. So she did not try. Instead she grabbed for and tugged at the cannon's lanyard. Dragged across the priming compound, the rough surface of the iron striker ignited the highly combustible substance. Flame flashed from the friction-primer, through the vent hole and detonated the ten pounds of black powder that formed the main charge. Turning into a vast mass of gas, the charge thrust a solid lead ball, seven inches in diameter and weighing 42·7 pounds, along the ten foot nine inch long smoothbore tube. Emerging, it struck Tollinger—who stood well within the 1,955 yards maximum range—and blasted him, revolver still not lined on the girl, from in front of the muzzle.

Avoiding the piece's wicked recoil slam, Belle let the lanyard fall from her fingers. The murder of her parents had been at least partially avenged. Maybe fully, for she had heard and seen nothing of Barmain after he fell from the wall. Bracing herself on the breech of the cannon, Belle fought down the nausea that threatened to engulf her.

Voices rose, shouting questions or comments, as the thunderous roar of the cannon shattered the air. Pouring out of their room by the main gate, the off-duty members of the guard rushed towards the source of the disturbance. The sentries on the north and south walls converged on the double, racing along the terreplein with rifles at the ready. A stream of men and women burst out of the mess hall. Soldiers quit their quarters in the casemate's rooms.

Already suspicious at Belle's non-arrival in the hall, the four Texans led the rush. Racing across the barrack square ahead of the others, the Kid looked to where Belle was walking slowly down the terreplein stairs.

'What the hell?' growled the youngster, staring from the girl to the shape by the pyramid of cannon-balls. 'How—Why——?'

'Somebody lied to me,' Belle replied and looked to where a soldier was shining a lantern's light on Barmain. In French she continued, 'Is he dead?'

Kneeling by the still figure, the sergeant of the guard answered, '*Oui, mon colonel.* I think his back is broken.' He used the formal mode of address without any hint of sarcasm, speaking as politely as if addressing one of his own officers. 'Did you——?'

'*Oui,*' Belle agreed. 'He and his friend tried to kill me.'

'That's one of 'em, huh?' growled the Kid. Although unable to follow the conversation between Belle and the sergeant, he guessed what had happened. Reaching for his knife, he went on, 'Is the other son-of-a-bitch around?'

'No,' Belle replied quietly. 'I shot him.'

Vociferous chatter rose in three languages as Belle's words were relayed or translated through the crowd. A bellow brought the torrent of French exclamations to a ragged halt as Caillard and von Bulow made their belated appearance. Watching the two senior officers force a way through the crowd, Belle noticed that Sylvie was not with them. That came as a surprise, for the girl would have expected the blonde to come and discover the result of the fight. Everything pointed to Sylvie having organised the meeting, yet she seemed to be displaying a surprising lack of interest in its outcome.

'What happened, Colonel Boyd?' Caillard demanded, watching one of the guard gather up and return the girl's weapon belt to her.

'Somebody laid a trap for me,' Belle answered as she buckled on the belt. 'It didn't work.'

'A trap!' Caillard repeated and his shock appeared genuine enough. Throwing a look at von Bulow, who maintained an air of icy, calm, detached innocence, the general seemed to be on the verge of making further comment. With an almost visible struggle, he refrained from doing so. Instead he glared around and barked in French, 'Back to your quarters, all of you. Sergeant of the guard, clear this area and return your men to their duties. Doctor, see if that one is dead and remove him.

Is the other here, Colonel Boyd?'

'No,' the girl replied. 'He was standing in front of the cannon when I fired it.'

'Then we needn't worry about him,' Caillard said indifferently.

'Gentlemen,' von Bulow remarked in Spanish, the inevitable sneer in his voice as he made use of the honorific mode of address to the guests. 'If you return to the main hall, food and *drink* will be waiting.'

Discipline drove away the French soldiers, except for the surgeon's party. After making certain that Barmain was dead, he asked Belle if she required his professional services. On being told that she did not, he told his assistants to carry the body away. Guessing that there would be few, if any, further developments to interest them, the guests headed back to their interrupted feeding and drinking in the mess-hall. Only the four Texans remained. Ignoring the scowls directed at them by Caillard and von Bulow, they formed a grim-faced, uncompromising half circle behind the slender girl.

'Did you know those two bastards'd got here, general?' Ysabel growled.

'No!' Caillard barked and, again, Belle believed that he spoke the truth. 'Did you, Otto?'

'They arrived just before we closed the gates at sunset, *mon général*,' von Bulow replied. 'I had them quartered in one of the casemate rooms, wishing to avoid an incident until after I had spoken to you about them. But I couldn't get you alone to speak privately.'

Ysabel could not argue with that point. At no time during the evening had Caillard been separated from his guests. Clearly the various *bandido* leaders were becoming restive and wanted some definite action. None of them being willing to trust the others, they had swarmed around the general all evening. If von Bulow was sensitive to atmosphere, he might have hesitated to ask Caillard to leave the men for a private conversation.

About to take the matter further, Belle saw Sylvie hurrying across the parade ground. The girl's lips tightened and her right hand rested on the rapier's hilt as she prepared to challenge the blonde with being implicated in the trap. Coming up to the group, Sylvie gave Belle no chance of doing so.

'Thank God you're safe, M—Colonel Boyd!' the blonde

ejaculated.

Instantly Belle's suspicions increased. Until that moment, Sylvie had steadfastly refused to address her by her military rank. The lantern held by von Bulow did not give sufficient illumination for Belle to see Sylvie's face clearly. It almost seemed that the blonde was standing away from the light.

'Didn't you think I would be?' Belle countered coldly.

'I didn't know what to think. When I heard that the two men had reached the fort and you didn't come to dinner, I became suspicious. So I went to your room to make sure all was well with you. That Caterham woman was quarrelling with one of the *cantinières* about how much she should pay for the girl luring you out here to Tollinger and Barmain.'

'Where are they now?' Belle asked.

'Caterham knifed the girl before I could get into the room and stop her,' Sylvie answered. 'I had to run her through with my sword when she tried to kill me. There was no other way of doing it. Caterham is dead.'

CHAPTER FOURTEEN

YOU'LL PAY THE PRICE OF FAILURE

'What do we do now, Belle?' asked the Ysabel Kid as the Texans and the girl returned to the fort after Eve Coniston's funeral.

Although the Rebel Spy had exhibited an attitude of indifference, or at most annoyance at being deprived of a maid, her companions sensed the hidden grief that filled her. Through the days following their latest meeting, Belle had formed a growing admiration and respect for the Yankee agent. Suffering far worse than the girl from the after-effects of the fight, Eve had never once forgotten to play her part. Every day she had served Belle's breakfast in bed, washed and pressed the girl's clothes. When in Sylvie's presence, Belle had treated Eve like dirt and piled indignities on her in the hope that the blonde would make advances to a possible ally. Working to the same end, Eve had heaped vituperation on her 'employer's' head in Belle's absence. In the end, that had worked to Sylvie's advantage.

Going to Caillard's office the previous night, Belle's party had attended the inquiry that the general had insisted in holding. Brought from his post, the guard commander had explained why his sentries had failed to prevent the fight. The dead *cantinière* had delivered a message, claiming it to have originated from Caillard, ordering him to remove the man from the east wall and keep the guards on the north and south terrepleins away from that area. According to the story he had been given, two of the garrison's officers intended to fight a duel and wanted privacy.

Duelling was still permitted in the French Army, but it had been restricted to the *au premier sang* fight in which the drawing of first blood, no matter how little, brought it to an end. That ruling did not meet the approval of the hot-blooded young officers. If two of them quarrelled, they often settled the matter far more permanently. To avoid wrecking the winner's career, the loser's injuries would be written off as an accident. In the interests of diplomacy, such duels were invariably carried out away from possible witnesses. So the sergeant of the guard had seen nothing suspicious in his instructions. Even the *cantinière* delivering them could be classed as understandable. She would be less likely to be suspected of complicity should the duel have fatal results.

Bitterly Belle had accepted that she could not prove anything against Sylvie. Eve's threats had been recalled by the blonde, establishing a motive for her aiding the two soft-shells. It had been suggested by von Bulow that 'Caterham' could have been a traitor to the South, or hired by Tollinger and Barmain after the end of the War, to account for how she had known the soft-shells. An examination of the women's bodies yielded nothing except proof of Sylvie's thoroughness. The *cantinière* had been knifed in the back by a weapon still gripped in Eve's hand. Pain had so distorted Eve's face that it had wiped away the emotions she had felt an instant before the rapier pierced her heart. Every point that had occurred to Belle had also been expected, countered or explained away by the blonde. So, wisely, Belle had forced herself to make the pretence of accepting Eve's guilt.

Excusing herself from joining the other guests, Belle had

retired to her room at the end of the inquiry. The bodies had already been removed and their blood washed away. Left alone, behind the locked door, Belle had sobbed long and bitterly; the first time for many a year. She had spent a very restless night. In addition to the emotional strain of having finally avenged her parents, she had felt a deep and gnawing sense of loss over Eve's death.

Despite the fact that they had twice fought each other with primitive savagery, Belle and Eve had become good friends. So much so that Eve had suggested that Belle should forget the War, swear the oath of allegiance to the Union and apply for acceptance as a member of the Yankee Secret Service. Having lost a number of its best operatives, who had retired to join a private detective force formed by Allen Pinkerton, Eve's organisation could use a woman of Belle's ability.

Knowing the precarious nature of her assignment, Eve had insisted on making preparations for the worst. She had told Belle the name of her superior in Brownsville and given the girl a password that would ensure her admission to him. More than that, Eve had told the Ysabels of her offer to Belle. To her surprise, when discussing the matter, Belle found that the Texans were agreeable to her accepting it. As Sam Ysabel had said, conditions in Mexico would remain too chaotic for profitable smuggling until either the *Juaristas* or the French gained full control. So he and the Kid would go back to mustanging, catching and breaking wild horses, for a living while awaiting more settled times below the border. Belle had suspected that her male companions were relieved to know that she could find gainful, and well-paid, employment.

All that ran through Belle's head as she walked at the Kid's side and tried to decide on an answer to his question.

'You're not going to let her get away with it, are you?' the Kid demanded impatiently.

'Not if I can help it,' Belle stated and her voice held a grim, purposeful note the listening men recognised. They had last heard it when she spoke of her determination to find her parents' murderers. 'I'm going to make Sylvie Caillard wish that she'd never been born.'

'Looks like they've decided to stay loyal to Maximilian, Miss Belle,' Cactus remarked. 'They'd never've tried to set you up that-aways if they didn't.'

'Unless I'm sadly mistaken, that was Sylvie's idea,' Belle

objected. 'I don't think Caillard, or von Bulow, knew anything about it.'

'She'd want that forged money if they aim to set up on their own,' Ysabel pointed out. 'And with you dead, they'd not get the other half of that letter.'

'That's why she killed Eve and the *cantinière*,' Belle answered. 'She knows that you know where it is, Sam. With me dead, and the people you'd blame for it killed, you would hand my half over to Caillard. It's no use to you without his part. Probably they'd have let you kill Tollinger and Barmain. Then they'd go ahead with setting up their own private kingdom.'

'You mean they'd hope I'd hand it over,' Ysabel corrected and the girl nodded her agreement. 'How're you fixing to play it now, Belle?'

'Let's go and have a showdown with Caillard,' Belle suggested. 'If you're willing to gamble on me being right, that is.'

'You've been right often enough for us to take a chance,' drawled the Kid and the others rumbled concurrence.

'If I'm wrong this time,' Belle warned, 'we're all likely to get shot.'

'How about if you've guessed right?' asked Ysabel.'

'Not *if*,' amended Rache. '*When!*'

'I stands corrected,' Ysabel grinned. 'What happens *when* you're right?'

'We'll have a choice,' Belle replied. 'Either we side him all the way, or we do what Eve wanted and save the United States from a whole mess of bad trouble.'

'Eve warn't a bad gal,' Rache commented. 'And I don't cotton to foreigners.'

'And I never did take to the notion of owning no big *hacienda*,' Ysabel went on. 'Man has to work a whole heap too hard running one.'

On that note, the discussion ended. Passing through the gates of the fort, they went to the main building. In the small hall at the rear, they found the sergeant major and asked if they could see the general. With the minimum of delay, Belle and the Texans were ushered into the office. Flanked by his wife and von Bulow, Caillard sat behind his desk. Interest showed on the two men's faces as they stood up. Sylvie remained seated and scowled at Belle while attempting to avoid meeting the girl's eyes.

'I was just going to send for you, Colonel Boyd,' Caillard declared. 'Would you care to be seated?'

'That depends, general,' Belle answered.

'On what?' Caillard asked, aware of the grim, businesslike note in her voice.

'On whether you intend to strike out on your own, or follow the plan your superiors made with Tollinger and Barmain's crowd.'

Startled exclamations broke from the Caillards and von Bulow. Thrusting back her chair, Sylvie started to rise. Her husband's right hand snapped downwards to pull open the desk's drawer. Reaching across his torso, von Bulow began to thumb open the flap of his holster. None of the hostile gestures reached fulfilment. Knowing Belle, the Texans had been ready for her to spark off a grandstand play. At the end of her speech, their hands were already resting on gun-butts. Steel rasped on leather, followed by the clicking of hammers riding back to full cock and four revolvers lined across the desk. Although a Lefauchex revolver lay in the drawer, Caillard kept his hand away from it. Freezing, von Bulow allowed his Army Colt to remain in its holster. Once more Belle locked eyes with Sylvie and the girl's sword hand tapped the rapier's hilt. Sinking back on to her chair, the blonde turned her head away.

'Put up your guns, boys,' Belle said. 'I'm sure the general and Count von Bulow are willing to listen to reason.'

'We are,' Caillard confirmed, watching the Texans' weapons return to leather. He sat down and closed the drawer of the desk. 'Would you explain your comment, Colonel Boyd?'

'Certainly,' Belle obliged. 'Either you will make your defection a fact, or you'll pay the price of failure.'

'In a way?' Sylvie spat.

'Before General Smethurst can replace Tollinger and Barmain, the Yankee Secret Service might learn what's going on,' Belle replied. 'And even if they don't, your high command aren't going to take kindly to learning they were killed before they could be of any use.'

'You know a lot that you shouldn't!' Sylvie hissed.

'Blame Tollinger and Barmain for that,' Belle said calmly. 'They just couldn't resist boasting to me about what they hoped to do.'

While Belle and his wife were talking, Caillard sat scowling at the top of his desk. Inadvertently, the girl had struck a nerve with her reference to his paying the price of failure. During the Napoleonic Wars, his grandfather had paid such a price. A colonel of *Gendarmerie*, and one of the Emperor's personal *aides-de-camp*, Jean-Baptiste Caillard had allowed two British naval officers to escape from his custody.* Doing so had caused Bonaparte great inconvenience and humiliation in the eyes of the world. In the tyrannical First Empire, there could be only one penalty for such an act. Colonel Caillard had been court martialled, found guilty and shot.

If General Caillard knew anything about his rivals in the French Army, the failure of his grandfather would be remembered when he was called to answer for the ruin of a carefully laid plot to remove the menace of United States intervention. He would be lucky to avoid his grandfather's fate. That was another factor to sway him along the path that had already been suggested by his wife and von Bulow.

'We made an agreement, Colonel Boyd,' Caillard announced. 'As Tollinger and Barmain are dead, I have kept my part of it.'

'And I'll keep mine,' Belle replied, accepting the seat brought to her by the Kid.

Greed flickered on Caillard's face as the girl took out and spread her half of the letter on the desk before him. Producing his section, he married the two portions. Then his head jerked up sharply.

'The forging plates are in New Orleans!'

'Of course,' Belle answered calmly.

'Then how do we get them?' Sylvie spat out.

'Matt Harvey has a fast boat,' the girl pointed out. 'On receipt of this letter, and a pass-word, Madam Lucienne will hand over the whole consignment.'

'And, of course, Harvey will bring it back here,' Sylvie mocked.

'He won't know what he's carrying,' Belle replied. 'Cactus, Colonel von Bulow, or another of your trusted men will accompany him, general.' She flashed a look at Caillard. 'There are men in the garrison you can trust?'

'There are some,' Caillard admitted. 'I can send one with your man and Harvey, but collecting the plates will take time.'

'I agree,' Belle said. 'How long will we have, do you think,

* Told in C. S. Forester's *Flying Colours*.

before your superiors become suspicious?'

'Two weeks, not more than three,' Caillard guessed and von Bulow gave a confirmatory nod.

'Good,' Belle enthused. 'Before then, the gang leaders can have their men assembled. It will give us time to think up some reason to send away all but the trustworthy members of the garrison and make ready to repel any attack Maximilian launches.'

'The gang leaders will need something more substantial than promises in the way of payment before they bring their men,' von Bulow warned. 'And not in French or Mexican money. That is why we hoped to get the forging equipment quickly.'

'Would they accept Yankee gold?' asked Belle.

'Of cour——' the Austrian began, then he stared at the girl. 'You mean the money that was to be paid to Klatwitter?'

'I do,' Belle confirmed. 'It could be collected and brought here in—eight days, would you say, Sam?'

'Eight days easy enough, Colonel,' agreed Ysabel. 'Fact being, me 'n' the boy could get it in less.'

Once again Belle felt admiration at the way the big Texan had not only followed her lead, but improved upon it.

Clearly Ysabel's suggestion did not meet with the Caillards' or von Bulow's approval; not that he had expected it to. Watching the general, Belle could see him struggling to decide upon the best line of action. With fifty thousand dollars in gold at stake—the actual amount had been much less, but legend had increased the quantity—Caillard felt disinclined to trust any of his subordinates. Certainly he could not contemplate allowing the Texans to make the collection unescorted. Nor did he regard his wife or von Bulow as suitable candidates. Given that much money, either or both of them would probably slip across the border and disappear into the United States.

'Why not let Count Otto take a small escort and Sam Ysabel or the Kid to guide him?' Belle suggested, knowing that Caillard would not agree.

'Or you could come with me, general,' Ysabel went on. 'Colonel Belle, Lon 'n' Rache'll stay on here and help get the fort ready for a fight. Lon knows Mexicans and Injuns better'n most, he'll likely be able to tell you which way them gang leaders're really thinking.'

'Eight days, you say?' Caillard breathed, looking calculating.

'Less with good hosses 'n' riders,' Ysabel corrected. 'A cavalryman like you could maybe cut it down to six if the others don't slow us.'

'Your presence would encourage greater speed, Gautier,' Sylvie remarked. 'Otto and I can take care of things here, with *Colonel* Boyd's help. There is one thing puzzling me, though.'

'And that is?' Belle challenged, guessing the words were directed at her.

'You have killed Tollinger and Barmain,' Sylvie explained. 'So why are you willing to pour your own money into this venture?'

'For very good reasons,' Belle answered. 'I wanted my revenge, but I knew that getting it wouldn't be the end. Smethurst and his crowd won't forget that I've ruined their plans. Nor can I use that money north of the border; it was originally looted from the Yankees. So I may as well invest it. In return, I want a good share of the profits. Sufficient money to set me up comfortably for life in Europe. I developed a taste for living there during the War.'

Going by their reaction to the words, Belle had presented motives that her audience could appreciate. She saw the Caillards and von Bulow exchange glances and knowing, satisfied nods. Apparently the reasons for her participation in the defection had been debated and she had now cleared up any lingering doubts on the matter. Most likely Sylvie still did not approve of Belle's inclusion in the plan, but she was willing to accept it—at least, until such time as Belle's usefulness came to an end.

'I will see Captain Harvey straight away,' Caillard decided and looked at Cactus. 'My sergeant major will accompany you, Mr. Jones.'

'Count on me to take care of him, general,' the old-timer promised soberly. 'How soon can we go?'

'If Harvey is agreeable, you should be able to leave this afternoon,' Caillard replied. 'Yes, Mr. Ysabel?'

'Might be best if you got them gang leaders off afore you send any of your soldiers away, general,' Ysabel suggested. 'Was I you, I'd not have them knowing how many soldiers you'd got left.'

'That is wise,' Caillard praised. 'Sylvie, my dear, we have men—and a lady—with intelligence as well as courage here.'

'Yes,' Sylvie sniffed shortly.

'How about the Mexican intellectuals, general?' Belle inquired. 'Will they be a significant factor in our revolution?'

'I doubt it,' Caillard snorted. 'Like all their kind, they don't mind the meek inheriting the earth; as long as somebody else takes all the risks and does all the fighting for them to get it. They'll be of no use to us.'

'That leaves Hoxley and the others Tollinger hired,' von Bulow remarked.

'Don't worry about them,' Belle said. 'They're in this for money and will fight for us as long as they are paid for it.'

'Then all we have to do is collect the money, and we are ready to win ourselves an empire,' Caillard enthused.

'I can hardly wait to make a start,' Belle assured him, with such sincerity that she might have been speaking the truth.

CHAPTER FIFTEEN

ARE YOU LOYAL TO FRANCE?

Sitting on her bed, nursing her Dance under the tunic draped across her knees, Belle looked at the two French *cantinières*. It would soon be evening on the day after the plot had been put into motion. Everything now depended on a question she was about to render. If she received the correct answer, her departure from Fort Mendez should become considerably easier.

Once the decision to defect had been taken, Caillard had lost no time in setting it into motion. Called into the office for a private consultation, Matt Harvey had agreed to transport Cactus and a small party of French soldiers to New Orleans, supply them with civilian clothing *en route*, then return them and their unspecified cargo to the fort.

The increase in the sergeant major's escort had been Belle's idea, ostensibly to guard against treachery on Harvey's part. In reality, she wanted to cause a further drain on Caillard's limited manpower. Pressed for information before they had interviewed Harvey, the general had admitted that he could only rely upon a small portion of the garrison. Hard, arrogant, and a martinet, Caillard possessed none of the qualities needed to inspire loyalty or devotion among his subordinates. Those he could count on to support his defection were the malcontents in search of easy promotion or wealth and others disenchanted with the latest Bonaparte to establish himself as ruler in France. They were not the material for grand conquest, but that had been a point in Belle's favour when she insisted that they should prevent the gang leaders discovering Caillard's exact fighting strength.

If presented with the opportunity, Cactus would slip away from Harvey and the sergeant major before boarding the ship. Should he be unable to do so, he would travel with them to New Orleans. Once a very capable member of the Confederate States' Secret Service, Madam Lucienne—returned to her successful dress shop at the end of the War—ought to possess the means to help him escape and organise his return to Texas.

With Harvey's party dispatched, Belle had supervised the other stages of the plan. Gathering the other gang leaders, Caillard had announced that he meant to start his revolution in two weeks' time. Questioned about the reason for the delay, he had explained that he needed a respite to obtain firearms from north of the border. However, he had promised every leader an advance payment depending on the size of the contingent he brought back. Having the full force of the garrison to enforce his decisions, he received a few arguments to the arrangement. Hoxley and his men had been sent to Brownsville so that they could spread the word along the border that gun-fighters could find employment at Fort Mendez. By evening, all the guests had taken their departure. At Belle's insistence, the Kid had left the fort and made a wide circle around it to ensure that none of the gangs remained in the vicinity.

Soon after breakfast the next morning, bugles blew assembly and the cry of 'Aux armes!' was bellowed. Parading ready for any eventuality, the garrison had been addressed by their general. According to Caillard, a message had just been received from the French forces holding San Luis Potosi saying that they were facing the attack of a large Juarista army. Reinforcements must be rushed there immediately.

The major assigned to command of the relief column had barely been able to hide his surprise at learning that neither

Caillard nor von Bulow would accompany it. Also he had looked dubious as he considered the wisdom of leaving the fort so poorly manned. Caillard was keeping only fifty men, and not the pick of the garrison. However, discipline had prevailed and the major had held back the objections he undoubtedly felt. So much the better, Belle had thought, he would be the more inclined to listen and believe when a messenger reached him with information about the true state of affairs.

To Caillard's way of thinking, everything was going his way. San Luis Potosi lay a good week's march to the west, for a force comprised of foot soldiers, a couple of 12-pounder gun-howitzers and a small cavalry screen. The way led through territory where *Juarista* activity could be expected to add delays. By the time the major arrived, reported and returned, Fort Mendez would be defended by men from the various *bandido* gangs. Already faced with a long, difficult task in subduing the *Juaristas*, the French Army might easily decide to ignore the defection until able to give it their full attention. In which case, the revolution could go ahead.

By noon, the relief column had left the vicinity of the fort, followed by Rache, at Belle's insistence. In the early afternoon, Ysabel had led Caillard and ten well-mounted men to the north-east. That left Sylvie and von Bulow with forty men and the *cantinières*. From what Belle had seen, the blonde intended to make sure that she and the Kid remained within the fort until Caillard and Ysabel returned.

So Belle had decided to take a chance. Originally *cantinières* had been mere camp-followers, picking up discarded items of regimental clothing to replace their own worn-out garments. By the time of the Franco-Austrian War in Italy, a change had come. The *cantinière* became an established member of the French Army, with a uniform of regulation pattern and subject to military discipline. Of course, some of them were no more than prostitutes taking advantage of an assured market for their wares; but many others were dedicated to their work and felt as great a pride in their regiment as did its male members. The problem facing Belle was to which category Marthe and Alice belonged.

Taking a chance, she had asked them both to come to her quarters. Sylvie had made it plain that she did not trust Belle. In the Rebel Spy's presence, the blonde had told the guard commander that *nobody*—with a pointed glance at

Belle and the Kid as she laid emphasis on the word—must be allowed to leave the fort. Granted the *cantinières'* help, the girl and the young Texan hoped not only to escape, but to take their horses and property with them.

'Are you loyal to France?' Belle demanded, watching the two women's faces.

'Of course!' Marthe stated immediately and stiffened to attention as she said the words. Before doing so, she flashed a knowing look at the other *cantinière*.

'My father, husband and two brothers all gave their lives in the service of our country, colonel,' Alice went on. 'Why do you ask?'

'There is treachery afoot,' Belle replied. 'No messenger came from San Luis Potosi——'

'Then the men have gone on a wild-goose chase!' Marthe said grimly.

'Hah!' Alice ejaculated and glared triumphantly at Marthe. 'I told you——'

'No more than I already suspected——!' the blonde *cantinière* interrupted.

'This is no time to quarrel with each other,' Belle pointed out. 'Unless something is done, *madame la général*, her husband and the Austrian will betray your country and may even bring about the defeat of your Army in Mexico.'

'*Madame la général!*' Alice blazed, going on to describe the blonde's ancestry in obscene detail.

'I'll scratch her eyes out!' Marthe declared furiously. 'I'll tear her bald-headed and have her heart with my bare hands!'

There could be no doubting the sincerity with which the two women spoke. During her stay at the fort, Belle had come to know the two *cantinières* well enough for her to be able to read their emotions correctly.

'She'd have you shot if you tried,' Belle warned Marthe, cutting across the women's tirades. 'If you will do as I suggest, you might still save the situation.'

'How?' Marthe inquired, and Alice stopped speaking to listen attentively.

'Can either of you ride?' Belle asked.

'I can,' Alice admitted.

'You know that the old one, Rache, left the fort this afternoon?'

'*Oui, mon colonel.*'

'He is waiting along the river,' Belle explained, blessing the forethought that had caused the old-timer to ask for two horses so that he could ride relay and make better speed if he had to come back in a hurry. 'If you can find some way of joining him, he will take you after Major de Redon's column and you can explain what is happening here.'

'What *is* happening, *mon colonel*?' Marthe said.

Naturally the *cantinières* had been interested in the continued presence of the *bandido* gang contingents and not entirely satisfied with the official explanation that they had come to be hired to fight against the *Juaristas*. Such was the respect which Belle had built up, that the women accepted her explanation of how she had become involved in the affair. According to Belle, she had come, like many Confederate supporters, to offer her services to the French. The arrival of two Yankee enemies, along with other details, had combined to arouse her suspicions. So she and her Texas companions had played along with Caillard, learned what he planned to do and set about devising ways of circumventing him.

'You have done well, *mon colonel*,' praised Marthe. 'I will help you.'

'And me,' Alice promised. 'But leaving the fort will not be easy. *Madame la général* has ordered that nobody is let through the gates and the guards will obey.'

'As long as they can,' Belle agreed. 'Have you wine?'

'Yes,' Marthe confirmed. 'But not enough to make the men drunk.'

'I've something that will make them *sleep*,' Belle said. 'It won't harm them, and by morning they will be awake. I think that when they learn the situation, the men will change their minds about deserting.'

'It could go badly for you when the column returns, *mon colonel*,' Marthe warned. 'Perhaps you should get away to-night.'

'I mean to,' Belle assured her. '*Cabrito* will saddle our horses and, as soon as the way is clear, we will leave. Before we go, we will help you arrest *madame la général* and the Austrian. With them locked up, the others will make no trouble.'

'If they try, I think we can persuade *madame* to talk them out of it,' Alice said grimly. 'A knife against her pretty face will do that.'

Having decided upon co-operation, the *cantinières* put

themselves wholeheartedly at Belle's disposal. Sending Alice to collect the Mexican girls, Belle asked Marthe to help her pack.

Before the first trunk had been filled and fastened, Belle heard the call of a whip-poor-will outside her window. Only the fact that that particular bird was not found in Mexico told Belle some other agency had given the call. Going to the window, she looked down. The Ysabel Kid had completed his preparations at the stables and stood below, awaiting further orders.

'Where's *madame la général*, Marthe?' Belle inquired.

'With the Austrian,' the *cantinère* replied. 'Probably sharing his bed.'

Although Belle felt that the hour was too early for the latter possibility, she knew von Bulow's quarters faced the front of the building. So there seemed little likelihood of her being overheard by Sylvie. For all that, she pitched her voice as low as possible as she addressed the young Texan.

'They're with us, Lon. Wait until Alice comes out, then see her on her way. As soon as she's safe, we'll move out.'

'Yo!' drawled the Kid, giving the traditional cavalry response. 'I'll do that easy enough.'

'Marthe and I will get my packs to the stable,' Belle went on.

'Hosses're saddled up and ready to go,' the Kid assured her. 'I'll be around ready for her.'

Assembling the *cantinières* in the passage, Alice confirmed that von Bulow was entertaining Sylvie in his quarters. Bringing the kegs in one at a time, so that the Mexican girls did not know what happened to them, Alice watched Belle give each a dose of a sleeping-powder. Produced by Confederate chemists during the War, the powder had been of use to Belle on other occasions. Quick-acting, it left the recipient with a bad headache but had no serious effect. With the additions made, the girls were sent to present wine to the depleted garrison. Alice told the Mexican *cantinières* to include the men on guard at the gates or patrolling the terrepleins in the issue.

After the girls had departed, Marthe and Alice helped Belle to complete her packing. Having worn it since the day following the fight, Belle retained her uniform. She wondered if she should wear her gunbelt, but decided against doing so. Changing her clothes or armament might arouse unwanted interest and comment. So she put the belt and Dance into her second trunk.

'We'll take them to the stables for you, colonel,' Marthe offered as Belle turned the key in the trunk's lock.

'Can you do it without being seen?'

'Yes. If we go down the back stairs and across the parade ground.'

'Then do it,' Belle said. 'Let Alice get out of the fort, Marthe, then ask *Cabrito* to meet me in the main hall.'

Fortunately the Frenchwomen had well-developed muscles, for Belle's two pack-saddle trunks were not light. Watching them being carried off, Belle breathed a sigh of relief. Maybe Marthe and Alice would have raised no objections to what she intended to do next, but the girl wished to avoid letting them know about it. Belle was going to search Caillard's office in the hope of finding documentary evidence of the plot. If she could do so, it would be of the greatest use. Not only would such proof prevent a repetition of the scheme and prove the innocence of the United States' Congress, it would remove the softshells who had originated from it from their influential positions.

Belle did not hear any alarm raised, warning her that Alice and Marthe had been detected, as she descended to the small reception hall. Entering it, she found the hall illuminated in the usual way. A single chandelier hung from the centre of the roof, the rope for raising or lowering it passing across and down to a hook in the wall alongside the door to Caillard's office.

Crossing to the office, Belle glanced towards the unlit mess hall. She tried the handle and the door opened to her push. Much to her surprise, she found that the office's lamp had been lit. Stepping inside, she decided that it had been done as a matter of routine. Or, maybe, Sylvie had been down to fetch something and not troubled to turn out the lamp on leaving. Whatever the reason, it would simplify Belle's search. Closing the door behind her, she stepped inside.

An examination of the desk's drawers yielded nothing. Not that she really expected to find incriminating papers in such a vulnerable location. Closing the last of the drawers, she went across to the safe in the corner of the room. One glance warned her that if the papers were inside, she had little chance of reaching them.

More in hope than expectancy, she tested the handle. A low hiss broke from her lips as it moved. Quickly Belle manipulated the handle and drew open the heavy door. Dropping to her left knee, she reached in and lifted up some of the papers.

At first, she felt that the reason the safe had not been locked was because it contained nothing of value. The documents inside might be of a confidential nature, but were only to do with the organisation and running of the fort. Perhaps a supporter of the *Juarista* cause could have found use for them, yet Belle regarded the papers as of no importance. About to close the safe, she noticed a sabretache on the bottom shelf. Picking it up, she raised its flap and took out a sheet of paper. As she started to read her find, she knew that she had hit pay-dirt.

Then she heard the door open and somebody step inside!

Turning her head, still kneeling, Belle saw Sylvie had entered. Although clad in her Hessian boots and scarlet breeches, she did not wear her tunic. Open considerably lower than, convention and modesty accepted, her white silk blouse clung like a second skin, with nothing separating it from her white flesh. In her right hand, she held the rapier.

'We didn't like your *cantinière*'s drink, Boyd,' Sylvie spat and kicked the door closed.

'Perhaps the rest of the garrison found them more acceptable,' Belle replied.

'You'll not live to find out!' Sylvie warned and sprang across the room.

Thrusting herself erect, Belle hurled the sabretache towards Sylvie's face. Twisting aside, Sylvie interposed her sword-filled fist between her head and the missile. Belle watched the blonde knock the sabretache aside as she leapt away from the safe. Down and across flashed the girl's right hand, finding the hilt of her rapier and sliding the blade from its sheath. Releasing the paper, she sent her left hand flying to her belt's buckle. Immediately after the point emerged from the sheath, she set free and cast aside the belt.

The girl did not act an instant too soon. Already Sylvie had evaded the sabretache and commenced another assault. Around lashed the rapier's blade in a savage cut to the flank more suited to a sabre than to the weapon she held. Suitable or not, the blow would have inflicted a near-fatal wound had it landed. Throwing herself to the rear, Belle passed beyond the arc of the blonde's blade. She missed being ripped open by inches, caught her balance and rapidly adopted the on guard stance best suited to the sword in her hand.

About to follow Belle for another try, Sylvie read the danger signs. Any further such wild attempts might easily prove fatal to the blonde. The Rebel Spy had recovered from her surprise, gained sufficient time to arm herself, and now stood ready to fight back. Having seen Belle in action at the *salle des armes*, Sylvie was all too well aware of the other's ability. Only an objection to the chance of being seen at a disadvantage, however, had prevented Sylvie from crossing swords with Belle in mere competition. Faced with serious stakes, the blonde did not hesitate. Married to a poor, undistinguished French general, Sylvie had seen a chance of obtaining riches, either through her husband, or von Bulow. The slender American girl threatened her chances. If Belle escaped with that damning paper, Sylvie would lose her opportunity—and maybe even her life.

CHAPTER SIXTEEN

DOUSE THE LIGHTS, BELLE

Balancing herself gracefully in the on guard position, Belle studied the blonde. Everything the girl saw warned her that she faced an opponent of considerable ability.

While the weapons they held were generally called rapiers, *épée de combat* would have been a more correct name. Shorter and lighter than the traditional rapier, each sword had a bell-shaped *coquille* guard, but no knuckle-bow on the hilt. Ending in a needle-like thrusting point, the triangular, fluted blade carried razor-sharp edges to permit the use of a slash or cut. Handling them required a special technique which Sylvie had clearly mastered.

Raising her left hand level with her head, the blonde turned her torso sideways to Belle. Sylvie stood pointing her slightly bent right leg in the girl's direction and turned her left foot outwards. Held in a near classic well-covered *sixte* with a low point, the *coquille* shielded her sword-hand, wrist and forearm in a position ideally suited to offence or defence. However Sylvie used neither for a moment. Instead, she flicked a glance towards the safe.

'I've told Gautier so many times about forgetting to lock that door,' the blonde hissed angrily. 'He always was a fool.'

'That shows in his choice of a wife,' Belle answered.

Fury twisted in Sylvie's face and she attacked. Their blades met, in a rapid hissing clash of steel, feeling out the other's potential. For all her anger, the blonde refused to be led into rashness. The first passes were in the nature of a *sentiment du fer*, feeling the opponent's reactions through the contact of the blades. Nothing in that exchange caused Belle to revise her opinion of Sylvie's skill, nor the blonde to decide she had overestimated the girl.

Belle feinted low and Sylvie accepted the bait, trying for a stop hit. Deftly Belle parried it by *sixte* and went into a straight thrust. Despite its swift and capable conception, the girl's second-intention attack failed to reach flesh. Again Sylvie parried and began a *prise-de fer*, taking Belle's blade on her own to carry it in a circle ready for the delivery of a thrust. Apparently yielding, Belle allowed her blade to be rotated. By bending her arm and raising her point at the completion of the rotation, Belle brought off a well-timed parry in *quarte*. She followed it with a swift riposte that caused the blonde to make a rapid leap to the rear.

Hissing through her teeth like an enraged cobra, Sylvie launched a savage *flèche*. Almost running to the attack, she forced Belle to retreat. Changing from pure *épée* fighting, the blonde whipped around a vicious cut towards Belle's head. Going below Sylvie's blade in a graceful, effective *passata sotto* evasion, Belle sent her point leaping towards the tight-stretched, pulsating front of the white silk blouse. Twisting aside, Sylvie felt a needle-prick sensation against her ribs. The silk split as the Rebel Spy's blade grazed her flesh.

Cutting back as she turned, Sylvie's sword slit through the shoulder of Belle's tunic. Delivered from almost out of range, only the point and last two inches of the foible* made the contact. Like Sylvie, Belle had received a scratch that would not seriously incapacitate her.

Certainly neither showed any sign of flinching or hesitation.

* *Foible*: half of the blade nearest to the point.

144

Facing each other, they met in a rapid exchange which took them twice across the room. The engagement halted when Sylvie performed a parry of *septime* and turned both blades upwards. Sliding together, the *coquilles* brought the move to a halt with the opponents almost breast to breast. For a good twenty seconds they remained locked *corps a corps*, using strength in an attempt to bring about a separation. The blonde's voluptuous body had an advantage of weight that counteracted the steel-spring power of the girl's slender frame. So much so that it seemed that they had reached a stalemate. Sweat trickled down their faces. Each girl tried to push the other off balance, escape and make the most of the advantage she gained.

Suddenly Sylvie brought down her left hand, bunching it into a fist that drove for Belle's stomach. Just in time, the girl braced herself. Grunting in pain as the blow landed, she reeled to the rear. With a spat-out, triumphant curse, the blonde leapt and cut for Belle's head. Again a *passata sotto* saved Belle from injury. However, she not only went under the blade, but thrust herself to the left. Snapping a side-kick in passing, Belle spiked the heel of her right boot into the top of Sylvie's thigh. Changing from triumph to pain, Sylvie's voice faded as she stumbled against the wall.

For all that, the blonde had returned to the on guard position before Belle could reach her. Approaching Sylvie, the girl changed her style of attack and handled her sword as if it was a sabre. Partially taken by surprise, the blonde also changed style to match her assailant's. Clearly Belle had a slight, yet significant edge in a cut-and-thrust engagement. Enough to make Sylvie put up a defensive box for her protection, guarding the vertical lines of her magnificent torso and from above the top of her head to below the waist. It was a blockade through which nothing could break—but expensive in energy. Sweat soaked the blonde's face and caused her blouse to cling in an even more revealing manner to her body. Her hair, let down in preparation for a love-making session with von Bulow, straggled untidily and wetly.

Back and forward the fight raged across the office, with neither girl gaining a definite advantage nor scoring further hits. Both had come very close. A lunge by Belle had torn Sylvie's left sleeve from wrist to armpit without touching flesh. Later, only a leap to the rear had saved Belle from worse damage than that caused by a cut opening up the front of her tunic.

Reaching the centre of the room, they again attained a state of *corps a corps*. Recalling Sylvie's last escape from the position, Belle prepared to deal with a similar attempt. This was no friendly—or rivalry-induced competition. Nor could it be classed as a formal duel. It was a fight to the death in which all thoughts of fair play could be forgotten. Seeing the blonde knot her left fist, Belle kicked her hard on the front of her right shin. Sylvie let out a squeal, falling back a little. Bringing down her own left hand, Belle laid it against the perspiration-soddened bosom of Sylvie's blouse. Combining the thrust of her left arm with the pressure already being exerted against the blonde's sword, Belle hurled Sylvie from her. Going backwards, Sylvie collided with the desk. Unable to stop herself, the blonde went over the top. The sword flew from her hand, clattering to the floor in the corner of the room. Then the woman fell from Belle's sight beyond the desk.

Driven back a few short steps by the force she had applied to pushing Sylvie away, Belle caught her balance. What she saw sent her bounding towards the desk. In falling, Sylvie had landed kneeling and twisted in the girl's direction. Down went Sylvie's right hand, entering her breeches' pocket and emerging holding a four-barrelled Sharps Triumph metal-cartridge pistol.

At the first hint that the blonde had another weapon, Belle forced herself into motion. Reaching the desk, she hurled herself across it. Still kneeling, the blonde began to raise the little hide-out pistol and thumb back its hammer. With the quadruple muzzles, looking far greater than their actual ·32 calibre, lifting to point at her, Belle glided over the desk on her stomach. Held ahead of her, the blade of Belle's sword reached the blonde. Perforating the top of Sylvie's left breast, the point of Belle's sword continued its downwards and rearwards advance. Driven on by the girl's weight, the sword spiked through its recipient's heart.

Sudden, violent agony ripped through Sylvie, preventing her from keeping the pistol aimed at Belle. Jerking uncontrollably, the little weapon tilted upwards at the instant its user involuntarily pressed on the exposed, guardless trigger. Belle heard the crack of the shot, felt the muzzle-blast lightly on her face, then she collided with Sylvie and they both crashed to the floor. Belle felt the sword's hilt torn from her grasp and saw the Sharps spin out of the blonde's hand. Rolling clear, the girl snatched up the little pistol. Twisting into a sitting position, Belle swung her feet around until she was facing Sylvie. Impaled by the sword, the blonde sprawled upon her back. Even as Belle watched, holding the Sharps ready for use, *madame la général*'s body gave a final convulsive shudder and slumped limply, with hands falling from the blade of the girl's sword. A low gasping sigh of satisfaction broke from Belle. The murders of Eve Coniston and the Mexican *cantinière* had been avenged and repaid in full.

Taking a few seconds to recover her breath, Belle stood up. She lowered the Sharps' hammer to half-cock and dropped it into her own breeches' pocket. Reaching over with her right hand, Belle touched the gash in her tunic's left shoulder. Under the separated edges of cloth, she found a shallow groove in her flesh. It was still bleeding a little, but she knew that the wound was not serious.

Going to the blonde's body, Belle retrieved her sword. The girl experienced no remorse or regret at killing Sylvie. There lay a ruthless, cold-hearted woman who had used the attributes of her sex so generously provided by nature to ensnare and delude men. Sylvie had been willing to kill to gain her ends and had met the fate she deserved.

About to leave the office, Belle saw the discarded sheet of paper. Crossing, she picked it up. In her hands, she held Caillard's orders. Clearly the general did not trust his superiors, for he had insisted on the whole scheme being outlined and signed by Maximilian's second-in-command. So the girl possessed evidence of the plot. Unfortunately it did not name the accomplices from the United States, other than Tollinger and Barmain.

'It's better than nothing, though,' Belle told herself, as she folded the paper and slipped it into the inside breast pocket of her tunic.

Ignoring the dead woman, Belle collected and buckled on her belt. Keeping the sword unsheathed, she went to the door. Even as she stepped out, she wondered where von Bulow—was—and very rapidly discovered the answer.

Along the hall, the Kid came through the rear door. At the same moment, von Bulow and four of his men appeared out of the darkened mess-hall. By sheer reflex action, Belle emerged from Caillard's office and closed its door; which proved a mighty fortunate action. All the men held revolvers, while von Bulow carried his sabre in addition to the hand-gun. The Kid reacted first and fastest to the unexpected multiple confrontation.

'Douse the lights, Belle!' the youngster roared, throwing his Dragoon into an instinctive alignment on what he hoped would be von Bulow.

Touching off the shot, the Kid hoped that Belle would show her usual effective grasp of the situation and rapid response to it. Caught in the chest, the man at von Bulow's right screamed and pitched backwards into the mess-hall. The shriek sounded so loud and unexpectedly that the other men—all Austrians—froze on hearing it. Taking her chance, Belle lashed around with her sword. Striking the rope, the blade sliced through and the chandelier plunged down. Impacting against the floor, its candles were extinguished and the hall plunged into darkness.

Just before the blackness descended, Belle saw the Kid fling himself towards the centre of the room. Instinctively the girl thrust herself rearwards, to pass before the door of Caillard's office in her companion's direction. Four shots roared from von Bulow's party. Belle heard the deep 'whomp!' of lead striking the wall behind her. Only one bullet came, the others having been aimed at the young Texan's recently vacated position.

'Get down and lie still, Belle!' ordered the Kid's voice, coming with an almost ventriloquial quality that made pinpointing its location difficult.

Obediently, without thought of objecting, Belle prepared to obey. They were playing the Kid's kind of a game; a deadly version of blindman's bluff in which a single whisper, a loud breath, or an incautious movement, could be fatal.

Another shot bellowed from across the corridor. It's muzzle-blast momentarily flared bright enough to illuminate all von Bulow's party except for the wounded man. He made his presence felt by groaning piteously. No answer left the Kid's old Dragoon. After the brief glow of light had gone, a hurried scuffling of feet warned the listening girl and Texan that the Austrians had split up as soon as the darkness returned to shield their movements.

With infinite care, Belle grasped the sheath of her sword. Feeling about her with it, she moved so slowly that, even if the steel-tipped case had struck the wall or the floor, it would not have raised a warning sound. Equally carefully, she lowered herself into a prone position. Reaching out with the toe of her right boot, she touched the wall. Showing even greater caution, she laid down her sword and extended its free hand to feel at the jamb on the hinges side of the door. Having established her location, she crept silent fingers over the floor until she regained possession of the rapier's hilt. Armed and recumbent, she listened, waiting to hear anything to tell her how she might best help the Kid.

Each succeeding moan from the stricken soldier decreased in volume, until he lapsed into unconsciousness. Then a deep, utter silence closed over the hall, one that seemed charged with electric menace.

Taking advantage of the noise made by the injured man, the Kid had advanced to the centre of the hall. In his right hand, he held the cocked Dragoon Colt. Almost without the need for conscious direction, his left hand had produced and now gripped the bowie knife. When the sounds ended, he stopped and his ears started to pick up other faint noises previously smothered by the groaning. The Kid stood like a statue; except that no statue had ever possessed such latent, deadly preparedness. Nor was a cougar, crouched upon a limb above a deer-trail, more alert, wary or ready for instant action than the Kid.

'Come on, you stinking Austrian *pelados*!' thought the Kid. 'Make some more noise, 'n' right now, blast you.'

Unfortunately, the Austrians proved unreceptive to thought suggestions. Instead, they continued to keep quiet. Not that they remained motionless. Displaying a skill at silent movement that the Kid found hard to credit to members of a European army, von Bulow and his remaining men advanced stealthily through the darkness. The Kid could hear them, but not sufficiently well to permit him to shoot with any hope of making a hit. So he did not try. To cut loose under the prevailing conditions offered too good an indication of one's whereabouts to be contemplated.

Seconds ticked by, or dragged away on leaden, crawling feet, and Belle guessed at the reason for the Kid's inactivity. She also wondered how she might be of use. It was not in the nature of the Rebel Spy to crouch passively in the dark and let a friend take all the risks. Rising and moving around did not provide an acceptable answer. Yet something had to be done. Perhaps the *cantinières* had failed to deliver the drugged drinks to the garrison. If so, men carrying lamps or lanterns would soon converge on the main building. Once the hall was illuminated again, Belle and the Kid could count their life expectancy in seconds. Von Bulow would show them no mercy.

Something hard dug into the girl's thigh and after a moment she realised what it was. Setting down her sword, she eased the little Sharps Triumph pistol from her breeches' pocket. Hardly daring to breathe, she inched the hammer to full cock. Nobody gave any indication of hearing the faint click. Making sure that she did not touch the rapier, she eased her torso upwards a little. Supporting herself on her left forearm, she hurled the Sharps so that it would strike the wall some distance away and above her. She did not know if the pistol carried a full load, but hoped that it did. Already the upper right barrel had been discharged in Caillard's office. Given luck, the remaining three tubes each held a cartridge.

Even if the gun did not go off, Belle hoped that the clatter of its arrival against the wall might bring about the desired result. Not until the Sharps had left her hand did she realise that the Kid would not know who had thrown it. However, she hoped that he would make the correct assumption and act accordingly.

Turning in its flight, the bottom of the pistol struck the stone of the wall. The Sharps Triumph did not have a guard around its trigger, an omission noted for a lack of safety. Slammed back by the impact, the trigger set the hammer free. Rotated by the action of the hammer being taken to full cock, the striker slammed against the base of the cartridge in the upper left barrel. Flame spurted and powder's gas ejected the bullet at roughly the height a man might hold the pistol when shooting.

Four guns roared from scattered points in the blackness, echoed by a fifth. From her place on the floor, Belle could tell that the first quartet had been aimed towards where her pistol had detonated. The fifth man had fired in the direction of the shooter nearest to him. Due to the ringing, confused, ear-shattering concussion of the gun-play, Belle could not decide which type of revolver had fired which shot. Anxiety gnawed at her as she wondered if the Kid might have become a victim of her trick.

Hearing the faint clink caused by the Sharps striking against the wall, the Kid started to turn his Dragoon that way. When he saw the comparatively minute jet of flame, and considered the noise made by the light powder charge erupting, he knew that they did not originate from the revolvers of his enemies. Yet, to the best of his knowledge, Belle did not own a firearm capable of producing the sound.

If one of the Austrians had tried to trick the Kid into revealing his position, the scheme was backfiring. Automatically, the youngster noted the places from which the shots roared. One in front of the door to the mess-hall; most likely fired by von Bulow, who was letting his men take the chances of stalking the two Americans. Two, down to the other end of the hall. Three, over in the centre of the floor and about level with Caillard's door. Which left number four.

He stood not six feet from the Kid!

There was one European who possessed a real quiet set of feet. Likely his other senses were not equal to the softness with which he moved. Clearly he was unaware of the Kid's proximity to him. He learned soon enough, but the knowledge came too late to be of use.

Up swung the Dragoon, lining on the spot from which the muzzle-blast had glowed. Pressing the trigger, the Kid sent a bullet on its way and flung himself aside. He heard the unmistakable sound of a round lead ball driving through a human chest cavity. Losing all his earlier silence of movement, the stricken man blundered back a few steps before crashing to the floor.

Only three shots came in answer to the Kid's Dragoon. Directed to the spot from which he had fired, nine of the bullets came anywhere near him. Although he had cocked his revolver on its recoil, the young Texan refrained from attempting to down another of his assailants.

'Colonel Boyd!' called von Bulow, confirming the Kid's guess as to his position. 'I suppose *Madame* Caillard is dead.'

'Right where I figured you to be!' breathed the Kid, pleased that Belle did not reply. 'Keep talking, soldier-boy, and you're right soon going to wish you hadn't.'

'Come now, Colonel Boyd,' the Austrian obliged. 'Sylvie came down to her husband's office to make sure that he had left the safe door locked. She must have found you there and, as you came out, I assume that she cannot. I believe a change of command is in order for our little enterprise. Two colonels are better than one inefficient general.'

Silently as a snake crossing soft grass, the Kid glided in the speaker's direction. All the time the youngster was advancing, moving slowly, he kept all his Indian-keen senses at work. His every instinct warned him that something was wrong. At first he could not imagine what it might be.

Then the realisation struck home and brought him to a halt, ears, eyes and even nostrils working with increased care. Nothing the Kid had seen about von Bulow led him to like the Austrian, but he could not honestly claim he believed the other to be stupid or incompetent. A man with von Bulow's training and knowledge of warfare did not endanger himself by giving away his location unless he had a valid reason to do so. Certainly the Austrian did not intend keeping to the offer he was making. Nor would he expect Belle to accept it.

'Come on, Colonel Boyd!' von Bulow continued and the Kid resumed his ghost-like approach. 'We can carry out this plan without the help of the Caillards.'

By that time the Kid had come close to the place from which the voice originated. Estimating how far he had moved, the youngster knew that he was close to the connecting door to the mess-hall. Two more strides, three at most, ought to bring him into contact with von Bulow. With their leader dead or captured, the other Austrians might be induced to give up the fight.

Tensing to launch his final attack, the Kid heard a creaking of hinges. The door to Caillard's office began to open. Light flooded across the small rear hall, illuminating the Kid. It also showed him von Bulow, standing partially concealed on the other side of the mess-hall's entrance.

Listening to von Bulow, Belle almost mirrored the Kid's train of thought. Aware that von Bulow did not make the offer with an expectancy of acceptance, she wondered what his motivation might be. Then she heard a faint sound, barely audible above the Austrian's voice, very close ahead.

A man was approaching Belle's position, feeling his way along the wall; which raised a point. Who was it? The Kid—or one of the Austrians? Knowing the dark youngster's ability at silent movement, Belle doubted if it would be the former. Which meant the man must be an enemy, probably searching for her.

Displaying the same caution that she had shown in all her movements since the chandelier had fallen, Belle unbuckled her belt and removed it. Then she eased herself upwards until she assumed a posture almost like that adopted by a splinter awaiting the signal to start the race. The faint sounds before her came to a halt and Belle froze. Had the man located her? Bringing up her sword, she extended its point in the direction she figured him to be.

Just an instant too late, the girl became aware of what her neighbour was planning to do. The door of Caillard's office opened and, before the glow of light dazzled her, Belle saw that von Bulow's burly sergeant was gripping its handle. Either von Bulow had signalled instructions in some way, or the sergeant had shown a shrewd grasp of the tactical situation. Under cover of his colonel's words, the man had crept across the room. Reaching the wall, he had felt his way along it, found and pushed to open the door.

Not that Belle wasted time considering the sergeant's motivation. By good luck, she was crouching in the darkness beyond the door's light. Either the sergeant was half blinded by the glare, or concentrating his attention on locating the Kid, for he did not look the girl's way. Driving herself forward, Belle heard the soldier's startled curse. Then she lunged and her blade passed between his ribs. Pain and surprise caused him to rock backwards and release the door's handle. Discarding the rapier's hilt as she felt its point driving home, Belle grabbed for the handle and jerked the door closed to cut off the light which endangered the Kid. Guns thundered as Belle completed her work and flung herself away from the door.

Fast as Belle moved, the effort would have been wasted but for the lightning speed of the Kid's reactions. An expression of shock came to von Bulow's face as he discovered how close the young Texan had come to him. Bringing up his Army Colt as he lunged through the mess-hall door, the Austrian fired. So did the last of the soldiers, sighting and turning lead loose with commendable speed if not accuracy.

Flinging himself out of the lighted area, the Kid felt a burning sensation across his right forearm. Pain caused him to open his fingers and drop the Dragoon. Cursing von Bulow's lucky shot, the Kid propelled himself towards the shadows beyond the cone of light. Another bullet passed over his head. Then Belle had dealt with the sergeant and closed the door to bring back a darkened state to the hall.

Feet pounded as von Bulow's remaining man ran along the hall towards where he had last seen the Kid. That, as anybody along the bloody border could have told the man, was no way to tangle with *Cuchilo*, grandson of Long Walker. Shaking his stinging right arm, the Kid satisfied himself that it still worked. While painful, he had suffered no more than a graze.

'I allus said shaped bullets're no good,' the Kid mused as he transferred the knife to his right hand.

Guided by his ears, the Kid went to meet the soldier. Blundering on through stygian gloom, the man kicked his foot against the chandelier. At the same moment, he felt something strike his stomach and sudden, shocking, numbing pain blasted into him. Doubling over, he let his revolver clatter to the floor. His hands clawed at the terrible gash torn into his lower body. Crumpling to his knees, he fell forward on to his face.

'*A:he!*' grunted the Kid. He had delivered a savage, raking chop with his bowie knife, showing the same deadly aim as when he could see his target.

Hearing the commotion, von Bulow took a chance. He sighted and fired towards it, hoping for a hit or a sight of his enemy in the muzzle's flash. Although the latter materialized, the former failed. The red glow illuminated the Kid, and the last of the soldiers tumbling to the floor with blood gushing from his slit-open stomach. Leaping clear of the dying man, the Kid heard and saw another chamber of von Bulow's Colt emptied. Its discharged bullet came nowhere near the youngster and he had avoided the glare of the muzzle-blast.

'You all right, Belle?' called the Kid, sounding almost at von Bulow's left elbow.

Twisting around, the Austrian restrained his first impulse to squeeze the Colt's trigger. A scuffling sound came from his right, causing him to swivel rapidly in that direction. Still he refused to shoot.

'I'm fine, Lon,' Belle answered. 'How about you, Otto?'

'He's sweating, Belle,' the Kid declared. 'I can smell it on him.'

Von Bulow became uneasily aware of the sweat that ran down his face. His clothing seemed wet with it and he wondered if the Kid could smell it. Slowly, a step at a time, the Austrian eased himself towards the mess-hall's wall. If he

could get that at his back, he would be comparatively safe
until help came——

What help?

Clearly the other *cantinières* had been more successful than
the one who had visited his men. She had failed because the
Austrians cared little for wine and the sergeant possessed a
suspicious nature. Forcing the girl to drink from her keg, he
had observed the results and reported his findings to the
colonel. Aware of what kind of men Caillard had attracted to
his cause, von Bulow doubted if any—even those on duty—
would have refused to drink. So the whole revolutionary garrison was probably lying in a drugged sleep.

For the first time in his life, von Bulow must stand or fall by
his own efforts. He must——

A savage screech shattered the silence!

It came from very close. So close, in fact, that von Bulow
could not prevent himself firing the Colt. To the extreme edge
of the muzzle-glow, he saw a fast moving figure. Such was the
savagery of its features that he could not resist cocking the
Colt and pressing the trigger. Only a click rewarded his action.

'Your gun's empty, Count von Bulow,' Belle called. 'Throw
it down and surrender.'

'To a woman and a half-breed?' the Austrian answered,
letting the Colt drop and taking the sabre in his right hand.
'Never!'

With that, he raised the sabre and commenced to move it in
a defensive box before him. If that damned young Texan
came too close, he would meet with a length of cold steel far in
excess to that of his bowie knife.

Somebody entered the hall, carrying a lantern that threw a
cloud of light through the blackness. In it, von Bulow saw the
young Texan ahead of him. With a bellow of mixed rage and
triumph, the Austrian sprang and lashed a blow intended to
take the Kid's head from the black-clad shoulders. Expecting
no trouble in dealing with the Indian-dark youngster, von
Bulow received a rapid disillusionment.

Throwing himself forward and down before his attacker, the
Kid let the blade pass over his head. He struck upwards, slicing the bowie's great blade through the inside of von Bulow's
left thigh. Blood burst from the femoral artery and the great
saphenous vein as the knife severed them. Bringing his blade
free, the Kid twisted himself over and rolled along the floor

155

clear of von Bulow's down-swinging sabre. Before he could strike again, the Austrian staggered and crashed forward in a faint induced by a rapid loss of blood. Thirty seconds later, he was dead.

'Colonel Boyd!' Marthe croaked from behind the lantern. 'Are you all right? Did I come soon enough?'

'You almost came too soon,' Belle replied, standing up and walking across to the Kid.

CHAPTER SEVENTEEN

WE CAN USE YOU, COLONEL BOYD

'After that, leaving the fort was easy,' Belle told General Philo Handiman, repeating the story of her exploits in Mexico some six weeks after they had ended. 'All Caillard's men had been drugged, so Lon Ysabel and I had our injuries treated and rode out before midnight. Rache caught up with us near Matamoros and said that Major de Redon had accepted the *cantiniere*'s story, then turned straight back. De Redon sent his cavalry screen ahead and Rache had been close by to see what happened. They reached the fort and were admitted, either by the garrison or the *cantinières*. So the French are still in possession of it and can't even blame the United States for its loss.'

Big, heavily-built, capable-looking, Handiman was in uniform. He looked at the slender, beautiful girl who sat erect on a chair in the sitting-room of his suite at Bannister's Hotel. Nodding his head, he signified his approval. It seemed that the Rebel Spy had performed a dangerous task and very thoroughly ruined a plan that might have involved the United States in another costly war.

Despite the hectic nature of her last visit, the hotel's manager had not recognised Belle when she had taken a room under his roof. On her arrival in Brownsville, the girl had visited the address given to her by Eve Coniston. Being granted an interview on sending in Eve's password, Belle had

156

given a full account of the happenings at Fort Mendez to a U.S. Army colonel. Requesting that the girl should stay in town, he had passed the information with all speed to his superior in Washington. To avoid attracting attention, Belle had become a blonde, dressing and acting the part of a young officer's wife waiting to join him at his regiment along the Rio Grande.

'The time wasn't wasted,' Belle assured Handiman when he mentioned the matter. 'The Ysabels and I spent it checking out a few things that had been troubling us; such as where Tollinger and Barmain hid in Matamoros.'

'Where?' asked Handiman hopefully.

'With the French garrison. The last place we would have expected them to be, not knowing about the plot. It seems they didn't trust their hosts enough to mention me. Or it may have been that there were Southerners around.'

'In which case, they wouldn't dare to make trouble for the Rebel Spy,' Handiman grinned. 'Unfortunately we've only your unsupported statement to use against Smethurst, and I'm afraid that wouldn't be enough. Wishing no disrespect to you.'

'I understand,' Belle smiled, pleased that she had an excuse not to mention one aspect of the affair.

Receiving the names of some of the intellectuals, Don Francisco Almonte had stated his satisfaction. Belle had not troubled to learn to what use he placed the knowledge gathered by her party.

'Did all your men escape?' Handiman inquired after a moment.

'All my *friends* escaped,' Belle agreed. 'Cactus slipped away from his party before they boarded the ship. Sam Ysabel deserted Caillard three days' ride from the fort. We haven't heard what happened to Caillard, but I should imagine he met with a warm reception on his return.'

'Where are your friends now?' Handiman asked, accepting the rebuke implied by the girl's emphasis and correction.

'Rache and Cactus decided that they'd like a spell of quiet living and have gone to work on a friend's ranch in the San Garcia country.* The Ysabels planned to start mustanging again and left two weeks ago; when they felt sure that they

* More of Cactus and Rache's story can be read in *McGraw's Inheritance*.

could trust you Yankees enough for me to be safe in your hands.'

Although Belle did not know it, the Ysabel family's plans had been changed. The discovery of a plot to assassinate Juarez had caused them to return to Mexico. Doing so would cost Sam Ysabel his life and send the Kid on a danger-filled hunt for revenge.*

'That's a pity,' Handiman said. 'We can use you, Colonel Boyd, and could have found employment for them. Will you join the U.S. Secret Service?'

Ever since her arrival in Brownsville, Belle had thought about how she would react if she received such an offer. Faced with it, she could not bring herself to make an immediate answer. Yet, at the bottom of her heart, she knew that there could only be one reply.

As she had told the sailors in the hotel's dining-room, on the night of her meeting with the Ysabels, the War was over. Her experiences with Eve Coniston and the courtesy shown by the woman's superiors had reminded Belle that not all Yankees belonged to Tollinger and Barmain's breed. The Confederate States no longer existed. Nothing remained of Belle's pre-War way of life. If it came to a point, she would find things too dull if she stopped being a spy. So she might just as well put her skills to use for the benefit of her reunited country.

'It will be a honour, general,' Belle said sincerely.

Crossing the room, Handiman picked up a bible on which the Rebel Spy could at last swear her allegiance to the United States.

* How the Kid avenged his father and the effect doing so had upon his life is told in *The Ysabel Kid*.

THE QUEST FOR
BOWIE'S BLADE

For Douglas 'The Red Baron' and
Anne 'Injun-Lover' Revell

AUTHOR'S NOTE

Once again, to avoid repetition for my regular readers, the histories of the floating outfit and Belle Boyd are given in the form of appendices.

The dimensions of James Bowie's knife are those of William Randall Junior's Model 12 'Smithsonian Bowie Knife' which is an identical copy of the original.

CHAPTER ONE

GIVE ME *THE* KNIFE

From the plaza came a rising cacophony of shouts, shots, the clashing of steel against steel, all intermingled with screams of men in mortal agony. They told a grim story to the two occupants of the room in the hospital.

Clearly at last, on March 6th, 1836, the defences of the Franciscan Order's disused *Mission San Antonio de Valera*—which was more frequently referred to as the 'Alamo' Mission on account of it once having been surrounded by a grove of *alamo*, cottonwood trees—had been breached. Although as yet it had not reached the hospital building, a savage, bloody hand-to-hand, no-quarter conflict was raging on the plaza and in the convent. The bitterness of the fighting was, in part, caused by memories of the events which had preceded it.

For the past thirteen days, one hundred and eighty-three men under the joint command of Colonels William Barrett Travis, Davey Crockett and James Bowie—although the latter was bedridden with a broken leg sustained in an accident while helping to mount a cannon on the parapet—had contrived to hold the Alamo Mission against a Mexican army which had grown until it was over four thousand strong. By making their stand in what had always been as much of a fort as a place of worship, the small band of defenders were hoping to gain sufficient time for Major General Samuel Houston to gather together a force which would be strong enough to liberate the newly created Republic of Texas from the tyrannical clutches of the Mexican dictator, *Presidente* Antonio Lopez de Santa Anna.

Right from the beginning, Travis and his co-commanders had been realistic enough to admit there could be only one ending to their efforts in spite of the heavy casualties which they were inflicting upon their assailants. Long before a relief column could arrive, even if Houston had had one to dispatch, Santa Anna and his second-in-command, General Cos, would have assembled enough men to launch such a massive assault that the garrison—which had also suffered losses, if on a much smaller scale, during the fighting—would be swamped under by sheer weight of numbers. Once that happened, there would be little or no hope of survival for any of the defenders. They had been left with no doubts on that point.

Soon after his arrival on the scene, being desirous of bringing the siege to an end without further loss of life among his army and wishing to avoid being delayed in his pursuit of Houston, Santa Anna had instructed General Cos to present the men inside the Alamo Mission with an opportunity to lay down their arms and leave. Travis, Crockett and Bowie had guessed what had motivated the offer and had realized that, by continuing their resistance, they might improve the Republic of Texas's chances of throwing off the yoke of tyranny and oppression. What was more, they had doubted whether the Mexicans would honour the terms of the capitulation.[1] In view of what had happened a few months earlier, they had not regarded Cos's word of honour as being a satisfactory guarantee of their safety.[2] Nor had the despotic

1. Although the defenders of the Alamo Mission would not live to hear of it, their distrust was well founded if a later incident was anything to go by. When Colonel Fannin and four hundred men surrendered to a vastly superior number of Mexicans at Goliad on March 27th, 1836, General Urrea—possibly without Santa Anna's knowledge—ordered that they all were shot. Only twenty-seven of the Texians—as the American-born citizens of Texas called themselves at that period—survived the massacre.

2. On December 10th, 1835, General Cos and his entire force of eleven hundred Mexican soldiers had surrendered to the Texians at

8

Presidente Santa Anna ever been noted for his compassion or mercy towards those who opposed him. So, after having had the situation explained to them, the defenders had elected to carry on with the fight. A warning that they would be granted no quarter if they did not accept Cos's offer had served to stiffen their resolve rather than sway them from their purpose.

Such was Santa Anna's rage over the defenders' defiance in the face of his ultimatum, the reply having been deliberately phrased in insulting terms so that it might produce the required reaction, that he had allowed it to cloud his judgement. Ignoring the advice of his senior officers, he had refused to follow what would have been the most sensible line of action. Instead of leaving a small force to contain the occupants of the Alamo Mission until starvation had driven them out, while he followed Houston with the rest of his army, he had sworn that he would not move on as long as one of the defenders remained alive.

There had been several attempts at dislodging the garrison during the days which had followed their refusal to surrender. Made for the most part by the poorly armed, badly trained Militia regiments—comprised of *peons* who had little desire to fight, but who had nevertheless been forced into Santa Anna's service—they were not carried out with any great resolution, and each had been repulsed.

However, with each succeeding day, the size of the Mexican army around the Alamo Mission had continued to increase in numbers. In his anger, Santa Anna had insisted upon calling on the services of two other columns which could have been put to a much more effective use elsewhere. By doing so, he had fallen into the trap which Travis, Bowie and Crockett had laid for him.

San Antonio de Bexar. All had been released on giving their parole that they would take no further part in the fighting. Cos had gone back on his word and resumed hostilities almost immediately.

9

From the walls, the defenders had watched the preparations being made for a major assault. Scaling ladders had been manufactured in large numbers and brought forward. Batteries of cannon had been assembled and sited. Lastly—and most significant—a vast pile of wood had been collected to be used as their funeral pyre. Obviously, *el Presidente* had been determined to crush their resistance no matter what the cost to his own men.

Although the price in dead and wounded had been high, the mass of Mexicans who had swarmed forward from every side would not stop. When the defenders' positions on the parapets had become untenable they had fallen back. Now the walls had been breached, they were continuing to sell their lives as dearly as possible.

Sitting on the bed in his hospital room, with his left leg held rigid by the splints which secured it, James Bowie knew that the end was drawing near. Not five minutes ago, having been sent to take care of Captain Dickinson's wife and daughter, Travis's Negro servant, Joe, had arrived to say that his master had been shot and killed on the northern wall. However, Dickinson and his men were still fighting. So, according to Joe, were Davey Crockett's Kentuckians and Bowie's own Texas Volunteers. For all that, Bowie realized, it was only a matter of time before it was all over.

A big man, well over six foot in height and broad with it, Bowie was still hard-muscled, strong and powerful despite his grey hair. Accepting that he was going to be killed, he was determined to go out fighting. There were two cocked pistols on the chair at the right of the bed and a big knife was sheathed on the belt which was hanging over its back.

'Get me on my feet, Sam,' Bowie ordered, as the sounds of the fighting grew nearer. 'I'm damned if I'll let them kill me lying on a bed.'

'Sure thing, Massa Jim,' the tall, well-made, white-haired Negro replied, setting down the double-barrelled shotgun which he had been holding as he stood by the window and reported on the progress of the battle.

Hurrying across the room, Sam helped his master to rise. Bowie grunted as, in spite of the Negro's assistance, pain shot through his broken leg. However, he braced his back against the wall and allowed Sam to slip a crutch under his left arm. While that took most of the strain from the injured limb, Bowie knew he would be unable to move from his position.

'That's better,' Bowie gritted. 'Now give me *the* knife.'

There was an expression of reverence almost on the old Negro's face as he slid the knife from its sheath and handed it to his master. He knew what the great weapon meant to Bowie.

Closing his fingers around the concave ivory handle, specially made to suit his massive hand, Bowie flipped the sheath on to the bed. There was just the trace of a smile on his lined, tanned face as he looked at the great knife and felt the perfect way in which its forty-three-ounce weight balanced in his grasp. Razor sharp, the clip-pointed blade was eleven inches long, two and a quarter inches broad and three-eighths of an inch thick where it joined the brass-lugged hilt. James Black, the blacksmith and master cutler from Arkansas, had never produced a finer piece of work. While the knife had been made to an original design which Bowie had devised, it was Black who had turned it into more than just a superlative weapon. It was, in fact, unique.

So unique that Bowie wondered if he should have tried to send the knife and a letter of explanation to his friend Sam Houston. Unfortunately, as the siege had progressed, no man could have been spared from the ever-decreasing garrison. That was a pity, for the knife carried a clue which could make the fortune of anybody who knew its secret and could exploit it.

There was, Bowie realized, no time to spare for futile regrets over the lack of an opportunity to pass on his

11

information. Probably James Black would be able to find some other way to attain the goal towards which they had been working. Bowie hoped so, remembering the number of times that the great knife created by the other's skilled workmanship had saved his life.

Thrusting all such reverie from his head, Bowie swung his gaze towards the pistols which Sam was holding. He spiked the point of the knife, with its cutting edge upwards, into the adobe wall alongside his left ear so it would be readily available when it was needed. Then, nodding his gratitude, he grasped the butts of the pistols.

Hearing approaching footsteps, Sam hurried across the room. Even as he was snatching up the shotgun, there was a crash and the door burst open. Before Sam could turn, he saw several men coming towards the window. Armed with old flintlock rifles and bayonets of the long, spike variety, they wore straw *sombreros*, ragged white shirts and trousers, white leather cross-belts, red sashes and had home-made sandals on their feet. That meant they were soldiers of the Mexican Militia and not *Chicano*[3] members of the Texas Volunteers arriving to try to defend their colonel.

Facing inwards and holding their weapons in what bayonet fighters called the 'high port' position, two more of the Militiamen entered the room. From all appearances, they had been expecting considerable resistance as they had shoulder-charged at the door and were taken by surprise when it had yielded very easily. However, they were not allowed to recover their equilibrium.

Bowie's right-hand pistol bellowed, vomiting smoke and propelling its heavy ball into the centre of the taller man's forehead. As he spun in a half circle, dropping his rifle and clawing spasmodically at the wound, the big Texian's second weapon hurled death just as surely at his companion. With the lead tearing open his heart, the stricken Mexican was twirled around to blunder a few

3. *Chicano*: Mexican-born citizen of Texas.

12

helpless steps before sprawling face down on the floor.

Already the next attacker was coming through the door, and one glance warned Bowie that he was likely to prove a much tougher proposition than the *peons* who formed the unwilling rank and file of the Militia. Big, burly, hard-faced, he had on a better-quality version of the previous pair's 'uniform', with three stripes on the sleeves of the shirt and his trousers tucked into boots. What was more, unlike his predecessors, he was in control of his movements and held his rifle and bayonet ready for use.

Glaring at Bowie, the sergeant started to raise his weapon. At that moment, Sam's shotgun thundered and one barrel's charge of buckshot slashed through the window to tumble two of the approaching men as limp as rag dolls to the ground. Instantly, the sergeant swung his attention from the big Texian.

Deciding that the old Negro might pose a greater and more immediate danger than the crippled *gringo*, who was dropping what were obviously empty pistols, the sergeant acted to counter it. Swivelling at the hips, he whipped the butt of his rifle to his shoulder and took aim.

'Look out, Sam!' Bowie roared, reaching up and across towards the hilt of his knife.

The warning came too late.

Lining his sights, the sergeant squeezed the trigger. From the fully cocked position, the simple mechanism propelled the flint in the jaws of the hammer so that sparks were struck from it as it met and tilted forward the steel frizzen. Falling into the now exposed pan, the sparks ignited the priming powder. There was a puff of white smoke from the pan and a tiny streak of flame passed through the touch-hole to detonate the main charge in the chamber. Spat out of the muzzle, the round lead ball flew to catch Sam in his right temple and burst out at the left. Pitched sideways, Sam was dead before his body landed in the corner.

Having dealt with the Negro, the sergeant returned his gaze to Bowie and took note of his actions. Raising the rifle's butt above his shoulder, he drew it back so that he would be able to drive home the bayonet. Although the big *gringo's* right hand was closing on the hilt of the knife that protruded from the wall close to his head, the sergeant did not expect any difficulty in killing him. Handicapped as he was by the broken leg, the Texian seemed likely to be easy meat. Once he was dead, the sergeant would be able to claim the pistols and the knife as his loot.

Plucking his knife free as the burly, savage-featured Mexican bore down upon him, Bowie acted with the deadly speed which had made him famous and feared. Whipping the weapon around to the right before him, he directed its blade in an arc that was calculated to meet and deflect the attack.

Knife and bayonet converged before the latter, moving with all the sergeant's strength behind it, could reach its target. Such was the quality of the steel used by James Black to manufacture Bowie's already legendary weapon that its blade not only pushed aside, but actually cut into and snapped the greatly inferior metal of the bayonet when they came together.

Awe, amazement and alarm began to flood through the sergeant as he realized that in addition to his rifle being turned away from its intended mark, the bayonet had been snapped like a rotten twig. Before he could decide upon what defensive action he might take, his momentum carried him onwards to his death.

Having diverted the attack, Bowie rotated his right hand until its knuckles were pointing towards the floor. Even as the ruined bayonet went by him and impacted against the wall to halt its user, he chopped upwards in a circular motion to his left. Showing no evidence of having been dulled, or even affected, by its cutting into the bayonet, the blade sliced the lobe from the sergeant's left ear and gashed open the side of his neck. While painful, the injury was not fatal.

Realizing that he had not incapacitated his attacker, Bowie reversed the knife's direction. Passing beneath the sergeant's chin, the five-and-a-quarter-inch-long concave upper portion of the clip point made the contact. Being just as sharp as the main cutting edge, it laid his throat open to the bone. Blood spurted in a flood over Bowie's hand as he twisted the sergeant aside. Releasing the rifle, the dying man took a long, involuntary stride before he crumpled and went down.

At that moment, Lieutenant Arsenio Serrano arrived on the scene.

The son of a wealthy Northern Coahuila *haciendero*, Serrano was in his mid-twenties, tall, slender and good looking. Bare-headed, having lost his hat during the advance on the walls, his brown, waist-length, double-breasted shirt-jacket was decorated with silver braid and buttons. His brown, bell-bottomed trousers and spur-bearing boots seemed better suited to riding than marching.

With the ever-present threats posed by the local Yaqui Indians and frequent raiding by Comanches or Apaches from north of the *Rio Bravo*,[4] Don Pascual Serrano had insisted on retaining all his *vaqueros* to defend the *hacienda*. So his son had had to be content with taking twenty *peons* when he had gone to answer *Presidente* Santa Anna's call for support to quell the rebellion in Texas. That had meant he was given a commission in the Militia, instead of being allowed to join one of the elite volunteer cavalry regiments. Like all the Militia's officers, although he was fighting on foot, he had done all his travelling on horse-back while his men walked.

If Arsenio Serrano had given thought to the matter, he might have considered himself a very lucky young man. Having been among the first arrivals outside the Alamo Mission, the Northern Coahuila Militia Regiment had suffered heavy casualties in the previous assaults. In fact,

4. *Rio Bravo:* Mexicans' name for the Rio Grande.

their strength had been so decimated by death, wounds and desertion that they could muster only two companies for the final attack. There had been a high mortality rate among the regiment's officers. The Texians and Crockett's Kentuckians were experienced Indian fighters and had known the strategic value of removing their enemies' leaders. Although Serrano had taken part in all the previous assaults and had had a few narrow escapes, he had come through them unscathed. That morning, because of their losses, his regiment had been held in reserve. So, much to his annoyance, Serrano had not reached the walls until after they had been breached.

On entering the plaza, hot and eager to play his part, Serrano had found that all the visible defenders were already being engaged in combat by the attackers who had preceded him. So he had led his men towards the hospital building. His luck had still held, although he did not regard it in that light. Flying from one of the savage, violent melees that were taking place all around the plaza, a bullet had struck his sword to shatter its blade and knock it from his hand. Surprise, alarm and not a little pain had caused him to drop his pistol and clutch at the stinging fingers with his left hand. While he had been delayed by retrieving and checking that the pistol had not lost the powder from its priming pan when it had struck the ground, Sergeant Ortega had led their men towards the hospital.

If it had not been for the chance destruction of the sword, Serrano and not the sergeant would have followed the two men into the room.

As it was, Serrano had seen the entry effected as he was running to join his men. He had watched Ortega following the pair who had broken open the door, heard the shots from inside and had witnessed the number of the party who had accompanied him from his home being reduced to four by the blast of Sam's shotgun. Calling upon the quartet to follow him, Serrano had set off to find out what was happening inside the building.

Having crowded through the door on their young officer's heels, the four *peons* were—like him—brought to a halt as they stared at the spectacle which was confronting them. There was something terrible and frightening about the big *gringo* who had, despite being incapacitated by his injury, already killed three of their number. If the grim, savage determination on his face was anything to go by, he was all too willing to continue with the slaughter.

Being descended from a family which had always produced brave fighting men, Serrano recovered quickly from the shock of his first real contact with one of the enemy. Up to that moment, they had always been at least a hundred yards away and no more than small, briefly seen shapes beyond the walls. So, momentarily, he had found coming into such sudden and close proximity to be disconcerting and alarming.

Then, having met Bowie at the home of a mutual friend, the young Mexican realized with whom they were dealing. For all his broken leg and even when armed only with that huge knife, Bowie would be terribly dangerous adversary at close quarters.

With that in mind, Serrano raised and took aim along the barrel of his pistol. However, he could not bring himself to shoot without first having made what he guessed would be a futile and unacceptable demand for Bowie to surrender. As one of the men responsible for the rebellion, he would not allow himself to be taken alive.

Given what they regarded as guidance by the officer, the *peons* also lined their weapons at the big white man. If he was afraid of the rifles and pistol which were being pointed in his direction, he gave no sign of it. In fact, lifting the bloody knife in a menacing fashion, he swung his crutch forward as if he was meaning to advance and attack them.

'Surren——!' Serrano began, watching what Bowie was doing with something that was close to superstitious awe.

The feeling was duplicated by the *peons*. Before their officer could even complete the first word, the man at the left tightened his right forefinger and his weapon roared. His almost involuntary action proved to be infectious. With their nerves already stretched taut, the other Mexicans responded automatically. Three more rifles and the pistol thundered like a rolling echo to the first shot and clouds of smoke gushed from their muzzles. Eruptions of pulverized adobe on either side of Bowie showed that at least two of the men had missed. However, the rest were more fortunate.

Slammed away from the walls by the impact of the bullets—not one of which was smaller than .69 in calibre —ploughing into his head and torso, Bowie crashed to the floor. The knife left his hand and his fingers relaxed and slid almost to Serrano's feet. Wild with excitement that was mingled with relief and fear, the *peons* rushed forward. Time and again, their bayonets were thrust into the big Texian's body; but he could feel no pain.

Bending, Serrano picked up the knife. Although its handle was too large to be gripped comfortably with his fingers, he realized that he was holding a superlative example of the cutler's art. From outside, the noise of fighting was being replaced by cheers and shouts announcing that the enemy were finished. For a moment, Serrano felt disappointed over having been able to play only a minor part in the final battle of the siege. Then, looking at the knife which he was holding, he decided that he had still obtained a most worthwhile piece of loot.

What the young officer failed to appreciate was that something unique and *very* valuable had come into his possession. However, realizing that the knife would attract the envy of his superiors, he decided to keep it hidden and to avoid mentioning the part he had played in Bowie's death. By doing so, he hoped that he would be able to take it home with him at the end of the campaign.

CHAPTER TWO

IT *SOUNDS* STRAIGHTFORWARD ENOUGH

'Our family is willing to pay any reasonable price for the return of Uncle James's knife, which we now have good reason to believe is in Don Arsenio Serrano's possession. And so, sir, in view of the fact that you were able to render such a service to Don Arsenio, we feel that you may be able to help us in this matter. I cannot emphasize too strongly that we are not asking you to intercede directly on our behalf, but merely want your assistance in opening negotiations with Don Arsenio.

'I appreciate that your regretted disability will not allow you to visit Don Arsenio Serrano personally, but hope that you can see your way clear to allow a member of your family to accompany our representative, Mr. Octavius Xavier Guillemot. He will arrive at the Sandford Hotel in San Antonio de Bexar on, or about, April 24th and will await your answer.

'Mr. Guillemot has our full confidence and is empowered to carry out all necessary negotiations with Don Arsenio on our behalf. However, we and he believe that our request will have more likelihood of receiving favourable attention if he can be vouched for by you. The is why we would like the services of your personal, accredited representative.

'In view of the unusual nature of this request, I offer as proof of my bona fides the fact that my father told me, in the strictest confidence, of the part Miss Melissa Cornforth played in the incident at Crown Bayou.

'Trusting that you will give this matter your consideration and that we may look forward to a favourable reply,
Sir, I remain,
Yours in anticipation,
Resin Bowie II.'

Having read aloud for a second time the most relevant
portion of the letter which had just been delivered from
the post office at Polveroso City, seat of Rio Hondo
County, General Jackson Baines Hardin—who was better
known as 'Ole Devil'—raised his eyes and looked, without really seeing, at the other occupant of the comfortably furnished, gun-decorated study in the OD Connected ranch's main house.

In his mind's eye, Ole Devil was picturing a valley
about five miles north of Eagle Pass about thirty-nine
years earlier. A group of Texian hard-cases had been on
the point of murdering a young Mexican Militia officer
whom they had captured as he was fleeing from the
Battle of San Jacinto[1] and trying to return to his home
below the border. Ole Devil and a small party of the
Texas Light Cavalry, who had been attending to a confidential assignment for Major General Samuel Houston,
had arrived and intervened.[2] Ole Devil had been compelled to kill the leader of the mob before they would
disperse. Introducing himself, Lieutenant Arsenio Serrano had thanked Ole Devil for saving his life. As the two
young men had shaken hands, each had known that a
debt had been incurred. If at any time in the future Ole
Devil chose to ask for something in return, he had felt
sure that Serrano would give it without hesitation. On
giving his parole not to take up arms against the Texians
in the future, Serrano had been loaned a horse and pistol
to replace those which he had lost and allowed to go on

1. April 20th, 1836.
2. What the assignment was is told in: Get Urrea.

20

his way.

The years since the meeting had been very full for Ole Devil Hardin. They had been action-packed and eventful years, in which he had fulfilled the promise which he had already been showing of becoming a prominent factor in the affairs of Texas. Nor had being crippled in a riding accident and confined to a wheel-chair[3] shortly after the War Between The States—in which he had played a not inconsiderable part as a general in the Confederate States' Army—lessened to any great extent the influence which he had come to wield.

It is probable that Serrano would have recognized his rescuer if they had met. In spite of the accident, Ole Devil had aged gracefully and with little change. While the once black hair was now grey, the lean face's crooked eyebrows and aquiline nose still gave it a Mephistophelian aspect which in part had been responsible for his nickname.[4] The strong features displayed no bitterness or despair over the disability but for which he might have held high public office in the State of Texas. His lean body might be wrapped in a blanket from the waist down, but the shoulders under his dark-blue smoking jacket retained much of their military stiffness.

'Well, Dustine?' Ole Devil said, laying the letter on the table. 'What do you make of it?'

The young man to whom the question had been addressed had attained much the same position in comparison with Ole Devil, in the esteem of their fellow Texans —the 'i' having been deleted from the name after independence had been won from Mexico—as Ole Devil had been to James Bowie, William Barrett Travis, General Houston or Davey Crockett back in the mid-1830s. Yet, taking into consideration the reputation which Captain Dustine Edward Marsden Fog had earned during the

3. Told in the 'The Paint' episode of: *The Fastest Gun in Texas.*
4. Another reason was the reputation he had gained for being a 'lil ole devil in a fight'.

War Between The States and since,[5] his physical appearance was mighty deceptive. By popular conception, a man capable of the deeds which he had performed should have been a veritable giant and exceptionally handsome to boot.

Not quite five foot six inches in height, Dusty Fog had a tanned, reasonably good-looking face which was far from impressive when in repose and curly, dusty blond hair. Although his clothing—that of a working cowhand —tended to hide rather than show it off, he had the muscular development of a Hercules in miniature. His garments were functional, of excellent cut and quality, but he contrived to make them look like somebody else's cast-offs. Even when wearing his gunbelt—which he was not at that moment—with the matched, bone-handled Colt Civilian Model Peacemakers in the cross-draw holsters, he was likely to go unnoticed unless danger threatened. *Then* his true potential suddenly became all too obvious.

Not that Ole Devil needed any convincing about the capability of the young man who was his *segundo*, the leader of his ranch's floating outfit[6] and his favourite— although he would never admit it in so many words— nephew.

'It *sounds* straightforward enough, sir,' Dusty replied, his voice a quiet, well-educated Texas drawl. 'Only I seem to remember when Tommy used to tell us about you rescuing *Senor* Serrano, he always allowed that he wasn't armed and you had to lend him a pistol.'

'I did,' Ole Devil agreed, knowing that his Japanese valet—who had been on the mission—had told the story to the younger members of the Hardin, Fog and Blaze clan.

'Then it doesn't seem likely that he could have had

5. Details of Dusty Fog's history and special qualifications are given in Appendix 1.
6. New readers can find an explanation of a floating outfit's function and purpose in Appendix 2.

Colonel Bowie's knife with him,' Dusty stated. 'Lon's old toad-sticker was made by James Black to Colonel Bowie's pattern. If it is anything to go by, *Senor* Serrano couldn't've been wearing it, even hidden under his clothes, without you seeing it.'

'It could have been in his saddlebags,' Ole Devil pointed out. 'A young officer wouldn't want to show off such a valuable piece of loot for fear that one of his superiors, or even Santa Anna, would take it from him. He explained that he wasn't armed as he hadn't thought it would be necessary, he was only going to ride across and take breakfast with a friend who'd arrived the night before with Cos's column. His horse bolted when the powder wagon we'd set a fuse in blew up and, by the time he'd brought it back under control, the battle was so close to over that he knew it would be no use going back. So he set off for home.'

'Hadn't the fellers who'd caught him searched the saddlebags?'

'No. We arrived before they could. And, as we weren't after loot, we didn't bother. He explained why he wasn't armed. They'd shot his horse from under him, so I lent him another and turned him loose.'

'Then he could have had it, sir,' Dusty admitted, showing no surprise at his uncle's chivalrous behaviour. It was what he expected of Ole Devil Hardin. 'Thing that puzzles me, though, is why the Bowie family have waited for so long before trying to get the knife back?'

'According to the letter, they've only just recently learned of its whereabouts.'

'Didn't they try to find out what had happened to it when they first heard of Colonel's Bowie's death?'

'They could have and probably did,' Ole Devil admitted, 'although I never got to hear about it.'

'Didn't *you* ever wonder what had happened to it, sir?' Dusty inquired.

'I suppose that it must have crossed my mind at some

time or another,' Ole Devil answered. 'But I had plenty other, more important things on it in the days that followed the Alamo. Probably I was like everybody else and accepted that it had been carried off by whoever had killed him. I wasn't at San Jacinto for long after the battle. Then before I'd rejoined General Houston after settling accounts with Urrea, Santa Anna and his army had left Texas and there were other things needing my attention. If it comes to a point, I never even heard who had killed Bowie. Houston wouldn't allow any extensive investigation into that aspect of the siege, so that he could avoid refusing demands for reprisals against the men concerned. I suppose that Serrano could have been responsible, he admitted to having been at the Alamo.'

'Peña, Navarro and the others whose accounts of the siege I've read never named him as Colonel Bowie's killer,'[7] Dusty said pensively. 'But, especially after word got around about how you dealt with Urrea, they could have had much the same notion in mind as General Houston about avoiding reprisals and kept quiet.'

'That's true. Or, if I was right about why he was hiding the knife, they wouldn't have known,' Ole Devil replied.

'You never saw him again, sir?'

'No. He sent back the horse and pistol, along with a message saying that I'd always be welcome if I cared to visit *Casa* Serrano and explaining how to get there. I had a letter during the Mexican War assuring me that he'd honoured his word and hadn't taken up arms against Texas. We've written back and forth maybe a dozen times since then, but I never got around to paying him a visit.'

'Huh huh,' Dusty grunted, then another thought struck him. 'I wonder how the Bowies learned about you

7. Colonel José Enrique de la Peña, Captain Sánchez Navarro, Colonel Almonte, Captain Fernando Urizza and other Mexican officers published statements, or stories, about the siege, and these were translated and circulated in Texas.

helping *Senor* Serrano?'

'Well, I've never made any special effort to keep it a secret, although there was never an official written report about the mission I was on when we met,' Ole Devil answered. 'There were eight of us on it. One of the others might have mentioned what happened, but I've never hear of it if they did.'

'I've never come across any mention of it in a book, sir,' Dusty declared. 'Not that I could lay claim to having read everything which's been written about that period. Thing being, what're you going to do about this letter, sir?'

'Like it reminds me in the paragraph about the incident at Crown Bayou being verification of his *bona fides*, I owe the Bowie family a favour,' Ole Devil replied. 'And what they're asking of me doesn't seem too much in repayment. All they want is for me to help get their man to *Casa* Serrano and vouch for them having sent him.'

'Which'll be easy enough done,' Dusty said quietly. 'Just so long as the Bowie family *did* send him.'

'How do you mean?' Ole Devil wanted to know, although he guessed that his nephew was duplicating his own line of reasoning.

'How can we be sure that this letter's really from Resin Bowie the Second, sir?' Dusty challenged, tapping the sheet of paper with his right forefinger and unconsciously confirming his uncle's judgement.

'Why wouldn't it be?'

'Jim Bowie's original knife would be a mighty interesting curio, sir, and *real* valuable. It'd be something any collector would pay mighty high to lay his hands on. Or go to some trouble to get hold of.'

'That's true enough,' Ole Devil conceded. 'I've never met Resin Bowie the Second, or had cause to get to know his handwriting. I can't even be sure that this is his real address, although it was posted in Baton Rouge, his father's home town. On the other hand, he knows about what happened at Crown Bayou. Some of it's been made public, but not about Melissa Cornforth's part in it. Only myself and the Bowie brothers knew that she was involved. So I'm inclined to believe that the letter is genuine. In which case, I'm honour bound to do as he asks.'

'He could've picked a better time to ask for help, sir,' Dusty drawled, accepting the decision without question and starting to consider how to have it carried out. 'Cousin Red and Mark[8] aren't back from delivering that herd to fill our Army beef contract. Waco's pulled out yesterday to help Tom Blevins up to Clinton City.[9] Not that it's going to need all of them. Lon's not doing anything, except rile Cousin Betty,[10] so I could send him.'

'You're my nephew and my segundo, Dustine,' Ole Devil pointed out. 'The letter asks me to send a member of my family. Even if it didn't, it would be more tactful and polite if I have you there to speak for me.'

'It would, sir,' Dusty agreed. 'There's nothing happening around the spread that needs me to handle it. I can leave tomorrow and be in San Antonio by the twenty-fourth, even without pushing my horse—— Damn it!'

'What's wrong?' Ole Devil asked, as his nephew uttered the last two words with an expression of annoyance.

'I'd clean forgotten for the moment, sir. But Colin Farquharson's[11] bringing in some of his best mares to be bred, and he'll be here before I can get back.

'You don't need to be here for that. Betty and Colin

8. Red Blaze and Mark Counter, members of the OD Connected's ranch crew who appear in various books from the 'Floating Outfit' series.
9. Waco, youngest member of Ole Devil's floating outfit. What his task in Clinton City entailed is told in the 'The Hired Butcher' episode of *The Hard Riders* and the 'A Tolerable Straight Shooting Gun' episode of *The Floating Outfit*. He later became a well-known peace officer, as is told in the 'Waco' series of books.
10. Betty Hardin; Ole Devil's granddaughter. She takes a prominent part in: *Kill Dusty Fog*, *The Bad Bunch*, *McGraw's Inheritance*, *The Rio Hondo War* and *Gunsmoke Thunder*.
11. Colin Farquharson's connection with the floating outfit is told in: ·44 *Calibre Man* and *A Horse Called Mogollon*.

can handle it.'

'She'd probably say better than with me here,' Dusty grinned, for his cousin was a high-spirited and very capable young lady. 'But I won't be able to use my paint. He's one of the stallions that Colin's wanting to use for stud.'

'Can't you take one of the other horses from your mount?'[12] Ole Devil inquired.

'Yes, sir,' Dusty conceded. 'There's that big claybank gelding I've just taken in. He's not trained for cattle work, but he's got stamina to burn and a bit of hard work won't do him any harm.'

'I'll leave that to you,' Ole Devil stated. 'Now, while I'm nearly certain that this letter is genuine, it might not be. So I'll send a telegraph to Resin Bowie the Second——'

'It'll be at least two days before we can hope for an answer, sir,' Dusty reminded his uncle respectfully, although he was sure that the point had already been considered. 'Even riding relay, I couldn't reach San Antonio by the twenty-fourth if I wait until it comes.'

'There's no need for you to wait here for the answer,' Ole Devil replied. 'The Bowies seem to think highly of this Octavius Xavier Guillemot——'

'Like Lon'll probably say,' Dusty drawled. 'There's a mighty high-toned name.'

'Very impressive,' Ole Devil admitted with a frosty grin. 'Don't let it influence you when you're sizing him up, which I want you to do *very* carefully. If you're satisfied, take him to *Casa* Serrano and fetch him back safely to San Antonio, with or without the knife.'

'Yo!' Dusty answered, employing the cavalry's traditional response to an order.

'I'll forward the answer to my message and it will be waiting for you at the Sandford Hotel on your return,'

12. Most Texans used the word 'mount' for their string of work horses.

27

Ole Devil went on. 'You can take whatever action you consider necessary after you've read it.'

'Yes, sir,' Dusty said thoughtfully, and his gaze went to where his gunbelt was laying on a small table near the door. 'Only, if the letter is a fake, this Guillemot feller's not going to be too eager to hand over the knife.'

'That's true,' Ole Devil conceded, following the direction in which the small Texan was looking and guessing what he had in mind. 'However, the letter doesn't say I shouldn't send more than one man. And, after all, even if it is genuine, Guillemot's likely to be fresh from east of the Mississippi River and new to the West. You've got some mighty rough country to cross between San Antonio and *Casa* Serrano. The Ysabel Kid knows Mexico and would be very useful as a guide.'

'I was thinking that myself, sir,' Dusty admitted, then grinned. 'Only Lon's not going to be any too pleased when he hears about it?'

'Why not?' Ole Devil challenged. 'He's always complaining about having to be around the ranch.'

'Yes, sir,' Dusty replied. 'But Colin's using his old Nigger horse as a stud, too.'

CHAPTER THREE

SOMEBODY'S LAYING FOR US

'Wouldn't want to go a-worrying you, Dusty, it being such a pleasant afternoon 'n' all,' the Ysabel Kid remarked, showing no change in his conversational tone nor difference in the relaxed posture with which he was sitting the big brown, spot-rumped Appaloosa gelding that he was riding instead of his magnificent white stallion. 'But I just saw somebody peeking at us from the top of that right-hand knob ahead.'

Without making his actions obvious, Dusty Fog looked in the required direction. The terrain over which he and his companion were passing, following the stagecoach trail that ran roughly north-west from Polveroso City to San Antonio de Bexar—a distance of slightly over one hundred miles—was typical open range for that part of Texas. Mainly grassland, it was scarred by coulees and draws as well as being punctuated by numerous rocky outcrops, clumps of bushes and groves of trees. Although the small Texan studied the 'knob' to which his companion had referred, he failed to detect the watcher.

'He's not there now,' Dusty declared, sitting his sixteen-hand claybank[1] gelding with an equally relaxed and effortless-seeming grace.

'Nope,' the Kid agreed. 'Just come up and ducked down again *pronto*.'

'Land's sakes,' Dusty ejaculated. 'I never did see such an all-fired suspicious-natured and untrusting a feller as you, Lon. We're not yet thirty miles from home and

1. Claybank: a yellowish colour produced from breeding a sorrel and a dun.

you're already figuring that somebody's laying for us.'

'I was born and raised that way,' the Kid answered. 'And staying like it's helped me to keep on living so's I'll grow to be old, honoured and respected.'

'Honoured and *respected*!' Dusty repeated, almost snorting the words out. 'That damned old *you* could *never* live to be.'

Despite the undertone of friendly derision in the small Texan's voice, he did not dismiss his companion's warning as being unworthy of serious consideration. Nor, despite the 'knob' being over half a mile away, did he doubt that the Kid had seen somebody looking at them over the top of it. As well as having instilled a sense of alert, wary and ever-watchful caution into him, the Kid's upbringing and early training had left him with an exceptionally keen eye-sight and powers of observation of a high quality.[2]

While Dusty did not have any reason to anticipate trouble, particularly so close to home—they had only gone about a mile beyond the stream which formed the boundary of Rio Hondo County—he knew that he and the other members of the floating outfit had made a number of enemies; any of whom would be willing to try to take revenge if presented with an opportunity. However, if an attempt was to be made upon their lives, he could not ask for better, more loyal nor capable backing.

Black haired, around six foot in height, lean as a steer that had grown up in the greasewood country and possessing much the same kind of wiry, tireless strength and endurance, Loncey Dalton Ysabel—to give the Kid his full name—was a fighting *man* second to none. Yet, as in Dusty's case, first appearances could be very misleading. The Kid's Indian-dark, handsome face, with its expression of almost babyish innocence, seemed young and harmless. A closer examination of his red-hazel eyes, or his

2. Details of the Ysabel Kid's history and special qualifications are given in Appendix 2.

features in times of stress, gave a warning that the innocence, like beauty, was only skin deep.

From the low-crowned, wide-brimmed J. B. Stetson hat tilted at a jack-deuce angle on his head, through bandana, shirt, vest and trousers to his low-heeled boots, the Kid's attire was black in colour as if to match his hair. Even his gunbelt, with an old Colt Model of 1848 Dragoon revolver butt forward in a low cavalry-twist holster at the right and an ivory-handled James Black bowie knife sheathed on the left, was of the same hue. A Winchester Model of 1866 rifle was cradled across his bent left arm. The lead-rope of a pack-horse, carrying Dusty's and his bed rolls and supplies, was secured to the low horn of his double-girthed[3] range saddle.

'Maybe not, company's I'm keeping these days,' the Kid conceded, favouring the small Texan with a quick and pointed glance before continuing his scrutiny of the 'knob'. 'But I sure's hell don't aim to change my ways none.'

'That's what I meant,' Dusty countered, raising his left hand to thumb back his black Stetson. 'He alone, or does he have some *amigos* on hand?'

'If he has, I don't see 'em,' the Kid answered, transferring his attention from the 'knob' to a similar rocky outcrop at about the same distance—slightly over two hundred yards—from the left-hand side of the trail. 'But I'm willing to bet there'll be at least one more up there. I could cut around a ways and scout a mite.'

'It wouldn't do any good,' Dusty objected. 'If it is somebody wanting to do a meaness to us, they'd see what you're fixing to do and light out. I'd sooner have them stay put and get it over with than have the worry of who they might be and when they'll be making another stab at killing us.'

'And me,' the Kid admitted.

3. Because of its Mexican connotations, few Texans used the word 'cinch'.

31

While speaking, the Kid was hooking the Appaloosa's loose-hanging reins over the first and second fingers of his left hand. Still keeping his movements just as unobtrusive, he unfastened the lead rope's knot and replaced it with a dally.[4] By doing so, he knew that he could part company with the pack-horse in a hurry if necessary. However, he did not follow a dally-roper's practice of retaining the loose end in his hand. The horse was sufficiently well trained to accompany the Appaloosa and would neither hang back nor attempt to pull free under normal conditions.

With the dally applied, the Kid let his right hand move in a casual-seeming manner until it enfolded the wrist of the Winchester's butt and its finger entered the triggerguard and the ring of the loading lever.

'It's lucky you've already got your rifle out,' Dusty remarked, having watched the precautions with approval.

Apart from the twin outcrops, there was little cover closer than a quarter of a mile on each side of the trail. Certainly none in which an enemy, knowing with whom he was dealing, would care to entrust himself when laying even an impromptu and unanticipated ambush which would involve the Ysabel Kid. So the would-be assailants were almost sure to be at a distance over which a revolver, even in Dusty's expert hands, would be hard put to make a hit. For the Kid to have drawn his rifle from its saddleboot without having any apparent reason to do so would have warned the watcher that his presence had been detected.

'Lucky!' the Kid yelped, adopting the air of one whose virtue had been maligned. 'I did it so's I could do a kindness for a friend 'n' feller Texan.'

For all the banter, the Kid secretly agreed with Dusty

4. Dally: to take a half-hitch around the saddlehorn, usually after a catch has been made, so that the rope can be released quickly in an emergency. Texans rarely employed a dally when roping, preferring to 'tie-fast' with a knot and so hang on to their captive no matter what happened.

that it was fortunate he had the rifle in such a readily accessible position. Normally, unless he had reason for expecting to need it, it would have been in the saddle-boot under his left leg with the butt pointing to the rear for easy withdrawal on dismounting. However, they had heard that Watson Weller—an old friend and owner of the stagecoach relay station at which they were planning to spend the night—was being plagued by a pack of Texas grey wolves. Having found signs that the animals had been on the bank of the boundary stream recently, he had drawn his Winchester ready for use if he should see them.

Although the opportunity to help rid Weller of the troublesome animals had not presented itself, the Kid's willingness to help was paying an unexpected dividend. If he and Dusty should be attacked, he was already holding the means with which he could start fighting back immediately. That would allow the small Texan to extract the new Winchester Model of 1873 from his saddle-boot and bring it into use.

As the Kid had claimed, his education as one of the *Pehnane*—Quick-Stinger, Wasp, or Raider—Comanche band had taught him the value of constant vigilance. Nor had the events in his subsequent life been calculated to have reduced his faith in the lessons of his childhood, rather they had tended to sharpen his appreciation of what he had learned. So, holding the Appaloosa and pack-horse to a pace which matched that of his companion's claybank, he continued to scour the terrain ahead with eyes which had won him acclaim in the Comanches' training game of *Nanip'ka*[5]

'How'd you handle it, was you laying for somebody from them?' Dusty inquired, studying the outcrops with the eye of a strategist.

'That'd depend on how many he was, what kind of rifles

5. A description of how to play *Nanip'ka*, 'Guess Over The Hill', is given in *Comanche*.

we'd got and *who* we was laying for,' the Kid replied.
' 'Less we'd got buffalo guns and could count on making a
hit—knowing who we're after—I'd let you and me get by
and take us from behind.'

'That's how I see it,' Dusty admitted. 'Knowing it's *you*
they're tangling with, they'd not want to chance showing
themselves as we're riding towards them.'

'So how do we play it, *amigo*?' the Kid wanted to know,
accepting the compliment with becoming false modesty.

'There's only one way, happen they don't show their
hand sooner,' Dusty decided soberly. 'Keep riding until
we're right between them, then use our spurs and go like
the devil after a yearling.'

'Sounds reasonable,' the Kid drawled. 'Only let's sort of
spread out a mite.'

Accepting his companion's suggestion, Dusty set about
implementing it. As they continued to ride along at the
same leisurely pace, giving little visible evidence of their
watchfulness, they gradually separated until they had the
width of the trail between them. Apart from that, to the
watchers, it would have appeared that they were completely unaware of their danger.

However, Dusty and the Kid kept their eyes constantly
on the move. Being skilled fighting men, at no time were
they both looking in the same direction. While the Kid
was subjecting the terrain on the left to his eagle-eyed
and Comanche-trained scrutiny, Dusty was watching the
right. When the Indian-dark youngster turned his gaze in
that direction, the small Texan kept the left-hand outcrop under observation.

'I'm damned if I can see 'em,' the Kid stated in an
aggrieved fashion, as he and Dusty were within fifty yards
of passing between the outcrops. 'And I'll *never* hear the
end of it happen I was wrong about seeing——'

As if wishing to save the young Texan from such an
embarrassment, a man rose from where he had been
crouching in concealment on top of the left-hand out-

crop. In doing so, he was ignoring the instructions which he had been given by his companion across the trail. While he had refrained from stating his objections, he had not approved of the way in which they were supposed to act. So, instead of allowing their victims to pass by before opening fire, he stood up. He was raising his rifle towards his shoulder when he realized that he had under-estimated the calibre of the men he was up against.

The moment that he saw the top of the man's high-crowned *sombrero* appearing, the Kid started to swing up his Winchester. While doing so, he shook free the reins and, as they fell, his right toe tapped the Appaloosa's right shoulder in the signal which he had taught it to mean 'halt'. Although the gelding obeyed instantly, the pack-horse continued to walk by on the left.

Catching a movement on the summit of the right side's outcrop and noticing the Kid's behaviour, Dusty set into motion the plan of action which he had decided upon. Slipping his right foot from the stirrup iron, he swung it to the rear. He intended to drop to the ground and slide the carbine from its boot.

Moving with smoothly-flowing speed, the Kid lined his sights and, when satisfied—which only took just over a second—he tightened his right forefinger. There was a crack as the waiting bullet was detonated. Down and up swung the loading lever, to toss out the empty cartridge case, cock the hammer and replenish the chamber in a single motion. Again and for a third time, making a small alteration to its point of aim between them, the Winchester flung out a ·44 calibre bullet. Through the powder-smoke, he saw the slender, *charro*-dressed figure on the outcrop jerk violently. Firing his rifle into the air, the man twirled around and tumbled from view. The Kid could not have said which of his bullets had found its mark. Nor did he give the matter much thought.

The danger was not yet over, and Dusty was in serious trouble!

While the small Texan's plans for dealing with the situation were basically sound, he had made one miscalculation. He had failed to take into consideration that he was *not* riding his reliable and trustworthy paint stallion.

Unused to having firearms discharged so close to it, the claybank gelding gave an alarmed snort and made a violent rearing plunge forward as the Kid's Winchester went off. Caught unawares, with his right leg passing over the cantle of the saddle and his torso inclined to the left ready to dismount, Dusty felt the horn snatched from beneath his left hand. Deprived of that support, there was no way, excellent rider though he was, in which he could prevent himself from being thrown. In fact, he had barely time to snatch his left foot out of its stirrup and release the reins before he was pitched sideways. Trying to break his fall, as the horse bolted, he crashed to the ground. A searing agony numbed his senses as his ribs struck a boulder and all the breath was driven from his body, leaving him numb and helpless.

Although the Kid was aware of what had happened, he could not attempt to ascertain the extent of his *amigo's* injuries. Not while he was conscious of the possibility of there being other assailants to be accounted for.

Realizing that Dusty would not be able to do so, the Kid set about dealing with the problem. Part of the Appaloosa's training had been to accept being mounted or dismounted on the right as well as from the left. Taking advantage of that fact, the Kid slipped his left foot from the stirrup and swung it forward and up without taking the butt of the Winchester from his shoulder or his left hand off the wooden foregrip. As he did so, the wisdom of his having changed the means of securing the pack-horse proved its worth.

Like Dusty's claybank, the pack-horse was displaying its resentment over the shooting. However, it was backing away instead of running forward and, but for the precautions taken by the Kid, would have prevented him from carrying out his scheme. Rising so as to pass over the saddlehorn, his left leg hit the lead-rope. A knot would have held, but the half-hitch of the dally performed its function by giving way. Freeing his other foot as the leg thrust the rope aside, the Kid leapt to the ground. He not only alighted facing in the required direction, but with his rifle still held ready for use.

Slanting the Winchester upwards, the Kid saw that there was a figure sky-lined at the top of the right side outcrop. Clad in Mexican fashion like his companion, he was still in the process of raising his rifle.

Something about the man struck the Kid as being vaguely familiar. However, he was not given the opportunity to make an accurate identification. Clearly the man had a healthy respect for his ability with a Winchester. Without making any attempt to use his own weapon, he swung around and, before the Kid could draw a bead on him, sprang back out of sight.

The man's abrupt departure placed the Kid on the horns of a dilemma. While his first inclination was to go and make sure that their assailant did not mean to resume the attack from another position, he also wanted to find out if his *amigo* had been seriously injured. The latter impulse won, but he did not permit his anxiety to over-ride caution. Lowering his rifle, but holding it ready to be raised and used if the need arose, he backed across the trail. He continued to keep the outcrop under observation until he was by Dusty's side. Looking down, he found to his relief that the small Texan was conscious.

'How bad is it?' the Kid asked and the concern in his voice was not simulated.

'I—I—think—bust—some—ribs!' Dusty gasped, rolling on to his back with his right hand pressed against his left side. Although his face showed he was in agony, he tried to sit up and looked at the outcrop. 'Wh—where's —the—feller?'

37

'He lit out,' the Kid replied.

'Best—take—after—him,' Dusty gritted. 'I—'ll—make —out—until—you've—made—sure—he's—not—about— to—come—back.'

'I'll tend to it,' the Kid promised, glancing to where the claybank was still running. However, the pack-horse had not gone far and was grazing at the side of the trail. 'Don't you go 'way, mind.'

Much as the Kid wished he could give his *amigo*'s injuries immediate attention, he was equally aware that their remaining attacker might be lurking in the vicinity to try to finish off his work. Collecting the Appaloosa, he fastened its reins to the saddlehorn and guided it with his legs so as to leave his hands free for handling the Winchester.

Although the Kid was ready to take any action which might become necessary, none was called for. On passing around the side of the outcrop, he found that the man apparently did not intend to renew hostilities in the immediate future. Nor had he wasted any time since diving out of sight. He was already galloping away as fast as his horse would carry him and did not even look back.

Realizing that the man had already built up such a lead that any attempt to catch him would entail a long chase, the Kid signalled for his Appaloosa to halt. Although the horse stood like a rock as he snapped the butt of the Winchester to his shoulder, he did not fire. He knew that, with the would-be attacker at least half a mile away and travelling at such a pace, he could only expect to make a hit if he took very careful aim. Before he could do so, the man had disappeared into a coulee. By the time he had emerged, he was far out of range and still riding at a gallop.

'Go on, you bastard, keep running!' the Kid growled disgustedly and lowered the Winchester. 'There's not a thing I can do about you right now. I just hope that you come back for seconds, so's I can find out if I *do* know you.'

Having made the comment, the Kid looked for Dusty's horse. Although it had slowed down, the claybank was still running. Letting out a curse over the animal's behaviour, he reached for the Appaloosa's reins with the intention of untying them. Even as he did so, he saw a man riding from a clump of trees on the other side of the trail and heading to cut off the claybank. On the point of raising the Winchester, the Kid refrained from doing so when he identified the newcomer.

However, despite recognizing Watson Weller, the Kid knew that he still could not pursue the departing attacker. Much as he would have liked to satisfy his curiosity, he accepted that it would not be possible under the circumstances. If Dusty was correct in his diagnosis, he would not be able to complete the assignment they were engaged upon. In all probability, the Kid would have to handle it for him. Otherwise, the Kid could have set off after the man, relying upon the Appaloosa's speed and endurance, or his own skill at following tracks, to bring them together. As it was, he reluctantly conceded that he would have to let the other get away.

'I just wish I knowed who you was and why you was after us,' the Kid mused, riding to meet Weller—who had caught the claybank and was approaching. Then another thought struck him. 'And how the hell did you know we'd be using this trail today?'

CHAPTER FOUR

DON'T KILL HIM JUST YET

'Why howdy there, Kid, I ain't seen you-all in a coon's age,' greeted the bald-headed old hostler of Shelby's Livery Barn on the fringes of San Antonio de Bexar, beaming delightedly at the trail-dirty young man who was walking out of the darkness leading a big Appaloosa gelding. 'How's General Hardin, Cap'n Fog 'n' all the folks back home to the OD Connected?'

'Fit's frog's hair, most of 'em, Milt,' the Ysabel Kid replied, although he wished that the hostler had drawn the correct conclusion regarding the manner in which he was dressed and had refrained from announcing his identity so openly.

Watson Weller had been hunting for the pack of wolves when he had heard the shooting. On joining the Kid and learning what had caused it, he had forgotten all about the animals. While the Kid had gone to examine the man he had shot, Weller had attended to Dusty Fog. As the small Texan had suspected, three of his ribs were cracked. Fortunately, there had been no more serious internal damage.

When the Kid had arrived to say that his victim appeared to be of mixed American–Mexican parentage, but was carrying nothing to identify him or suggest why he had taken part in the attack, Weller had been able to furnish some information. He had said that the young man had arrived at his relay station late the previous afternoon, accompanied by another half-breed; a *pistolero valiente* called Matteo Urizza, who the Kid knew slightly. They had taken a room for the night and left shortly after breakfast that morning. Although Urizza had called his companion 'Enrique', Weller had not learned his surname. As far was he was aware, they had asked no questions about other users of the trail. While they had studied the horses in the corrals and barn and had shown interest every time anybody had entered the house, he had put that down to nothing more than the watchful nature that was a vital necessity in their line of work.

On hearing why the ambush had failed, Weller had declared that he was not surprised by 'Enrique's' behaviour. He had struck the old timer as being eager to prove that he was a real bad *hombre*. Such a man might have considered that, although he was going up against Dusty Fog and the Ysabel Kid—or perhaps even because of *who* they were—he did not want to follow the comparatively safe and easy course that had been proposed by his more experienced and cautious companion.

While awaiting Weller's return with the buckboard which he had gone to fetch from his relay station, to transport Dusty—who was unable to ride—there, the two young Texans had dismissed the ambush. On learning from the Kid that Urizza made his headquarters in Rosa Rio's notorious *cantina* at San Antonio, Dusty had wondered if the letter received by his uncle was merely intended to lead them into a trap. Although the contingency might have been remote, they had considered it as explaining how Urizza could have known they would probably be on the trail. He would have reasoned that, if Ole Devil had agreed to do as 'Resin Bowie II' had requested, the men who were to carry out the assignment would leave the OD Connected shortly after the letter's arrival. As the stagecoach which delivered the mail from San Antonio had reached Polveroso City the previous day, Urizza would expect his would-be victims to be approaching Weller's relay station during the afternoon and had laid his ambush accordingly. That he had merely been contemplating a robbery of the first travellers to pass was out of the question. While his and 'Enrique's horses had been hidden from the view of riders approaching from Rio Hondo County, they would have been seen by anybody who was coming from the other direction.

Another possible explanation for the attempt had occurred to Dusty and the Kid. The letter was genuine, but somebody did not want Ole Devil's representatives to contact Octavius Xavier Guillemot. If that was the case, it would clear up the point of why only two men had been involved in the abortive interception. Such an apparently simple task would hardly warrant the services of the whole floating outfit. In fact, particularly as spring was always an exceptionally busy period on a ranch, probably only one, or at the most two of them would be dispatched by Ole Devil.

With that possibility in mind, it had been decided that the Kid should take a few precautions during the remainder of the journey. Although Urizza had fled, he might obtain assistance and try again. Or there might be other men with similar orders watching the trail. To lessen the chances of being recognized at a distance, the Kid was to change his all-black garments for a grey shirt, multi-coloured bandana and a pair of old Levi's trousers. He always carried the spare clothing in his war bag, so that it could be used for a similar purpose. He worked on the assumption that by the time he was close enough for his Stetson or armament to be identified he would already have located whoever was studying him.

Having spent the night at the relay station, the Kid had set off for San Antonio the following morning. He had left the pack-horse behind, preferring to travel light, carrying his bed roll strapped to the cantle of his saddle. Not only did he have a copy of Bowie's letter and the letter of introduction which Ole Devil had written to Don Arsenio Serrano, but Dusty had given him a note

42

which would explain to Guillemot who he was and what had happened. His instructions were basically those which Dusty had received from Ole Devil and he had been confident that he could carry them out.

The journey to San Antonio had been so uneventful that the Kid might have—but did not—considered the change of attire a waste of time. Except when approaching a relay station, he had travelled parallel to the trail at a distance of around half a mile. His visits to the stations had been of short duration, merely long enough for him to take a meal and to acquire what in every case had proved to be almost negative information. While Urizza and his companion had passed through, even less was known about their purpose than Weller had discovered and the *pistolero valiente* had not called in on his return journey. If he had picked up another helper, so that he could make another attempt at earning his pay— he had had no personal reason for wanting to kill either Dusty or the Kid—there had been no mention of it. Nor had the Kid discovered anything to have led him to assume that other men were hoping to intercept him. The Kid's arrivals had aroused no curiosity. Like Weller, the men with whom he had talked had assumed that he was going to San Antonio to enjoy the festivities of the Bexar County Fair which was in progress.

Refusing to allow himself to be lulled into a sense of false security by the lack of hostile activity, the Kid had decided against resuming his all-black clothing for the time being. He had also considered it was advisable to delay his entrance into the city until after nightfall.

Not until the Kid had been approaching Shelby's Livery Barn had he wondered if he might be making a mistake by going there. The floating outfit always used it when in San Antonio. However, he had balanced the chance of anybody who was looking for him knowing that against other factors. With so many people in town for the County Fair, all such places would be filled. If it was at all possible, Shelby's staff would find accommodation for the Appaloosa. In addition, he would be among friends there and they would warn him of any danger. Lastly—and not the least important to his way of thinking—he could rely upon his horse being well cared for.

'Got any room for this fool critter, Milt?' the Kid inquired, glancing around.

Apart from one other person, the Kid and the hostler had the big building to themselves. A thin, unshaven and poorly dressed man was staring at the newcomer while sluggishly sweeping the floor with a broom. He looked like a typical range-town idler, the kind who could be found swamping a saloon or performing any such menial task which required neither skill nor a great deal of effort.

'You can have that 'n',' Milt answered, indicating an empty stall. 'T'other empty 'n's took already. Hey though, where's your ole Nigger hoss?'

'Left him back to home, having his pleasure with a bunch of Colin Farquharson's mares,' the Kid replied, making his way towards the designated stall.

'Is this'n 's mean 'n' ornery's that big white goat?' Milt inquired, eyeing the Appaloosa with wary caution as it approached on its master's heels.

'Nigh on, but not quite.'

'That being the case, 'I'm staying well clear of him. Is anybody else coming down from the spread?'

'Nobody. What with the spring round up and all, they're all needed. I sort of snuck off. Looks like you're keeping busy.'

'Town's busting at the seams,' Milt admitted, closing the gate behind his visitor and the Appaloosa. 'You got someplace in mind to sleep?'

'Was counting on getting a room at Ma Laughlin's,' the Kid drawled. 'Can I leave my gear here until I've seen her?'

'Time you can't ain't likely to come. Put it in the

office,' Milt answered and, studying the state of the other's clothes, went on, 'You look like you've been doing some sage-henning[1] recent.'

'Why sure,' the Kid agreed, having already anticipated such a question and thought up an acceptable answer. 'Happen I'd called in at Watson Weller's, or some other place on my way down here, I might have been given a telegraph message saying I was wanted back at the spread.'

'That's sneaky,' Milt pointed out with a grin.

'Don't you-all go telling me you never did nothing like that when you rode with the Texas Light Cavalry against Santa Anna,' the Kid challenged.

'Hey, Milt,' the man called, before any denial could be made. 'I've done. Can I get going? There's that whing-ding across town and I'd like to see what's doing.'

'You might's well,' Milt confirmed and, as the man slouched out, continued, 'For all the work he does, it wouldn't be much worse if he never came. I'll fetch you some water, hay 'n' oats.'

'*Gracias*,' the Kid answered, conscious of the honour which was being done him. Usually the hostler would have had to be asked to render such assistance. 'I won't be sorry to get a bath and changed into some clean clothes.'

While attending to the Appaloosa's welfare, the Kid continued to talk with Milt. Hostlers ran barbers a close second in willingness to gossip, and the old timer was no exception. However, although he commented upon the way the town had been behaving during the Bexar County Fair and the number of strangers who were attending it, he did not give any useful information. Nor did he mention, as he was sure to have done if it had happened, that anybody had been making inquiries about the possibility of the floating outfit arriving.

With his mount settled in, the Kid was free to see to his own needs. First, however, he carried his saddle and bridle into the office annexe. Setting the former upon the

1. Sage-henning: sleeping in the open.

45

inverted V-shaped 'burro', he slid the Winchester from the boot but left the bed roll fastened to the cantle. He knew that he could do so in safety and without fear of anybody trying to interfere with it. Although he was carrying the two letters in a pouch built into the inside of his gunbelt, he was not expecting to need them that night. Not only was Guillemot unlikely to be in town until the following day, he had some other business to which he hoped to attend.

'You can allus come and bed down in the hay loft, happen Ma's got the good luck to be full up,' Milt offered as the Kid headed for the main entrance.

'I'll take you up on it,' the Kid promised.

Strolling leisurely in the direction of the small rooming house owned by Ma Laughlin, the Kid was as alert as always. He was soon passing through the business area of the poorer white section of the town. Although a few of the establishments were still open, he appeared to have the street to himself. That did not surprise or disturb him unduly. Commenting upon the unshaven man's eagerness to depart while helping to care for the Appaloosa, Milt had said that some of the local ranchers were throwing a barbecue to which everybody who wished to attend had been invited.

Carrying the Winchester across the crook of his left arm once more, the youngster was as prepared to bring it into action swiftly as he had been while riding towards the twin outcrops. His right hand moved on to the wrist of the butt as a figure emerged from the alley that he was approaching. Both the building which he was passing and its neighbour beyond the alley were closed and in darkness. However, there was sufficient light from the windows and open door of a store across the street for him to decide that the person in front of him was a middle-sized, plumpish woman clothed in a respectable fashion.

Even as the Kid relaxed and took his right hand away

46

from the weapon, the woman appeared to stub her toe against an uneven board of the sidewalk. Whatever the cause, she stumbled and went down on to her bent right knee almost at his feet.

'Here, ma'am,' the Kid said, bending forward and extending his right hand. 'Let me help you.'

The attack came so unexpectedly and fast that not even the Kid's Comanche-trained and lightning-sharp reflexes could save him from it.

Giving no outward indication of her intentions, probably because she kept her head bent forward and did not look up, the woman reached with both hands as if intending to accept the youngster's offer. Instead, she clasped hold of his wrist with a surprisingly strong grip. Surging upright as she gave a sudden and powerful tug at the trapped limb, she caught the Kid off balance. What was more, from the deft way in which she thrust her right foot between his legs to complete the ruin of his equilibrium, she must have pulled a similar trick on more than one occasion.

Unable to save himself, even though he dropped the Winchester so as to try and catch hold of the hitching rail with his left hand, the Kid reeled forward. He was already resigned to sprawling face down as he passed the end of the building. Although he saw the lurking and—under the circumstances—menacing shape in the alley from the corner of his eye, he knew that he could do nothing to protect himself.

Hissing through the air in an arc, the wicked, leather-wrapped sap in the waiting man's hand struck the Kid on the head. His Stetson robbed the blow of some of its force, but he was still pitched forward into what appeared to be a pool of brightly flashing light. As everything seemed to be swirling around him and he crashed on to the boards of the sidewalk, he heard his assailants talking.

'Are you sure he's the right one, Slippers?' demanded a

harsh male voice.

'That dirty old bastard from the livery barn said it was,' was the answer in tones which, although somewhat effeminate, were also masculine. 'Drag him into the alley, Vern. I'll bring his rifle.'

Even as the blackness started closing in about the Kid, he felt his wrists grasped and the man called 'Vern' carried out the 'woman's' instructions.

'Is he dead?' Slippers asked, the words coming faintly to the Kid as the dragging motion ended.

'If he ain't, I'll soon change it,' Vern promised.

'No!' Slippers contradicted sharply. 'Don't kill him just yet. If he doesn't have a letter, we'll need to find out how he's going to identify himself to the Ox.'

Although the Kid could still hear the words, he could not attempt to struggle. Then, before Vern could reply, he slipped into unconsciousness.

Crouching over their victim's supine and motionless body, the two men started to go through his pockets. So engrossed were they in their task that neither of them saw the slender, somewhat boyish figure which was approaching from the rear end of the alley. Although armed with nothing more than what appeared to be a slender stick about eighteen inches in length, the newcomer made no attempt to raise the alarm.

'There's nothing in his pockets,' Slippers complained, sounding aggrieved by the Kid's lack of consideration.

'Ain't got no money-belt on neither,' Vern went on. 'We'd best take him some place where we can make him answer some questions.'

'Come on the——' Slippers began, the words ending as he heard a slight sound from farther along the alley. His head swung around and, seeing the slender shape, he started to straighten up, saying, 'What do——?'

Once again, Slippers failed to complete a sentence. Darting closer, the newcomer brought up a kick which propelled the toe of a riding boot towards the effeminate man's jaw. Slender and boyish the figure might look to be, but there was considerable strength in its leg. So much so that Slippers might have counted himself fortunate he did not receive its full power. As it was, the foot caught him in the chest with sufficient force to lift him erect. The padding which he was wearing in that region as an aid to his disguise saved him from what would otherwise have been a painful injury. Even so, he was sent reeling backwards from the alley and across the sidewalk. Letting out a screech which was almost in keeping with his feminine attire, he fell from there to land rump-first on the hard-packed, wheel-rutted surface of the street.

Letting out a snarl of anger, Vern lurched upright. For a big, bulky man, he could move with a fair amount of speed. He had returned the sap to his jacket's pocket after striking the Kid down, but did not take the time to draw it. Nor did he anticipate the need for such an aid to deal with what he took to be a slim and very imprudent youth.

Thrusting out his right hand, Vern caught hold of the newcomer. He felt his fingers grasping the material of a jacket's lapel and what appeared to be a fancy, frilly-bosomed shirt such as professional gamblers frequently wore; except that it was a darker colour than the usual white. Then he became aware that beneath the garments was a protuberance which ought not to have been present on a *boy*. What was more, unlike the material with which Slippers had produced his 'bust', the mound was flesh and blood.

Almost as soon as the realization that he was holding a woman's left breast impacted itself on Vern's mind, causing him to slacken his grip involuntarily and to hold back the punch which he had been on the point of launching with his left fist, his captive responded in a very effective manner. Crouching slightly, she plucked herself from his grasp before he could tighten it again and pivoted her torso to the left. Reversing its direction, she drove back her bent left arm so that its elbow rammed hard into his *solar plexus.*

Taken unawares, Vern expelled all the breath from his lungs in an agonized croaking gasp and stumbled back a few steps. Then, spluttering what were meant to be curses, he stabbed his right hand beneath the left side of his jacket. It emerged enfolding the bird-head butt of the nickel-plated Colt Cloverleaf House Pistol—a four-shot revolver despite its trade name—which had been thrust into his trousers' waistband. Cocking back the hammer as the weapon came clear, he curled his forefinger across the exposed trigger.

Taking warning from Vern's actions, the girl came towards him swiftly. Her right hand, holding the thing like a short piece of stick, swung across and upwards. Then it whipped around and down at a somewhat gentler angle. There was a vicious whistling sound and, although the 'stick' seemed to be an inadequate weapon, something which had the solidity of a steel ball struck the man on the tip of his right clavicle. A sudden shattering pain tore through him, causing him to snatch at the Cloverleaf's trigger which had emerged from its protective sheath when the action was cocked. Although the revolver fired, its three-and-a-half-inch-long barrel was pointing away from the girl. Flying above Slippers' head as he was starting to rise, the bullet smashed through the window of the store across the street.

Vern's Cloverleaf slipped from his numb and inoperative fingers as his hand fell limply to his side, but he found that his troubles had not ended. Halting, the girl swivelled with the grace, speed and agility of a ballet dancer. The kick which she delivered caught him in the ribs and sent him reeling towards the mouth of the alley.

Coming to his feet, wild with fury over the attack upon him, Slippers heard shouts from behind him and saw his companion stumbling into view. There was, he realized, only one thing they could do under the circumstances.

'Run, Vern!' Slippers screeched, hitching up his skirts and starting to sprint along the street.

Clutching at his torment-spitting shoulder, the burly man saw the wisdom of his companion's advice. The occupants of the store were sure to come out to investigate the cause of the shooting. In fact, even as he swung on his heel to dash after Slippers, the first of them appeared at the doorway of the building.

Instead of following the two men whom she had attacked, the girl glanced at the Kid. He was already groaning his way back to consciousness. Satisfied that the sound would attract the attention of the men who were coming from the store, she turned and hurried silently back in the direction from which she had appeared.

Although one of the trio to leave the store was a deputy town marshal who held a revolver, he did not fire. Before he could draw a bead on either of the fleeing pair, they had darted down an alley and out of his range of vision.

'That feller come from across the street,' the storekeeper announced. 'Hey! Somebody's lying in there!'

Half an hour later, suffering from a headache, the Ysabel Kid was welcomed by Ma Laughlin and told that he could have a small room on the ground floor and at the rear of the building. Accepting, he asked if he could take a bath.

'I was going to insist on it,' the plump, motherly woman declared. 'And I'll have young Mick fix it.'

On entering the bathroom, the Kid waited until Ma's grandson had filled the bath-tub with hot water.

'You do something for me, *amigo*?' the Kid inquired.

'You can count on it, *Cuchilo*,' Mick answered, using the Kid's Comanche man-name which meant 'Knife' and had been granted in tribute to his skilled use of one.

'I want you to go to the store and fetch me two cans of

51

kerosene.'

'Is that all?'

'Nope,' the Kid replied and any member of the floating outfit who had heard the gentle, almost caressing mildness of his voice would have known that it boded ill for somebody. 'Happen you-all can get hold of a lil ole horned toad[2] for me, I'll pay you a dollar.'

2. Horned toad: a small, short-tailed, scaly lizard of the genus *Phrynosoma* which is somewhat toad-like in appearance. The species in question would be *Phrynosoma cornutum*, The Texas Horned Lizard.

CHAPTER FIVE

IT COULD'VE BEEN A SIDEWINDER

Rosa Rio was in a fairly contented frame of mind as she crossed the passage to her private quarters on the ground floor at the rear of her *cantina*. Business had been very good that evening. With so many visitors in town, the petty thieves had been reaping a rich harvest and the majority of their plunder would eventually find its way, at far below its actual value, into her hands.

If there was one thing to spoil Rosa's sense of well-being, it was her failure to discover why Matteo Urizza had been hired and sent out of town. She always hated for something to happen without her knowledge, particularly when she sensed that it might be important and, more to the point, a source of further revenue for her.

While Rosa had put the men who hired Urizza in contact with him, receiving a good sum for her services, she had found them very reticent over what they would want him to do. Nor had she attempted to press the matter too far, knowing that to do so with them could create a bad impression and might have an adverse effect upon similar transactions in the future. Instead, she had hoped to satisfy her curiosity through other sources.

The hope had not materialized. Selected by Urizza to accompany him, young Enrique Escuchador had needed only to know that they were going to kill somebody. That was enough for him. Craving to gain a reputation of being a killer, such as his Mexican *bandido* uncle, Juan, possessed, he had been content to follow Urizza without bothering even to find out the name of their victim. Nor had Urizza's girl friend, Elena, who worked for Rosa, produced any further information. When she had attempted to raise the matter for a second time, he had given her a beating and threatened to do worse if she continued to poke her nose into his affairs.

To Rosa's way of thinking, one thing was obvious. Urizza's victim must be a person of considerable influence and consequence. Somebody whom it would be most inadvisable for him to be known to have killed. Unfortunately, she told herself as she reached towards the handle of the door to her quarters, by the time she had discovered the victim's identity, the news might be so public that she could not turn the knowledge to her financial advantage.

'Except maybe if they put a bounty on whoever did it,' Rosa mused and opened the door.

The thought of betraying Urizza for such a reward brought a gold-toothed leer which made Rosa's normally unpleasant face—the passing of the years and general dissipation had ruined what, according to those who had known her in her youth, was once a great beauty—seem even more repulsive. Tall, bloatedly fat in a way that made her expensive black satin gown hang lumpily and shapeless, she was a force of evil in and around San Antonio. Yet, for all that, the town marshal and the Texas Rangers had never been able to prove her connection with, much less participation in, a single illegal activity. All that they knew for sure was that her *cantina* served as a meeting place for hired guns—especially those of mixed racial ancestry—and on occasion was visited by outlaws.

Stepping into her spacious and opulently furnished sitting-room, Rosa found it was only illuminated by the lights of the passage. Scowling angrily, she stalked towards the table in the centre of the room. If the stench of kerosene which assailed her nostrils was anything to go by, her maid had filled the lamp and forgotten to light it. In fact, there was such a powerful smell from the fluid that it almost seemed the maid had been splashing it around the room.

Suddenly, for no apparent reason, the door closed. Letting out a low curse, Rosa decided that she was nearer to the table and so would light the lamp instead of returning and opening it. Even as her hands were fumbling for the box of matches, which were left on the table with the cigar humidor she kept for use by important visitors, she thought that she heard a click from behind her.

It was, Rosa thought, the sound a key would make when turned in a lock.

Yet she knew it could not be that.

While there was a key in the door, Rosa very rarely made use of it. Nobody would dare to enter without her permission, much less try to rob her.

With that comforting thought arrived at, the woman's fingers touched the matchbox and there was a faint rattling sound from its contents.

'Wouldn't go lighting no matches, was I you,' said a gentle, almost mild voice. 'Not with all this kerosene scattered hither and yon.'

'What——!' Rosa began, so startled that she could neither say nor do anything more practical.

'And don't go yelling for help,' the speaker continued. 'The door's locked 'n' it'd be all hell for 'em to bust it open. On top of which, *I've* got me some matches, one of 'em ready to strike. I know where the kerosene's at—and I don't mind if I have to set your place on fire.'

Recovering from her shock with commendable speed, Rosa moved slowly and as silently as she could manage around the table as the unseen speaker was delivering his warning. On reaching the place where she usually sat—facing the door—when receiving visitors, she felt for and started to ease open the drawer in which she kept a loaded and cocked twin-barrelled, ten-gauge shotgun which had been cut down to little over a foot in length.

However, try as she might, the woman could not pinpoint her unseen visitor's exact location. Obviously he must have been standing behind the door when she entered, so that he would be unseen until he had closed and locked it. Yet there was a strange ventriloquial effect—although Rosa would not have known how to express such a term—which rendered her unable to be sure whether he was still there or had moved.

'Just who the hell are you?' the woman demanded, speaking English as fluently as the visitor. However, she was far less interested in learning his identity than in discovering his exact whereabouts.

'The name's Loncey Dalton Ysabel,' came the reply, but it seemed to be far from where she had last heard it.

'Loncey——!' Rosa began, then realization struck her and she felt as if she had been touched by an icy hand. She went on in Spanish, '*C-Cabrito!* Is that *you?*'

At one time or another, Rosa had had practically every dangerous killer or badly wanted outlaw in Texas under her roof. Yet none of them, not even Bad Bill Longley, John Wesley Hardin or the savage and murderously unpredictable Ben Thompson, had filled her with the alarm which she was now experiencing. She remembered the Ysabel Kid all too well from the days when he had ridden the smuggler trails with his father. Young as he had been, the toughest and most ornery hard-cases had grown silent and uneasy in his presence. Many had been the tales which were told about his terribly effective way of dealing with his enemies. Nor had his taking employment on the OD Connected ranch changed his ways, if all the stories that were still being circulated did not lie. Rosa was one who believed that they were true.

However, no matter what her enemies might say about her complete lack of moral scruples, Rosa Rio was no coward. So she reached into the drawer in search of the sawed-off shotgun. Once she had it in her hands, she felt confident that she could deal with even the Ysabel Kid. All she needed to know was roughly where he was standing. The weapon held nine ·32 calibre buckshot balls in each barrel, and they would spread in such a manner that some at least were sure to find their mark.

With that in mind, Rosa waited anxiously for a reply to her question.

'It's me,' the Kid confirmed, in just as excellent Spanish. Moving on silent feet through the darkness, he made his way towards the window which he had opened as part of his preparations for extracting information from what he had known would be a *very* reluctant source. Reverting to English, he continued, 'Only, from now on, it's me's'll do the asking and you the answering.'

While her unwelcome visitor's voice once again seemed to be originating from somewhere entirely different to its last position, Rosa felt sure that she had located it. At that moment, her little finger brushed against an object and she knew what it must be because there was never anything except the shotgun in the drawer.

Sucking in an anticipatory and satisfied breath, the woman grabbed for the object which she had touched.

After having taken his bath, the Kid had donned his all black clothing. However, he had replaced his boots with a pair of *Pehnane* moccasins. As most of the Kid's work entailed some form of scouting, much of which was of necessity performed on foot, he did not require the high heels that cowhands found necessary. The task which he was proposing to carry out that night was such as to require a greater silence of movement than would be permitted by his boots.

Young Mick Laughlin had produced the items which the Kid had requested, but had not been told of the purpose they were to serve. Fortunately, their conversation had been curtailed by the arrival of Town Marshal Anse Dale.

Having been told about the attack on the Kid, Dale had sensed that there might have been more than a mere attempted robbery behind it. So he had come in search of further information. Knowing the marshal to be a shrewd, honest peace officer and also a good friend of his employer, the Kid had been frank in his explanation. Without disclosing its nature, he had said that he was on Ole Devil Hardin's business and had described the partially successful ambush. Dale had always made a habit of trying to keep in touch with any happenings in San Antonio which could end in criminal activity. So he had heard from an informer that Matt Urizza had left town accompanied by Enrique Escuchador, but—until that moment—he had not known the nature of their business.

Turning to the subject of the more recent attack, Dale had drawn conclusions which had come close to matching the Kid's thoughts regarding its purpose. The two assailants had probably had more than a chance robbery in mind, for they would have been unlikely to consider the Kid a lucrative prospect as a victim. Which had implied that they had known who to look for and where to find him.

Although at that time the Kid had forgotten the conversation which he had overheard while drifting into unconsciousness, he had been able to offer an explanation as to where they had gathered their information. Only two people had known of his arrival and intentions. As he trusted the hostler, Milt, the man who had been sweeping out the livery barn was the logical suspect.

Knowing something of the Kid's forthright way of dealing with such matters, Dale had stated that he would personally find and question the man. Having had other things in mind and being satisfied that the marshal was better able to locate the man, if restricted in the methods he could use to elicit the required answer, the Kid had not argued. He had described as best he could the assailant whom he had seen, but had realized how little use the description would be as the man would have already discarded his female attire. Promising to do all he could, but warning that finding the attackers would not be easy with so many strangers in town, Dale had taken his departure.

The time had been close to midnight when the Kid had left Ma Laughlin's rooming house. Equipped for the task which lay ahead, he had made his way to the Mexican quarter. He was not carrying his Winchester, having concluded that the bowie knife and old Dragoon Colt would be adequate for his needs and more suitable in an emergency.

Waiting for his opportunity with the patience of a *Pehnane* brave on a 'raiding'[1] mission, the Kid had entered Rosa Rio's *cantina* by its rear door. He had been there on several occasions in his border-smuggling youth and had found that the interior layout was much as he had remembered it from those days. Going into the owner's private quarters, having already checked through the window that they were unoccupied, he had closed the door and made ready for her arrival.

All in all, the Kid considered that everything was going as he had planned. Finding herself in darkness, Rosa had crossed to the table with the intention of lighting the lamp instead of returning and opening the door. That was what he had hoped would happen. If she had done the opposite, she would have spoiled his arrangements and made his task more difficult.

Thinking of the surprise which she was going to hand to the invader of her privacy, Rosa closed her fingers——

But not upon the smooth metal or wood of the sawed-off shotgun!

Instead, her hand was enfolding something cold, scaly——

And which moved!

Feeling whatever she had taken hold of struggling in her grasp, Rosa knew that she was most certainly *not* touching the weapon. Considering the person with whom she was dealing, her imagination suggested the nature of the thing which she was gripping. That belief was given

1. Raiding: a polite name for the Comanche pastime of horse stealing.

what she regarded as complete confirmation when she heard—sounding shockingly loud under the circumstances—the patter caused by spots of liquid striking the side of the drawer.

Like many women of her day and age, Rosa had a dread of snakes and reptiles. The thought that she was probably grasping a deadly poisonous, venom-spitting creature completely unnerved her.

Snatching away her hand, the woman gave a screech and staggered back until she was halted by the wall. Her whole body was shaking with the violence of her reaction to what she believed to have been a narrow escape from a particularly unpleasant death.

'Don't know what you're taking on like that for, Rosa,' came the Kid's voice, but from an entirely different region to that in which she had estimated he would be. 'It wasn't nothing but a lil ole horned toad. I've got some pack-rat in me and I just couldn't take that sawed-off ten gauge from the drawer without putting something in its place. Now could I?'

Cold rage drove through the woman as she listened to the sardonically drawled words, driving out something of the terror. She knew that such a creature as the Kid had mentioned was completely harmless, although apt to be disconcerting due to its habit of squirting drops of blood from the forward corners of its eyes—for distances of up to three feet—when alarmed.

'Y-you—son-of-a-bitch!' Rosa croaked, but realized as she spoke that she would have fired in entirely the wrong direction if the shotgun had been available.

'Don't take it too hard,' the Kid advised. 'I didn't want to do you no hurt.' Then a subtly different timbre crept into his voice and he went on, 'But it could've been a sidewinder just's easy.'

'What the hell's all this about, *Cabrito*?' Rosa demanded, struggling—but not entirely succeeding—to conceal her growing sense of trepidation.

'I've been jumped twice just recently,' the Kid replied, getting down to the reason for his visit. 'First time it was by Matt Urizza and Enrique Escuchador——' He heard a low gasp from the woman and knew that he was justified in coming to see her. 'They put lead into Dusty Fog——'

'So that's who——!' Rosa began, before she could stop herself, appreciating the reason for Urizza's reticence and knowing that she had guessed correctly at its cause. No man in his right mind would openly boast that he was setting off to try to kill Dusty Fog. 'Is he dead?'

'Do you reckon I'd be playing fool games with *horned toads* happen he was?'

For all her hardness, the woman shuddered as she listened to the gently spoken—yet, somehow, chillingly menacing—reply.

'Nope, he was just hurt a mite,' the Kid went on. 'Escuchador's dead though. But Urizza got clean away. Which's a pity, 'cause I was wanting to ask him what he'd got against a couple of good-hearted, loving-natured lil ole Texas boys like Dusty 'n' me.'

'Wh-what do you want from me?' Rosa asked, conscious that her voice was displaying anxiety.

'Who sent them after us?'

'I—I didn't!'

'You know who did.'

'How would——?'

'This room'll be on fire happen you can't do better than that by the time I've counted five,' the Kid warned. 'And I'm starting at "three".'

'On the Holy Mother's name, *Cabrito*!' Rosa wailed, certain that she was not hearing an idle threat. 'I don't know!'

'Day anybody hires a feller like Urizza in San Antonio and *you're* not in on it, I'll start to vote Republican.'

'It's true, *Cabrito*——'

'Four!' said the Kid. 'Fi——!'

'I don't know his name!' the woman almost shrieked. 'I only saw him the once!'

'Who?' the Kid insisted remorselessly.

'This *hombre*! A dude! You know that I *never* ask for a name!' Rosa explained, spluttering the words out almost incoherently. 'He said he'd got word that I could tell him where to hire a *pistolero valiente*——'

'And you admitted all honest and true that you could —to a *stranger*.'

'The feller he said sent him was Ram Turtle, so I knew he was all right. Anyway, he paid me and I sent Matt Urizza over to his table.'

'And then what?' the Kid prompted.

'That's all I know,' Rosa replied in an almost pleading manner. 'Honest to God, *Cabrito*. Sure, I knew Urizza was wanted to kill somebody, but neither of them let on who. Would *you* have, knowing *who* you was after?'

'I'm not real likely to be fool enough to go after Dusty, much less *me*,' the Kid pointed out, sensing that he was being told the truth. He also conceded that Urizza would be unlikely to make public names of such victims as he had been hired to kill. 'What's this *hombre* look like?'

'Big, thickset, wore range clothes with a hat so big it hid his hair and had got a false black beard,' the woman answered. 'He wasn't no Texan, sounded German or some such.'

'You'd want to know more about him than that, even if he did come with Ram Turtle's backing,' the Kid stated. 'Where's he staying at in town?'

'I only wish I knew!' Rosa declared bitterly and almost indignantly. 'The sneaky son-of-a-bitch must've guessed I'd have him followed. He bust the skull of the boy I sent afore they was out of the Mexican quarter. So I don't know where he is, or even if he's still in town.'

'He could be,' the Kid drawled, thinking of the second attack.

Neither of the speakers' voices had been Germanic in accent or timbre, but the man who had struck the Kid down had conveyed an impression of possessing size and bulk. Anybody smart enough to disguise his appearance would also be likely to change the manner in which he normally spoke.

'Where's Urizza now?' the Kid inquired, keeping his summation to himself.

'I've not heard about it if he's come back,' Rosa answered.

'Happen you see him,' the Kid requested, 'tell him I said, "*Ahi te huacho*."'[2]

'I'll do that,' the woman promised, guessing the meeting was coming to an end and, boiling with anger at the way she had been treated, starting to consider how to take her revenge upon her unasked and unwanted visitor.

'One thing, though,' the Kid's voice cut in, and Rosa for the first time felt sure that it was coming from several feet away, near the window. 'Happen you've got any fool notions about trying to get even with me for coming calling all uninvited this way, I wouldn't do it was I you. If I get just the teensiest call to think you have, there's going to be word passing 'round that *somebody* told Dusty 'n' me how Urizza 'n' Enrique Escuchador was gunning for us, which's how we knowed and poor ole Enrique got made wolf-bait. Why his Uncle Juan might even figure's it was you's done it. 'Specially as I'll have said it was.'

'You bastard!' the woman spat out, being able to foresee the possible consequences of such a rumour. Juan Esuchador would feel compelled to take revenge upon whoever was responsible for his nephew's death. However, she was not over-perturbed about it, having considerable strength of backing if he should come looking for trouble.

2. *Ahi te huacho:* colloquial Mexican–Spanish term meaning, 'I'll be watching for you.'

'Happen that don't make you see reason,' the Kid continued, apparently from the same place. 'Make good and sure whoever you send kills me as dead as a six-day stunk-up skunk. 'Cause if he doesn't, you'll never dare to go out of doors, nor even sleep at night, for wondering when I'll be coming to pay you back. No matter what you'd do, nor how many men you had around, one night you'd feel my hand on you—— Like this!'

Listening to the quiet, menacing speech, Rosa had no idea that the speaker was drawing closer. Yet, with a final exclamation, a hand pressed on her shoulder. Letting out a squawk of terror, she sprang away. Stumbling on to a chair, which collapsed under her weight, she was precipitated to the floor and winded by her landing. By the time she had recovered her breath, the Kid had gone.

Rising, Rosa fumbled her way unsteadily to the table. With shaking hands, she found the matches and lit the lamp. As she stared around the room, she could not hold back a shudder. There were several heaps of kerosene-soddened paper on the floor and the shotgun was half buried in one of them. Sinking into her chair, she glanced into the open drawer. The horned lizard had apparently climbed out, but the spots of blood it had ejected showed plainly on the wood. Shivering involuntarily, she reached a conclusion. No real harm had been done. Even her dignity would not suffer if she made no mention of the visit. So, having no desire to engage in a feud with the Kid, she decided to forget her plans for trying to take revenge upon him.

CHAPTER SIX

THE MOST DANGEROUS MAN IN EUROPE

Although the Ysabel Kid believed that he would have no further need for concern over Rosa Rio's objections to his visit, especially so soon and after the fright he had given her, he maintained his usual wary vigilance as he walked back towards Ma Laughlin's rooming house. He was satisfied that the woman had had neither part in organizing nor knowledge of the second attack, which indicated that somebody else might be after the bounty on his scalp. He still did not know how, or why, his assailants had been driven off; except that he had had nothing to do with it. Whatever the reason had been, they were still at liberty and might even now be searching for him in the hope of having another stab at earning their pay. If *that* happened, their next attempt could be made with guns.

For all the Kid's thoughts on the subject, he came into sight of Ma Laughlin's without having had need for his constant alertness. However, despite the comforting feeling that he would shortly be climbing through the window into his room—having left through it when setting off to visit Rosa Rio, so as to have an alibi if necessary—he did not relax.

Which proved to be fortunate.

Stepping over the picket fence, the Kid moved quietly across Ma Laughlin's truck garden towards the window. Even as his hands went towards it, he realized that something was different from when he had taken his departure.

The window was fully closed!

Yet he had left it open just enough to be able to insert his fingers to facilitate his return!

Even in the unlikely event of Ma, or her grandson, entering and discovering that their guest was absent, they would not have touched anything.

Nor was it likely that the window had slipped into the closed position during his absence.

All of which added up to one thing, to the Kid's way of thinking.

Some unauthorized person had arrived after his departure, entered the room and was now awaiting his return.

Scowling, the Kid gave very rapid consideration to what he should do. One thing was instantly apparent. He could not stand for any length of time thinking about the matter. If he did, whoever was in the room would become suspicious and realize that his—or their—presence had been detected.

Bearing that aspect in mind, the Kid reached his decision. While his left hand began to ease the window open, his right turned palm outwards to enfold the worn walnut grips of the old Colt Dragoon. He would have preferred to use his bowie knife, so as to avoid disturbing the whole household, but he might have been observed as he reached across to extract it.

'Ma's going to be riled's all hell happen there's shooting,' the Kid mused as he curled his thumb across the Dragoon's hammer-spur and prepared to twist it from its holster. 'How the hell do I get into things like this?'

'I didn't know that the Ox had arrived yet, Lon,' announced a gentle, well-educated Southron woman's voice which the youngster recognized even as he had started to move aside and clear of the window. 'What did you make of him?'

'Belle!' the Kid ejaculated, too amazed to offer an answer. Coming to a halt, he allowed the half-drawn Colt to slip back into its holster and went on, '*Belle Boyd!* Well

I'll be damned!'

'According to Betty Hardin, who should know, there's nothing more likely than that,' replied the woman in the room and her voice was bubbling with suppressed laughter. 'Come on in and close the drapes so that I can light the lamp and we'll have ourselves a talk.'

Shaking his head in bewilderment, the Kid did as his as yet unseen visitor requested. Climbing through the window, he closed it and pulled the drapes together. A match rasped and the stench caused by its phosphorus and sulphur head igniting came to his nostrils as the lamp was being lit. Turning, he looked across the room.

Standing by the small dressing table, the young woman was about five foot seven in height, slender—but far from skinny—with black hair that was cropped almost boyishly short and a very beautiful face. She had on a black, two-piece tailored costume of the current severe cut and lines that still emphasized her shapely figure. The jacket covered a dark blue blouse with a frilly bosom and a man's black bow-tie. The flared skirt was long, although it did not hide the toes of what the Kid guessed would be a pair of serviceable riding boots. On the bed, alongside a closed parasol, lay dainty 'jockey' hat which was pinned to a wig of fashionably-styled blonde curls.

'Surprised to see me, Lon?' the girl inquired, with a smile.

'Oh *no!*' the Kid replied. 'I allus expect to find you in my room after midnight. It happens so often, I can't rightly get to sleep the times you're not there.'

'I saw *you* earlier tonight,' Belle said, shaking hands and still showing amusement at his perplexity. 'But you were in what Betty says is your usual state.'

'What might *that* be?'

'Sleeping.'

'*Sleeping?*' the Kid repeated, wishing that he could stop sounding so puzzled. Then he remembered what he had been told about the attack. The deputy had suggested that he had been fighting with his assailants until he had been clubbed down and they fled, which he had known all along was impossible. At last he knew the real explanation. 'So you cut in, huh?'

'Betty will never forgive me,' Belle answered, sitting on the end of the bed. 'But I have to confess that I cut in.'

That a slender girl would even consider trying to defend him by physical means against two men did not surprise the Kid. Not when she was Belle Boyd; who had won the name the Rebel Spy during the War Between The States and now worked as an agent for the United States' Secret Service.[1] With her somewhat unconventional upbringing,[2] she was well able to defend herself.

'And started to whomping them evil-doers with your lil ole parasol's handle, huh?' the Kid suggested.

Nor was the comment made in a facetious manner. He knew that, telescoped into the detachable handle, the parasol concealed a powerful coil-spring billy with a round steel ball for its head.

'I kicked Slippers where it would really have hurt him if he'd been a woman instead of only dressed like one, although I was aiming at his head,' Belle corrected. 'I admit I did take a swing at Vernet, but I only got him on the top of the shoulder.'

'Sounds like you know them,' the Kid commented.

'I do. They work for Roger de Leclerc.'

'Who'd thishere de Leclerc *hombre* be?'

'Although he'd hate for you to call him anything so crude, he's France's best spy,' Belle replied.

'Happen he set them two jaspers to abusing me that ways, I'll call him something a whole heap cruder 'n' that,' the Kid declared. 'And then I'll ask him real polite-like why he done it. 'S far's I know, I've never done nothing to give a French spy cause to be riled at me. I've

1. How this came about is told in: *Back to the Bloody Border*.
2. Details of Belle Boyd's history and qualifications are given in Appendix 3.

never even called him one.'

'He may have wanted to stop you meeting the Ox,' Belle suggested.

'Who-all's thishere "Ox" *hombre* you keep talking ab——' the Kid began, then remembrance flooded back. 'Hell's fire! One of them jaspers said something about wanting to find out how I was going to identify myself to the Ox. I've never heard of any such feller.'

'He's the most dangerous man in Europe,' Belle said soberly. 'Or was. Right now he's in the good old U.S. of A. and coming to San Antonio to meet you. His full name is Octavius Xavier Guillemot.'

'*Octavius Xavier Guillemot!*' the Kid spat the words out. 'But he's——'

'Yes,' Belle interrupted. 'He's the man who you're going to take into Mexico so that he can ask Don Arsenio Serrano to give back James Bowie's knife.'

'Nope,' the Kid corrected. 'After what you've just told me, he's the *hombre* I'm *not* going to take.'

'Why not?'

'Ole Devil said we should do it for Resin Bowie's man. Which, according to you, this "Ox" *hombre's* not all that likely to be.'

'I'd still like you to go, Lon,' Belle requested. 'And to take me with you if we can find a way to do it.'

'I don't follow your trail,' the Kid declared.

'It's like this,' the girl elaborated. 'General Handiman is *very* interested in learning why the Ox is going to all this trouble to obtain Bowie's knife.'

'He can likely sell it for over a thousand dollars,' the Kid suggested, knowing that the officer mentioned by Belle was the head of the United States' Secret Service.

'A thousand dollars would hardly cover his expenses. And he wouldn't look at any deal unless there was well over fifty thousand dollars clear profit in it for him. He's the biggest of the international criminals and I don't just mean his size.'

'If he's such an all-fired big owlhoot, how come he's roaming around on the hoof and not in a hoosegow some place?'

'Why weren't you and your father ever put in jail?' Belle countered.

'We was never caught doing anything wrong,' the Kid replied.

'The same applies to the Ox,' Belle told him. 'Every police force and Secret Service in Euopre knows about him, but they've never been able to prove a thing.'

'Could be that's 'cause he's never done nothing 'cept make out he had,' the Kid drawled, crossing to sit with his rump hooked on the corner of the dressing-table. 'I knowed a feller like that once. Allus telling about how he'd ridden with owlhoots. Only he'd never done no such thing.'

'The Ox has done plenty,' Belle stated. 'And most of the Secret Services could prove it, because they've all used him, or bought things from him which they knew he didn't own and had no right to be selling.'

'Including you-all?' asked the Kid.

'Anyway,' Belle went on, neither confirming nor denying the question. 'The General was very interested when he heard that the Ox was over here. I can't tell you how, but we found out that he'd gone to see Resin Bowie the Second, then contacted General Hardin to ask for help in collecting the original bowie knife from Don Arsenio Serrano. What we're just dying to know is, why does he want it? The French and the Germans want to know, too.'

'I hear tell that them French and Germans don't get on too well,' the Kid remarked quietly.

'The war between them ended back in seventy-one,' Belle replied, studying the young Texan's Indian-dark features in a speculative manner. 'But I wouldn't say that they're friendly.'

'So they'd not be likely to team up together to find out what's going on?'

'From what I've heard about Leclerc and Horst von Uhlmann, I'd think it would be most *unlikely*. Why do you ask?'

The Kid told Belle of the ambush and its aftermath, assuring her that Dusty Fog had suffered only comparatively minor injuries even though they had been sufficient to prevent him continuing with the assignment. Then he went on to give her the information which he had extracted from Rosa Rio, without offering to explain the means he had used to acquire it. Nor did she ask. After her inquiry about the small Texan's condition, the girl listened without interrupting.

'I didn't realize that the Germans were here already,' Belle remarked at the end of the Kid's story.

'Huh?'

'I thought I was here ahead of them all until I saw Slippers and Vernet this evening. But I suppose one of the Germans could have made even better time than I did.'

'How'd they know where to come?'

'Perhaps the same way that I did,' Belle answered. 'Or they could have had another source of information. I've been doing this kind of work for too long to be surprised over learning that other people have found out as much as I have.'

'Do you reckon one of them French jaspers pretended to be a German while he was hiring Urizza so, happen there was trouble, they'd get blamed?'

'It's possible. Vernet would fit the description. But, according to the register at the Henry Hotel, they only took their room there this morning. Which, before you tell me, doesn't mean that they couldn't have been in town earlier.'

'I never said a word,' the Kid protested. 'Hey though! How come you was on hand and didn't do nothing until *after* they'd whomped me on my poor lil ole head?'

'I thought Betty would prefer it that way,' Belle replied with a smile, then became serious. 'I'd seen them leaving their hotel and was following them hoping to learn what their game was. But I was too far away to hear what the man from the livery barn was telling them. And I couldn't chance going closer while they were waiting in the alley. Of course, I assumed that they were waiting for *somebody* and might have guessed who it was if I'd known then who the man from the livery barn was. By the time I found out it was you, it was too late to do anything except stop them doing anything worse to you.'

'Why'n't you stick around after they'd lit out?'

'I wasn't dressed for it,' Belle answered. 'If I'd been seen without my skirt, it would aroused the kind of attention I want to avoid. So, as soon as I saw that you'd be looked after, I dressed and went to find Slippers and Vernet.'

'Did you do it?' the Kid asked and something in his gentle words brought the girl's eyes to his face.

'Yes,' Belle said flatly.

'Where're they at?' demanded the Kid and it was all of that, despite his gentle tones.

'Back at their room,' Belle replied.

'Are they now?' the Kid drawled, looking as innocent as a fresh-scrubbed choir-boy, as his right hand drifted towards the hilt of the bowie knife. 'I reckon I'll sort of drift along and say "howdy".'

'Call it evens, Lon,' Belle requested.

'Call it *evens*!' the Kid snorted indignantly. 'After they whomped me on the head 'n'———'

'I think I broke Vernet's collar-bone,' Belle interrupted. 'They sent for a doctor as soon as they got back to the hotel. I'd say that's a fair trade for an itty-bitty tap on the head. It wasn't as if they hit you anywhere they could've damaged.'

'I'll let *that* pass,' the Kid growled. 'Only they could've sent Urizza after us, which's another thing entirely.'

'They *could* have,' Belle conceded. 'But, if they did,

they weren't showing much faith in him.'

'How come?'

'They had a man watching out for whoever came from the OD Connected at the livery barn,' the girl pointed out.

'Just to make sure we didn't get by Urizza,' the Kid countered.

'I'm not gainsaying it,' Belle assured him. 'All I want you to do is let it ride, at least until we know who-all else's in the deal.'

'You mean there might be more of 'em?'

'If France and Germany are interested, it's possible the English are too and other European countries.'

'Damn it all!' the Kid grunted. 'You mean all of them countries might be wanting to lay hands on ole Jim Bowie's knife?'

'If that's what the Ox is really after,' Belle agreed.

'But you said he wasn't likely to go after something unless it's real valuable,' the Kid reminded her.

'I did,' Belle admitted. 'And that's why I've been sent to find out what he's after. Will you stay clear of Slippers and Vernet for the time being, Lon?'

'Going after 'em could make fuss for you, huh?'

'It won't make things any easier. How about it?'

'I was hoping you'd talk me out of going,' the Kid declared, rising and unbuckling his gunbelt. Placing it on the chair by the bed, he went on, 'Hey though, how did you know where to find me.'

'That was easy,' Belle replied. 'I just came here——'

'Why *here*?' the Kid wanted to know.

'Because I remembered when I was on vacation at the OD Connected, one of you said that you all always stayed here when you came to San Antonio,' Belle explained. 'So I came to see Ma as soon as I arrived and was lucky enough to get the next to last empty room. Nobody had taken the other when I left this evening, but it was occupied when I came back.'

'Why didn't you come and see me——? the Kid began.

'I did, except that, due to trying to find the man from the livery barn and all, it was gone midnight when I arrived. I wasn't absolutely sure it was you in the room, so I came around the back to find out. The window was open a little and the room deserted, but your rifle, saddle and bed roll were in it. So I decided that you'd gone out to look for the Ox and, with you being away for so long, that he'd arrived. In fact, I was just thinking about coming to try to find you when you returned.'

'I was like to come in shooting when I figured there was somebody in here,' the Kid warned.

'And I was all set to shoot, if it hadn't been you,' Belle countered, lifting her hat and wig to show that they had been concealing a pearl-handled, nickel-plated Remington Double Derringer. Then she gestured towards his gunbelt. 'May I?'

'Feel free,' the Kid assented.

'James Black made this, didn't he?' Belle asked, having drawn the knife from its sheath.

'Why sure,' the Kid agreed. 'It's modelled exactly on Jim Bowie's.'[3]

'It's excellently made,' the girl commented, turning the weapon over in her hands, then tapping the blade with her left thumbnail.

'They do say old James Black made the best steel in these United States,' the Kid replied. 'And he did even better than his best when he whomped up that toad-sticker for Jim Bowie.'

'In what way?'

'Story is that Jim Bowie took him along a carved-out wooden model and asked him to copy it with the best steel he knew how to make——'

'Of course!' Belle interrupted. 'The legend is that

3. Although the Kid did not know it, his knife—having an eleven and a half inch long, two and a half inch wide, blade—was slightly larger than Bowie's original model.

74

James Black made the steel by melting down a piece of a star that had fallen near to his forge.'[4]

'So I've always heard,' the Kid agreed. 'And they do say that the blade it made was so tough 'n' sharp that it'd cut through any other knife——Hey! Maybe that's why all these jaspers want to get hold of it.'

'How do you mean?'

'Happen the steel's that good, it'd sure's hell be worth a heap of money anybody's knowed how to make it.'

'There's only one thing wrong with that,' Belle objected, returning the Kid's weapon to its sheath. 'If the legend is true and the knife was made from a piece of a star, there wouldn't be any way that the steel could be duplicated. Unless, of course, you had a whole lot more pieces.'

4. Further details of this legend are given in Paul I. Wellman's: *The Iron Mistress.*

CHAPTER SEVEN

A MISTAKE LIKE *THAT* COULD GET YOU SHOT

'Mr. *Octavius Xavier* Guillemot—*sir?*' asked the plump, pompous-looking clerk at the Sandford Hotel, lifting his gaze from the brass-framed Winchester Model of 1866 rifle which had been placed on the well-polished top of the reception desk and glancing uneasily at its owner. The final honorific had clearly been an after-thought.

Although the black-dressed cowhand—or so the clerk, having only recently arrived in the West, assumed the Ysabel Kid to be—had appeared very young and unsure of himself as he had stepped into the opulent lobby of San Antonio de Bexar's most luxurious hotel, a closer inspection had left its doubts. The clerk had been on the point of delivering a sharp protest when the rifle had been laid in front of him, and the words had gone un-uttered. There was a sardonic glint, almost a mocking challenge, in the newcomer's red hazel eyes which the clerk had found disconcerting and even unnerving. The glint had suggested that he should not attempt to be too high-handed.

However, being consious of the dignity of his position, the clerk had tried to throw off the sensation. His query-ing of the name given by the 'cowhand' had been a vain attempt to re-establish the correct relationship between them. Even as he had started to do so, he had been won-dering if an insistence on social standing was a good idea in this case.

'There's not *real* likely to be more than one gent name

of "Guillemot" staying here, even in a fancy, high-toned place like this, now is there?' challenged the Kid, who was rarely influenced by atmosphere and impervious to unwarranted disapproval. 'I mean, they're not running around all over the range like "Smiths", "Joneses" or "Rileys".'

'Is Mr. Guillemot expecting you, sir?' the clerk asked stiffly.

'I reckon he just might be.'

'May I inquire your name?'

'It wouldn't do no good, even if I told you,' the Kid declared. 'But General Hardin sent me.'

'From the OD Connected ranch, sir?' the clerk inquired and there was a slight change in his attitude.

'Like you said,' the Kid drawled. 'From the OD Connected ranch.'

'I see,' the clerk said, glancing at the rifle and returning his gaze to the centre of the Kid's chest. He could not meet the coldly mocking scrutiny of the red-hazel eyes. 'Mr. Guillemot is in Room Twenty-One, sir. I'll have a boy show you up.'

'Shucks, I found my way from the spread to here without having no "boy" lead me by the hand,' the Kid protested, picking up his rifle. 'I reckon I mught just about make it the rest of the way.'

'It—It's the rule of the establishment, sir,' the clerk said nervously.

'Wouldn't want to go busting no rules in a fancy place like this,' the Kid stated, watching the flicker of relief cross the man's sallow features as he rang the bell on the desk and a boy wearing a bell-hop's livery came forward. 'Howdy, *amigo*. Looks like you're my scout over thishere trail.'

'Number Twenty-One,' the clerk ordered, glaring at the grinning and apparently unimpressed boy. As he watched them walking away, he took out a handkerchief and mopped daintily at his brow, thinking, 'I should never have left Baltimore. People knew their place there.'

Oblivious of the clerk's sentiments, which would not have worried him even if he had been aware of them, the Kid accompanied the youngster upstairs. He was conscious of the way in which the bell-hop was studying him, with particular attention to his clothes and armament.

'Hey,' the boy said, having scrutinized the Winchester and Dragoon Colt. 'Aren't you the Ysabel Kid?'

'Don't you go telling anybody,' the Kid replied, knowing that he would obtain information by admitting the truth. 'But I am.'

'Wowee!' the boy breathed. 'Wait until I tell the other fellers about *this*!'

'What's this gent I'm going to see like, *amigo*?' the Kid inquired.

'He's a dude,' the boy replied, but his voice did not hold the kind of contempt which would normally have accompanied such a term. 'A hard cuss, 'less I miss my guess. Walks 'n' talks like a bow-necked Army officer, but he could be a Pink-Eye.'

'Huh huh,' the Kid grunted, comparing the information with Belle Boyd's description of Guillemot the previous night. Although they had not come any closer to solving the mystery, they had formulated a plan which might help them do so before she had returned to her own room. He was on his way to put the first stage of the plan into operation. 'What makes you reckon that?'

'He's got that big *hombre* who's been hanging around all week up there with him.'

'Which big *hombre*?'

'He's another dude. A big square-head. Got papers saying he's a Pink-Eye's 's been sent down here to keep watch for owlhoots's might've come in for the County Fair.'

Although nothing showed on his Indian-dark features, the Kid found the bell-hop's information very interesting. It was, he realized, possible—even probable—that the Pinkerton National Detective Agency might send their

'Pink-Eye' operatives to San Antonio to keep watch for wanted men or known criminals, particularly any with sufficient money to stay at the Sandford Hotel. They might even have heard of Guillemot's intention to visit the town and hoped to achieve what the official law enforcement organizations of the world had failed to do, catch him committing a crime. Or somebody might have hired them to try to find out what had brought him from Europe. It was even possible that he had hired them to watch out for his various enemies.

However, the term 'square-head' was applied to men of Teutonic nationality. All came under the same ethnic classification in the Old West, whether they be Danish, Dutch, Norwegian, Swedish—or German!

According to the bell-hop, the 'square-head' had been in town for at least a week. Which meant that he could have been the man who had hired Urizza.

There was no time for the Kid to consider the matter too extensively. They were already approaching the door marked '21'.

'Say one thing,' the boy went on, oblivious of the disturbing possibilities his news had produced for the Kid. 'Them Pink-Eyes sure live well. Thishere suite's the best in the house.'

Before any more could be said, the bell-hop knocked on the door.

'Come in!' called a hard, commanding voice.

'Means you, not me,' the boy remarked. 'Said for me to fetch whoever come up and let 'em go in.'

Opening the door, after tipping the boy and watching him scuttle away, the Kid entered. He was carrying the Winchester in his right hand as he walked in and looked around. There was a door at either side, giving access to the rest of the suite. The one at the left was slightly ajar. Noticing that, while closing the door behind him, he turned his attention to the occupants of the sitting-room.

One, standing by the window, was a tall, lean, hard-looking man with close-cropped brown hair and clad in expensive Eastern riding clothes. There was, as the boy had said, something of a military air about him. It was the look of a hard martinet officer, which the smile on his face did little to soften.

Seated at the table, the second occupant of the room came as a surprise to the Kid. Brown haired, dressed in a dark-grey two-piece travelling costume which set off a richly endowed figure, the beautiful young woman met his gaze. However, she neither moved nor spoke.

'You have come from General Hardin?' the man asked, speaking English with an accent with the Kid could not identify.

'Why sure,' the youngster replied, taking his gaze from the woman.

'I'm pleased to meet you,' the man stated, extending his right hand. He did not, however, offer to advance.

'Same with me,' the Kid drawled, transferring the Winchester to his left hand as he took his first step forward. Flickering another glance at the young woman, he noticed that she gave what might have been a quick, but definite negative shake of her head. Walking across the room in a very leisurely fashion, he allowed the Winchester to slide until he held it at the wrist of the butt and with the muzzle pointing at the floor. At the same time, he continued speaking in a matter-of-fact manner. 'Know a feller name of "Limping Joe" who allus used to squeeze 'stead of just shaking hands. Just for a joke, 'cept he hurt, way he did it. Only one time he started squeezing when t'other feller was holding a rifle and the feller couldn't stop his-self pulling the trigger. Which's why they call him *"Limping* Joe".'

So well had the Kid coordinated his words and movements that his story came to an end just before he reached the other man. However, he glanced downwards as he thrust forward his right hand.

The man's eyes followed the direction in which the Kid

was looking, then snapped up to stare hard at his face. The quick examination had disclosed that the muzzle of the Winchester was almost touching the centre of his well-polished brown Hessian-type riding boot. More significantly, not only was the rifle's hammer at the fully cocked position, the youngster's little, third and second fingers were inside the loading lever's ring while his forefinger was curled over the trigger. Nobody who had any experience with firearms—which Ole Devil Hardin's representative was certain to possess—would commit such a blunder unintentionally. Although nothing in his visitor's guileless young face gave any inkling of whatever thoughts might lie beyond it, the man swung his head momentarily towards the partially open door and shook it in an urgently prohibitive manner.

'So *you're* Mr. Guillemot,' the Kid drawled, in an amiable tone which gave no indication of his true feelings. Then, without actually looking at the young woman, he jerked his head in her direction and went on, 'And this'll be Mrs. Guillemot, I reckon.'

Although the Kid had done so to prevent the man from suspecting, he did not need to guess at the young woman's identity. In spite of her normally blonde hair having been dyed brunette and fixed in a different style to their last meeting, he had recognized her at first sight. Belle Starr, the lady outlaw, was on very close and intimate terms with his *amigo*, Mark Counter, and the Kid had met her on more than one occasion.[1]

Already alerted by the bell-hop's description of 'Guillemot' to the possibility of something being wrong, the Kid had been worried about the absence of the 'big square-head'. Taken with Belle Starr's warning head-

1. How Mark Counter's romance with Belle Starr started, progressed and ended is told in: the 'The Bounty On Belle Starr's Scalp' episode of *Troubled Range*, *The Bad Bunch*, *Rangeland Hercules*, the 'The Lady Known As Belle' episode of *The Hard Riders* and *Guns in the Night*. Two occasions when she met the Ysabel Kid are told in: *Hell in the Palo Duro* and *Go Back to Hell*.

shake, the partially open door had offered an answer to that question. Her signal had also been warning that it might be inadvisable for him to shake hands with 'Guillemot'.

'Without wishing to offend you,' the man said, without acknowledging the Kid's suggestion regarding his and Belle's identities, 'but you have proof that you are General Hardin's representative.'

'Nope,' the Kid answered, moving around so that he could keep the left side door under observation; but doing it in a casual and, apparently, accidental manner.

'You haven't?' the man growled.

'I didn't reckon I'd need any,' the Kid explained, 'seeing's my boss, Cap'n Fog'll be along soon. Him being Ole Devil's nephew 'n' all, he's the one who'll be doing all the talking.'

'And where is Captain Fog now?' the man asked, his face showing no emotion.

'Down to Shelby's livery barn,' the Kid lied, with such an air of sincerity that he might have been telling the truth with his hand on a bible. 'We've only just now hit town and he sent me along to let you know he's coming.'

'*Ach* so!' the man ejaculated. 'And he will be here soon?'

'Why sure.'

'I trust that you had an uneventful journey, Mr.——' Belle put in.

'So peaceable I was like to sleep all the way for want of something to do, ma'am,' the Kid replied. 'Why wouldn't we have?'

'One hears such terrible stories about this wild frontier country,' Belle explained, with a wide-eyed awe which was amusing to anybody who knew her true nature. 'What with marauding Indians and outlaws lurking behind each and every bush.'

'We didn't see a one of either, ma'am,' the Kid declared. 'Which doesn't surprise *me* none.'

82

'Why ever not?' Belle inquired.

'Without wanting to sound boastful, ma'am,' the Kid elaborated, looking at the girl and sensing that the man was paying very keen attention to the conversation, 'any body's knows Cap'n Fog 'n' me, which most folks out here do, wouldn't want to lock horns with us.'

'You think so, huh?' barked the man.

'Mister,' the Kid replied, turning coldly mocking eyes back to his challenger. 'I *know* so for sure. Was a feller once tried to have us gunned down. Hadn't the guts, or was too smart, to try it his-self, so he hired him a couple of *pistolero valientes*—happen you-all know what they are——?'

'I know,' the man conceded.

'Well, sir,' the Kid went on. 'He paid 'em real good money to do it. Only, once they'd got that money, why they just headed over the border and he never saw them —or his money—again.'

For all his surreptitious, but keen-eyed, scrutiny, the Kid could not detect any trace of concern on the man's hard face. Yet he sensed that his comments had aroused some emotion.

'Well,' the Kid continued, deciding against forcing the issue. 'I've done what I was sent for, so I'll be drifting along. There's this lil Mexican *senorita* I know——'

'How long will it be before Captain Fog comes?' 'Guillemot' interrupted.

'About an hour or so,' the Kid replied. 'His Cousin Betty's coming in on the noon stage 'n' he wants to be on hand to meet her.'

'Very well,' 'Guillemot' said, glancing at the partially open door as if trying to make up his mind. Then he shrugged and went on, 'Will you go and tell him that I'd be obliged if he could come to see me straight away? We can attend to our business in time for him to meet his cousin.'

'I'll do that,' the Kid promised. '*Adios*, Mrs. Guillemot,

83

ma'am. It's been right pleasant making your acquaintance.'

While speaking, the Kid was crossing the room. He
walked in such a manner that at no time was the left side
door out of his range of vision. Returning the Winchester
to his right hand, but taking the precaution of grasping it
in the same way, he nodded to the man and Belle, then
left.

After the door had closed, the second man came out of
the bedroom. Burly, with close-cropped blond hair, his
town suit was of a cheaper quality than 'Guillemot's'
garments. Scowling, he thrust the short-barrelled Webley
Bulldog revolver he was holding beneath his open jacket
and into the cross-draw holster on the left side of his
waist-belt.

'Shall we wait for Fog?' the man asked and, although
he spoke English very well, there was a trace of a hard
Germanic accent in his voice.

'You can,' Belle Starr replied, before 'Guillemot'
could speak. 'But *I'm* leaving right now. And, if you've
any sense, you'll do the same.'

'What do you mean?' 'Guillemot' demanded.

'When Ram Turtle asked me to come down here with
you and lend you a hand, I don't think he knew—and I
certainly didn't—that the people you were after was the
OD Connected,' Belle answered, standing up and lifting
free the reticule which was dangling by its draw-strings
from the back of her chair. Holding it in her left hand,
she slipped the right into its mouth and went on, 'That's
one outfit I don't intend to lock horns with——'

'We came here to "lock horns", as you put it, with the
man who has been sent to act as guide for the Ox,' 'Guillemot' protested. 'And you being here was to lull his suspicions.'

'That's true,' Belle conceded. 'And it was a good plan,
or would have been if it had worked. Now I've seen who
we're up against, I'm not surprised that Urizza either

backed out or failed. If I'd known who was involved, I could have told you that there'd be more than one of them coming and no two-bit *pistolero* like Urizza would stop them.'

'The Ox only asked for one man to be sent,' 'Guillemot' objected.

'Or so you were told,' the girl countered. 'Have you seen a copy of the letter?'

'No,' 'Guillemot' admitted. 'But my informant knew what was in it.'

'Maybe he only *guessed* at what was said,' Belle suggested. 'He might not have had a chance to read it.'

'*He'd* have the chance all right,' the burly man put in. 'Are we going to wait for Fog to come and catch him like——'

'Like you *didn't* catch the Kid?' Belle corrected, although the words had not been directed at her.

'You *knew* him?' 'Guillemot' growled, eyeing the girl suspiciously.

'I've seen him and all the rest of Ole Devil's floating outfit,' Belle replied.

'When Fog comes——' the second man began.

'He'll be ready for trouble,' Belle interrupted. 'Hasn't it sunk into your head yet that the Kid knew Mr. Ehlring isn't the Ox?'

'How could he know?' the burly man asked worriedly.

Maybe your informant didn't know as much as you think,' Belle answered. 'There could have been a description of the Ox in the letter, or perhaps there was supposed to be a password.' She looked at Ehlring and continued, 'You saw the way he acted. He either guessed, or knew, that Werra was in the bedroom.'

'I should have come out——!' Werra barked.

'If you had, there'd have been shooting,' Belle assured him. 'Which's what we were trying to avoid. I tell you, he *knew* he wasn't meeting the Ox. Now he's gone to tell Dusty Fog. And I don't aim to be here when they arrive.'

'There'll only be the two of them,' Werra declared truculently. 'Let's wait for them and——'

'A mistake like *that* could get you shot,' Belle warned. 'You'll be up against the fastest gun in Texas and the Kid's nearly as good. There'll be no way you can take them by surprise, or catch them without shooting. Even *if* you survived, the Ox would hear about it when he gets here and the letter of introduction from General Hardin wouldn't do us any good.'

'So what do we do?' Ehlring wanted to know, gritting out the words angrily.

'Get out of here,' Belle answered, backing towards the door with her right hand still concealed in the reticule. 'And out of San Antonio.'

'We came here to do a——!' Ehlring commenced.

'Then you can stay on and try to do it,' Belle told him, halting at the door. 'But I'm going somewhere that's a whole heap safer than this town's going to be.'

'Damn it——!' Ehlring snarled, taking a step forward in a menacing fashion.

'You're not going to *try* to stop me, are you?' Belle challenged, showing neither alarm nor fear although her right hand came nearer to the top of the reticule and was clearly grasping something. 'I wouldn't advise *that*.'

'All right,' Ehlring grunted, after having studied the girl's coldly determined face and attitude for a few seconds. 'Go if you want.'

'I thought you'd see it my way,' Belle declared. Then she tightened the draw strings so that the reticule would remain on her right hand while she used the left to reach behind and open the door. 'There's *no* way you can make your idea work and, if you've any sense, you'll get out of town as quickly as possible. That's what I intend to do.'

'You think it's *that* serious?'. Ehlring inquired, impressed despite his aversion to receiving even sound advice from a woman.

'I *know* it is,' Belle assured him. 'Which's why I'm

pulling out. *Adios*, gentlemen. If you don't think I've earned my pay, see Ram Turtle and tell him I said to let you have half of it back.'

With that, the girl stepped into the passage and closed the door. Looking each way, to satisfy herself that she was unobserved, she released the Remington Double Derringer with which she had ensured her safe departure and brought her hand from the reticule. Going to the main staircase, she gazed down at the reception lobby. However, although she saw nothing to alarm her, she glanced at the door of the suite and turned to go up to the second floor.

'She's right,' Ehlring admitted to his companion, after Belle had left. 'Let's get out of here.'

'Shall I go and see the desk clerk?' Werra inquired, as they crossed the room.[2]

'No,' Ehlring replied. 'There's no need. We can't get a man with the Ox now. He'll have to go through Eagle Pass, so we'll wait there and follow him when he arrives.'

2. If the plan had worked, Werra was to have interviewed the desk clerk and told him that, having learned of a plot to rob Guillemot, he and his partner had taken steps to prevent it. So his partner had pretended to be the victim and had acted as bait. To avoid the kind of publicity which would have been detrimental to the hotel's reputation, they had already dealt with and would remove the would-be robber. However, if Guillemot was to learn of the attempt, he would leave immediately, losing the hotel a valuable and influential guest. The only way this could be avoided was for the clerk to ensure that no mention of the 'Pinkerton agents'' activities was made when Guillemot arrived. From what they had seen of the clerk, they had felt sure that he would do as they wished. Then they would have sent a man, hired by Belle Starr and supplied with whatever means of identification the Kid had been carrying, to pose as Ole Devil Hardin's representative.

CHAPTER EIGHT

I'M *VERY* FAST WITH A GUN

'Good afternoon,' Belle Boyd greeted, as a tall, handsome and well-dressed young man opened the door of the Sandford Hotel's Room 21. 'I'm Betty Hardin and I've come to see Mr. Guillemot.'

'Show the lady in, Silk,' called a booming voice.

'He's with me,' Belle explained in an off-hand manner, as the man looked pointedly at the Ysabel Kid. She contrived to sound as if she regarded her companion as being of no importance. 'He can wait out here if you wish.'

'Aw, Miss Hardin,' the Kid protested. 'You know your granpappy said I should stick with you——'

'All right, Silk,' the booming voice went on. 'Show them both in.'

Moving aside, the young man allowed Belle and the Kid to walk by. Then he closed the door and followed them. They ignored him for the moment, being more interested in the room's second occupant.

There was something almost bovine about Octavius Xavier Guillemot which might have accounted for his nickname, even without the coincidence of his initials. It was not the sleek, awesome majesty of a longhorn bull, but more of the massive yet placcid solidity of a draught oxen. Six foot in height, he was built on an enormous scale. His face was bland, with bulbous pink cheeks, lips and chins set on a thick neck. The eyes, made to look small by the rolls of fat around them, were dark but alert and his curly brown hair was tinged with grey yet still luxurious. Obviously his excellently cut black town suit had been tailored to his measure, for it covered his ample body perfectly without lessening the bulk underneath.

While studying Guillemot, Belle and the Kid were conscious that he was subjecting them to an equally careful scrutiny. The girl was dressed as she had been during her meeting with the Kid, except that she no longer wore a wig. For his part, the Kid had left his rifle behind at Ma Laughlin's rooming house.

Finding Belle Starr with the two impostors had presented the Kid with a dilemma in how he should deal with them. While his first instinct had been to find some way to capture and question the men, he had seen a major objection to such an action. It was unlikely that he could bring it off single-handed without gun play. Yet to call on Town Marshal Anse Dale for assistance would have meant involving the lady outlaw. The Kid had been disinclined to do that. Not only had she given him a warning which had steered him out of a trap, she had been of the greatest assistance to Dusty Fog and himself in the town of Hell.

With that thought in mind, the Kid had waited in concealment and followed the two men when they had left by the rear entrance. They had gone to a smaller hotel. Reappearing in a few minutes carrying carpetbags, they had gone to a livery barn and collected a rig. Although the Kid had not followed them, he had felt sure that they were leaving San Antonio and would not be coming back.

Discussing the matter with Belle Boyd, while they were on their way to meet Guillemot, the Kid had found that she approved of his decision. They would, she had said, be able to turn his failure to do anything about the men to their advantage.

On arriving at the hotel, Belle and the Kid had been informed by a clearly perturbed clerk that Mr. Guillemot had arrived. Although it had been apparent that he would have liked to say more, he had made no reference to the Kid's previous visit. Instead, he had ordered the same bell-hop to take them upstairs. The youngster had been just as obviously bubbling with curiosity, but had restrained it.

Passing the visitors, the young man halted slightly to the rear of Guillemot's chair. Dark haired, swarthily handsome, he moved with a swift economy of motion which implied that he would be capable of even greater speed. His brown town suit was expensive and well tailored. Its jacket almost, but not quite, concealed a slight bulge under the left arm-pit. Studying the man, the Kid gave the bulge more attention than the Smith & Wesson American Model of 1869 revolver which was riding in the low-tied fast-draw holster of his Western style gunbelt.

'Miss Hardin?' Guillemot said, advancing around the table and offering a huge right hand.

'I am, sir,' Belle lied, noting the way the greeting had been expressed and wondering if the deception would fail.

'I hope you'll pardon me,' Guillemot went on, after shaking hands. 'But I wonder if you would object to showing me proof of your identity.'

'I beg your pardon, *sir?*' Belle snapped, displaying haughty indignation.

'I assure you that I mean no distrust, nor disrespect, my dear young lady,' the Ox stated blandly. 'But I have good cause for displaying caution.'

'I should hope so, indeed!' Belle snorted, then waited with the air of expecting an explanation.

'I discovered, on arriving, that an impostor had come——' Guillemot commenced.

'Hey!' yelped the Kid, with well-simulated alarm. 'You mean that feller wasn't working for you?'

'Which fellow?' Belle demanded, turning on the Texan.

'I come 'round earlier, to see if this gent was here——' the Kid began, adopting a sullen and resentful tone.

'Why?' Belle interrupted. 'You knew that I would be

arriving——'

'What happened, young man?' Guillemot put in, then swung his gaze to Belle who was registering disapproval. 'My pardon for interrupting, Miss Hardin, but you will appreciate my eagerness to learn more about this matter.'

'I suppose so,' Belle conceded stiffly and, with the air of granting a favour, went on, 'Very well, Ysabel, tell Mr. Guillemot all about it.'

Watching the by-play the Kid found himself most impressed by the way in which Belle was acting the part she had selected as suitable for their needs. Every word and gesture was that of a rich, arrogant, spoiled and snobbish young woman who was filled with an over-inflated sense of her own importance. He also found amusement in contemplating how Betty Hardin was going to react on hearing about the type of person—one who was completely the opposite to her true nature, in fact—that the Rebel Spy was making her out to be.

However, the Kid was less amused by the way in which the younger of the men was looking at him. There was more than a hint of contempt and mockery on the swarthily handsome face, the emotions clearly having been brought about by seeing the Texan treated in such a fashion by a woman.

'Like I said,' the Kid explained and the younger man's thinly veiled disdain did much to help him attain the right kind of attitude. His voice and general bearing conveyed—to the two men at least—an impression of his annoyance over the manner in which the girl had addressed him. 'I come 'round here to see if you'd showed up, Mr. Guillemot——'

'Why?' Belle demanded indignantly. 'You knew that I was coming.'

'Your telegraph message hadn't got to me,' the Kid answered sullenly, then returned his gaze to the Ox. 'Anyways, I come and asked for you. Got showed up and this feller was in here. He allowed he worked for you and's

91

you'd just gone for a walk. Asked who I was and if I'd gotten anything to prove's I'd been sent by Ole Dev— General Hardin——' The alteration in the name had been made in response to Belle's frown and, having made it, he went on, 'When I said I hadn't——'

'Why hadn't you?' the younger man put in.

'He wasn't supposed to come here at all,' Belle answered, glaring angrily at the Kid. 'And the letters wouldn't have been of any use to him. They were to introduce my cousin, Captain Dustine Edward Marsden Fog.'

'Why isn't Captain Fog here?' Guillemot inquired.

'He was ambushed on the trail and injured,' Belle replied, glancing pointedly at the chairs around the table.

'My dear Miss Hardin, how remiss of me!' Guillemot ejaculated, having noticed and interpreted the look correctly. 'Please have a seat. You must be tired after your journey.'

'A five mile ride is nothing,' Belle sniffed, allowing herself to be seated on the chair which the Ox drew out for her. Resting her parasol against it, she dropped her reticule on to her lap.

'*Five* miles——?' the younger man began.

'I was visiting out at the Schofield ranch, *sir*,' Belle told him, showing her disapproval at the interruption and then scowled at the Kid. 'You were supposed to come and fetch me. The first thing I knew was when the General's telegraph message arrived.'

'I was aiming to——' the Kid commenced, although his attitude suggested that he had had no such intention.

'Tell me about the ambush, *Mr*. Ysabel,' Guillemot requested.

'There's not a heap to tell,' the Kid declared, but obliged with a description of the affair.

'It could have been somebody with an old score to settle,' Guillemot suggested, having resumed his seat.

'Why sure,' the Kid agreed. 'And that's all I figured it

to be, until I got jumped last night here in San Antonio.'

'Who by?' Guillemot demanded.

'A feller dressed's a woman was all I saw for sure, and him not plain,' the Kid replied. 'Was another one, 'cording to the deputy's happened by and chased 'em off. Big and heavy built jasper.'

'Could he have been the man who was here?' Guillemot wanted to know.

'Not 'less the deputy called it wrong. The jasper here was tall, but not hefty. Looked like he'd been in the Army. Real bow-necked officer, I'd say.'

'They could have been trying to rob you,' Guillemot remarked, after darting a questioning look at his companion and receiving a negative shake of the head.

'I'd've thought that, 'cepting they left my money in my pocket,' the Kid countered. 'Which's one of the reasons I wasn't carrying Ole—the General's letters this morning when I come around.'

'Here they are, Mr. Guillemot,' Belle said, opening her reticule and extracting three envelopes without allowing its other contents—particularly her Remington Double Derringer—to be seen. 'These are the General's letters introducing Cousin Dusty to you, along with a copy of the letter which he received from Resin Bowie the Second, a letter of introduction to *Senor* Serrano and the telegraph message telling me to take Cousin Dusty's place. How soon do you wish to start?'

'*You* want to go with *us*?' the younger man put in.

Instead of answering, Belle slowly ran her gaze over the speaker. Then she turned an interrogatory glance at the Ox.

'May I present Mr. Anthony Silk, Miss Hardin?' Guillemot inquired, lifting his gaze from the first of the letters. 'He is my secretary, companion and strong right arm.'

If the cold scrutiny which the girl returned to Silk meant anything, she felt that the introduction was hardly worth acknowledging as the person in question was of little or no consequence. However, she nodded briefly before finally deigning to reply, 'No, *Mr.* Silk. I don't *want* to go with *you*. I intend to take your *employer* to visit *Senor* Serrano, as Resin Bowie the Second requested. You *may* be coming along.'

'Shucks, Miss Hardin,' the Kid put in, deriving some satisfaction in watching a red flush creeping into Silk's cheeks and anger showing on his face. 'I can handle it easy enough. There's no call for you to come along.'

'Mr. Bowie asked for the General to send his *personal* representative,' Belle reminded the young Texan in her most haughty and overbearing manner. 'That means one of his kin, not just a hired hand. All we need from you is that you guide us there and back.'

'Ah! So you are to be our guide, young man,' Guillemot boomed, watching in a speculative fashion as the Kid's Indian-dark features registered resentment over the girl's words. 'Do you know how to find *Casa Serrano?*'

'It's easy enough done,' the Kid replied, noticing that Silk was showing pleasure at the way Belle had spoken to him. 'We'll cross the Rio Grande up Eagle Pass way, then head south until we hit the *Rio de la Babia*. From there, we'll go up the *Rio Ventoso*. *Casa Serrano*'s maybe fifty miles along it.'

'There doesn't seem to be any great difficulty in finding it,' Silk remarked, addressing the Ox.

'Well now,' the Kid drawled. 'I'd say that depends on who-all's going.'

'I intended only a small party,' Guillemot answered, as once again the words had clearly been directed at him. Just myself, Silk and General Hardin's representative. But in view of what has happened——'

'I can assure you that Ysabel is a very competent guide,' Belle declared, deliberately misinterpreting the cause of the Ox's and Silk's eyes swinging towards her.

'I don't doubt *that*——' Guillemot began.

94

'And if you're concerned on my behalf, don't be,' Belle advised. 'I've been handling and riding horses practically all my life.' Her gaze flickered at the younger man in an insultingly challenging way and she continued, 'It won't be *me* who you have to worry about slowing us down.'

'That's for sure,' the Kid confirmed, before he could stop himself. 'Only it's not being slowed down's'll be all we have to worry about.'

'Why?' Guillemot asked. 'Is the terrain difficult?'

'Nope,' the Kid replied. 'Fact being, most of the way it'll be real easy going.'

'Then what——'

'Mexican *bandidos*, Mr. Guillemot. Could even be some Yaqui Injuns. We're likely to run into 'em between the Rio Grande and *Casa Serrano*, even if that jasper who was in here when I first came doesn't figure on cutting in again.

'I don't follow you,' Guillemot stated, although his attitude suggested that he had an idea of what the Texan was driving at.

'He was here after *something*——' the Kid began, having decided that—with his 'resentment' over 'Betty Hardin's' treatment made noticeable—he should let the Ox see that he had qualities which might be useful.

'Just what does that mean?' Silk demanded, drawing a disapproving frown from the older man.

'Just what it says, mister,' the Kid answered, matching the other's thinly concealed hostility. A glance at Belle told him that she felt he was doing the right thing. 'He wasn't in here, letting on's how he worked for Mr. Guillemot, just so's he could get out of the sun.'

'Possibly he was a thief and said what he did when you surprised him,' the Ox suggested blandly.

'It that's all he was, he sure's hell knew some mighty smart questions 'n' answers,' the Kid responded sardonically. 'Anyways, Marshal Dale's a pretty slick lawman. Is that what he reckons the feller was?'

'We haven't reported the matter to the marshal,' Guillemot confessed.

'Why not?' the Kid wanted to know. 'If I'd got word that somebody'd been in my room and letting folks think's he worked for me when he didn't, I'd sure's shooting want him found.'

'I'd prefer not to have anything which might draw attention to me,' Guillemot explained. 'After all, I hadn't even arrived. So there was nothing here for him to steal——'

'There could've been, happen I'd've been toting along those letters from General Hardin,' the Kid pointed out. 'Happen that feller'd've jumped me then took them 'n' my body out of here, you could be talking to one of his *amigos* right now.'

'We might be,' Silk remarked.

'Happen you think so, go send for the marshal to tell you who I am,' the Kid offered. 'I won't stop you.'

'I don't think we need do *that*,' Guillemot stated, waving a fat hand at the letters. 'These are satisfactory evidence of your *bona fides*.' Then he eyed the Kid with a greater interest which its recipient and Belle found satisfying. 'And *you* certainly don't strike me as being a *man* who it would be easy to "jump" as you put it. What do you think, Miss Hardin?'

'I wouldn't care to be the man who tried it,' Belle said and, for almost the first time in the conversation, was completely sincere. 'But I must also agree with Ysabel. You should have told the marshal. The desk clerk or the manager is sure to——'

'That isn't likely,' Guillemot contradicted politely. 'I have left them in no doubts as to my feelings on the matter. And for a good reason. The impostor may have been here, as Mr. Ysabel so shrewdly deduced, to replace General Hardin's representative with a man of his own. Which implies that others know of what we hope to achieve.'

'Then surely you should tell Marshal Dale,' Belle suggested.

'I think *not*, Miss Hardin,' Guillemot stated and there was hardness under his bland tones, giving the girl and the Kid their first insight of his true nature. 'Once he started his inquiries, they would attract attention and could cause still other people to suspect that my visit might be for more than just a hunting trip. *That* could only increase our difficulties.'

'You mean that somebody else'd figure on getting ole Jim Bowie's knife from you,' the Kid put in.

'If they knew we had it,' Guillemot agreed. 'We are dealing with something of considerable historical value. Such things command high prices.'

'And folks're likely to try *real* hard to get 'em,' the Kid went on. 'Fact being, they've already started at it.'

'So it seems,' Guillemot conceded.

'So it *is*,' the Kid corrected. 'Maybe more'n one bunch of 'em. The *hombre* who got away after the bushwhack wasn't the same's I met here, nor with them's jumped me on the street——'

'Go on,' Guillemot prompted.

'That being so,' the Kid obliged. 'I reckon we should telegraph the General and have him send the rest of the floating outfit along.'

'We don't need them,' Silk commented.

'Comes trouble and we will,' the Kid answered. 'Because, even if all these yahoos aren't in cahoots, there's more of 'em than I can handle on my lonesome.'

'I'll be with you,' Silk pointed out.

'*You?*' the Kid sniffed, wanting to see what kind of a reaction he could evoke.

'I'm *very* fast with a gun,' Silk announced, showing anger. 'Perhaps you think differently?'

'I wouldn't know,' the Kid answered. 'Never having seen you use one.'

'Perhaps you'd like to see me now?' Silk suggested icily,

lifting his right hand as if to let it hover over the butt of the Smith & Wesson, but held horizontally. His left rose slowly, as if in a nervous gesture, to stroke at the lapel of his jacket.

Taking in his challenger's appearance, the Kid drew rapid conclusions. He had grown up around gun fighters and had met many of the best. So he could differentiate between the real thing and a show-off. Unless he was much mistaken, dude or not, Silk came into the former classification. There was the indefinable aura about him of a man who was capable of killing without hesitation.

'Well now,' the Kid drawled at the completion of his summation, sounding so mild that Belle—if not the two men—realized he was at a state of complete readiness for action. 'Happen you're so all-fired fast, I don't reckon's I would at that.' Then, as he saw the mocking twist which came to Silk's lips, he hooked his thumbs into his gunbelt and went on, 'Only I never took to looking like I've backed down, neither.'

Even if Belle had not duplicated her companion's estimation of Silk's potential, she would have sensed it. So she glanced at Guillemot, who was sitting with both hands resting before him on the table. She could read nothing on the bland, pink face and wondered if she should intervene immediately or wait to see what he would do.

The decision was taken from Belle's hands by a knocking on the door.

'Will you see who that is, Silk?' Guillemot requested, still without giving any evidence of his feelings.

For a moment, the younger man neither moved nor spoke. Belle, for one, could sense that he wanted to force a showdown.

Then, making an almost visible effort, Silk relaxed and walked with short, angry steps across the room to open the door.

'Good afternoon,' said a feminine voice from the passage. 'Mr. Turtle of Fort Worth asked me to drop by and say "hello" to Mr. Guillemot for him.'

Belle and the Kid exchanged glances!

Instantly, in a casual-seeming manner, the girl lowered her hands to the reticule on her lap.

Although the Kid had not done so while confronting Silk, he let his right hand drop and turned it palm outwards alongside the worn walnut grips of his old Dragoon Colt.

Even without being able to see the speaker, they both knew that she was Belle Starr.

CHAPTER NINE

THE SON-OF-A-BITCH *IS FAST*

'Ask the young lady to come in, Silk,' Octavius Xavier Guillemot requested, as the swarthily handsome young man looked at him for guidance.

Once again, after briefly studying their host, Belle Boyd and the Ysabel Kid exchanged swift glances. Neither of them knew what to make of this latest and most unexpected development. However, they had failed to detect any suggestion that the fat man had discerned something of their perturbation and had given the order so as to try them out. So each was seeking assurance that the other appreciated the situation and was prepared to meet any eventuality. Having satisfied themselves on that point, they turned their attention towards the door.

There was, Belle and the Kid realized, a considerable threat to the success of their deception. While they were now sufficiently forewarned to be able to conceal the fact that they recognized Belle Starr, the same did not apply with her. Finding herself suddenly confronted by them and being aware of the Rebel Spy's true identity,[1] she might inadvertently say or do something to betray them.

Or, in view of how the lady outlaw had announced herself, the betrayal might be deliberate. Her reference to 'Mr. Turtle of Fort Worth' had been as significant to Belle Boyd and the Kid[2] as it had appeared to be to the Ox. Ram Turtle was a man of considerable importance

1. How Belle Boyd and Belle Starr first met is told in: *The Bad Bunch.*
2. How the Ysabel Kid came into contact with Ram Turtle is told in: *Set Texas Back on her Feet.*

to the criminal element of Texas, owning a saloon on the outskirts of that city at which wanted men could find shelter or leave messages. According to Belle Starr, she had been sent by Turtle to make contact with Guillemot.

All of which raised two vitally important points for Belle Boyd and the Kid.

Why had the Ox asked the lady outlaw to come in, guessing what she must be, while they were present?

Could he suspect them and hoped that Ram Turtle's agent would be able to confirm or deny their identities?

Thinking fast, before Silk could carry out his instructions, Belle Boyd started to stand up, raised her voice and said, 'If it isn't convenient for Ysabel and I to stay, Mr. Guillemot——'

By doing so, the Rebel Spy had two things in mind. She hoped to give a warning to the lady outlaw, in case Belle Starr might have no desire to expose them. Or to be in a better position to protect herself if the need should arise.

'It isn't, Miss Hardin,' the Ox boomed in tones loud enough to accidentally, or deliberately, give the girl who was entering further information.

Belle Starr had changed her clothes since the Kid had last seen her and, from all appearances, had been doing some travelling. She had on a black Stetson, a tight-rolled scarlet bandana knotted around her throat, a fringed buckskin jacket over an open-necked grey shirt and a doeskin divided skirt from beneath which emerged brown riding boots. All the garments were spattered with a coating of dust. The reticule had gone, being replaced by a leather quirt which was dangling by its carrying strap from her left wrist.

'I'm sorry, Mr. Guillemot,' the lady outlaw said, coming to a halt and looking at the two men and the girl around the table. 'If I'd realized that you had visitors, I wouldn't have come.'

Watching the other young woman, Belle Boyd was impressed by her self control. Either she had recognized the Rebel Spy's voice and understood the warning it was giving, or she was exceptionally good at concealing her emotions. No matter which it might be, she gave no hint of knowing Belle Boyd or the Kid.

Nor of betraying them.

'I'm pleased you did, Miss——' Guillemot answered, coming to his feet and advancing with his right hand extended.

'Beauregard,' Starr replied, shaking hands. 'Magnolia Beauregard.'

'This is a pleasure, Miss Beauregard,' Guillemot stated, then indicated his other guests. 'Perhaps you know Miss Betty Hardin and Mr. Ysabel?'

'We haven't met,' Starr lied, but without any evidence of it showing in her voice or actions. 'But of course everybody has heard of the Ysabel Kid. It's a pleasure to make your acquaintance, sir. And yours, Miss Hardin.'

'I hope that you haven't heard of Mr. Ysabel in your official capacity, Miss Beauregard?' Guillemot inquired, then swung his gaze to the Kid. 'Just a little joke, sir, with no offence meant or, I hope, taken. You wouldn't think it to look at her, but Miss Beauregard is a detective from the Pinkerton Agency.'

'Wee dogie!' the Kid ejaculated, guessing that Starr was as surprised as himself to learn of her employment. 'I ain't never yet met a real-live lady detective before.'

'A *lady* detective,' Boyd went on, having duplicated the Kid's summation. It ruled out the possibility that Starr had attempted to pass herself off in such a capacity as a means of pulling a confidence trick or robbery with the Ox as its victim. Wanting to give Starr a clue to the part she was playing, her voice expressed thinly-veiled disdain and snobbish disapproval. 'My! Whatever next.'

'A girl has to earn her livings as best she can, Miss Hardin,' Starr answered in chilly tones. 'Or *some* of us do.'

'I suppose so,' Boyd sniffed, then turned away from the other girl. 'If you have things to discuss with this—*lady*—Mr. Guillemot, I can come back later.'

'There's no need for that, as our business also concerns you,' the Ox replied. 'Please be seated. And you, Miss Beauregard.'

'Very well, if you're sure that we're not intruding,' Boyd consented, although her attitude displayed that she did not care for the idea of sharing the same table as the 'lady detective'.

While the Kid was satisfied that the danger of being exposed had passed, at least for the time being, he did not relax in his vigilance where Guillemot's secretary was concerned. Anthony Silk had closed the door and crossed the room to take up his position behind his employer's chair. Although he darted a challenging glare at the young Texan, he did not attempt to resume the situation which had been developing before Belle Starr's arrival. Sensing that any furtherance of it might need to be pushed to the limit, the Kid was willing to let things ride. Something warned him, however, that he and the secretary might have to lock horns in the future. Nor did he sell Silk short. Dude or not, there was a *very* dangerous man.

'I suppose you are wondering why I have hired a member of the Pinkerton Agency, Miss Hardin, Mr. Ysabel?' Guillemot remarked, after the girls had taken their seats and he was settled on his chair.

'I am,' Boyd agreed, wondering what excuse would be made.

'Wouldn't be to keep a look out for folks's might have a hankering to lay hands on old Jim Bowie's knife, would it?' the Kid inquired, wanting to carry on with the process of impressing the Ox.

'It would, sir,' Guillemot admitted and his expression suggested that the process was producing the required result. 'I don't know to whom, but I have reason to believe

103

that a rumour of what I hope to do—for the Bowie family —has been circulated.'

'You mean somebody's been talking out of turn, huh?' asked the Kid, having noticed that the reference to the Bowie family appeared to have been an afterthought.

'It would appear so,' Guillemot confirmed.

'Perhaps your *lady* detective could find out who did it,' Boyd suggested and received a frown from Starr that was surprisingly genuine.

'There's no need for her to waste time on *that*,' Guillemot declared, just a shade too quickly Boyd thought. 'Silk has already found out that my valet was responsible.'

'Where's this here "valley" at now?' the Kid inquired, deciding against casting doubt on the secretary's judgement.

'I discharged him without a reference, naturally,' Guillemot answered, but there was something in his bland tones which implied that the subject was closed as far as further discussion was concerned. 'He refused to say to whom he had sold the information, unfortunately. That was why I consulted the Pinkerton Agency.'

'Have you found out who it is, Miss——?' Boyd inquired, her attitude suggesting that a 'lady detective's' social standing was not sufficient to warrant remembering her name.

'*Beauregard*,' Starr supplied icily, guessing what kind of a character the Rebel Spy was portraying and sharing the Kid's view on the excellence of the performance. 'And my findings are confidential, *Miss Hardin*.'

'Come come, Miss Beauregard,' Guillemot boomed jovially. 'You can speak freely. Miss Hardin, Mr. Ysabel and Silk are all in my confidence.'

'Well, if that's how you want it, all right,' Starr replied, sounding as if she disapproved but felt she was absolved of all blame if things should go wrong. 'As far as I can make out, there are two separate groups involved, one

French and one German. In fact, the Germans were in this room this morning.'

'We know all about that,' Boyd declared haughtily, having noticed an exchange of glances between the Ox and his secretary. 'I suppose you learned in the same way we did, from the desk clerk?'

'Not exactly,' Starr answered. 'I'd come to see if you'd arrived, Mr. Guillemot, and was told that you had. So I came up and was just in time to see Ehlring and Werra leaving the suite.'

'Why didn't you stop them?' Boyd demanded, feeling such a comment would be expected from her.

'I didn't know that Mr. Guillemot wasn't here and they weren't behaving suspiciously,' Starr told her. 'For all I knew, they could have been paying him a visit. Of course, as soon as I'd knocked and didn't get an answer, I went downstairs. The clerk told me that "Mr. Guillemot" had just left, so I went to look for them. They were driving away in a rig, so I got my horse and followed.'

'Why didn't you fetch the marshal and have them arrested?' Boyd wanted to know.

'Because Mr. Guillemot had said that he didn't want any attention drawn to him,' Starr countered. 'And the way I see it, if there's any complaint about how I've handled things, it should come from my employer.'

'Well *really*——!' Boyd squealed indignantly, starting to rise.

'Ladies, *please*,' Guillemot put in soothingly. 'Although I don't condone how she answered you, Miss Hardin, I am satisfied that Miss Beauregard acted for the best.'

'Very well,' Boyd sniffed, sitting down.

'Where did they go to, Miss Beauregard?' the Ox inquired, with peace restored.

'Out of town, on the south-bound trail,' Starr replied. 'I followed them for as long as I dared and they weren't showing any sign of turning back.'

'Do you-all reckon they will be, ma'am?' asked the Kid.

'They *might*, but they didn't look like they meant to as they'd got baggage in the rig,' Starr answered. 'They'd know that Mr. Guillemot would hear about what they'd been up to when he arrived and might figure that the town marshal'd be set to looking for them. So they could just keep on going.'

'You say there were *two* of them, Miss Beauregard?' Guillemot asked and glanced quizzically at the Kid.

'I only *saw* one of them,' the young Texan admitted, in response to the unasked question. 'Which the other could've been in one of the other rooms. Fact being, the door to that 'n——' he pointed a finger to the left, 'was open a mite. So that's where he likely was hidden.'

'*Two* of them,' Silk put in, 'and they let you walk out.'

'Why not?' countered the Kid. 'I wasn't carrying the letters's they was after—but I did have my ole "yellow boy".'

'Your what?' Guillemot asked, throwing a cold scowl at his secretary as he spoke.

'Winchester,' the Kid explained. 'Folks call it that 'cause of its brass frame. Anyways, I reckon that, seeing's I didn't have what they wanted, they figured it wasn't worth chancing making a fuss.'

'That's true enough,' Guillemot said firmly and, clearly wanting to change the subject, he looked at the lady outlaw. 'So you don't think they'll be coming back, Miss Beauregard?'

'I'd be surprised if they do,' Starr answered. 'Especially if they think you've told Marshal Dale. He's a well-deserved name for being an efficient lawman.'

'Then we'll hope that we've seen the last of them,' Guillemot declared.

'We may have seen the last of *them*,' Starr conceded. 'But not of the other two.'

'Which other two?' the Ox barked.

'The Frenchmen,' Starr replied.

'Haven't *they* left town?' Boyd asked.

'Not unless they went since I came up here,' Starr assured her.

'What do you mean?' Guillemot demanded.

'They're in the Bon Ton Restaurant across the street,' Starr explained. 'Seated by a window, so that they can watch the front entrance of the hotel.'

For a moment, none of the others spoke. The Kid looked at Belle Boyd, then turned his gaze towards the two men. Nothing showed on Guillemot's face. However, Silk seemed pensive and his left hand was once more rising to stroke at the lapel of his jacket.

'Are you sure that they're watching us?' Guillemot finally asked.

'I am,' Starr confirmed. 'They call one of them "Slippers", he's a swish——'

'A "swish"?' the Ox repeated, sounding puzzled.

'It means he likes men, not girls,' Starr interpreted. 'If Miss Hardin doesn't mind me saying so.'

'Does he dress up like a woman, too?' Boyd inquired, before she could stop herself. Then she contrived to look coy, although apparently pretending to act broadminded. 'I've heard people like that sometimes do.'

'I've never *seen* him doing it,' Starr confessed, wondering what had prompted such a question. 'The other one's name is Vernet. He seems to have broken his arm, at least he's wearing it in a sling.'

On the point of speaking, the Kid caught a quickly delivered warning shake from Belle Boyd's head. For a moment, he was puzzled. Then he realized what the prohibitive signal had meant. As he had told the other two men that he had been knocked unconscious by his attackers the previous night, he should not have known about Vernet's injury.

'One of the feller's jumped me just after I hit town was dressed like a woman,' the young Texan drawled, revising his comment. 'That'd be the sort of thing a swish'd do happen he was wanting a disguise. Anyways, I don't reckon it'll do any harm happen I drift over 'n' take a look at 'em.'

'Would you recognize them?' Guillemot inquired.

'Likely not,' the Kid admitted. 'But they just might think I had 'n' do something to give 'em away. I figure it's worth taking a look.'

'So do I,' Silk remarked. 'If they are after us, it will be worth knowing.'

'There's more to it than that,' the Kid pointed out. 'Happen they did jump me, we can get 'em off our trail.'

'How?' Guillemot asked.

'Easy enough,' the Kid replied. 'The marshal'll toss 'em in the pokey.'

'And keep *you* here as a witness,' Guillemot protested.

'He won't if *I* ask him not to—in the General's name,' Boyd put in.

'What do you intend to do, Mr. Ysabel?' Guillemot inquired.

'Just go on over, like I was fixing to have a meal, and look 'em over,' the Kid explained. 'Then, happen I reckon it was them, I'll pass word for the marshal. Like Miss Hardin says, he'll do a favour for General Hardin and'll hold 'em. Then he can turn 'em loose tomorrow after we've pulled out.'

'It's possible that they know our destination,' Guillemot warned. 'If so, they could follow us.'

'Let 'em,' the Kid stated. 'They might be real he-coons where they came from, but I figure I can hand them their needings once they get out on the range. That's *my* kind of country.'

'It's certainly worth trying,' Guillemot admitted.

'I'd better come with you, Ysabel,' Boyd remarked, rising as the Kid turned to leave. 'Cowhands don't usually eat at the Bon Ton.'

'Perhaps you and I had better go, too, Miss Beauregard,' Silk suggested.

'Sure,' Starr agreed, dusting off her clothes. 'I could use a meal. How about you, Mr. Guillemot?'

'I think not, young lady,' Ox replied. 'They could become suspicious if we all arrive.'

Although the Kid did not agree with the comment, he kept his thoughts to himself. Leaving the suite with the two girls and Silk, he suggested that they should try to avoid being seen crossing the street. To do so would either scare off the men, or at least allow preparations to be made for their arrival. It was Belle Starr who proposed that they went out by the rear entrance and kept the neighbouring buildings between them until they were beyond the pair's range of vision, entering the Bon Ton Restaurant by its side door instead of from the front.

There was little conversation as the party left the building in the way that the lady outlaw had suggested. The Kid was wondering why Silk, who had shown some animosity towards him, had offered to accompany them. However, he put the matter from his thoughts as they approached the side door and entered the Bon Ton Restaurant.

The dining room was, the Kid noted with mixed feelings, almost empty. While that reduced their chances of remaining unnoticed by the men they were seeking, it lessened the danger of harmless bystanders being hurt in the event of gun play. Only a few people and a single waitress were present, none of them near to the pair who were of such interest to the Kid's party.

The two men were still sitting at the table by the window. Both were well-dressed, the shorter of them almost fussily so. As the two Belles, the Kid and Silk came through the door, the taller and more bulky of the pair glanced in their direction. Stiffening noticeably, he spoke in a low tone to his companion. Then both of them gazed briefly at the front of the hotel. It was obvious that they found the quartet's arrival disconcerting. What was more, from the way they were acting, the Kid decided that—despite his change of clothing and being much cleaner than on the previous night—they recognized him as their would-be victim.

'They know you, L—Kid,' Starr said quietly, changing the name just in time as she remembered that there had been no mention of the young Texan's full name.

Darting a look at Silk, Belle Boyd concluded that he had not noticed the lady outlaw's near error. Having removed his hat, he was hanging it on the rack by the door. Then he turned his gaze to the Kid, who was placing his Stetson alongside it.

'Let's go over,' Silk suggested, although the words came out more as a command. 'Keep well behind us, ladies. There could be trouble.'

Without waiting for the Kid to say whether he approved or not, Silk started to walk across the room. Following, the young Texan moved until he was at his companion's left side and about a yard away. While he approved in general of the other's instructions—if not of the manner in which they had been given—he could see one basic flaw in them. Under normal conditions, neither of the girls would have needed to be relegated to a position of safety. Each of them was fully capable of taking care of herself and knew better than to get in the way if there should be any shooting. He accepted that such standards would not be applicable in the case of 'Betty Hardin', as the Rebel Spy was portraying her. So she and, probably, the 'lady Pinkerton agent' would be better kept out of the possible line of fire.

Against that, the sight of the Kid and Silk approaching, while the girls fell behind, was almost certain to confirm any suspicions the two men might be experiencing over the possibility of their having been identified as his assailants.

Watching Slippers and Vernet, the Kid concluded that his summation on the latter point was correct. As he and Silk continued to draw nearer, with the girls falling even further to the rear and moving aside, the pair started to display agitation.

Glancing at Silk, the Kid found that he was once again stroking the lapel.

No, not *stroking*!

He was *grasping* it!

Something told the Kid that his earlier thoughts had been correct. Silk's action was not merely a nervous gesture.

Slowly, the two men at the table eased back their chairs. They stood up in such a way that they confronted the Kid and Silk. Vernet's right arm was in a sling, but his left hand was reaching underneath it and the side of his jacket. Acting in just as apparently a casual fashion, Slippers raised his right forearm towards the horizontal and its elbow pressed against his ribs. Instantly, a Remington Double Derringer attached to the end of a metal rod was propelled into his palm.

'Look out!' Silk shouted and his left hand drew open the lapel.

From the corner of his eye, even as he responded to the danger, the Kid saw his companion's right hand whip across and under the jacket. It had barely disappeared when it gave a rapid forward twisting motion and emerged holding a short-barrelled revolver.

Although the Kid's right hand had already turned palm outwards and enfolded the Dragoon's butt, making the movement without the need for conscious guidance, he still had not cleared leather when Silk's weapon crashed.

'The son-of-a-bitch *is* fast!' was the thought which passed fleetingly through the Kid's mind.

It came and went in a flash, for there were other and far more important matters to occupy the young Texan's attention.

Silk was undoubtedly fast and certainly deadly, as the Kid had suspected he might be during their confrontation in Guillemot's suite. However, he appeared to possess a very poor tactical sense.

With the Remington Double Derringer already in his hand and pointing towards the Kid, Slippers was far more dangerous than his companion. Clearly hampered by his injury, Vernet had not even brought out the revolver which he was attempting to draw when Silk's bullet struck him between the eyes and slammed him lifeless against the wall.

Only two things saved the Kid. The lightning speed of his Comanche-educated reflexes and Slippers' momentary indecision.

Obviously the dapper man had considered that the young Texan posed the greater and more immediate threat to his life. However, with his right forefinger commencing to tighten—the hammer was already cocked when the Remington had appeared—he saw and heard Silk open fire. For a vitally important split-second, Slippers wavered between which of his assailants he should deal with first.

Seeing his opportunity, the Kid took it by diving sideways and to the left. He had just—and only just—moved when Slippers' weapon spat. Its bullet passed where his body had been an instant before, ending its flight harmlessly in the wall.

Landing on his side, the Kid had completed his draw as he was going down. Lining the big Dragoon, he squeezed the trigger. Forty grains of black powder—an equivalent load to that fired by a Winchester Model of 1873 *rifle* and twelve grains *more* than his 'old yellow boy' could handle —expelled a ·44-calibre soft lead ball which ripped into Slippers' left shoulder.

Hurled bodily against the wall, the dapper man was badly injured and helpless—but that did not save him.

Silk's weapon, a British-made Webley Royal Irish Constabulary ·450-calibre revolver with its barrel reduced to two inches and the lanyard ring removed from its butt as an aid to concealment, roared twice as fast as he could operate the double-action mechanism.

The stricken man jerked under the impacts, as the bullets ploughed their way into his chest and through his heart. He was dead before his body struck the floor. Watching him go down, the Kid wondered what Marshal Anse Dale would say about the shooting. There was, he realized, also the danger that the peace officer might recognize Belle Starr or expose Belle Boyd as a fake.

CHAPTER TEN

HE KNOWS I KILLED HIS NEPHEW

'Hello down there,' called the shorter of the two riders who sat their horses on the rim above where the Ysabel Kid and his party were setting up camp on the third night after their departure from San Antonio. 'Can me 'n' my nephew come in?'

Contrary to the Kid's fears, Marshal Anse Dale had neither recognized Belle Starr nor exposed the Rebel Spy. On the peace officer's arrival at the Bon Ton Restaurant, the girls had kept in the background and allowed the Kid to make the explanations. He had told what was basically the truth. Omitting the fact that he and Silk had already known about the Frenchmen, he had stated that they were compelled to defend themselves when the pair had started to draw on them. There had been sufficient independent witnesses to corroborate the story without the need to involve either of the Belles. Nor had there been any difficulty in establishing a motive for the unprovoked attack. In fact, Dale himself had provided it.

The idler from the livery barn had been found murdered earlier that afternoon. In the course of his investigation, the marshal had discovered that—as he and the Kid had suspected—the victim had been hired, along with a man at every other livery barn, to report on the arrival of any members of the OD Connected. Having obtained a description of the men who had done the hiring, Dale was satisfied that they were the Kid's and Silk's victims. He had also assumed that, having recognized the young Texan and been afraid it might be mutual, the pair had tried to kill him and escape. So the marshal had not pressed the matter any further, beyond asking pointedly when the Kid would be leaving. He had been assured that the departure would be in the near future and that to the best of the young Texan's knowledge, there was not likely to be any more trouble. Dale had said that he hoped there would not be.

Even without the marshal's hint that—due to the shooting—he was not too popular in San Antonio, the Kid had already realized that too long a stay would be inadvisable. Being equally aware of the risk of meeting somebody who knew the real Betty Hardin, Belle Boyd had turned the incident to their advantage. On returning to the Sandford Hotel, she had suggested that—as they disposed of both sets of watchers—it might be wise to leave for *Casa* Serrano before any more could arrive.

Octavius Xavier Guillemot had seen the wisdom of making an early departure. Asking Belle Starr how soon they could leave, he had been told that it would be possible to go at sun-up the following morning. Acting upon the instructions which she had received at the start of her assignment from the 'Pinkerton National Detective Agency', she had already hired a buckboard, horses, supplies and had employed a leathery old timer called Salt-Hoss to act as wrangler. Pointing out that 'Miss Hardin' would need a chaperone, the lady outlaw had contrived to have herself included in the party. As the Rebel Spy had wanted to find out why the other girl was so interested in the affair, she had—pretending to be reluctant—allowed the men to 'persuade' her that it was for the best and had agreed.

Learning that 'Miss Hardin' had not yet arranged for any accommodation, Starr had suggested that Boyd shared her room at the hotel and the offer had been apparently grudgingly accepted. Ordered by the Rebel Spy to help collect her baggage, the Kid had left with the girls and Silk had insisted upon accompanying them. Once out of the suite, the secretary had started to display gallantry towards and interest in 'Miss Hardin'. Hoping that it might be productive, Boyd had encouraged him to continue along those lines. However, no matter what might develop out of the situation in the future, Silk's presence had prevented the Rebel Spy and the Kid from satisfying their curiosity regarding the lady outlaw's behaviour during the collection of the baggage.

That night, in the privacy of her room, Starr had been reasonably frank with Boyd. She had claimed that she had not betrayed the Rebel Spy or the Kid, who could not be present during the interview but was told of it later, because of their previous friendship.

Having settled that aspect satisfactorily, Starr had gone on to explain how Guillemot had hired her—through Ram Turtle—to do more than organize the transport for their journey to *Casa* Serrano and to discover the identities of the men who were following him. She was also to try and find out who had passed them the information that had set them on his trail, which had suggested he was not so certain as he had pretended to be regarding the guilt of his valet. Realizing that the most logical suspect was Silk, Boyd had understood why Starr had shown such disapproval when she had suggested the 'lady detective' should attempt to learn the traitor's name. When dealing with a man who was as dangerous as the secretary had proved himself to be, it did not pay to take chances or to arouse his suspicions.

Either as evidence of her good faith, or to show that it could not be used as a lever against her, Starr had discussed her presence in Guillemot's suite during the Kid's first visit. Shortly before she had been hired by the Ox, Ehlring and Werra had asked Ram Turtle for advice on hiring gun-hands in the San Antonio area. Turtle had learned enough to suspect that they were involved with Guillemot. So Starr had seen a way in which she might obtain the information required by the Ox. She had been too late to prevent Werra from leaving Fort Worth, but with Turtle's help had been accepted as a useful contact by Ehlring. Although she had prevented the Kid from falling into the trap, she had failed in her main purpose. She had claimed—and Boyd believed her—that she had not known the identities of the Germans' victims.

However, after having been so forthcoming, Starr had been less so regarding her motives for accompanying the party. Her explanation—that she had been hired to do a job and wanted to see it through—had not been over-convincing. Seeing that the Rebel Spy was sceptical, she had admitted to being intrigued by the vast amount of interest which was being shown in Guillemot's activities. Being aware of his status in international criminal circles, she had decided that an investigation into them might be worth-while. Like Boyd and the Kid, she had no idea of what made the recovery of the original Bowie knife so important; but had accepted that it must be very valuable for the Ox to be involved.

One thing Starr had refused to comment upon was how she would act if their mission was successful. Knowing that to continue to press that point would be futile, Boyd had let it drop. Nor had she been communicative regarding the United States' Secret Service taking so much notice of the affair. With other countries' agents involved, it was obvious that her department would want to find out why. Although a truce had been declared between them, the Rebel Spy had decided that—past friendship notwithstanding—she would have to keep a wary eye on the lady outlaw if the Ox achieved his purpose.

Setting off early the following morning, the party had headed south along the stagecoach trail which would eventually lead them to Eagle Pass and a ferry across the Rio Grande. While the girls rode horses, Guillemot and Silk—clad in clothes suitable for their pose as hunters—travelled in a buckboard which also carried their baggage. Leaving Salt-Hoss to handle the spare horses, the Kid had spent the day either behind or ahead of his companions. He had seen nothing to suggest that the Germans might have returned to San Antonio and were following, or were waiting along the trail for them to arrive with the intention of ambushing them.

The day had passed uneventfully and the night had been spent at the hotel in Hondo, seat of Medina County. Silk had continued to show great attention to 'Miss Hardin', leaving Salt-Hoss and the hostler at the livery barn to deal with the buckboard's team and luggage so that he could help her unsaddle and care for her horse. From all appearances, Guillemot had not approved of his secretary's behaviour towards the girl. Although he had not commented on the matter, the Kid had sensed that the Ox was perturbed by such a development.

During the evening, the Kid had sought to find out if anybody answering the two Germans' description had passed through the town. While the answers had been negative, he had remembered noticing the tracks of a buckboard leaving the trail about a mile from Hondo. At the time, he had thought nothing of them. However, in the light of a later discovery, he had considered it was possible that—wanting to avoid their presence being disclosed—they had gone around the town. He had located the place where the vehicle had rejoined the trail shortly after they had set off the following morning, but had decided against mentioning the matter to his companions.

The party had passed the second night at Uvalde. Once again, the Kid had found the tracks of the same buckboard leaving the trail at an angle which would keep its occupants out of sight of the town. So he had felt even more certain that it was carrying the Germans and guessed that, having anticipated the point at which the party would cross the Rio Grande, they were heading for Eagle Pass.

There had been little opportunity for the Kid to discuss his findings with Belle Boyd. Continuing to play her part as the snobbish, arrogant and spoiled 'Betty Hardin', she had harassed him to such an extent that it would have been highly suspicious for them to be seen indulging in a lengthy conversation. What was more, the opportunity to do so had been limited by Silk monopolizing so much of her time.

In one way, the latter aspect had been advantageous to the Rebel Spy and the Kid. Guillemot had started to show a growing interest in the young Texan's background and abilities. Most of the information had been supplied by Belle Starr and Salt-Hoss, the latter having known the Kid slightly and by reputation during the days when he and his father had ridden the border-smuggler trails. From them, the Ox had formed a fairly accurate idea of the young Texan's ability as a very capable and efficient fighting man. He had also learned that the Kid possessed considerable knowledge of the border country. That he was impressed had been obvious, also he appeared to have a reason for his curiosity. On the second night, after the Ox had gone to bed and Boyd was seated elsewhere with Silk, Starr had told the Kid that she had been asked to sound out the extent of his loyalty to the OD Connected.

While the Kid had felt sure that the Germans would refrain from taking any action until after the party was in Mexico, he had decided against taking chances. So, on the pretext that to do so would shorten their journey and give them an opportunity to obtain practical experience which would prove useful once they had crossed the Rio Grande, he had suggested that they should go directly to Eagle Pass instead of following the trail via Crystal City in Zavala County.

Accepting the Kid's suggestion, the party had realized that they would be compelled to spend the night out of doors. However, as doing so would be the rule rather than the exception during the journey from the border to *Casa* Serrano and back, they had all agreed that it would do them no harm to start becoming accustomed to such conditions.

Scouting ahead of his companions in the late afternoon, the Kid had selected a suitable camp-site for the party. In a valley which would offer shelter from the elements if the weather should take a turn for the worse, on the banks of a stream that offered grazing for the horses and water to satisfy all their needs, it was a pleasant location. They had made most of their preparations for the night when the two riders had appeared on the rim.

'How about it, Mr. Guillemot?' the Kid inquired, without either raising or lowering the rifle which he had picked up on hearing the horses approaching. 'It'd be's well to find out who they are and what they're doing hereabouts.'

'I agree,' the Ox replied, before any of the others could speak. 'But there's probably nothing to worry about.'

'Nope,' the Kid drawled. 'They're likely just a couple of cowhands wanting to pass the time of day and have a meal.' He raised his voice and went on, 'Come ahead, gents!'

For all his casual words, the Kid subjected the riders to a careful scrutiny as they came down the slope. They and their horses—a big blue roan and an equally large, powerful iron-grey—showed signs to his range-wise eyes of having been travelling hard very recently. What was more, for all his comment to Guillemot, the Kid suspected that they were something other than merely chance-passing cowhands. The way in which they had studied their back trail before commencing the descent into the valley had given a warning of that.

One was of medium height, in his mid-thirties, with a sun-reddened face of almost cherubic appearance. He had thinning, curly brown hair and gave an impression of being corpulent. A white 'planter's' hat sat on the back of his head. He had on a fringed buckskin jacket, open-necked blue shirt with a matching bandana, Levi's pants and low-heeled boots. While there was a Winchester rifle in his saddleboot, he neither wore a gunbelt nor showed signs of being armed in any other way.

Topping the six foot level by maybe two inches, the second man looked to be in his very early twenties. He had wide shoulders and a lean waist, being clad—with the exception of a black J. B. Stetson hat—in the same general fashion as his companion. Rusty-red hair topped a face which, despite a badly broken nose, a scar over the left eye-brow and a thickened left ear, was ruggedly handsome. He too had a Winchester in his saddleboot and was carrying in the low-tied, fast-draw holster of his gunbelt a Colt 1860 Army revolver that had been re-chambered so that it would fire metallic cartridges.

Bringing their horses to a halt, the newcomers sat for a moment looking at the members of the party. There was, however, nothing hostile in the scrutiny.

'Sorry about barging in on you-all like this, folks,' the smaller man announced in a pleasant and amicable voice. He swung from his saddle and left the blue roan standing ground hitched by its dangling reins. 'The name's Brady Anchor and this here's my nephew, Jefferson Trade.'[1]

'Good evening, gentlemen,' Guillemot acknowledged, rising from the trunk upon which he had been seated since its removal from the backboard. 'I trust that you will join us for supper?'

'That's right neighbourly of you, sir,' Brady Anchor declared. 'We've got some victuals——'

'They won't be needed,' Guillemot assured him. 'We have more than sufficient, if the ladies don't object to the little extra work.'

'*Gracias*,' Brady drawled. 'That being the case, we'll lend a hand to 'tend to your hosses.'

1. Brady Anchor and Jefferson Trade had made some changes to their armament by the time they became involved in the incidents recorded in: *Two Miles to the Border*.

'Ysabel!' Belle Boyd called, adopting her usual tone. 'Go and collect some wood, then make a fire.'

'Sure, *Miss Hardin,*' the Kid answered, scowling as if angry at the way in which she had addressed him before the newcomers.

'I'll come with you,' Brady suggested as the young Texan turned away. 'You help the gent with the stock, Jefferson.'

'Yo!' Jefferson Trade responded.

'Way you was holding that old yellow boy's we rode up,' Brady remarked in conversational tones, after the Kid had placed his rifle on the buckboard's seat and they were walking towards the nearby trees in search of firewood, 'I'd say you could be expecting trouble.'

'Not more'n mostly,' the youngster replied.

'You wouldn't have done nothing to get Juan Escuchador riled up at you then?' Brady inquired.

'Would you have call to think's I might?' the Kid countered, letting his right hand drift in a casual-seeming fashion towards the butt of the old Dragoon Colt.

Having made a closer examination of the stocky man as they were walking, the Kid had drawn further conclusions. What appeared to be corpulence was merely the effect caused by the clothing, he had decided. Under the garments lay a hard and powerful body, for the man walked with a rubbery bounce which did not go with a load of fat. In addition, there was a distinct—if unobtrusive—bulge below his *right* armpit that suggested he might be carrying a weapon concealed beneath his jacket.

'Not so much me's Marshal Dale from back to San Antonio,' Brady replied, giving no hint that he had noticed the motions of the Kid's hand although the young Texan did not doubt that he had. He reached with his right hand into the jacket's left breast pocket. 'Gave me this letter to show's he'd asked me 'n' my nephew to drift down this way and tell you's Escuchador's looking for you.'

Accepting the envelope, the Kid extracted and read the letter:

'*Lon,*
Rosa Rio's sent word that Juan Escuchador is gun-
ning for you. The man who is bringing this is Brady An-
chor. He knows as much as I do and you can trust him
and his nephew like you would me.
Yours faithfully,
Anse Dale.'

'Me 'n' my nephew'd just dropped by to say "howdy" to the marshal, us being old friends,' the stocky man explained, when the Kid turned a quizzical glance at him. 'One of Rosa Rio's bouncers came in and asked where you might be. When Anse said you'd left town, the feller asked him to send somebody after you and say that she hadn't sent Juan Escuchador on your trail, nor told him nothing. That was all the feller would, or could—which comes out the same way—tell. Anyways, Anse told me who you was and asked if I'd come by to give you the word.'

'I'm much obliged,' the Kid declared, folding the letter and returning it to the envelope.

'Escuchador's one bad *hombre*,' Brady warned. 'Has he got something against you personal, or against those folks you're travelling with.'

'Just me,' the Kid replied. 'I reckon he knows I killed his nephew.'

'Whee-dogie!' Brady breathed, although the Kid guessed that Marshal Dale had already supplied that information. 'He's not going to take kindly to it. You're lucky in one way, though. He's only got half a dozen men at his back.'

'You've seen 'em, huh?'

'Passed 'em early this morning. We circled 'n' got ahead of 'em without being seen. Found where you'd turned off and followed, but not close enough to your tracks for our sign to be seen.'

'Maybe they're figuring that we'll stick to the trail,' the Kid suggested.

'I wouldn't count on it, because they haven't,' Brady answered. 'They turned off where you did. Maybe they won't have caught up by nightfall, but they'll not be far behind and you sure's hell can't lick 'em to Eagle Pass. They'll be on to you afore then.'

CHAPTER ELEVEN

I'LL STAND BY MR. YSABEL

Having collected wood and returned to the rest of the party, the Ysabel Kid told them the news which Brady Anchor and Jefferson Trade had brought from San Antonio de Bexar. As he was speaking, he watched his companions' faces to see how they were reacting to what he was saying.

Seated on the trunk, Octavius Xavier Guillemot frowned and glanced to where a Sharps 'Old Reliable' buffalo gun—which he had brought from the East as an aid to his pose as a hunter and had already proved that he could use with some skill by shooting a deer at long range on the second day of the journey—leaned against the buckboard. Although he swung his bland, emotionless face back towards the Kid, he did not offer any comment.

Belle Boyd and Belle Starr stood just as quietly, although they showed that they appreciated the gravity of the situation. While neither of them was wearing the gunbelt and revolver which the Kid knew each was carrying in her travelling bags, they both had a Winchester Model of 1866 carbine in their saddleboots. He knew that they were capable of using the weapons. However, they too did not speak. Both appeared to be waiting for somebody else to open the conversation.

Spitting out a spurt of tobacco juice, Salt-Hoss dropped a gnarled right hand to the butt of his holstered Colt 1860 Army revolver. Then he began to scrutinize the rim down which they had come.

Standing near to Belle Boyd, as had become his usual

habit, Anthony Silk looked briefly at her. While clad in a light coloured, thin suit and wearing his gunbelt, he still retained the Webley in what the Kid now knew to be a split-fronted, spring-retention shoulder holster. Being aware of the secretary's continued, thinly veiled, hostility, the young Texan did not doubt that he would try to turn the situation to his advantage.

'This Mexican is after *you*, Ysabel,' Silk stated, a calculating glint coming into his eyes.

'He's after me,' the Kid conceded, guessing what was coming.

So did the rest of the party, if the way they were watching Silk was anything to go by.

'In which case,' the secretary continued, his left hand rising to stroke at the jacket's lapel, 'he has no quarrel with the rest of us.'

'*You* might say that,' the Kid said quietly.

'So if you leave now, when he arrives we can tell him that you've gone,' Silk explained, selecting his words with care. He wanted 'Miss Hardin' to believe that, although his primary concern was for herself and the others, he was also thinking of her 'grandfather's' employee whom she had told him was regarded as being of considerable use around the ranch. So he continued, 'By the time he gets here, you'll be too far away for him to catch you. But he'll leave us alone and go after you.'

'I wouldn't want to count too hard on that, was I you, mister,' Brady Anchor warned, from where he was standing alongside his nephew. 'Escuchador's just about's mean and ornery a *bandido* as ever slit a throat. No matter what you told him, him and his boys'd praise the Saints for giving 'em such good pickings as they was gunning you down.'

'They'd kill *you* quick, mister,' Jefferson Trade supplemented. 'Only with the ladies, it wouldn't likely be so quick—although they soon enough get 'round to wishing it had been, what'd happen to 'em.'

'I'll go along with Brady and Jeff on that,' Belle Starr declared, glaring coldly at Silk. 'Good as you are with a gun, you couldn't handle seven like Escuchador's gang. I don't know about Miss Hardin, but much as I'd hate to be killed, I'd hate even worse to be taken alive by them.'

'I agree with Miss Beauregard,' Belle Boyd went on, with the air of conveying a favour to the other girl by even considering her opinion. Then she continued in her current haughty fashion, 'If I thought that it would do any good, I'd send Ysabel home straight away. But, from what I know about Mexicans, they wouldn't just ride off after him and leave such valuable loot as our belongings would be.'

'I was only thinking of *you*, Miss Hardin!' the secretary assured her hurriedly, but he was clearly annoyed by the dismissal of his suggestion. 'If you weren't with us, I wouldn't have said that he should go. But if there's going to be shooting——'

'I've never been one for billing in on something that isn't rightly any of my never-mind, mister,' Brad Anchor injected, with every evidence of politeness and apology for his lapse. Refusing to be silenced by the glowering look which Silk directed at him, he went on, 'But there'll be shooting whether the Kid goes or stays.'

'I don't suppose that we could buy him off, could we?' Guillemot inquired, studying the stocky, cherubic-looking man with interest and appraisal.

'Nope,' Brady replied. 'Even if he let you make the offer——'

'We could be waiting, with our weapons ready,' Silk interrupted, 'so that he'd rather listen than chance being shot.'

'You *could*,' Brady admitted, but showed that he had reservations regarding the idea. 'Only he'd gun you down after he'd taken your money. If he didn't do it straight away, he cut ahead and bushwhack you. Escuchador's never been one for taking less than all he can get when all that's standing between him and it are a few killings.'

'You say that they're some way behind, Mr. Anchor?' Guillemot asked, rubbing at his multiple chins with an enormous hand.

'Two-three miles back and not a-rushing,' the stocky man agreed. 'But coming for all of that.'

'Then we could start moving and outrun them to Eagle Pass,' the Ox suggested. 'They're hardly likely to dare follow us into a town, are they?'

'Nope,' Brady conceded. 'Trouble being, you'd never make it. They can travel a whole heap faster on horseback than you'll be able to do with your rig, especially after it gets dark.'

'Damn it!' Silk ejaculated, glaring at the Indian-dark young Texan. He had noticed how the others were exchanging perturbed glances, which told of their understanding of the precarious nature of their predicament, and saw in it a way of reducing his employer's regard for the man who was responsible for it. 'If you hadn't killed his nephew, none of this would be happening.'

'Likely,' the Kid answered, so quietly and mildly that anybody who knew him would have taken a warning from his tones. 'Only it seemed the reasonable thing to do at the time, him being set on killing Dusty and me. 'Specially seeing's how he was trying to stop us coming to help your boss.'

'We can hardly blame Mr. Ysabel for defending himself, Silk,' Guillemot supplemented. 'And talking about what should, or shouldn't, have happened isn't going to get us anywhere. Our problem is to decide what to do for the best.'

'I've got some notions on *that*,' the Kid declared, standing on spread-apart feet and with his right hand turned palm-outwards *very* close to the butt of the old Dragoon Colt. Taken with the challenging way in which he was looking at the secretary, it was a provocative posture. 'And so has Mr. Silk—happen he'd like to spit 'em out.'

'I don't want to see Miss Hardin endangered——' the secretary began sullenly.

'Nor do any of us,' Guillemot put in, standing up. 'I think *that* goes without saying. However, I'm satisfied that asking Mr. Ysabel to leave won't achieve anything.'

'Then what do we do?' Silk demanded.

'Suppose we ask somebody who *knows* just how serious the situation is?' the Ox answered, but the way in which he was speaking showed—particularly to his secretary, who had come to know him very well—that he was giving an order. 'After all I've seen of him, I'll stand by Mr. Ysabel and do whatever he thinks will be best.'

'Well, sir,' the Kid drawled, ignoring Silk's angry hiss and obvious disapproval. 'First off, I'd say offer Brady and Jeff maybe fifty dollars a-piece to stay with us for a spell.'

'*Fifty dollars each!*' Silk spat out. 'You're damned free with our money.'

'I didn't know it was *your* money, mister,' the Kid answered, looking relaxed despite being ready to spring into instant motion if he had pushed the secretary too far. 'But if——'

'I think that I'm quite capable of deciding how to spend *my* money, Silk,' Guillemot interjected coldly, before the other could make any response. 'Do you know these gentlemen, Mr. Ysabel?'

'Nope, not per——' the Kid admitted, but was not allowed to continue.

'How did you get involved in this?' Silk demanded, scowling at the newcomers.

'I don't know's how we are involved in it, mister,' Brady Anchor replied. 'We were Anse Dale's deputies three years back. When he heard we was headed down Zavala County way, he asked us to drop by and warn you folks about Escuchador. Which's what we've done and, having done it, we'll be moving on.'

'Just a moment, Mr. Anchor,' Guillemot boomed. 'I

think Mr. Ysabel was going to say something more.'

'Why sure,' the Kid agreed, darting a triumphant glance at Silk. 'Happen these gents're the same Brady Anchor 'n' Jefferson Trade's worked for Colin Farquharson on the Upper Nueces early last year, they'd be good men to have around.'

'We worked for Colin,' Brady conceded. 'Only it was on the Middle San Saba. Which means you're testing us, or don't know as much's you let on.'

'Colin allowed you was left-handed, Brady,' the Kid replied with a grin. 'And that you tote your gun in the damnedest rig he'd ever seen. In a shoulder-holster that hangs cross-wise instead of down.'

'Like this?' Brady inquired, drawing open the right side of his jacket to show that his holster was suspended horizontally instead of the more usual vertical.

'Just like that,' the Kid confirmed. 'No offence meant, Brady, Jeff.'

'None took, Kid,' Brady assured him and Jefferson Trade muttered agreement.

'You can rely upon them, Mr. Guillemot,' Belle Boyd announced, concealing her satisfaction at the way the Kid was playing Guillemot against Silk. It would help her own efforts with the secretary. 'Colin has always spoken highly of them.'

'Very well, Miss Hardin,' the Ox replied and looked at the newcomers. 'As you have been deputies, that suggests you have considerable proficiency with your weapons.'

'We both know which end the lead goes in and where it comes out,' Brady confessed off-handedly. 'And, happen what we're shooting at's stood still and's big enough, we can most times hit what we're aiming at.'

'Only if it's real close,' Jeffer supplemented.

'I think you're being modest,' Guillemot smiled. 'May I ask if you are going to Zavala County on a matter of urgency?'

'Not especially,' Brady admitted.

'Would it be taking you out of your way to come to Eagle Pass with us?' the Ox went on. 'I'd be willing to reimburse you.'

'We'd rather get paid,' Jefferson stated. 'See, mister, we're just a couple of lil ole country boys who're trying to make enough money to live in a manner we've always been too poor to get accustomed to.'

'And you would advise that I hire them to join us, Mr. Ysabel?' Guillemot asked.

'I reckon you'd be making right good sense,' the Kid confirmed.

'Very well,' Guillemot said, taking no notice of Silk's obvious disapproval. 'I'll pay you fifty dollars each to accompany us to Eagle Pass, gentlemen.'

Watching the men, Belle was delighted by the further evidence that Silk hated the way in which Guillemot was showing preference for the Kid's judgement. She had sensed from the beginning that the 'secretary' was dissatisfied with his subordinate's capacity and now saw a threat to it in the way the Ox was treating the young Texan. That was, she supposed, why Silk had started to cultivate 'Betty Hardin'. He hoped to use her as the means of improving his situation. So she had been playing him along with the intention of discovering if he knew why Guillemot was going to so much trouble and expense to obtain James Bowie's knife. From the scowl on Silk's face, she believed that he might be receptive to sympathy and, as a result of receiving it, could possibly be persuaded to divulge at lest some of the required information.

Always providing, Belle told herself, that the Mexicans could be prevented from interfering. She did not underestimate the threat which Escuchador was posing to all their lives. However, she felt sure that the Kid would be able to supply a solution to the problem. If he did, he would strengthen his position with Guillemot and render Silk even more susceptible to her wishes.

'Sir,' Brady drawled. 'You've just hired yourself two men.'

'One thing, though,' the Kid drawled, before any more could be said. 'For that kind of money, I'd say you ought to be willing to do something a mite harder than just riding along with us to Eagle Pass and collecting it.'

'I don't understand——' Guillemot began, showing that he was puzzled.

'Escuchador's no fool,' the Kid elaborated. 'He's not about to try anything when he sees we've got two extra men riding along. He'll just follow until after they pull out and then jump us.'

'Are you suggesting that we should hire them to come all the way to *Casa*—where we are going?' Guillemot asked.

'Well, no sir,' the Kid replied. 'That wasn't exactly what I had in mind.'

'Then what——!' the Ox commenced.

'Hey, Salt-Hoss,' the Kid interrupted, glancing at the old timer. 'How's about lighting up a fire so's the ladies can make us a meal?'

'A *fire!*' Silk snorted, certain that his rival was committing an incredibly stupid blunder which would convince Guillemot that he was of no use as an ally. 'If we do *that*, the smoke will tell the Mexicans where we are.'

'Well I'm damned!' the Kid ejaculated, sounding exasperated as he slapped his left thigh with his near hand. 'I just hadn't thought it'd do *that!*'

'Hello the fire!' called a voice from the fringe of the post oak trees that surrounded the clearing in which Juan Escuchador and his gang had camped for the night. 'Can I come on in and share it?'

Every man in the villainous-looking group gathered around the fire had already heard the rider as he had come from the north-east. However, at the evidence that he was approaching their location, they started to reach for holstered revolvers or the various rifles which were leaning against their saddles.

'No shooting!' the burly, brutal-featured and best-dressed member of the party commanded. 'We're too close to where *Cabrito's* camping and he doesn't know we're around. Let this feller come in, then one of you can use your knife.'

'*Si*, Juan,' responded one of the gang, relaxing, and the rest muttered their concurrence as they also settled down to either sit or squat on their haunches.

'Come ahead, *amigo*,' Juan Escuchador called, standing up. He glared as some of his companions sought to emulate his example and resumed speaking in their native tongue after having addressed an invitation in English. 'Stay down there, damn you. Don't do anything to scare him off.'

Obeying their leader's command, the Mexicans remained in passive postures. Their saddles and bed rolls were set out for the night and their horses were either picketed or hobbled around the clearing. All of them peered with considerable interest at the rider who was approaching. Sufficient moonlight was filtering through the trees for them to make out various details of his appearance.

If his voice had been any guide, the man riding towards the clearing was a Texan. Tall, slim, seated on a big, dark-coloured horse, he had on a fringed buckskin jacket, open-necked white shirt, multi-hued bandana and Levi's pants. However, the brim of his white 'planter's' hat threw a shadow which obscured his features. A gun-belt was strapped about his lean waist, but the jacket prevented the Mexicans from seeing the kind of weapons it was supporting. However, he kept both of his hands in plain sight and did nothing to make them suspicious.

On coming to the fringe of the area illuminated by the fire, the newcomer reined his horse so that it halted with its right side towards the Mexicans. Still acting in a casual manner, although without allowing them to see his face, he dismounted with the animal between himself and them. Having done so, he gave its rump a slap with his right hand and it walked forward. As he came into full length view once more, he proved to have a Winchester rifle in his hands and, advancing a couple of paces, he allowed them to take their first unimpeded sight of his young-looking, Indian-dark face.

'Howdy, *Senor* Escuchador,' the Texan greeted in fluent Spanish. 'I hear that you're looking for me.'

'*Cabrito?*' Escuchador gasped and his right hand started to move towards the butt of the low-tied Colt Civilian Model Peacemaker that he was wearing.

'Easy, all of you!' the Ysabel Kid commanded and, although his left hand was grasping the wrist of the butt—with his right holding the foregrip—he lined the rifle at waist level with deft and practised ease. 'That's right. I'm *Cabrito.*'

Watching the Winchester's muzzle swinging in an arc which encompassed them all, the men carried out the order which the Kid had given. They were all too aware of *Cabrito's*—as Mexicans translated 'Kid'—deadly skill with such a weapon and doubted if handling it left-handed would make him much less effective.

'Now that's a lot better,' the Kid went on, still employing the kind of Spanish which the *bandidos* could understand. 'It'll let me tell you what happened to your nephew, *Senor* Escuchador.'

'How did you know what I was after you for?' Escuchador demanded, having moved his hand well clear of the holstered revolver.

'It figured,' the Kid answered and his voice hardened as he went on to prove that he was keeping *all* of the group under observation. 'Just like it figures that *hombre* with the scar's going to be scratching himself near his gun with a hole in his head, happen he don't quit doing it.'

'Stop that, damn you!' Escuchador commanded, glaring at the man in question, although he had not needed to give the order as it had already been anticipated. 'Go on, *Cabrito*.'

'Feller you should be all riled up about is Matteo Urizza,' the Kid obliged. 'It was him who brought your nephew after us, only he didn't let on it was Dusty Fog and me they'd be going up against.'

'Just the *two* of you?' Escuchador asked.

'Did Matt allow there was more?' the Kid inquired, turning the Winchester's barrel slightly and allowing his tone to take on the menacing timbre again. 'Damn it, Juan, I've never seen such a bunch for fidgeting and fussing near their guns. It's making me so nervous, I swear I'll shoot next time—regardless of who I'm lining up on when it happens.'

'Sit still, all of you!' Escuchador snarled, taking *very* careful notice of the way that the rifle had halted so that it was lined on his chest. He undestood the Kid's meaning all too well and continued in a milder voice. 'I'm sorry about that, *Cabrito*, only you've got them jumpy coming in like you did.'

'I figured it'd be best done that way, so's we'd get a chance to talk things out peaceable instead of throwing lead,' the Kid drawled. 'Thing that worried me was Matt might've told you I wasn't wearing my usual clothes and am riding the Appaloosa.'

'There was a lot Urizza didn't tell me, it seems,' Escuchador gritted. 'He said that a whole bunch of you jumped him and Enrique for no reason.'

'Well now,' the Kid replied. 'That's not exactly the way it happened. Dusty and I were riding along, wasn't anybody else with us, when Enrique came up from behind a rock and started to throw down on us. Urizza didn't show at all. He lit out just after your nephew died, without even trying to burn lead.'

'*Hijo de puta!*' Escuchador spat out furiously.

'I allus figured that's what his mother must have been,'

the Kid commented, knowing that the expression meant 'son of a whore'. Then he went on with such sincerity that he might have been speaking the truth, 'Enrique wasn't quite dead when we got to him and he was some surprised when he learned who he'd been up against. Seemed like Urizza had forgotten to tell him.'

'And I let the bastard ride off!' Escuchador spluttered.

'I just bet he told you I was headed down to San Antonio on my lonesome,' the Kid continued. 'Was figuring after all the lies he'd told you, you'd come gunning for me. Which's what he wanted, having took pay to get me but being scared to try again. Point being, Juan, I'm right sorry about what happened. But when Enrique come up shooting, there wasn't anything else I could do but cut loose back at him.'

'That's understandable,' Escuchador conceded.

'And, seeing you fellers coming,' the Kid went on, 'I could guess what you had in mind. So I figured I'd best drop by, explain and try to save us all a heap of grief. If I hadn't and you boys had tried to jump us tomorrow like you planned'—he could see that he had guessed correctly—'there'd have been some of you dead when the smoke cleared.' Watching the Mexicans, he could see that he had made a telling point and elaborated upon it. 'I know it's hard on you, Juan, losing your nephew and all, and how you'd want to try to avenge him, way you was told it happened. But is it worth getting some of these fellers killed over now you know the truth?'

'Is it hell,' Escuchador declared, having glanced at his men and decided that they expected such a response. 'I had to try to do something, you know that, *Cabrito*.'

'I'm not holding it against you,' the Kid assured him. 'Just as long as you don't keep on with it.'

'I won't,' Escuchador promised. 'Hell, he only got to be my kin because some *gringo* priest took a fancy to my sister Maria and sired him one night after confession. Now you've explained, I can tell her why I didn't try to avenge him.'

'*Bueno*,' the Kid drawled, lowering the muzzle of his rifle out of alignment. 'I'm right pleased it's been settled peaceable and I'll be on my way.'

'Why not stop for a meal?' Escuchador offered.

'I'd like to, only I've got one waiting for me when I get back to our camp,' the Kid replied. 'Which *isn't* where you saw the smoke coming up.'

'You're a crafty son-of-a-gun,' Escuchador chuckled. 'How about a cup of coffee before you go?'

'I'd like to, but it's the boss lady who's cooked the meal and she'll get riled happen I let it get cold,' the Kid answered. '*Adios*, Juan, *amigos*, I'm real pleased things've worked out right and peaceful between us.'

With that, the young Texan turned on his heel. Before he had taken his second step, Escuchador reached towards the butt of the holstered Colt. Clearly his men had been expecting some such action in spite of the way the conversation had progressed. Every one began to grab for a weapon and started to rise.

CHAPTER TWELVE

YOU COULD GET THE KID KILLED

'You did realize that I was only thinking of *you* when I suggested that the half-breed should clear out this evening, didn't you, Miss Hardin?' Anthony Silk asked earnestly, taking the opportunity which had been presented to him for a private conversation with the girl.

'Of course I did,' the Rebel Spy assured him, having hoped for such a development when bringing him a cup of coffee from the camp. 'And I feel much safer with *you* up here keeping watch.'

'It wasn't that I minded doing this,' Silk insisted, wanting to clear away any ideas that the girl might be harbouring to the contrary. 'I just didn't care for the way that damned half-breed was giving orders.'

'Mr. Guillemot seemed to approve of them,' Belle pointed out, controlling the irritation she was experiencing over the secretary's references to the Ysabel Kid's mixed blood and selecting a comment which she felt sure would add fuel to his sense of discontent.

'He did,' Silk gritted, gripping the cup tighter and moving restlessly as he remembered how he had failed to discredit the young Texan.

Despite the Kid's comment when Silk had warned him about the danger of lighting a fire, he had gone on to show that it might not have been such a foolish suggestion after all. He had claimed that, knowing with whom they were dealing, the Mexican *bandidos* would be disinclined to chance an attack in the darkness. Once they had seen the smoke rising, they would make camp themselves—selecting a spot from which the glow or smoke of their own fire would not be seen—and wait until the next day. As Brady Anchor and Jefferson Trade had agreed with the Kid's summation, Guillemot had gone along with the line of action which the young Texan had proposed.

While the Kid had been pretty certain that Juan Escuchador would hold off until the following morning at least, preferring to catch the party on the move, he had suggested that precautions should be taken during his absence. One of them, which Silk had disputed, was that he should stand guard on the uppermost edge of a clump of bushes overlooking their camp. Much to the secretary's annoyance, Guillemot had once again backed up the young Texan and had insisted upon the order being obeyed.

Having decided that the rift between Guillemot and Silk might offer possibilities, Belle had waited for what she believed would be a good time to set about exploiting them. Allowing the disgruntled secretary almost three hours in which to brood alone on his grievances, she had brought him a cup of coffee. From the way in which the conversation was going, she sensed that it might possibly shed some light upon the mystery she was trying to solve.

'I can't say that I approved of how Ysabel was behaving,' Belle declared, letting a note of haughty indignation creep into her voice. Showing a keen grasp of the situation, the Kid had given her orders so that she could pretend to resent and object to them. 'He's already acting above his station. And if he brings this off, Mr. Guillemot is going to keep on listening to his suggestions. You and I might not have been here for all the notice he took of our opinions.'

'Your grandfather sent him to act as our guide,' Silk pointed out, glancing at the bushes to make sure that he and the girl could not be seen from the camp. Satisfied that they could not, he looked along the bushes without seeing any sign of 'Magnolia Beauregard' who was keeping watch from the other end.

'Yes,' Belle Boye agreed. 'But *not* to take charge as he's doing. Guillemot certainly seems impressed by him. Look at the way he let himself be persuaded to hire those two men in spite of your comments.'

Although Silk sucked in a deep breath, he did not comment on the girl's statement. So she too stood silent, allowing him to consider the implications of what she had said.

'You know, Anthony——' Belle began, after almost a minute had passed. 'You don't mind if I call you Anthony when we're alone, do you?'

'No,' Silk answered, jolted from his reverie.

'And you can call me "Betty",' the girl instructed. 'You know, Anthony, I'm puzzled——'

'What about?' Silk wanted to know.

'Mr. Guillemot is going to a lot of trouble and expense to collect the knife for the Bowie family,' Belle remarked, watching his face.

'They're paying for it,' Silk reminded her.

'I don't doubt that. But Mr. Guillemot doesn't strike me as the kind of a man who would make such a long and uncomfortable journey just to collect a knife for somebody else. Surely he could have let you fetch it for him. You could have made much better time on horseback than it's possible to do with him riding the buckboard. And, after all, you *were* his "strong right arm" I think he called you.'

'He likes to handle things personally,' Silk said coldly, showing that he had taken notice of the way she had emphasized the word 'were'.

'Obviously,' Belle sniffed. 'One might almost think that the knife is so valuable that he doesn't trust even his "strong right arm" to collect it for him. Yet I don't see how it *could* be. Possibly it might have a certain value as a trophy, but that hardly warrants so many men having been hired to try to get it.'

Instead of replying, Silk studied the girl's beautiful face for several seconds. A keen student of human— especially feminine—nature, he had already come to revise his original impression that she was a somewhat naïve, if spoiled, arrogant and self-opinionated snob who would fall easily under the spell of his sophisticated charm. During their acquaintance, he had decided that she was far more intelligent and worldly than he had at first imagined. The way that the conversation was progressing gave him a hint that she suspected Guillemot of having an ulterior motive for collecting the knife. Silk wondered if the time had come for him to carry out the intentions towards which he had been working since leaving San Antonio. However, his plan might need to be changed in the light of the latest development. 'Betty Hardin' might not be the dupe that he had envisaged and hoped for.

Silk did not know the whole secret of Bowie's knife, but he had learned sufficient to realize that he would need powerful financial backing to utilize its full potential. Meeting 'Betty Hardin' had seemed to offer the means by which he could obtain it; and from a source that was ideally suited to make the most of it. Not only was her 'grandfather' a very wealthy man, but he also wielded considerable political influence in Texas. The latter would be of tremendous importance. So Silk had been hoping to use the girl to attain the General's confidence.

While satisfied on those points, Silk was wondering if the time was right for a disclosure of his knowledge. He was aware of how dangerous double-crossing the Ox would be. Certainly he would never dare return to Europe once he had done so. However, he wanted to be sure of the girl before he shared his knowledge with her.

'That's true,' Silk finally admitted, trying to sound as if the idea had not occurred to him.

'And if it *is* so valuable,' Belle went on, 'perhaps Mr.

141

Guillemot doesn't intend to return it to the Bowie family.'

'Maybe he doesn't,' Silk answered non-committally.

'In which case, Ysabel would be of great use to him,' Belle continued. 'Knowing that the men are after him, or will be waiting when he returns, he might intend to avoid going back.'

'How do you mean?' Silk challenged.

'Haven't you noticed the interest he's been showing in Ysabel's knowledge of Mexico?' Belle demanded. 'It could be because he's hoping to go to the coast and take a ship, instead of returning to the United States.'

'He wouldn't need Ysabel for that,' Silk growled, but his voice showed uncertainty. 'All we'd have to do would be return to the Rio Grande and follow it to the coast.'

'Through some of the worst *bandido* and cut-throat infested country that you'll ever see?' Belle challenged. '*You* couldn't do it, Anthony, but Ysabel could. And I think Guillemot knows it.'

'He can't do without *me*!' Silk growled, but it was obvious to the girl that he was trying to convince himself as much as her.

'He seems to have been doing so recently,' Belle pointed out. 'Look, Anthony, I don't pretend to know what makes the knife so valuable, although I'm sure that *you* do. What I do know is that Guillemot can't get it without my help and, if I had a better idea what it's all about, well, I could make up my mind what to do.'

'How do you mean?'

'*Senor* Serrano will be doing the favour for the General, not the Bowie family, if he hands over the knife.'

'So?' Silk prompted and, try as he might, he could not entirely restrain his eagerness.

'So, if it would be worth the General's while, I could suggest that Serrano sends it to him for disposal,' Belle suggested. 'And, if it is so valuable——'

'It is,' Silk assured her.

'Why?' Belle asked and felt sure that she would be told what she wanted to know.

Before Silk could reply, they heard shots from the north-east—the direction in which Jefferson Trade, who had been sent to investigate, had claimed that the *bandidos* were bedding down for the night.

'It looks like the half-breed didn't manage to talk the Mexicans out of killing him,' Silk remarked, not without a suggestion of satisfaction. 'You'd better go back to the buckboard in case they come after us.'

'But——!' Belle began, fighting down her concern for the Kid's welfare.

'Do it. You'll be safer down there,' Silk ordered. 'I'll stay and keep a watch in case they come.'

'Very well,' Belle replied, accepting that she would not receive any further information at that moment; but knowing she had implanted the seeds of doubt in Silk's head and that they might provide the required results in the future. 'Take care of yourself, Anthony,' she continued, stepping closer and kissing him lightly on the cheek. 'I wouldn't want any harm to come to you.'

With that, the Rebel Spy began to back away. She went slowly, watching Silk turn and stare to the north-east. The shooting had ended, but they had no way of knowing what the result might have been.

'Hard luck, "Miss Hardin",' Belle Starr's voice remarked quietly from the bushes as the other girl was passing the lower fringe of them on her way back to the camp. 'You were handling it real well. Of course, the way you were doing it, you could get the Kid killed—unless Escuchador's already done it.'

'Turn!' a voice shouted from the darkness as Escuchador started to draw his gun.

Not only the *bandidos* had expected their leader to behave in such a treacherous fashion.

Although the Ysabel Kid had told the other members of

his party that he hoped to explain about Enrique Escuchador's death, he had realized that the chances of it doing any good were almost non-existent. So he had taken precautions. While he had approached the gang openly from the opposite direction to where his companions were camping, Brady Anchor and Jefferson Trade had been taking advantage of the distraction which he was providing. Having left their horses some distance away, with Salt-Hoss present to keep the animals quiet, they had moved in on foot.

Hearing the not unexpected warning, the Kid responded like lightning. Swivelling to his right, as being the shorter distance for his Winchester to move into alignment, he discovered that—in spite of his precaution—he was still in very serious peril. Already Escuchador's revolver was close to clearing the lip of its holster and, grabbing for weapons, the rest of the Mexicans were coming to their feet as swiftly as they could manage.

Aiming by instinctive alignment, with the Winchester still at waist-level, the Kid began to fire as fast as he could operate the lever and produced the three shots per second which the manufacturer's advertisements claimed was possible. He swung the barrel as he did so, pouring a fan of flying lead in Escuchador's direction.

Shock twisted momentarily across the *bandido's* face as he realized that his trick had failed. Then the Kid's fourth, fifth and sixth bullets tore through his chest and flung him backwards to collide with one of his men.

Selecting the Mexican who was moving fastest and so posed the most immediate threat to the Kid's well-being, Brady Anchor—who had delivered the one-word warning—sighted and fired his Winchester, directing its bullet with deadly effect. Even as the *bandido*, hit in the head, twirled around and fell, Jefferson Trade displayed a comparable accuracy by tumbling the next swiftest in an equally lifeless heap. Then the two Texans turned their respective attention to the other Mexicans.

Although the remainder of the gang must have realized just how small were their chances of surviving, none of them offered to surrender. Only one of them escaped.

Having contrived to stay on his feet, the man who had been struck by Escuchador's body made no attempt to duplicate the actions of his companions. While they tried to bring their weapons into use, he let his fall and spun on his heel. Alarmed by the shooting, the horses were rearing and plunging. Darting to where one had contrived to tear free its picket-rope, he managed to vault astride its bare back and to cling on as it dashed away into the darkness. Only one of the men he had deserted succeeced in firing a shot. Its bullet sent Brady's hat spinning from the Kid's head. Then the Mexican followed his companions as Texan lead caused them to crash to the ground.

Coming out of the darkness with their rifles held ready for further use, Brady Anchor and Jefferson Trade converged on the Kid. Although four of the Mexicans' horses had fled, the other three had been brought down by their hobbles as they had attempted to do so. However, the Kid's well-trained Appaloosa was standing at the edge of the clearing where it had come to a halt after obeying his signal to walk away.

'*Gracias amigos,*' the Kid drawled, moving forward with the intention of ensuring that none of the gang could resume hostilities.

'*Es nada,*' Jefferson Trade answered, advancing to help with the examination. At its conclusion, he looked to where his uncle was attending to the three hobbled horses. 'They're all cashed in.'

'I'll not do much mourning for them,' Brady replied. 'Happen you don't have any notions contrary-wise, Kid, we'll deliver 'em to the sheriff at Eagle Pass.'

'It'd be's well to,' the Kid conceded. 'I'm right obliged to you for helping.'

'You don't need to be,' Brady answered, as he and the two young men walked from the clearing. 'We saw what they did to a rancher and his family over to Val Verde County just afore Christmas. Which's one reason we brought word that they was gunning for you.'

'Figured's how odds of seven to two was just a lil mite higher than we could handle,' Jefferson continued frankly, 'and's how you'd likely be willing to help us whittle 'em down a mite. Only we never thought you'd want to do it the way you did.'

'I allowed it was the only way, 'cept for bushwacking 'em and I didn't reckon you'd've stood for that,' the Kid replied. 'In spite of what I told the folks back there, I knew that Escuchador'd try to kill me no matter how much explaining I did. At least, doing it my way gave him the chance to change his mind.'

'There's one thing puzzling me, though,' Brady remarked. 'Likely it's none of my never-mind, but—knowing who and *what* she is—why did Rosa Rio pass word to the marshal that Escuchador was gunning for you?'

'Maybe she's got religion and did it out of the good of her heart,' the Kid suggested mildly.

'It *could've* happened that way, just like I *could've* voted Republican,' Brady admitted. 'Only I'd be inclined to think there was a mite more to it than that.'

'Fact being,' Jefferson went on, 'if we didn't know it wasn't likely, Uncle Brady 'n' me'd've thought she was scared you'd reckon she sent him after you and wanted to make sure you knew it wasn't so. Only Rosa Rio wouldn't be scared—would she?'

'Like I said, Kid,' Brady continued. 'Maybe it's none of our never-mind and we hope you'll forgive us for acting nosey. But, not that we'd like too many folks to get to know about it, we're Texas Rangers and it makes us act that way when there's something's we don't understand.'

'Happen you can wait until we get back to the camp, seeing's how the folks're to have heard the shooting and'll be worrying,' the Kid drawled. 'I'll tell you when we get there.'

'Well, by gad!' Guillemot boomed, slapping a fat thigh appreciatively as the Kid completed the story of his visit to Rosa Rio's *cantina*. 'If that doesn't beat anything I've ever heard! You *are* a remarkable young man, Mr. Ysabel. Wouldn't you say so, Mr. Anchor?'

'I reckon you don't know just how remarkable,' Brady Anchor replied, being able to imagine what such a visit must have entailed.

Sitting on her opened-out bed roll, Belle Boyd had been watching Guillemot's and Silk's reactions as they had listened to the Kid. She had noticed that the secretary's face had grown more surly as his employer had shown interest and approbation.

The Rebel Spy had not been particularly surprised to discover that Belle Starr had contrived to eavesdrop on her conversation with Silk, although she had appreciated the other girl's skill in having passed through the bushes so silently that her presence had not been detected. However, they had not been able to debate the matter upon which the lady outlaw had commented due to Boyd being in a position where Guillemot could have seen her. So Boyd had descended the slope to join him and Starr had gone back to her position.

Boyd had been relieved when the Kid, Brady Anchor, Jefferson Trade and Salt-Hoss had arrived unharmed. While Guillemot and Starr had shared the Rebel Spy's sentiments, Silk had barely been able to hide his disappointment over the young Texan's safe return. Having insisted on hearing what had happened, the Ox had clearly been impressed by the way in which the Kid had handled the situation and was even more so on learning why Rosa Rio had been so obliging as to send the warning.

'There's some riders coming,' Jefferson Trade remarked, standing up with his rifle in his hand.

'Five or six of them,' the Kid supplemented. 'They're not trying to sneak up on us, noise they're making, but you ladies'd maybe best move back out of the firelight until we know for sure who they are.'

Although the girls obeyed, the precaution proved to be unnecessary. Even before they appeared on the southern side of the valley, the riders had announced themselves as being the sheriff of Maverick County and his posse.

'You folks wouldn't happen to've seen or heard a rider in the past hour or so, would you?' the peace officer inquired, after he and his men had dismounted in response to Guillemot's invitation.

'No,' the Ox replied. 'Who are you after?'

'A *pistolero* called Matt Urizza,' the sheriff answered. 'He walked into the Eagle Pass Hotel and threw down on a couple of dudes who were having a meal. Killed 'em both, but got hit in the shoulder afore they went down. He still managed to light out, though, and we're after him.'

'Dudes, you say,' Guillemot remarked. 'Do you know why he did it?'

'Nope,' the sheriff admitted and eyed the fat man in a speculative manner as he gave further information. 'Seems like Urizza walked in, they saw him, started to get up and he threw down on 'em. No offence meant, but you wouldn't know 'em by any chance?'

'I'm afraid I can't help you,' the Ox lied, after the sheriff had described the victims in a way which suggested that they were the Germans, Ehlring and Werra. Then he indicated Belle Boyd who had returned from the darkness along with Belle Starr. 'This is General Hardin's granddaughter, she is acting as my hostess on a hunting trip.'

'I didn't reackon I'd be lucky enough to meet somebody who knew the dudes,' the sheriff drawled, when Guillemot had introduced the rest of his party. 'What brought us out this way was we heard shooting a while back and concluded we'd best find out what it was all about.'

'We had a run in with Juan Escuchador and his bunch,' the Kid explained.

'Looks like you come off easy,' the sheriff declared, glancing around. 'Which way'd they go when they lit out?'

'They didn't exactly light out, 'cept one,' the Kid replied and explained why the gang had failed to do so.

'Can't say's I blame you for handling it like you did,' the sheriff stated at the end of the story. 'They'd've gunned all of you given a chance.'

'We couldn't fetch the bodies in with us,' the Kid went on. 'All their hosses either ran off or got hurt through being throwed by their hobbles, so we came back to borrow some of Mr. Guillemot's.'

'We'll go and fetch 'em for you,' the sheriff offered. 'And if you'll let me use some of your stock, I'll send 'em back to you, sir.'

'You can use them and welcome,' Guillemot answered. 'But you don't need to send them back, we'll collect them on our way through Eagle Pass.'

Accepting Brady Anchor's suggestion that he and his nephew would guide the posse to the bodies, the sheriff had set off with them after having some coffee.

On returning to the fire, after having helped the sheriff select three horses to be used for transporting the bodies to Eagle Pass, the Kid sensed there was trouble in the air.

Looking angry, Belle Starr was confronting Silk. Belle Boyd was standing near Guillemot, who sat studying the lady outlaw in an appraising manner. However, Silk swung his attention from Starr. Looking at the Kid, he raised his left hand towards the lapel of his jacket. Taking a warning from the hint of malicious satisfaction on the secretary's face, the Kid came to a halt by the back of the buckboard. In a casual-seeming fashion, he dropped his right hand on to the Winchester which he had placed there when satisfied that the posse were who they had claimed to be.

'You look like a man with something on his mind,' the Kid remarked, adopting a provocative attitude.

'I'm wondering how the Germans knew enough to be waiting for us at Eagle Pass,' Silk answered. 'As Miss Beauregard pointed out, *she* didn't know where we were going. And only one other person here saw, or spoke to, them.'

'That'd be *me*, I reckon,' the Kid said quietly.

'It would,' Silk agreed.

'And *you* figure's I told them?' the Kid asked, just as gently.

'You're the only one who spoke to them——!' Silk began, hoping that he could provoke the young Texan into a hostile move which would justify him in drawing.

The hope materialized, but not as the secretary would have wished.

Given no hint of his intentions, the Kid scooped up his Winchester. Although he did not point the barrel in Silk's direction, his left hand closed on the foregrip and his right forefinger was inside the triggerguard.

Taken by surprise, as the Kid made the very rapid and unexpected transition from apparent unpreparedness to complete readiness, Silk allowed the comment to die away unfinished. He was painfully aware that the Indian-dark Texan held a weapon which was far more readily available for use than was his own holstered revolver.

'Go on,' the Kid challenged and his face had the cold, hard, menacing savagery of a *Pehnane* Dog Soldier. '*Spit* her out, *hombre*.'

'*Ysabel!*' Boyd shouted, stepping forward; but, as Starr noticed, halting before she had come between the two men. 'How *dare* you threaten Mr. Silk?'

'I wouldn't say I'm threatening anybody,' the Kid contradicted. 'All I'm doing is making sure I'll get a chance to say my piece. That *hombre's* too jumpy and handy with a gun for me to want him suspicioning me of having sold out to the Germans.'

'I don't think that Silk meant it quite like that, Mr. Ysabel,' Guillemot put in soothingly. 'And Miss Beauregard gave us a perfectly satisfactory answer to how they knew where we'd be crossing the river.'

'That's right,' Starr agreed, glaring indignantly at the secretary. 'They'd guess that Mr. Guillemot wouldn't be riding a horse and Eagle Pass's the nearest place to San Antonio that we could take the rig across.'

'And I'm inclined to believe that is what happened,' Guillemot declared. 'So I'd be obliged if you would let the whole matter drop, Silk.'

Turning away angrily, the secretary faced Belle Boyd. The look which she gave him said as plainly as any words, 'I told you he was on Ysabel's side against you.'

CHAPTER THIRTEEN

THE KNIFE IS YOURS, *CABRITO*

'Tomorrow I will show you some really exciting sport, gentlemen,' Don Arsenio Serrano promised his guests after they had finished their dinner on the night of their arrival, and he waved a hand towards the weapon which his senior servant had placed on the table. 'And then we will talk further about the knife.'

The remainder of the journey to *Casa* Serrano had been almost without incident. Although Anthony Silk had clearly been displeased and embittered over Octavius Xavier Guillemot's acceptance of Belle Starr's theory regarding the Germans, he had kept his objections to himself. Moving on the following morning, the party had collected the horses which had been loaned to the sheriff at Eagle Pass and had heard that Matteo Urizza had been shot by a rancher while attempting to steal a fresh mount.

Crossing the Rio Grande on the ferry which operated between Eagle Pass and the Mexican town of Piedras Negras, the party had followed the route which had been suggested by the Ysabel Kid. Wanting to avoid attracting unwanted attention, which might have brought *bandidos* down upon them, the Kid had insisted that they did not stay on the trail that would have taken them through Zaragoza. He had had another, unmentioned, reason for going across country.

There had been no further confrontations between the Kid and Silk, only a smouldering, thinly-veiled hostility which had threatened to erupt without actually having done so. Belle Boyd had been responsible for that, having warned Silk that they could not hope to reach their destination without the Kid's aid. Becoming aware of the difficulties once they had left the trail, Silk had appreciated the girl's point of view and had held his temper in check. For his part, realizing that an extra gun might make the difference between life and death if they should be attacked by *bandidos* or Yaqui Indians, the Kid had been content to allow the peaceful conditions to continue. However, his every instinct had warned him that Silk intended to force a showdown eventually.

While the Rebel Spy had been successful in keeping the peace, she had been less fortunate in another matter where Silk was concerned. As they could not find an opportunity to be alone, she had been unable to resume the conversation which had been interrupted by the shooting on the night that the Kid had dealt with Juan Escuchador.

On reaching the *Rio de la Babia*, the party had made the crossing by floating the buckboard over supported by logs. They had then spent the night in a deserted adobe house near to the edge of a very deep and narrow chasm through which the river poured in raging, churning rapids. Going upstream for a couple of miles, they had turned along the *Rio Ventoso* and had followed it to their destination.

Despite their unexpected arrival, the party had been made welcome by Don Arsenio Serrano. He had grown into a silver-haired, distinguished-looking man with the courtly manners of a Spanish *grandee*. Apologizing for his inability to speak English, he had suggested that they might like to refresh themselves before dinner. So they had been assigned to rooms in his magnificent, well-protected house. After the girls—each of whom had brought a stylish dress and jewellery in her baggage—the Kid, Guillemot and Silk had bathed and changed into clean clothing, they had joined their host in the dining-room. The secretary was at a disadvantage, as he alone could not speak Spanish. At Salt-Hoss's own request, he had been accommodated with and was being entertained by the *vaqueros*. They were, as the old timer had pointed out, his kind of people.

Learning of the reason for the visit, Serrano had hidden the surprise which he must have felt. He had remarked, somewhat wryly, that he would not have thought anybody had read his uncle's history of the family. Beyond Guillemot admitting that the book had been his source of information, the comment had gone unexplained. However, Serrano had shown no hesitation about ordering his *majordomo* to fetch the knife from his study.

'May I look at it, Don Arsenio?' Guillemot requested, accepting his host's promise to consider the matter of its return to the Bowie family without question.

'Of course,' Serrano agreed, drawing off the sheath and holding out the knife.

Watching Guillemot turning the great knife over and over, the Kid was impressed by his self control. While the young Texan—and, probably, the girls and Silk—could sense his great excitement, nothing of it showed on his now sun-reddened and bland features. To all appearances, the Ox might have been examining something in which he had only a marginal interest rather than the goal of a long and costly quest.

'With all respect, *Senor* Guillemot,' Serrano remarked, watching the fat man holding and studying the hilt of the knife, 'I wish that my hands were as large as yours. I can't hold the handle comfortably, nor can any of my men.'

'Couldn't you have had it cut down to size, Don Arsenio?' Belle Boyd inquired and noticed that Guillemot stiffened slightly.

'I thought of having it done when I came home,' Serrano admitted. 'But our blacksmith, who was very good at his work, warned me that to do so would ruin the knife's balance. As I didn't wish for that to happen, I kept it untouched as a memento of a not unimportant period of my life.'

'Did your blacksmith dismantle it to make his examination?' Gullemot inquired and it was obvious to the other members of his party, if not to their host, that he found the possibility disturbing.

'No,' Serrano replied. 'He just looked and felt at it. Then he said it was the finest weapon he had ever seen, which was no mean compliment, and warned me that any alteration would spoil it. So I left it as it was. To be quite honest, it was far too big and heavy for my taste.'

'I can see that you would like to look at it, Mr. Ysabel,' Gullemot commented, acting more relaxed now that he had received a negative answer to his question and offering the weapon to the young Texan.

'Whee-dogie!' the Kid ejaculated in English, as he took the massive and gleaming knife. He found it to be somewhat heavier and, with its enlarged handle, not so well balanced in his grasp as his own product of James Black's forge. 'Old Jim Bowie must've had a real big fist——' Then, remembering where he was, reverted to Spanish and continued politely, 'My apologies, Don Arsenio, but I never thought that I'd be holding Colonel Bowie's own blade. I've heard about it all my life. Is it true that it can cut through an ordinary knife?'

'It can,' Serrano answered, smiling at the normally impassive young Texan's enthusiasm. He picked up one of the table-knives and went on, 'I have heard of your ability as a knife-fighter, *Cabrito*. Would you care to try?'

'How about you doing it, Mr. Gullemot?' the Kid suggested, holding out Bowie's knife. 'You can use it one-handed.'

Watched by the men and girls, Gullemot grasped the big weapon's hilt in his right hand. Accepting the table-knife with his left, he held it with the end of the cutting edge resting on the table. Tentatively at first, he brought the blade of the bowie knife into contact. Then, making a sawing motion, he caused it to sever the other knife without any great difficulty.

'*Whee-dogie!*' the Kid breathed, the comment brought from him before he could prevent it. Not that he needed to be concerned over his display of emotion. The rest of the party were duplicating it in their own individual fashions.

'You might not believe me,' Serrano remarked, clearly enjoying the response created by the experiment and watching Guillemot examining the bowie knife's cutting edge, 'But I have never done more than rub up the edge on a razor-strop a couple of times a year and yet it stays as sharp as ever.'

'I'm most impressed, sir,' Guillemot declared, returning the knife to its owner. He intended to go on with a comment about the impossibility of duplicating the steel due to it having been created from a solitary fragment from a 'star'.

'So were Pascual and the other leaders of the Ventoso Yaquis when they saw me cut one of their lances' head in two,' Serrano replied, before the Ox could continue, sliding the knife into its sheath.

'Do you get much trouble with the Yaquis, *senor*?' the Kid inquired, knowing that the tribe in question were to Mexico what the Comanches had been to Texas and the Apaches still were to New Mexico or Arizona.

'None,' Serrano replied. 'At least, not since I armed all my *vaqueros* with Winchester repeaters. After one attack, which cost them many lives, the chiefs agreed to talk peace. Now we trade together and some of their people even work on the *hacienda*. Of course, to save the chiefs' faces if some hot-headed young brave wants to attack us, I pay them a small tribute of horses, mules and cattle twice a year.'

'You say that they've seen you cut through the head of a lance, senor?' the Kid asked.

'That was during the first meeting,' Serrano answered.

'Since then, I've repeated the trick at each visit. It amuses them.'

'Have any of them ever tried it?' the Kid wanted to know.

'Several have, over the years,' Serrano admitted offhandedly, clearly attaching no importance to the matter. 'However, the Yaqui tend to be of middle height and stocky and only one of them has been able to use the knife one-handed. A young brave called *Manos Grande* can do so.'

'Big Hand,' the Kid translated, half to himself, then addressed his host. 'You say *he* can do it, *senor*?'

'He cut through a knife with it during the Christmas visit,' Serrano confirmed. 'His companions were highly delighted to see him do it.'

'Yes, sir,' the Kid said soberly. 'I can see how they might be.'

'What kind of sport are we to have tomorrow, Don Arsenio?' Guillemot put in, wanting to change the subject before the Kid reminded Serrano any further about the knife's value.

'It is something that a cousin from Spain who had been to India taught to us when he paid me a visit,' Serrano explained. 'The *vaqueros* enjoy it very much. It is called "pig-sticking".'

'There one goes!' Serrano yelled excitedly, reining his big white gelding to a halt and pointing to where a swiftly-moving brown animal burst from a clump of bushes ahead of the line of *peons*, who were acting as beaters, and fled at considerable speed across the rolling terrain. 'After it!'

Elaborating on his answer to Guillemot's question the previous evening, Serrano had told his guests how a number of pigs had escaped during a Yaqui attack in the early 1830s. Many of the animals had never been recovered and, finding conditions on the range to their liking,

157

had gone feral. Subsequent generations had gradually reverted to the physical appearance and behaviour patterns of wild swine, increasing in numbers until they had become the cause of considerable damage. However, the visit by a cousin from Spain had shown a way in which the animals could not only be controlled, but would also provide an exciting kind of sport which the *vaqueros*, natural-born horsemen, had found very much to their liking.

Serrano had said that the hunt would be conducted in a similar manner to that developed by the British 'tent clubs' in India. However, there was one variation. Hunting over fairly open country, the Mexicans had found that lances of between eight foot six inches and nine foot in length were more suitable than the six foot six inches variety used by the British.[1] The participants would be formed into three-man 'heats', taking turns to pursue the pigs once they had been flushed by the beaters.

On being asked if he would care to take part in the hunt, Guillemot had pointed out that his bulk precluded him from horseback riding. So Serrano had offered to put a buggy at his disposal and he could follow in it. Although both of the girls had proclaimed willingness to participate, they had been told that doing so would be too dangerous and they were to be restricted to the role of spectators. That had left the Kid and Silk to uphold the honour of the visitors. With his Comanche upbringing and Dog Soldier's regard for a lance as a weapon—he had been initiated into full membership of the supreme *Pehnane* war lodge as a boy—and despite the years he had lived among white people, the Kid had been delighted by the opportunity to do so. Silk had clearly been less enamoured by the prospect, but could hardly have refused when Serrano had suggested that he acted as representative for his employer.

1. With the exception of the Calcutta Tent Club, the British eventually adopted a longer type of spear.

Soon after dawn, the party had assembled. While they were eating breakfast, Serrano had told the Kid and Silk that they would be members of his heat. He had also placed horses which had been trained for, and gained experience in, the business of pig-sticking at their disposal. From all appearances, he had gauged his guests' potential as riders with some accuracy. He had assigned a steady-looking brown gelding to Silk. The Kid had been supplied with a smallish, ugly *bayo-cebrunos*[2] stallion. Studying it, he had decided that it possessed the indefinable quality known as *brio escondido*,[3] and would be a most reliable mount for what he suspected would be tricky and dangerous work. Watched by the grinning and appreciative *vaqueros*, he had quickly asserted his dominance over the horse. By the time they had reached the area over which they would be hunting, he was in full control and had known that he was sitting an animal upon which he could place complete dependence.

Being guests of Serrano, it had been accepted that the Kid and Silk should have the opportunity to chase the first pig. So, having delivered his command, the *haciendero* set his mount into motion.

'Hee-yah!' whooped the Kid, feeling the little stallion quivering with readiness beneath him and allowing it to spring forward.

With the young Texan to his left and Silk on his right, fanning out so they had room to manoeuvre, Serrano led the way through the line of beaters. For all his years, he set a hard pace across the anything but smooth and even country.

Keeping the *bayo-cebrunos* under control, the Kid once again tested the weight and balance of the lance in his right hand. Nine foot in length, with a needle-pointed and diamond-shaped head counter-balanced by a lead-

2. *Bayo-cebrunos:* a dun shading into a smokey-grey colour.
3. *Brio escondido:* 'hidden vigour', stamina and endurance of a high quality.

loaded butt, it compared favourably with the type of Comanche weapon which he had handled as a boy and since. So he was eager to test it in the sport of pig-sticking. His every instinct gave warning that such a pastime would call for riding skill of a very high order and, even to a person who possessed the requisite ability, it might become a dangerous and exciting occupation.

For all his eagerness, the Kid did not forget the rules which Serrano had explained as they were riding to the hunting area. Once the prey had been flushed by the beaters, the members of the heat had to decide whether or not it was 'rideable'. As neither he nor Silk could claim sufficient knowledge to make such a decision, they had agreed that it should be their host's prerogative. What was more, they had suggested that Serrano should take the centre position and demonstrate how the sticking was carried out. Of course, as he told them, if the designated animal should 'jink', or swerve aside, the rider in front of whom it was moving would be permitted to deal with it—or to try to.

Watching Serrano, Silk was hoping that he would hold out his lance horizontally at arm's length to signal that the pig was unworthy and would not be 'rideable'.

The hope did not materialize.

'On! On! On!' Serrano yelled, lowering his spear's tip to the vertical and giving the traditional order for the pursuit to continue.

'He's "rideable"!' the Kid yelled, excitement causing him to forget his dislike of the secretary and to explain their host's decision.

Having passed on the order, the Kid turned his full attention to the fleeing animal. Although originally descended from domestic stock, the big boar neither looked nor acted like its ancestors. About thirty-four inches in height at the shoulder, it weighed close to two hundred and sixty pounds; which did not make it slow or clumsy. Just the opposite in fact. Short-backed, tapering to the hips from a long-snouted head that was armed with a pair of curved and very sharp tushes, it was a solid mass of steel-hard muscles which propelled it across the range at a very high speed. Its wild nature and agility showed in the way that it selected the roughest ground over which to flee.

Half a mile of fast and furious galloping was needed before the heat began to close with their quarry. However, by that time Silk had fallen well behind the other two. Being unwilling to accept the risks involved in such a reckless chase, he restrained his mount's eagerness and held it forcibly to a much safer pace than that of his companions.

Although the Kid could tell that he had the swifter horse, he refrained from forging ahead of his host. Not only did he have the rules to consider, but he had talked with the *vaqueros* on the journey to the hunting area. They had told him about the sounder of pigs which they were expecting to find. Its leader, the big boar which Serrano and he were now pursuing, had evaded several previous attempts to ride it down. As the *vaqueros* had mentioned that their *patron* had set his heart on doing so, the Kid considered that it would be impolite to circumvent him. Only if the animal jinked to the left, or something untoward happened, could the young Texan intervene.

'He's tiring, *Cabrito*!' Serrano called, flickering a brief glance to his left as the boar sped towards a small clump of bushes. He did not look to the right as he had already discovered that Silk had fallen behind. 'It won't be long before——'

Instead of going into the bushes, the boar swerved around them. However, as it went by, a second pig erupted from beneath them and dashed, squealing in alarm, in front of Serrano. Startled by the pig, the white gelding swung violently to the right. Taken by surprise, the elderly Mexican was thrown from his saddle. Letting the lance fall, he crashed into the top of the bushes and went onwards over them. While they lessened the force of his fall, he was winded by his impact with the ground.

At that moment, having grown tired of fleeing, the big boar seemed to reverse direction in its own length. Letting out an awesome snorting screech, it charged towards the dazed and helpless man.

Dropping the head of his lance, the Kid was on the point of trying to take the second pig when he saw Serrano thrown and the boar swirling around to return. So, realizing that his host was in terrible peril, he forgot the smaller pig. Guiding the *bayo-cebrunos* in the required direction, he let out a *Pehnane* war yell and kicked its ribs. Although already galloping at a good speed, the little horse increased its pace as it hurled at a tangent towards the boar.

Seeing its new assailant, the boar swung to meet the challenge. Relying upon his mount, the Kid concentrated his attention towards the bristling beast which was rushing in his direction. Holding the lance in an underhand grip, he aimed the point as he had been taught by his maternal grandfather.

From the way in which the two animals were converging, it seemed that they would collide and the horse be ripped open by the boar's great tushes. Knowing its work, the little stallion swerved at the last moment and just sufficiently to avoid being disembowelled. Hearing the fearsome chomping as the boar's jaws opened and closed, the Kid thrust with the lance. Its diamond-shaped head passed between the boar's ears to sink home just behind the shoulders. Such was the impetus that it impaled the powerful body. Allowing the lance to slip from his grasp as he was carried by the stricken animal, he concentrated both hands on the work of turning his speeding mount. Responsive to the instructions which it was receiving, the stallion went into a rump-scraping turn. Transferring his right hand from the reins to the butt of the old Dragoon

Colt, the Kid was ready to draw and fire. The need to do so did not arise, for the boar was sprawled lifeless on its side some feet from where Serrano was lying.

Riding towards his host, the Kid saw the other members of the party approaching. Silk was nearest, pushing his horse faster than he had done during the chase. The rest were coming as swiftly as they could, with Belle Boyd and Belle Starr among the leaders. Showing considerable driving skill, Guillemot was bringing up the rear at a good speed. Bringing the stallion to a halt, the Kid dropped from his saddle. To his relief, he saw that Serrano was staring at the boar and trying to rise.

'Are you hurt, *senor*?' the Kid inquired, helping the Mexican to his feet.

'Only my pride,' Serrano confessed with a wry smile. 'I think I'm getting too old for this kind of sport.'

'I wouldn't say that, *senor*,' the Kid said with a grin, glancing to where Silk was dismounting from the brown gelding. 'You were unlucky, nothing more. I apologize for taking what should have been your kill.'

'If you hadn't——' Serrano began, nodding towards the impaled carcass of the boar. 'You saved my life, *Cabrito*.'

'You'd have done the same for me, *senor*,' the Kid pointed out.

'Perhaps,' Serrano smiled. 'Anyway, the knife is yours, *Cabrito*.'

'What?' the Kid gasped.

'I have no son or grandson to whom I can leave it when I die,' Serrano explained. 'So I give it to you. Do what you will with it.'

CHAPTER FOURTEEN

A WHOLE *HILL* OF SUCH STEEL

'Well, sir,' Octavius Xavier Guillemot said, as he sat on the chair which had been offered to him and wasting no time in getting down to the business that had brought him to the Ysabel Kid's room after the rest of the household had retired for the night. 'I hope that you will not think it forward of me if I suggest that you ignore Miss Hardin's uncalled-for and unjustifiable ultimatum.'

'How do you mean?' the Kid inquired, glancing to where James Bowie's knife lay on the dressing-table.

Although Don Arsenio Serrano's gift had placed the weapon in the Kid's possession, he still did not know why the Ox was attaching so much importance to it. So he and Belle Boyd had staged a little scene which they had hoped would produce the required information. On their return from the hunt, she had waited until only Guillemot was close enough to hear and had stated that the Kid must turn the knife over to her 'grandfather'. On the Kid pointing out that it had been presented to him by their host, she had warned that unless he acceded to her demand General Hardin would fire him and make sure that nobody in Texas would give him employment. Then, apparently becoming aware of the Ox's presence, she had stalked away.

'If you will accept the advice of an older, more experienced man,' Guillemot replied, 'you will not hand the knife over to her grandfather.'

'Well, I don't know about that,' the Kid said soberly. It's not a whole heap of use to me, seeing that I can't use it and to have it cut down to my fit'd spoil it. On top of that, Ole Devil could make things mighty bad for me happen I crossed him.'

'You mean that he would discharge you?'

'Likely. And there's not many in Texas's'd dare go against him if he passed the word I wasn't to be taken on. So I might's well let him have it. Likely he'll give me a couple of hundred dollars for it.'

'If that's all he gives you, you will be cheated,' Guillemot stated. 'The knife is worth much, *much* more than a paltry few hundred dollars in the right circles.'

'I'm listening,' the Kid drawled.

'Come, sir,' the Ox boomed. 'You are an intelligent young man. Surely you don't believe that I have travelled from Europe merely to collect and return the knife to the Bowie family?'

'I'd sorta got a notion you could have something else in mind,' the Kid admitted. 'And I'd a sneaking feeling that Jim Bowie's blade must be worth plenty of money, there being so many fellers trying to take it from you. So, afore we do any hoss-trading, I'd like to know a lil mite more about the stock.'

'I'll do better than that, sir,' Guillemot promised. 'I'll tell you the full story. Then you will be able to judge for yourself how valuable the knife is.'

'That's right obliging of you, sir,' the Kid declared and sat on the bed with an air of expectancy.

'I suppose you know the story of how the knife was made?' Guillemot began.

'Well, I've allus heard's how it was made from a piece of a star that James Black found near his forge in Arkansas,' the Kid answered. 'Which can't be why it's so valuable, as the only way you could make steel like it was if you'd more lumps from the same star.'

'The story is true, sir,' Guillemot insisted, neither confirming nor arguing against the young Texan's comment. 'But only up to a point. While the knife was manufactured from a fragment of what you refer to as a "star", it came into Black's possession in a somewhat different manner. The ore came into his hands when a badly injured man arrived at his forge. Despite all Black could do for him, the man died. However, before he did, he gave Black several pieces of metal and told him where they had come from. Apparently he was an English geologist who had been on an expedition in Texas and had made a find of such magnitude that he had been coming to visit Black with the hope that they could exploit his discovery, but was waylaid by thieves and shot as he had escaped. After he died, Black examined the pieces and realized that he had come into possession of something unique. They were lumps of raw ore, sir, but of steel and of such a quality that it was far in advance of anything which could be produced in the 1830s—or today for that matter——'

'That'd be right useful, happen there was more of it,' the Kid commented.

'There is, sir, there is!' Guillemot stated and the excitement in his voice was far from being assumed. 'A hill which, under the soil, is a solid piece of it. Can you imagine that, sir, a whole *hill* of such steel?'

'How'd it get there?'

'Possibly as Black said, by falling from the sky. Such things have been known to have happened, sir, but on a smaller scale. To go on, though, Black had the information to guide him to the hill, but he lacked the means to do so. Then fate brought a solution. James Bowie arrived at Black's forge, bringing a wooden model from which he wanted a knife to be created. One with special features and made to fit his massive hand. As you no doubt know, sir, in addition to being a knife-fighter par excellence and an adventurer, Bowie was also a shrewd businessman. Black took him into his confidence and they became partners. However, each of them realized that to exploit the hill to its full advantage would require far more capital than they could put out. They also knew that they

166

would have to have some more concrete evidence before any businessman would condescend to back them. So Black carved the directions which he had been given into the handle of the knife which he was making from the largest piece of the "star". With the ivory grips in place, the carving could not be seen. Nor would their presence be suspected. I believe that the idea may have come from Bowie. While nobody would think twice about a man with his reputation carrying the knife, they might have grown suspicious if he was seen examining a sheet of paper. Or it could have been lost, or destroyed, with far more ease than the knife could. Anyway, Bowie went to Texas and found the hill——'

'I've never heard tell of it happening,' the Kid objected.

'He did not speak of his find, naturally, sir,' Guillemot replied. 'Not even to his brother and the other men who had accompanied him. They suspected that, while he was off on his own, he had discovered a lost Spanish mine and never imagined that the actual find was something infinitely more valuable. Knowing the nature of the Mexican authorities, Bowie was aware that one hint of the truth would cause himself and Black to be deprived of any benefits which they might otherwise have hoped to accrue. That was one of the reasons why they decided to seek financial support in Europe rather than from the United States.'

'Seeing's how nobody's ever started to dig up the hill and make this kind of steel,' the Kid drawled and indicated the knife, 'I'd say they didn't get it.'

'That's true,' the Ox conceded.

'Folks in Europe wouldn't believe them, huh?' the Kid asked.

'They believed Black, who came over, to a certain degree,' Guillemot corrected. 'I tell you, sir, his arrival created a sensation in England, Germany and France. In addition to having brought pieces of the ore, he had four clasp-knives which he had made from it. Two were from the raw ore and the others blended with it and the best steel he could manufacture. Even the latter were vastly superior to any steel Europe had ever seen. This is one of them.' Reaching into the pocket of his smoking jacket, he produced the knife and offered it to the young Texan, continuing, 'It came into my possession when I was commissioned to obtain either the location of the hill, or to discover Black's system of smelting and producing the steel if he should be doing so by other means. I must confess that, due to the bungling of an assistant, I failed in my mission. While she learned the story which I have just told you, her informant did not supply her with the knowledge that was required.'

'Then you still don't know whether there is a hill, or if James Black was making it?'

'He wasn't making it. That was the respective, but unanimous decision of experts from the major steel manufacturing companies of Great Britain, Germany and France. However, all of them told him basically the same thing. While interested in his proposition, none was willing to incur the heavy expenses of mining the ore and working it with conditions so unstable in Mexican-controlled Texas. Although disappointed, Black did not despair, for he knew that the Americans in Texas were already commencing their struggle to establish independence from Mexican rule. So he returned home to await developments. When they came, they were not of a satisfactory nature. Bowie was killed at the Alamo and a few weeks later Black died in a hunting accident. Neither of them left any written record of their arrangement, nor of the hill's location.

'I must confess that my interest in the affair waned when I heard of this. The only means by which the hill could be discovered, without a *very* long search, would have been to obtain Bowie's knife, which I assumed, correctly, had been carried off by one of the Mexicans who had been responsible for his death. I tried to discover who it might be and failed.'

'That's not what *I'd* say, seeing's we're sat talking here like this,' the Kid objected. 'It looks to a half-smart lil Texas boy like me's you must have found out.'

'I did, sir,' Guillemot admitted. 'But not for a number of years. In fact, it was only last year that a brilliant young acquaintance of mine, Professor James Moriarty, re-aroused my interest. A remarkable young man, James, I'm sure that he will go far in our way of business.[1] Anyway, he was hired as tutor for the youngest son of a Squire Holmes in Yorkshire. Apparently James and the son took an instant dislike to each other, but James stayed in his father's employment for a time. Holmes had travelled extensively on the Continent and had a size-able library to which James had access. More to test his knowledge of Spanish than for any other reason, he started to read *A History of the Serrano Family*, by Eugenio, Duke of Zamora. In it, James read of how our host had served in the North Coahuila Militia under Santa Anna at the Siege of the Alamo. He had been re-sponsible for the death of James Bowie and had carried off his famous knife as a trophy of war, taking care that nobody knew so that his superiors could not take it from him. Fleeing from the Battle of San Jacinto, he was way-laid by Texian ruffians and his life was saved by *"Diablo Viejo"*, Old Devil Hardin, to whom he expressed grati-tude. I saw in this last piece a way in which I might gain possession of the knife. Coming to the United States, I located Resin Bowie the Second and won his confi-dence by pretending to wish to write a history of his fam-ily. I also told him of my discovery and suggested that I should visit Serrano with the dual objective of learning how James came to die and, if possible, to secure the re-turn of his knife to his kin-folk——'

1. According to Sir Arthur Conan Doyle's Sherlock Holmes stories, Professor James Moriarty justified Guillemot's faith in his abilities.

'Without mentioning about the hill of steel,' the Kid guessed with a grin.

'As he clearly knew nothing about it, I saw no reason to say anything which might cause him to doubt my motives,' the Ox replied, also smiling. 'At my instigation, he wrote to General Hardin and you know the rest.'

'Huh huh,' the Kid grunted as the Ox sat back and looked at him expectantly.

'I have, of course, more in mind than just satisfying your curiosity,' Guillemot warned.

'I sort of figured you might have,' the Kid admitted.

'Having come so far and expended a not inconsiderable amount of money on the quest for Bowie's blade,' the Ox went on, 'I was naturally perturbed to learn that Serrano had given the knife to you. But then I told myself, "Mr. Ysabel is an intelligent young man and will appreciate my being completely frank with him." So I have been.'

'And I'm right obliged to you for doing it.'

'May I ask, in the light of what you now know, what you intend to do with the knife, sir?'

'One thing's for sure,' the Kid stated firmly. 'I'm not going to hand it over to General Hardin.'

'How will you dispose of it?' Guillemot inquired.

'Sell it, I reckon.'

'To whom?'

'There seemed to be plenty of folks after it,' the Kid began hesitantly.

'And they are all dead,' the Ox reminded him. 'No, sir, *you* can't dispose of it.' He raised a fat hand to silence the young Texan's protest before it could be uttered. 'Capable as you are in many ways, sir, handling the financial ramifications of a matter like this would leave you as lost as I would be alone on the range.'

'You could be right at that,' the Kid conceded.

'Then, sir, as your ownership of the knife was in part at least brought about through my efforts, and as I am

170

eminently qualified to make the most advantageous negotiations, I wonder if you would consider a partnership?'

'That'd depend on how we'd cut the pot,' the Kid said cagily.

'I have expended a considerable sum already——'

'I'm not gainsaying it.'

'And I assure you that no small amount is involved——'

'Would a sixty-forty cut, your way, suit you?' the Kid asked.

'By gad, sir!' Guillemot boomed and extended his right hand. 'You have a deal.'

Carrying the Winchester rifle with his left hand grasping the lower end of the foregrip so that it was parallel to the floor, and with his saddle supported on his shoulder with the right, the Kid walked into the main room of the adobe house near to the chasm of the *Rio de la Babia*. As the afternoon was fairly well advanced, he and his party had elected to stay there and make the crossing of the river in the morning.

Although the Kid had apparently accepted Guillemot as his partner, he had contrived to avoid letting him learn the information that was engraved on the handle of the knife. He had achieved this, without arousing the Ox's suspicions as far as he could tell, by pointing out how neither of them possessed the necessary tools or knowledge to remove and replace the ivory grips and conceal the fact that they had done so. Accepting the comment, Guillemot had also agreed that the Kid should retain the knife and they would leave its examination until after they had parted company with the others in Texas.

The Kid had been adamant regarding the matter of ensuring 'Betty Hardin's' safe return to Eagle Pass, stating that—while the money which he obtained as his share from the knife's sale would make him independent of Ole

Devil's employment—he intended to continue living in the United States and could not hope to do so if he had allowed harm to come to the General's granddaughter. Having stated that he could understand the Kid's point of view and discussed a few other minor details, Guillemot had returned to his own room.

Waiting until he was sure that the rest of the household could be sleeping, the Kid had visited Belle Boyd and had told her what he had found out. The girl had agreed with the arrangements which he had made and had suggested that they should take no action until they were north of the Rio Grande. They had not attempted to examine the handle, for the same reason that he had given to the Ox.

Spending another day at *Casa* Serrano, the party had commenced the return journey. Wanting to avoid arousing Guillemot's suspicions, the Rebel Spy had carried on with her pose of being 'Betty Hardin'. She had also continued to cultivate Silk, in the hope that she could learn his plans for gaining possession of the knife. As he had clearly regarded her as playing part in whatever scheme he had in mind, she had persuaded him that it would be unwise to implement it until he was certain he could guide them to safety without the Kid's assistance.

For his part, the Kid had discovered that his 'partner' apparently was not content to rely solely upon the binding effect of their hand-shake and verbal agreement. Guillemot had asked Belle Starr to become more friendly with the young Texan and, if possible, to ascertain if he had any ideas about reneging on their arrangement. The lady outlaw's attitude had puzzled the Kid. While warning him of what she was supposed to do, she made no attempt to discover what made the knife so valuable. He doubted that she was as disinterested as appeared on the surface, but had not been able to confirm his suspicions. It was, he had realized, possible that she had no desire to do anything to antagonize a man as influential as Guillemot in criminal circles.

Although there had been some tension, with Boyd acting haughty—but avoiding any action which might have resulted in a confrontation between the Kid and Silk—the journey to the *Rio de la Babia* had been comparatively uneventful. Nor did the Kid anticipate any trouble from the secretary until they were much nearer to Piedras Negras. Certainly Silk had not given Belle Boyd any indication that he might be considering putting his plan into operation.

Having helped Salt-Hoss to attend to the horses, the Kid was the last member of the party apart from the old-timer to enter the house. He found that the girls had already gone into the back room which they would be occupying for the night. As usual, Silk had carried Boyd's saddle for her and was evidently in the girls' quarters. Guillemot was kneeling and opening out his bed roll.

Crossing the room to set his saddle on its side in a corner,[2] where there would be no danger of anybody stepping on it, the Kid glanced at Silk who was coming from the girls' room. There was something in the secretary's attitude which warned the young Texan against laying down his rifle as he had intended. Not only did Silk's face show vicious satisfaction, but his left hand was caressing the jacket's lapel in what had become a familiar and *very* significant manner.

Moving slowly, with the Winchester still held at its point of balance in an apparently negligent fashion, the Kid turned until he was facing the secretary.

'All right, half-breed!' Silk said, every word dripping with sadistic pleasure. 'I've been waiting for this. Go for your gun!'

'Is this *your* idea, Mr. Guillemot?' the Kid inquired, without taking his eyes from the secretary.

'No,' the Ox replied.

2. No cowhand ever threw down his saddle, or stood it on its skirts.

173

'Are you backing him on it?' the Kid wanted to know.

'It appears to be a matter between the two of you,' Guillemot answered evasively, lurching erect much in the manner of a draught-ox coming to its feet. 'So I can hardly take either side. You must see that, sir.'

'There you are, half-breed,' Silk mocked. 'It's just between you and me.'

'I won't draw against you,' the Kid declared, with deceptive mildness which gave no indication of how prepared he was to spring into instant action. 'You're too damned fast for that.'

Even as he was answering, the Kid noticed that the girls were standing in the doorway of their room. However, neither of them offered to move or speak. He did not allow their presence to distract him, for he knew that to do so while dealing with a man as fast and as deadly as the secretary would be fatal. The Kid had little enough chance of survival as it was, without reducing it any further.

'You don't have any choice,' Silk warned, enjoying what he took to be the other's fear of him. 'I'm going to kill you one way or the other.'

That was, the Kid conceded mentally, all too likely under the circumstances. He was aware of his limitations. It took him well over a second to draw and fire the old Colt Dragoon, while Silk could do the same with his short-barrelled Webley in half of that time. So he could not hope to match the secretary's speed.

There was, as the Kid knew all too well, only one second prize in a gun fight—death!

'Like I said, you're way too fast for me to draw down on,' the Kid finally answered, moving his right hand away from the Colt's butt and conscious that Silk was watching it. Then, playing for time, he went on, 'You'll be next, happen I go down, Mr. Guillemot.'

'Why should I be?' the Ox countered, having no intention of being forced into taking a stand. 'Silk is my strong

174

right arm and I trust him implicitly.'

'Could be you're trusting the wrong feller,' the Kid drawled, standing apparently motionless. Silk's mocking eyes had returned to studying his face and he wanted them to remain there. 'I've been thinking a fair bit about those two French *hombres*'s we gunned down in San Antonio. We all figured's they jumped us because they thought I knew it was them who'd whomped me on the head and was coming for 'em.'

Drawing a malicious and sadistic pleasure from the situation, Silk did not wish to terminate it too quickly. He was supremely confident in his ability and certain that he could allow the young Texan to make the first move, then kill him before he could bring the heavy old revolver from its holster. So he made no attempt to stop the other from talking, although keeping a careful watch on the Indian-dark features for any suggestion of the thoughts that were concealed by their lack of expression.

Behind Silk, the two girls exchanged worried glances. Each of them had her Remington Double Derringer in her jacket's pocket, but neither offered to take out the weapon. The click of its hammer being drawing to full cock would be heard by the secretary and might—almost certainly would—cause him to draw. So they too stood still and awaited developments.

'If they didn't recognize you——' Guillemot began.

'It wasn't *me* they recognized,' the Kid interrupted. 'It was Silk, which's why he had to side me instead of letting them gun me down. And why he killed the feller after I'd already wounded him, to make sure he couldn't tell what had happened. I'd say it was your "strong right arm" and not your "valley" 's sold you out to them.'

'You're too smart to live, half-breed!' Silk taunted and his right hand flashed across while the left drew open the side of the jacket for it to reach the Webley's butt without impediment.

175

While speaking, unnoticed by the secretary, the Kid was allowing the muzzle of his Winchester to sink towards the floor. Then he let the weapon slide very slowly through his fingers until its butt was braced against the rear of his forearm. Still drawing Silk's attention on to his face or, by flickering glances making sure that his right hand was not going any closer to the Dragoon's butt, he contrived to grasp the rifle ready to be fired with his left.

As soon as Silk made his move, so did the Kid. Setting his weight upon his slightly separated feet, he bent his knees a little and, inclining his torso to the rear, adopted much the same posture that combat shooting experts of the future would use when completing a 'speed rock' draw.[3]

There was, however, one vital difference in the way that the Kid moved. He had no intention of attempting to circumvent Silk's speed by pulling out the Dragoon. Instead, he pivoted the Winchester into alignment with his left hand. Even as the right was reaching for the foregrip, the rifle bellowed. The bullet took the secretary between the eyes and, bursting out of the back of his head, ploughed into the wall not a foot from where Belle Boyd was standing.

It must be confessed that luck played a considerable part in the Kid making such a supremely effective shot. He had hoped to hit Silk somewhere in the body, or at least to distract the secretary for long enough to permit a more careful aim. Instead, he had been fortunate enough to make an instant kill. Hurled backwards, with the Webley R.I.C. falling unfired from his hand, Silk caused the girls to jump to the rear out of his way and measured his length on the floor of their room.

'I told him that he was too fast for me to draw against,' the Kid remarked, swinging his gaze towards Guillemot and ignoring the sound of running feet approaching the front door.

3. A detailed description of the 'speed rock' draw is given in: *The ½-Second Draw*.

'Thank god you're alive, Lon!' Belle Boyd said fervently, walking towards the Kid although Belle Starr did not follow her. Instead, the lady outlaw retreated into their room. 'I'd no idea that he was planning anything like this.'

'*Lon!*' Guillemot repeated, taking note of the change in the girl's attitude.

Before any more could be said, Salt-Hoss dashed into the room with his Henry rifle held ready for use. Skidding to a halt, he looked at the body and up to where Starr was walking by it with her Winchester carbine in her hands.

'Put your rifle down slow and easy, Kid,' the lady outlaw commanded, lining her own weapon at the young Texan. 'Then unbuckle your gunbelt and let it fall.'

'Do it, *Cuchilo*,' Salt-Hoss supplemented, also elevating his Henry into alignment. 'We figure what we'll make on selling old Jim Bowie's knife'll set me up in a comfortable ree-tired-ment.'

CHAPTER FIFTEEN

IF LON DOESN'T GET YOU, I WILL

'What do you think you're doing, Miss Beauregard?' Octavius Xavier Guillemot demanded, his florid face darkening with anger as he started to step towards the lady outlaw.

'Stand still!' Belle Starr commanded and her Winchester carbine turned towards the fat man's chest as if it had been drawn by a magnet. 'Salt-Hoss just told you. We're taking Jim Bowie's knife.'

'You do just what Miss Belle tells you, *Cuchilo*,' the old-timer advised, keeping his Henry rifle lined on the Ysabel Kid. 'I don't want to see you get hurt, but that won't stop me happen I have to. I'm getting a mite too old for out-running posses and that old toad-sticker'll bring enough money to set me up comfortable some place.'

'You'll never get away with it,' Belle Boyd warned, speaking to Salt-Hoss as she looked straight at the lady outlaw and kept perfectly still. 'I don't think she's told you who I really am.'

'We'll take our chances for all of that,' Starr declared, before the old-timer could make any comment. 'So you start doing what I told you, Kid. You know I'm not bluffing.'

'If I might make a suggestion, Miss Beauregard,' Guillemot put in, having come to a halt as he had been requested. 'You appear to have the upper hand, so I will make you a liberal offer for the knife and, of course, the pleasure of your company as far as Texas where we can close our deal.'

'Am I in on that, *partner*?' the Kid inquired, without

offering to comply with the girl's order.

'Hardly, under the circumstances,' the Ox replied. 'I will, of course, reimburse you for your services—always assuming that Miss Beauregard intends to leave you alive.'

'If they'll let me, I do,' Starr stated. 'I'll leave your horses a couple of miles away, Kid. If two old hands like us can't get away with that much of a head start, we deserve to get caught.'

'*Two*, Miss Beauregard?' Guillemot asked. 'Do I take it that you are not going to accept my offer?'

'You might say that,' Starr admitted.

'I don't think that Mr. Turtle will be kindly disposed towards you if I am compelled to complain about your actions,' the Ox warned.

'He won't give a damn if you do,' Starr corrected cheerfully, glancing at the left side window as the horses in the corral began to snort and move restlessly. 'Your friends in New York riled him when they said "You will" instead of "Will you?" when they passed the word that you needed help. Kid, I'm getting awful tired of waiting for you to do what I said. And you stand *real* still, Belle Boyd!'

'*Belle Boyd!*' Guillemot repeated, staring at the slender girl. 'Then you're not——'

'She's no more "Betty Hardin" than I'm "Magnolia Beauregard",' Starr replied, deriving pleasure at the startled and baffled expression which came to the fat man's face after the superior and condescending way in which he had treated her ever since they had met.

'That's true, Mr. Guillemot,' the Rebel Spy agreed. 'And, seeing that introductions are in order, "Miss Beauregard" is better known as Belle Starr.'

'You asked Ram Turtle for the best help he could give,' Starr pointed out, then her voice hardened. 'Time's wasting, Kid. Start doing what——'

'You'll never get away with it, Starr,' Boyd cautioned, watching for some way in which the hold upon them might be broken. 'If Lon doesn't get you, I will. And I've got the whole of the United States Secret Service to back me in it.'

'Hell's fire!' Salt-Hoss ejaculated. 'You didn't say we'd be up against anything like *this*, Miss Belle——'

'What's spooking the horses?' the Kid interrupted, for the animals were still displaying evidence that something was disturbing them.

'Best take a look, Salt-Hoss,' Starr ordered. 'And don't you worry, we'll pull through like I promised.'

Without taking his Henry out of alignment, the old-timer started to move in a crab-like fashion towards the window. Looking through it over his shoulder, he stiffened and tried to turn, yelling, 'Hell, it's Ya——'

A shot crashed from outside the house, before Salt-Hoss could either finish his warning or complete the turn. Passing through his right temple, a bullet shattered out at the right in a hideous spray of bone splinters, brains and blood. Pitched across the room, he went down.

Springing forward, the Kid reached the window with his Winchester held ready for instant use, which was fortunate. He saw several stocky, thickset young Indian braves rushing towards the building. Their black hair was held back by head-bands, but without decoration by feathers. Dressed in breech-clouts and a variety of garments, they were armed with bow and arrows, or muzzle-loading and antiquated firearms. Lining his rifle, the Kid fired. Working the lever as one of the warriors fell, he changed his point of aim and tumbled another. Then Starr was at his side and her carbine dropped a third as he was raising his bow.

Putting aside her anger over Starr's attempted theft of the knife, Boyd darted forward. As the lady outlaw was running towards the Kid she snatched up the Henry which Salt-Hoss had dropped. With the weapon in her hands, she went to the door of the back room. Nor did she arrive a moment too soon. Several young Yaqui brave-hearts were approaching. Swinging up the rifle, she drove a bullet into the head of one of the attackers and was throwing the lever through its reloading cycle when the barrel of another weapon was thrust by her and roared to send a second brave to the Land of the Good Hunting.

Showing surprising speed for one of his bulk and normally lethargic movements, Guillemot had bent and snatched up his Sharps 'Old Reliable' buffalo gun. After glancing out of the right side window to make sure that no danger was threatening from that direction, he had lumbered rapidly to join the Rebel Spy and take his part in the fighting.

Realizing that the Ox was armed with a single-shot rifle, Boyd thrust the Henry towards him. She opened her mouth to speak, but found that an explanation was unnecessary. Taking his left hand from the foregrip of the Sharps, he accepted the repeater. Then, paying no attention to Silk's body—having seen more than one corpse during her eventful young life—she ran to where the secretary had placed her saddle and slipped the Winchester carbine from its boot. However, by the time she had crossed to the window, and Guillemot—who had leaned his Sharps against the wall and moved forward—joined her, the Yaquis were running back up the slope.

'Are they pulling out, Belle?' the Kid called from the other room.

'Yes, up the slope at any rate,' the Rebel Spy answered. 'We dropped two, though.'

'Can we come in and join you, Mr. Ysabel?' Guillemot requested.

'Should be all right,' the Kid replied. 'Only stop at the door so that you can keep an eye on them.'

Backing from the room, Boyd and Guillemot looked at the remaining members of their party. Much to their surprise, they found that the Kid had rested his rifle against the wall, removed his hat and was unfastening his ban-

181

dana. Starr had turned and was staring at the old-timer's body.

'Poor old Salt-Hoss,' the lady outlaw sighed, raising her eyes to Boyd and showing genuine sorrow. 'All he wanted was to get enough money to buy a spread somewhere that he wasn't known as an outlaw.'

'May I ask what you're doing, Mr. Ysabel?' Guillemot inquired, watching the Kid dropping the bandana into the crown of his hat and starting to unbutton his shirt.

'Hey, *gringos*!' called a voice in Spanish. 'Hey, *gringos*. Do any of you speak Mexican?'

'I do, *Manos Grande*,' the Kid replied, drawing off his shirt.

'You know my name?' the speaker yelled and there was surprise in his voice.

'My medicine told me you'd be coming,' the Kid answered, freeing the pigging thong which connected the tip of the Dragoon's holster to his right thigh. He lowered his voice, looking at Boyd and addressing her in English. 'Get the knife from my war bag and——'

'No white man has medicine,' *Manos Grande* interrupted, before the rest of the instructions could be given.

'I'm a man of two people, like you,' the Kid explained in Spanish, then reverted to English while unbuckling his gunbelt. 'And the moccasins and my rifle's medicine boot.'

'Yo!' Boyd responded, not knowing why the request had been made but setting off to carry it out.

'What are you——?' Guillemot commenced, staring in amazement as the young Texan laid his gunbelt on the floor by the hat and shirt.

'What tribe do you belong to?' *Manos Grande* demanded.

'The *Nemenuh*,' the Kid explained, starting to lever off his left boot. 'Or, as others call us, the *Tshaoh*.'

'Just what is going——?' Guillemot tried again.

'I'd leave him to it, whatever it is,' Starr advised, guessing what the Kid had in mind and knowing just how dangerous it would be. 'He's trying to save our lives.'

'Are you of the Enemy People?' *Manos Grande* wanted to know, translating the word '*Tshaoh*'.

'My grandfather is Chief Long Walker of the Quick-Stingers,' the Kid stated with pride. 'My man-name is *Cuchilo*. I have taken and have never broken the oath of the *Pehnane* Dog Soldiers' war lodge.'

'Does your medicine tell you why I have come, *Cuchilo*?' the Yaqui leader challenged.

'You have brought your men to be killed *trying* to take the big knife from me,' the Kid answered, selecting his words with deliberate care and completing the removal of his boots.

'Not to try!' *Manos Grande* corrected. 'I'm going to take it.'

'Are these what you wanted, Lon?' Boyd inquired, bringing the knife, a pair of moccasins and a long pouch made of fringed buckskin and decorated with red, yellow and blue patterning.

'Sure,' the Kid agreed and unfastened his waist belt. While opening his trousers' fly buttons, he replied to the Yaqui. 'You'll lose many men before you even get near the house. Every one of us has a repeating rifle and many bullets. Don Arsenio gave me the knife——'

'And I am going to take it, then lead the *Ventoso* Yaqui to drive the old one from our lands,' *Manos Grande* announced. 'If you give it to me, I will let you ride away.'

'You can't do it!' Guillemot protested in alarm, as the Kid removed his trousers and socks to stand clad only in the traditional blue breech-clout of a Comanche which he always wore instead of underpants. 'Why not let him have *your* knife?'

If the Ox's suggestion was caused by seeing Starr bending to slide the Kid's weapon from its sheath and thinking that she had the same idea, he was rapidly disillusioned.

'He'd know what we'd done as soon as he touched the

handle,' the lady outlaw pointed out. 'Leave it to Lon, he knows what he's doing.'

'Well, *Cuchilo*?' *Manos Grande* bellowed impatiently. 'Will you bring it to me, or do I come and fetch it?'

'Got you, you son-of-a-bitch!' the Kid enthused quietly yet vehemently and in English as he donned the moccasins. Resuming the use of Spanish and speaking louder, he went on, 'Dare *you* come and fetch it, *Manos Grande*?' While speaking, he draped the *Pehnane* medicine pouch over his bare left shoulder and accepted the knives from the girls, his left hand shaking the sheath from Bowie's blade. 'Not your brave-hearts, just *you* yourself.'

'What are you trying to do?' Guillemot demanded.

'He's counting on making strong medicine with the knife,' the Kid explained. 'And if he doesn't get it, then he's through. So I'm betting he'll take up my challenge. Fact being, he'll have to.'

'Then why not shoot him as he comes?' the Ox suggested.

'If you do, we'll never get out of here alive,' Starr warned angrily. 'I've told you that Lon knows what he's doing.'

'Happen things go wrong,' the Kid drawled, strolling to the front door, 'save a bullet for yourselves.'

'Count on it,' Starr promised grimly. 'Good luck, Lon. I'm sorry I tried to take the knife.'

'You will be, if we come through,' Boyd assured the lady outlaw. 'Take care, Lon.'

'I'll do my damnedest to,' the Kid declared. 'Let's hope there's a few old hands along with him.'

'What did he mean?' Guillemot inquired, after the young Texan had left.

'If there're older warriors, they'll be more inclined to accept that *Manos Grande*'s medicine was bad if he fails and will take the party away,' Starr explained and managed a weak grin at Boyd. 'I might even take you up on it, if we come through.'

Strolling out of the house in an apparently unconcerned fashion, the Kid made his way towards the edge of the chasm. However, as he was walking, he kept his eyes open and was alert for treachery. The Yaquis were moving into sight on the rim, but did not offer to advance towards the building. Instead, all were looking expectantly at one of their number; a well-built young warrior astride a big paint stallion and with a rifle cradled across his arm.

Coming to a halt facing the Indians, the Kid took the medicine pouch from his shoulder without relinquishing his hold on his weapon. Then he raised it and Bowie's knife into the air so that both could be seen.

'Here!' the Kid yelled. 'I offer you the big knife—if you can come and take it. Or is *Manos Grande* like a woman who waits while the brave-hearts do the fighting and bring home the trophies for her to take?'

From his first sight of the attackers, the Kid had suspected that they were *Ventoso* Yaquis and had guessed what they were after. One of their people who worked on the *hacienda* must have taken them news of Serrano's gift to the Kid. So *Manos Grande* was taking the opportunity to gain possession of the big knife, which he alone could use one-handed, that had previously been unobtainable as it was kept in the well-defended house.

The words which the Kid had just spoken were a direct and deliberate challenge, one that no self-respecting warrior could ignore; particularly if he had asperations towards leading the other brave-hearts of his people into battle.

There was one danger. As the Kid had discovered while talking about the Indians with the *vaqueros* on the last afternoon at *Casa* Serrano, *Manos Grande's* mother had been a Mexican *peon*. So he might not respond to the challenge in the fashion of a pure-blooded Yaqui. However, the Kid was gambling that he would. A man who was trying to live down what he regarded as the stigma of mixed parentage, which was how the *vaqueros* had described *Manos Grande*, was likely to be determined to uphold his people's traditions and beliefs rather than to go against them.

Sure enough, the warrior on the paint was handing his rifle to the grey-haired man who was nearest to him. Then he passed over his powder horn and ammunition bag. Peeling off the buckskin vest which he was wearing, he dropped it. Having done so, he set his horse into motion. None of the other braves offered to follow him, the Kid noted with relief. If the worst should happen, Guillemot and the girls would at least have an opportunity to sell their lives dearly.

'It's working!' Starr breathed, having watched what was happening.

'Surely if we shot him, the rest——' Guillemot began, but the words trailed into nothing as the girls glared furiously at him.

'If you even try, we'll shoot you in *both* arms so that you'll be alive when they get you!' Starr threatened. 'Our only hope is that the Kid comes through.'

Satisfied that all was going as well as could be expected, the Kid tossed Bowie's knife about thirty feet in the approaching rider's direction. Then he laid the medicine pouch on the ground at his feet and stood waiting for *Manos Grande* to arrive.

Letting his mount increase its pace, the Yaqui studied the tall, lean figure. He was not fooled by the relaxed-appearing way in which the *Tshaoh*—for that was how he now thought of the Kid—was standing, knowing that he was alert, watchful and ready to meet any eventuality. What was more, to have earned the man-name '*Cuchilo*' implied that he had attained considerable efficiency in and acclaim for wielding a knife in combat; no mean feat that, among the very capable ranks of the *Pehnane* Comanches' Dog Soldier war lodge.

Noticing the shape and dimensions of the weapon

which the Kid was holding, *Manos Grande* frowned and stirred uneasily on his horse's back. He wondered if he was being tricked. The knife on the ground might not be the same that had excited his envy at *Casa* Serrano and upon which he was basing his hopes for the future. It looked as if it was, but he was too far away to be certain.

What was more, being so much alike, perhaps the *Tshaoh*'s knife possessed similar magical properties. That was a sobering and disturbing thought. However, *Manos Grande* knew that he could not turn back without a complete loss of face. He had many enemies, including a few who had joined his raiding party. If he should return without the knife, even if his sole intention was to collect and use his rifle as a means of dealing with the *Tshaoh*, they would claim that his medicine was bad and leave him.

Accepting that he had no other course except to go on, *Manos Grande* gave thought as to how to deal with his enemy. He discarded the idea of using the knife which hung sheathed on his belt. If the *Tshaoh*'s weapon was made from the same kind of steel as the one from *Casa* Serrano, it would be capable of breaking his own blade.

With that in mind, *Manos Grande* urged his paint to a faster pace. It would never do for his rivals, or the waiting man, to think that he was suffering from doubts and uncertainties. Quitting the fast-moving animal's back, he alighted with a cat-like agility. Advancing on foot, he reached for the knife. The moment his right hand— which was unusually large for his stature, hence his man-name—closed on the hilt, he knew it was the weapon which he required as a means of becoming the war leader who would guide his people to victory over the Mexicans.

Watching the Yaqui pick up the knife, the Kid noticed that he did not grasp it in the usual Indian fashion. Instead of the blade extending from the bottom of the hand —which allowed only two types of blow, a downwards chop at the side of the neck and a horizontal hacking slash—it protruded ahead of his thumb and forefinger. The Kid held his own weapon in the same manner.

Coming closer, *Manos Grande* showed how—for all his hatred of the Mexican side of his blood—he was not averse to adopting that nation's methods of knife-fighting.

Moving lightly on spread-apart feet and well-flexed knees, their torsoes inclined forward so as to offer a smaller target, each man kept his right arm bent and the knife at hip level. He held his left hand extended slightly to one side as an aid to retaining his balance and to help with his protection from his enemy's weapon.

Circling for a few seconds, watching each other's eyes for any hint of what action was being considered, the Kid and *Manos Grande* were like two great cats. However, the Texan was in no hurry to start. Time was on his side, to a certain degree, as he did not have a reason for preventing his companions from thinking that he was afraid to make an attack.

While aware of the urgency and the inadvisability of delaying from taking the offensive, *Manos Grande* was unwilling to allow it to drive him into being rash. The knife was very heavy and, despite its excellent balance, seemed somewhat awkward after the weapon to which he had become accustomed. So he would be worse than foolish if he was to take chances with such an obviously competent enemy.

Guessing what was causing *Manos Grande* to act in such a cautious manner, the Kid feinted a cut towards his forward knee. Out thrust the Yaqui's left hand in an attempt to either grasp or deflect the Texan's knife arm. Like a flash, the Kid changed the direction that his blade was taking and he succeeded in opening a narrow, shallow gash on the other man's left forearm.

Manos Grande could not restrain a low hiss of surprise and pain, but he realized that the injury was only minor and would not incapacitate him. So he responded swiftly with a backhand swing at the Kid's head. Although the Texan had no wish to allow his own blade to meet the Yaqui's in an edge to edge clash, he reacted before he could stop himself. Just in time, he contrived to parry the attack with the flat of the blade.

Recoiling a long pace, the Kid saw that *Manos Grande*'s right arm was exposed. However, the cut at it which he launched failed to connect due to the speed with which the Yaqui withdrew. In doing so, *Manos Grande* straightened his torso. Unfortunately, by the time that the Kid had recovered his own balance, *Manos Grande* was once more in the 'on guard' position.

Once again, the two men circled each other. Watched by the girls and Guillemot—who had left the door from where he had been keeping the Yaquis on the rim under observation—and the men who had joined *Manos Grande* on the raid, the fighting pair decided upon their next moves.

'Your medicine is bad, *Manos Grande*,' the Kid mocked as he avoided a raking slash aimed at his chest.

Goaded to recklessness by the taunt, the Yaqui attempted an uppercut. However, although the Kid twisted rearwards at the waist, he did not attempt to counter the blow. Instead, he bounded aside and crouched low, using his left hand on the ground for support. At the same moment, he made a swing as if trying to rip open his enemy's forward leg. Whirling his own knife downwards and to the left in an attempt to parry the blow, *Manos Grande* discovered just a fraction too late that it had been another feint and not a serious attack.

Straightening up, the Kid changed the direction in which his weapon was travelling. As it flashed to the left, his greater reach and the extra half inch's advantage offered by his knife over Bowie's blade proved their worth. Although *Manos Grande* tried to move clear, he failed to go quite far enough and he received a raking gash across the forehead.

For all the pain which the wound must have caused him, the Yaqui responded with some speed. His own knife was pointing towards the ground and to his left, but he reversed its course. Seeing the concave swoop of the false edge rising in his direction and being aware that it was just as sharp and deadly as the main cutting edge, the Kid twisted to the left and clear. Still displaying the same rapidity of movement, *Manos Grande* pivoted into a kick. The ball of his foot caught the Kid in the small of the back with considerable force, propelling him towards the chasm.

Only by an effort did the Kid manage to bring himself to a halt. Even then, he was teetering on the very edge of the sheer wall which dropped almost a thousand feet to the raging rapids of the *Rio de la Babia*. However, in his struggle to regain his equilibrium, he released his knife and it fell a short distance away.

Despite the blood which was running from the wound on his forehead and into his eyes, *Manos Grande* could see that his enemy was disarmed. Letting out a wild victory whoop, he charged and thrust forward with his weapon. By that time, however, the Kid was in full control of his movements. Weaving aside, he caught the Yaqui's knife-wrist in both hands and, pivoting, heaved. As *Manos Grande* was rung by him, he released his hold. Unable to stop, the Yaqui went over the edge—and took James Bowie's knife along with him.

Moving forward, the Kid watched *Manos Grande* plunging downwards. There was a tiny splash which might have been caused by the knife, having slipped from his hand, falling into the torrent. It was obscured as he arrived and was instantly swirled along by the racing current. There was over half a mile of violent rapids, speckled with jagged and sharp-pointed rocks. Not that *Manos Grande* knew much of them. He was dead before he had gone a hundred yards.

Turning away, the Kid saw the other Yaquis talking

among themselves on the rim, after which they swung their horses around and rode away. Sucking his breath in, the young Texan gathered up his knife and medicine boot. Then he walked slowly towards the house. The girls and Guillemot came out to meet him.

'We don't need to worry about anybody else trying to steal old Jim Bowie's knife any more,' the Kid told them '*Manos Grande* took it over the edge with him.'

THIS TIME I CAN REALLY FIGHT!

'I've been looking forward to this ever since I caught you pretending to the Bad Bunch that you were me,' Belle Starr remarked in a matter-of-fact manner which gave no indication of her intentions, then swung her left fist across to catch the right side of the Rebel Spy's jaw.

The blow sent Belle Boyd reeling several steps, but she did not go down. Catching her balance, she weaved aside just in time to avoid Starr's follow-up attack. As the lady outlaw blundered by, unable to stop herself, Boyd drove an elbow hard into her back and brought an involuntary squeak of pain.

Although Octavius Xavier Guillemot had been angry over the loss of James Bowie's knife, he had grudgingly conceded that the Ysabel Kid could hardly be blamed for how it had come about. There had been little discussion on the matter, however, as the Kid had warned that they might still be in danger from the Yaquis. The death of their leader had caused them to withdraw, but some other warrior might assume command and wish to test his medicine by trying to avenge the braves who had been killed.

Going back into the house, the girls, the Kid and Guillemot had made ready to continue the defence. The need to do so had not arisen. Just before dark, a party of Don Arsenio Serrano's *vaqueros* had arrived. Word of *Manos Grande*'s intentions had reached their *patrón* and he had sent them to help deal with the Yaquis. On learning of the fight, the *vaqueros* had commiserated with the Kid and agreed with him that the knife was beyond any hope of recovery.

Having spent the night with the party, after breakfast that morning the *vaqueros* had helped move the buckboard and horses across the *Rio de la Babia*. However, their offer to help bury Anthony Silk and Salt-Hoss had been refused by the Kid. He had claimed that Guillemot was so filled with remorse over their deaths that he wished to dig the graves himself. On the Ox starting to object, the Kid had remarked pointedly that it was a *very long walk* to the nearest town. Looking at the grim expression on the Indian-dark young face, Guillemot had known that he was not listening to an idle threat and had done the Kid's bidding.

There had been no mention of Starr's attempted theft of the knife the previous evening. When the Kid had raised the matter with Boyd that morning, she had said that she would attend to it.

After the *vaqueros* had departed, Boyd had suggested that—like a drowning man was said to clutch at a straw —*Manos Grande* might have clung to the knife and, if so, they could perhaps find it with his body downstream from the chasm. Although none of them had believed it was likely, the Kid had offered to make a search. Guillemot had agreed to accompany him, but Boyd had said that she and Starr would wait with the horses. The lady outlaw had not raised any objections, much to the Ox's surprise.

Once the two men had ridden out of sight, Starr and Boyd had secured the horses and went to the sandy edge of the river. As the lady outlaw had guessed what the Rebel Spy had in mind, she had taken the offensive.

Rubbing at her back as she swung around, Starr walked straight into a jab from Boyd's right fist. Its knuckles caught her on the nose, hard enough to sting and make her eyes water even though it was almost at the end of its flight. Pivoting like a ballet dancer, Boyd demonstrated the skill at *savate*—French foot boxing—

which had served her so well on numerous occasions. Like the lady outlaw, she had donned a pair of moccasins that morning. For all that, the kick which thudded against Starr's ribs was hard enough to send the heavier girl staggering. While she gasped, she retained her upright posture.

'The thing is,' Boyd commented, gliding forward as the other girl came to a halt, 'this time I can really fight.'

'So can I!' Starr warned, lowering her head and charging with hands reaching to take hold.

On the occasion to which the lady outlaw referred, although they had tangled, neither had been able to display her true ability in fighting.[1] Both had frequently wondered what the result would have been if they had, and so were not averse to finding out.

Instead of allowing the lady outlaw to come into contact with her, Boyd leapt into the air. Her hands slapped on to the brunette head as she leap-frogged over. Letting out an angry squeak, Starr turned. Boyd had twirled around on landing. Once again she bounded into the air, using the technique which would become known in wrestling as a drop-kick. Seeing her danger, Starr jumped backwards. Boyd's feet caught the other girl's full bosom, but once again were just too far away to arrive with their full impact. However, gasping in pain, Starr was forced to continue her retreat.

Rebounding, Boyd landed rump first on the sand. Flinging herself forward, Starr meant to land on the other girl and make the most of her weight advantage. Tilting over so that she once again avoided Starr's hands, Boyd brought her feet under the lady outlaw's body and thrust upwards. Turning half a somersault, Starr landed supine. The soft sand broke her fall and, expecting to be attacked, she rolled rapidly on to her face. From there, she forced herself on to her hands and knees. While doing

1. Told in: *The Bad Bunch*.

so, she found out why her expectation had not been fulfilled.

Finding that the skirt was impeding her agility, which would be needed to off-set Starr's extra pounds of weight, Boyd freed her skirt as soon as she had bounded up from foot-rolling the other girl. It was sliding down, revealing that she was wearing her riding breeches, as Starr dived at her. The brunette head rammed into Boyd's mid-section, then Starr's arms locked around her waist and bore her to the ground.

At first female instincts sent Boyd's fingers into Starr's brunette locks, taking a healthy hold and tearing at them as she was crushed against the sand. On releasing the Rebel Spy's waist and duplicating her actions, Starr found that the boyishly short black hair offered a far less effective grasp for pulling upon. Bracing herself, as the torment she was inflicting caused Starr to writhe in agony, Boyd managed to roll her from the top. Boyd hoped to be able to escape and rise, having no desire to fight at such close quarters as doing so would favour the other girl. As she released the hair and tried to get up, Starr gave a heave which toppled her over and regained the upper position. Straddling the Rebel Spy's slender waist and kneeling over her, Starr started to rain slaps at her face.

With her head rocking from side to side as the blows landed, Boyd wriggled and squirmed with furious desperation. Fortunately for her, Starr had not been able to trap her arms. After making a few abortive attempts to grab the brunette's wrists, Boyd acted in a more effective manner. Scooping up a handful of sand, she flung it into the other girl's face. Then, while Starr was still half blinded, she surged her body upwards like a bow. Although the lady outlaw was pitched from her perch, Boyd did not resume the fight on the ground. Instead, she rolled free and, with her cheeks reddened by the slaps, jumped to her feet.

Staying clear until Starr was also up, Boyd moved into the attack. Clenching her fists, the lady outlaw advanced to meet her. The fight went on for another half an hour. Some of the time, they used their fists like a couple of men. In between, they wrestled in feminine fashion. There were occasions, such as when Starr held her head in chancery and pummelled at her face with the other hand, that Boyd came close to regretting the decision to inflict summary punishment for the attempted theft of Bowie's knife. However, the Rebel Spy managed to escape and launched a swift-moving *savate* attack which more than repaid what she had received.

Starr had been in more than one rough-house, but not even Calamity Jane had proved to be as tough as the Rebel Spy. There were muscles which felt like steel springs in Boyd's slender arms and legs. Not only was she extremely competent at *savate*, which made use of punching as well as kicking, but she showed that she could hold her own when it came to old-fashioned knock-down-and-drag-out brawling.

Gradually Boyd began to gain the upper hand. Her speed and knowledge of *savate* slowly swung the balance of the scales in her favour. To the dazed, exhausted and suffering Starr, it seemed that every other second a bony fist was impacting against her face, naked breasts—the brawling had left both of them clad in nothing but their breeches—and stomach. They were punctuated by the kicks which the Rebel Spy seemed to be able to launch from any angle and as high as her head. Starr might have felt grateful that Boyd had not been wearing riding boots, for the results with her bare feet were sufficiently painful.

Staggering on wobbly legs, the girls were trading exhausted punches and slaps. At last, making a final desperate attempt to get her hands on Boyd, Starr found they flopped limply to her sides and her knees began to buckle. She made a despairing effort to carry on, stumbling forward with her mouth trailing open and bosom heaving as she tried to drag air into her tortured lungs.

The sight gave an almost equally spent Boyd the fillip that she needed. Summoning every last dreg of energy that she could muster, she put all her rapidly failing strength behind a roundhouse swing with her left fist. Obligingly, if inadvertantly, Starr reeled into range. Caught alongside the jaw, she spun around and crashed face down on to the sand. A moment later, Boyd collapsed on top of her.

'Good heavens!' Guillemot ejaculated, staring at the two girls as he was climbing laboriously from the largest of the harness horses which he had been riding. 'Have you been fighting?'

There was good cause for the Ox's comment. Almost ninety minutes had elapsed since Boyd had delivered the *coup de grace* to Starr. Recovering first, the Rebel Spy had dragged her beaten opponent into the water and revived her. After having ascertained that the lady outlaw had had enough, Boyd had suggested they should try to make themselves look more presentable before the men returned. Although they had washed away the sand which perspiration had caused to adhere to them, done the best they could to alter the tangled messes in which their hair had been left, stopped the bleeding from noses and lips, and changed into fresh clothing, their bruised faces left little doubt as to what they had been doing.

'It seemed like a good idea at the time,' Starr answered, speaking somewhat thickly, and touched her jaw with a delicate finger. 'Now I'm not so sure.'

'Who won?' the Kid asked with a grin, having suspected what might happen when he had accepted Boyd's suggestion and taken Guillemot in search of the knife.

'Boyd got lucky,' Starr explained, throwing a wry grin at the Rebel Spy.

'Sore loser,' Boyd sniffed, but with no greater show of

animosity. 'Did you have any luck, Lon?'

'Nope,' the Kid replied. Having dismounted, he jerked a thumb towards the fat man. 'Mr. Guillemot allows that we can't put him in the hoosegow for what he's done.'

'I doubt whether you could,' the Ox declared. 'And, more to the point, as I have not committed any crime— no matter what my intentions might have been—I'm sure that, in view of my past and, possibly, future services to them, I don't think Miss Boyd's organization would want me to be incarcerated.'

'You could be right,' the Rebel Spy conceded. 'But you might have notions about getting revenge on us——'

'Perish the thought, dear lady,' Guillemot boomed. 'Much as the loss of Bowie's knife rankles, I wouldn't think of wasting time, money and effort on idle revenge——'

'Particularly when trying to do it might mean that word would get out how the Ox was fooled by a girl and a Texas cowhand,' Starr continued. 'It'd make him the laughing stock throughout the criminal world.'

Watching Guillemot's face, the Kid saw anger flicker briefly across it to be replaced by grudging admiration.

'By gad!' the Ox boomed, slapping a fat thigh with the palm of his hand. 'By gad! And to think that I expected to be dealing with dull-witted rubes! I must be getting old.' Then he ran his appreciative gaze over the three young people and went on, 'I don't suppose you would care to accompany me to Europe and assist me in a venture which had interested me for several years. One which, if it is successful, will be at least as profitable as the sale of Bowie's secret.'

'What'd that be?' the Kid inquired.

'Locating and acquiring a statuette of a falcon, sir,' Guillemot replied. 'It is made of solid gold and encrusted with the finest jewels to be looted from the Crusades.[2]

2. Full details of the statuette can be found in Dashiell Hammett's *The Maltese Falcon*.

198

Its value, sir, in the right circles, is immense.'

'Sounds like it might be,' the Kid drawled.

'Then you'll accompany me?' the Ox asked.

'I don't reckon so,' the Kid replied. 'I'm not saying's I don't reckon you'd play fair, even if I don't, but I'd sooner stay on my own range.'

'And work as a forty-dollars-a-month cowhand?' Guillemot challenged.

'Why not?' the Kid countered. 'Ole Devil's a damned good boss and Betty Hardin's nothing like Belle pretended. You might not believe me, but even after you'd told me about Bowie's knife, I'd still have taken it back for his kin.'

'I *do* believe you,' Guillemot stated and there was respect in his voice. 'How about you, ladies?'

'I'm satisfied with what I am,' Boyd replied. 'Why don't you go, Belle?'

'Like Lon says, I'd sooner stay on my own range,' Starr answered.

'Tell you what, sir,' the Kid drawled. 'Just to show there's no hard feelings, on the way back to San Antonio, I'll show you some mighty fine hunting.'

'You may as well, sir,' Guillemot boomed enthusiastically. 'I might as well get *something* out of the quest for Bowie's blade. And to show *you* that there are no ill-feelings on my part, I'll give you the clasp-knife which James Black made.'

APPENDIX ONE

During the War Between The States at seventeen years of age, Dustine Edward Marsden Fog had won promotion in the field and was put in command of the Texas Light Cavalry's hard-riding, harder-fighting Company 'C'.[1] Leading them in the Arkansas Campaign, he had earned the reputation for being an exceptionally capable military raider the equal of the South's other exponents, John Singleton Mosby and Turner Ashby.[2] In addition to preventing a pair of Union fanatics from starting an Indian uprising which would have decimated most of Texas,[3] he had supported Belle Boyd, the Rebel Spy,[4] on two of her most dangerous missions.[5]

When the War had finished, he had become the segundo of the great OD Connected ranch in Rio Hondo County, Texas. Its owner and his uncle, General Ole Devil Hardin, had been crippled in a riding accident[6] and it had thrown much of the work—including handling an important mission upon which the good relations between the United States and Mexico had hung in the balance[7]—upon him. After helping to gather horses to

1. Told in *You're in Command Now, Mr. Fog*.
2. Told in: *The Big Gun*; *Under the Stars and Bars*; *The Fastest Gun in Texas* and *Kill Dusty Fog*.
3. Told in: *The Devil Gun*.
4. Further details of Belle Boyd's career are given in: *The Hooded Riders*; *The Bad Bunch*; *To Arms, To Arms in Dixie*; *The South Will Rise Again* and *The Whip and the War Lance*.
5. Told in: *The Colt and the Sabre* and *The Rebel Spy*.
6. Told in: *'The Paint'* episode of: *The Fastest Gun in Texas*.
7. Told in: *The Ysabel Kid*.

200

replenish the ranch's depleted remuda,[8] he had been sent to assist Colonel Charles Goodnight on the trail drive to Fort Sumner which had done much to help the Lone Star State to recover from the impoverished conditions left by the war.[9] With that achieved, he had been equally successful in helping Goodnight to prove that it would be possible to take herds of cattle to the railroad in Kansas.[10]

Having proven himself to be a first class cowhand, Dusty went on to be acknowledged as a very capable trail boss,[11] round up captain,[12] and a town-taming lawman.[13] In a contest at the Cochise County Fair, he won the title of the Fastest Gun In The West, by beating many other exponents of the *pistolero* arts.[14]

Dusty Fog never found his lack of stature an impediment. In addition to being naturally strong, he had taught himself to be completely ambidextrous. Possessing fast reflexes, he could draw and fire either, or both, of his Colts with lightning speed and great accuracy. Ole Devil Hardin's valet, Tommy Okasi, was Japanese and from him Dusty had learned *ju jitsu* and *karate*. Neither had received much publicity in the Western world, so the knowledge was very useful when he had to fight bare-handed against larger, heavier and stronger men.

8. Told in: *·44 Calibre Man* and *A Horse Called Mogollon*.
9. Told in: *Goodnight's Dream* and *From Hide and Horn*.
10. Told in: *Set Texas Back on Her Feet*.
11. Told in: *Trail Boss*.
12. Told in: *The Man From Texas*.
13. Told in: *Quiet Town*; *The Making of a Lawman*; *The Trouble Busters*; *The Small Texan* and *The Town Tamers*.
14. Told in: *Gun Wizard*.

APPENDIX TWO

The only daughter of Long Walker, war leader of the Pehnane—Wasp, Quick Stinger, or Raider—Comanche Dog Soldier lodge and his French Creole *pairaivo*[1] married an Irish Kentuckian adventurer called Sam Ysabel, but died giving birth to their first child. Given the name Loncey Dalton Ysabel, the boy was raised in the fashion of the *Nemenuh*.[2] With his father away much of the time on the family business of first mustanging, then smuggling, his education had been left to his maternal grandfather.[3] From Long Walker, he had learned all those things a Comanche warrior must know; how to ride the wildest, freshly caught mustang, or when raiding—a polite name for the favourite *Nemenuh* sport of horse-stealing—to subjugate a domesticated mount to his will; to follow the faintest of tracks and conceal traces of his own passing; to locate hidden enemies, yet remain concealed himself when the need arose; to move in silence through the thickest of cover or on the darkest of nights; and to be highly proficient in the use of a variety of weapons. In all these subjects, the boy had proved an excellent pupil. He had inherited his father's rifle-shooting skill and, while not real fast on the draw—taking slightly over a second, where a tophand would come close to half of that time—he could perform adequately with his colt Second Model Dragoon revolver. His excellent

1. *Pairaivo*: first, or favourite, wife.
2. *Nemenuh*: 'The People', the Comanche Indians' name for their nation.
3. Told in: *Comanche*.

handling of one as a weapon had gained him the man-name *Cuchilo*, 'the Knife' among the *Pehnane*.

Joining his father on smuggling trips along the Rio Grande, he had become known to the Mexicans of the border country as *Cabrito*; which had come from hearing white men referring to him as the Ysabel Kid. Smuggling did not attract mild-mannered, gentle-natured pacifists, but even the toughest and roughest men on the bloody border had learned that it did not pay to tangle with Sam Ysabel's son. His education and upbringing had not been such that he was possessed of an over-inflated sense of the sanctity of human life. When crossed, he dealt with the situation like a *Pehnane* Dog Soldier—to which lodge of savage, efficient warriors he belonged—swiftly and in a deadly effective manner.

During the War, the Kid and his father had commenced by riding as scouts for the Grey Ghost, John Singleton Mosby. Later, their specialised talents had been used by having them collect and deliver to the Confederate States' authorities in Texas supplies which had been run through the U.S. Navy's blockade into Matamoros, or purchased elsewhere in Mexico. It had been hard, dangerous work and never more so than on the two occasions when they had been involved in missions with Belle Boyd.[4]

Sam Ysabel had been murdered soon after the end of the War. While hunting for the killers, the Kid had met Dusty Fog and, later, Mark Counter. Engaged on a mission of international importance, Dusty had been very grateful for the Kid's assistance. When it had been brought to a successful conclusion, learning that the Kid no longer wished to continue a career of smuggling, Dusty had off-ered him work at the OD Connected ranch. When the Kid had stated that he knew little about being a cowhand, he had been told that it was his skill as a scout that would be required. His talents in that line had been most useful to

4. Told in: *The Bloody Border* and *Back to the Bloody Border*.

the floating outfit.[5]

In fact, the Kid's acceptance had been of great benefit all round. Dusty had gained a loyal friend, ready to stick by him through any danger. The ranch had obtained the services of an extremely capable and efficient man. For his part, the Kid had been turned from a life of petty crime —with the ever-present danger of having it develop into more serious law-breaking—and became a useful member of society. Peace officers and honest citizens might have been thankful for that as he would have made a terrible and murderous outlaw if he had been driven into such a life.

Obtaining his first repeating rifle while in Mexico with Dusty and Mark, the Kid became acknowledged as a master in its use. In fact, at the Cochise County Fair he won the first prize—one of the fabulous Winchester Models of 1873 'One Of A Thousand' rifles—against very stiff competition.[6] Also it was in a great part through his efforts that the majority of the Comanche Indian bands agreed to go on to the Reservation.[7] Nor could Dusty Fog have cleaned out the outlaw town of Hell without the Kid's assistance.[8]

5. Floating outfit: a group of four to six cowhands employed on a large ranch to work the more distant sections of the property. Taking food in a chuck wagon, or 'greasy sack' on the back of a mule, they would be away from the ranch house for weeks at a time. Because of General Hardin's prominence in the affairs of Texas, the OD Connected's floating outfit were frequently sent to assist his friends who found themselves in trouble or danger.

6. Told in: *Gun Wizard.*

7. Told in: *Sidewinder.*

8. Told in: *Hell in the Palo Duro* and *Go Back to Hell.*

APPENDIX THREE

Wanting a son and learning that his wife, Electra, could not have any more children, Vincent Charles Boyd had insisted that his only daughter, Belle,[1] be given thorough training in several subjects which were not normally regarded as being necessary for a wealthy Southron girl. At seventeen, she could ride a horse—astride or side-saddle—as well as any of her fox-hunting male neighbours; men who were to supply the South with its superlative cavalry. Not only that, but she was a skilled performer with a sword, an excellent shot with handgun or rifle, and expert in *savate*, French fist and foot boxing. All of which were to stand her in good stead in the future.

Shortly before the War Between The States had commenced a mob of pro-Union rabble had stormed the Boyd plantation. They had murdered her parents and wounded her, setting fire to her home before being driven off by the family's Negro servants. On her recovery, Belle had joined her cousin, Rose Greenhow, who was operating a spy ring. However, wanting to find the two leaders of the mob, who were serving with the Union's Secret Service, she had taken the active and dangerous task of delivering her fellow agents' findings to the Confederate States' authorities. Gaining proficiency and acquiring the name, 'the Rebel Spy', she had graduated to handling risky and important assignments. On two of

1. According to American fictionist-genealogist Philip Jose Fraser's researches, Belle Boyd is related—the aunt of—to Jane Porter, who married Lord Greystoke, Tarzan of the Apes.

them, she had been assisted by the already legendary Dusty Fog[2] and a third had brought her into contact with the equally famous young Texan called the Ysabel Kid.[3] However, her quest for the murderers of her parents did not come to its successful conclusion until shortly after the War had ended.[4]

On signing the oath of allegiance to the Union, Belle had been allowed to join the United States Secret Service. Despite her enmity for that organization during the War, she had served it loyally and with efficiency. She had been responsible for the breaking up of the notorious and deadly Bad Bunch,[5] assisted by lady outlaw Belle Starr and Martha 'Calamity Jane' Canary.[6] Then she had brought to an end the activities of the Brotherhood For Southron Freedom, with the help of Ole Devil Hardin's floating outfit.[7] Her latest assignment, before becoming involved with Octavius Xavier Guillemot's attempt to gain possession of James Bowie's knife, had brought her together with Calamity Jane for a second time and they had contrived to prevent what might have developed into a war between the United States and Great Britain.[8]

While the Yankees might have had every reason to hate the Rebel Spy during the War, they had no cause to feel other than gratitude to her once it had ended.

2. Told in: *The Colt and the Sabre* and *The Rebel Spy*.
3. Told in: *The Bloody Border*.
4. Told in: *Back to the Bloody Border*.
5. Told in: *The Bad Bunch*.
6. Details of Martha Jane Canary's career are given in the author's 'Calamity Jane' series of books.
7. Told in: *To Arms! To Arms, in Dixie!* and *The South Will Rise Again*.
8. Told in: *The Whip and the War Lance*.

J.T. EDSON OMNIBUS VOL.10

THE BIG GUN
UNDER THE STARS AND BARS
THE FASTEST GUN IN TEXAS

He was small and unassuming. The sort of man you'd dismiss as just another cowhand. But Dusty Fog was one of the brightest officers in the Confederate Army. Promoted in the field, he commanded the roughest, toughest, and most ornery fighting company in the Texas Light Cavalry.

Three Civil War stories starring Dusty Fog.

Also available from Corgi Books:
J.T. Edson Omnibuses Vols 1-12

J.T. EDSON TITLES AVAILABLE FROM CORGI BOOKS

THE PRICES SHOWN BELOW WERE CORRECT AT THE TIME OF GOING
TO PRESS. HOWEVER TRANSWORLD PUBLISHERS RESERVE THE RIGHT
TO SHOW NEW RETAIL PRICES ON COVERS WHICH MAY DIFFER FROM
THOSE PREVIOUSLY ADVERTISED IN THE TEXT OR ELSEWHERE.

☐ 13602 6	**EDSON OMNIBUS VOLUME I**		£3.99
☐ 13603 4	**EDSON OMNIBUS VOLUME II**		£3.99
☐ 13604 2	**EDSON OMNIBUS VOLUME III**		£3.99
☐ 13605 0	**EDSON OMNIBUS VOLUME IV**		£3.99
☐ 13606 9	**EDSON OMNIBUS VOLUME V**		£3.99
☐ 13607 7	**EDSON OMNIBUS VOLUME VI**		£3.99
☐ 13608 5	**EDSON OMNIBUS VOLUME VII**		£3.99
☐ 13609 3	**EDSON OMNIBUS VOLUME VIII**		£3.99
☐ 13863 0	**EDSON OMNIBUS VOLUME IX**		£3.99
☐ 13864 9	**EDSON OMNIBUS VOLUME X**		£3.99
☐ 13865 5	**EDSON OMNIBUS VOLUME XI**		£3.99
☐ 13541 0	**MARK COUNTER'S KIN**		£2.50
☐ 13341 8	**J.T.'S LADIES RIDE AGAIN**		£2.50
☐ 13623 9	**RAPIDO CLINT STRIKES BACK**		£2.99

All Corgi/Bantam Books are available at your bookshop or newsagent, or can
be ordered from the following address:
Corgi/Bantam Books,
Cash Sales Department,
P.O. Box 11, Falmouth, Cornwall TR10 9EN

UK and B.F.P.O. customers please send a cheque or postal order (no currency)
and allow £1.00 for postage and packing for the first book plus 50p for the
second book and 30p for each additional book to a maximum charge of £3.00
(7 books plus).

Overseas customers, including Eire, please allow £2.00 for postage and packing
for the first book plus £1.00 for the second book and 50p for each subsequent
title ordered.

NAME (Block Letters) ....

ADDRESS ....

....